Anthony Burgess was born in Manchester in 1917. After six years in the Army he worked as an instructor for the Central Advisory Council for Forces Education and as a grammar school master. From 1954–1960 he was stationed in the Far East, where he was an education officer in the Colonial Service.

He became a full-time writer in 1960, although he had already published three novels and a history of English literature, as well as composing several full-length works for orchestra and other media.

His work includes *A Clockwork Orange* (later filmed by Stanley Kubrick), *Honey for the Bears*, *The Long Day Wanes*, *Time for a Tiger*, *Earthly Powers*, the 'Enderby' novels and *The Kingdom of the Wicked*.

D1328650

Also by Anthony Burgess in Abacus:

ENDERBY'S DARK LADY
THE KINGDOM OF THE WICKED
FLAME INTO BEING:
THE LIFE AND WORK OF D. H. LAWRENCE

Anthony Burgess

HOMAGE TO QWERT YUIOP

Selected Journalism 1978–1985

This selection first published in Great Britain by
Century Hutchinson Ltd 1986
Published in Abacus by
Sphere Books Ltd 1987
27 Wrights Lane, London W8 5TZ

Copyright © 1985 Liana Burgess 1986

This book is sold subject to the condition that it shall not, by way of trade
or otherwise, be lent, re-sold, hired out or otherwise circulated without the
publisher's prior consent in any form of binding or cover other than that
in which it is published and without a similar condition including this
condition being imposed on the subsequent purchaser

Set in Compugraphic Baskerville

Printed and bound in Great Britain by
Collins, Glasgow

Per Liana
non per abitudine

Contents

Preface: Homage to Quert Yuiop

The title is not altogether facetious. As every hammerer at a typewriter knows, QWERTYUIOP is the blazon on the second bank of the keyboard from the top. I have earned my living with a typewriter for the last twenty-five years, and I have developed an affection for the instrument analogous to my love for my old Gaveau piano, which once belonged to Josephine Baker. But whereas a piano, once acquired, becomes a permanent article of furniture, typewriters break down irreparably and have to be replaced. Yet the old loved name – Qwert Yuiop – reappears and proclaims a continuity of identity, minimally modified when it gets into Italy or France and becomes Qzert Yuiop. Without Qwert Yuiop's willingness to submit to my punishing fingers I doubt if I could have sustained the profession of author. I know how to use a pen, but ever since I took my last written examination, the pen has always been for me a musical instrument: I still write orchestral scores with it but, associating it as I do with the shaping of notes and dynamic signals, I find it difficult to put it in the service of any written statement longer than *allegro ma non troppo*. Still, I do not have to make excuses for not being a literary penman (except in so far as they say that typewriterese is a recognized and debased type of prose). Nobody is nowadays, and thralldom to Qwert Yuiop persists even when the writer graduates from the neolithic technology of the typewriter to the electronic mysteries of the word processor.

As I write, an IBM word processor with daisywheel sits malevolently waiting for me in a customs shed. I am scared of making the transition from clattering Qwert Yuiop to his velvety successor, even though I am beginning to be warned that publishers will soon accept from authors only floppy discs. I have not even made the hop from manual to electric typewriter. I do not like the low hum which says 'Get on with it, you're wasting power', and I do not like my hammering to be muffled. When you hear your own clatter you know you are at work, as a blacksmith is. More, the rest of the household knows you are at work and does not suspect you of covertly devouring a *Playboy* centrefold.

Qwert Yuiop in his traditional form, which is not much different from the way he was in the pioneering Remington days, when Yost and Soule thought of a writing machine as a kind of gun (hence 'Chicago type-writer'), not only relates authorship to artisanship; he separates the written from the writer (a pen is too close to the heart) and brings him closer to that objectification which only the final printed copy can bestow. A writer does not pour out his heart or even talk on paper. He creates an artifact. Even a newspaper article is an artifact, a thing for use. When used it is discarded, having done its work. It is not like a book or a symphony, which the creator submits, with little hope, to the notice of posterity 'Sufficient unto the day is the newspaper thereof,' says a character in Joyce's *Ulysses*. He means primarily the news, but he must mean also the kind of thing represented by what I have assembled here – chiefly comments on books, the writings of a writer on other people's writing, which – since a publishing event is a new thing that happens – may be considered news about the unnewsworthy.

Why trouble to collect such ephemera and put them to bed between hard or soft covers? Chiefly because of writer's guilt. A novelist like myself brings out a novel occasionally, and it is assumed by some that he does nothing between novels. Writers are supposed to be lazy (H .G. Wells admitted to an idleness that kept him glued to the chair; glued to the chair, he felt he might as well write), but a collection of a writer's journalism is meant to convince the reading world that, like everybody else, he gets on with what the French call the *boulot*. In this book you will find evidence that, in the last seven years, I have not been altogether idle. The pieces I have collected amount to about one third of my total journalistic output during that period. It has been a period spent mostly on the Côte d'Azur, a region dedicated to that rich idleness which former President Nixon inveighed against, and my response to other people's sybaritic laziness has been to work hard.

Another thing – and one to be admitted with a certain shame: the rewards of the serious novelist are meagre, and he needs journalism to augment his insufficient earnings from art. I consider that the novel is an important and serious art form, but most readers of novels wish to reduce it to a mere diversion. Harold Robbins, who lives up the coast from myself, does not have to produce journalism, since he gives the public what it wants – sex and violence under the guise of a lesson in morality. So long as I produce novels with a more complex content and technique than, say, *The Carpetbaggers*, I shall have to produce also fodder for the up-market press.

I do not mind doing this work; indeed, I enjoy it. It is a means of keeping in touch with a public that does not necessarily read my or anybody else's fiction. The reading and reviewing of books which, in the covenant I have always insisted upon, have been selected not by myself but by a literary editor, keeps my mind open to fresh ideas in both literary creation and criticism. And the need to keep within the limit of a thousand words or so is, as with the composing of a sonnet, an admirable formal discipline. Qwert Yuiop helps me here: when I have typed three pages of typescript and a bit over, I know that my allowable quota has been filled.

The bulk of the work here presented has been addressed to a European audience, but a certain amount has also been commissioned by American editors. With the increasing unification of the world of western literature and ideas, I do not feel that American readers are likely to dismiss me as an unintelligible foreigner. But it sometimes happens that I refer to persons better known in Europe – or, more specifically, Great Britain – than in the United States. Names like Lord Longford, Barbara Cartland and Mrs Mary Whitehouse appear because they stand for a kind of philistinism universally known but given sharper definition to a British reader through pronouncements that have already made them news. They are concerned with cleaning up the arts, taking homosexual poets to court, denouncing blasphemy, recommending the blandly safe (like *The Sound of Music*) and warning against the subversive (*Ulysses* or *The Waste Land*). Mr Bernard Levin and Mr Malcolm Muggeridge also appear, the first because of his Johnsonian prose style in the London *Times*, the second because, before his conversion to Catholicism and the discovery of charity, he preferred knocking people to praising them. For the rest, the mythology is part of our common Anglo-American stock.

The arrangement of the essays is a loose one. The author begins by brooding on smarts from women and ends with a meditation on woman raised to the condition of music. In between he thinks about travel, language, film, music and, overwhelmingly, literature. You are to open the book at any page and take what comes. The author took what came in living his journalistic life, and it would be pretentious to suppose there was a pattern in it. The author wishes to thank the dedicatee and her secretary, Bettina Culham, for their help in putting the book together and the editors of the *Times Literary Supplement*, the *New York Times* and the *Observer* for their kind permission to reprint these pieces.

A.B.
Monaco
1 October 1984

Grunts from a Sexist Pig

Cleaning out my son's bedroom the other day (he has gone to Paris to work as an apprentice fish chef in the all-male kitchens of Le Fouquet) I came across a partly eaten pig in pink marzipan. It had come, apparently, in the Christmas mail and was so ill-wrapped that neither its provenance nor purpose was apparent. My son thought it was an eccentric gift from one of his friends. Now, quite by chance, I discover (a matter of an old *Punch* in a thanatologist's waiting room) that it was a trophy sent by the Female Publishers of Great Britain to myself as one of the Sexist Pigs of the year. I forget who the others were, but I think one of them published a picture book on the beauty of the female breast. What my own sin against woman was I am not sure, but I'm told that it may have been a published objection to the name the Virago Press (women publishers publishing women) had chosen for itself.

Now all my dictionaries tell me that a virago is a noisy, violent, ill-tempered woman, a scold or a shrew. There is, true, an archaic meaning which makes a virago a kind of amazon, a woman strong, brave and warlike. But the etymology insists on a derivation from Latin *vir*, a man, and no amount of semantic twisting can force the word into a meaning which denotes intrinsic female virtues as opposed to ones borrowed from the other sex. I think it was a silly piece of naming, and it damages what is a brave and valuable venture. The Virago Press has earned my unassailable gratitude for reprinting the *Pilgrimage* of Dorothy Richardson, and I said so publicly. But I get from its warlike officers only a rude and stupid insult, and I cannot laugh it off. Women should not behave like that, nor men either.

It has already been said, perhaps too often, that militant organizations pleading the rights of the supposedly oppressed – blacks, homosexuals, women – begin with reason but soon fly from it. On this basic level of language they claim the right to distort words to their own ends. I object to the delimitation of 'gay'. American blacks are not the only blacks in the world: the Tamils of India and Sri Lanka are far blacker. 'Chauvinistic' stands for excessive patriotism and not for other kinds of sectional arrogance. 'Pig' is an abusive word which libels a clean and tasty animal: it is silly, and it can be ignored. But 'sexist' is intended to have a precise meaning, and, on learning that I was a sexist pig, I felt it necessary to start thinking about the term.

As far as I can make out, one *ought* to be a sexist if one preaches or practises discrimination of any kind towards members of the other sex. In practice, a sexist is always male, and his sexism consists in his unwillingness to accept the world view of women in one or other or several or all of its aspects. This means, in my instance, that if I will not accept the meaning the Virago Press imposes on its chosen name, I qualify, by feminist logic, for the pink pig. But I cannot really believe it is as simple as that. The feminists must have other things against me but none of them will speak out and say what they are.

In the *Harvard Guide to Contemporary American Writing*, Elizabeth Janeway, discussing women's literature, considers a book by Mary Ellmann called *Thinking About Women*. She says: 'It is worth being reminded of how widespread and how respectable has been the unquestioned assumption of women's inevitable, innate, and significant "otherness", and Ellmann here collects utterances on the subject not only from those we might expect (Norman Mailer, Leslie Fiedler, Anthony Burgess) but from Robert Lowell, Malamud, Beckett, and Reinhold Niebuhr.' Note both the vagueness and the obliqueness. There can be no vaguer word in the world than 'otherness'. The vagueness is a weapon. Since it is not defined, the term 'otherness' can mean whatever its users wish, rather like 'virago'. The position of people like Mailer and Burgess and Fiedler vis-à-vis this 'otherness' does not have to be defined either: we have an intuitive knowledge of their qualities, and, between women, no more need be said.

That women are 'other', meaning different from men, is one of the great maxims of the feminists. They are biologically different, think and feel differently. But men must not say so, for with men the notion of difference implies a value judgement: women are not like us, therefore they must be inferior to us. I myself have never said or written or even thought this. What I am prepared to see as a virtue in myself (as also in Mailer and Fiedler and other pigs) is – because of the feminist insistence on this damnable otherness – automatically transformed by such women as read me into a vice. I mean the fact that I admire women, love the qualities in them that are different from my own male ones, but will not be seduced by their magic into accepting their values in areas where only neutral values should apply. Here, of course, the trouble lies. Women don't believe there are neutral zones: what males call neutral they call male.

I believe, for instance, that in matters of art we are in a zone where judgements have nothing to do with sex. In considering the first book the

Virago Press brought out – the masterpiece of Dorothy Richardson – I did not say that here we had a great work of women's literature, but rather here we had a great work which anticipated some of the innovations of James Joyce. I should have stressed that this was a work by a woman, and the womanly aspect of the thing didn't seem to me to be important. I believe that the sex of an author is irrelevant, because any good writer contains both sexes. But what we are hearing a lot of now, especially in American colleges, is the heresy that *Madame Bovary* and *Anna Karenina* can't be good portraits of women because they were written by men. These are not aesthetic judgements: they are based on an a priori position which refuses to be modified by looking at the facts. The feminists just don't want men to be able to understand women. On the other hand, women are quite sure that they understand men, and nobody finds fault with the male creations of the Brontës or of Jane Austen.

Let's get out of literature and into life. I think I am quite capable of seeing the feminist point of view with regard to men's sexual attitude to women. I am strongly aware of the biological polarity, and it intrudes where women say it shouldn't. I am incapable of having *neutral* dealings with a woman. Consulting a woman doctor or lawyer, shaking hands with a woman prime minister, listening to a sermon by a woman minister of religion, I cannot help letting the daydream of a possible sexual relationship intrude. That this diminishes the woman in question I cannot deny. It depersonalizes her, since the whole sexual process necessarily involves depersonalization: this is nature's fault, not man's. Women object to their reduction into 'sex objects', but this is what nature decrees when the erotic process gets to work. While writing this I am intermittently watching a most ravishing lady on French television. She is talking about Kirkegaard, but I am not taking much of that in. Aware of her charms as she must be, she ought to do what that beautiful lady professor of mathematics did at the University of Bologna in the Middle Ages – talk from behind a screen, meaning talk on the radio. But then the voice itself, a potent sex signal, would get in the way.

This awareness of the sexual power of women, I confess, induces attitudes which are, from the feminist angle, unworthy. At Brown's Hotel a woman porter proposed carrying my bags upstairs. It was her job, she said, but I could not let her do it. Old as I am, I still give up my seat to women far younger when on a bus or tube train. This is a protective tenderness wholly biological in origin. How can I apologize for it when it is built into my glands? Women are traditionally (but this is, I admit, possibly a man-imposed tradition) slower to be sexually moved than are men, and this enables them to maintain a neutral relationship with the other sex in offices and consulting rooms.

I believe what women tell me to believe – namely, that they can do anything men can do except impregnate and carry heavy loads (though this latter was contradicted by the girl at Brown's Hotel). Nevertheless, I have to carry this belief against weighty evidence to the contrary. Take music, for instance. Women have never been denied professional musical instruction – indeed, they used to be encouraged to have it – but they have not yet produced a Mozart or a Beethoven. I am told by feminists that all this will change some day, when women have learned how to create like *women* composers, a thing men have prevented their doing in the past. This seems to me to be nonsense, and it would be denied by composers like Thea Musgrave and the shade of the late Dame Ethel Smyth (a great feminist herself, the composer of *The March of the Women* as well as *The Wreckers* and *The Prison*, which the liberationists ought to do something about reviving). I believe that artistic creativity is a male surrogate for biological creativity, and that if women do so well in literature it may be that literature is, as Mary McCarthy said, closer to gossip than to art. But no one will be happier than I to see women produce the greatest art of all time, so long as women themselves recognize that the art is more important than the artist.

I see that most, if not all, of what I say above is likely to cause feminist rage and encourage further orders to pink-pig manufacturers (did the Virago Press search for a *woman* confectioner?). But, wearily, I recognize that anything a man says is liable to provoke womanly hostility in these bad and irrational times. A man, by his very nature, is incapable of saying the right thing to a woman unless he indues the drag of hypocrisy. Freud, bewildered, said: 'What does a woman *want*?' I don't think, despite the writings of Simone de Beauvoir, Caroline Bird, Sara Evans, Betty Friedan, Germaine Greer, Elizabeth Janeway, Kate Millett, Juliet Mitchell, Sarah B. Pomeroy, Marian Ramelson, Alice Rossi, Sheila Rowbotham, Dora Russell, Edith Thomas, Mary Wollstonecraft and the great Virginia herself, the question has yet been answered, except negatively. What women *don't* want is clear – their subjection to the patriarchal image, male sexual exploitation, and all the rest of it. When positive programmes emerge – like the proposed 'desexualization' of language – we men have an uneasy intimation of the possible absurdity of the whole militant movement. I refuse to say Ms, which is not a real vocable, and I object to 'chairperson' and the substitution of 'ovarimony' for 'testimony'. And I maintain (a) that a virago is a detestable kind of woman and (b) that feminist militancy should not condone bad manners. If that pink pig had not been thrown in the garbage bin I should tell the women publishers of Britain what to do with it.

Evil Eye

Mal Occhio: *The Underside of Vision*, by Lawrence di Stasi, North Point Press, San Francisco

'F*orza malefica,*' says *Le Monnier's Dictionary,* '*attribuita dalla superstizione popolare ad una forma di ostilitá sorda, ostinata, e peccaminosa,*' and it sets the word solid: *malocchio*. Mr di Stasi's separation of the two elements, like electrical leads that must not touch, seems in itself an apotropaic act, but it signals a concern with the *occhio* in general, from which evil may be dissociated only to disclose a large, impersonal and primordial *mal*. Some people have the evil eye; all of us have evil eyes.

Mr di Stasi is an American of Neapolitan origin on his father's side, and the *malocchio* sturdily crossed the Atlantic along with Saint Januarius, pasta, and the tradition of the protective *padrone* or *padrino*. Innocent non-Italian Americans assume that Italo-American culture represents the peninsular totality, forgetting that the North never went in much for emigration. Italian food in New York means Mamma Leoni's, with its monstrous gross loads of spaghetti, and not the pastaless refinements of Bologna or Milan. And so it is assumed also that all Italians make the sign of the horns or carry an amulet against the wicked eye, whereas this is a southern speciality, like pizza and tomato sauce. On the other hand, the South infects the North more than the other way, because of immigration in search of work. The Milanese scorn the tomato, preferring a patrician white diet, but Napoleon found tomatoes, or his cook did, for a famous dish on the eve of the battle of Marengo. The Mafia is in Turin, and the evil eye operates in the shadow of the Alps.

I have seen Roman prostitutes make the apotropaic horn-gesture in the presence of a priest. This is not, as some say, because a priest is a monster – a mixture of skirted woman and celibate man – but because, having given up the joys of copulation, priests have received the malocchial gift in compensation. To possess the milk-turning or cow-killing endowment does not argue of necessity a studied malevolence. One has to guard against the effects of the *malocchio*, but one bears no ill will against the *iettatore* or thrower of the maleficent beam. Some people are clumsy, others accident-prone, others have the evil eye. Pope Pius IX, a kind and clever and probably holy man, had it in abundance. Driving through Rome after his coronation, he looked at, among other things, a nurse holding a child at an open window. At once the child fell to the street and was killed. From then on his reputation as a prime *iettatore* was secure. One of his contemporaries said:

If he had not the *iettatura*, it is very odd that everything he blesses makes fiasco. When he blessed our cause against Austria in 1848, we were winning battle after battle, doing famously. Suddenly, everything goes to pieces. The other day he went to Santa Agnese to have a great festival, and down goes the floor in collapse, and the people are all smashed together. Then he visits the column to the Madonna in the Piazza di Spagna, and he blesses it and the workmen, and of course one of the workmen falls from the scaffolding the same day and kills himself. There is nothing so fatal as his blessing.

Mussolini did not have the *malocchio*, though he is said to have feared it. One of the most distinguished of modern Italian scholars, whose books on English romanticism will be well known to readers, had reputedly the power of the *iettatura*, and to say this was not to libel him. I was forbidden to mention his name in Italian literary circles, though his initials were harmless. This was Mario Praz, who died while I was writing this essay. Like grace or rain, the *malocchio* falleth where it listeth.

Usually the bad eye is feared for innocent children, and the admiring gaze of a childless aunt can cause a brief fever or headache – nothing lethal – but envy can operate very nastily with pregnant women, just as it can with a fine milch cow. To ward off the effects you can carry an amulet. The reader may believe this or not, but at the moment of typing the word a *malocchio* amulet rolled out on to the central plain of my desk from the space beneath a trough of reference books. It must have been there some time: I cannot remember buying it. It is a twisted horn in red plastic surmounted by a gold-painted coronet. It resembles a large red pepper, and it is comfortingly ithyphallic in the hand. It is noteworthy that the response to the *malocchio* is a phallic gesture or symbol – the power of male generation against female destruction. And yet the ceremonies and diagnostics which operate when the eye has struck are all handed down from mother to daughter.

My wife saw recently in Romagna, which is pretty far north, a performance of the oil-and-water ritual to keep the eye off a calving cow. Drops of olive oil were poured by a farmer's wife on to a bowl of water. Oil and water proverbially do not mix; when the oil unnaturally spreads and mingles with the water, then the *malocchio* is at work. When the globules reassert their independence and float on the surface, then the spell has been broken. The ceremony my wife saw denied that the evil eye was at work at all.

Mr di Stasi is no floating globule. He wants to get below the surface of the superstition, always a dangerous thing to do, since it leads to anthropological depositions which are finally more baffling than the evil eye itself. The oil and water lead us to the *Rosarium Philosophorum*, through Jung (Mr di Stasi gets most of his sources at second hand), and to the god Mercury, called *aqua permanens* and *unctuosum* (why this nominative neuter or masculine accusative?). 'Life is soul, that is, oil and water. . . . Olive oil was considered by both Greeks and Romans to be the vegetable equivalent of soul-stuff. . . . The use of olive oil as a soul symbol in the *malocchio* ritual thus makes eminent sense.' The reasoning is somewhat elliptical, but it seems to have something to do with the symbolization of vital tension – between spirit and matter – in the pouring of oil on water, and the evil eye's dissolution of that tension.

But why the eye? Why not another organ? The touch of an envious hand or the ripe hogo of gumrot would appear to be more dangerous than ocular *invidia*. Mr di Stasi takes us all the way back to the Fall, an anomalous description of man's deciding to stand upright. All-four humanity was more concerned with smell than with sight; the genitalia were hidden. With the upright stance came exposure of the genitals and the birth of shame as well as the primacy of the eye, a primacy to be associated with shame. There is truth in this, and we need no anthropologist to demonstrate it to us. As a social organ the eye is treacherous and a nuisance. We keep it averted from others, lest it be interpreted as a challenge: animals rightly resent the insolent stare, though they will tolerate cameras. In a railway compartment it is safer to train the eye on a book. When we look at something it appears that we want it, and this is *malocchio* enough. Admiring and envious eyes eat the children in their prams and the cows in their pasture. Cows give milk and children are nourished by it. The commonest act of the evil eye is to turn the milk sour. The *malocchio* is a milky thing. The eyes of those who see too much, like Homer and Milton and James Joyce, are turned into miniature saucers of milk. Oedipus, who had looked on his mother with desire, tore out his eyes rather than let the gods make them lactiform.

In the Balkans milk has everything to do with the evil eye. Its possessors are those who, having been weaned, go back to their mothers' breasts. Thus they learn of the dual, or Melanie Kleinian, mother – the one who comforts them with milk and the one who strikes them when they bite. But the *malocchio* tradition only exists in ectolactic communities, steady static societies which till the fields and keep cows. Their goddess is the non-biting mother, fat and blind. The goddess of the pastoral nomads and the hunters is a sharp-eyed mother, and the building of a pluralistic society in which cow's milk is drunk and mutton and venison eaten (though not, in Semitic societies, at the same meal) entails some kind of reconciliation of acute-sighted Artemis and the static blind mother too old to have a name. The eye has to be accepted, but with qualifications: some eyes are evil.

Thus, anyway, I interpret the phenomenon, but this would be somewhat superficial – meaning insusceptible of grandiose holistic expression – for Mr di Stasi. 'Alongside the familiar and familial binding in *mal occhio*,' he says, 'there must equally exist that other, that subterranean intimation: that all Mercurial phenomena – the visual, the phallic, the egoic – are at some stage to be unbound or unwound, to yield at last to that more complete, that more all-embracing vision.' Meaning, I think, that the *malocchio* is a symptom of our sick separateness (is Mr di Stasi serious when he seems to derive *sick* from *siccus*, or, for that matter, when he ties *matter* up with *mater*?), our inability to enjoy the prephallic world to which drugged youth, our stoned or blind mentors, would lead us. Mr di Stasi's publishers have done him proud – a sewn book and acid-free paper. Its content stimulates only to obfuscate; he has not fully digested the many things he has read; the evil eye leads him to an entire mystical cosmology. I am satisfied to grasp my plastic amulet.

Writer Among Professors

In the summer of 1940 the Luftwaffe was dropping bombs on Manchester and distracting me from typing my thesis on Christopher Marlowe. The copying out of Faustus's penultimate line – 'Ugly hell, gape not, come not, Lucifer' – forced on me the realization that even melodrama could be relevant to life, but the objective appraisal of Marlowe's technique seemed, as the bombs drew nearer, somewhat frivolous. Empson had suggested that the weakly placed negatives indicated a scholarly desire on Faustus's part to experience, for learning's sake, even the ultimate horrors. An interesting speculation in a cool time, but not when Trafford Park was being bombed. 'I'll burn my books – ah, Mephistophilis . . .' No ambiguity there. For many of my generation the war meant the figurative burning of variorum editions and Middle English grammars. Before September 1939 there was the possibility of postgraduate study and a life of scholarship. In 1946, when those of us who had survived were coming home from the theatres of war, it was evident that the future lay elsewhere – in exploiting a first degree in the teaching market, making a fair copy of our war poems, supporting a wife, finding somewhere to live. But a nostalgia for the scholarly life was to remain.

Dr Johnson could, in his letter to Lord Chesterfield, refer to himself as a scholar, even though he had left Oxford without a degree. In those days scholarship could be extramural, and it was possible to conduct chemical experiments on the kitchen table. But today we recognize that the university is the closed shop of research, and that everything outside it is amateur and dilettante. I have taught, both at home and abroad, a kind of applied linguistics, but always with the knowledge that I was cut off from the heart of revelation and innovation. We have grown to expect that the great advances, whether the discipline be scientific or humane, should come from the universities. Literary criticism, as opposed to mere reviewing, is a preserve of the academics. It is not just a matter of new ideas coming out of the dialectic of the seminar and being confirmed in the huge specialist libraries; the very atmosphere of the university is conducive to leisurely speculation and cautious discovery.

I am not, however, so nostalgically foolish as to grant a special magic to the university. Professors can themselves be foolish. I remember being appalled, while working in Malaysia, to read in a book on semantics by the late Professor Ullmann an assertion to the effect that the Malay language had no specific terms to denote personal relationships when, as I knew well, what it really lacked was general terms. He had copied the canard from Professor Conklin, who had copied it from somebody else. But this is not what we usually expect from professors. The right attitude of the unscholarly to the scholarly is that of Dylan Thomas to I. A. Richards: he was scared of meeting him. He recognized in him what was not in himself – a well-stocked, disciplined, systematic mind. Such minds make universities. Universities are only bricks, red or brown or black, sheltering libraries and laboratories. They may encourage the development of the scholarly mind, but they cannot create it.

When I took up, twenty-eight years ago, the novelist's career, I became aware that this entailed the abandonment of any dormant inclinations to scholarship that I possessed. Fiction is a lying craft and it has no pretensions to exact knowledge. Plausibility is very nearly all. A novelist may check in a cheap encyclopedia such objective data – details of the sinking of the *Titanic*, the formula for sodium glutamate – as he needs for his narrative, but his art is a very tentative one and depends largely on guesswork as to how the human mind operates. As structure is important – meaning the imposition of a beginning, a middle and an end on the flux of experience – there has to be a large element of falsification. Nothing could be less scholarly than the average novel, even when its basis is historical fact. A number of twentieth-century novelists, copying Nabokov and Borges, make parodic scholarship an aspect of their artistic seriousness. The novelist is a confidence trickster, while it is the task of the scholar to abhor trickery and teach scepticism.

It is not surprising then to find, in the universities of Europe, very few scholars who practise seriously the craft of fiction. True, we have in England David Lodge and Malcolm Bradbury, who satirize from the inside the life of the campus, but before they appeared there seemed to be only Professor J. I. M. Stewart, who wrote detective stories under the pseudonym of Michael Innes. Stewart, who has written profoundly on the modern novel, has much of the born novelist's equipment – a fine ear for dialogue, a freshness in handling the *récit*, a sense of humour, a capacity for dealing surprises – but he lacks seriousness. If he had taken the novel seriously he would have disqualified himself for scholarship. The detective story is the ideal form for the don, whether as writer or reader: it is neat, witty, cruel, dispassionate, merely diverting. For a professor of literature to take seriously his own quasi-literary efforts might entail his taking seriously contemporary literature as a whole. This, for the most part, he dare not do, and his instinct, or reasoned judgement, is right.

Whatever happens in the English departments of the newer universities, the older ones have a tradition of wariness of approach to the study of contemporary letters. The first Scottish professor of English literature could say: 'Now, gentlemen, ye'll concern yersels wi' Milton's *Paradise Lost* and Thomson's *Seasons*. Pope's Homer's a guid buik too,' but he was too close to Thomson to be able to evaluate him. My own professor of English regarded, in 1937, the poems of Gerard Manley Hopkins (died 1889, first published 1918) as too dangerously contemporary even for a session of practical criticism. He was probably right. If a writer ceased writing sixty years ago we are conceivably in a position to judge his worth. I have enough of the aborted scholar in me to express doubt about the advisability of studying Iris Murdoch or William Golding or Philip Larkin or Seamus Heaney in a university course. By about AD 2030 we shall know how we stand with regard to these writers. In 1982-83 we are wise to beware even of Joyce, Conrad and Lawrence. It is in the European academic tradition to stick to the safe past, and the past is a couple of days before yesterday.

Clearly, with such a situation, there has to be a gulf between the literary academic and the literary practitioner. Academics will occasionally, in the columns of literary weeklies, condescend to review new fiction or verse, but reviews are rarely serious criticism. Such academics may meet the writers they review in pubs or at publisher's parties, but the writers are rarely welcome in senior commonrooms. If a writer occasionally finds himself invited to lecture at a British university, it will usually be under some aegis that admits the general public and thus ensures a lack of high seriousness. Professors are right to distrust living poets and novelists. Such people are of their nature unscholarly and the value of their work is, by vice of its very contemporaneity, much in doubt.

The situation is very different in the United States. I cannot speak much for the Ivy League universities, which have inherited British cautiousness, but the state universities, as I know well, live all too cheerfully in the present. I have given two lectures at Harvard – one for a summer course of teachers, the other for a student society whose cheque bounced – and I spent a year at Princeton in which I was rigorously excluded from serious academic work and confined to courses in Creative Writing. This in itself was a daring adjunct to the stricter disciplines and, one might say, not typically hederal. The state universities are as prepared to train writers as to create physicists, and it is logical to invite writers in to do the training. Whether such training is in fact possible is a matter for discussion. It is boring work, to be relieved only by the concession of the odd lecture on Whitman or Milton, usually to be given when the regular instructor is ill or being interviewed for another post. Creative Writing courses tend to attract exhibitionists, activists and admirers of Tom Wolfe. The students usually wish to teach the instructor who, being an established writer, clearly belongs to the past and understands little of the literary tastes of the young. He is sometimes expected to learn through smoking marijuana.

Still, there is contact between two worlds of a kind not yet current in British academia, and not only through sessions in which girls recite feminist *vers libre* and are praised by their friends ('Wow, that's great, Janice'). For the study of literature in many state universities is the study of the up-to-date. A course which offers class discussion of *Slaughterhouse Five* or *Portnoy's Complaint*, or, since those novels already belong to the past, *The White Hotel* or *The Hotel New Hampshire* is more likely to appeal to the young than one which offers *Walden* or *The Scarlet Letter*. Universities which depend on fees must be even more trendy and, moreover, dare not oppress the prospective student's attention span with books either long or difficult. That cautiousness which is at the heart of British literary academicism is sometimes learnt, though too late, by the more thoughtful of the instructors and even students: Ken Kesey and Richard Brautigan, much studied in the seventies, were discovered to be not worth studying. But the time better spent on a book of *Paradise Lost* or a canto of *The Rape of the Lock* was now past and irrecoverable.

It often seems reasonable to invite a writer to lecture on his own work, if that work forms part of the course. But writers are rarely good at understanding their own work, let alone discoursing on it. There are those who dream of Shakespeare's suddenly appearing in the classroom to talk about *Troilus and Cressida*. One cannot doubt that he would be less than enlightening on it and would recall mostly Burbage's cuts and the audience's indifference – facts interesting in themselves but not useful for term papers. If the writer is to be on the campus at all – and many American universities in their kindly wisdom understand this – it should be with the investment of a sinecure that subvents his writing. The fact that, in the odd semesters I have spent in American colleges, I have been able to write little does not invalidate the philanthropic principle. British writers, once there, need to get to know America; they can do their writing better at home. For Americans it is different. John Barth, for instance, could not produce his fictional monsters without a professorial subsidy. Yet such a subsidy need be only adventitiously academic: Exxon or IBM could, much more reasonably, supply it.

But I think British universities are wrong in not welcoming writers for a brief time – not a year, not even a term – to talk to students. Writing is a desperately lonely life, and the author too often has the impression of throwing his work into a great silence. The acerbic review and the manic letter are no substitute for meeting informed and serious readers, actual or potential, among the young. The young are at the colleges and can be brought into classrooms and lecture halls and salons where weak punch is served. The author needs them probably much more than they need him. I have just returned from Penn State, where, having been absent from universities for several years, I had an opportunity to find out what today's young think of my work. I should welcome such chances in Europe, but I rarely get them. Dickens did not know the term feedback, but he knew the reality of a kind of discourse with his readers. Writers today are working too much in isolation, and our universities and colleges could help to build causeways to the mainland.

But I think the older tradition is right – that of excluding the modern from academic studies – and I note that this tradition often touches American professorial writing on the living. I myself have been treated as though already dead, laid out on the slab, incapable of moving and kicking, contradicting the careful thesis by speaking out or branching into new artistic directions. Which means, probably, that the casual review is good enough for the contemporary author but the doctoral dissertation is too much. The professors should leave us alone and we, like Dylan Thomas, should be scared of the professors. There is nothing the professional writer can give to the university – as opposed to the young readers of books who just happen to be in it – except certain insights about literature derived from his own practice. But these insights are of little academic value, especially when the post-structuralists are forcing the separation of the text from its creator. The concern of the academics should be with the safely dead who are undoubtedly important. The rest of us will never know whether we are important or not: we leave the sifting to time and the evaluation to an academic grove which has not yet been planted.

Endtime

W e have had the end of the wor'd with us ever since the world began, or nearly. As we are all solipsists, and all die, the world dies with us. Of course, we suspect that our relicts are going to live on, though we have no proof of it, and there is a possibility, again unprovable, that the sun will heartlessly rise the morning after we have become disposable morphology. Perhaps it is rage at the prospect of our ends that makes us want to extrapolate them onto the swirl of phenomena outside.

When I was a small Catholic boy living in the Middle Ages, the end of the world was likely to come any time: I had sinned so much that the Day of Judgement could not be much longer delayed. But there were periodic doomsday threats for Protestants too, as in 1927, the year of fancy garters and the eclipse of the sun, when the Sunday papers had double-page apocalyptical scare stories. I remember a sudden puff of smoke bursting from a back alley and my running like mad: this was it. At school, with the nuns, the end of the world was in Christ's promise to the disciples – he would be with them till then though not apparently after – and yet the finish of things was contradicted by the 'world without end' of the Paternoster. That though, I was told, was another world, post-terrestrial and not easy to envisage. Without benefit of biblical prophecy, much popular culture in my youth dealt with the end. The *Boy's Magazine* had a serial about it that excited me so much that my father burned it. The BBC, whose expressionistic drama was so brilliant in the 1930s and all without recorded sound effects and with only wind-up gramophones, put on a play about the consummation of all things, with an angelic bass singing *Sic transit gloria*. Terminal visions are not a speciality of the nuclear age. There seemed to be far more of the end of the world around before we learned how to bring it on ourselves.

The difficulty of writing subliterature about the end of the world (for it is almost entirely that: in *Ulysses* the End of the World is a kilted octopus that sings 'The Keel Row') lies in the point of view. There has to be somebody to witness it. Having refugees looking down on it from a spaceship is cheating, and so might be thought the bland narrative of Nevil Shute's *On the Beach* if that narrative were not so impersonal, like some dimwitted archangel's chronicle. There is a 717-page novel by Allan W. Eckert called *The Hab Theory* ('You'd better pray it's only fiction,' says the blurb) in which the weight of the polar icecaps causes the earth to capsize. This has happened before, states the President of the United States in his address to the world, and it is the duty of mankind to preserve all knowledge so that civilization can be reinitiated by the possible handful of survivors. ' "I therefore call on all governments and all people –" And *then* all the power went off . . . *all over the world.*' So the book ends, and clearly Allan W. Eckert is still there with a typewriter. It won't do.

There never was a time when it would do. Not even Charles Dickens, who worked in the white light of theocentric fiction, would have sent the whole world up in comic spontaneous combustion and ended with a resounding moral paragraph. Mary Shelley, the mother of contemporary science fiction, established the principle of the solitary survivor in her little-read eschatographical novel *The Last Man*. This is a story of a monstrous plague killing everybody off except a doomed personage wandering companionless like Percy Bysshe's moon. There is thus an observer, though he is not going to observe much longer. (Incidentally, I must deplore in my old-fashioned way the custom, to which the author of *Terminal Visions** adheres, of presenting women writers with neither first name not honorific. Mary Shelley becomes Shelley, as Doris becomes Lessing. There is only one Shelley, and he was a poet; there was only one Lessing, and he was a German.) H. G. Wells's *The Time Machine* looks at the imminent extinction of the sun, but it is only an apocalyptic vision, St John the Divine on a bicycle. The point is, if I read Professor Wagar's book right, that most of our literary world's ends are clearings away of old rubbish to make way for fresh starts. The world's great age begins anew, as Shelley wrote. St John the Divine's vision is of the end of pagan Graeco-Roman civilization. The end of the world was for that; world without end was for the new faith.

The virtue of Professor Wagar's book on the endtime is that he has read so much rubbish, old and new. He is an academic historian and does not have to worry about literary considerations: indeed, style would only get in the way of the vision. He has read books we have only heard of, and some not even that – books like Robert Hugh Benson's *Lord of the World* (1908); Poul Anderson's *After Doomsday* (1962); Léon Daudet's *Le Napus: Fléau de l'an 2227* (1927). He has read every book called *The Last Man*, of which there are a fair number, though he does not mention one that was very nearly called *The Last Man in Europe*. Strictly, Orwell's *Nineteen Eighty-Four* is very much a novel of the end with no resurrection. When Winston Smith is shot the visions of collective solipsism will take totally over, and the world as objective reality will cease to exist. This is a far more terrible prophecy than anything in Professor Wagar's long bibliography can provide, if we except *Brave New World*, where the last man hangs himself. It is the vision of stasis, of the impossibility of change, that is so terrifying. William Blake shuddered at heaven's sempiternal marble and reflected that in hell there is at least energy and motion. Shaw's *Back to Methuselah* (again unmentioned here) sees life itself as the great mutable élan: the human world may end, but, as servants of the life force, we should regard this consummation with indifference. Even Wells, who had begun as a scientific optimist and ended by presenting no future for humanity, saw the vital torch handed to other creatures too wise to destroy their environment. Professor Wagar's visions do not perhaps range wide enough.

More than halfway through he gives us the meaning of his title:

> Terminal visions are not just stories about the end of the world, or the end of the self. They are also stories about the nature and meaning of reality as interpreted by world views. They are propaganda for a certain understanding of life, in which the imaginary end serves to sharpen the focus and heighten the importance of certain structures of value. They are games of chance, so to speak, in which the players risk all their chips on a single hand. But games just the same.

* By W. Warren Wagar, Indiana University Press, 1982.

In other words, test the *Weltanschauung* that happens to be in vogue by pushing it to the limit. Some world views have a theory of catastrophe, some don't. That of the Enlightenment did not, though the Marquis de Sade and Malthus had visions springing out of theories of sexuality which, by reason of the very atavism of their subject, had to admit catastrophe. After the Enlightened came the Romantics, who abandoned the steady-state model of reality drawn from mathematics and mechanics and thought, felt rather, in terms of volcanic changes, catastrophe for good or ill. They were succeeded by the followers of Comte and his doctrine of positivism. Without positivism there would have been no Mill, Darwin, Spencer, Engels or Marx and, in literature genuine or sub, no science fiction. Certainly no Jules Verne or H. G. Wells.

Since positivism is, except in socialist states and departments of sociology, generally discredited today, how is it that science fiction flourishes and by some writers, notably Ballard and Asimov, is regarded as the really significant imaginative florescence of our time? A cruel answer might be that practitioners of the form are hopelessly old-fashioned and do not see how the world has changed since 1914. Certainly, in respect of the techniques and insights of modernism, they cherish a peculiar blindness: there is not one S F writer whom we would read for the freshness or originality of his style. A writer who proclaims that subject matter is all, as most S F writers do, is clearly already admitting a rejection of modernism, but since modernism arose with a rejection of positivism this is probably in order. Now world catastrophe is one of the themes of science fiction, and yet science fiction is a child of positivism, which rejects catastrophe. We must leave it to Professor Wagar to resolve the anomaly.

Where there is a 'positivist terminal vision' the blame for world catastrophe is to be placed not on science but the abuse of science by people who do not understand science, or else on the blind forces of unscientific nature, which might include items like messianic Ludditism. But there is a post-positivist 'anti-intellectualism' or 'neo-Romanticism' or a new *Weltanschauung* which Professor Wagar, with misgivings, calls 'irrationalism'. This posits a new beginning after disaster, a system which rejects science and accepts superstition, primitive pastoralism, pragmatic cannibalism of technological debris. What both kinds of vision find impossible to accept is total and irreparable destruction, which is an extrapolation of the individual's inability to accept the death of consciousness. Sleep is in order, but death is only a kind of sleep. Nothing, thou elder brother e'en to shade, cannot be a conclusion for even the lowest order of literature.

It is the fact that Professor Wagar's survey covers only the lower order which makes one unwilling to grant too much importance to his theme. Frank Kermode saw, in his *The Sense of an Ending*, that what Professor Wagar calls the public endtime had to be 'radically immanentized . . . reduced merely to an individual's death or to a time of personal crisis or of waiting for crisis, a waiting for Godot.' That 'merely' is surely out of order. The end of the world is, alas, a very trivial theme. If Henry James had written a story about a group of people awaiting the end in an English country house, his concern with personal relations would have rendered the final catastrophe highly irrelevant, the mere blank part of the page after the end not of time but of the story. When Professor Wagar writes of Moxley's *Red Snow*, Southwold's *The Seventh Bowl*, Spitz's *La Guerre des Mouches*, Vidal's *Kalki*, Vonnegut's *Cat's Cradle*, George's *Dr Strangelove* (or *Red Alert*), Moore's *Greener than You Think*, Disch's *The Genocides* and Roshwald's *Level 7*, he is dealing with electronic games. The genuine crises that face us – the death of the topsoil, the population explosion, the chance of the wrong button being pressed – are not strictly material for fiction. Fiction is not about what happens to the world but what happens to a select group of human souls, with crisis or catastrophe as the mere pretext for an exquisitely painful probing, as in James, of personal agonies and elations. If books have to be written about the end of the world, they should be speculative as science and not as subliterary criticism.

And if H. G. Wells emerges in this survey as the only giant in a genre which he virtually invented, it is, almost in spite of himself, because he was interestingly ambiguous, which few of his successors are, and because he dealt in the minutiae of human experience. The man in *The War of the Worlds* who, facing the probable endtime, mourns the loss of tinned salmon with vinegar remains more memorable than the Martian death rays. Only very minor literature dares to aim at apocalypse.

Thoughts on the Present Discontents

When I was a soldier I was taught: 'If it moves, salute it; if it doesn't move, whitewash it.' Today's militant, if unsoldierly, extremists have a simpler philosophy: whether it moves or not, kidnap it. We have seen the kidnapping of a Goya, a Fellini film, the corpse of a great comedian, an Italian political leader. We are shocked, but perhaps some of the shock comes from awareness that we are not shocked enough. We have already imagined most conceivable outrages against law and decency, or had them imagined for us in drugstore bestsellers or films. We are more than ready for the kidnapping of the Pope. Our emotional response to the reality will be a mere carbon copy of what we felt when contemplating the idea or the fiction. We are overprepared, as we were for the moon landings.

Still, I am certain that, if Moro had been shot outright, like the members of his bodyguard, our outrage would have been even fainter. Since the assassination of Kennedy, we seem to have no more shock to register about the killing of a public man. We all shot our bolts in Dallas. The killing of the President's brother caught us with little fresh feeling to give: we were watching a PBS teleplay about the fall of the house of Atreus. Besides, there is a sense in which an assassination is less of an affront to morality than a kidnapping. The great man is knifed. Revenge is accomplished or unholy ambition thwarted. This is only a rerun of *Julius Caesar*, without the blank verse. Long live, for a time, Brutus. With kidnapping you have torment direct and referred – the waiting, the humiliation, the delivery of an earlobe, the blackmail which tempts us all to wish to compromise with justice and make a fool of the law. 'Free those undoubted, or figurative, criminals or we kill this figurative, or undoubted, one.' But once we give in, the law is finished for ever.

It is all too easy for one unworthy to be kidnapped to proffer lofty advice to those whose position puts them perpetually in danger. But I nevertheless counsel preparedness to die rather than put the law in jeopardy, to make willingness to be a sacrifice to the law a condition of rising to greatness. There is a price to be paid for the luxury of ambition. Consider a scenario. Hitler, Streicher, the whole Nazi gang have been captured by the Allies and await trial. Churchill, or Truman, is kidnapped by a clever Nazi rearguard. I need not go on: the plot is too obvious to merit commercial exploitation. The brutality of this view (here is suffering flesh and blood; the law is only an abstraction) is, however, less reprehensible than the assumption we have all started to make, and not just because of kidnappings – that law and order are already at an end. This belief – which we are often too scared to articulate – makes us at one with the kidnappers, rapists, torturers, vandals and murderers.

We all look back to a golden past when there was no kidnapping, skyjacking, mugging, raping, gratuitous street murder. Such a past never perhaps existed, but there was a time when New Yorkers could, on hot nights, sleep safely in Central Park, when citizens of all cities regarded it as a right to be able to walk the streets of an evening, when air travellers were not searched for weapons, when the safety of the great, and even the generality, did not shakily depend on bodyguards, armed janitors, closed-circuit television. There are various ways of explaining the breakdown of order, but all seem to rest on the twentieth-century realization that repression of the atavistic in ourselves was not divinely ordained and, anyway, was not necessarily a good thing. With the removal of sex taboos the way was open for the free expression of other, cognate, primitive urges. It is good to be sexually free; it is correspondingly good to be aggressive, intolerant, even murderous. Of course, certain inhibitions remain which move us to justify our atavistic urges in terms of myths or ideologies – Bakuninian anarchy, neo-Maoism, Palestinian liberation, what we will: they mostly add up to a mere vague blessing from the superego on the acts of the ego. We just want to have things our own way and to hell with oppression, suppression, repression.

And yet men spent slow centuries learning how to build societies which would function peaceably and happily with the minimum of punitive sanctions. That democratic government was, if not perfect, the system of rule which best balanced the claim of the citizen to be free and happy and the need for the State to maintain order took a long time to discover. Essentially democracy depends not on law and the law-enforcing arm of the State, but on the willingness of citizens to accept an unwritten contract – a contract between the rational and the atavistic in themselves. When democratic order, what the British call the Queen's Peace, has to depend on police repression of the antisocial aggressive, then democracy itself is impaired. The more draconian become the measures whereby kidnappers and skyjackers are kept under, the more the democratic State itself is moving towards an acceptance of the principles, or lack of them, which sustain crime.

The most conspicuous aspect of democratic order is the assumption that government, or certainly the making of laws, depends on the free dialectic of opposed political views. Britain, having learned in pain and effort the need for such dialectic, taught the principle to her colonies. Some colonies have been quick to unlearn it; their independence from the British yoke is marked by one-party rule enforced by police suppression of dissidence. The element of suppression has to exist in any State, but a democracy depends on a sophisticated citizenry that regards the suppression of intolerance as the duty of the individual soul. The duty is, or should be, a thing taught at one's father's knee, and the structure of the family gently enforces it. But Freud taught that the son had to fight the father, that the family was not an emblem of bigger order but the cast of a Greek tragedy. Transposing the liberation of the psyche to the social level, we have killed our neuroses and now live in a permissive world. But permissiveness turns out to be very naive, and the world today is in danger of being taken over by the naive. Many newly liberated peoples are astonished at how easy it 's to rule, or be ruled: all that is needed is a single party and a brutal police force. But rule was never meant to be easy.

Two great powers – Russia and China – and the new States that are their satellites or apes provide, for Red Brigades and other naive dissidents, a living witness to the validity of bloody revolution and subsequent one-party government. Shibboleths, half-baked doctrines based on Marx and Bakunin (who always contradicted each other) provide the pseudo-intellectual superstructure for such acts of aggression as the kidnapping of Moro. In a sense, we can do nothing about it except lessen the possibility – by the kind of anti-democratic surveillance of which all democrats are heartily tired – of its happening again. But we need more than armed guards, house-to-house searches and airport checks. What we all want is the freedom we have lost. We may not get it again for a long time, but we have to devise democratic means of getting it sooner or later. Otherwise we shall have to say to the Brigate Rosse, the Mafia, the neo-Bakuninians and the rest: you are justified in denying democratic order, since democratic order no longer exists.

We all have to be made more aware, through propaganda and education, of how flimsy the basis of democracy actually is: it rests on the free association of individual men and women who have learnt how to suppress intolerance and aggression. It rests, ideally, on all members of society being intelligent or at least having a notion, however primitive, of what democracy means. To keep hammering home the lesson – the task of anybody who cares, the duty of those who are in charge of the media of mass communication – is not an act of oppression: it is the administering of a prophylactic against oppression. We may even have to learn how to be a pre-Freudian society again.

I may seem to be offering a naive solution to the eruptions of violence which are the fruit of political naiveté. But I can see no alternative to reiterated insistence that the way of tolerance is the only one acceptable to human societies. Unfortunately, tolerance seems to mean tolerance of the intolerable – like political kidnapping – but it is a price that, for the moment, has to be paid: we know the alternative. Our democratic systems may not be working very well – indeed, look at Italy – but they are still preferable to anything the Red Brigades wish to instal. They will work better when the heads of the democratic families become more trustworthy fathers, not dithering uncles or bullying big brothers. And we ourselves must become better sons and daughters.

A Greene Trilogy

1 MONSIEUR GREENE OF ANTIBES

I don't know how many British novelists live on the Côte d'Azur these days, but I am certainly in the Condamine of Monaco and Graham Greene certainly, when he is not in Paris or Anacapri or on his remoter travels, lives on the Avenue Pasteur, Antibes. He is hospitable to fellow-novelists, and I see him less than, for the good of my soul, I should. I don't mean just the spiritual organ I cart occasionally to my confessor, as he his to his, though the theological authority of Greene's works of the imagination has led more than one troubled priest to go looking for him; I mean the sense of exaltation, or reassurance, or the sheer stimulation of communion with a superior artist.

This has been a dull winter for me. Torpor has kept me in bed till noon and driven me back to it after dinner. The waking patch of the day has been devoted to the hammering out of one thousand words of fiction. I have been lame with an excess of cholesterol (which Greene believes is a fiction, like phlogisten). To get to Antibes was like plotting a major campaign. I would get the dawn train, which meant I was awake for most of the night. I limped up the hill to the station, sprayed by the hoses of the darkling street cleaners, and started my pilgrimage. Stations of the Cross: Cap d'Ail, Eze, Beaulieu-sur-Mer, Nice, St Laurent-du-Var, Cros-de-Cagnes, Cagnes-sur-Mer, Villeneuve-Loubet, Biot. Antibes is quiet at this season, though its harbour is full of small shipping. The sun is bright and mild, the air liked chilled Pouilly-Fumé. Greene's apartment is a hundred metres up the hill. I have, blast this left leg, to take a taxi.

Greene is on the fourth floor. His balcony overlooks the crammed shipping (like teeth so close set you couldn't twang dental floss between them). In summer the noise of motor traffic is as loud for him as for me. The days of authorial seclusion, Maugham and the Villa Mauresque, are long over. Writers live in small flats and hope to have a daily help. The best décor in the world, which you can't get in London or Paris, is marine sunlight. Greene looks well in it. Seventy-five years old, he is lean, straight, active. The blue eyes are startling, especially in all this light. We are to talk about his work, especially his new novella, *Doctor Fischer of Geneva*.

A.B. Graham, you've practised all the literary forms – verse, drama, the novel, the short story, the essay, even biography. Speaking as one who started his artistic career as a musician and took to literature fairly late, I wonder if you ever wanted to practise any other art.
G.G. I'm tone deaf. I can't draw or paint. I've worked in the cinema, of course – as critic, scriptwriter, even in the cutting room – that was

when I was a co-producer. All my novels have been filmed, with one exception – *It's a Battlefield*. Ironically, that was the one book I wrote with the intention of adaptation to the screen.

A.B. *Doctor Fischer* cries out to be filmed, doesn't it? It's short, so no director is going to want to cut it. There's a fine scenic background – winter Switzerland – and a climax, an elaborate dinner party in the snow with great bonfires, which you must have seen as film even while you were writing it.

G.G. Well, yes, the preliminaries to filming it are already under way. I suppose you could say that, just as landscape painting was behind Sir Walter Scott, film is behind or before me. It's the great visual art of our day, and it's bound to influence the novelist.

A.B. With all except one of your novels filmed, and several short stories, you're exemplary as the filmable novelist. How many of the films do you find satisfactory – I mean, as saying in dialogue and image exactly what you've already said to the reader's imagination?

G.G. *The Third Man* certainly works, but of course I wrote that as a film – having first done a kind of literary treatment which reads well enough as a story in its own right. I saw *The Third Man* again recently in Paris. There's a whole new generation discovering it. Yes, it still works. *The Fallen Idol* too. I'm not happy about a good number of the others. Endings get changed. *Travels with My Aunt* stops before the story I wrote really gets started. When *The Heart of the Matter* was filmed we weren't allowed to show a suicide on the screen. That ruined the whole point – self-elected damnation on the part of Scobie. Seeing a preview of *The Human Factor* just recently, I was disappointed that so much of the book just couldn't find a correlative in cinematic images.

A.B. Without having seen it, I'd say right away that it wasn't possible to deal with Buller, the boxer dog, who needs the devices of literary description to turn him into a character –

G.G. Both Kim Philby and Harold Acton said that they liked Buller better than anyone.

A.B. No wonder. Buller licks his testicles with the juicy noise of an alderman drinking soup. He leaves trails of spittle on the bed like a bonbon. You can't film the phraseology. I'd say also that you can't translate that bit about the alderman into another language. We make literature out of our own traditions as well as our own language. Which brings me to the Graham Greene style, which is wholly a matter of words. What is it that's peculiary Greeneish in the way you use words?

G.G. I started off with the desire to use language experimentally. Then I saw that the right way was the way of simplicity. Straight sentences, no involutions, no ambiguities. Not much description, description isn't my line. Get on with the story. Present the outside world economically and exactly.

A.B. You're a strongly visual writer. I mean, I see things clearly when I read your work. I don't feel that the vision had to be fulfilled in cinema adaptation – which is what people usually mean when they talk about 'visual possibilities' in a story. The cinema images are redundant. It's all in the book.

G.G. You think that? I think there are solidities – I mean I try to be accurate. Then someone comes along and says that boxers don't salivate like Buller. Or (it was you who said this) there are no carrots in Lancashire hotpot. Or there isn't an ABC on the Strand.

A.B. I see you have a volume of Borges here, the man who kindly calls himself the Argentine Burgess. He seems to think a fiction writer ought to be able to make the external world out of his head and then, if he wishes, just make it collapse into nothing.

G.G. Yet Borges is devoted to the very writers I admire so much. Chesterton, for instance, and Stevenson. I was walking on a crowded street with him in Buenos Aires. Totally blind, he was clinging to my arm. I mentioned Stevenson's best poem and he stopped, in all that roar of the traffic, and recited it from beginning to end.

A.B. If Borges had written your new book, or Nabokov for that matter, the critics would start wondering why its hero has an artificial hand.

G.G. The best answer would be because he lost his real hand in the London Blitz, which he did. The artificial hand's there so that the ghastly Dr Fischer can insult him by referring to a 'deformity'. Also to stimulate the reader's imagination, make him wonder about the problems of making love with a false hand. But there's no deep symbolism – or if there is, it's not my job to find it. Critics and university professors rejoice in the *sous-texte* these days. The study of fiction has become less the study of the narrative art than a search for arcane meanings. Take *The Third Man*. One distinguished critic looked for arboreal significance in the names Harry Lime and Holly Martins. Now the original name of Martins was Rollo, which the actor Joseph Cotten wouldn't accept. If Lime has a connotation it's to do with quicklime, the disposal of bodies. No, it's dangerous to dig too deep. I try to be a straight writer.

A.B. A highly readable one – not like Joyce or Faulkner. I approach your books in two ways. I swallow a new Greene novel whole, with great speed. Then I slow down for a second reading and taste it. Then three months later go back to it for the various aftertastes I've missed.

G.G. I'm happy to think that I'm read that way. The more I think of it, the more I worry about this division of literature into the great because hard to read, the not so great – or certainly the ignorable by scholars – because of the desire to divert, be readable, keep it plain. You don't find Conan Doyle dealt with at length in the literary histories. Yet he was a great writer. He created several great characters –

A.B. Eliot admired him but didn't think him worthy of a critical essay – not like Wilkie Collins. And yet Eliot lifted a whole chunk of *The Musgrave Ritual* –

G.G. Where?

A.B. In *Murder in the Cathedral*. You remember – 'Whose was it?' – 'His who is gone.' – 'Who shall have it?' – 'He who will come.' 'What shall be the month?' And so on. In the Sherlock Holmes story we have 'Whose was it?' - 'His who is gone.' - 'Who shall have it?' - 'He who will come.' - 'What was the month?' Almost identical.

G.G. Something ought to be done about this double standard. I admire writers like Stanley Weyman. Victor Pritchett had the nerve to write about Rider Haggard after reading only two of his books. Haggard has to be read entire. H. G. Wells too. I've been seeking out the novels of the so-called middle period in old bookshops and I find them remarkable. There's also Bulwer Lytton. His *Pelham* deals with an illicit love affair in a throughly contemporary way.

A.B. Why not write a book, or certainly an essay, on the literary snobbism which prefers symbols and ambiguities to the straight art of story-telling?

G.G. I leave that to you.

A.B. In the same way, Eliot admired *My Fair Lady* but wouldn't take it with the right literary seriousness. Otherwise he wouldn't have accepted lines like 'I'd be equally as willing for a dentist to be drilling than to ever let a woman in my life.' Only Auden took Lorenz Hart seriously.

G.G. He wrote songs with Richard Rodgers, didn't he? I met Rodgers and Hammerstein when they were doing a stage adaptation of *The Heart of the Matter* -

A.B. Not a musical, for God's sake?

G.G. No, a very bad straight adaptation. I may not be musical but I've written popular songs. I like to put them in my novels, as you know. Now some of them have been set to music. They're broadcasting three of them on French radio.

A.B. Write the book of a musical and I'll be happy to do the music.

G.G. Oh, I had this idea of a musical in which a band of girls steal chasubles and croziers at an episcopal conference and then get themselves up as bishops before the Archbishop of Melbourne arrives. Melbourne falls in love with Canterbury. There's a good telephone song there - 'Cantuar calling Melbourne'.

A.B. Do it, please. Auden, who took Hart seriously, was responsible for the lines

Is this a milieu where I must
How grahamgreeneish! How infra dig!
Snatch from the bottle in my bag
An analeptic swig?

He's referring to a college where he's going to give a lecture, and there may be nothing to drink. Why should the analeptic swig be grahamgreeneish?

G.G. I don't think he means my drinking habits. I can take alcohol - a couple of Scotches or dry martinis and a bottle of wine a day. My liver was vaccinated against cirrhosis by my undergraduate thirst. No, grahamgreeneish seems to refer to a particular kind of fictional character I've created - white men going to seed in outlandish places. Unshaven, guilt-ridden, on the bottle. One word I seem to be associated with is *seedy* – characters I mean, not myself. It's not a happy term, a bit vague. There are such people. But they seem to have become, in their transference to my fiction, symbols of something. Of mankind after the fall, perhaps.

A.B. Would it be right to say that your novels were the first fiction in English to present evil as something palpable – not a theological abstraction but an entity symbolized in glass-rings on the brothel table, joyless sex, dental caries (Mexico in *The Power and the Glory*), hopeless and empty men in exile?

G.G. Evil's in Hitler, not in dental caries. I see we're getting on to myself as a Catholic novelist. I'm not that: I'm a novelist who happens to be a Catholic. The theme of human beings lonely without God is a legitimate fictional subject. To want to deal with the theme doesn't make me a theologian. Superficial readers say that I'm fascinated by damnation. But nobody in my books is damned – not even Pinky in *Brighton Rock*. Scobie in *The Heart of the Matter* tries to damn himself, but the possibility of his salvation is left open. The priest's final words are that nobody, not even the Church, knows enough about divine love and judgement to be sure that anyone's in hell.

A.B. Last time we met you said you no longer believe in hell. And then Pope John Paul II, before going off for the summer to Castel Gandolfo, reaffirmed the doctrine. You've got to believe in hell as you've got to believe in the resurrection of the body.

G.G. I've no difficulty in accepting the idea of the transfigured flesh. As for hell, God's love goes on getting in the way of God's justice. Hell may be necessary, but I don't think there's anybody in it. Like a seaside hydro out of season. Purgatory I begin to understand more and more – progressive purification, the divine vision getting nearer and nearer.

A.B. I'm a cradle Catholic – ridiculous phrase; who invented it? – and you're a convert. Do you see much difference between the two kinds of believers?

G.G. Very little. Since Pope John, converts and cradle Catholics – ridiculous phrase; who invented it? – have had to grow accustomed equally to a new kind of Church. Converts can be rigorous, of course. Evelyn Waugh showed great theological rigour when attacking some of my earlier work.

A.B. I admired him greatly, but he scared me. I wanted to visit him but never dared. The daughter of his I met in America said he was approachable, no monster. I remain scared even of his shade. If he had a son I suppose I'd be scared of him too.

G.G. He had a son.

A.B. I never knew that. What do you think of the present state of the novel in English?

G.G. Beryl Bainbridge is very good. Muriel Spark too, of course. I used to be able to read Frank Tuohy. And William Golding. R.K. Narayan I still love.

A.B. Don't you find the British novel parochial?

G.G. There was a time, in the nineteenth century of course, when it could be both parochial and universal. Not now perhaps. I don't read much American fiction. Bellow? I liked *Henderson the Rain King* – a remarkable picture of Africa for a man who'd never been there. John Updike, no. The Southerners, no. Faulkner is very convoluted. Patrick White? I liked *Voss*.

A.B. Both Bellow and White got the Nobel Prize. When are you going to get it?

G.G. Yes, I was asked that question in Stockholm. How would you like the Nobel Prize? I said I look forward to getting a bigger prize than that.

A.B. Which one?

G.G. Death. Let's go and eat lunch. As you can't walk far with that leg we'd better go to La Marguerite, just round the corner. It's terrible, but it's near.

It was not, in fact, terrible, but it was the parodic *haute cuisine* at its most vulgar – the thick floury sauces that Escoffier condemned, the *faux-filets* toughish and swimming in an unnecessary goo, the *glaces* vulgarly crowned with *Chantilly*. But the cocktails and burgundy and armagnac and calvados were all right.

A.B. I like things plain. I prefer to eat over the border, in Ventimiglia. I miss English pub food.

G.G. I miss English sausages. I don't like them all meat, on French lines. I like a bit of bread in them.

A.B. I've been tempted to fly to Heathrow just to pick up sausages and then fly back again. Which reminds me – back again to Dr Fischer and his banger party. Here you have a man who loves to humiliate and finds his humiliands among the greedy, who will even eat cold porridge for dinner for the sake of the munificent presents they get afterwards. Who are prepared, at the end, to play a kind of Russian roulette with Christmas crackers. One contains a bomb which explodes on pulling. The others have cheques for two million Swiss francs. Fischer is misanthropic and cruel. Is he also evil?

G.G. No, he's just a very sad man. The big Catholic verities like good and evil – you won't find these in my later work.

A.B. I find compassion.

G.G. Yes, I think you're meant to. We're the last. We'd better leave. Can you walk as far as the station?

A.B. With the help of my stick.

G.G. That stick makes you look venerable. (*With glee*) See, the patron shook your hand, but not mine. He's impressed by your venerability. You look venerable, Anthony.

A.B. (*sourly, in pain*) And you still have something of the look (Jesus Christ, my leg's going into spasm) of the (God help me) the (blast the bloody thing) juvenile delinquent.

G.G. Yes, yes. Yes, something of that. The station's just there, see. If you miss your train, come back to the flat. We can talk more about God and literature and so forth.

A.B. The horror, the horror.

G.G. The juvenile delinquent, yes.

2 HOW TO DEFECT

The Human Factor, by Graham Greene

Our defectors of Moscow have become an established mythology, to be exploited not only by biographers and social historians but by inquirers into the semantics of 'treason' and the morality of a nation, a class and a generation. Graham Greene, an Englishman and an Oxonian of the age group of Maclean, my namesake, and other sputniks from the fringe of the British ruling class, was perhaps bound sooner or later to make a fictional study of a defector, and this book is it. Let me say at once that *The Human Factor* is as fine a novel as he has ever written – concise, ironic, acutely observant of contemporary life, funny, shocking, above all compassionate.

The Secret Service he presents is the one we have already met in *Our Man in Havana*. C, who runs it, is not the glass-eyed C to whom Wormold sent drawings of secret weapons that were really vacuum cleaners, but that C is well remembered by older members of the firm. When Maurice Castle, reliable, dull, and past retiring age, buys two copies of *Clarissa Harlowe* or *War and Peace*, we suspect that he is using book-codes for transmitting secret messages. As he buys the books himself, and does not have them issued by SIS, we must suppose that he is acting as a double agent. This is not a thriller, with an unexpected final disclosure, the good guy turning out bad. The very title warns us of the roots of Castle's treason, and the epigraph from Conrad spells it all out: 'I only know that he who forms a tie is lost. The germ of corruption has entered into his soul.' How good, by the way, Greene's epigraphs have always been.

Castle hardly at all fulfils the Oxford traitor paradigm. He has taken a third in History at what Oxonians call the House, but he has displayed no epicene glamour and shown no leaning to either Catholicism or Communism. That a Catholic can become a Communist more easily than an Anglican can has already been demonstrated in *The Comedians*, and Greene's own observations on the detestability of American consumerism and the goodness of Fidel Castro indicate his own, rather passive, sympathies. But this novel is not about faith, either political or religious. Readers who expect theology will be disappointed, or relieved. A Catholic priest makes a mandatory entrance – someone Castle tries to talk to – but he is a brief thumbnail horror. Castle has neither belief nor doubt: he merely loves his wife and son, and it is human loyalty that sends him over the wall.

Sarah, his wife, is a black African, and the boy Sam is her child by another black African, believed dead. Castle loves the child, in a Greenean paradox, because he is *not* his own flesh and blood. In another sense, though, he is, since Castle, after service in South Africa, has made himself an honorary black. He got Sarah out of South Africa with the help of a Communist who was a kind of saint, and certainly a martyr, like Dr Magiot in *The Comedians*, and his passing on of secret information to the Communists is the payment of a debt. When he learns of the plan called Uncle Remus (African gold, tactical atomic weapons, the wicked Americans, his former investigator and Sarah's oppressor Cornelius Muller now an official friend) our sympathies are all with the dull quiet traitor of King's Road, Berkhamsted.

A leak occurs in his subsection, and the suspect, his harmless colleague, is killed by his own masters, English sporting gentlemen, members of the Reform and the Travellers'. If there is no overt Catholic eschatology here, there are various hells. Castle ends up in Moscow. Sarah and Sam stay in England – a hell of British niceness for the one, of British savagery for the other. The men who do their duty are in the deeper hell of their own innocence, and Muller, who expects to go to an apartheid heaven, is in the deepest hell of all. If you want full-flavoured Greene you have to have hell.

For those who don't merit hell there has to be a nasty quietus. Castle's colleague Davis, whose only crimes are to like port and to be in hopeless love with his secretary, is poisoned with *aspergillus flavus*, the mould on bad peanuts, and has a week to die. Castle's boxer dog Buller has to be shot before his master can make his getaway, and the job is done messily. Buller is a major character in the story, though he does nothing except dribble tributes of spittle on the trousers of strangers and kill cats. There is so much affectionate expenditure of Greene wit on Buller that we know he has to die – like the dachshund Max in *Our Man in Havana*. Buller licks his genitals 'with the gusto of an alderman drinking soup'. As he drops his *crotte* (Greene lives in Antibes), 'the eyes stared ahead, inward-looking. Only on these sanitary occasions did Buller seem a dog of intelligence.'

The novel is full of the kind of jolting apophthegm we expect from Greene, and the bizarre yoking of the banal and the profound which confers moral significance on the inert and ordinary. 'The depth of their love was as secret as the quadruple measure of whisky. To speak of it to others would invite danger. Love was a total risk.' Again, 'A prejudice had something in common with an ideal.' South African gold is not immune from the corruption of bad men. Captain Van Donck, of the South African Security Police, polishes his gold ring with a finger 'as though it were a gun which had to be kept well oiled. In this country you couldn't escape gold. It was in the dust of the cities, artists used it as a paint, it would be quite natural for the police to use it for beating in a man's face.' The trout fishing of Dr Percival, who kills Davis, becomes as sinister as the snow of Moscow – 'a merciless, interminable, annihilating snow, a snow in which one could expect the world to end'. There is no neutral property in the Greene scene. I cannot even return to Brighton without thinking of Pinky.

This capacity to change experience for us is the mark of the major artist. I shall be unhappy if *The Human Factor* is mentioned in the same breath as Mr Le Carré's best-selling deadweights. Greene's book is about people and love and loyalty, not just about spies and Secret Service bureaux. Every character invites sympathy, even identification. *The Honourable Schoolboy* has no character that is not either dull or unlovable. But, if we accept the Secret Service novel as a genre, Greene must be acknowledged its master. He is too big, however, to be approached in terms of genre. Unless, that is, *Hamlet* is a murder mystery and *Lord Jim* a rattling good yarn of the sea.

3 HIDALGO INGENIOSO

Monsignor Quixote, by Graham Greene

When Mr Greene's new novel is adapted to the screen it will hardly be distinguishable from one of those *Don Camillo* films which, because Fernandel is in them, regularly turn up on French television. There is a simple village priest, bizarrely promoted to monsignore because of acts of corporal charity to a visiting bishop, and there is a communist mayor, or ex-mayor. The innocence of the priest gets him into trouble, and the ex-mayor becomes his protector. The two men amiably wrangle about their respective faiths, the ex-mayor finding a Marxist moral in the parable of the prodigal son and the priest discovering a certain spirituality in the *Communist Manifesto*. Much of the dialectic between these two, as they munch cheese and chorizo and swill wine under a cork tree, is predictable and entertaining. They have adventures on the roads of Spain, not on the huge picaresque scale of Cervantes but diverting enough. Why, I wish to know, does Mr Greene bring Cervantes into the story?

His Monsignor Quixote is descended from the mad hidalgo, and the ex-mayor's name is Zancas, which is what Sancho Panza was originally called. Monsignor Quixote's old car, a Seat 600, is inevitably nicknamed Rocinante. The fancy is harmless enough, prompting speculations about reality and fiction. We may all be, as our priestly hero puts it, fictions in the mind of God, and hence it is in order to regard the knight of the woeful countenance as a personage real enough to breed descendants. But since no filmgoer or TV gawper is likely to know anything about Don Quixote, save perhaps as a bearded incarnation of Peter O'Toole warbling 'Impossible Dream', no scenarist is likely to transfer the Cervantes element to the screen, and, indeed, Mr Greene's little novel could discard its quixotry without great loss. I ask again: why did he put it in?

For it harms his book to remind his readers of the great comic epic which lies behind it, and the ponderous attempts to find parallels between the adventures of one Quixote and the other are productive of no great enlightenment. True, Monsignor Quixote's Christianity is as outmoded in our age as was Don Quixote's chivalry in his, and to tussle with the computerized Guardia is a kind of tilting at windmills. When priest and ex-mayor take to the road in Rocinante (a little holiday pending transfer, since a monsignore cannot be permitted to rule over a mere parish), holy innocence confronts a fallen world and has to be judged by that world – Monsignor Quixote's bishop is a fair stupid unimaginative hypocritical representative of it – and there the parallel ends.

The holy innocence, our age being what it is, most typically manifests itself in sexual naiveté. Monsignor Quixote spends a night in a Salamanca brothel and considers it a most charming hotel. He takes one of Sancho's condoms and blows it up like a balloon. He inadvertently goes to a pornographic film – misled by the title, *A Maiden's Prayer* – and finds it very amusing. His innocence is taken by the Guardia to be a kind of criminality (he hides a robber in the boot of Rocinante), and by his bishop a kind of irresponsible madness. He is brought home, locked in his room and suspended from priestly duties. But, like his ancestral namesake, he escapes for a second bout of adventures.

In Galicia, Monsignor Quixote and his Sancho meet a community of Spaniards repatriated from Mexico, men who worship money and buy their way into carrying the processional statue of the Virgin Mary. This statue is covered with thousand-peseta notes, and Monsignor Quixote protests at the simony. He causes a riot to which his anti-capitalistic Sancho cannot be unsympathetic, and he is injured by the Guardia. Ill, he finds refuge in a Trappist monastery. Deliriously somnabulistic, he says mass in Latin and consecrates sheer nothingness (can this, Berkeleyianly, be taken as bread and wine?). Sancho, to humour him, takes the nonexistent wafer on his tongue. Our mad Christian knight dies and Sancho wonders, perhaps implausibly, at the fact that hate can die with its object (his own hatred of Franco has died) but that love, since it is always directed at the spirit, can live on. The new Don Quixote lives on posthumously as does the old. The immortality of the soul is, in a sense, attested by the immortality of fictional characters.

Mr Greene will be the first to admit that he finds it hard to avoid sentimental endings. This here, compared with Cervantes's sternly comic death scene, is something of an embarrassment. It provokes no healthy tears, whereas Cervantes never fails – even in his transmogrification into a Strauss symphonic poem – to open the cathartic floodgates.

The virtue of the little book lies less in what happens than what is said. Mr Greene has done his theological homework, and his citations from the fathers of both Christian orthodoxy and Marxist heresy are apt and, as his intention, sometimes dramatically surprising. We have all forgotten that Marx had a burning nostalgia for the Middle Ages, condemned the Henrican dissolution of the monasteries and deplored the death, under capitalism, of the free life of the spirit. We have also forgotten that St Augustine was capable of scabrous humour (musical farts in *Civitas Dei*). The parallels between the Christian and communist ideals are well worked out in fascinating dialectic, but Mr Greene's whimsical intentions do not accommodate any profundities about the mystery of evil: he is much more interested in the morality of coitus interruptus (permissible on the unannounced entry, into the room that is, of a third party). His Don Quixote and Sancho Panza alike are committed to a kind of optimism: some day true Communism will come; some day the word of the Lord will prevail.

This is the second novel of Mr Greene's which presents a priest as a hero. The first, now forty-odd years old, was *The Power and the Glory* and dealt with the tribulations of a whisky-priest in atheistical Mexico (Monsignor Quixote makes reference to a priestly second cousin in that country). Mr Greene has come a long way since that novel in the direction of tolerance, and he is now prepared to find good in godless Communism, if not in godless (literally, inevitably) teetotalitarianism. There is no hopeless searching for wine in *Monsignor Quixote*; the book is flooded with it. It was for wine that Mr Greene put down his roots in France. In France he has, recently, been his own Don Quixote. He may in old age be ceasing to care about the novel but he continues to care about justice and humanity and the memorable trope. 'So many of his prayers had remained unanswered that he had hopes that this one prayer of his had lodged all the time like wax in the Eternal ear.' That is good Greene.

Christography

The Foreigner: A Search for the First Century Jesus, by Desmond Stewart

Desmond Stewart's recent death was untimely. He was only fifty-seven and he had much still to do, in fiction as well as in Middle Eastern scholarship. His biographies of Theodor Herzl and T. E. Lawrence were both remarkable, and this final essay in Christography, whose proofs he lived just long enough to correct, is learned, daring and compulsively readable. One would have loved to argue out some of the more blazing audacities with him, but those who read the book – and I hope they will be many – must, alas, be content to argue among themselves.

Stewart calls Jesus Christ 'the foreigner' because he believes he was brought up in Egypt, probably Alexandria, and, under the necessary guise of an explicator of the Torah, took to Galilee and subsequently Judea an exotic doctrine strongly opposed to the faith of the Hebrews. That Jesus, with his mother and fosterfather, fled into Egypt to escape the slaughter of childermas is what most Christians are prepared to take or leave: it is a mere decoration on the essential biography. Nowadays few will accept the historicity of either the mass infanticide or the imperial census which brought Joseph and Mary to Bethlehem. If the holy pair went to Egypt at all, it would be straight from Nazareth. Joseph knew his betrothed was pregnant and, being a humane man who had no love of the strict Mosaic law, wished to get her out of a narrow community given to scandal and stone-throwing. There was a large and cultivated Jewish population in Alexandria, Hellenized out of a ghetto mentality. Joseph was no mere carpenter. The Aramaic *naggar* means literally that, but it has also connotations of skill, learning and wealth. A trip to Alexandria could be doubly convenient – a matter of business as well as a salvatory act.

Whether Jesus was conceived by parthenogenesis, or was the illegitimate son of a soldier named Tiberius Julius Abdes Pantera (a belief the Nazis held, since it half-Aryanized the Saviour), there is no doubt that he is the first great man in history to bear a metronymic – not Jesus bar-Joseph but Jesus Son of Mary (or Miriam). Free of the Oedipal guilt which lies heavily on Hebraism, Islam, and the Puritanical perversions of the faith he himself taught, Jesus was able to preach more love than original sin. He had no Pharisaic inhibitions. He was able to elevate woman – lowly and unclean in Jewish tradition – to a status shocking to the Sanhedrin, and it was wholly typical of the risen Christ that he should appear first to a reformed prostitute. Blessed by a tolerant Egyptian Hellenism, he was able to absorb elements of wholesome sun worship. It is possible, thinks Stewart, that his last words on the cross were not *Eli, eli, lama sabacthani* but *Elie, elie*. . . . This is the vocative of *helios* in its demotic unaspirated form. He was calling on the sun.

This sounds like paganism, but *helios* can be taken as a metaphor of the ultimate light-giver. Certainly the God whom Christ worshipped was not the Yahweh of the Hebrews. He is closer to the Egyptian Rê, sweetened into total benevolence by Hellenic Alexandria, and standing at the opposed pole to the jealous, blood-loving, unpredictable, always fearsome deity of the tribes of Israel. The tempter whom Christ encounters in the desert is closer to this God than to the horned *diabolos* of medieval fancy. The Paternoster addresses *our* father, not theirs. Christ makes no claim to Jewish messiahship. He came to the Jews bearing a Greek name – probably Chrestos, meaning good, gentle, and not Christos, meaning the anointed one. He should have called himself

Joshua, but Iesous denoted the Hellenic bringer of a new religion.

His parables, notes Stewart, are essentially those of a foreigner. The tale of the Prodigal Son tells of famine in the land – more likely in Egypt than in Israel – and of pig-keeping, anathema to the Jews. There are allegories about absentee landlords and land agents, pointing perhaps to his fosterfather's concern with property in Galilee which he could not well look after from Alexandria. The miracles are of an Egyptian order. The raising of Lazarus (the friend of some probable wealth whose name Jesus ironically bestows on the beggar whose sores the dogs lick) may be less a miracle than an exercise in ritual necromancy. Whatever it was, it was the alleged magic with which the Sanhedrin sought to secure his condemnation by Rome, whose laws were as opposed to its practice as were those of the Jews.

Stewart denies the Resurrection as pious Christians know it. He thinks it possible that Christ's corpse was burned on the rubbish dump outside Jerusalem known as Gehenna – a name whose signification has been expanded into the hell that Pope John Paul II refuses to have humanized out of existence. The story of Christ harrowing hell may be an heroic distortion of his being cast into the smaller inferno of an incinerator. If the body was not to be found, here is a plausible explanation. If he appeared to many after death (about five hundred, says St Paul), it may have been in the manner of any other revenant. We have all had the experience of the dead returning – in dreams, shadows, noises in the kitchen, our name's being called (Dr Johnson's dead mother woke him up crying 'Sam!') – and a personality as powerful as that of Jesus was not easy to expunge from the living world. Needless to say, such suppositions will not be acceptable to orthodox Christians, but I doubt if many would deny to Stewart the right to speculate. Even St Thomas Aquinas had to begin his *Summa* by speculating that God did not exist.

This is a book shocking, stimulating, finally heartening. Of the earth-shaking importance of the Christian message Stewart has no doubt, nor of the superhuman stature of the intellect and sensibility that delivered it. The Middle East which Stewart lived in for so long is alive on the page. His familiarity with its climate alone bids him reject the spring death and resurrection of Jesus. Why blast a fig tree that nature has not yet permitted to produce its summer fruit? The young man who leaves his single garment behind in the hands of the police in Gethsemane was clad for high summer. To follow reason is no heresy; Christ was crucified in great heat.

We are informed but also moved. Stewart ends: 'As history proceeds down its highway of crime, Jesus points upward to a knowledge which frees the self. In the darkest night he is hidden, not extinguished. To each generation he speaks in glittering fragments. Every morning, like Helios, he is born again.' These are the tones of a believer.

Sang Réal

The Holy Blood and the Holy Grail, by Michael Baigent, Richard Leigh and Henry Lincoln

The following is, roughly and briefly, the argument of this book. The Knights Templar were founded as the military and executive arm of a secret organization known as the Prieuré de Sion. Though the Knights were disbanded between 1307 and 1314, after charges of heterodoxy, corruption and sexual irregularities had been made to stick, the Prieuré de Sion has continued quietly to function as an organization whose aim is to restore the Merovingian dynasty to France and to other European countries besides. This dynasty claims divine right of rule on the grounds that the widow and offspring of Jesus Christ left Palestine after his crucifixion, settled in the South of France, and sustained their lineage through intermarriage with the royal house of the Franks, thus engendering the Merovingian dynasty. In AD 496 the Church of Rome made a pact with the Merovingians, guaranteeing the perpetuation of their rule, but eventually broke the pact when it colluded in the assassination of Dagobert. The Carolingian usurpation sought legitimacy through marriage into the deposed house, but the true survival of the line, and the fulfilment of one of its aims, was ensured by the descendants of Dagobert, one of whom was Godfroi de Bouillon, who, taking Jerusalem in 1099, regained the heritage conferred by the Old Testament on the House of David.

The authors offer some things as historical fact, others as legitimate speculation. That Christ married and had children is a thesis that Christians may reasonably reject only on lack of evidence: there is no blasphemy in the image of Christ as a married man. The writers of this work are prepared, which few others would be, to name his bride. She was, they think, the Magdalene, no virgin, far from it, but the true Notre Dame of the Gothic cathedrals – 'those majestic stone replicas of the womb . . . shrines to Jesus's consort, rather than to his mother'. She was the grail, or vessel of Christ's blood. Alternatively, there was no grail: the *sangraal* is the *sang royal*: the title of the book is a pleonasm.

The fact of the Prieuré's continuing existence is vouched for by certain *Dossiers Secrets*, ascribed to Henri Lobineau, a man of very obscure identity whose name, indeed, may be that of a Paris street. These contain a list of Grand Masters, among whom are Robert Boyle, Isaac Newton, Victor Hugo, Claude Debussy and Jean Cocteau. Our authors find a plausible liaison between the father of gravity and the Languedocian Camisards, Gnostics and neo-Cathars suppressed by Rome and looking for refuge in Restoration London. They, presumably, passed the Merovingian secret on to the greatest thinker, and occultist of the day. Of Cocteau our authors say 'A most unlikely candidate', and one agrees at once. Drugtaker, pederast, minor poet, collaborator – what has he to do with the blood of Christ? We are asked to consider the occult symbolism of *Orphée* and *The Eagle Has Two Heads* and examine the Rosicrucian décor of the church of Notre Dame de France, just off Leicester Square, all Cocteau's work. There is another church in Villefranche, a few kilometres from where I write, which has the same weird Crucifixion. As for Debussy – well, he was tied up with occultists, meaning men like Mallarmé and the author of *Axel*. But the authors are wrong in thinking that he proposed an opera on *Axel* which his death in 1918 frustrated. He composed one scene in 1888 and then suppressed it. He did not 'set' *L'Après-Midi d'un Faun* [*sic*] by the 'enigmatic magus of French symbolist poetry': he merely evoked its mood in an orchestral prelude. Too many of the reasons adduced to justify qualification for Grand Mastership are impressionistic. The authors seem to want to believe.

All the Grand Masters took the name John, and Cocteau appears as Jean XXIII. Cardinal Roncalli, assuming the pontificate during Cocteau's seigneury, also took the name John XXIII – name and number of an antipope who abdicated in 1415, hence flavoured with anathema. Why? Was Roncalli really a member of the Rose-Croix, concerned with having an identity of name and ordinal in both the Vatican and the Prieuré? He revised the Church's attitude to secret societies, lifting the ban on Freemasonry. This meant, presumably, that there was no harm in helping along the benign Merovingian conspiracy. He stressed, in an apostolic letter of 1960, the redemptive powers of Christ's blood and this, think the authors, rendered otiose a belief in his resurrection. There are some dangerous things embedded in this book, and here is one of them.

The whole business – the 'quest', as they term it – began when Mr Lincoln, in 1972, made a BBC television film about Bérenger Saunière, curé of Rennes-le-Château in the Pyrenees, and his mysterious wealth. This area is Knights Templar country, with a church devoted to Mary Magdalene that, so Saunière discovered, had coded messages hidden under its altar stone. One of them said: A DAGOBERT II ROI ET A SION EST CE TRESOR ET IL EST LA MORT. Was Saunière's suddenly acquired wealth the treasure referred to? With the young American novelist Richard Leigh and the New Zealand psychologist Michael Baigent – who came to England to do research on the Knights Templar – Henry Lincoln got down to the inquiries which resulted in this book. It will seem to some a crackpot enterprise, but these young men are no fools: they have learning, energy, enthusiasm tempered by scepticism. If their material had been presented in a blockbuster novel like Irving Wallace's *The Word*, or cooled into a structuralist game, it might have been easier to take. One needs a lateral approach; facing the findings head on is embarrassing.

For what is the authors' conclusion? We're hungry for belief, but we don't want either a Führer or a Billy Graham, rather 'a species of wise and benign spiritual figure, a "priest–king" in whom mankind can safely repose its trust. . . . Such an atmosphere would seem eminently conducive to the Prieuré de Sion's objectives. . . . How might the advent of Jesus's lineal descendant be interpreted? To a receptive audience, it might be a kind of Second Coming.' So we await the banners of the rearisen Merovingian line, the new knights, or, as in Iran, the consuming fire of a Christian ayatollah with the Redeemer's blood in his arteries. It is typical of my unregenerable soul that I can only see this as a marvellous theme for a novel. Perhaps Irving Wallace or Morris West is already writing it.

Telejesus (or Mediachrist)

The notion of making a six-hour television film on the life of Jesus Christ was proposed by an ennobled British Jew, with the golden blessing of an American automobile corporation. The project struck some as blasphemous, others as ecumenical. Lord Grade, who was then merely Sir Lew Grade, presided over a massive press conference in the Holy City (viz. the one that crucified St Peter upside down before making him pope) and said all that was available to be said – namely, that there would be this film, that Franco Zeffirelli would direct it, and that Anthony Burgess would write it. Fired by this announcement, the Romans laid on a great, as it were, First Supper, which the Chief Rabbi of Rome attended, as well as odd cricket-playing British ecclesiastics. Sir Lew Grade was made a Cavaliere of the Republic. The Pope was noticeably absent. The ball was slammed into my court, and there was a long silence while I got down to work. This meant loading my typewriter and the New Testament into my motor caravan and setting off for the Alps. It was a sweltering summer in the Italian lowlands.

I took the New Testament in Greek, in order to get a fresh or original look at it. There are four versions of the life of Christ, and the most popular version is the least reliable. This is the highly romantic fable written by St John, too long after the historical events, which has the wedding at Cana and the raising of Lazarus. The stories of Matthew, Mark and Luke are not like that of John, but they are so like each other that they can be studied as a single book called the Synoptic Gospels. Zeffirelli, being a romantic, was naturally drawn to John, but I stood out for the plainer evangelists. The result, as you'll see, was a compromise: no wedding at Cana, but a spectacular raising of Lazarus.

The gospels, I knew, were not enough. I had to read Josephus's *History of the Jews*, histories of the Roman Empire, manuals on the technique of crucifixion. The traditional image of Christ carrying the whole cross flouts true tradition: he would merely have carried the crosspiece, which would, at the execution site, be attached to a permanent upright. Televiewers seeing this adherence to historical fact may be outraged, but truth must always be one's master. The more I read Matthew, Mark and Luke the more I became dissatisfied with their telling of the story. They're good propagandists but bad historians, and they'd never make a Fiction Writers' Union. 'Now Judas was a thief.' How stupidly inadequate. Whatever Judas was he wasn't a thief.

Judas, in fact, had to be remade from scratch. I made him first as a decent American college boy, well read, devoted to his widowed mother, charmed at first by Jesus, later wholly convinced of his divinity, but so politically innocent that he runs to the Sanhedrin and says: 'This man is the Messiah.' The Chief Priest nods gravely and says: 'Ah, the Messiah, is he? The Zealots think he's a political leader come to free Israel from Roman rule. They'll kill him when they hear his true mission. Help us, dear Judas, to have this Jesus put away in a safe place until the time is ripe for his instatement as Messiah.' And so the arrest in the garden, Judas's shocked loss of innocence, his suicide following the flooding in of awareness of his involuntary betrayal of the one man he would never have wished to betray. That was my first Judas. The final Judas is a palimpsest of Judas as sweet innocent, as Higher Zealot, as indiscreet blabber, as disappointed man, but never as easy melodramatic villain.

Certain characters, key characters too, appear in the film who have no place in the gospels. Judas has to have a primary contact in the Religious Council, a priest believed to be imaginative and progressive but in fact highly reactionary. This character, whom I call Zerah, is seen, as the story progresses, to be a necessary wheel in the machine: he even has the last word, a bitter and baffled one. Again, if Pontius Pilate refuses to sign Jesus's death warrant, there has to be someone willing to sign it – a deputy procurator friendly to the Jews. There was another way of legalizing Christ's execution, one which I toyed with but eventually abandoned. Barabbas's full name was possibly Jesus bar Abbas, and his name may have been set down in a portmanteau death warrant without the patronymic. 'Here we have a Jesus. It doesn't matter about the rest of his name – bar Joseph or bar Abbas. His Excellency has already signed. As long as there's a Jesus up there on the cross this afternoon the record will be quite in order.'

The twelve apostles are not well characterized in the Gospels. I had to bestow qualities on them which would make them clearly recognizable, even when they were all there in the round dozen. Not easy; far too easy to let them blur together into twelve interchangeable bewildered bearded artisans in dirty smocks. Matthew-Levi the reformed taxman comes through, I think. Doubting Thomas is a kind of gnarled Scot with the dour scepticism of a highland race. Thaddeus plays the flute. Bartholomew is an amateur physician with a bad stomach. The gospels give us a clear enough Peter. One had to be careful with the beloved disciple John, especially in a permissive age only too anxious to augment cautious hints of a possible pederastic relationship with his master into the cover story of a 'gay' magazine. Our disciples are tough and heterosexual, though uneasily celibate. They may be saints, but they wear no haloes.

The various versions of the script I wrote fill a whole long shelf. A script is very much the humble servant of a medium only marginally verbal, and it must submit not only on the set but also in the cutting room to the exigencies of the director's vision. Unfortunately, it's not only a matter – with so dangerous a subject – of pleasing director, producer and the men who pay the bills. There are the theologians, professional and amateur, to satisfy; there is the need to reconcile a myriad sectarian images of Christ (including, in this post-Joannine age, the Jews if not the Arabs). Wherever I went with my caravan, typewriter and Greek Testament, I was hounded by the religious experts of Radiotelevisione Italiana (one of the bodies involved in the making of the film) with requests, orders, ultimata. They pursued me from Rome to Ansedonia to Siena to Bracciano to Rome, telling me what to write. 'Write it yourselves, for Christ's sake,' I said reverently. 'No, no, you're the writer. Now write *this*.' One remarkable suggestion was that Jesus, in formulating the Lord's Prayer, should stumble over the word *padre*, stuttering *papa papa* in involuntary homage to His Holiness. I pointed out that in English this would have to be *fafa fafa*, which is a homage to nobody. Theological advisers were ten a penny, all seeking commemoration in the credits. I said I would trade them all for an adviser in carpentry. The absence of amity and love could be justified by Christ's own words: 'I don't bring peace – I bring a sword.'

The language of the script marries timeless colloquial with the Authorized and Revised versions. It's as though Hamlet chatted in supermarket English and then, for *To be or not to be*, switched to Shakespeare. The story is terrifyingly topical and cries out against reverential remoteness. Here are people saying the answer to life's problems lies in political reorganization, while Christ infuriatingly replies that we have to change ourselves before we can change the world outside. It's a message still generally rejected because not well understood, and the injunction to practise charity as a deliberate technique is too horrible for most to take seriously. As I worked on the presentation of Jesus Christ, the traditional image of gentle flaccidity receded, and a tough irritable indiscreet overcandid muscular intellectual emerged. 'In the juvescence of the year,' said T. S. Eliot, 'came Christ the tiger.' This Christ is tigrine enough.

The pedant within me could not resist writing one scene foredoomed to extinction. When Christ says it's as easy for a camel to pass through the eye of a needle as for a rich man to get to the kingdom, he uses the Greek word *kamelon*, which means camel. But a Greek word very close to *kamelon* is *kamilon*, which means a rope. The rope to many sounds more plausible than the camel. It seemed to me a good idea to have Jesus say the whole apophthegm to a young Greek, courteously using the young man's own language. Nobody except the Greek and Judas the scholar understands, and when Judas translates for his fellows' benefit, he is not sure whether he heard *kamelon* or *kamilon*. Jesus smiles and shrugs Jewishly, leaving the semantic problem to posterity. This was not considered cinematic enough.

John Allegro, a scholar from my own university of Manchester, wrote a book proving that Christ was a mushroom. The more I worked on my scripts, the more convinced I became that this man existed in dusty torrid Palestine, a disregarded colony of a great empire, and that he probably had divinity in him. He was no fungus. Of the revolutionary nature of his programme and its feasibility, given hard work and self-denial, I became more convinced than ever I had been when I was a good son of the Church. Whether this telejesus will indent the brains of American viewers in a way that Barbara Walters does not remains to be seen. But the ennobled British Jew was right: it had to be done.

Quiet Waters

Psalm 23: An Anthology, compiled by K. H. Strange and R. G. E. Sandbach, Saint Andrew Press, Edinburgh

Most people know some version or other of Psalm 23 by heart. It is a potent mantra or cantrip. You put off fear along with free will: the Lord (or Controller, or Probation Officer, or Pacesetter, or Great Spirit) takes over. But, woolly and baaing as you are, you can still stay human enough to have a good gloat at your enemies, who have to grind clean teeth while you dine amply and alone at high table, holding your cup with care for it is running over. As Frank Shaw's Scouse version puts it:

> Dem as ates yew, dey see me sittin down to good scoff, you get me all poshed up and toney, I just can't say ta enough. No argin about it, s'long as I live the gear tings and the elpin and'll be durr. An' in the nex world.

The opening words, from Coverdale to 1611, possess immemorial magic, but they are not in the Vulgate – *Dominus regit me, et nihil mihi deerit* – nor in the Wycliffe and Douai translations, which have respectively 'governeth' and 'ruleth'. The Douai has also a literal rendering of the line about the full cup – 'my chalice which inebriateth me, how goodly it is!' – which was evidently unacceptable to Protestants. But 'The Lord is my shepherd' and 'my cup runneth over' are sentimental enough to retain a large secular popularity (the latter phrase is the title of a contemporary love song), and Winston Churchill found 'the valley of the shadow of death' rhetorically valuable.

After 1611 it might be thought that any other English version of the psalm would be supererogatory, but it was necessary to put it into rhymed strophes for hymn-singing purposes. It has never worked, not even with George Herbert:

> Nay, Thou dost make me sit and dine
> Ev'n in my enemies' sight:
> My head with oyl, my cup with wine
> Runnes over day and night.

And then there is the Rous and Barton perversion of English word order – 'he leadeth me /The quiet waters by' – as well as the Isaac Watts evasion of the contents of the cup, which with vague 'blessings overflows'. But this was the age when Oliver Goldsmith could describe ale in a country pub as 'mantling bliss'.

A Japanese version by Toki Miyashina was translated near-literally into English and broadcast by the Rev. Eric Frost in 1965. The cup, in keeping with Japanese industrial and technological enterprise, over-flows 'with joyous energy', but the Lord will not allow this to lead to excess and debilitating effort:

> The Lord is my Pace-setter, I shall not rush;
> He makes me stop and rest for quiet intervals.
>
> He provides me with images of stillness, which restore my serenity;
> He leads me in ways of efficiency through calmness of mind. . . .

The inebriating cup has turned into its opposite – no cup at all – in a version called 'The Lord Is Like My Probation Officer', made for a book for young delinquents, *God Is for Real, Man*, by Carl Burke, chap-lain of Erie County Jail, New York:

> He makes sure I have my food
>   And that Mom fixes it.
>   He helps her stay sober
>   And that makes me feel good
>   All over.

The Rev. Eric Hayman, Vicar of Wrabness, Manningtree, goes even further in pastoral ineptitude with his version for the Space Age:

> The Lord is my Controller, I shall not deviate;
> He places me in true orbit around my planet Earth.
> He plotteth my course across the vacuum of Space. . . .

These people do not lack piety, but they certainly lack taste, as well as talent. It is not enough, alas, to be holy.

E. C. D. Stanford, in a foreword written for the 1969 edition of this anthology, says: 'I have been looking at the Top Ten for last week, and wondering how long these best-selling songs will last.' Then he goes on to say that Psalm 23 has been going strong for two and a half thousand years. This reads strangely in a week when Psalm 137 seems to be in the pop charts. It is not clear what distinction he is drawing – between the literary excellence of King David's Hebrew (of which we do not know the tune, and it is songs Stanford is evidently on about) and the ephemeral trash of today's pop lyrists? Apparently not, since he does not object to the transposition of the shepherd theme 'into other keys for those who know nothing about sheep but all about support and care and guidance'. It's the 'original message' that counts, apparently. Also, 'some of the versions in this collection are fun'. What, then, is this anthology all about? The 'sheer enjoyment', it seems, to be derived from comparing bad paraphrases with a noble English original.

But there is a good point almost obliquely made – that of a kind of liturgical continuity. 'The early Christians went to martyrdom with

"The Lord is my shepherd" on their lips: Augustine loved it: George Herbert paraphrased it: Ruskin learned to say it for his mother.' It is good to have a link between Ruskin and the Christian martyrs. And even between them and the anonymous Yorkshireman who gives us

> T'owd Boss luks after mi; ah want for nowt.
> 'e sees as 'ow there's fields weer ah c'n sit missen dahn,
> or tek a walk alongside o' t' dams.

But all the rest – the Lord is my Pilot, or Shop Steward, or Benign Housemaster – is just evasion of what the psalm is about. It is very Old Testament, with its sheep and eating fit to burst and getting drunk and a tribal god on your side and a sneer at your enemies and your hair dripping with oil. The Rev. William Wye Smith, whose head has been cheeptit wi' yle and whose cup is teem-in' fu', has no right surely to say: 'David is aye unreelin' a pirn aboot Christ.' David is unreelin' a pirn aboot the God of David.

Preparing for the Pope (1982)

Introducing John Paul II, by Peter Hebblethwaite
Pope John Paul II and the Catholic Restoration, by Paul Johnson
Pope John Paul II: His Travels and Mission, by Norman St John Stevas
Pope John Paul II: An Authorised Biography, by Lord Longford

Business is business, and the publishers are entitled to cash in on the impending papal visit as much as the toymen and medallion-makers. Still, it has been something of a burden for this reviewer to have to read four adulatory works on Jean-Polak (as the irreverent French call him) in rapid succession. I feel surfeited with sweetness and theology. I should have welcomed a scarlet-woman diatribe from a literate Orangeman, of whom, unfortunately, there are few, or a MCP denunciation from an unfrocked nun.

Mr Hebblethwaite thinks there is a certain kind of adulation, close to idolatry, which does the Pope no good. 'If anyone wants to know the secret of the success of the pontificate,' said *L'Osservatore della Domenica*, 'I would say that it is enough to watch how and how much the Pope prays. He is in continual contact with God. He cannot fail.' Mr Hebblethwaite says: 'This is exactly the tone used by *Pravda* in speaking of President Leonid Brezhnev.' And he cites Orson Welles's remark that there are two things that can't be filmed – prayer and sexual intercourse. The Pope on his knees may, for all we know, be going through his English irregular verbs. Hebblethwaite also refers to pope-struck nuns, and rapture at touching the hem of his garment. Paisley and Enoch Powell are right to wish to vomit; some of the faithful feel nausea too.

Both Hebblethwaite and Paul Johnson are very lucid on those aspects of the present pontificate which bid us view John Paul II as a forceful intellect, a stringent theologian and metaphysician rather than as a mere pop pope suffering for Poland, getting shot, singing in a fine baritone and jetting his charisma round the world. To the disappointment of a great number of the faithful, the new pontificate has made no concessions at all to the forces of alleged progress: immaculate contraceptives for the populace, infanticide *in ventro*, women priests, the abolition of hell are not merely not on the papal agenda but have been decisively rejected. John Paul, who once had Auschwitz in his diocese, sees no difference between abortion and the Final Solution. For those who wish for copulation without population he affirms that the two go together, but there is always the Malthusian way out – self-control. The unrepentant sinner is shut away from God for ever but he has to face public judgement in his rearisen flesh first. There has been absolutely no change in fundamental doctrine, and I for one do not see how there ever could have been. If you can accept the papal premises you will find no fault in his logic. Masses in Scowse with pop singers may look like progress (and one feels that if John Paul had his way we'd be back to Latin tomorrow), but the truth is the truth and progress is a heretical word.

Paul Johnson makes sound points about possible future relations between the Church of Rome and that of Canterbury. If British members of one communion or the other expect the Pope's visit to signal closer sorority or even affiliation, then they are likely to be disappointed. The Pope looks East, not West, and Britain remains an offshore sanctuary of empiricism. The big task is not only the safeguarding of Christian rights in Poland but the tugging of Russian Catholics, who were dumped by Stalin into the arms of Eastern Orthodoxy, back to the fold. The Orthodox Church in Russia supports the State since the State allows it to live, but this collaborationism John Paul interprets as the bad dream of 'a slumbering giant, which might be roused by the sacral kiss of brotherhood from Rome'. Constantinople regards Rome as heretical, and for Rome to get closer to Canterbury would compound the schism. There is no question of the papacy looking westward.

Mr St John Stevas's Latin is not good – '*Sint lacrimae rerum,*' he says, '*et mentem mortalium tangunt,*' but that is a venial sin in these vernacularist days. He covers the same biographical ground as Lord Longford but, since his concern is primarily with the jetting and helicoptering Pope, he is speedier and, as he has the coming visit very much in mind, he has something to say about English attitudes to the papacy in general, as well as to papists. As the editor of the great Walter Bagehot, he has relevant dicta of 'the nineteenth century's most perceptive critic' to dole out, such as 'The English have ever believed that the Papist is a kind of *creature*; and every sound mind would prefer a beloved child to produce a tail, a hide of hair, and a taste for nuts, in comparison with transubstantiation, wax candles and belief in the glories of Mary.'

Lord Longford, who, as a convert to Catholicism, has had that best of both worlds which we persecuted cradle Catholics have missed, thinks that Catholics are doing well in Britain today. Mr St John Stevas has been Leader of the House of Commons and Mr Paul Johnson editor of the *New Statesman* (a reconciliation of Pelagianism and Augustinianism I have never been able to understand), and it is not impossible that we may some day have a Catholic prime minister. It may gently be suggested that Catholics did even better before 1534, and that once even a monarch could be a Catholic. This rejoicing comes at the end of an extremely well-illustrated biography (Mrs Thatcher at the Vatican in black mantilla; Queen in same place with black mantilla and crown) which, as it was my last piece of enforced reading about the hero of the Vatican, served to bang home with final authority an image of holy virility reinforced by knowledge that the Pope was once an actor and a poet and had girlfriends.

Everybody except Mr Johnson has something to say about the poems. As a crash course in Polish is not offered as one of the apparatuses of preparation for the visit, most of us have to take these in translation and admire the ideas, since we are debarred from assessing the language. Karol Wojtyla is a poet as the Emperor Nero was a poet: his eminence or holiness impels awe: if it is not done well it is amazing to see it done at all. But the aesthetics of Catholicism are always dangerous, and Evelyn Waugh's Lord Brideshead will remind us that, if God is present, beauty must be present too.

A final point. If the Pope's visit to Britain is to have any meaning for Protestants and free thinkers, if it is possible to separate the two, it must be in the area of that *liberum arbitrium* which Calvinism and communism equally deny. I have said often enough in the Italian press that if the Pope's sacred function spills over into the secular world it must be through reiteration of the fundamental truth that men and women are free to make moral choices. There seems to be nobody else in the world today who has that basic authority. To tell the British that they are free is justification enough for John Paul II's visit, but how many of the British will believe him?

Jebbies

The Jesuits – A History, by David Mitchell

The Dominicans, the Franciscans and the Jesuits argued long and bitterly about which of the three orders was dearest to the Lord. Finally they asked the Lord Himself to resolve the conflict. He sent a letter: 'My dear children, you are all equally worthy in my sight, so cease this unholy wrangling. Yours affectionately, God SJ.' Many a Protestant has nodded bitterly at this story. Many a non-Jesuit Catholic too, the occasional pope even. The Jesuits have an ayatollah quality. If the Catholic Church ever seems dangerous to the children of reform, it is invariably because the Jesuits are grimly at work. Jesuitry, in the English lexis, carries no amiable connotations. It means militancy, fanaticism, equivocation, unscrupulousness, apologetic brilliance, terrible erudition. No jolly fat friars there: lean men rather, with blue jaws, who curiously reconcile the ascetic and the worldly, men who will stop at nothing. They will pose, as they did in Elizabethan London, as rakes and dancing masters for the sake of the sacred word. Orwell's Inner Party might as well be Jesuit. Did not the founder, Ignatius Loyola, say: 'To arrive at complete certainty I will believe that the white object I see is black if that should be the decision of the hierarchical Church'?

It is the image of Loyola which has been stamped upon the order since its creation at the time when Christendom had split itself into Lutheranism, Henricanism, Zwinglianism, Calvinism and God, or the Jesuits, knew what else besides. The Catholic Church itself, despite the horrid warnings from the North, was not disposed to initiate reform from within. Pope Paul III got where he did because his sister was Alexander VI's mistress. His own mistress gave him a daughter and three sons, one of whom was accused of ravishing the Bishop of Fano. He gave drunken parties with naked dancing girls. He made cardinals of his grandsons, whom he called nephews. The Church needed a singleminded soldier, dour, disciplined, unseduced by the joys of the flesh or Renaissance art. It needed, in fact, a Spanish aristocrat.

Loyola came from the Basque border, son of a fighter, a fighter himself. He might not have got his sharp blade into the soft flesh of Italic Catholicism had not, about 1540, the Vatican accepted the Spanish scourge as a kind of castigation of its sins. Charles V descended on easygoing Rome; the Papal States were enclosed in Spanish-conquered territory: the *Iniguistas*, as the first followers of Ignatius were called, were seen as an aspect of the Spanish doom, what with their puritanical rigour and military organization. When they were established the papacy could never be the same again. Ignatius called his order a sword in the hand of the Head of the Church. The hand had to be capable of grasping and wielding it. Ignatius created the Church Militant.

If the wielder and the wielded have not always got on well together, this has been because the Society of Jesus is an army, and armies notoriously tend to autonomy. Jesuits have rarely been absorbed into the general hierarchy of the Church: they have their own hierarchy, headed by a Black Pope. Popes and cardinals have to compromise somewhat with the world. About the papacy there is always an air of the empirical; the Jesuits, disciplined by the Loyolan *Exercises* and an exceptionally lengthy novitiate, professionals, specialists in the crafts of communication, go in for unyielding intellectual rigour. If they use the skills of diplomacy, it is cunningly to impose their own thesis, not, through dialectic, to arrive at a synthesis with their opponents. It is not the way to be loved, though it is the way to be, usually reluctantly, admired.

Mr Mitchell gives us the whole story from the foundation to the present day when the Jesuits, like everybody else, are in crisis. It is not always an inspiring story, but then the chronicle of any religious order is tainted with the consequences of the all too human tendency to ignore ends while concentrating on means. Even the Franciscans, whose founder was a gentle pantheistic mystic, have been responsible for blatant cruelty: they tortured Father Garnier, for instance, during the Loudun scandal. The Jesuits are associated with unsavoury machinations (the murder of King Alexander of Yugoslavia and the French foreign minister Louis Barthou; the shameful support of Franco and Salazar; the pogroms of Serbia). They have been stained too by association with the fascist philosophy. Himmler modelled the SS on Jesuit principles and Hitler called him 'our Ignatius Loyola'. Pius XII's condonation of the slaughter of the Jews was believed to have Jesuit influence behind it. We need not go so far as to believe, with Edmond Paris, that *Mein Kampf* 'was written by the Jesuit Father Staempfle and signed by Hitler', but we cannot evade the political implications of Jesuit rigour. On the other hand, we must not forget the Témoignage Chrétien group, founded in 1941 in occupied France, and the Jesuit martyrs of the Maquis.

One does not automatically praise a religious movement for becoming involved with the world. The worker–priest movement in postwar France meant factory and tavern evangelization, but it gained more publicity – and quite irrelevant left-wing approval – for its syndicalist activism. Fr Berrigan SJ said: 'The worker-priests radicalized me, gave me a vision of the Church as she should be.' In other words, he became politically aware. When the spiritual and secular meet, however, it is usually the secular which prevails. Jesuits have been notable for the acquisition of important secular skills, and these means have tended to obscure ends. I read recently an American Jesuit publication on communications, brilliantly erudite, which nowhere mentioned any person of the Trinity. A Swiss Jesuit spoke of the dangers of secularism: 'The effect is to turn the service of God into the service of man, to regard evolution as the source of revelation, and to degrade Christianity to a mere method for the improvement of human relations.'

The Society of Jesus is trying to shed the aristocratic elitism which is an inheritance from its founder. Its younger members want to get into the ghettos and the dirty bars, even to face the firing squads. They want to cut down the desperately long novitiate and start work earlier. But it would seem that any attempt to soften the discipline, modify the professionalism must quell the very nature of Jesuitism. Mr Dedalus wants young Stephen to be educated by the Jesuits, learned men of the world, and not by Paddy Stink and Mickey Mud of the Christian Brothers. The aristocratic aura has been one of their glories, as has the tradition of military discipline with its instant obedience. 'If you are a Jesuit and you are given a job to do, you just get on with it. If you are obeying orders you presume that Divine Providence has something to do with it.' So said an old priest before dying in the saddle at ninety.

There must, the layman ought to think, be something even for the ungodly in a movement which produced Baroque, a fine stage tradition, the greatest English poet of the nineteenth century and the greatest Irish novelist of the twentieth. Mr Mitchell has produced a fine compact history. His impartiality is praiseworthy. He promotes no new love for the Jesuits but he does nothing to impair four centuries of somewhat fearful admiration.

Thoughts on Travel

The time has come for me to speak with the right objectivity, meaning the right lack of personal interest, on the putative joys of travel. I decided the other day that I would travel no more, if, that is, travel means air travel and I think it does. I can cope no more with the lack of legroom, the plastic meals, the insolence of customs and immigration officials, the eccentric hours of flight (which, for me, always seem to be at 0745 or 0059), the calf ache induced by long walks through terminal buildings, the endless waits at check-in desks while the people in front of me argue about excess baggage on trunks containing cadavers. The sea is out, it seems, except for cruises, which are not travel, and the area I can cover in my ancient Bedford Dormobile or second-hand Mercedes is limited by parking facilities – which no longer exist in conurbations – or by the growth in the car-stripping industry, which means that towns like Marseilles, Avignon and Naples are out. Nevertheless, I would say that travel is an excellent thing for the young, though the young are too young to see quite why it is excellent.

Clearly, the jeaned and rucksacked young I see on Continental trains or thumbing rides on motorways are not in search of the exotic. They are seeking confirmation that their own kind exists everywhere and denies the racial and cultural variety that used to be one of the joys of the world. If they want the exotic at all is in the form of what they know well in their own lands through regular, though usually illegal, importation. 'Welcome to Tangier,' I heard one young American say to another just getting off the boat, 'land of the great grass.' There used to be young Americans who saved up money just to fly to Liverpool, not because the Beatles were there but because the Beatles had long left there. I taught a group of American students in Deyá, home of Roberto the Heavies or Robert Graves, who could not stomach a diet of wine and fish and rice but seriously suffered because of a lack of Coke and burgers. Foreign travel is essentially foreign diet, but the young will not have this. It is also the squitters and appropriate medicaments, but not even the mature think it fair that a trip to Athens or Cairo should entail enteric agony.

Why go abroad then? There is no general answer. Travel for the sons of the eighteenth-century British aristocracy meant chiefly Italy, and Italy was an education in the visual arts. It still is, and it is also a series of lessons in human ingenuity – in town planning, tax evading, and living by one's wits. But there is no point in going to Italy if one does not prepare in advance by studying a little of the history of art, which includes urbifaction and terrace agriculture. And if one absorbs something of Italy, has one become a better educated person? Only in the sense that one is dissatisfied by the Bolton or Bury or Ealing to which one returns. In the first Elizabeth's reign Italians exposed to the travelling English used to say: '*Inglese Italianato, diavolo incarnato,*' meaning that Englishmen turned into incarnate devils after their Italian education. They ceased to be mere English puddings; under a grey Midlands sky they yearned for flashing eyes and hot sunlight and wine by the bucket. They became, in a word, dissatisfied.

If one does not wish to be dissatisfied with one's lot at home, one ought to go where the flies and the stinks are, which means the Middle East. This is also a good way of reconciling oneself to one's laws and police force and the probity of one's magistrates. The really great British travellers, like Charles M. Doughty for instance, to say nothing of 'Eothen' Kinglake, always went East, but not too far East. When you get to Southeast Asia you find no dirt or flies but the suspicion that you are in a tropical paradise, and then you go to pieces. It is essential, when travelling, to feel that you belong to a superior civilization, and the lands of the Arabs lavishly grant opportunities to nourish this conviction.

For the young who have never been further than Broadstairs I grant with few reservations that they ought to have a look at France, even if they go no further than Ambleteuse or Wimereux. At least they will be encouraged to drink wine and perhaps develop the elements of a palate for it. But it is no good their going without mastery of a few French phrases. These may be useless in practical terms and even enigmatic – like *Tout passe, tout casse* or *O flots abracadabrantesques, prenez mon coeur qu'il soit lavé*. Tourist's French is hopeless and makes one despised and cheated. For practical purposes remain dumb and point, but then, apropos of nothing, come out with your perfect line of Rimbaud and smile mysteriously thereafter.

The same procedure applies to any foreign visit. A verse of Pushkin will take you a long way in Leningrad; after it you can turn into a Dostoevskian fool. But you must never appear to be a tourist. Before going to see the Sons of the Prophet, even the lowliest, have a phrase of the Koran ready and learn to read and write Arabic script, which is not difficult. With it you will be able to interpret Coca-Cola signs.

I do not think Italy is really for the young, unless they are exceptionally well educated and know Etruscan and Roman history. Too many young British girls go to Rome to be picked up by dark-haired louts whose mothers have ensured that they know nothing about sex. There are plenty of dark-haired louts at home who know quite as little. Spain is better, since the only history you have to know has to do with the Moors and their conquest, and you can smell the dual tradition of the country as soon as you lug your knapsack off the train or dusty lorry. It is quite legitimate to go to any of the sunnier countries for the sake of the sun. My wife, who is Italian, finds the grey skies of autumnal Scandinavia correspondingly fascinating. Exotic is a relative term. When a Tangier night spot offers 'exotic dances' these should really be the Okey-Cokey and 'Knees up Mother Brown'.

What we used to think of as exotic can only now be found in countries that cannot afford Americanization. Meaning no home comforts, peppers, unleavened bread. It is a kind thing to take one's bit of tourist money there, to the deserving, and not put it in the hands of the disdainful Niçois or Cannois. If you can get into a country which is politically oppressed, that too is a good thing for the natives, for you are bringing a breath of freedom. Increasingly, perhaps, one ought to be travelling for the benefit of those who cannot afford or are not permitted to travel. We all belong to one another now, and no foreign country ought to be merely a sideshow.

Let me return, finally, to this business of travel as an education. Frankly, I believe one learns more about a country by reading about it, especially in its fiction, than by visiting it. I have never been to Japan, and I do not intend to go, but I have heard enough travellers' tales to be convinced that, if it came to the pinch, I could write a fairly convincing novel with a Tokyo setting. There is only one thing that cannot be brought back, despite these canisters of Dickensian fog you could once buy in London shops before the atmospheric revolution, and that is the smell of the place. I have smelt Leningrad and Singapore and Adelaide (which had no smell) and there is no literary trick I know which can convey them.

If by travelling we mean the existential process of being on the move and not yet arriving, I think this is an excellent thing, and soon, with videotapes and wallsize screens, we ought to be able to reproduce it in our living rooms. The essence of being on the move was hope – hope of change, perhaps even change for the better – and to travel hopefully was better than to arrive. But as the term 'hopefully' has changed its meaning, that is no longer possible. Go where you like, be assured that it will effect minute alterations in your psychoneural structure as well as making you ill, but don't tell me any of your stories and for God's sake don't show me your photographic slides. From now on I live where I am (which may include the inside of my Bedford Dormobile) but my travelling days are over. This may mean that my larger education is just beginning.

Not So Grand Tour

Travels through France and Italy, by Tobias Smollett, edited by Frank Felsenstein

We like Smollett less than Fielding, finding him less digestible, dourer, more pessimistic, conceding great fictional merits in him but insufficient fantasy. He fails for us mostly in his lack of humanity; he is solid but sour. When he took to recording his travels he had to stand comparison with Sterne, whose *Sentimental Journey* is pure quicksilver (Joyce said that Sterne and Swift should have swapped names). Sterne, who had read Smollett's grumpy account of his European journeys, portrayed him as 'the learned Smelfungus . . . the man who can travel from Dan to Beersheba and cry, 'Tis all barren.' Smollett, in the two years between the publication of the *Travels* and the instant *réclame* of Sterne's book, became the type of the worst kind of Englishman abroad – full of spleen, dyspepsia, insularity, xenophobia, longing for a good cup of tea and a clean toilet.

Yet Smollett was not English but Scots, which explains the tough dourness, and he went abroad already laden with misanthropic gloom, to say nothing of ill health. In 1759 he had been jailed and fined for a libel; in 1762 he edited *The Briton* and failed resoundingly with it; in 1763 he was 'in such a bad state of health, troubled with an asthmatic cough, spitting, slow fever and restlessness' that he decided to seek a cure in the South of France. He had practised as a surgeon both at sea and on land, and he had a healthy disdain of professional diagnoses. So he denied the obvious verdict of a slow consumption and, in the manner of Clarence Day's father, tried the therapy of bad temper, which the French and Italians were, with their filth and dishonesty, only too ready to aggravate. He also tried sea bathing, which did him a lot of good.

In the manner of all travellers abroad, he made monstrously unfair generalizations out of monstrously limited observations. He skims over Florence and says: 'I would not hesitate to pronounce the Italian women the most haughty, insolent, capricious and revengeful females on the face of the earth.' *Mia moglie l'ha letto inorridita.* 'For my part, I would rather be condemned for life to the gallies, than exercise the office of a cicisbeo, exposed to the intolerable caprices and dangerous resentment of an Italian virago.' Even the *lingua Toscana* excites his spleen: '. . . disagreeably guttural: the letters C and G they pronounce with an aspiration, which hurts the ear of an Englishman. . . . It sounds as if the speaker had lost his palate. I really imagined the first man I heard speak in Pisa, had met with that misfortune in the course of his amours.' Note the humour, though – sour but solid.

It is the sour solidity of his record that sometimes satisfies more than the wit and fantasy of *A Sentimental Journey*. He goes to the trouble of setting down in an appendix the daily state of the weather in Nice for eighteen whole months, complete with temperatures (Réaumur and Châteauneuf), and, with Scots bang-went-saxpence particularity, he puts down the cost of everything. The obsession with facts is partly temperamental, partly the product of desperate concern: he was not a rich man and was naturally sick of the imputation of wealth that, before 1939, was applied to all the British abroad; he believed that his cure depended on climate, air, water, the redisposition of the humours (the medicine of the Enlightenment was still Galenian).

A sick man was inevitably obsessive about diet and hygiene. The French, who earn, as they always have done and always will, more travellers' spleen than the Italians, do not let Smollett down in his apprehension of stinking cloacae and unwashed, though perfumed, bodies. The inns are always frightful, but Smollett is fair enough to impute their horrors less to the defects of the nation than to the principle of monopoly. All post houses come under the State, and there is not, as in dear unsocialized England, that healthy spirit of competitive enterprise which ensures a clean bed and decent victuals. Towards the end of his book Smollett says: 'You cannot imagine what pleasure I feel while I survey the white cliffs of Dover. . . . I am attached to my country, because it is the land of liberty, cleanliness, and convenience.' One cannot but feel that the mention of liberty is wholly conventional: it is the other two properties which really count.

As for convenience, it is therapeutic to read Smollett before recording one's next grouse against Alitalia, Air France, or the traffic on the Corniche. Travelling to Nice, where he established himself long enough to give the mild air a chance to work, he tells us of broken axles, villainous ostlers against whom he has to raise his whip, starved Rocinantes. He goes from Nice to Monaco and thence to the Italian Riviera ports in leaking feluccas with cheating boatmen. Disunited Europe is full of small unshaven bureaucrats and exorbitant imposts. Fleas leap, bugs bite. Peasants are nice in the tasting of human ordure to see whether it is fit for their fields. Goats are kept but not milked: the Smollett family has, by God, to drink its tea black. Nice, where he stayed long enough to pay it the tribute of a fine dissection of its diet, morals and lavatories, ought still to be smarting under his lashes. 'Here superstition reigns under the darkest shades of ignorance and prejudice. . . . All the churches are sanctuaries for all kinds of criminals . . . and the priests are extremely jealous of their privileges in this particular. . . . The husband and the cicisbeo live together as sworn brothers; and the wife and the mistress embrace each other with marks of the warmest affection. . . . I cannot open the scandalous chronicle of Nice, without hazard of contamination.' And so on. David Hume said that if Smollett were to return, the 'People would rise upon him and stone him in the Streets.' This must be the only travel book ever written which incited to violence.

It is a vastly entertaining and informative book, sharp-eyed and even daring. Smollett knows nothing of art and hence feels free to deliver artistic judgements. If the Riviera has radically changed since his time, Rome is much the same, and on the treasures of Rome he is refreshingly free from cant and prejudice. Of Michelangelo's *Pietà* he says: 'The figure of Christ is as much emaciated, as if he had died of a consumption: besides, there is something indelicate, not to say indecent, in the attitude and design of a man's body, stark naked, lying upon the knees of a woman.' John Knox could hardly have said it better.

The Hard Way

Slow Boats to China, by Gavin Young

There is nothing fanciful about the title. Mr Young, who has been various kinds of correspondent for the *Observer* (foreign, Paris and New York), took various kinds of slow boat from Piraeus to Canton, evidently being unsated of the dangers and discomforts into which his journalistic assignments had already led him. The willingness to suffer storms, fleas, pirates, bad food and bureaucrats must not be ascribed to sheer masochism. Mr Young wished to write a travel book, and it was only by taking slow boats that he could do it. Mr Theroux has exhausted, in two admirably flavoursome and witty works, the possibilities of the world's railways. No one, unless he had arranged skyjacking and engine failures in advance, would want to write about the wearisomeness of flying. The big ships now only do cruises. It had to be slow boats, a category of travel very charitable to boats that cease to function in the Red Sea or are overrun by gunmen or capsize or do not sail at all.

I have covered most of Mr Young's route but, to my shame, in P & O and Rotterdam Lloyd liners as well as by a mixture of airlines. I could never hope to make a book out of it: there was absolutely no danger and the only discomfort arose from gorging, swilling and sexual guilt. Mr Young suffered what he did in order to entertain us and, through diversion, to instruct. What we chiefly learn is that most seamen are good, unless they are pirates, and that there is too much bureaucratic tyranny in the ports; that the solitary travelling man is now deeply suspect and that only groups are trusted; that the Near East is filthy and Southeast Asia clean; that anyone looking nostalgically for what Conrad and even Somerset Maugham knew on the oriental seas is probably going to be disappointed. Needless to say, Mr Young takes those authors with him, as if to probe the nostalgic ache to see if it is still there.

A citation from *The Nigger of the Narcissus* heads Mr Young's chapter about sailing on *Al Anoud* from Cyprus to Alexandria: 'Ships? . . . Ships are all right. It's the men in them!' He does not mean the crew but the mob of deck passengers, brutal Egyptians, the lowest of the low, 'forty or fifty unemployed riffraff to travel on *Al Anoud* to handle the cargo and divide it into parcels, which they will carry ashore at Alex,' thus evading the heavy charges on bulk freight. Knives, urine, vomit, fights. Rather Mr Young, who is enduring this for us, than us. Compared with these dregs the pirates are kings.

The pirates came aboard the *Allimpaya* from a 'narrow, nippy out-rigger with a Japanese outboard motor in the stern,' the *Allimpaya* being a kumpit plying, with bronchitic engine, from Sandakan to Zamboanga in the Philippines. They were Moros growling 'Goddam fuckin' Marcos government,' armed, ready to slit throats, surprised but not awed to find a white man calmly reading Edith Wharton. Mr Young comes out of the ordeal as a white man should, losing fifty Malaysian dollars and his fieldglasses but refusing to hand over his watch and his jacket, maintaining the fixed smile or ivory shield which wards off violence in jungle, desert and kumpit alike. The thing we have to remember is that pirates are not for television Sundays but are very much there in the Sulu Sea and elsewhere, and that there is no Rajah Brooke to sweep the waters clean of them.

Mr Young says nothing about the liquidation of our imperial navy or naval empire, but we can't help letting a sigh escape when we read about sea rats, undisciplined Arabs, haughty immigration officers and insolent emirs. The British consul at Jedda, wretched gate to Mecca, has to get up in the middle of the night to provide visas for Saudi princes who have suddenly decided to fly to London. 'You mean to say,' asks Mr Young, 'that our ambassador gives in to this bullying?' He is sadly told: 'As we all know, they have all the money. And, as we all know, we need it, don't we?' None of this is a legitimate part of the entertainment.

Indeed, when you forget about the relief of being at sea with decent Baluchis or Goanese or Pakistanis, instead of fretting in high humidity in front of locked offices or sneering officials, you get an overall impression of a bad world of internecine hatreds, gratuitous violence, filth, shut-down docks and desperate migrants. The shark-filled sea is an escape. Mr Young reads Ford Madox Ford's *Memories and Impressions* in Skala and finds:

> In the nineties in England – as indeed in the United States, France, Germany, Spain and Italy, and subterraneously in Russia . . . there were Anarchists . . . Irish Fenians, and Russian Nihilists. . . . The outrages in London and the North of England were mostly committed by Fenians. Their idea was to terrorise England into granting freedom to Ireland. They dynamited successfully or unsuccessfully underground railways, theatres, the Houses of Parliament and docks.

This, and other things, primes Mr Young's memories of his own experiences in Vietnam and Cambodia, and other people's memories of the Japanese occupation of the East. Things don't get better; may we justly say that they are getting worse? Yes, in the sense that the sea voyager is losing amenity as well as facing danger and, above all, that the lone traveller is being scorned or computerized out of existence. That was not true in the time of Conrad and the man who wrote so much of Conrad (as well as, in *Parade's End*, the greatest British novel of our century).

Mr Young, typing his last pages, remembers, as is right, the people who defy the dehumanization of the world and are the true ports of his journey – Walid from Pakistan, sex-starved, who begged for a sex doll (but what would the customs men of Saudi Arabia have done to Mr Young?); Mr Missier, who arranged passage to Tuticorin and was a kind of saint; Hentry in a three-master on the Malabar coast – others who have so far evaded the politicians promising 'universal salvation' but leading men and women to madness and destruction. The book is a testament of a particular kind of sanity – that which Kipling's 'For to admire and for to see' sums up.

Call, Call, Vienna Mine
(or Yours)

I had previously known Vienna in spring and autumn – the right seasons for, respectively, Johann and Richard Strauss (*Voices of Spring*; last act of *Der Rosenkavalier*). This time I arrived just before Shrove Tuesday and in the bleak fag end of the Central European winter. I'd travelled by train from Hamburg, by way of Cologne, Stuttgart, Zürich and Munich, and the whole of Germanophonia was covered in snow, which I loathe. Snow, indeed, was the only black spot on my journey. German trains are wonderful, dead on time to the second, their efficiency unimpaired by strikes or the bloodymindedness of railroad scrimshankers, their shining galleys ready all journey long with anything from a sausage to a carpetbag steak. In winter it is perhaps better to travel than to arrive. It was not Vienna's fault if the weather was chill and dank and the Danube (which you have to get outside the city to see, anyway; what you see in the city is the Danube Canal) looked like grey slops.

It is, of course, unfair to Vienna to expect it to fulfil dreams about love under the lindens and open-air string orchestras discoursing schmalz salted with the faint clang of the zither. There is the city of *The Third Man*, where it is too cold for pigeons to brood on the head of a statue of Franz Josef. (Anton Karas, by the way, who played the zither music for that film, started his own restaurant, called inevitably *Der Dritte Mann*, but jealous rivals shut him down because they said it was unfair for the same restaurateur to serve both goulash and zitherstuff.) The winter city looks grim, but it knows how to keep carnival, which starts well before Christmas. I got to Vienna in time for the sumptuous pre-Lent ball held in the Opera House.

This was an affair of white tie and tails, pearly bosoms, flashing jewels, damnably expensive, with the whipped cream of Central European society sweating under the chandeliers as they jigged to rock or swirled to Strauss. Yet there was something artificial and nostalgic about it. It evoked a dead empire, when the imperial metropolis Vienna was a point of the triangle completed by Budapest and Prague. It is not easy to get into Prague these days: in the old days the elite thought nothing of going there for the premiere of Mozart's *Le Nozze di Figaro*. Budapest, which is only a brief drive away, opens ready enough gates and is perhaps the most tolerable capital of the whole Communist Bloc. Nevertheless, one is aware of a cold eastern wind blowing onto Vienna. Losing its Empire, it went into a decline. With Hitler's *Anschluss*, it participated in the prospect of a world *Reich*. After Yalta it became, like the imperial port Trieste, a door opening on to the Russian steppes. Sightseeing in Vienna is mostly snooping on the glorious past. The good architecture is impressive Baroque and wedding-cake Rococo, and it all celebrates the Hapsburg dynasty. The modern age is typified by anonymous office blocks, which dimly glorify commerce, and by the statue to the Red Army, whose liberation of the city (meaning looting and raping) the Russians will not allow the Viennese to forget.

The Austro-Hungarian Empire was, some of us believe, far superior to the Roman or the British. By its fruits shall ye know it – Metastasio, Haydn, Mozart, Beethoven, Schubert, all the Strausses; Hofmannsthal and Rilke and Schnitzler; Freud and Adler; the uneasy Jewish atonalists. Joyce's *Ulysses* was perhaps its last great literary product – started in Trieste as it was, at the edge of a crazy elegant ambience where the secret police was omnipresent but inefficient. Vienna thrilled all Europe and was a staple of popular ballads. It jetted out the spicy aroma of goulash or Turkish coffee. The goulash is still there, flavoured with caraway, and the coffee houses are crowded, but you will find no new Freud at a *Stammtisch*, nor see a new Schubert scribbling songs on the backs of menus.

Still, a coffee house is a fine place to be in snowy weather. It is a typical Viennese institution springing from two unexpected sources. The first was the old apothecary's trade, which held the medicinal monopoly of sugar: this became the stuff of exquisite pastries, once munched only by the aristocracy but later, as the revolutionary spirit blew in from France, turned into a democratic right. The retreating Turks left a sack of coffee beans behind, which spilled their heady scent on to the cobbles. The breakfast croissant, pride of the Parker-Meridian Hotel, is more Viennese than French: it has rendered the once threatening moon of Islam merely esculent. Viennese pastries are too good: the heart and soul of the *Jause* or snack, they silt up the arteries very satisfactorily, abetted by the *Schlagobers* or whipped cream that crowns the coffee.

We had better dispose of the Viennese cuisine before we go any further. It's a heavy cuisine which renders Viennese evenings quiet and torpid: after the meal, the solider citizens climb slowly to bed. It's different for the young, of course: they flock to Hamburger King and Macdonald's. Soup is a meal in itself. Take *Brandteigkrappeln*, with its milk, butter, eggs, flour, semolina, and nourishing floating bits of fat meat. Or *Brösel* or *Gries* or *Leberknödel*. There is a fine *Gulaschsuppe* which you can eat at five in the morning if you have been out on the town. You can eat *Apfelstrudel* after dinner, but you can have also bits of *Strudel* (salted, not sweetened) floating in your soup. The greatest of the main dishes is the beefy *Tafelspitz*, which seems purely Austrian – a necessary thing to say when you consider that, like most imperial capitals, Vienna has drawn on the provinces or even outlying foreign territories for its kitchen. Thus Wiener Schnitzel comes from Milan, and paprika from Hungary. There is even a dessert called *Powidldatschkerl*, which name turns out to be a corruption of 'Poor Little Dutch Girl', triangles of pastry with jam in them, beloved of a resident English family. The Austrians don't like to serve things without sauces, whose spiciness points eastwards when they're not homely compounds of chopped leeks or onions, dill or gherkin.

You can still eat well at the old places – the Weisser Rauchfangkehrer in Rauhensteingasse, in the centre of the city, or the Deutsches Haus near Saint Stephen's Cathedral (a very old place with a garden), or, of course, the Sacher, whose *Tafelspitz* is superb and prices abominable to young American students like John Garp Irving (not now, of course): the Sacher gives its name to the delectable *Sachertorte* which Americans with circulatory problems ought merely to gaze upon. The Drei Husaran is pure Hungarian, and the Zum Stadtkrug, very close to it, has light music, which you've a right to expect in a Viennese eating house. The conservative, if cosmopolitan, cuisine of the city and its environs (Grinzing, for instance) have not been severely dented by the fast-food cult (which is aflame in Paris) or the impatience of the young, who see food as instant fuel and the hell with the taste.

Vienna displays charm still, even in winter, though capitalist pragmatism and socialist dogmatism alike regard charm as old hat and time-wasting. This means, I suppose, that charm has something to do with flirtatious leisure, a property of the pretty ladies in Schnitzler's novels, and that Vienna, like Paris but unlike London, is a woman's city. The sharp aggressiveness of women's liberation (which puts them in the prison of an ideal) is not manifest here: women are women, and aware of the reality of sexual magnetism. It would be dangerous to think in terms of a *type* of Viennese woman, though I carry away with me, now as before, images of svelte dark-haired sirens rather than big-boned Brünnhildes. This, after all, is not Germany. The men, like everybody in Europe these days, look Irish or Turkish and probably are; the women are not quite Slav and not quite Italian. You will see them shopping in Kärntner Strasse, which leads from the Opera House to the Cathedral, or in the Graben, just off St Stephen's Square, where there are boutiques and fashion stores. This is still a city where women buy evening dresses or ball gowns (and, by the way, it is the only city in the world which still manufactures top hats for men). It is also a place where striptease cabarets are not picketed by women's libbers, and where the advertisements for escort services (some of them in Arabic) promise, perhaps, more than you will get. 'If you wish nice company?' says one coyly. 'Come and meet the most charming and elegant ladies of Vienna.' (The telephone number is 45 31 25.) This invitation is illustrated by a charmer too nude to be elegant. Oh, I don't know, though.

The masculine aspects of the city can, as a prelude to wandering, be best seen from the Pummerin – second highest belfry in Western Europe – at the top of the Cathedral. I climbed up there and agonized in a shark-toothed wind. There it all is to the west – the Ring and the Hapsburg palaces, the Rathaus and the Burgtheater, the Staatsoper and the museums. And to the east is the Danube Canal and the Franz-Josefs-Kai. To the north-northwest is the Black Spaniard Street or Schwarzpanierstrasse, leading into Freud territory. Number 19 Berggasse (a *Gasse* being smaller than a *Strasse*) is a Freud museum. The street, with its parked cars and gaudy sport shops, is not what the master knew. The master, exiled from a city which he had always regarded as anti-Semitic and obscurantist, died in London, and you can buy a phonograph record in which he speaks from the dead in precise English tortured by the clicks of his prosthesis. But he is alive, more alive than ever, though the museum was empty when I went to see it.

I said earlier than Vienna is not, despite the memory of the *Anschluss*, German territory. Austrian is not High German, and Germans need a glossary to tell them that *a*, as in English, means *ein* and *eine* alike, and an *Achterl* is *ein kleines Glas Wein*. With an Austrian ruling the Third Reich, the Viennese could feel they had a stake in it; now they joke about sending to Berlin an Austrian they didn't particularly want. There is the kind of perky inferiority complex, expressed as contempt, towards Germany that Australians feel towards England. The Austrians are not as efficient as the Germans, and they know it: they have too much charm, a concern with *dolce far niente*, and they are still touched by the breath of a great dead civilization. But they are aware of no longer being in the middle of things, of that cold Soviet blast from the east. The native name for Austria, Österreich, like the Nazi Ostmark, refers to an eastern empire, but the Latin name Austria, like Australia, refers to the south wind, which is warm and ripens the grapes. Incidentally, American spelling is becoming sketchy: too many letters intended for Australia end up in Austria, and the Viennese are getting tired of saying that they have no Alice Springs or Wagga Wagga. Perhaps there are so many Australians in the city because they have come for their mail.

English is a second language here, and the Blue Danube radio discourses in English. There is an English bookshop called, like the Left Bank protonym in Paris, Shakespeare and Company. There is even an English theatre. But the Viennese patois seduces even the anglophones, who will call for a *Mokka* (black coffee) while they sit in a *café-konditorei* with a *Funsn* or *dumme Frau*. It was, I think, pleasant for this particular anglophone to go back to Vienna, but I needed the spring or autumn and my own language of nostalgia, which is also the language of Vienna's past. It's a pretty old past – the Romans called the city Vindobona and Marcus Aurelius died here – but one segment of it crowns the rest: the period that began with the Haydn symphonies and ended with the exile of Arnold Schoenberg and Sigmund Freud. And, whether we like it or not, we can't separate even the high literary and musical achievements of the city from the schmalz of throaty tenors burbling: 'Call, call, Vienna mine.' Vienna ends up as a congeries of flavours and memories; the reality of stone and limetree and river is somewhat insubstantial. We can thank God that it didn't join the new Russian Empire and become grim and purposeful: it belongs to the capitalist West, with all its self-indulgence, consumerism and sensuality. But, even in summer, we're aware of that chill wind.

Malaya

1 TANAH MELAYU

anah Melayu is the Malay for Malaysia and means 'Malay Land'. It is more than Malay land: it is Bengali, Tamil, Eurasian, Sikh and Chinese land as well, and you can add to the deeds of proprietorship other, smaller, races, including Buginese and such aboriginals as the Temiars and Negritos. But the Malays call themselves the *bumiputra* or sons of the soil, and they call their language the *bahasa negara* or national tongue. Malaysia is confirmed as the country of the Malays, and this is causing trouble among the Malaysians who are not Malays. I served in Malaysia (which the British then called Malaya) in the 1950s when what had been a British protectorate was moving towards independence. I went back two years ago to make a television film. I noted changes, and these had much to do with the new assertiveness of the Malays. But the physical impact of that lovely country remained much what it had always been – hot, humid, green, jungly, fruity, snaky, the yodelling of the *bilal* on his minaret punctuating loud pentatonic Chinese song on the radio, the ringing of the trishaw bells, the hawking and spitting of the long fasting day of Ramadan, the cry of the fever bird.

In the days of Somerset Maugham, Malaya relaxed in the warmth of a May afternoon that seemed likely to last for ever. It was wealthy then as it is now. Rubber had been taken from Brazil to Kew Gardens, and from Kew Gardens to the state of Perak, where it flourished and bled endless latex to be processed into tyres and contraceptives. In that same state of Perak (which means silver) tin proved more abundant than the costlier metal. Tamil immigrants worked on the rubber plantations all over the peninsula; the Chinese came to mine the tin. Both industries supported a commercial structure which led cultural transplantations from India and China. The Malays had nothing to do with either industry or commerce: they stayed in their kampongs, growing rice (three crops a year), catching fish, training *beroks* or rhesus monkeys to hurl down coconuts. The British took care of secular government for all the races. The Malays, whom Arab traders had converted to Islam, gave sultans and rajas to oversee the administration of Moslem law. Islam and British paternalism supported each other in a bizarre compromise which worked.

There were nine Islamic states, and there still are – Perak, Selangor, Johore, Trengganu, Kelantan, Pahang, Kedah (all with sultans), Perlis (which is too small to have anything but a raja), and Negri Sembilan (which means Ninth State and has a strange matriarchal system which seems able to reconcile itself with patriarchal Islam). The Islamic rulers had British advisers and cultivated British habits, sending their sons and daughters to Oxford or the London School of Economics, serving alcohol, though not pork, at state banquets, drinking brandy on doctor's orders. There were three states ruled directly by the British and termed the Straits Settlements – Penang, Malacca and Singapore. Malacca, first colonized and Catholicized by the Portuguese, decayed with the silting up of its harbour. Penang, a lovely island called the Pearl of the Orient, replaced Malacca as a port. During the Napoleonic Wars the British needed a southern territory to keep an eye on the Dutch in Java and Sumatra. This was hacked out of mangrove swamps by Sir Stamford Raffles and was called Lion City or Singapore. Malacca and Penang have now been absorbed into independent Malaysia. Singapore remains a great free port with a large Chinese population and a Chinese prime minister who has authoritarian leanings.

The Malays were always the favoured racial group. After all, they might not have sprung out of the soil like the animistic naked aboriginals, but they had been in the peninsula a good deal longer than the other races. Their national history was more fiction than truth, accommodating Alexander the Great, with his tutor Aristotle, among the first settlers, but their religion and its laws were well established long before the British arrived. The British arrived with no intention of conquest: the East India Company had set up trading posts on the western seaboard, and its officers were called on by the native sultans to help with the putting down of rapacious river barons. The parallel with India is exact, and Stamford Raffles is a perfect analogue of Robert Clive. First came trade, then the amateur protective army, finally the flag. The Union Jack flies now only above the offices of the British High Commission; the flag of independence features the moon and star of Islam.

The stories of Somerset Maugham deal only with the lives of the British planters, miners and administrators. The natives are reduced to quacking voices in the distance or padding feet on the verandah. I wrote a trilogy of novels some twenty-odd years ago which attempted to drag the Malays, Chinese and Indians into the foreground. Perhaps the best of all Malayan fiction is, strangely, by a Frenchman – *Malaisie*, by Henri Fauconnier, a Prix Goncourt winner of the twenties. Its strength lies in the author's knowledge of the Malays, which naturally entails a knowledge of the Malay language. Maugham was a mere visitor and did not have to take any language examinations; a civil servant like myself was forced to reach degree level in Malay. The insistence on the expatriate's learning this language rather than Chinese or Tamil was an aspect of the Malay hegemony which was, with independence, to worry the other races. I knew only one man who learned to read and write Tamil: he became adept at forging Tamil signatures on cheques and was asked to leave. A fellow education officer, sent like myself to teach at the Malay College, insisted on learning the Hakka dialect of Chinese and was punished by being posted to an obscure Malay territory where nobody spoke Hakka. Malay was the chief language; the Malays were the top race.

They are very much the top race now, and they insist on imposing their language on the others. Chinese lawyers prefer to conduct their cases in English, and they want their children to learn English too. Malay is a kampong tongue, not well able to cope with the demands of international law or electronic computers. There is not even a word for *you* in Malay, which is subtly ceremonious in its modes of address and cannot conceive of *you* as a general concept. On my recent visit to Malaysia I saw Chinese advertisements in this Moslem land which tried to tell the passer by who Guinness was good for. *Guinness baik untoh anta. Anta?* I had never met the word before, nor had any Malay whom I spoke to. It was an Indonesian importation and was meant to mean an unceremonious democratic *you*. Malay is not yet ready to be a tough modern language, but the independent Malay rulers think it is. Meanwhile educated Chinese and Indians want to get to places where a more civilized language is spoken.

But the Malays are not backward headhunters, despite the limitations of a language which they try to modernize (with the help of foreign scholars: I myself devised a system of phonetic description for them). They read the Koran and claim cultural kinship with the Arabs and the Iranians. But they have a temperamental disinclination to work, especially in occupations which require high modern skills. The Chinese man their airline and their warships, repair their television sets and tap their computer keyboards. The Indians join the Chinese in the humane professions – medicine, dentistry, law, education, veterinary surgery. All that the Malays can do is run the police force and the army. They are not an aggressive people, but they tend to the hysteria which is expressed in the disease called *amok*, and I never feel happy when I see a Malay with a gun in his hand. They are not fitted even to the lowlier mechanical skills, such as car maintenance. They are essentially a people who have been pulled out of the kampongs into the towns, and the town in Malaysia seems essentially a Chinese creation. The young have taken to the towns, which mean Lambrettas, cinemas and electronic games: the new Malay prosperity is unimpressive compared with that of the Chinese, but it is a sufficient badge of political power. They have become boastful and rather shrill, as though ready to run amok, and when they insist on being called *tuan* (formerly the honorific of white men and Moslems who had made the trip to Mecca) the Chinese and Indians do not argue.

Any visitor to Malaysia will probably fly to Kuala Lumpur (which André Gide called *Kouala l'impure* because of its brothels) and will meet a modern capital whose roots, like those of Teheran, seem not to have struck deep soil. I mean this literally: even the drains are not far below the surface. The American-style hotels offer American-style food, but the electricity fails without warning and old people die of heat stroke in the halted elevators. The town is polluted with motorcycle exhausts and cheap entertainments. But the Selangor Club, still known as the Spotted Dog, attests to an unkillable British influence. The former clubs of the white man are run by Chinese and Indians of the trading and professional classes: there are not many Malay members, though the royal houses and their hangers-on drop in occasionally to play billiards or get drunk. Afternoon tea is served, and people brought up on bare hands and chopsticks eat roast lamb and mint sauce with a knife and fork. There is a profound middle-class nostalgia for the days of British protection. There is a profound fear that Moslem Malaya will suddenly throw up an ayatollah and cut off the hands of thieves. The British Empire was not, after all, such a bad institution.

Despite the threatening tonalities of this new politicized Malaysia, it still remains one of the most delightful countries of the East. No white visitor has to feel guilty here, as in India or Latin America. There is prosperity, planted by the British and confirmed by the Chinese, and no beggars exhibit leglessness in the streets. This is not the Third World. Penang is a paradise, and east coast Kelantan has beautiful Malay women who walk proudly ahead of their husbands and scorn Koranic purdah. *Dallas* is watched, but old entertainments like the *wayang kulit* or shadow play draw crowds, as does *bersilat*, the Malay art of self-defence, and crowds of men wait their turn to dance with Malay beauties in the *joget* halls. The Malay kitchen is not interesting, but the Chinese restaurants exhibit all the cuisines of the ancestral land, and Indian curries are hot. The fruit is delicious – *pisang mas* or tiny golden bananas, papaya and pomelo, rambutan and that king of fruits the durian which sheds its delicious fetidity in the season of durians. It is a country for pampering the senses. The heat is never oppressive and, to use Fauconnier's phrase, Malaya takes a daily shower bath at teatime. If you want European cool, you need do no more than drive up to the Cameron Highlands, where log fires are lighted before dinner and you eat your roast beef dressed in a thick European jacket.

It is also a safe country where you are not likely to be kidnapped or raped. True, there is the tradition of the *orang minyak* or oily man who comes out of the jungle to molest young girls, but, if the police could get hold of him, they would cool him down with strokes of the traditional bamboo rod. It is a country of large courtesy and overwhelming hospitality. The Indians will get you drunk on Tiger beer and brandy, and the Chinese will lay on banquets which begin with snake wine – the blood of serpents slain at table and drunk in small cups to promote sexual appetite. With such exquisite women there is little need for aphrodisiacs. There are exquisite animals too, such as the banana-eating *musang* and the *pelandok* or mouse deer. The tigers keep their distance and roar from afar, but the snakes have a high profile and can bite. In the tiny state of Perlis there are state elephants. *Chichaks* or geckos chirp on the walls. The birds have little song – the fever bird sings a small segment of the chromatic scale, the copperhammer bird strikes treetrunks with its bill and sounds like a plumber on overtime – but they are highly coloured.

Somerset Maugham refers more than once to the pleasure of the Malayan morning – papaya and eggs and bacon and strong British tea taken while the air is cool and the sun awaits its sudden thrust into the green land. But the nights have their own magic when the huge moon is at the full. There is literal magic too, engineered by *bomohs* and *payangs*, and there are ghosts and evil spirits: the *hantu tilam*, which is shaped like a mat, causes havoc among the crockery if it is not invited to a party, and there is a nasty ghost called the *penanggalan* which is a head and dangling entrails: it drinks the blood of the newborn. There is no shortage of superstition, despite the television sitcoms from Britain and the computerized hairdressers. After all, the jungle is the great source of magic, and the heart of Malaysia is jungle. Here the nice little people worship river gods and count only up to two. The jungle would march to the coastline if it could, but Western pragmatism, Allah, *yin* and *yang* and the Indian pantheon keep the dark forces at bay. Everything is, for the moment, under control.

Singapore is not Malaysia. It lies beyond the Johore causeway and claims few affiliations with its big northern neighbour. It has no natural resources except a harbour whose usefulness Stamford Raffles was quick to spot. But it is a triumphant assertion of the virtues of free trade, and it trades in everything. One becomes weary, however, of its rootlessness, the sybaritic range of its pleasures, its rejection of its own history. It is not even a place where a white man is permitted to go to pieces. But Malaysia remains a blessed land of head-spinning contradictions of race and culture, warm, green, fertile. Perhaps we were fools to let it go.

2 WHITE MEN SWEATING

The British in Malaya 1880–1941: The Social History of a European Community in Colonial South-East Asia, by John G. Butcher

Francis Light got Penang (now, as heretofore, Pulau Pinang) from the Sultan of Kedah in 1786; Stamford Raffles established a trading post on Singapore Island in 1819; Malacca, or Melaka, became British through the Anglo-Dutch treaty of 1824. These three Malayan, now Malaysian, territories were for years to be known as the Straits Settlements. The lure of tin took the British, following the Chinese, to the Malay sultanates of the hinterland. What began in blood – the assassination of the first Perak President, J. W. W. Birch, in 1875 – was to end with the establishment of a pacific multiracial society under British rulers who were termed advisers. That society is still moderately pacific without the British presence. The Malays, now called the *bumiputra* or sons of the soil, run an elective federal kingdom, impose the Malay language, or *bahasa Malaysia*, on a narrow minority of Chinese and Indians, and bask in a prosperity of tin, rubber and oil which the British did much to establish. When the Japanese took over the Federation of Malaya in 1942, they found much to praise in the colonial system they briefly inherited – much too liberal, of course, but delightfully incorrupt; good roads, good hospitals, well-trained teachers quick to learn to instruct in the imperial tongue of Nippon. Mr Butcher's purpose is to inquire into the manner of men these colonial British were. He is right to regard 1941 as the year of their sunset. The British who returned, somewhat shamefacedly, in 1945 presided over a crepuscular regime. I was myself in Malaya, as a colonial officer, to help with the handing over of power to a Malay cadre which, in the Malay College of Kuala Kangsar, I had tried to train in the ways of a world bigger than the river kampong (now called *kampung*). The year of British withdrawal was fixed as 1957: one worked to that deadline. Up to the humiliating debacle of 1942 the British in Malaya had no sense of an ending.

Apart from the box wallahs, or *orang perniaga*, British expatriates worked either in government or on the rubber estates. Somerset Maugham thought that the planters could be divided into two classes: 'The greater number of them are rough and common men of something below the middle class, and they speak English with a vile accent, or broad Scotch . . . There is another class of planter who has been to a public school and perhaps a university.' This observation was inaccurate. The background of planter and civil servant alike was well-spoken middle class; the vile accents were to be found among railwaymen and, later, notoriously, among the police lieutenants recruited from the Palestine Police who served during the Emergency of the fifties. The Residents knew what they wanted of their Malayan Civil Service cadets as early as 1883: 'What we require out here are young public school men – Cheltenham, for preference – who have failed conspicuously at all bookwork and examinations in proportion as they have excelled at sports.' As Resident of Perak, Swettenham 'kept an eye out for men who would do credit to both the civil service and the state cricket team, which one sporting official judged as the equal of a good English county team.' Oliver Marks, who performed brilliantly for a visiting Ceylon eleven, was at once urged to come and work for the Perak government.

As for the apprentice planters, or 'creepers', the major qualification was negative – failure to become something else. The Kindersley brothers, famous planters, had been plucked in the army entrance examination; C. R. Harrison had not been up to the medical. Some creepers had grown tired of studying for medicine or professional competence in the violin; others had been unsuccessful solicitors. In my time I have met on the rubber estates, or, more typically, maudlin at the club bar, a planter who had played the guitar with Geraldo, one who had been shot at on his banana grove in South America, two who were surfeited with Ceylonese tea, three who had failed at ranching in the United States, one who had pipped his second MB seven times.

Planters and MCS men got on well enough together: they were of the same tastes as well as background and used the same jargon – *satu empat jalan* (one for the road), take a pew, damn good *makan* at Foo Ong's. There was jealousy sometimes about pay differentials, but both cadet and creeper tended to despise equally the richer dealer in frigidaires or Ford cars. When it came to getting a room in a rest house, the civil servant was able to show his muscle. He took pride in dislodging a Dutch commercial traveller even when he was settled down for the night. In the white man's club it was understood (and still is, to judge from the Ipoh Club, July 1980) that the hairy legs and shorts of the visiting planter should not be juxtaposed to the pressed linen slacks of the government man. A small room was frequently set aside as a rubberman's bar.

Mr Butcher stresses the importance of the club in the lives of the expatriates. That it was a precious preserve where the British could get away from the natives and read the six-week-old magazines (never, of course, the *TLS* or the *New Statesman*) over a *pahit* or a *stengah* was not necessarily a gesture of fancied racial superiority. If Chinese and Indians could not get into it, though the better class Malays could, it was because of the need for an exiled Britisher to be refreshed with the illusion of drinking in his own culture, such as it was. After all, Chinese did not mix with Malays, nor Indians with either. An Englishman could not visit a Musical Gong Society, whatever that was. The virtue of the club as a centre of sequestration from the multiracial hurly-burly is still recognized in independent Malaysia. The great Selangor Club, or Spotted Dog, flourishes. It is a place where Indian and Chinese professionals speak English together over *stengahs* or Anchor beer. They play cricket, and a European cuisine is served. There are not many Malays, or *bumiputra*, about: the lawyers and real-estate specialists see too many of them during the day. The sultan, of course, is a different kind of *bumiputra*. At the little Idris Club in Kuala Kangsar, the Sultan of Perak has a tiny gambling room, plastered with Chinese nudes, for the use of himself and his cronies. At the Ipoh Club he takes over the dance band, blowing a fair tenor saxophone. The clubs of Malaysia, like the Church of England, glory in a continuity of tradition which ignores the age of reform. They are noisier than they used to be, perhaps. A Malayalam lawyer will get drunk and rowdy. The Chinese perpetuate the old British spirit of decorum.

Mr Butcher recognizes that the long pacific summer of the British *kerajaan* could not subsist without occasional cloudbursts. It is astonishing that there were, in fact, so few storms. At the beginning of the First World War rumours got around among Moslem Indian troops that they were to be sent to fight the Turks, their co-religionists, but the riot was quickly contained and it did not spark off disaffection for different causes among the other races. The business of segregating races in the carriages of the FMS railway caused minor trouble, and it was usually white women who were involved. Hoicking Chinese and betel-chewing Indians could not be allowed to defile the presence of the travelling *mems* and *missis*. The expatriate women were always a nuisance as well as a blessing. Single women were goddesses in the club, and they knew it. Wives got bored and, after reading Maugham, committed adultery. Husbands, away on outstation treks, aware of the lack of civilized comforts in a bungalow where life was mostly shivering with ague or yawning over novels, became guilt-stricken. Wives were always going home, and the provision of an adequate family allowance was a problem.

Some young men could not afford to marry or were statutorily forbidden to do so, and then their visits to Japanese brothels engendered guilt as well as VD. The official attitude to taking brown mistresses was always ambivalent. It let the side down, but a sleeping dictionary was the only way to learn the language. Mr Butcher is good on all this, and he gives such tables as one headed 'Ethnicity of Women from whom European Men Treated at the Sultan Street Clinic Contracted Venereal Disease, 1927–1931.' The girls of Siam were the great infectresses, but the Malays came a close second. The Japanese, who had regular medical inspections and lived in brothels cleaner than hotels, were down with the Eurasians to 0.4 per cent in 1931. This damnable sex, by no means to be tamed by quinine or cricket. Guilt guilt guilt.

In an appendix Mr Butcher gives us the true story behind Somerset Maugham's 'The Letter'. Mrs Proudlock, who had emptied a revolver into the body of her lover, William Steward, was sentenced to death by hanging. Outrage expressed in fiery petitions to the Crown gained her a free pardon. The reputation of all white women in the FMS was at issue. 'We have an idea,' said the *Malay Mail*, 'that nowhere at Home are English women more honoured and esteemed than here.' Yet it was the existence of Englishwomen in the tropical colonies that was responsible for the greatest measure of disquiet among the men. They were temptresses as well as goddesses. When white female flesh appeared on the cinema screens of Malaya, to be drooled at by hot-blooded Asians, the status of the governing British seemed threatened. A white woman tipsy in the club, discoursing sexual needs unsatisfied by an overworked and debilitated husband, was a great topic of scandal in the bazaar. It was a man's world, and a realistic planter or government officer should have been content with beery sodality and the odd session with a geisha or *perempuan jahat*. But these men had been to decent schools and were romantic. It was the same in Burma, as Orwell reminds us. The French suffered less.

Whether the French were better colonists than the British is an academic question, but at least such Frenchmen as were planting in Malaya (Pierre Boulle, for instance, and Henri Fauconnier) were kept sane by their own culture and some of them (those two, anyway) produced memorable novels based on their Malayan experiences. The British were mostly philistines, and they have left behind a heritage of philistinism. Kampung culture is dying, and a metropolitan culture of art galleries and orchestras seems unlikely to arise. What there is, and flourishing too, is a materialist consumerism which is threatened from the north by the communists and from the west by the militant Islam of the ayatollahs. Mr Butcher's book deals with a race of people who may well be surveyed in terms of anthropological generalities. There was no room for the brilliant or the eccentric. British Malaya was created by courageous and suffering mediocrities. The building of Singapore in 1819 was a rather different affair.

Homage to Barcelona

One good thing about living in the Condamine of the Principality of Monaco – midway between Monte Carlo where the Casino always is and Monacoville where Princess Caroline frequently is – is that Europe is almost literally on one's doorstep. The railway station is ten minutes' walk up the hill from our apartment on the rue Grimaldi. You can flop into bed in a wagon-lit that rocks you gently from Monaco to Rome or Paris. You can take the noon train, whose provenance is Milan and which is blazoned with T E E, for Trans-Europe Express, and get to Avignon in mid-afternoon. Then you pick up the Spanish Talgo from Geneva and end up in Barcelona in time for an earlyish dinner, meaning about ten at night (though the Barcelonan taxi drivers are having dinner too and the earlyish dinner may become a latish one).

Today my wife and I are going to this jewel of Catalonia, which officially lies outside the new Europe (the community specially created to benefit big business men and malefit ordinary people through high prices and the inexplicable exportation of butter mountains to Soviet Russia) but is our nearest great city – much nearer than our mother Paris and a good deal nicer. Also cheaper, but that won't be for much longer. Spain's entry into the Common Market will take care of all that. Spain will export oranges cheap to Israel and import them dear from Iceland. But, even without prospects of that kind, inflation gallops. This is modish and proves that Spain has achieved the first step in Common Marketdom. The shut-in days of Franco are over; Spain, like Britain, is a democratic monarchy and looks out at the big world of pan-European culture, meaning mostly unhandy Americanism.

We're going to Barcelona because the aged Catalonian leader, Josep Tarradellas, is at last back from exile and he has assumed the presidency of Catalonia's regional government. Franco killed regional autonomy as he put to sleep regional languages. Spain was strongly centralized, unsyndicalized, heavily policed – in a word, was fascist. In the fifteen months since the Prime Minister, Adolfo Suarez, took over the leadership of the Spanish government, he has – with the help of King Juan Carlos – moved the country a fair distance along the democratic road. Political prisoners have been freed, political parties – including the communists – made legal, there have been parliamentary elections and a national referendum. The province of Catalonia wants nothing less than total autonomy, but that must lie either in the distant future or in the region of unrealizable dreams. There are reasons why Madrid doesn't want Catalonia to turn into an autonomous republic, and we'll come to them later. Let's get to Barcelona first.

My wife and I carry our bags up the hill in a sudden downpour, but the trip to the station is too short for a taxi. The bags are light, or near-empty: we expect to buy things in Barcelona. My pockets are heavy, however, being crammed with pesetas. I obtained these earlier in the season from my Spanish publisher, who had them waiting for me in the seaside resort of Sitges, neatly enveloped in bundles of *mil* notes. What Spain gave, Spain may now take back in return for fish dinners, shoes, clothes, and little models of Don Quixote. We have other purposes than shopping and politics, however. We want to speak Catalan; we want to see certain pictures of Picasso and architectural fantasies of Gaudí.

The train from Milan is twenty minutes late but, says the loudspeaker, lost time will be made up by, at latest, Marseilles. It wouldn't matter, anyway: I'm prepared to forgive trains most things, being so thankful to have them. I recently made up my mind not to fly any more – not just a matter of airport strikes and go-slows and the indignities of the security search: I've clocked up more flying hours than is right for one lifetime and I have a recurring nightmare of what Henry James called the Distinguished Thing. The train arrives and we go to the dining car. The stewards are Tuscan and full of the wry fatalism that two thousand years of misrule have taught all Italians. How are things in Italy? So bad, they say, that even the cats are leaving. We eat antipasto, spaghetti alla Bolognese, veal in wine sauce with sauté potatoes, cheese, apple tart; we drink Chianti, acqua minerale, espresso, grappa. Then, back in the compartment, I read a story in Catalan:

> Van pujar al restaurant a un quart de dues. Hi havia moltes taules buides i pogueren escollir. 'Caram,' va pensar el senyor Joaquim, 'jo em creia que estaria ple com un ou . . .'

Catalan is the mother tongue of some eight million people: it's spoken in Catalonia, Valencia, a part of eastern Aragon, the Balearic Islands, Andorra, the French province of Roussillon and the city of Alghero in Sardinia. Franco's tyranny meant the banning of the language in those regions where he could enforce a ban; to the Catalonians the unshackling of the language is hardly separable from the notion of political freedom. It's clearly an important language, and not only to those to whom it's a political banner. In one form or another it's a kind of underground language of the entire Mediterranean, and even the Monegasque that's spoken up in the bars of Monacoville has affinities with it. '*Ple com un ou*' – full as an egg: you can get away with the phrase all over the Mediterranean.

Kids in America who deign to learn French or Spanish – which the Catalonians always refer to as Castilian – turn up at their noses at Latin. Yet without some knowledge of Latin you can't really find a way into the culture of the *langue d'oc* which the centralizing tyrannies of

Madrid and Paris have spent centuries trying to push down. French of Paris is a fixed formalized bureaucratic instrument, much given to abstractions and imposed principles of correctness. The lisping tongue of Madrid has given the world *Don Quixote*, but it tends, like Paris French, to the fixed, the formed, the lapidified, the heavily authoritative. We call these like the Tuscan dialect which has become Italian, great Latin languages, but the greatness is an applied property, derived from political power. The tongue spoken by the Roman legionaries has taken many forms, with literatures almost as impressive as those of Castilian and Parisian French, but none of these forms has ever been an imperial instrument. Try the Castilian lisp in Barcelona – *lapith* for *lapiz* or Thervantes for Cervantes – and you will find your interlocutor politely trying not to wince. In Andalusia I once saw and heard a conjurer hissed off the stage for saying that a trick was fathil instead of facil. Your way into the Latin Europe away from the big capitals is through the history of the classical tongue that university students everywhere are starting to disdain. Entering Barcelona, I must forget *buenas noches* and remember to say *bona nit* – not difficult, since we say 'Good neet' in Lancashire.

We reach Avignon and wait for the Talgo from Geneva. I detest Avignon, where I was once more thoroughly robbed than in any other city I know, except perhaps Los Angeles. There are no travelling students around at this season, but the bluejeaned ghosts of the summer still haunt the station. Why did they come? To examine the architecture, sample the wine and cuisine? They all drank Coca-Cola, read Irving Wallace, kept on the move, believers in travelling rather than arriving. The kids now back in America will perhaps still be reeling off the names of the towns they've visited – swallowed pills which never had a taste but whose brand-name is approximately remembered. We start off. Soon we pass churches of Catalan Baroque and come to the frontier at Cerbere. Is the name derived from Cerberus, the dog that guarded the frontier of hell? *Passeports* now become *passaportes*, and the ghost of a disgruntled fascism comes aboard with the police. We have a long stop, something to do with a jewel robbery. Dinner is rushed but good: asparagus soup, a ham tortilla (why do the French claim the omelette monopoly?), chicken with green peas and zucchini, wine like bullfighter's blood. No time for coffee, except for an American lady who screams that she'll die without it. And then Barcelona. No disciplined line-ups for taxis, no taxis. '*Caram*,' I swear in good Catalan. Eventually we get to the Avenida Palace Hotel, bath, bed, television. Gary Cooper swears '*Caramba*' in good Castilian. It will be a long time before Barcelona gets down to the craft of dubbing in Catalan. Damn it, they've had forty years of the Falange: you can't get cultural self-determination overnight.

30 October

It is Sunday, but we are up early. Between the hotel and the Comedia Cinema is a bar-cafeteria called the Self Comedia. This 'Self' is a great

European importation, and with it 'Service' is understood. In Paris there is a restaurant called the Self Grill, which, except for Saint Lawrence, seems to take things too far. On the door leading to the cafeteria is a whimsical line-up of movie stars with trays – Karloff, Chaplin, Marilyn, Groucho, Gable. The barman, with the rest of Spain, thinks highly of Groucho's art. The Falangists regarded the name Marx as inflammatory, but they couldn't keep the Brothers out. My first venture into lengthy Catalan – or pan-Med or tortured Latin – is an account, for the barman's benefit, of my having lunch with Groucho in Cannes, how he loped to the men's room and back (loped – no Hispanic word; I had to mime) much in his screen manner, how he gave me a Romeo and Juliet cigar which I kept till it fell to shreds. Then, a little sad, to the Cathedral. Would it be in order to pray for the repose of Groucho's soul while mass is being said in Catalan? Probably not. Catalan is Catalonia's own thing and excludes strangers. I feel a certain uneasiness at that, especially in a temple of the Universal Church. One can't altogether approve of the exclusion of strangers.

Behind the Cathedral's aspiring Gothic, presiding over the Barrio Gótico, is the Plaza Nueva, where you can frame your view of a piece of open-air Picasso with a pair of lone Roman columns. Picasso, who started his career in Barcelona, has decorated the façade of the College of Architects with a frieze of kings and kids and horsemen, in the infantile style of the ultra-sophisticated. 'Salvador Dali,' says a helpful passer-by. Picasso's graffito manner fits in well with the anonymous political daubs on the walls nearby. The Barcelonans are great graffitists. They are good sloganists too. VIVA EL REY, someone has written, and someone else has added: POCOS DIAS. Freedom from Franco's Falangist violence has opened the door to democratic violence: there is rape about in Barcelona these days, and the response of the new *feminismo* is: CONTRA VIOLACION CASTRACION.

We walk the Ramblas, the wide-avenued district leading to the sea, crammed with strollers at noon, full of flowers, caged birds and bookstalls. As was to be expected, the new era of liberty has not resulted in a rush of periodicals devoted to free thought but to a rash of crude publications about sex. Nude covers; frank pictures inside of Spanish teenagers in alfresco fornication, jeans well down for it; articles on how the sexuality of Spanish woman compares with that of her long-democratic sisters. You look in vain for Orwell's *Homage to Catalonia*; the Barcelonans have forgotten their old British friend and have taken to American neutrals like Harold Robbins. In the Franco time, magazine covers showed kittens in ribbons and little girls in communion frocks; the new popular journalism is franker but ranker. The Barcelonans have discovered, along with democracy, the delights of the soft-porn film. I never expected to see the *Pamela* of the great Samuel Richardson turned into a period eroticon, but there it was in the summer at Sitges in the open air, the women in the audience giggling where their American sisters would yawn. *Sexo* is new; the latest interviews with nymphomaniacal pop singers and homosexual bullfighters set people panting; the new *Interviu*, with its nippled cover, is in every man's briefcase. But, in the *plazoletas* of the Barrio Gótico, a chaster tradition is being upheld at noon – the dance called the Sardana, young men and women in a circle holding hands high, prancing with sedate vigor to music with a panpipe flavour.

The Ramblas, stretching from the sea-looking statue of Columbus to the Plaza de Catalunya, is a fine wide green artery just right for the *paseo* – the showing-off evening stroll – but Barcelona goes in for treed avenues everywhere. It is a city of firm street lines and very satisfactory contemporary architecture. When a commercial block is thrown up, its façade is tastefully lozenged with Aztec-type abstractions. No architect dare go too far in either dull boxiness or fussy neo-Baroque: he has behind him and in front of him, not to say above him, the warning example of Gaudí.

After lunch, in sudden rain, we go to see Gaudí's masterpiece – the still unfinished church of the Sagrada Familia or Holy Family. There is nothing in the world like it. It is Disney whimsicality raised to the level of soaring nobility. It is metaphysical conceit humanized with crockets and pompoms. It is scrawl and mysticism, vision and fancy, an evanescent dream hammered into sempiternal solidity. New York knows Gaudí: it even has a chapter of Amigos of the great mad sane genius. Probably only Spain could have produced him; most probably only Barcelona.

Gaudí started the cathedral in 1884, and the work was still proceeding when, in 1926, he was run over by a streetcar and died. The difficulty of getting the whole structure completed has partly been due to Gaudí's unwillingness to plan *in toto*: he approached the work rather in the manner of a novelist, letting new notions effloresce as he proceeded, and not even the close collaborators who survived him have been able to guess at his final vision. Spain, as the world knows, is a Catholic country, and was once aggressively Catholic, but Barcelona has long been given to republicanism, socialism, anarchy and various kinds of godlessness, so that there is a very ambiguous kind of pride in these flying towers and the flowery sculptural façades out of which, like visual hosannas, they soar. But never in the whole history of ecclesiastical architecture has there been so idiosyncratic, indeed eccentric, a creation, and collective collusion in the stone and concrete hymnody can easily be excused: Gaudí was one of Barcelona's great men, and here's one of the great things he did; we don't share his faith, but we let him dance in our sky; this is a city of energetic individualism, and it's always possible to see that as Gaudí's true credo. Besides, the bulk of his work is secular.

We must postpone a trip to the biggest of the secular Gaudís – the Park Güell – but we can at least take in the Casa Batlló, with its balconies like carnival masks, its lizardy rooftiles, its little ogre's tower, its second-floor picture windows framed in stone vulvae. The stark rectangular is anathema to Gaudí; hard stone must appear not merely soft but edible. Roughcast walls are stuck all over with big fairy money pieces, pillars ape limbs, stone overhangs drip like stalactites. *Edibility* will always do as one of the Gaudí keywords. Those great towers of the Sagrada Familia are long rolled waffles, foraminated, crunchy, with pinnacles of crisp sugar. Enough, or too much, as Blake said.

31 October

The eve of All Saints, Hallowe'en in Anglo-America, All Souls here, the Day of the Dead. The streets are full of the living, and one wonders if there is a Catalonian physical type. There are as many thin hard streaky blondes as hippy lacquered creamy flamingos or flamencas: this could be New York, except for the courtesy and the good temper. We take a taxi to what we would think of as out-of-town, though ten miles up in the hills you're still within city limits. The taxi driver is Andalusian, saying *E'pañole'* for *Españoles*, and he has come to Catalonia because that is where Spaniards who want to work always come: the rest of Spain, he says, is bone idle. He takes us up to El Tibidabo, high on the Sierra of Collcerola, from which you can look down on the entire city and the sea beyond. Another way up would have been by funicular from the Columbus statue. The name Tibidabo comes from Christ's promise to Peter in the Vulgate: *Tibi dabo clavia regni caelorum*, or 'To thee I will give the keys of the kingdom of heaven'. To justify the religious intitulation of a park of secular attractions – ferris wheel, huge Meccano seesaw, museums, observatory, bars – there is the great Templo Expiatorio de España (suggesting that there is always guilt beneath gaiety), topped by a Christ with arms spread winglike to the sea and city.

I am beginning to understand now the nature of Catalonian pride. The creative energy that could provide a Tibidabo is not what the ignorant world would call a typically Spanish property, and the Catalonians, rightly or wrongly, see it as a very unusual growth of the Iberian earth. They don't want their own achievements to be part of the general Spanish glory, with Madrid pointing to Catalonia and saying: 'See what the Spanish can do.' The Spanish can't do it, say the Catalonians, but the Catalonians can. Our Andalusian taxi driver agrees. What do you find in the South? Only bullfights, guitar-twanging, Islamic architecture, unshaven *mañana*.

If Tibidabo is a wonder, Montjuich is a marvel. I take the Catalan name to be the equivalent of Montjoie or Mountjoy or heaven and, like heaven, it has no truck with space and time. For a complete artificial city called the Pueblo Español was built for the Exposición Internacional of 1929, and in it you can literally walk through the whole of Spain, if by Spain you mean not dusty distances on donkeyback but the cultures, cuisines, architecture of all the Spanish provinces. There is also the Museo de Arte de Cataluña, which shows very firmly that Catalonian painting and sculpture go back a long way, autonomous, indigenous, a straight line from the Byzantine-like Christographs to Miró and Picasso. This pride in an ancient and continuous culture has, of course, profound political implications.

We discuss this later over jugs of sangría with Mario Muchnik, Russian in origin but a son of Argentina. He published a book on how he felt about Michelangelo, and I supplied the preface. Spain, these days, is full of South American exiles: the old mythology of the western land of promise and the corrupt mother country has been reversed. Mario says what they all say here: that Catalonia's desire for total independence, based on history, language, culture, industrial potential and achievement, is likely to be thwarted because Madrid can't afford to see the virtual secession of the province which provides so much of Spain's wealth. It would be like nineteenth-century Lancashire cutting free from London, or present-day New York declaring independent nationhood. A measure of autonomy, yes, but never the whole hog.

Catalonia has had her own government, or Generalitat, ever since 1289. The Castilio-French occupation of 1714 put an end to that for a time. It struggled for revival until the whole idea of an independent government was brutally quashed by Generalissimo Franco in 1938, complete with head-lopping of some of the Catalonian leaders. The Honorable Tarradellas went into exile, along with surviving members of the Generalitat, and has had to wait in Saint Martin-le-Beau, France, until this year, the *annus mirabilis* of amiable and fruitful negotiations with Premier Suarez. Catalonia has, in effect, gone back to the 1932 situation, when the Spanish parliament in Madrid voted 334 to 24 for a quinquennial Catalonian assembly, an elected head of the executive, and the coexistence of Catalan and Castilian. *Un Estatuto de Autonomia para Cataluña* – it sounds good. But Mario Muchnik shakes his head. Catalonia will be like Wales – eisteddfodau and signposts in the regional language. Autonomy strictly means power of total secession, perhaps with Catalonia coaxing Roussillon to break away from France and join the Catalan-speaking Union. Besides, Catalonia will soon have a leadership problem. Tarradellas is an old man (born in 1899) who's never known real power. There's been no chance to breed leaders. Political optimism is a commodity that died in the thirties, not only in Catalonia.

2 November
Shopping – clothes, shoes, leather. The couture of Barcelona need feel no inferiority in the face of boastful Paris. Isn't Berhanyer at least as great a name as Saint Laurent? The boutiques are superb, the service courteous and efficient. But I, a dedicated smoker, note a great shortage of tobacconists. Children set up soapboxes in the narrower streets and sell stolen panatelas and Lucky Strikes. Barcelona tolerates smoking but doesn't seem to encourage it.

A visit to the Museo Picasso, preceded by lunch near the street where he painted some of the *Demoiselles d'Avignon*. Many of his admirers continue to believe that these girls came from the French city. They did not: they were denizens of the Calle de Aviño. Picasso did his early work in Barcelona and kept up contacts with the town throughout his long life. The gallery covers all the periods and has the embarrassing surprises of a sentimental *First Communion* (1896) and an academic anecdote (1897) called *Ciencia y Caridad* (woman ill in bed, doctor – *ciencia* or science – taking pulse; nun – *caridad* or love or charity – offering nourishing cup of something). Then come the bright blues and reds, Cézanne-type fruits, Toulouse-Lautrec-style stage performers, the displaced physiognomies, bulls, doves, *meniñas*. *Meniñas* are properly attendants on Spanish royalty. Picasso uses the term to cover a recognizable curtseying wide-skirted Velasquez skit and several red and yellow dot-eyed square-heads.

Food. Barcelona is good for eating. I have had *butifarra con judías* – beans with sausage – and *habas a la catalana* – broader browner beans in a rich sauce with a variety of thick-sliced pig-meats – and *paella a la marinesca* – rice with olives and lemon and mussels and big prawns. There are odd charcoal-grill shops tucked away off the main streets, where you can get a course of grilled fresh seafood followed by a course of grilled meats – chicken, beef, lamb. The best dessert is *crema catalana* – a many-egged custard with an ice-sheet of caramel on top. Tonight we meet Jorge Edwards, a Chilean diplomat and writer whose *Persona Non Grata* is devastating about Cuba, and whom I want to translate a book of my own. This book has just appeared in French, but not in English. It is the only book I have written which was intended for a Latin language and is, in its original tongue, not quite what I wanted to write. We go to dinner in an Aragonese restaurant near to the place where Joan Miró was born and the Hôtel Oriental where George Orwell stayed. Edwards (whose grandfather was a British adventurer, probably Welsh, of the kind that helped build South America) has a marvellously attractive blonde girl with him who is fiercely Catalanophone and would rather listen to French than to Castilian. We drink, he nostalgically, a thin dry yellow wine of the Chilean kind. He eats squid cooked in its own ink, the rest of us not. We talk about the future of Catalan.

The way to encourage a new Catalan literature is to translate into it. The professors of Catalan at the university, who are also Catalan poets, are getting the Romans and Greeks into Catalan. I am delighted to learn that there is a Catalan translation of James Joyce's *Ulysses*. When I complain, long and loud, about the death of the Lancashire dialect, I am not really getting off the point. I think that world literature has come to a phase where it needs a return to the smaller unofficial languages. Look at Hugh MacDiarmid, perhaps the greatest modern poet. He taught himself the Scots language, Lallans, the tongue of Robert Burns, and fools regard that as a contractive rather than an expansive thing to do. Who was the greatest Italian poet of the nineteenth century? Belli, who wrote in the dialect of the Roman streets. The point about writing in Lallans or Lancashire or Romanesco or Provençal is that you can get away from the abstractions which increasingly burden a big central official language. In England the chance to use the dialects has gone for ever. I can get away in a poem or novel with a word like *kecks* for trousers or *oxters* for armpits, but who would read a book in the dialect of Lancashire? Lancastrians? No, they speak the language but don't read. If Catalan is taught in schools – which English dialects are not – there will be the substructure of an audience for the eventual Catalan Cervantes or Ibañez.

On the way to the parked car we pass again the hotel window from which Orwell watched the fighting in the Plaza del Rey. Edwards sadly says that the Orwell of *Homage to Catalonia* has nothing to give to the new age. You see Hemingway everywhere on the bookstalls, but not Orwell. What did Hemingway do for Spain except write about bullfights and get drunk in Pamplona? Orwell was wounded in the throat for Catalonia as well as in the heart. History is always unfair.

3 November

Lunch with Paco Porrua, my publisher, another exile from Argentina. We eat in Los Caracoles, which not only serves snails but has them carved on the banisters and even has cochleiform bread rolls. This is the restaurant where all visitors go, whose *patron* is a polyglot 'character', whose walls are covered with signed photographs of Marlene Dietrich, Vittorio Gassman and, of course, the great Hispanic hero Hemingway. My wife eats zarzuela, a very inclusive seafood anthology, Paco paella, myself a great wedge of grilled toughish succulent bull. Still on about the little languages, I describe my meeting with Borges at the Argentine Embassy in Washington DC and how, to the mystification of the watchful officials, we talked Anglo-Saxon. Barcelona, not just the wine, is making me drunk. Cultural fringes are obsessing me; I dream of a new Latin empire stretching from the Atlantic to the Alps, with *langue d'oc*, in some form or another, presiding over a renascence of troubadours and courts of love.

But Paco Porrua's trade is the promotion of imperial Castilian – though the spoken Spanish of Argentina is derived from Andaluz. He publishes books in Latin America as well as Spain and thanks God for a *big* language. Past imperial wickedness goes on paying fruitful dividends to both Hispanophone and Anglophone publishers, possibly also even some authors. No publisher could survive on Catalan. Glory in the world-spread of Spanish, as of English. Portuguese has spread too, but Lisbon has been unlucky. Brazilian has become the major tongue, metropolitan Portuguese a mere dialect. If I publish a book in Rio I can't publish the same version in Lisbon – the differences in nuance are too great. But Spanish is Spanish everywhere. Catalan? A political toy, no literary (viz. publishing) future in it. Big business has spoken; you can't fight economics.

Later in the day we drink with Alfonso Quintá Sadurni, a very considerable Barcelona journalist, head of the Catalonia bureau of *El Pais*, himself Barcelona-born. He knows his city and his fellow Catalonians too well to be unrealistic about the future, knows too the industrial wealth of the province – steel, textiles, natural gas on its way – and the improbability of Catalonia's being allowed to dispose of its own riches for its own benefit. Besides, it is the rich themselves who do the disposing. Since 1960 Spain has moved rapidly to the forefront of the European industrial nations. There are a lot of millionaire capitalists about, and they look after themselves in the way the great timocracy America has taught them. There are no direct taxes – they legally exist,

of course, but everybody evades them – and this overwhelmingly bene-
fits the rich. It is difficult to be radical in the old pre-bellum manner.
There are too many examples around of the dreadful consequences of
turning into a socialist state.

'It's funny about Franco,' says Alfonso Quintá Sadurni. 'It's as
though, as a personality, he never existed. You British retain a very
distinct image of Churchill, but Franco has just been vaporized,
become, in Orwellian phrase, an unperson.' The King? The King is a
more complex personality than is generally realized. That early accident, in which he shot his brother while fiddling with a gun, led him into
psychoanalytical labyrinths and voyages of self-discovery that don't fit
in easily with the view of a constitutional monarch as a rubber stamp. He
has a mind of his own; circumstances have forced him to put that mind
together, very painfully. Is fascism really dead? Fascism is never really
dead. So long as you have an army and a police force brought up on the
techniques of easy and brutal authority the fascist pot is always sim-
mering on the stove. How do you feel about the Church? Alfonso
Quintá Sadurni says he has no strong feelings one way or the other.
That big spiritual right arm of fascism has lost its muscle. The intellectual dignity has gone, along with the ability to oppress. With Catalan as
one of the permitted vernaculars since Vatican II, churches can be
regarded as active cells of Catalonian nationalism. I remind him of what
I saw once in the bellum days – a statue of the Virgin Mary endued with
the sash of a captain-general in Franco's army. Those days will never
come again, he thinks, doubtfully.

Barcelona kept her Avenida Generalissimo after the death of Franco.
Now it will be Avenida Tarradellas. But the grim fascist name seemed to
disturb no one. To the young, Franco has the same kind of reality as
Snow White's stepmother. Avenida Genghis Khan. Avenida Attila el
Huno. The name won't bite you.

4 November

A busy day. There is a great deal of Barcelona still to see, and there is
also the complicated business of getting tickets back to Monaco. You
can't buy them at Thomas Cook's or even at the offices of the railroad
authority. You have to ride to the Estación del Nord – even though
you'll leave Spain by the Estación de Francia – there to find an armed
policeman protecting small bureaucrats ready to bark at you, as though
taking a journey were still something illegal or vaguely suspect. We
apply at one counter and are barked off to a second and then have hopes
of buying a ticket at a third. When the ticket is eventually and reluctantly filled out, there are at least ten carbon copies. I run off clutching
the prize, fearful of being called back again to hear of its cancellation by a
suddenly revived Falange. We plunge again, with relief, into the modern city.

And also the ancient one. The city's historical museum, for instance,
with its busts of the Empress Agrippina and Antonino Pio, and the
Cathedral, with its black Christ of Lepanto, and the Basilica de la

Merced, with its fourteenth-century statue of the crowned Our Lady of Mercy, who is Barcelona's patroness – though, in the manner of most ancient sea ports, she is sometimes confounded with the goddess Venus. And. There is a great deal to see, but our final sightseeing date must be with Gaudí, the true mythic patron or incubus of Barcelona. We go to the Park or Parque Güell, whose architectural fancies took Gaudí from 1900 to 1914 to erect or exude.

A gingerbread pavilion for the concierge, spiked and nippled and fox-eared. Surfaces are undulant jigsaws of pebblework. Stairways azured and aurified out of dreams, with guardian dribbling dragons. Colonnades whose ceilings erupt into large boils, lanced by multifaceted columns. Stone seats like circular railroads, the backrests all frozen kaleidoscope. Viaducts imitating caverns, pillars and roofs dragon-scaly with stones stuck onto brick. It's a huge park, once the property of the great rich family Güell but now a playground for the people. But you don't play; you drink black coffee and Fundador and gawp at the curlicues of Gaudí's brain.

Barcelona by night, with fountains raging and bursting with fire in the Plaza de Catalunya. There are few cities left in the world where you can walk the nocturnal avenues without too much fear. There are rape and robbery in the city, but the city doesn't shrug its shoulders: appalled at the defiling of its own image of itself, it acts often very cunningly against crime – decoy policewomen rapees, for instance – and yet it does not seem to be a city of swaggering gunned constables. 'Vengeance of the wronged' was an item in the litany of praise that Cervantes, through his *ingenioso hidalgo*, showered on the city. We have our last dinner at the Carballeira, in a street by the port crammed with timepiece shops. Millions of watches for sale, cigarette lighters too, but not a cigar anywhere. The Carballeira isn't all it's cracked up to be. My plate of ham is rilled with white fat-streaks as though designed by Gaudí. The grilled fish floats in oil. But they give me a very good vanilla *helado* or ice soaked in whisky. There is, I see too late, an *estofado de toro* on the menu, and I wonder if this is at all like the son-of-a-bitch stew (pizzle, testes and all, washed down by Bloody Marys) that I met in Montana.

5 November

The train for Avignon leaves at 10.15. An ancient bureaucrat awaits us at our reserved seats, with the news that a mistake was made at the booking office (what steel whips await them?) and that we have to pay another 1000 pesetas. Then we move off, sorry to leave. It would be wrong to talk of taking a nostalgia for Spain back with us to Princess Caroline territory; it's rather a sense of southern Europe being new-made here, and our being barred, except very remotely, from participation. Barcelona doesn't want foreign residents: there are quite enough refugees from Latin America to fill up spare spaces. But my wife and I have been in search of a city ever since 1968, when I decided that London was no longer my town. We tried Malta and were appalled by a censorship that prevented my practising my trade; Rome, and Rome has erupted into high prices, violence and more theft than a civilized person can conceivably tolerate; Monaco, safe enough for a growing son but philistine despite its enlightened prince; New York, but you all know about New York. I'm sick of spending my evenings watching television, and I need something more than this perpetual typewriter-hammering during the day. Barcelona has the sort of rich day and night life one used to associate with Paris. Call it the Paris of the Mediterranean and you won't go far wrong. It's not netted into Spain but free to queen it over the varied middle-sea culture out of which we all ultimately spring. The discoverer of America stands on his plinth looking out to sea and wondering where the Americans are.

That Sweet Enemy

I have been living in Monaco, which is as much as to say France, for the last two years. French is my language of daily intercourse with shopkeepers and bureaucrats and police, but I avoid the language, and hence the intercourse, as much as I can. I huddle over my typewriter, which, though German, disgorges only English, as I would over a Sussex fire of pearwood or a gasfire in Camberwell. And yet French is my second language; I have known it for forty-five years. I try to explain to myself my seemingly volitional rejection of part of my culture and communicative equipment, a rejection expressed not only in avoiding its use but also in refusing to understand it when others speak it. I watch French television and reduce its voices to an unintelligible nasal babble. Why?

It may have something to do with the nature of the language itself, which seems to me to be morbid. The Latin *aqua* became Italian *acqua* and Spanish *agua*, but in French it has become *eau* (the word that the man in the Water Board in *Nicholas Nickleby* rightly scowled at). *Eau* is one vowel, as short a word as you can get, but I feel that if the French could have truncated it further they would have done so. French words are at their most French when they are monsters with heads but no tails. I was on a television programme in Paris before Christmas, and I had to turn Jesus Christ into *Jésu' Cri*. I have heard this shortening process in Lancashire pubs, but only with the one word *pint*, which moves through *pin'* and *pan* to nasalized *pa*. In French, unless there is a restraining *e* at the end, all words tend to be swallowed, just like that *pint*.

When I was a boy, you could hear the difference between *parlé* and *parlais*, but not any more. There used to be two kinds of o-sound, but they are becoming one. Spoken French is far closer to Eskimo, with all words glued together like deep-frozen shrimp heads, than it is to Italian or Spanish, where all sounds are clear and the endings click sharp as a belt buckle. General de Gaulle was the last of the clear, slow public speakers of French. Nowadays we have the nasal babble.

French was always hard for an Englishman to speak, since he couldn't really take those nasals and round front vowels very seriously – the vowels in *feu, coeur, bleu, pu, cru*. Now it is more difficult to speak than ever, and the French are merciless to its inept speakers. No interviewer who comes to see me moderates speed or vocabulary for the benefit of a poor foreigner. If I make, which I frequently do, an error in gender, there is a wince from the listener, as though I was offering him a nice strong cup of tea. People, think the French, ought to know French; it is the primal language that came even before Latin; it is the language of culture and logic. If you don't know it well, you'd better not know it at all. Italians are different: they take your mangled Tuscan as a compliment. But the French are Cartesian and unforgiving.

The French language always sounds sure of itself. Indeed, it sounds dogmatic and arrogant. Even prostitutes speak like school mistresses, and waiters have no hesitation about correcting your grammar. The tone of arrogance is not an accident of intonation, like the sobbing of Germans; the French are expressing arrogance by means of the sounds of arrogance. The French are always right, and the English usually wrong. The Germans, whom the French got to know well from 1940 on, are sometimes wrong too, but more usually right. Can the French and the English really become friends, as opposed to customers? Was Winston Churchill's offer of common nationality a gift he knew he wouldn't have to deliver? Can France and England become sisters only through a new Hastings or Agincourt?

Sir Philip Sidney called France 'that sweet enemy'. That seems to be the position still. First World War soldiers, including Robert Graves, swore that the next war would be an Anglo-French one. It needn't happen ever, since nagging at Britain in *Le Monde* over her sense of insufficient responsibility to the EEC, anglophobia on TV and at customs barriers, sneering at linguistic ineptitude in post offices and restaurants is more attritive and satisfying to the French. Americans, who don't speak French at all, never get sneered at. When they do, Americanized French is regarded as rather chic, and is used in TV commercials.

The sweetness is there, as well as the inimical: the cuisine and the couture, both *haute*, though the wine, when cheap, is dreadful. When dear too, often. But the fundamental cat–dog relationship of France and England is, I should think, one of the eternal international verities. To say that the French are not my brothers is not, I think, a racist statement, since the French are not black, at least not all of them. We just have to face a fact of temperament, culture and history.

My thirteen-year-old son, who is Anglo-Italian, knows all about it, since he goes to a French school. He hears about the French near-victory at Waterloo, francophone Canada, the joke of the British cuisine. Christened Andrea, he is called André, but has now Scotticized himself to Andrew. He has never seen the Hebrides, but he teaches himself Gaelic and plays the chanter. There is evidently here a desperate attempt to get himself, in imagination, as far as possible away from French language and culture. Put off by Gallic arrogance, he craves the porridgy warmth of the Gaels. He makes himself porridge for breakfast, though from French oats.

M. Peyrefitte has written a book called *Le Mal Français* – the French disease. This is neither syphilis nor arrogance but excessive logicality, which is called Cartesianism. He thinks the French must be more like the English – empirical, pragmatic, self-disciplined, patriotic, adaptable to change. Let's nourish no illusions. The French will never be like the English. The Channel remains the Great Divide. Concord and Concorde fly parallel and will never meet.

If you're superstitious, delete that final statement.

Yves and Eve

I have paid in my time many visits to Paris, and for many purposes. These have ranged from serious business to the most flippant and vulgar self-indulgence, with what is termed *culture* in the middle. But perhaps only in Paris can the notion of culture embrace the entire spectrum of living, so that Parisian vulgarity always has a kind of intellectual frigidity about it, the intellect can cope warmly with vulgar appetites, and big business is not incompatible with high art. In the *haute cuisine* and the *haute couture* you can see best how Paris effects its reconciliations of the vulgar flesh and the intellectual imagination, making money out of both with the kind of detached eagerness you associate with exalted philosophical inquiry. There's no city like it, except perhaps New York. But there's more honest animal drive about New York than refined aesthetic imagination. New York excels in short-order cookery and the rag trade, or clothing business. For anything *haute* it has the sense to go to Paris.

I went to Paris towards the end of July to have a look at the *haute couture*. I have always been as interested as the next man in the way women dress, but I never thought I would tiptoe round an atelier or sit with hard-faced fashion editors at a *défilé*, much less line up to give a French general's kiss to a couturier. I had very little time in which to build up the right enthusiasm. I caught the Train Bleu from sweltering evening Monaco and arrived in a cold wet Paris the following morning, a sixty-year-old sour man limping with sclerotic calf ache, in no mood for the fripperies of the season of fashion shows. The hotel room wasn't ready, so I took a taxi from the Place Vendôme to the Palais Galliera on the Avenue Pierre Premier de Serbie, where there is now a *Musée de la Mode et du Costume*. Between what the French call breakfast and the midday *croque monsieur*, I gave myself a crash course in thirty years of high fashion.

Paris was arbiter of modes as far back as Marie-Antoinette, who had a kind of minister of *haute couture*, and it was everybody's dress centre even in the Revolutionary period: my stepmother, I remember, wore *Directoire* lingerie. Hippolyte Leroy dressed the entire Napoleonic court and cost Joséphine, or the imperial exchequer, a fortune. But the tradition now flourishing really began with Charles-Frédéric Worth, who invented the *modèle* – the standard of dress elegance – and was the first to use mannequins. The name Worth is still a great one. Gabrielle Chanel, no less great, showed that the art need not be an exclusively male preserve: indeed, it was Madeleine Vionnet who revolutionized the craft of cutting and handed on her skill – much in the manner of a medieval painter – to pupils like Marcelle Chaumont and Jacques Griffe. The notion of apprenticeship in a distinguished school of dress design has characterized the art ever since. The great Irishman Molyneux taught Pierre Balmain and Marc Bohan. Robert Piguet produced Christian Dior, Antonio del Castillo and Hubert de Givenchy.

Balenciaga, Carven, Jean Dessès and Jacques Fath all opened their houses in 1937. Madame Grès, who had started off with her husband Alix in 1934, kept the couture flag flying during the German occupation as her own mistress. When the post-liberation efflorescence came, there had no been real break in continuity, but the thirty years since 1947 constitute an epoch whose professionalism obeys hard rules proper to a period of syndicalism, in which the competition is stiff, the stakes high, and the big names have to carry an aura of quality which can be attached to more than a mere dress design. The distinction of perfumes like Chanel No. 5 and Miss Dior has only a kind of mystical affinity with the magic of *turban* and *jupe*, but it is assumed that whosoever can dress a woman's body elegantly can also impart the right smell to it. And, in the primary field, a durability of character is as necessary as a powerful imagination. The professional couturier has to present two Paris collections every year, showing a minimum of sixty models at each: this is laid down by the *chambre syndicale*. In the Saint-Laurent show on 28 July 1977, there were ninety-seven distinct and separate creations. This is no work for lily-handed dilettantes.

The big name in 1947 was Christian Dior, and it was America that gave the name 'new look' to his euphoric confections, with their ample long skirts, strangled waists and pigeon bosoms. From 1950 on, skirts grew shorter and waists vaguer: Balenciaga was the big name now. In 1954, Dior responded with the Y-line – narrow skirt and wide shoulders – and 1957 saw the advent of Yves Saint-Laurent, with the *ligne-trapèze*. The couture of the sixties showed the first spectacular capacity of the art to reflect the times. Social and economic change in France (symbolized by the student uprising of May 1968) forced what had been a preserve of the wealthy to open up for the comparatively poor. What the French call the *prêt-à-porter* and we the ready-to-wear dress became very much the concern of the big fashion houses. The age of the restless young had arrived, and this meant also the young couturiers. Hubert de Givenchy, Guy Laroche, Pierre Cardin, André Courrèges all realized that the *haute couture* had to abase itself, to come out of the ivory tower and engage the mass markets. Of all the young names, the most considerable is that of Yves Saint-Laurent, Dior-trained, who left the Dior studios in 1962 after the death of his master (Marc Bohan took over there) and is now universally acknowledged *roi de la mode*.

Universally? Paris is perhaps a little less enthusiastic about him than Munich, Rome, Tokyo, New York. In this late wet July, with the foreign press and the foreign buyers coming in to see the winter fashion parades, it seemed to me that it was Saint-Laurent they were all after. The German ready-to-wear folk swear by him. Did not John Fairchild of *Women's Wear Daily* say that his spirit hovers over Fifth Avenue and that he's at the peak of his influence? Coco Chanel proclaimed him as her successor in 1968, but it is New York chiefly that has jammed on the crown. Saint-Laurent has responded to American enthusiasm by saying that he wished he'd invented blue jeans. He is a friend of *le grand new-yorkais* Andy Warhol (who has taken photographs of him which make him look just like Andy Warhol). On behalf of New York I set myself three aims: to watch him at work, to see the hundred fruits of his latest creative agony, to board the man himself artist to artist.

Fearful, a china-shop bull who happens also to be colour-blind, I went to 5 Avenue Marceau, centre of the YSL empire. It is all mirrors there and the decor is Second Empire. Wearing my YSL foulard like a hopeless gesture of propitiation (nobody, naturally, noticed), I was told by charming ladies of deliberate dowdiness that I would have to wait before I could see the master at work. This I had expected. So I waited, feeling like Dr Johnson in the antechamber of the Earl of Chesterfield. Beyond that mirrored door, I was breathlessly told, the final preparations for the *défilé* of the next day were proceeding: nerves were like overtuned E strings; work would have to go on all night; the master (and I thought of Mozart composing the overture to *Don Giovanni* while the audience was already arriving) had left things a little late. Ladies of the entourage peeked in to see how things were going. At length – now, you may enter. I don't want to stay long, I said (meaning it). So I went in. It was as though I were being admitted to a royal accouchement or some delicate ancient rite of erotic initiation. Actually, it wasn't as frightening as I'd expected.

There were chairs laden with rolls of silk and satin, and I succeeded, as I'd expected, in knocking some of these over. There were the master's designs, methodically arranged, with patches of material pinned to them. There were, of course, mirrors. In the middle of the room was one of the mannequins, or *jeunes filles* as Saint-Laurent prefers to call them, having what looked like a plaid travelling rug draped over her shoulders. I would have put it on her like an old coalsack, but the master, with deft twists of hands I could see were both strong and delicate, made an instant sonnet of it. His coadjutors were all around – Jean-Pierre the cutter, Anne-Marie Mugnoz the guardian of the temple, Gabrielle Buchaert of public relations, Loulou de la Falaise the muse or *inspiratrice* – but it was clear who was in control. I had a chance to shake the strong hand swiftly and exchange an *enchanté*. The smile was shy. He is fair, slight, very myopic. Thick big glasses rest on a John Gielgud nose that bespeaks strong will. The mouth is wide, the chin firm. In handling his *jeunes filles* he exhibited a gentleness, even a tenderness, that indicated a respect for the female body not far from worship. Later, in a rare flash of English, he was to say to me that he looked on women as – The word sounded like 'dolls'. '*Des poupées?*' I said, unbelieving. No, no, no, not dolls – idols. It is only homosexuals who are capable of this near religious awe. We heterosexuals, alas, want to get too close for worship.

Pierre Bergé came in, the man in charge of the YSL empire that goes far beyond the *haute couture* – small, stocky, bearded – carrying a long-playing disc: tomorrow's music, to be approved by the master. I tried to see what the music was to be, but Bergé hugged the secret. Bergé is a formidable man who shares a house as well as a life with Saint-Laurent. He is forty-six and looks it, while Saint-Laurent, forty-one, conserves the bodily meagreness and blue-eyed gaze of a boy. While he keeps the artist's innocence, the exploiter of his talent has been sophisticated by the hard world of *affaires*. Bergé believes passionately in the talent he sells and regards the Saint-Laurent label, or *griffe*, as a precious badge not to be distributed lightly like a joke decal. The name is attached to thirty-five products, including spectacles, stockings and umbrellas, all of which may be regarded as accessories to the primary couture image. It is a lot, though only half of the number of commodities which bear the *griffe* of Pierre Cardin. Bicycles, candy, wine – that probably goes too far for a great couturier's label. 'A name,' says Bergé, 'is like a cigarette. You draw on it and use it up, till only the fag end is left. I have to refuse franchises. In America they want Saint-Laurent automobile tyres. No, nothing doing.' With Bergé the world of the name starts to get in the way of the more immediate world of pins and stitches.

I did not stay long in this world, but I found it unexpectedly soothing. If I expected to see delicious young girls waiting to have their near-nudity draped, I was disappointed. They came in dressed for a final going-over – the set of a hat, the snip at a ribbon. Backstage the army of sewers (so the handout in English calls them – disgusting ambiguity; why not seamstresses?) was undoubtedly needling away still like fury: here we were close to the reality of the *défilé*. I understood that, the work going on all night, tantrums might be possible in the small hours. It did not seem likely to me that Saint-Laurent would throw tantrums. I knocked some more rolls of material over and left. Nobody, of course, noticed. I felt gently elated, as though I been let in on a mystery, the mystery being that there was no mystery – just a talent for enhancing beauty with cloth, stitches, and a genuine devotion to the female body. In an age when women yell for equality and would gladly jettison all their inborn glamour to get it, I had been given a little lesson in an older value: that female beauty is a kind of eucharistic tabernacle, not a man-made cage.

The following morning I walked from the Place Vendôme to the Hôtel Intercontinental on the rue Castiglione. The show was to be held in the Salon Impérial. I always find seat numbers hard to see, so I was there early. There were others there earlier than I – buyers and ladies (chiefly) of the press. Japanese photographers had their Leicas at the ready; a big Moroccan with a tarboosh greeted women he knew, or perhaps did not know, with kisses of excessive enthusiasm; there were exquisite men with silver hair in safari outfits. Everybody knew everybody, except me. I sat surlily down next to an old Byzantine lady who proved criminally quick with a pencil. They looked a tough lot, these fashion correspondents, with hard eyes and hard lines round the mouth, devotees of elegance but scorning to be elegant themselves. A long raised walkway stretched the length of the salon, separating press and buyers as the Red Sea separated Egyptians and Israelites. We glared at each other across it. The photographers clung like crabs to its shores. We waited long but without rancour. Nobody, apparently, ever expects these sessions to begin on time. I lighted a Schimmelpenninck and there was the usual French chorus of expostulation, like the frogs in Aristophanes – Brekkekekekk koax, with the odd *oo là là*. I smoked it stolidly to the butt, a brutish Britisher who won at Waterloo.

Then the music started – Nino Rota or Morricone or somebody. Without preamble a disembodied voice chanted a number from the catalogue, and then the first *jeune fille* strode along the walkway like Helen on the ramparts of Troy. From then on it was nonstop – always two of these goddesses on stage, stalking with superb panache, crossing each other under the central chandelier with never a greeting. 'Why,' I asked Saint-Laurent later, 'do they carry their visages so immobile?' It was ritual, he replied. Would I expect a wink or a smirk from a priest at the altar? Yet the beautiful hostile impassivity did once break down. One of the blonde goddesses dropped her swirling foulard in her whirling passage. A plain little Japanese camera girl picked it up and handed it to her on her proud march back. She was rewarded with a smile of such opulent radiance that my heart turned into Atlantic City taffy. After that, I noticed, model occasionally deigned to grin at model at the point of crossing.

That damned chandelier. There was a metal knob like the fist of heaven, ready to crack at all this female hubris. It hit one girl's hat; she turned her temporary disconcertment into a lovely little hand ballet of multiple apology. The iron fist was grudgingly appeased. It left them all alone from then on, except for swiping humorously twice at long hat-feathers. All? There seemed to be a girl for every confection, but of course there were only ten. Black, Asiatic, English rose – Saint-Laurent likes them exotic. When he told me later that his *haute couture* was a matter of 'nostalgia', he was not referring to homesickness for the past so much as for lands as remote as the past and yet quite as easily recoverable. He was born in Oran and has a house in Marrakesh. All the dresses of this collection – with the exception of a wedding gown and a very intrusive Edwardian bustle – looked firmly East. Last year he was Caucasian (not in the sense of the US immigration form); this year there is a lot of China about. The old conical coolie hat sat at least three times like, I thought, an impertinent candle snuffer. The opulence of material was of a mandarin order; provocative harem pants flowed like brown champagne out of boots; capes swung; furs defied all of France's save-wild-life committees. It was gorgeous and unreal. You cannot go through a Métro turnstile in these, people complain. Saint-Laurent says: 'These are not for women who use the Métro.' He also says: 'My dresses are for women who travel with forty suitcases.'

How is this reconciled with the Saint-Laurent who put women elegantly and practically into pants suits and constellated jeans with twinkling brilliants? We have to go back to Worth to understand the philosophy of it. The creation is a model, an ideal that can stand undiluted only on the screen or the stage. It is in order to dress Catherine Deneuve for *Belle de Jour* or *La Sirène du Mississippi*, or to design for Zizi Jeanmaire at the Casino de Paris, but we must not confuse the art of fictive extravagance with the craft of utility. The models I saw on the burlesque-type stage of the Salon Impérial express an élan, a spirit, an inspirational force. They say: this is the trend of the coming autumn and winter. If women start wearing coolie hats, we shall know that they have been listening to Saint-Laurent or his avatars. When women stride Fifth Avenue in harem pants stuffed into boots, the shy grin of Yves will hover for an instant, Cheshire-catwise. Nobody has to swallow the whole rich draught; nobody could. But you can sip; you can make your own mild cocktail with his ingredients. In other words, the heavy brew has to be filtered gently into ready-to-wear.

I don't know how many of the crammed five hundred were listening to the music as the parade proceeded; I certainly was. It was a strange medley, but apparently there was nothing arbitrary. We heard the voice of Mae West, but twice we went through the closing scene of *Tristan and Isolde*. The fat juiciness of the orchestration was right for what we were looking at, the restless chromatic language made up for the colour we mostly missed in the subfusc materials, but what did the tragic love-death have to do with it all? I wasn't convinced by Saint-Laurent's later assurance that the tragic was not inappropriate to the expression of joy in a woman's body: does a piece of couture have to subsist only on the level of comedy? This was the stageman talking. But Wagner was certainly brought low, bent to serve an applied art. Fashion shows need their own musical scores, and the man best capable of writing them is long dead – I mean Erik Satie. He would have contrived piquant *musique d'ameublement* for flute, oboe and cello, set the musicians at a distance from each other, and made sure that each of the ninety-odd confections had its proper accompaniment.

The show ended with a *robe de mariée* in which ritual reached its limit. I cannot describe the bubbling white with its butterfly bows and street-long train in the right technical language, but I do know that the face of the generic bride was totally obscured by a trellis of veiling. The influence of North Africa? Hardly, since the purpose of the yashmak seems to be to enable its wearer to make with the doe-like eyes. No eyes here. This creature met you at the altar like an ambulant sybil, and it might not be at all the girl you courted. I daydreamed that afternoon of undressing it to find wires, laths, a simple piece of clockwork. Or, nearly as bad, the living reality of the ideal mannequin, all legs and no breasts. Let me light another Schimmelpenninck and be coarse. A friend of mine slept with one of these exquisite dream figures and said it was like going to bed with a bicycle.

The show was over. The applause that had greeted the creations had had a precise graduation of appraisal about it, no mere politeness. Now ecstasy, decently held in before, cracked and burst as the shy creator emerged among banked lilies. I went to fight for free gin and, when the time came, to smack my felicitations on the master's cheeks. I was really felicitating myself. I had been to the greatest *défilé* of the season and come through unemasculated. But I was tired out for the rest of the day.

The following afternoon I was due to see Saint-Laurent at home. I spent much of the morning going round the YSL shops, probing the nexus between art and big business. There are two kinds of *magasin* or *boutique*, and you have to distinguish between those called Yves Saint-Laurent – with the distinctive typeface that I look down now to see on my crumpled *carré* or foulard – and those, with a more pedestrian typeface, named Saint-Laurent Rive Gauche. The first has its headquarters at the 5 Avenue Marceau I had already visited; the second at 26 rue d'Aboukir. The first sells scarves, belts, cravats, men's stuff, kids' stuff, and has a separate shop for each commodity. It also runs two shoeshops – one for men, one for others. Saint-Laurent Rive Gauche has four shops that sell ready-to-wear to women, and one that does the same thing for men: I have passed it often, since it is on the Place Saint-Sulpice, near my publisher Laffont. These retail outlets, I know, are reproduced in all the great cities of the world. I had a close look at the Saint-Sulpice shop and was not impressed. Odd letters had become detached from the legends on the windows; inside it was morgue-like; service was at its most Parisianly disdainful. As for the goods, they were merely goodish, like anybody else's. Distinction resided only in a large photograph of the master, arms folded, grim in a context of well-hung burly statuary. And, of course, in the name itself, what there was of it left to read on the window.

Couturiers' names have become holy, magical, a sufficiency in themselves. If the couturier's product (I do not now mean his individual creations) were really distinctive, it would not need his name. Fabergé needs no label; when you listen to Beethoven you don't have to have a quiet voice cutting in every ten bars to tell you who this is. But only when you literally flaunt the name on scarf or aftershave is the mirage of special quality evoked. I have a very ordinary black dressing gown which cries GIVENCHY on its waist rope. If that name were not there to impress the mailman, the garment itself would be nothing. There are inevitably exceptions: I can spot certain great perfumes with the nose alone; Gucci products never let one down as leather, though as articles for use (I'm thinking particularly of the huge travelling satchel Fellini gave me) they are not always as efficient as the compartmented plastic junk you can pick up for a dollar or two in your drugstore. There is talk of retailing Saint-Laurent cigarette lighters. I'd like one of those out of sheer snobbery, but I don't expect it to burn with a special hard gemlike flame.

With such thoughts in my mind I went to Saint-Laurent's home on the rue de Babylone. The street is not distinguished, and he doesn't see much of it, though it must be a comfort to have a police barracks close by. He is not, for instance, an habitué of the Café de Babylone opposite. I asked the *patron* there if he knew of the great man at Number 55. Great? he said. Pouf, there are greater. Neighbours, of course, are always big disparagers. Frankly, I expected no large revelations from a tête-à-tête with the man himself. Oscar Wilde said that minor poets are always more fun to meet than major ones. The major poet is fulfilled in his work and has nothing to say outside it; the minor one's talk coruscates with all the poems he'd like to create but can't. When the *simpatico* sixty-seven-year-old Spanish manservant showed me in and led me to the bottle of Beefeater (it was again Dr Johnson visiting Lord Chesterfield), I knew that I would learn something from the decor, bibelots and books.

Jean-Michel Frank designed the place for a great American lady who crashed on Wall Street in 1929. It retains a twenties aura which matches its present owner's literary tastes. There is a complete leather Proust in the library; there are pictures of Jean Cocteau, of whom Saint-Laurent was a protégé. The vast mass of solider possessions is eclectic – ivory, shagreen and parchment tables, a Siamese Buddha wondering what the hell all those lamé cushions are doing there, a Csaky bronze, Greek statues thoroughly balled, a Modigliani drawing willed to him by Cocteau, Ballet Russe frivolities, heavy elegance from Napoleon III, chairs in the form of full-grown sheep created by Lalanne, a Le Corbusier console. I envied only the pastel Burne-Jones pentatych picked up at a sale. I saw, sadly, how little taste I really had, what a failed artist as well as business man I was. I live in dust among old newspapers, I hide marks on the wall with askew *Playboy* playmates, I must scrub the kitchen floor tomorrow: where have I gone wrong? There was a small mitigant, though. He has a drawing of prancing nude Josephine Baker, but I have Josephine Baker's Monte Carlo piano. His own baby grand has no stool and is desperately out of tune. When he arrived I played part of the *Liebestod*, ironically. It jangled, ironically, like an Isolde made of tinfoil. We talked.

I knew the main facts of his career. He was born on 1 August 1936, in Oran, Algeria – a provincial, a *pied noir*, the only boy of a family of Alsatian origin. He has two sisters, both married, living in Paris. His mother lives in Paris too, and he adores her, a woman of vivacity and, naturally, elegance, one to whom he could run as a child, the abettrix of his dreams. The desire to escape from the exterior world – a very hard-lined one in Oran, all sun and inky shadows, full of brutal boys – was with him early. He wanted the softer lights of the theatre, Maeter-linckian shadows, the fantasy of decor and costumes. He was also strongly aware not only of being in the French provinces but of being in a colony; even as a child, he had a Pépé le Moko hunger for Paris, where the action, or the couture, was. Tastes which American meat-and-potatoes men would term effeminate were helped to develop in an encouraging female ambience. His father was a tough man of law but 'he let me do what I wanted. . . . I was greatly attracted to costumes and the theatre and fashion. . . . I used to do whole collections for myself.' When he left school he went to Paris, where, at seventeen, he got some sketches into *Vogue*. In 1953, after attending a school of dress design, he won the prize offered by the International Wool Secretariat for a black, asymmetrically cut, décolleté cocktail dress. Michel de Brunhoff, the director of *Vogue*, introduced him to Christian Dior, and he joined the Dior house. Dior took 'my mother aside,' said Yves, 'and told her that one day I would be doing his entire collection.' The prophecy was fulfilled with unexpected speed. Dior died when Yves was only twenty-one; something had to be done quickly for the spring collection; Yves came up with the trapeze line – the most original dress concept since Dior's own 'new look' of 1947. It was, as they say, a sensation.

Then came an experience which he tells me, still gives him *cauchemars*. The Algerian war was on and he was called into the army. The directors of Dior, following the precedent of Brigitte Bardot's husband Cheri, pleaded that bad nerves make bad soldiers (one of the catchphrases surrounding Saint-Laurent is 'He was born with a nervous break-down'). The dithering young couturier was dragged off, but he never had to suffer the banal cut of a military uniform. His nerves broke, he was thrown into hospitals and prison cells, but he did not become a soldier. The army authorities let him go. My well-read readers will remember that Shakespeare has a couturier among his minor characters. The 'woman's tailor' in *Henry IV Part Two*, who is called Feeble, joins Falstaff's army without protest. 'We owe God a death. . . . He who dies this year is quit for next': those untypical words of a couturier became a kind of mantra for Ernest Hemingway. There was nothing of the Feeble about Saint-Laurent.

When he got back to Dior, he found that Marc Bohan had taken over his job as artistic director. He demanded freedom from his contract. The Maison Dior said no. Yves fought. He won. Free but penniless, he and Pierre Bergé borrowed money and showed their first collection in a rented house on the Bois de Boulogne on 29 January 1962. It was a huge success. From then on the story has been one of fame and money.

I asked him if money meant much to him. No, he said, and he seemed to mean it. He is surrounded by expensive and lovely things, but these are eternal solidities, not the evanescent pamperings of the consumer. He smokes Kool cigarettes, which are cheaper than my own Schimmel-penninck. Food doesn't interest him, he could subsist on boiled rice. Bergé, who lives in the lower half of the house, goes to work in a chauf-feured Rolls; Yves drives his own Volkswagen. His tendency is to asceti-cism – the bare room and the uncluttered table. He has pared himself down to sheer function.

He'd been in the business for twenty years, I reminded him. Was it time for a change? Yes, he said: he wanted to write. Do you love words? Yes, adore them: words are analogous to fine stuffs and colours, their arrangement into new patterns is the highest of the high couture. Degas, I told him, said to Mallarmé' that he had lots of ideas for poems, but he just couldn't get down to writing the poems. Mallarmé's reply is to be engraved on the hearts of all writers: 'Literature isn't made with ideas, it's made with words.' Saint-Laurent nodded and nodded (he is a great nodder) his profound agreement. He was shy about showing me the manuscript he's working on, but later, in his marvellously cluttered bedroom, I stole a glance at a page or two of his typescript. I didn't take in much of the content, but I was pleased with the intricacy of sentence construction, the love of rare words, the hints of a mental complexity not usually associated with the dress designer. I was also pleased that he crammed the page with words (though neatly) and didn't like margins: if it had been in English, I might have taken it for something of my own.

There can't be any real change of métier, I suggested. You can't get out of the cage, you're a prisoner of the talent by which the world knows you. He didn't accept the word *prisonnier*. It was rather, he said, a question of responsibility – for the people whose livelihood depended on his skill; he was not a *prisonnier* but a free man, free to go on choosing the responsibility. Do you, I asked, feel any responsibility for the peripheral things done in your name – the tatty boutique in the Place Saint-Sulpice, for instance? No, no responsibility; he was responsible only for the primary trade he practised. The name as a vague guarantee of quality in other, marginally related, spheres must look after itself.

And how does your art subsist, I asked, in relation to other arts? If there is a ladder of the arts, on which rung does the art of the great couturier stand? He has no delusions about its comparative lowliness. The word 'genius', so often attached to him, was an embarrassment. Compared to Beethoven, Flaubert and, yes, Cocteau, the achievement of the trapeze line was a very minor one. To make a dress is to practise an *art appliqué*. And so we came to the bodies of women, and more than their bodies – the mystery that inheres in the whole sex, the female numen that asks for worship, the way in which couture is a cult of adoration. Saint-Laurent was very serious, even religious, about this. Is there, I asked, a tension between nature and form in your art, as in other arts? He didn't at first understand; probably my French was at fault; I tried again. What I mean is: the task of the artist is to get the better of nature, to impose his own pattern upon it, and the tension we get from his struggle to do this is one of the excitements of art. He understood that well enough, and he was insistent in affirming that, in his art, nature must win. He hated the twisting and torturing of the *coiffeuse*, for instance: hair must be shining and free. The body must be free too; the aim of his art is to emphasize the freedom of the body, to glorify that freedom – no impositions, no constraints, no torturings.

If he has a religion, its deity is without doubt woman. I asked him about his more conventional beliefs. Did he believe in sin? No, no, no, no, never. He shuddered, much as we can imagine Rimbaud shuddering, at the iron doctrines and sour pieties of the French faith. They were part of his boyhood in Oran, and the escape he makes to his villa in Marrakesh – not in August, of course, August is far too hot – is an escape to an environment whose Islamic culture he finds very sympathetic. Yes, he is attracted by Islam, he says. I did not pursue this, but I could see that that sunlit faith, younger than Christianity, might have something to give to a homosexual whose concern is with a nonrepresentational art – the only art Islam allows, as Islamic ethics, especially in Morocco, does not frown on the pederast.

We talked of the agonies of art while his chihuahua, Hazel, slept on my knees. Artists, who get no end of a kick out of the trade they practise, are always eager to say what hell it all is. 'Art,' said Yves, 'is a poison.' It's well known that he's had his depressions, his cafards, and made his escape from reality into alcohol and drugs. But drugs are more than an escape, he says: they can open new imaginative vistas for the artist. I'd heard all that before, especially from junkie students of creative writing, and was pretty sour. Examples? Well, Cocteau. How about Shakespeare, Milton, Flaubert, whose visions were bigger than anything that bizarrely sparking synapses could throw up? He let that pass; his own tastes, as the decor of his house shows, don't encompass the gigantic thunderers. He had dressed Albee's *Delicate Balance* and Colin Higgin's

Harold and Maude, but one can't imagine his doing *King Lear*.

Did he ever desire to be something other than an artist? Oh, yes. A bartender, for instance? (My own dream, but I know I'd give too many drinks free.) Oh yes, by all means, *un barman*. I got an image of Yves's bar then – exquisite decor, baa-lamb bar-stools, strong cocktails of unbelievable ingredients, a link between the *haute cuisine* and the *haute couture*. Did he ever desire to get away from art and everything with a final quietus? Of course, suicide, why not? Everybody thinks of suicide sometime. But there's always the matter of one's responsibility.

I had a look at his hands, drawing on my village fête experience as a palmist. As I'd expected, the hands were heavy to hold, tough, soigné worker's hands. As I'd expected also, the right hand was almost an exact mirror duplication of the left: his career had all been worked out in the stars. Intellect and emotion were well developed and health was good, life a straight road; there were no signs of enemies. 'Enemies?' he said. 'Oh yes, I have enemies.' He is a Leo, and I know Leones – my own son is one of them: strong-willed, limpet-sticking to an aim against all opposition, nasty-tempered when he doesn't get his own way. There seemed to me to be no capacity for nastiness in this Yves who was worn out with work and the pressures of people, desperate for a vacation yet submissive to cameras and my own probing. He was going to Deauville for a holiday, but it would be no holiday. The imagination, as he said, takes no holiday: his pencil would be busy, new glorifications of woman were hungry for realization.

So there it was. I left the hermetic paradise and went out into a drizzling Paris whose taxi drivers seemed all to have gone on vacation, though probably not to Deauville. I trudged, wincing at the toothache in my calf, over the greasy pebbles to that Métro whose turnstiles could never admit a Saint-Laurent creation. What were my feelings, a Bottom who'd been introduced briefly to Titanian enchantments? Not envy, rather brotherliness. We were both committed to the enchantment of raw material into some sort of image of beauty. To hell with the material rewards – lavish with him, meagre with me. I have my name on books swift to go into the publishers' mincing machines; he has his on boutiques from here to Tokyo. In ten years, perhaps less, a bright new name will emerge from the French provinces, and Saint-Laurent will join history, like Worth. *Tout passe*, and not even art survives in the days of the new Goths. Yves, who prides himself on being a man of the present, knows all about the teeth of time. Couturiers come and go, like novelists, but woman remains. That is an abiding consolation. Use the priest till his vestments are rags, and then throw him on the sacerdotal scrapheap. The goddess lives, and that's all that matters.

Morbus Gallicus

Some years ago my former professor of modern history, Dr A. J. P. Taylor, caused a minor riot among British patriots by asserting that any reasonable Englishman would, *au fond*, prefer to be a Frenchman. You can see how this had to go against the Anglo-Saxon grain: France the traditional enemy (though Sir Philip Sidney called her 'that sweet enemy'), land of frog-eaters and dancing masters, of dirty sexual habits, rapacious and untrustworthy even as an ally, given to dipping teabags in tepid water, eating nothing for breakfast and too much for lunch, heavy-drinking but never honestly drunk. It had all been summed up earlier in a song in Gilbert and Sullivan's *Ruddigore*:

> Then our Captain he up and he says, says he,
>   'That chap we need not fear –
>   We can take her, if we like,
>   She is sartin for to strike,
> For she's only a darned Mounseer,
>   D'ye see?
> She's only a darned Mounseer!
> But to fight a French fal-lal – it's like hittin' of a gal –
>   It's a lubberly thing for to do;
>   For we, with all our faults,
>   Why, we're sturdy British salts,
> While she's only a Parley-voo,
>   D'ye see?
> While she's only a Parley-voo!'

It's hardly worth mentioning that the Englishmen who call themselves patriotic Anglo-Saxons are usually half-French, or half-Norman, and that there's a profound ambivalence in traditional British francophobia. Most Englishmen would be prepared to go along with King Henry V, who loved France so much that he wouldn't part with a single acre of her. Anglo-Saxons regard France, along with her culture, as something absorbable. She has many fine things, and these would sit well on an English mantelpiece, as her wines sit well in an English cellar. But to *be* French – horror of horrors.

How do Americans look at France? American aesthetes in the twenties were ready enough to be absorbed into French culture so long as the American Express remained open and the exchange rate was favourable. The French and the American Revolutions sprang out of the same libertarian philosophies; Ben Franklin could give the Parisians the title of a revolutionary song – '*Ça Ira*'. But to present-day Americans, even the most cultured, France is somewhere out there, usually to be confused with the special Paris of the Americans, and her influence on the American way of life is minimal. America is, *au fond*, a drunken country that is scared of drink. She has been reared on British pragmatism and is scared of ideas. She remains, despite the permissiveness, puritanical about sex. Although French is a mother tongue of the Laurentian Shield, few North Americans want to learn it or, if they learn it, learn it well. But why should they? Non-French learn French so that they can buy from Paris what Paris is only too willing to sell without a word spoken.

There is much talk in France these days of *le mal français*, and many Anglo-Saxons are glad to hear that the French are finding something wrong with themselves. The Americans and British have done enough breast-beating in the last twenty or so years, but the French have rarely been quick to be sorry for anything. Indeed, one aspect of the French character that has always been displeasing to Anglo-America is arrogance. It is a quality that, to English speakers, is attached to the very sound of the language. Even prostitutes sound like schoolmistresses. Taxi drivers use French with a precision that, to our ears reared on the hesitancy and sloppy syntax of everyday Anglo-American, seems positively academic. Whereas most nations are delighted that foreigners should wish to speak languages not theirs, however haltingly, the French don't take kindly to foreign garbling of the speech of Corneille and Racine. I remember in a restaurant pointing to the menu, where it said *Fruits*, and saying '*Fruits, s'il vous plaît*,' and the waitress instinctively correcting: '*DES fruits, monsieur.*' Though I live in French-speaking territory, I use French as little as I can. I don't like, even in a tobacconist's, putting myself *in statu pupillari*.

The language is, we all acknowledge, a fine intellectual instrument, and it carries, even in the street, the aura conferred on it by its literary and philosophical masters. It's cerebral, which Italian tries not to be, and it glories in its cerebrality. The French pride themselves on being Cartesian, though many of them are not sure what the term means. René Descartes was, of course, one of the greatest of the Renaissance philosophers, and his fellow-Gauls believe themselves to have inherited, through an educational system of extreme rational rigidity, his capacity for seeing everything with the sharp sight of the logician. To some extent this is true. All Latin countries go in for stifling bureaucratic systems, but whereas an Italian functionary can't explain why a form has to be filled in in septuplicate, his French counterpart always can. We can accept the logic, even if we can't always swallow the premise on which it's based. The lady who runs the café across the street recently had to fill in a form which had to do with her having a baby. Was her situation one of matrimony or of concubinage? The answer: concubinage. No shame, no hedging, no euphemism. An intellectual categorization, but somehow lacking in basic humanity.

The French have a great capacity for inventing philosophical systems; they are perhaps the finest theorists in the world. They can intellectualize anything, and frequently do. The last world war produced

Sartrean existentialism, which explained (somewhat belatedly, considering that France had surrendered to the Germans in 1940) how necessary it was for man to resist evil and, considering the yawning indifference of the universe, how absurd. Camus came up with the image of Sisyphus, rolling a rock for ever up a hill in hell, always seeing it fall down again. The French were at their usual business of thinking. Claude Lévi-Strauss devised a structuralist system which could combine into acceptable intellectual patterns riddles and incest, or menstruation and honey, or lunar eclipses and loud music. His disciple Roland Barthes could even intellectualize the *haute couture* and the *haute cuisine* into structuralist formulae.

All this is very clever, but a lot of it sounds like chess. In the field of art, as usual, the French have been propounding theory and expecting practice to follow, rather than – which is what Anglo-America prefers to do – theorizing out of art put together out of instinct. Thus, there has been the doctrine of the *nouveau roman*, or anti-novel, which, apart from the odd book by Robbe-Grillet and Nathalie Sarraute, has been more exciting to argue about than to see incarnated in an actual work of art. Indeed, France has had to leave it to England to produce genuine anti-novels – like those of Christine Brooke-Rose and Rayner Heppenstall – just as it has had to watch structuralism germinating in the American work of Thomas Pynchon and the British work of your humble servant. But your humble servant's novel *MF*, based sedulously on the doctrines of Lévi-Strauss, had to have these lines from Charles Péguy as epigraph:

C'est embêtant, dit Dieu. Quand il n'y a aura plus ces Français,
Il y a des choses que je fais, il n'y aura personne pour les comprendre.

Which, freely translated, goes: 'It's a nuisance, says God. When there are no more Frenchmen, there'll be nobody around any more to understand the things that I do.' I appended that as a sincere tribute; the French capacity for intellectualization must leave any stupid instinctual Anglo-Saxon dribbling with envy.

How do we tie Gallic rationality in with Escoffier and Yves Saint-Laurent? Frugality, parsimony, surprisingly, comes into it somewhere. The French are good logicians in that they hate waste: 'Entities must not be multiplied unnecessarily' (William of Ockham said that, and he ought to have been French). The arts of the cuisinier and the couturier alike begin with economy, with doing the best you can with the little you have. The eve of the battle of Marengo, Napoleon's cook could find only a scrawny chicken, some tomatoes, eggs and crayfish. The result was a classic dish, *poulet Marengo*. No classic Paris couture has ever succeeded through excess. At the end of the war British women looked dowdy but French women had never been lovelier. To make great art out of few materials is a supreme achievement, but the French tend also sometimes to believe in frugality for its own sake. They are not generous, as Americans are. In the First World War they charged their British allies abominably for accommodation and fodder. They save at the expense of others. The abhorrence of waste sometimes looks like human concern, but it is merely an instinct. Thus, some years ago, a careless gas-station attendant had failed to put back the cap of my gas tank, and I was dripping rich fluid all through the Var. Literally hundreds of French motorists pointed this out to me with shock and horror. They didn't give a damn about me; they just couldn't help it.

Why, with these gifts, should the French be suffering from a *mal* or a national illness? Alain Peyrefitte, the new Minister of Justice, has been discussing all this at length in a best-seller called, predictably enough, *Le Mal Français*. His method is anecdotal and full of rhetorical questions. There is an unspoken premise which even an intellectual Frenchman takes for granted – that it is terrible that the French, of all people, should have a *mal*. The British, the Germans, the Americans – well, what do you expect? But the French should be true to their history and destiny and, terribly, they have been failing. Peyrefitte finds the source of the *mal* in the gap between ideation and realization. The French father theories, but they are not always successful in putting these into practice. Intellectualization makes for rigidity; the French meet problems less in terms of what can be done than in terms of what ought to be done. Albert Schweitzer said the French were *vertrauenswürdig*, '*on ne peut pas compter sur les Français*' – they come to Africa and build a hospital which would be fine in Paris but is hopeless on the equator. '*Ils ont leurs idées toutes faites*' – they have their ideas already worked out. You can't trust them in emergencies. They're not pragmatic enough.

Peyrefitte, as a student in London, found virtues in the British impossible of transference to the French. Few things had to be *imposed* on the British; if there was not enough electricity in the grids of the age of austerity, it was left to the fathers of families to cut off the supply themselves. Peyrefitte calls it '*le civisme au breakfast*': 'Every morning, almost at nine, the head of the house would look nervously at his watch, then go off at nine on the dot and come back looking relieved.' He had done his duty; he had pulled the switch. As for the blackout during the war, 'If a neighbour,' said the paterfamilias, 'saw a sliver of light under my door –' 'He'd report you?' said Peyrefitte. 'No, but he'd be appalled.'

The French lack, apparently, the gift of governability. Their intellectualism created, with Rousseau and Montesquieu, the principles of contractual democracy which made the American Constitution. They love the notion of creating a State on the best rational principles, but they are temperamentally incapable of allowing it to work. The State is an intellectual glory, but it is also the enemy. An outsider would say that there is more than a gap between ideation and realization; of the holy trinity of mind, emotions and body, the two outer elements function well, but something goes wrong with the feelings that, in stupid races like the English (and it was Walter Bagehot who pointed out that such stupidity was England's salvation), spring to life when they are needed. A good question is: how far is the average Frenchman prepared to die for

France? The stupid British have died for England, but something terrible and baffling happened to the French in 1940. A kind of intellectual cynicism supervened at a time when intellect was not wanted, only patriotic guts. The French used to despise the Germans for their lack of Gallic culture – an attitude which, given the natural arrogance of the French, one might expect. But the French believed they could prevail over the Germans precisely because of this German lack. This was carrying the supremacy of the intellect too far.

There is no war on now, but much of Europe – Italy, Britain, France itself – is suffering from a common *mal* more depressing than war, since wars are sustained through hope. Intellectuals like Peyrefitte are wrong if they suppose that inflation, political unrest, strikes (I write this by candlelight with a deep-freeze full of incipient decay), growing unemployment spring out of a specific Gallic disease, although there is something very Gallic in the hard-spending consumerism – better, in France, thought of as hedonism – which accompanies the general social and economic mess. Britain's ghastly inflation, for instance, can be blamed not on abstract Cartesianism but on anachronistic syndicalism. Yet the basic French *mal* has to be referred to the way France is governed, to the administrative structure with which, it is believed, French Cartesianism can grapple.

A recent *sondage* or poll in the monthly *Comment* showed that 82 per cent of the pollsters believe that the French administration complicates rather than simplifies the life of the citizens; 66 per cent think that French justice favours the rich rather than the poor; 40 per cent don't think the French army capable of defending the country in the event of war; 68 per cent are dissatisfied with French education because it doesn't fit young French men and women for the practice of a profession; 84 per cent think their political representatives are more concerned with getting themselves re-elected than with doing their legislative job; 46 per cent believe that the Catholic Church in France is neglecting its office, that of guardian of the faith, and is too much concerned with *la vie matérielle*. But it is typical of the French that they should find a certain intellectual satisfaction in their own dissatisfaction and not be strongly disposed to putting things right. The old shadow between the idea and the reality. Peyrefitte has been greatly interested by this poll, which, he says, is of permanent import and shows that there is really a *mal français* which is basic and deep-rooted – no nonsense about a mere '*actualité mouvante ou personnalisée*' – a here-and-now animated by change and personality.

So the French have to refashion themselves, cutting out the tendency to dogma, abstraction, cultural arrogance, self-satisfaction. Their skills are undoubted – look at Concorde – but often frustrated. They began with a TV picture of 819 lines, only to see it lose to the German 625. When, with the help of the British (who naturally have to be kept, for rhetorical reasons, out of the picture), they get a Concorde off the ground, they have to cope with the obscurantists of Kennedy Airport. It is no good blaming the frustrators for their lack of knowledge of French culture; French culture itself – and that means more than a few thousand battered books and two score of broken statues – has to adjust itself to pragmatic need.

Thus speaks Cartesian France. As a CASC (Catholic Anglo-Saxon Celtic) outsider whose books sell somewhat better in France than they do in Anglo-America, I am both uninvolved and involved. I am also married to an Italian who is Sorbonne-educated, who finds in France what she does not find in Italy – a clarity of thought and enactment, a precision of languge which are no longer to be found in her own Latin culture. I therefore have to listen carefully to her when she says that there is a French tradition other than the vaunted Cartesian which needs to be revived and fostered. She means, and I agree, the Rabelaisian. The Abbey of Thelema, with its sign of the Holy Bottle, and its slogan 'Do what the hell you want', encourages the pragmatic, insists on toleration, frowns on intellectual pride. It is also quite as French as Descartes.

She, I and my young son are great readers of a series of books which, unmentioned by Alain Peyrefitte, are very popular in France and seem to stem from the Rabelaisian tradition. These are the illustrated adventures of Asterix the Gaul, written by Goscinny and drawn by Uderzo. The time is the time of Julius Caesar, who has overrun all Gaul except for a tiny pocket in the north. Here a happy village remains independent of Roman occupation because its Druid has discovered a magic potion that renders the taker physically invulnerable. Obelix, the mountainous friend of Asterix, was dropped into the magic brew by accident as a child, and he requires no special preparation for fisting a whole Roman platoon into pulp. He hunts in the same way and eats two whole roasted boar at a sitting. There is an attempt in this never ending fantasy to identify the essence of France with the pure Gallic, as opposed to the Latinized Gallic. It is a kind of national dream, a wish fulfilment, and one can see how it must appeal to a people (meant for children, it is mostly read by adults) still smarting from memories of the German occupation and uneasy about the encroachment of the foreign, from Franglais to Coca-Cola.

The Gauls have no wish to overcome Roman rule in Gallia; they only wish to be left alone to quarrel among themselves and be reconciled at great banquets of roasted *sanglier* and wine. They have a Bard, but they hit him senseless when he tries to sing. Their chief, Abraracourcix, is respected but henpecked. It is an idyllic vision of a France that does not take itself too seriously and enjoys life. When Abraracourcix has a liver crisis he attributes it to 'intellectual fatigue'. No cultural pretensions, and all battles defensive. The Asterix books are popular because their readers are well aware that the concept of an independent France, cultural beacon in a barbarous world, self-supporting, haughty, is as much an anachronism as the foreign-devil-despising China of the nineteenth century. France, like everywhere else, has to become a kind of small America. I think that Peyrefitte's readers know this well enough, that they are aware of their *mal*, but they just want to dream a little longer.

Unclean

No Laughing Matter: Rationale of the Dirty Joke: Second Series, by G. Legman

Receiving this huge book (1132 pp.) and seeing at first only the primary title, I thought for a mad instant that Angus Wilson had greatly enlarged his 1967 novel – a legitimate act, since what a writer does to his work is his own affair. But whose affair is titles? I published in 1960 a novel called *One Hand Clapping*. Much later came a biography of John Middleton Murry with the same name. Herman Wouk's hero Youngblood Hawke writes a first novel called *Alms for Oblivion*. Simon Raven comes along with a many-volumed *roman fleuve* identically titled. I know there's no law to forbid the duplication of titles, but I do wish authors and agents and publishers would check more carefully before committing a screaming duplication to the world. 'I want *No Laughing Matter*, please. I forget the author.' Trouble. Writing once from Malaya for a copy of Eliot's *The Family Reunion* I got Ogden Nash's. Anger.

Mr Legman's first tome in this series was merely called *The Rationale of the Dirty Joke*. I recognized, having with difficulty got the book through the toils of Maltese censorship, that the author's aim was not the building of a great anthology of sniggers; it was a scholarly attempt to uncover the motivations behind joke telling. Some reviewers objected, showing off, that they knew all the jokes already and that sometimes Mr Legman told the same joke more than once. They missed the point. We're supposed to know all the jokes he tells, but we're not supposed to know why the jokes exist in the first place. Mr Legman's name supported the fallacy that here was the ultimate bemerded Joe Miller. In the new grim volume Mr Legman says that he is of the other fraternity, and that is the end of joking.

The jokes here are the *dirty* dirty ones, the ones that anger and humiliate, that are based on our basest elements – hatred and contempt for foreigners, especially if their skins are not pink; desire to destroy our mothers and our fathers; gloating over excreta; scatophagy, pedication; bestiality; incest; sex, disease, eating, drinking and violent death rolled into a single nauseating pellet. In his long introduction Legman admits the difficulty of drawing a line between the 'outrageously dirty and marvellously vile' on the one hand and the ' "good" or normally dirty' on the other. There is a continuum, as also of audience response – 'from the polite *"titsa-de-bitsa"* smile-creating witticism, to the bellylaugh-creating *"hupcha-de-bupcha"* or *"hockcha-de-bopcha"* knock-down-&-drag-out prize jokes – abbreviated to "yocks" – of Yiddish-speaking professional comedians or *bodchonim*.' The laughter elicited by *foul* foulness is not, however, easily codified or transcribed. It is close to hysteria; it is a howl at the ghastliness of the human condition; it is a sob of frustration that the attempted catharsis of our horror at the Beckettian *merde universelle* cannot be effected through mere words. The end of the foul joke is not humour but foulness. The creation of what we may term picaresque foulness, in which every conceivable nauseant is cold-bloodedly put together, is analogous to a Loyolan composition of hell. 'The secret source of humor is not joy but sorrow; there is no humor in heaven' – words taken from Pudd'nhead, not Angus, serving Mr Legman as an epigraph.

The organization of the book recalls *The Anatomy of Melancholy*, with its members and sections and subsections. The 130 pages on jokes about homosexuality, for instance, are divided into Homosexual Recognitions, The Short-Arm Inspection, Fellation, Pedication. Pedication is subdivided into Bend Over, Pedication as Insult, Pedicatory Rape, Pedication through Misunderstanding, Rape by Animals, The Ganymede Revenge. But Mr Legman prefaces the whole member with a long essay on the origins of homosexuality, which he finds in a more than normally Oedipal fear of the father, the homosexual state itself being sado-masochistic and *dongiovannesco*, and most homosexual jokes bearing out these attributions. We are never very far away from Freud. Legman's own dislike of homosexuality is always evident. He seems, if I read him right, to find the British book-reviewing profession suffused with it. He is even, at a pinch, prepared to go along with the common American view that all British males are homosexual. This, and other quirky superstitions, bits of misinformation, and aberrations of taste do not, of course, invalidate his major theses. But sometimes the areas of alleged fact and joke fantasia overlap disturbingly. He says, for instance, that a newly elected pope has to sit on a special *chaise percée* to be examined for genital integrity. I doubt if John Paul II had to submit to this.

It was in the final section of *Seven Types of Ambiguity* that Professor Empson invited his readers to enter a world where black was white and things stood on their heads. In Legman's final member, Scatology, the arse or ass rules: we eat faeces, drink urine, crepitate and indulge in anal sadism. Man, top of creation, becomes mostly bottom. The privy chamber is the throne room. Reviewers sometimes deserve well of their readers. It has taken Mr Legman from 1934 to 1975 to gather his materials. I have had to read through his second thesis in a single day and night. It is the jokes one remembers, alas, and not his exegeses. I feel very unclean, all the more so when I consider that these menses-eating and pus-lubricating fantasies were already there in my soul, not to be realized until the bold or mad was cruel enough to put them into words. We meet the most ghastly filth with a sad nod of recognition. What oft was thought but ne'er so well express'd. This is hell, nor am I out of it.

A Deadly Sin – Creativity
for All

I was at the University of Nantes recently, and, after I had spoken of the rarity and sanctity of great art, a haired and barefoot pot-smoker said: *'Nous sommes tous des artistes ces jours.'* There was no noise of disagreement save from myself, and I was easily howled down.

That is a growing view and the consequence of misguided democracy. We all have a right to everything, to speak of the greatness of Shakespeare or Mozart is elitism, and we may all wear tee-shirts proclaiming that we went to Princeton or Harvard. Jangle guitar strings and you are ipso facto a musician, daub ordure on canvas and who will deny that you are a painter?, shout alliterative words of protest and you are bound to be a poet.

Some of the debasing of the term art began with the Surrealists, who regarded creation as a form of free association, letting the unconscious speak. Everybody has an unconscious, and one unconscious has as much claim to be heard as another. So if a dustman or car salesman comes out with 'Purple in vestige recoil cabbages derelict from polar outrage,' he is entitled to our attention as much as if he were Tristan Tzara.

We have abdicated strict aesthetics as much as strict ethics, and nobody is able to say, we are told, what is not art. I think I know what art is – the disposition of natural material to a formal end that shall enlighten the imagination – but many people would say there are too many indefinable terms there, and all we can be sure of is the disposition part. Change things and you are being creative. Change a living organism to a dead one, and you are creating by destroying. The IRA is in the service of the birth of a terrible beauty. No terrorist or thug would be displeased by the imputation of an aesthetic motive to his acts.

But, at a milder level, we may say that it is a combination of the difficulty of aesthetic definition and the invention of certain machines that has spread the view of the universal availability of creative fulfilment. We are told that there are great photographers, and I have even been photographed by some of them. But I cannot for the life of me see how mere recording can be creation. Ah, I am told, the creative skill lies in the framing of the eye, the balance of chance components, the disposing of light and shadow. This is a matter of *trouvailles*, I would say, not creation. Find on the beach a salt-eaten stick that looks like a Giacometti and you are not in the presence of art. Blind chance is no artist.

In the days of skiffle you could buy guitars with programmed tonic, dominant and subdominant chords. You can activate Moog synthesizers which will give you massed violins. You can drive a bicycle with paint on its wheels over a canvas. It is not a question of saying this is not art but of explaining why it is not.

We have had in recent years in London state-subsidized exhibitions in which groupings of farm boots, decaying turnips and hardened cow dung have been presented as creative efforts. The same was done, notoriously, with some bloodcaked sanitary towels. This is the new creativity of the collage or montage, and anyone can do it. One essential aspect of traditional art is clarified by surveying the ease with which it can be done. True creativity, we were always told, is difficult.

If the writing of a book still remains the most difficult task in the world, it is nevertheless possible to articulate inarticulately into a cassette recorder and get it all typed up. The ahs and ers and syntactical abortions will, in some views, add up to a precious spontaneity which, to his harm, you don't find in John Milton.

We need some Johnsonian or Ruskinian pundit to frighten everybody with near impossible conditions for true creativity. We have to stop thinking that what kindergarten children produce with pencil or watercolour, is anything more than charming or quaint. If you want to be considered a poet, you will have to show mastery of the Petrarchan sonnet form or the sestina. Your musical efforts must begin with well-formed fugues. There is no substitute for craft.

There, I think, you may have the nub of the matter. Art begins with craft, and there is no art until craft has been mastered. You can't create unless you're willing to subordinate the creative impulse to the constriction of a form. But the learning of a craft takes time, and we all think we're entitled to short cuts.

It's time, too, that parasitism were excised from the practice of true creativity – meaning the construction of works of art. There are too many hangers-on who are not satisfied with money but want to call themselves creative as well. I mean publishers' editors, literary agents, the *cadreurs* of French television. Art is rare and sacred and hard work, and there ought to be a wall of fire around it.

On the Cards

The Game of Tarot and *Twelve Tarot Games*, by Michael Dummett

T. S. Eliot, in his Notes to *The Waste Land*, airily admitted to an ignorance of 'the exact constitution of the Tarot pack'. Such ignorance was common in the 1920s but is far from common now, chiefly because Eliot's poem set people to searching for the exact constitution. While we deplore the presence in that poem of a man with three staves and a one-eyed merchant (neither of whom are to be found in the Tarot), we accept, because of the authority of the poet, the quasi-mystical status of the pack and its divinatory power. In 1949 I managed to get hold of a copy of Papus's *The Tarot of the Bohemians*, which exalts the cards as the 'absolute key to occult science', and, with its aid, turned myself into a fairly efficient Madame Sosostris of the charity bazaars. Michael Dummett now comes along to tell us that the Tarot is primarily for games, not cartomancy, and that there is nothing either venerable or mystical about it.

Let us consider first the thing that Eliot did not know, namely 'the exact constitution'. The Tarot is composed of seventy-eight cards, divided into a 'minor arcana' of fifty-six and a 'major arcana' of twenty-two. The fifty-six correspond to our own Anglo-American pack, with the additional court card of a knight. There are four suits – wands or sceptres (our clubs: this is where Eliot got the notion of the 'staves'); cups or goblets (our hearts); swords (spades, *spada* being Italian for sword); money or pentacles (ennobled with us to diamonds). In Italy, in the card-playing drinking shops, one still sees those old Tarot suits. The Anglo-American versions are to be found in the bridge-playing upper-class *circoli*. Tarot, incidentally, derives from the Italian *tarocco*, but nobody knows whence *tarocco* derives.

The major arcana is all picture cards, and some of the pictures seem to be of remote and terrible meaning. A dog and a wolf howl at a moon that drips blood, while a crayfish tries to crawl out of a pool. An angel trumpets the Last Judgement. A tower is struck by lightning and starts to crumble. A man is hanged upside down from a tree. *The Waste Land* has invested these last two cards with a poetic weight which they were not originally intended to carry. Mr Dummett does not use the term 'major arcana', finds in its cards nothing extraordinary, and asserts that the pictures have an arbitrary derivation. The figures 'are, in fact, just what someone of the time would be likely to pick up if he were asked to select a series of subjects for a set of twenty-one picture cards.' The time in question is the fifteenth century. What is important on these picture cards is not the picture but the number attached to the picture. The cards are no more than permanent 'triumphs' or trumps, and each has a fixed numerical value.

Mr Dummett mentions twenty-one picture cards, though the total is actually twenty-two. The twenty-second is the Fool. Its value is zero. 'The player who holds it can play it at any time, irrespective of the obligation to follow suit or to play a trump; it cannot take the trick, but it excuses the player from the normal constraints on playing to a trick, which is why it is often called the Excuse.' It is not the ancestor of the Joker, which is an American invention of the late nineteenth century.

Things are now becoming clear. The Tarot pack is for playing games. If we wish to use it for divination, that is entirely up to us, but we would be foolish to think, like Papus, that we have here an ancient mystical codex which, over the centuries, has been debased and reduced to the greasy pack once known as the Soldier's Prayerbook. The Tarot is an ordinary fifty-six-card pack of fifteenth-century Italy (we have dropped the knight), to which twenty-two extra cards have been added. The important thing, the one which gives a Tarot game its special fascination, is the existence of permanent trump cards with marked values. On the cover of Mr Dummett's paperback guide to twelve representative games card players are warned that, if they try some of them, they may lose their appetite for games played with the regular pack. It is a fair warning. After Grosstarock, Ottocento, Konigsrüfen or Cego, bridge and whist seem very insipid.

Let us now consider Mr Dummett himself, whose big and expensive book on the history of the Tarot is as exhaustive a study as one will find, scholarly, sceptical, worthy of the philosopher whose books on Frege have met with large acclaim ('Superb exegesis' – *The Times*; 'Monumental' – *The Listener*). Mr Dummett was more or less driven to this study by political events. An inveterate opponent of racism, he became sickened in 1968 ('the most terrible year that I hope I ever have to live through') by such horrors as the assassination of Martin Luther King and the Labour Party's promotion of racial discrimination in Britain. Emotional anxiety precluded rigorous work on philosophy or logic, so he fell back on a new hobby, of which this brilliant book is the scholarly fruit. I agree with Mr Dummett about the importance of the ludic in our lives and the hypocrisy of scholars who will not see games as an integral part of a culture. Of the world's great games, chess is approved because there is no chance and hence no gambling in it. Card playing, because of the aleatory element, is looked down upon. Dr Johnson, honest as always, wished he had learned to play cards, seeing in the ombre table a means of heightening human sodality. One might add that a card game brings us into contact with the unexpected, the unknown, the mysterious.

And so we come back to Papus and the division of the syllables of the Sacred Name among the suits, the Tarot as the sidereal book of Henoch, the astral wheel of Athor. Even though Mr Dummett puts our cartological emphases right, I still swear by the Tarot as an efficient engine of divination. Eliot, as a good Anglican, scorned Doris and Dusty, who drew the coffin, as well as the cartomancer with the bad cold. But it is evident that he was fascinated by those who 'report the behaviour of the sea monster, describe the horoscope, haruspicate or scry . . . riddle the inevitable with playing cards.' So are we all. These two books are intended to cool our fascination, interest us in the history of cards, and promote new pastimes. They succeed in the last two, but I am not persuaded to throw away my Papus.

But Do Blondes Prefer Gentlemen?

I was sitting in the sun in Oslo, having just read of Anita Loos's death, though not in a Norwegian newspaper. *Gentlemen Prefer Blondes* is not the only book she wrote, but it is the best known, and the title is known even to those who never saw the film. It has been taken as a true, or at least proverbial, statement. Do they really? Looking about me at the women of the North, I saw that, here at least, they had little choice in the matter.

But, in the world as a whole, there are very few blondes, and this grants them a scarcity value appropriate to the valence 3 of their tresses. In dark-skinned countries blondes are auriferous goddesses; in countries like our own, where there is a whole spectrum ranging from raven to pale wheat, blondes have been both desired and feared. They are supposed to be temperamentally different from brunettes, and this is a circumstance that was exploited long before Anita Loos. In her novel *Corinne*, Mme de Staël has a dark-haired genius of a woman heroine, a noble actress before whom all Italy prostrates itself, but, in matters of love, she fears defeat from a blonde rival. The *Corinne* tradition got into England in

George Eliot's *The Mill on the Floss*, where the brunette Maggie Tulliver has a similar blonde *bête noire*. But in both authors blondness is dangerous because it stands for the fire of the hearth, not of temperament; blondes are dolls wearing satin and laces and smelling of cologne, and men want to install them in houses. The nineteenth-century blonde is best typified in Lucy Manette, whom Sidney Carton first sneers at and then dies for.

The twentieth century has been responsible for the cult of the blonde siren, platinized in Jean Harlow but mocked by both Mae West and Marilyn Monroe. Blondness became more than colour: it was the slinky dresses of Carole Lombard and the arch look of Marlene Dietrich. There was no domesticity in it; blondes were there for men's ruination. When, in films, men have blondes for wives they are either endowed with the siren temperament which makes them unfaithful, or else they are of Scandinavian origin (probably Minnesota) and hence have totally cornfield associations. Blonde sirens are never from the deep North.

Reality as opposed to the cinema gives us two main kinds of blonde – the fraily anaemic and the Junonian. There is no woman more appealing to the protective in men, as Corinne and Maggie Tulliver realized, than the blue-eyed washed-out insomniac-looking doll with thin limbs and an aura of orphanage deprivation. Dark girls with the same physique seem at least to have blood in them and don't, as Fay Wray is in *King Kong* (or *Kong King* as it is called in Oslo), have to be rushed to the nearest hash joint to be fed. The Junonian blonde, or statuesque blonde as she is known in show business, represents the opposed pole, and blue-eyed fairness takes on a meaning with little of the seductive in it. Such blondes are either to be looked at from a distance or, brought close, permitted to be cruel, especially to blondes of the other types. They can parody the siren, as Mae West did, but they cannot be it. They make good, bad really, prison wardresses or orphanage mistresses. Their teeth are strong, while those of their washed-out sisters tend to be brittle: I have this on the best stomatological authority.

Of course, fashion comes into this blonde–brunette business, and it may be said that the cult of the blonde lost its validity – becoming something nostalgic for late-night movies – when Italian film stars evinced more allure than their rather rarefied counterparts from America. Gina Lollobrigida and Sophia Loren were obviously real women, while Doris Day was clearly a cleansed artefact. In Elizabethan England there was a taste for blondness which Shakespeare – unusually for a man of such conventional sentiments – defied by falling for a woman with black wires in her head. The oceanic in Shakespeare wished, we presume, to be overwhelmed by the dark sea of mystery that he foreheard rippling from her fingers as her midnight hair fell over her shoulders swaying to the tune she wrung from the virginals. Or perhaps he sought intelligence in a woman. Blondes are traditionally held to be less bright than brunettes. '*Molle à la fesse*,' as they used to say in France, '*mais folle à la messe*.' And yet Shakespeare's brightest heroine is blonde, with a golden fleece tucked under the cap of a doctor of laws.

The myth of the dullness of blondes probably started among their dark sisters. During the war I had to master a quiz for members of the Auxiliary Territorial Service. 'Blondes versus brunettes,' I suggested. There weren't enough blondes available, so a brunette was told off to join the blonde team. 'Coo, am I as dumb as that?' she said, undulating towards it. The lack of pigmentation suggests a lack of intelligence. It is there in men too, with the cunning swarthy set against the blond ox from the North. In Britain tall fair Celts superseded the small dark Silurians, taking their fields and leaving them to smelt iron (they are still there in the industrial Midlands as well as in Wagner's *Ring*) but also to steal blond babies and become malignant fairies. Blondness in Britain is at least *good*. It is also clean, and not only in Britain. Aldous Huxley's first wife Maria, appalled at Frieda Lawrence's filthy housekeeping, yet conceded that she must be fundamentally clean, being blonde. Dirty blondes are not, in fact, easily conceivable. Go to the Third World, and you will have your fill of dirty darkness. The blondes belong to the privileged races, such as the Germans. It is the blonde Gretchen of Goethe who is the eternal woman leading us upwards. The great dark women of literature, like Cleopatra and Anna Karenina, are goddesses of defeat.

These are some of the thoughts I had, sitting bemused in the Oslo sun. They make little sense really. For cosmetics can turn a woman into whatever she wishes. Anne Gregory, according to Yeats, could be loved not for her self alone but only for her yellow hair. The girl, very sensibly, said that she could buy a hair dye and make herself black or brown or carrot. All Yeats could do, with the obtuseness of a man, was to bring thundering religion into it, as well as palpable lies. To set up a polarity when we have only a spectrum is a silly thing to do. And we ought to remember that Anita Loos was having a joke at the expense of H. L. Mencken, that very German American who loved beer, sauerkraut and the goddesses of the North. She wrote a sequel to *Gentlemen Prefer Blondes*; it is called *But Gentlemen Marry Brunettes*. Meaning that gentlemen prefer both.

But, shortly before she died, Anita Loos proposed a novel more appropriate for today – *Gentlemen Prefer Gentlemen*.

Beneficent Poppy

Opium and the People, by Virginia Berridge and Griffith Edwards

M axim Gorky was not sure whether the slogan '*Religiya – opium dlya narodo*' ('Religion is the opium of the people') was well understood by ordinary citizens. He asked a Red Army man on guard: '*Chto takoye opium?*' ('What is opium?') and he replied: '*Znayu – eto lekarstvo*' ('I know – it's a medicine.'). So they changed *opium* to *durman*, which means any kind of unwholesome dope. The point of the story is that, to Karl Marx, who coined the phrase, opium was not so much a bad thing as a solvent of harsh reality: change the reality and the opium will not be needed. The common people, in Russia as everywhere else, saw opium as something good for an aching body and a depressed mind. The pejorative use of *opium* as a metaphor, which goes along with the condemnation of the drug itself, belongs to our century, and to the nineteenth-century social reformers who helped to bring our century into being.

Griffith Edwards is a physician and psychiatrist and an expert on drug addiction. Virginia Berridge is a social historian with two specialities – the history of the popular press and the use of drugs in the Victorian age. It is up to Dr Edwards, first, to tell us of the physical substances whose use and abuse merits such large historical research:

> The nineteenth century was engaging with a range of drugs which nicely represented the complete spectrum of drug types – opium as the source of opiates, with morphine and heroin later added, alcohol as the pervasive depressant and chloral as the new medical substance, cocaine as the first encounter of this society with a powerful stimulant, cannabis as a psychomimetic which received quite a lot of attention and mescaline as an exotic.

But the greatest of these was opium, the dried milky exudate of the capsule of the white poppy, known and revered for six thousand years, imported into Britain as freely as tea or coffee, and retailed in a variety of forms – laudanum, paregoric, Battley's Sedative Solution, Dover's Powder, Dr Collis Browne's Chlorodyne, Godfrey's Cordial, Mrs Winslow's Soothing Syrup, Atkinson's Infants' Preservative, Street's Infants' Quietness, and (friend of my Lancashire bronchitic boyhood) Owbridge's Lung Tonic. Some of the patent medicines are still around, but, while they once glorified their opiate content, now they deny all connection with the poppy.

Alethea Hayter's book *Opium and the Romantic Imagination* (listed in Dr Berridge's extensive bibliography) gives us information about the great named opium-takers. Coleridge, for instance, who had to employ two strong thugs to keep him out of druggist's shops in Bristol (where a nod and a penny were enough to have the stuff shoved over the counter for you), but who, nevertheless, enriched literature with 'Kubla Khan'. Inevitably, this work is now, by the enemies of opiates, regarded as a sober product of genius, with the story of the drugged dream broken by the person from Porlock as a self-publicizing lie. We are past finding any good at all in opium. But Dr Berridge is surely right in arguing that, if opium had remained solely the preserve of men of letters and other members of the bourgeoisie, no reformers would have come along to control its use and, finally, ban its sale. The faceless nameless proletariat, the slaves of industrialism, the seekers of a penny dream after a hundred-hour week of ill-paid back-breaking labour had to lose one of their solaces. Gin at a penny a pint had to become the rich man's martini; laudanum went off the market.

There were two areas of England where the use of opiates was widespread and, in consequence, their abuse spectacular. One was the Fen country, where the white poppy is indigenous and may be seen as the gift of a bountiful providence to a people climatically disposed to agues and fevers; the other was my own county of Lancashire. Lancashire, the cradle of world industry, bred an oppressed proletariat which Marx and Engels studied and mythologized in their *Communist Manifesto*; its damp climate favoured the growth of a cotton industry sustained by women operatives. Children had to be neglected and pacified with opiates, and sometimes these were administered to excess. Though De Quincey became an opium-eater in London, he was bred in Manchester and may be regarded as the patron saint of an entrenched Lancashire habit. Many of the patent opiates I list above were Lancashire products.

Victorian England was scared of the vast proletariat the historical process had forced it to bring into being. This proletariat was discontented, and no wonder, but there was no thought of resolving the discontent through better wages or more salubrious housing. Organize Sunday schools, make people sing Handel and Mendelssohn, put cornets and euphonia into the corned hands of miners, but deny them the easier palliatives of alcohol and drugs. The whole history of government in the industrial period is one of, to use J. B. Priestley's phrase, denying the materials of conviviality to the people: the process still goes on. And, of course, not merely conviviality – full pubs and the threat of riot – but nepenthe too. The people have to suffer, and governments exist to ensure that they do.

There is another factor stressed by Dr Berridge in her history of drug control, and that is the increasing professionalization of medicine, with the consequent urge to deny to the laity the right of self-prescription. Presumably doctors would if they could, as they do in Russia, keep even aspirin off the open shelves of the pharmacy. There is a jealousy in professionalism which expresses itself in, on the lower level, syndicalist restrictivism, and, on the higher, in a spurious kind of moralizing which sees suicide and murder lurking in processes and substances which only a highly trained priesthood can handle. But, while one group of drugs becomes the preserve of specialists, others get easily into the hands of those who want them. There is much talk nowadays of the legitimization of traffic in marijuana. You can sniff glue or chew privet leaves. Humanity needs drugs. Aldous Huxley, the LSD pioneer who died in an LSD euphoria, said rightly that chemical research ought to be seeking a cheap and harmless soma. Neither government nor priests of the other soma can legislate for Pelagian man. Man is Augustinian and needs his sinful apples.

Mr Graham Greene will tell you of the beneficent qualities of opium – obscured for the generality by *Edwin Drood* myths of squalid opium dens. I may testify myself, after six years in the Orient, to the soothing properties of the occasional pipe. But the very word OPIUM on the cover of this book strikes, as our rulers mean it to do, with terror. And yet six millennia have blessed the substance, and only a century ago the name exuded, like *heaven* or *nirvana*, the promise of peace.

The Whip

The English Vice, by Ian Gibson

I t is not homosexuality nor the habit of quotation but flogging and being flogged. Ian Gibson, who comes of a Dublin Methodist family and was brought up among Quakers, first developed an interest in *le vice anglais* when reading the appendix about Swinburne in Mario Praz's *La carne, la morte e il diavolo nella letteratura romantica*. There Praz speaks of the prevalence of sexual flagellation in England and the popularity of the theme in *fin de siècle* French literature, in which English milords indulge in acts of exquisite cruelty, concealing – according to Péladan – *'le couteau de l'assassin dans le lit de l'amour'*. There is probably another English vice there too, one not to be found in the Marquis de Sade, namely hypocrisy. The whole constellation of *vices anglais* is to be associated with the public schools. But, says Gibson, the French are being distressingly naive in assuming that the English are given to sadism. As all the world ought to know by now, they are profoundly masochistic.

The poet of the 'Hymn to Proserpine' hymned flagellation in the same metre under the pseudonym 'Etoniensis':

> Oh, by Jove, he's drawn blood at the very first cut! in two places by God!
> Aye, and Charlie's red bottom grows redder all over with marks of the rod.
> And the pain of the cut makes his burning posteriors quiver and heave,
> And he's hiding his face – yes, by Jove, and he's wiping his eyes on his sleeve!

'Charlie Collingwood's Flogging' is a very long poem, and it may be said to represent all the fladge poetry that a man could reasonably need. Mr Gibson's book also is very long, and it has to be repetitious, matching the art it expounds and condemns. We are left in no doubt as to the prevalence of flogging in England and the extent of its dissemination throughout an empire run by public school alumni. As for the navy, James Joyce made flogging its creed:

> They believe in rod, the scourger almighty, creator of hell upon earth,
> and in Jacky Tar, the son of a gun, who was conceived of unholy boast,
> born of the fighting navy, was scarified, flayed and curried. . . .

But why Britain? Why is it specifically *our* vice?

There is no real answer, except that, once the principle of corporal punishment was established in our schools and cognate institutions, there seemed little need to disestablish it. If, as foreigners allege, the English are sexually tepid or, thanks to Puritanism, shy of sex, whipping could be a surrogate or a stimulant, or both. The bare fundament is exposed, with the genitalia shyly visible; there is a literal whipping up of blood to the pudenda. A fairly recent novel by Mr Alec Waugh, *A Spy in the Family*, is a candidly jolly piece of propaganda for the use of the whip by the wife on sexually cool husbands. But, of course, the coolness itself is usually a symptom of prepubertal arrest, a fixing of sexual interest at the anal stage, one of the lifelong garments woven on the loom of youth.

Johann Heinrich Meiborn published a book in 1629 – *De Flagrorum Usu in Re Veneria* – in which, in Latin rather more elegant than Krafft-Ebing's, he expounds the connection between whipping and sex. On the unconscious, or symbolic, level the connection has traditionally been made through the preferred instrument of punishment. One of Mr Gibson's illustrations is an early fifteenth-century Flagellation of Christ, by the Catalan painter Luis Borrassá, in which the floggers use whips with phallic handles, holding them in such a way that the thongs look like discharges of semen. The cat-o'-nine-tails and the birch have, in English life, usually been preferred to the rod or the cane. Freud identified the witch's broomstick as a penis. On the cover of Mr Gibson's book there is a *Vanity Fair* cartoon of the Rev. J. L. Joynes, Swinburne's tutor at Eton, who is wielding a birch. You need not just a stick but a stick spurting. The headmaster of the imaginary school dreamed up by the pupils of Greyfriars, a dream within a dream, was named Dr Birchemall, mad phallic father.

I don't think we need to be told about a *lex talionis* operating in the relation between buttocks and breasts. 'You attack my breasts,' says the mother to the greedy suckling, 'and I'll attack your buttocks.' The buttocks are an obvious choice for voluptuous flagellation – big, wide, inviting – and less susceptible of real harm than other areas of the body. To go back to Mr Gibson's fellow-citizen, the description of the pandying in *A Portrait of the Artist as a Young Man* is far more terrifying than any bottom-spanking fantasy from Mr Gibson's copious bibliography. I, like Joyce, went to a hand-caning school and consider this brutal torturing of the quintessentially human organ, nervous and well supplied with blood, as a kind of sin against the Holy Ghost. In Clifford Odets's play, *Till the Day I Die*, the Jewish violinist is whipped on the hands by his Nazi tormentor, a cultivated man who knows by heart the 'Joachim' cadenza to Brahms's Violin Concerto. In comparison, all this English bottom-tawsing is trivial and, like the bottom itself, comic.

It seems to me that the real significance of flagellation in English public schools has resided in a kind of bond of shameful-shameless intimacy between the members of the ruling class those schools were concerned with turning out. To have beaten, been beaten, witnessed the same beatings is a red badge of something. There is an analogy to Freemasonry with its *rachbone* password and its secret rituals. As for Mr Gibson's book, I am reminded of Dr Skinner in *The Way of All Flesh*, who had meditated so much on the life and character of St Jude that there was no need for anyone ever to meditate upon them again. If the English vice is pleasurably exhausting, *The English Vice* is painfully exhaustive.

Futures

1 AFTER FORD

Brave New World and *Brave New World Revisited*, by Aldous Huxley

Huxley, as his biographer Sybille Bedford reminds us in her introduction, came closer to being a professional utopiographer than any writer except H. G. Wells. He wrote two forecasts of the future – both cacotopian – and, just before his death, a vision of a possible good place in the didactic novel *Island*. In 1947–48 he worked on *Ape and Essence*, a post-nuclear nightmare whose horrors are cooled by Huxleyan rationality and wit: its impact was deflected somewhat by the appearance of *Nineteen Eighty-Four*, whose importance Huxley at once recognized. Huxley's claim to be taken seriously as a cacotopian writer rests, however, on *Brave New World*, which he wrote in four months in 1931 'in the cool library at Sanary' in the South of France. 'The sun shines feebly in spite of our latitude,' he wrote, '– and as a gesture towards disarmament the French military authorities are preparing to make a battery of 14-inch guns almost in our garden. How awful people are!'

Orwell's complaint about *Brave New World* was, in effect, that Huxley didn't consider people to be awful enough. The world of AF 632 – six centuries after the birth of Henry Ford – has achieved the Wellsian goal of a World State under 'an absolute and rational dictatorship'. This is animated not by an Ingsoc metaphysic – a boot grinding in a human face for ever and ever – but by a doctrine of hedonism, a belief that the end of life is happiness (or, remembering Dr Johnson's unwillingness to debase a term appropriate for paradise, content). Orwell did not believe that a governing power could sustain a sufficient dynamic out of organized benevolence and, despite Pavlovian conditioning to render its citizens politically docile, the Huxley utopia would collapse. He was, in effect, ascribing a kind of liberal innocence to Huxley; Orwell's political experience had led him to a bitter recognition of the sadistic element in the dictatorial mind: states exist for the gratification of the power urge in their rulers. How right was he and how wrong was Huxley?

Huxley, in a letter to Orwell thanking him for a copy of *Nineteen Eighty-Four*, said:

'Whether in actual fact the policy of the boot-on-the-face can go on indefinitely seems doubtful. My own belief is that the ruling oligarchy will find less arduous and wasteful ways of governing . . . and that these ways will resemble those which I described in *Brave New World*. . . . Within the next generation I believe that the world's rulers will discover that infant conditioning and narco-hypnosis are more efficient, as instruments of government, than clubs and prisons. . . .'

But the question 'Why do some people wish to rule?' remains unanswered. Perhaps it cannot be answered.

It is notable, and ironic, that the 'Orwellian' future presented recently in so much popular journalism owes more to *Brave New World* than to *Nineteen Eighty-Four*. There is virtually no technology in Orwell's novel, and Pavlovian conditioning and brainwashing are alien to a metaphysic which depends on free will. Loving Big Brother is not a matter of infantile hypnopaedia: it is a question of intellectual choice reserved to an elite forming 15 per cent of the population. As an extended metaphor of the relation between the sadist and his victim Orwell's book has a large poetic value; as a political programme it has little relevance to any foreseeable future – even in the Soviet Bloc. That future depends on certain technological advances, and some of these are adumbrated in *Brave New World*. It also depends on how we treat the ecology – a theme unmentioned in that novel but given full consideration in the commentary that Huxley published on it in 1958.

Where Ingsoc goes wrong is in its assumption that reality can subsist entirely inside in the mind: external events like earthquakes can be ignored if the ruling party's solipsistic philosophy says so. Where *Brave New World* goes wrong is in its old Christian liberal assumption that the non-human environment is as controllable as the human. In his long essay Huxley admits this. We are rapidly wasting the resources of our planet – 'spending like sailors' – and at the same time breeding like flies. Any realistic political philosophy of the future must be based on a desirable relationship between demography and food and fuel supplies. Although Huxley satirizes the World State in his novel, he has to come close to accepting it in his commentary. The problem, as he sees it, is to reconcile control with individual freedom. Orwell never went so far as he in considering all the factors involved in building and sustaining a tolerable world. He did not know as much as Huxley, whose polymathy remains one of the wonders of the age. Where Orwell exhibits the sickness of a disillusioned liberal, Huxley shows the sanity of a philosopher who can take disillusionment in his stride. He reads like a man who can be trusted.

Brave New World remains as entertaining as it was in 1932, but it has inevitably dated. Huxley is puzzled as to why he left the possibilities of nuclear fission out of it – it was a big subject in the thirties – and he saw in 1958, and after, that he had not taken the potentialities of mind-control far enough. To his Savage, who comes from an Aztec reservation to the wonders of the hedonistic utopia with Miranda's cry on his lips, he gives no alternative to a world without sin, love or freedom except self-destruction. There is, after all, the way out of the heretic asylum or monastery to which Bernard and Helmholtz are banished. Even in a universe of total regimentation there is always the way out. Orwell did not believe this.

Huxley ends *Brave New World Revisited*, after a lengthy consideration of the horrors of a scientific dictatorship, with these words: 'Meanwhile there is still some freedom left in the world. Many young people, it is true, do not seem to value freedom. But some of us still believe that, without freedom, human beings cannot become fully human and that freedom is therefore supremely valuable.' Back in 1958, we note, he was worrying about the young. If he were alive today he would worry even more. He would worry about their acceptance of conformity, their distrust of thought and their rejection of the past. Both Huxley and Orwell affirm, in their different ways, the glory of human diversity, the need for pragmatic reasoning, and the danger of jettisoning tradition. They come together also in their profundity of human concern. They remain the two great sane men of our age.

2 AFTER ORWELL

1984 and After – Changing Images of the Future, by Nigel Calder

Prophets are rightly unhonoured: they very rarely get even a fragment of the future right. Knowing this, Orwell did not attempt prophecy in his *Nineteen Eighty-Four*, contenting himself with an uneasy fusion of a real 1948 and an impossible dream of British intellectuals running the government. He bequeathed merely his title to the amateur futurologists who needed a more solid calendar than *Brave New World*, with its A F 632, could give them. Twenty years ago Nigel Calder was responsible for a published symposium called *The World in 1984* – the year then seemed sufficiently remote for uninhibited speculation – and in this present book he looks at some of the predictions of his hundred scientists and sociologists. Most of them, naturally, have been proved wrong.

Mr Calder borrows from my own *1985* (whose prophecies are so fantastically wrong that I can justify them only by reference to an SF timewarp) a technique of dialectic. He, A or Author, converses with O'B, a computer whose full name O'Brien is an acronym for Omniscient Being Re-interpreting Every Notation. The name is, of course, that of Winston Smith's interrogator, but O'B is benign, helpful, ready to disgorge all the facts we need at the trip of a switch. This saves A from being stodgily omniscient himself, which he would have to be in a straight piece of expository prose. So when Ruth Glass was sceptical about Kingsley Davies's projection of a population for Calcutta of between 24 and 41 million by 1984, A has only to ask: 'What is the latest figure?' and O'B comes up with '9.165 million, for a larger geographical area than Davies had in mind.'

On the whole, the sociologists seem to have done better than the scientists. A is 'particularly proud' of Barbara Wootton, who said that social patterns in British life would not change spectacularly: 'it would still be news if a duke married a dustman's daughter, still be startling to find a truck driver at a lawyer's dinner party.' But collar colour would change increasingly from blue to white and 'in any increasingly competitive society I think we must expect rising figures of crime.' Nobody else said that, nor that 'by 1984 the practice of adult homosexuality will surely have ceased to be criminal, and only the deeply religious will be shocked by pre-marital unchastity.' The calm precision of the forecast, says A, is uncanny. The same cannot be said of Sir Herbert Read's conviction that poetry and the graphic arts would disappear by 1984. O'B quotes him: 'There will be lights everywhere except in the mind of man, and the fall of the last civilisation will not be heard above the incessant din.' That is pure biblical prophecy, which refers to no calendar.

If Lady Wootton can get some things right, we may conclude that some aspects of the future are 'broadly foreseeable over a timescale of twenty years', and, with the proviso that shocking errors are going to be made, we can make a stab at guessing at the world of 2004. But, says O'B, 'from the mistakes made one learns particularly to avoid wishful thinking in serious exploratory forecasting, as opposed to normative forecasting and mere advocacy.' It is left to this machine to predict the nuclear war we should already have had but haven't. The north temperate latitudes will be 'comprehensively disrupted' but the southern hemisphere will survive, particularly Brazil with its population in excess of 100 million and a huge potential GNP. At this point A demands an excision from O'B's memory bank of the whole conversation of 192 pages. 'A human cannot be a party to a no-hope forecast. It's not allowed.' Winston Smith said much the same thing to the other O'Brien.

A has hopeful formulae for the future. The artificial intelligence which O'B represents is dangerous, but there could be an agreement not to develop machines 'the full workings of which are not entirely transparent to human beings'. O'B cynically tells A to tell that to the Japanese, who are at work on their fifth-generation computer. How about unemployment? Create a welfare world, 'keep everybody busy meeting urgent human needs'. Pie in the sky, says O'B. How to avert nuclear war? Democratic pressure on the nuclear-weapon states to proceed towards disarmament. O'B counters all this with a program called SCARE – Systematic Consideration of All Relevant Excursions. Unemployment means war ('grandest Keynesian enterprise for employing the jobless'), means crime, means more surveillance, means more artificial intelligence, means more – 'You're in shit alley, Your Majesty,' O'B concludes coarsely.

Still, hope persists. 'My genes,' says A, 'go back billions of years, my culture tens of thousands of years, and they are case-hardened by crises without number.' The worst long-term consequence of a major nuclear war would be the triggering of a new ice age, but humanity has survived ice ages before. We can go further, I suppose (this is myself talking, not A), and join Bernard Shaw in believing that life itself, in some form or another, will survive everything that happens to man. Strange that the pre-nuclear liberals, Wells among them, looked farther ahead than Doomsday. Saving industrial civilization is, in the long run, neither here nor there. To see man destroyed would be a pity. But the old Bergsonian *élan vital* is not terrified by our trigger-happy Russo-Americans.

Dr Calder has the good sense not to leave everything to the scientists, sociologists and futurological thinktanks. The novelists have not done badly in presenting nightmares from which man may awaken. My forecast of 1962 in *The Wanting Seed* – artificial conventional wars whose purpose would be the provision of processed cadavers to keep man nourished – was derided before the Andes disaster, whose survivors kept fit though profoundly constipated through eating their unluckier fellows. O'B, unshocked by the cannibalistic taboo, accords it a little respect. Kurt Vonnegut's *Player Piano* is taken seriously. And Orwell's *Nineteen Eighty-Four*, the literary trigger of all this speculation, is not so hopeless as it sounds. Winston Smith is scared by the rats into loving Big Brother, but what happens to Julia?

Julia may not have undergone the Room 101 treatment. A garbage truck could pick her up outside the Chestnut Tree Café and transport her to Wales. 'One studies the rather primitive surveillance technology assumed by Orwell,' says O'B, 'and concludes that it cannot work very well in deep valleys.' And what would she find in Wales? Perhaps the slogan 'Anarchy will supervene'. A thinks this to be impracticable, but O'B has the last word: 'Julia would understand.' If we want to play at the game of prediction, Dr Calder's book gives us all the information we could possibly require. But the game is no more than that; the future continues to preserve its secrets.

Cry of Pain

Freaks – Myths and Images of the Secret Self, by Leslie Fiedler

In his list of acknowledgements Professor Fiedler kindly expresses thanks to myself for urging him to carry on with the book 'when I was reluctant to begin'. I was working in the State University of New York at Buffalo some years ago, and Fiedler holds the Samuel L. Clemens Chair in Literature there. He foresaw trouble with this work, but it seemed to me that it had to be written and that he, who has done so much to bring popular and elitist culture together, was the one man to write it.

What kind of trouble? Accusations of morbidity and bad taste and cruelty chiefly, and the trouble began with the title. In 1898 in London members of a travelling troupe from the Barnum and Bailey Circus held a meeting to protest against their being known as Freaks. The Bearded Lady called the meeting, the Human Adding Machine took the chair, and the Armless Wonder recorded the minutes with his feet. The Bishop of Winchester suggested that they be known as 'prodigies', and there was a near unanimous acceptance of the term, but it never caught on. 'Freak' is a mysterious word of obscure etymology, and it sounds like a cry of pain. To employ a term like sport, phenomenon, mutant or monster is to kill the pathos as well as the mystery.

Besides, the juvenile culture of our own age, which Fiedler knows well (too well, some have said) and to which he is sympathetic, has legitimized the use of the word, and with connotative ambiguities which accord well with its traditional meaning. Diane Arbus, who used to photograph dwarfs and giants and transvestites, once said: 'Most people go through life dreading they'll have a traumatic experience. Freaks were born with their traumas. They've already passed their test in life. They're aristocrats.' The young of the so-called counter-culture asserted their superiority to a drab conformist democracy by wishing to be physically different from their despised elders – more, say, like Hobbits – but all they could do was to adopt 'freakish' hairstyles and clothes, proclaim unisex, induce visions, listen to acid rock, and talk about 'freaking out'. At the same time, 'freak', if applied to a lifestyle not acceptable to all 'freaks', could be a term of opprobrium. The 'Jesus Freaks' did their own thing, but it was not everybody's. The ambiguity of the term fits a traditional ambiguity of attitude. Freaks – dwarfs, giants, Siamese twins, pinheads – are undeniably Other, but they are also ourselves.

Children know this. They are dwarfs in a world of giants, but they are told that they are growing into giants themselves. Their mythology contains talking animals, which they find more sympathetic than adults, and the *zoon phonanta* leads them not to the zoo, where the beasts are all too dumb, but to the circus and its sideshows. The attractions and repulsions of dog-headed boys and singing crab-ladies are about equally balanced. Most writers are childish – a kind of infantilism being one of the conditions for creating art – and Fiedler very skilfully, and out of a hard-earned erudition, shows us how much freakishness there is in our literature. *Gulliver* is primarily a freak dream (the kids are right) and only secondarily political satire. *The Old Curiosity Shop* ('curiosity' being a Victorian euphemism for 'freak') attests a fascination with human oddities that Dickens shared with his royal mistress. Mark Twain spent much of his life trying to find a place for Siamese twins in literature: the scars of the severed bond are all too clear in the normal twins of *Pudd'nhead Wilson*.

Fiedler's book is a freak show in itself. Potential readers who merely want the visual thrill of the Elephant Man and the Bearded Lady and not a load of professorial disquisition are not going to be disappointed. It is all here, from Bartholomew Fair to Todd Browning's great freak film, at last acknowledged as a classic, and there are pictures galore. But Fiedler would not be Fiedler if he did not try to make philosophical and, above all, sexological sense out of the freakishness that craves freaks. (Fiedler, by the way, had little hope of selling his book in Britain. It has come here late, and I think its publication rides on the success of *The Elephant Man*.) Why the dwarf should be a figure of such sexual power is a mystery hardly solved by referring to him as an animated phallus. We have a highly respected dwarf in this French village where I write, and he has shown me signed photographs and love letters from internationally known beauties. The potency of Siamese twins has evidently much to do with their sexual lives, but only John Barth, Fiedler's former Buffalo colleague, has had the courage to enter fictionally into their cloacal lives as well. All boys dream of copulating with the Fat Lady.

We need, even, to invent freaks who will not appear in any Ten-in-One. America has produced the Geek, eater of raw animal flesh, human faeces, live chickens, who represents 'not degradation but a mystery which transcends the very possibility of degradation.' For *The Geek*, Craig Nova's novel of 1975, gives us the ultimate dropout or freak-out – the black, the dull, the hopelessly alcoholic – who must make a virtue of necessity. Fiedler also has something to say about the freakish implications of the oral emphasis in contemporary American sexual mythology and its dangers in the context of radical feminism. A postcard published by the Berkeley Print Mart shows a young woman grinning down at a skeleton and saying: 'He asked me to eat him. And I did.' The final freak dream is of the cannibal.

Not everyone, however, even in the dying twentieth century chooses to play such dangerous games. Most congenital malformations, in fact, seek with hormones, surgery, and psycho-endocrinology to become for others the normals they suspect they are. And most of us most of the time consider theirs to be the better part – except when at the side show and not sure whether we wake or sleep, we experience for a moment out of time the normality of Freaks, the freakishness of the normal, the precariousness and absurdity of being, however we define it, fully human.

Meaning, I think, that we have never lost the glamour and horror of merely *becoming* that we knew in childhood, and that only the dull-witted apply the verb *to be* to themselves. The study of mankind is of a being absurd, pitiable, unstable, endlessly fascinating, and that is what we mean by a freak.

The British Observed

Speak for Yourself: A Mass-Observation Anthology 1937–49, by Angus Calder and Dorothy Sheridan

I well remember the children carolling in December 1936:

> Hark the herald angels sing
> Mrs Simpson's pinched our king.

That was the month of Edward VIII's abdication, a time in which the perspicacious began to perceive that there was a great gap between the rulers and the ruled. Paradoxically a large rapport was revealed between the nominal head of the State and the common citizenry – something that was supposed to have disappeared in 1689 – while our elected representatives were seen to be remote and mostly complacently ignorant of true public opinion. What was termed public opinion was what the press said; the pulse of the people was never properly taken and the proletariat had no voice. So while the executive and legislature, to say nothing of the Church of England, forced the King to abdicate, the commons, as opposed to their house, wanted him to stay on the throne and to create an Anglo-American union through a non-morganatic marriage to a Baltimore divorcee. It was clearly time to let the people speak out, and that was why Mass-Observation came into being. As it happened, the abdication question was old hat by the time, in 1937, the observers got to work, but the issue primed less portentous and more revealing epiphanies. The British people were anthropologized.

Tom Harrison, one of the founders of the movement, was an old Harrovian and a Cambridge dropout, a self-taught ornithologist, the eventual curator of the Sarawak museum in Kuching, where I met him before his death in a car accident in Thailand. Cut out of his father's will for his irregular career – he lived with cannibals on the island of Malekula; Douglas Fairbanks Sr signed him up in some vague Hollywood advisory capacity – he went native in Bolton and began to study the Lancastrian way of life. His colleague, Charles Madge, was a distinguished poet anthologized both in Yeat's *Oxford Book* and Michael Robert's *Faber Book*. Harrison stayed in Bolton – which is called Worktown in the surveys – while Madge organized a panel of inquirers in Blackheath. By the end of 1937 he had recruited over 500 unpaid observers. Victor Gollancz, whose proletarian sympathies had led him to commission Orwell's *The Road to Wigan Pier*, gave financial support to the venture and published its findings. Humphrey Spender, brother of Sir Stephen, took remarkable photographs, some of which are reproduced in this anthology; Tom Driberg took time off from being William Hickey in the *Daily Express* to question simple proles; William Empson looked into sweet shop windows; Julian Trevelyan did paintings of Bolton mill chimneys. Mass-Observation was part of my youth. Its surveys still fascinate.

Fascinate mainly because of their concentration on the trivial. Trivial, after all, derives from the word for a crossroads, which was where ordinary people used to meet to discuss the important things – the price of bread, the irrelevance of government, a good cure for warts. Some of the subjects listed for anthropological inquiry included aspidistras, bathroom behaviour, beards, armpits, dirty jokes, undertakers and funerals, female eating taboos, the private lives of midwives. The very first Observation presented here is about a pet tortoise which a man in a Bolton pub takes out of his pocket. 'How old is it?' – 'Only 36.' The conversation goes on about 'how you can't drown tortoises or suffocate them, only way to kill them is to cut off their heads. "But you can't get at their head." ' This is, when you come to think of it, Orwellian. Not only those superstitions which he used to mention in *Tribune* – a moustache makes your beer go flat; a swan's wing will break your arm – but Winston Snith's hopeless pub conversation with the old man who can only remember trivialities. Yet Orwell was, often in spite of himself, on the side of trivialities. So are most novelists.

Sex is as trivial as anything else, especially at Blackpool.'1 man, 1 woman. Kiss, arms clasped round shoulders. 35 secs.' Or, somewhat longer: 'He gazes into her eyes. Kisses her neck, rubs her nose with his moustache. They peck. She looks up. They talk. . . . They cuddle. She tries to press him to her lips. He kisses her neck. She rises from form, tightens her girdle. He presses her breast, drawing her down. They cuddle. He does not kiss her. They both get up, he towards station.' In Worktown the patterns are firmer, less tentative, with back-wall knee-tremblers and mattinay soffey enders (afternoon sessions on the sitting-room couch). 'Shop assistants who have Thursday afternoon off often have their mattinays then. And if a chap wants "a shot" during the week, O.K. "if the wife is willing." Decent men "won't take advantage" of their wives.' Worktown's morals are decent. One thing we all learned from the war was the almost heartrending blend of ignorance and decency in the other ranks ethos. The British soldier, from Worktown or else-where, was a saint. You can see from this anthology the extent of his patience, common sense, hard-headed scepticism, natural courtesy, courage. It seemed at the time that the working man and woman could only improve their lot through a revolution. But sanctity is not a revolu-tionary quality.

The popular press – the *Daily Mirror*, for instance – told its readers to be wary of the Mass-Observers, whom they called snoopers. Of course, they were partly right. When one reads half a page describing a 'male .25 cockney (Irish)' undressing for bed ('Time taken 8 mins. 40 secs.'), one feels that things are going too far. And, of course, the movement itself presupposed a social division, with both Madge and Harrison stepping down from the fringe of the ruling class, like Orwell himself, to stand, with pencil and notebook, on the fringe of the ruled. Yet if we accept the value of anthropology as a discipline which, observing primitive societies, tells us what *ho anthropos* is like, we ought not to resent over-much the application of its principles and techniques to our own, which may be more primitive than we think. Mass-Observation was on the side of knowledge in the service of social amelioration.

It stopped its work in 1949. Harrison, unable like many of us to settle in postwar Britain, went back to the Far East. Mass-Observation Ltd was founded, and much of the old spontaneous life went out of its activities. One of the last of its surveys, with which this excellent anthology ends, was on popular response to a government poster still well remembered – the widow with the slogan 'Keep Death off the Roads'. It was, like most government propaganda of the period, ill-timed and in doubtful taste. Too many husbands had died in the war; the hazards of driving seemed small stuff in comparison with Hiroshima and the death camps. The people, more articulate than before, defaced the poster with 'She Voted Labour' and 'Wot, no mouth, no make-up, no ambulance, no husbin'?' The mourning lady was called the Black Widow and the Merry Widow. 'A friend of mine,' said someone, 'an old chap of about 70, had an acci-dent in his car and killed his wife. And right opposite his window is one of those damned Merry Widows.' The people were speaking for themselves but, as ever, they were more enlightening to the anthropologist than to the statesman. And now they have been abstracted into material for the statis-tician and the sociologist. The people can never really win.

Kant and the Cripple

A Leg to Stand On, by Oliver Sacks

I did not want to go to Capri last September to receive the Premio
Malaparte. It is an island with sinister associations – Tiberius,
Norman Douglas, others. Nevertheless my wife and I went, and she
broke her back slipping in the enmarbled bathroom of the Hotel Pala-
tium. Shortly before she had smashed a leg in two places when trying to
save, with admirable loyalty, one of my manuscripts from the territory-
affirming musk spray of our cat. On Friday, 13 January, this year my
son had a car accident on the Corniche and converted his hip into a sack
of Scrabble pieces. I have all my life dreaded breaking something, and
one of my reasons for going to live in the south was to get away from icy
roads. In films characters break legs and are at once made whole, with
no boring nonsense about muscle wastage and physiotherapy. Losing
the use of a limb, as I now know well enough though only vicariously, is
a catastrophe, and it needed a thoughtful essay written about it. This
is it.

It is more than that. Oliver Sacks is a neurologist of wide lay reading,
a man of humane eloquence, a genuine communicator aware of the
damnable rift that subsists between doctor and patient. He deals with
what can only be termed the metaphysical implications of a somatic
crisis in his own life and he points the way towards a more holistic
approach to what, to the orthopaedist, is a matter of crass carpentry.

Briefly, what happened to Dr Sacks is this. He was climbing a steep
mountain path in Norway, and he met a white bull that, considering the
scant green fodder, should not have been there. Surprise and panic
caused him to plunge down the path, fall heavily, and end up lying with
a serious injury to his left leg. He examined it with professional
objectivity. 'Yes, gentlemen, a fascinating case! A complete rupture of
the quadriceps tendon. Muscle paralysed and atonic – probably nerve
injury. Unstable knee joint – seems to dislocate backwards. Probably
ripped out the cruciate ligaments,' and so on. But he was not addressing
students in the safety of a city hospital; he was alone on a mountain, and,
totally crippled, he had to get down. He had brought an umbrella
with him. He tore his anorak and improvised a splint. With immense
toil and pain, and the providential help of a couple of Norwegian
hunters, he made it. He was flown from Bergen to London. For the first
time in his life, a fit and muscular man much given to strenuous exercise, he had left the doctor's world and entered that of the patient.

'You've torn a tendon,' said Mr Swan, the orthopaedic surgeon. 'We
reconnect it. Restore continuity. That's all there is to it . . . nothing at

all!' But there was a great deal more to it than that. Dr Sacks, after the operation, was aware that he had become nightmarishly alienated from his leg. The leg had become an alien property, soft, inorganic, obscene. Despite physiotherapy he could not make it function. The cerebral image of the leg had disappeared, and he wondered for a time whether he had sustained an infarction in the posterior right hemisphere of his brain. The pink healthy wriggling toes beneath the alien limb gave the lie to that, but the sick bewilderment continued. Dr Sacks pondered on Sherrington's doctrine of 'proprioception' – the sixth sense by which the body knows itself, which confirms the totality of psychosomatic gnosis and denies the Cartesian dualism of mind and body. Aldous Huxley used to speak of that 'other self' which is in charge, to which all the games of consciousness are an impertinent frivolity. Dr Sacks now had the task of yielding to it.

He had to learn to walk again, and he didn't want know how to do it. 'It wasn't "my" leg I was walking with, but a huge, clumsy prosthesis . . . a leg-shaped cylinder of chalk.' Then there was a miracle. Mendelssohn's Violin Concerto came into his head, it seemed to stimulate an inner 'motor' music, a 'kinetic melody', and the leg suddenly felt alive again, it became his. He was able to walk, not like a robot activated by conscious effort, but like himself. The inner monitor had taken over.

During his convalescence Dr Sacks discovered that his case was not unique; his uniqueness lay in his own introspection, his articulateness, his capacity to relate the trauma of alienation to that area of discourse where the neural and the psychic meet. He corresponded with the great Dr Luria in Moscow, who affirmed that the human organism is a unitary system and 'might show a system-breakdown whether the original disturbance was central or peripheral'. Dr Sacks was drawn into a profound sense of companionship with the sick (and a corresponding though temporary loathing of the sound), a sympathy for those who felt what he had felt but could not, through inarticulateness or because of the damnable barrier between doctor and patient, make those feelings known where they ought to be known. A book had to be written by 'an unusual patient – perhaps a patient who was a physician, and a neuropsychologist, himself – to bring out the full character of the experiential disturbance.' This, of course, is the book.

Its value lies in its willingness to combine the technical and the demotic, to admit poetry and philosophy and the religious impulse, if not the ontology of religion. It is also intensely personal, but it affirms the community of human experience. It represents a 'third stage' in the discipline of neurology. The first, or classical, phase saw only fixed centres and functions, was essentially static. Neuropsychology, the newer development, is dynamic, and it affords an image of the human totality as 'a magnificent, self-regulating, dynamic machine'. It also encourages the emergence of what Dr Sacks calls a 'clinical ontology' or 'existential neurology', which does not disdain the metaphysical. This book ends with Hume and Kant.

Hume's empiricism was not enough. 'We are nothing but a bundle

. . . of different perceptions.' Personal identity had to be a fiction, but Hume knew it couldn't be. Kant put him right in *The Critique of Pure Reason*, where he proposed a priori intuitions of time and space capable of supporting an experiencing ego. Dr Sacks, nearing the end of his convalescence, exulting like a Blake or Traherne in the recovery of life and the world, was undergoing a holistic rebirth, a metaphysical remaking of the Kantian categories, a refashioning of time and space. We are a long way from Mr Swan and his simple carpentry.

Grace

Princess Grace, by Sarah Bradford

Ms Bradford has written the definitive work on the muddy grape of the Douro (Huxley's term), a life of Cesare Borgia which was traduced into a bad television series, and a very fine biography of Disraeli. The late Princess Grace of Monaco drank champagne and lived a life devoid of Roman excess and Levantine intrigue. Thus she sits oddly on Ms Bradford's short shelf, and the question may even be asked: does she deserve the attention of so intelligent and skilled a writer? As one who was for several years one of Grace's subjects, an admirer and even, in respect of certain artistic projects which were never fulfilled, a colleague, I find it hard to answer objectively. A year and a half after her death she is terribly missed. She was beautiful and elegant but, above all, good. She invites an attitude of *bondieuserie* which Ms Bradford tries to avoid. All her sources unite, however, in finding no fault in Grace, with the exception of Lady Docker. But Lady Docker was ejected from the Côte d'Azur by Prince Rainier for tearing up a paper Monegascan flag at a party. Not even Hedda Hopper could monger scandal in her regard. All her leading men fell in love with her. After a year's desperately hard work in her last role, that of a European princess, she made the hard-bitten unsentimental citizens of a bare Mediterranean rock love her too. They wept when she died, and they were not the only ones.

She was of Philadelphian stock, but not main line. German blood, evident in her colouring and facial structure, conjoined with Irish – devoutly enough Catholic, bitterly republican, hardworking – to produce an ambitious girl who got to Hollywood by no easy route. The beauty was already in the family, as well as, on her uncle's side, a proven theatrical talent. She studied drama in New York but refused to fall into the squalor of bohemianism: her father the builder, a tough self-made millionaire, trained a telescope on her from Germantown, Pa. She played with Raymond Massey in Strindberg's *The Father*, did her share of TV soap, acting and promoting it, and made her film name early for the wrong reasons. She was chosen for *High Noon* because a certain Quaker colourlessness was needed: an apparent emotional anaemia had to be set in contrast to the suffering of Gary Cooper (which, at that time, he did not have to act).

The colourlessness was, some thought, that of ice. Grace presented a patrician façade to the world, the blue-eyed Miss Frigidaire of *High Society*, innate 'class'. But the high-society accent had been cunningly learned at drama school, the poise was the product of innumerable lessons; it would not be hard, eventually, to give a few tips on royal deportment to the future Princess of Wales. Grace was a trained actress and remained it. As for the iciness, Alfred Hitchcock had the insight to see the warmth it hid and the skill to exploit, with a devastating effect no bosomy vulgarity could attain, a powerful if restrained sexuality. She remained his favourite actress, and Tipi Hendren would have got nowhere if Grace had been permitted to play Marnie. Prince Rainier was not averse to her discarding her crown temporarily and reverting to her hard-learnt trade; it was the public, meaning the press, that would not permit it. Princess Anne can be a professional horsewoman; Grace of Monaco dared not budge from her throne, except to preside over galas and flower shows.

There is a certain comedy, altogether cinematic, in the situation of the princely courtship of Miss Kelly: Ms Bradford brings it out to the full. Jack Kelly was a bigoted republican who thought an impoverished kind of foreign count with a probably phoney title was after his daughter's money. Plutocratic America was both shocked and tickled on learning how small Monaco was (get the goddam place into my back lot); some did not, and still do not – I include a US immigration officer I was forced to insult a year ago – know where Monaco was, is. As for matters on the Grimaldi side, how was it possible for an actress called Kelly to get into the act at all – into, that is, a dynasty probably the oldest in Europe? America thought it was doing Prince Rainier a favour; Quaker Pennsylvania believed that one of its sweetest flowers was being hijacked into becoming the madam of a high-class gambling saloon. It was an intriguing situation and the press, vulgar, lying, intrusive, insolent, drank deep of it. Having seen Grace married, it wanted the scandal of her unmarrying. But Grace stayed married, and happily, and she saved the principality from French appropriation by securing the dynastic line.

For though France ostensibly is committed to protecting Monaco from foreign usurpation, the great republic is dubious about having an independent monarchy as a southern enclave and would be quick to grab it if the succession was in doubt – as it was when Rainier, long a bachelor, decided to marry the star of *To Catch a Thief*. General de Gaulle did his share of threatening to cut off the principality's lifelines – gas, water, electricity, postal services, railway – when he saw Monaco welcoming French commerce to its tax-free shores. But Rainier is a tough and resourceful monarch as well as a skilled diplomat. Grace, being a sort of goddess – a higher rank than princess – did her share in securing a place in the sun for the *famille princière*. Monaco and its monarch were taken seriously at last: compare, contrast rather, the ranks of Grace's official mourners with those of her wedding guests.

I am quoted in Ms Bradford's book – one of her lesser but still primary sources – as a sincere admirer and continuing mourner and one who laments the frustration of a number of new cultural plans for the principality. Princess Grace was to preside over a kind of free open university in which I, and one or two others who cultivate the arts more than the bars, were to participate. The heart seems, for the time being, to have gone out of us. But there are certain monuments to her cultural interests – the Théâtre Princesse Grace, an admirable structure inspired by her still vigorous theatrical expertise, and an Irish library named for her which it is hoped will be inaugurated on her birthday. She had been an Irish American but, living in Europe, she became strongly aware of her cisatlantic roots – ready to rebuke the Hôtel de Paris orchestra at St Patrick's Day dinners for not knowing Irish songs, particularly 'The Fighting Kellys'.

This brief life for a sadly brief life is more than a dutiful and pious monument. Its facts are solid, its history very sound, and its supporting cast of characters – film stars, Onassis, the ebullient young Princess Caroline, the Prince himself – highly compelling. There are many photographs, attesting to a beauty that had attained its peak in the autumn of 1982, when she met with that damnable accident on one of the most dangerous roads in Europe. And Ms Bradford's account of her death ought to dispel for good the journalistic mythology that has been permitted to surround it. *Requiescat in pace*.

Sophia

I wish to celebrate the fiftieth birthday of one of the heroines of our time. That last phrase means, I think, what it has always meant – a woman who has achieved incredibly against incredible odds – but to be fifty years old is no longer what it used to be. At least it is not, for this heroine, what it was for my grandmother (my mother never reached that age). To be fifty not so long ago was to sigh resignedly at the loss of youth, beauty, energy and, worse, hope in the future. A woman who has chalked up the half-century today will find that youth (meaning gawky immaturity) has been well lost and that beauty has arrived at its true meaning. Physical beauty exists in three dimensions only; total beauty demands a fourth. This fourth dimension is hard to define but it is easily recognizable. The ancients used terms like soul and wisdom. We, being cleverer than the ancients, do not believe in the soul and think wisdom is a property of computers. Sophia Loren's beauty is now set firmly in its fourth dimension, whatever that is, and this has much to do with her having attained her fiftieth birthday. Her films celebrate the beauty more adequately than words can, but I hope, later, to use words about it. For the moment, let me go more deeply into this quality of heroinism. The term was coined by Thomas Carlyle, the Scots philosopher who wrote about heroes and hero-worship, and, in his day, it had no connotations of drug addiction. To use it in connection with Sophia, who is a paradigm of virtue and clean living, is to restore its plain Victorian meaning.

A heroine I define above as a woman who has won through. That is not quite enough. There are many men and women who have surmounted the obstacles of a slum childhood, a lack of formal education, the devastation of a war, the stigma of illegitimacy to arrive at wealth, high social status, universal respect. This does not necessarily make them heroes or heroines. The Greeks divided the rational or soul-carrying creation into gods, heroes and men. A hero was not quite a god but was above mankind. Mankind might, in its ignorance, confuse a god with a hero, seeing in him godlike attributes which were really human qualities raised to a higher power. For god read goddess; for hero read heroine. When I first met Sophia I was inclined to grovel on the carpet, but her humanity forbade it. She is not a goddess but a woman raised to a higher power. She demands admiration more than worship. But admiration never seems quite enough. How about love?

Love of a special kind, perhaps – public and universal rather than personal and intimate. She has this first love in large measure, and it is accorded primarily to an image on the cinema screen. Other film stars have had it but not quite in the same way as she. We loved and still love Marilyn Monroe, but we did not dare let our feelings spill over from the screen into the dangerous well of her private life, which we knew was disastrous, though we were shocked when it ended in disaster. There is, with most stars, a parallelism we do not care to think about too much. We don't want to know about the star's drinking, drug addiction, multiple divorces, bad temper; we are happier with the image up there. But with Sophia there has never been much tension between the real woman and the glamorized screen icon. Her true personality, in some measure, gets up there. When we meet the real woman we do not feel let down, rather the opposite. There is something of a unity, confirmed in the fact that some of her screen roles derive from phases of her own life. It was not difficult to make a convincing television drama out of her autobiography.

Because her vocation has permitted her to present woman raised to that higher power, the drama of her private life has become, for many women and not a few men, a set of poetic symbols summing up the pains and triumphs of the unknown and unglamorous. Her father behaved abominably, as many fathers do. She fell in love with an older man and has been far from diffident in admitting that filial deprivation had something to do with it. Her marriage to Carlo Ponti, who was still, in the eyes of the Catholic Church and the Italian State, a married man and hence a bigamist, initiated a melodrama whose intensity the whole world felt. Here was a pair of lovers against whom the brutal paternalism of civic and ecclesiastical authority battered but battered in vain: love won at the end. Married, but not yet a mother, Sophia was the battleground of a struggle between her own deepest instincts and the limitations of her biology. Again, she won through.

There have been other struggles. She and Ponti have been the victims of gross and vulgar publicity, of expropriation, of mad intruders and violent thieves. Despair has always been countered by the wisdom that only a deprived childhood can teach: naked we come into the world and naked we leave it. Sophia has been given much but has never asked for much. She cooks tasty meals out of scrag end. The destiny of too many women has been that of the Roman housewife she portrays in one of her best films, *Una Giornata Particolare*. When, in all her glamour, she acknowledged the plaudits of those who witnessed its premiere, it was clear that the glamour was a mere joke: the real woman shone through, ready to cook pasta and *fagioli* for the children. A good part of her heroism lies there: she is an ordinary woman who has fulfilled more than is given to ordinary women. At the same time, which puts the balance right, she has suffered more.

It is probable that her best films have been made with a fellow-Neapolitan – Marcello Mastroianni – and directed by another – Vittorio de Sica. Although she is universal woman, she is also a daughter of Pozzuoli. One has to know that deprived and lively part of Southern Italy to appreciate Sophia's special femininity. She is best when a film allows this quality to come through: de Sica encouraged it and Mastroianni abetted it. Like heroinism, it is not easy to define, but the common view of it, expressed in terms like tempestuous fieriness tempered with a hard sense of disillusion which yet allows room for hope, probably comes near enough. Naples and its environs are very old: a Greek city became Roman, a Roman city bred a people not at all like the obscene pagan philosophical underdogs of the Roman capital or the suave controlled citizens of Milan. Go to Pozzuoli and you will be aware of an unbroken line of poverty, of resignation broken by occasional dramatic pleas to heaven, which goes all the way back to the days when it was Puteoli. What beauty you will find in the women is not easy to paint or photograph: it depends on movement, on facial animation. There are beautiful girls enough, but very few are as beautiful as Sophia. It is this beauty which makes her not quite an ordinary woman.

Sophia herself is aware of its unanalysability. She is bolder than her worst critics in finding irregularities – mouth too wide, nose too long – but she would agree with Sir Francis Bacon that true beauty hath ever something of strangeness in it. She resisted the Hollywood professional prettifiers, who wanted to reduce her to the starlet's symmetrical banalities: beauty is not something imposed but something immanent. When she says that her best feature is her eyes, she is saying something about a Pozzuoli endowment, for there the eyes learn to speak. But the totality of her beauty, which sprang suddenly in her teens after an ugly duckling girlhood when the girls called her Sofia Stuzzicadente (a *stuzzicadente* being a toothpick), represents no stereotype. The body, of course, is beautifully made, but that is a generic gift. Though, in the Neapolitan manner, she may speak with her body, even in repose her face carries an eloquence very rare and very disturbing.

Her beauty may be regarded as an inheritance from her mother – the fact of that beauty if not its particular quality – since her mother won a national contest that was looking for an Italian Greta Garbo. We do not know how far the acting talent was also inherited: her mother's prize was a trip to Hollywood which she never took, since her own mother was full of dark warnings about Greta Garbo's probable jealousy and her setting of the Black Hand or American Mafia on to her. Certainly Sophia got into the film business, through her winning of a less specific beauty contest, with her mother's encouragement: it was a vicarious way of fulfilling a frustrated ambition. It was the beauty itself that was first exploited, not only in bit parts but in that now demoded Italian craze – the magazine photostory with its speech-balloons or *fumetti*: Fellini's film *Lo Sceicco Bianco* is the best memorial to it. It was, but is no longer, a beauty that could strike straight at the appetite: the beauty of the mature Sophia is of a different, less edible, order.

The women's liberationists object strongly to an attractive woman's being regarded as something to eat. Unfortunately, men being what they are and the god of biology having made them that way, the hunger that such a woman arouses cannot be wiped out by a decree against sexism. Look at Shakespeare's *Antony and Cleopatra*, and you will find that the poet makes a continual meal of the serpent of old Nile. She talks of her salad days when she was green in judgement and of being a morsel on Caesar's dish. Sophia has taken the esculent compliments with the pleasure of a realist. In her films she moves men – making Mastroianni howl with lust as she performs the most seductive striptease of all time; eliciting the drying up of saliva and the lump in the throat as she exposes what is, damn it, a delectable body. There is nothing wrong with being attractive and nothing unclean about sexuality. Seeing the younger, and even the older, Sophia on the screen has refocillated many a wilting male appetite. But the heroine in her is larger than the mere sex goddess. Still, this capacity to excite is part of her universal role: let us not be hypocritical about it.

It was soon recognized – paradoxically after she had mouthed for Renata Tebaldi in a film of *Aida* – that Sophia had a voice as well as a face and a body. Not a singing voice, though she has one and has exploited it, but a speaking voice which is allied to a fine ear. A musical faculty has to be somewhere around when we talk of the ear, and it is relevant to note that Sophia's sister Maria could have been a professional singer of high quality and that their mother was, as well as looking like Greta Garbo, a fine pianist. Her standards were so high that she rapped Sophia's hands when giving her piano lessons, thus quelling any desire to excel on the instrument. Sophia has mastered all the regional varieties of Italian – a truth you can only know by seeing her Italian films undubbed – and her English is good. I used to practise as a phonetician, and, on first meeting her, I listened carefully for italicisms in her speech: there were none. She can pick up sounds exactly. Carlo Ponti recalls that, when she was filming in the Soviet Union, she picked up enough Russian to give an impromptu speech in it at a public dinner. This is another aspect of heroinism – the ability to cross borders, to affirm the universality of a human appeal.

I have spoken of two natural gifts, beauty and a fine ear – both of which, naturally, have been tended conscientiously and brought to mature flowering. As for Sophia's acting skills, I am never sure how to take her affirmation that she is essentially an amateur, that there is not one ounce of Olivierian professionalism in her. Working with de Sica, she was happy to follow his gestures and mouthings from behind the camera. With Chaplin, in the disastrous *A Countess from Hong Kong*, she begged the old master to conduct her, literally, like an orchestra. She is certainly not one of those assertive actresses who know better than the director and, for that matter, the scenarist: she needs direction, she says, and she sedulously learns the lines she has been given, coming to the set word-perfect (unlike Mastroianni, whose fine nervousness is the fruit of his learning his lines while walking on to the set). In her early days in Pozzuoli, she took lessons from an old actor who, following the technique of the silent films, taught her bold facial gestures close to carica-ture. The lack of stage experience or training of the RADA or Lee Strasburg type has perhaps led her to denigrate what we may call an instinctive professionalism. But her confessed approach to a part – that of relating it to her own life – has produced results perhaps impossible to trained professionalism: they certainly help to explain what I describe above as the unity of her real-life personality and her filmed persona. She has achieved much but I think she still has to achieve more. She has won her Oscar as well as high praise for her work in films otherwise mediocre (*Man of La Mancha*, for instance, and the Chaplin disaster), but she still has to make a great film.

In 1962 I published a novel entitled *The Wanting Seed*. This is a fantasy set in an imagined future when the world's preoccupation is not with the coming nuclear holocaust but with the failure of the global food supply to match the growth of population. In my fantastic future England sterility is enforced by law and sexual inversion is encouraged ('It's sapiens to be homo,' say the posters). There is one female character in the story who stands for the ancient virtues of straight love and natural fertility. Her name is Beatrice-Joanna (taken from the heroine of Middleton's play *The Changeling*) and she is all woman. When I had finished writing the book I saw a film with Sophia Loren in it and realized that, without properly knowing it, she was the woman I had had in mind. During the past twenty-odd years there have been various failed attempts to get *The Wanting Seed* onto the screen. The possibility of success dawned when Carlo Ponti professed his interest. Here, whatever else the film would have, was an outstanding part for his wife. But the world of the cinema is crammed with frustration; the theme of the script I wrote (it ends with organized cannibalism) was considered too daring by potential backers; the project came to nothing.

I met Sophia Loren because of this proposal. It was a meeting in which I was charmed, overwhelmed because of her star status, but this quickly modulated into a more personal attachment: here was a fine woman of large honesty, few pretensions, genuine humility. *Una Giornata Particolare* had just appeared: she was as excited by the reviews as I had been with the notices of my first novel. I have not seen her since, though I worked remotely for her when I translated Lina Wertmuller's Sicilian blood-feud film into English. I do not know whether it was ever shown in English: it was no great success in Italian, or Sicilian, though Sophia, passionate and earthy, was as compelling as she always is. She is always around in my life – in television films, in the signed portrait (which has the humour of a parodic glamour) that hangs on my study wall. She never feels distant, and I think she has that effect on all who know and admire her work. She is now, at least in a statutory sense, middle-aged, while I decline into genuine old age. She has portrayed an eighty-year-old in a film (*Lady L*) and has said, 'When I am an old woman of eighty . . . I see myself surrounded by my two sons, daughters-in-law and grandchildren – and by my husband, who will just have turned one hundred.' I wish for that consummation, which I shall not see, and give my anticipatory blessing on thirty years of life in which she will continue to shed the glow of her femininity and the goodness of her Pozzuoli heart.

The *OED* Man

Caught in the Web of Words – James Murray and the Oxford English Dictionary, by K. M. Elisabeth Murray

When Becky Sharp threw away her copy of Johnson's *Dictionary* – Miss Pinkerton's invariable gift to her departing students – it was not the least of her gestures in the direction of modernity. That book was a dog walking on its hind legs and, moreover, walking backwards. It tried to fix standards of usage in terms of the undefiled wells from which writers from Sir Philip Sidney to the Restoration drank; it wanted to make a closed garden of the English lexis; it prescribed as well as described. It was also more of an autobiography than a work of lexicography. It was decidedly not a dictionary for the scientific age that would start to bloom after Waterloo. Noah Webster in America (starting in 1828), Charles Richardson in England (1836–37), Joseph Worcester (1846 and 1860) again in America – all learned from Johnson what not to be, namely subjective and quirky, but they learned too that no scholarly dictionary – as opposed to the pocket word list you bought for a penny – could do its work without ample citation. This was Johnson's real achievement, the provision of illustrative quotations drawn from his own reading, than which no man's had ever been wider. Richardson was so taken with this aspect of Johnson's *Dictionary* that he relied totally on citation, dispensing with definition. It is doubtful whether this can really be called lexicography. Moreover, Richardson's notion of etymology was derived from Horne Tooke's dangerous *Diversions of Purley* (1786), which went in for philosophical conjecture about the origins of words and was quite capable of deriving *hash* from the Persian *ash*, meaning stew.

1876 was a momentous year for British lexicography, though the impulse which made it momentous came from America. All that the English-speaking world then had in the way of dictionaries was Webster, Worcester and Richardson, and none of them was suitable for the age which had already seen *The Origin of Species* (1859) and *Das Kapital* (1867), to say nothing of the publications of the British Philological Society. Harper, the American publisher, wished to cooperate with Macmillan in London in the production of a new dictionary 'like Webster, in bulk, and as far superior in quality as possible'. He was not thinking of the 1828 Webster but of the huge and authoritative edition of 1864, so his conception was bold enough. Who should be editor? There was only one man, and his name was James Murray.

Murray was the consummate example of the self-made scholar. Born near Hawick in Roxburghshire, his father a small tailor of Covenanter stock, himself a godfearing teetotal non-smoking philoprogenitive bizarrely polymath dominie, he was at that time a teacher at Mill Hill School near London, one of the dissenting establishments set up as a pedagogic counter to places like Rugby and Winchester, where only Anglican pupils were admitted. Murray was suffused with a passion for learning which, if it ever needed justification, could find it in the duty to serve God through useful action and honour Him by trying to understand His Creation. But his temperament was naturally that of a man infinitely curious, especially about language. He seems to have had at least a theoretical knowledge of literally every language, living and dead. When the exiled Hungarian patriot Kossuth visited Hawick – a town passionate for national liberties – he was met not only by the town band but by a banner inscribed in Magyar – '*Jöjjön-el a' te orszagod*', meaning 'Thy Kingdom come'. James Murray had been at work. He always learned his modern languages from the Bible. He tackled a Chinese Book of Genesis as a boy, and he could still write its characters in whitebearded old age. He was a man intended for white-beardedness; he had a lot of the Old Testament prophet about him.

Brought up as he was on the English–Scottish border, he was struck while still a very young child by the failure of a political boundary to coincide with an isogloss. The Sassenachs down there spoke his kind of language. Language was a continuum, in time as well as space. Anglo-Saxon still existed, though Hengist and Horsa were long dead. Dialects were not 'incorrect' speech but survivals of earlier forms of the language. He became – passionately, as with everything – a member of that movement dedicated to the study of the English language as a totality – diachronic and synchronic, as they say nowadays. There were great men in this movement, and they joined together to form the Philological Society. One of them, Henry Sweet, has become, as Henry Higgins, a world figure of romantic myth. His nature belied his name. He had a right to be sour and prickly, especially in his attitude to the scholarly Establishment. Oxford and Cambridge despised the study of English. The new linguistic scholars were in a *Catch-22* situation, for they could not propagate the new learning without a degree in it, and they could not get a degree in what they themselves were creating. Frederick J. Furnivall, founder of the Early English Text Society, had started off as a mathematician. You always had to start off as something else. James Murray never went to a university, though Edinburgh gave him an honorary doctorate: he wore his doctor's cap even at meals. The philologists were a mixed and eccentric gang and among them was Prince Louis-Lucien Bonaparte, Napoleon's nephew. He was very interested in what a Berkshire farmer would say to his cow. Murray didn't think much of him as a philologist.

Murray was very modern in his approach to language, and the proponents of language laboratories would be unwise to find fault with his tackling new tongues through biblical texts. Where Dr Johnson would speak French with an English accent, Murray saw that the essence of a language was its sound and that, for instance, there was no point in transcribing a piece of Border English in the amateur orthography of a Robert Burns. (He had a lot against Burns, who compromised in his treatment of Scots grammar for the benefit of an English audience: 'Scots wha hae' should have been 'Scots 'at hae'. Phonetics was the key to accurate transcription, and he went to the lectures of Alexander Melville Bell, the inventor of the Visible Speech that is mentioned in *Pygmalion*. This system, which uses stylized depictions of tongue and lip positions, looks very fearsome, somewhat like Tamil, but, being rational and consistent, it works. There was also Broad Romic, based on conventional orthography, the ancestor of the International Phonetic Alphabet. While Murray sat at the feet of Alexander Melville Bell, Alexander Graham Bell, the teenaged son, sought lessons in electricity from this man who knew everything. Murray gave him lessons; Graham invented the telephone. The grandfather of the telephone, as Graham later insisted on calling him, was, in a distracted way, preparing himself for a task both thrilling and appalling. He had a Scots engineer's patience and integrity towards every aspect of linguistic research. He was an etymologist temperamentally incapable of tolerating *lucus a non lucendo* nonsense; his ear was tuned to the sounds of the world's languages; his knowledge of early English texts (gained through Furnivall's bullying him into doing most of the work for the EETS) was formidable; his capacity for hard work was impressive. He was destined to become the century's greatest lexicographer. This is where we came in.

Murray saw that the Macmillan–Harper proposal could bring Anglo-American lexicography into the modern mainstream of philology running strong in Germany, where Sweet had been trained. He knew also that the Philological Society had been for twenty years gathering materials for a new dictionary of its own. What he did not expect was that the Society, in the ebullient person of Furnivall, should decide to force its own concept on Macmillan. Harper had thought of a book of 2000 pages, the Society thought of 6000. Soon Macmillan and Harper grew frightened as the prospect of a dictionary unmanageable and unprofitable, possibly even ruinous, presented itself. The Delegates of the Oxford University Press took over the project, though not even they had any conception of how big the work was ultimately to be. Nobody knew, though the editor began to have his suspicions. We know, because we have the book. The OED, though Murray did not live to edit all of it, and though, through its supplements, it must be said to be always in the making, is as great a product of Victorian enterprise as the erections of Brunel or the Disraelian Empire. And, of course, far more enduring.

It seems incredible to us that this gigantic undertaking was conducted at first as a sparetime activity while Murray was still teaching at Mill Hill. Admittedly, he was given time off from the classroom, with a corresponding reduction in salary, but the emoluments from the Delegates were, by our standards, derisory. K. M. Elisabeth Murray, in this admirable biography of her grandfather, counts out the £ s d for us and shows us that there was more scholarly, or patriotic, martyrdom in it than profit. Not that Murray disliked the martyr's role, since it had honourable precedents and brought him closer to God. It also brought him, at the last, honorary doctorates and a worrying knighthood (the tradesmen might put up their prices), but it never brought him what he most wished – acceptance by the Oxford dons as one of themselves, the university's confirmation of a scholarly ability to which few of its members could pretend. Sweet had always warned him about Oxford:

> You must be prepared for a good deal of vexatious interference & dictation hereafter, liable to be enforced any moment by summary dismissal. You will then see your materials & the assistants trained by you utilized by some Oxford swell, who will draw a good salary for doing nothing. I know something of Oxford, & of its low state of morality as regards jobbery & personal interest.

In the garden of his house at Mill Hill Murray set up an iron shed which gained the name of the Scriptorium and lined it with pigeonholes. The idea of pigeonholes had come from Herbert Coleridge, first editor of the Philological Society's project, who had had fifty-four of these, adjudging them sufficient for the 100,000 wordslips the dictionary would need. Coleridge had died at thirty-one. Warned he would not recover from the consumption brought on by sitting in damp clothes at a Society lecture, he spoke heroic words: 'I must begin Sanskrit tomorrow.' Murray, who trusted God not to take him too soon, had a thousand pigeonholes, but these were soon crammed, words resisting the carpenter's taxonomy, and the two tons of paper slips that Murray got from Furnivall were a mere continental breakfast. Inedible, mostly. These, the contributions of voluntary workers over the years, consisted of head words with quotations. They came in sacks (a dead rat in one, a live mouse with family in another), parcels, a baby's bassinet, 'a "hamper of I's" with the bottom broken, which had been left behind in an empty vicarage at Harrow'. H was found with the American consul in Florence, though it had started life fifteen years earlier with Horace Moule, Thomas Hardy's teacher and friend. Fragments of Pa were found in a stable in County Cavan, but most of the slips had been used for lighting fires.

So little of the material inherited from the enthusiastic but slapdash Furnivall was of value that Murray had to start again, appealing for volunteer readers all over the anglophone world, laying down rules of admirable clarity for the making of slips, playing the dominie in letters of inordinate length to his co-lexicographers. Murray's children – Wilfrid, Hilda, Oswyn, Ethelwyn, Elsie, Harold, Ethelbert, Aelfric, Rosfrith, Gwyneth, Jowett (named for the great Benjamin) – got their pocketmoney from slip-sorting and, inevitably, acquired precocious vocabularies. In the Scriptorium the editor sat a foot higher than his fistful of assistants, doing with skill and delicacy the work he alone could do – contriving definitions of wonderful terseness, indicating pronunciation through a system that the Supplements still use, and demonstrating, by means of a brief historical procession of citations, the semantic complex we call a meaning. Despite his uprightness of life, reflected in a great chasteness of speech, Murray did not believe in omitting words because they were substandard or taboo. His approach to language was totally scientific: one could not apply moral judgements to words. But he yielded to the prejudices of the Victorian middle class, and nothing in the *OED* could bring a blush to the cheek of innocence. The recent Supplements are a different matter, of course. One can imagine Murray in heaven nodding his beard in approval at the scholarly treatment of *f**k* and *c**t*.

One excellent feature of the *OED* is typographical. Murray learned early in his schoolmaster's life the pedagogic value of a variety of types in a textbook. One of the set texts at Mill Hill (imposed by the examiners of the Cambridge Locals) was William Paley's *Horae Paulinae*, a worthy exposition of theological utilitarianism that Murray's pupils found baffling. Murray was a great maker of easy primers, though the only one he published was his *Synopsis of Paley's Horae Paulinae* (1872). This used different types to make Paley's arguments 'eloquent to the eye'. The *OED* is not only a triumph of philological engineering; it is a book satisfying to handle because of Murray's appreciation of the semiology of type – something that the Oxford swells, who had never taught children, were slow to see.

Elisabeth Murray's story of the setbacks, scholarly blindness, tyrannous demands, spurts of official indifference, unworthy commercialism that beset the road from A to T (as far as Murray got) makes painful and infuriating reading. Murray's transfer of home and Scriptorium from Mill Hill to Oxford, as much in the hope of a university appointment as out of a fancied need that Oxford would be more lexicographically nourishing than Mill Hill, is an episode not lacking in pathos. But no less pathetic character than Murray ever strode the new terrain of philology. Complaining to the cook that his porridge was too waesh or too brose, shouting for his wife Ada (a heroine of the age) with 'Where's my lovey?', stern but loving with the children, a great man to be with on holiday (he knew all about botany and marine biology and could make a lifesize Grendel out of sand), he is a supreme example of the virtues of the poor ambitious dissenting class. Samuel Johnson would have entertained very mixed attitudes towards him.

As good commercial drama could be made out of Murray's life as out of Sweet's. Indeed, there is hardly a personage in Elisabeth Murray's book who does not demand Shavian treatment (or more detailed Shavian treatment than some of the philologists get in the preface to *Pygmalion*). Frederick James Furnivall, whose doctor father attended Mary Shelley in her confinement of 1817, seems to have lent some of his characteristics to Henry Higgins:

He never understood, or attempted to understand, the quality of tact. It was a species of dishonesty. What he held to be true was to be enounced in the face of all opposition, with unfaltering directness and clarity; what he held to be false was to be denounced with Athanasian intensity and resolution.

Furnivall had learned to hate religion and didn't give a damn about convention. He married a lady's maid and later left her (this was so scandalous that Murray stuck stamp-paper over the signature of the correspondent who gave him the news). He would have married a flower girl as readily. Professor Freeman called him the Early English Text Society's madman and said he ought to be chained up or gagged. Then there was Alexander Ellis, who wanted spelling reform but only his own system. A rival proposal was 'bad from every conceivable point of view . . . a disgrace to the Committee . . . all bosh. . . .' Such men would willingly fight over the pronunciation of the Middle English yogh. Furnivall accused Murray of spending £5 of the Society's money to get a yogh specially made for *The Complaynte of Scotland*, but it was really the printer's fault. 'A beastly big ξ.' There are naive people around who regard philologists as dull, forgetting that the rogue-god Mercury presides over language.

It is true that Murray's preoccupation with the *OED* begot a kind of monomania, but it must be regarded as a beneficent or at least an innocuous one. It became difficult for him to make aesthetic judgements on literature: words kept getting in the way. Murray got into correspondence with Robert Browning, but only to ask about the meaning of *apparitional* in E. B. B.'s *Aurora Leigh*. When his son Oswyn later said how much he admired Browning's poetry, Murray's grave reply was: 'Browning constantly used words without regard to their proper meaning. He has added greatly to the difficulties of the Dictionary.' Was he perhaps thinking of the misuse of *twat* in *Christmas Eve and Easter Day*?

Murray died in 1915 at seventy-eight. He should have died thereafter. It took another thirteen years – under first Henry Bradley, later William Craigie and Charles Onions (to whom the Murray children would derisively sing 'Charlie is My Darling') – to bring out the final volume. The work continues to be Murray's monument: his pattern of approach will still be evident in the Supplements of 2077 and 2177, if Newspeak allows. But he did not want a monument – 'It is extremely annoying to me to see the Dictionary referred to as *Murray's English Dictionary*' – and he would have been horrified at the thought of a biography:

> I wish we knew nothing of Carlyle but his writings: I am thankful we know so little of Chaucer & Shakespeare. . . . I have persistently refused to answer the whole buzzing swarm of biographers, saying simply 'I am a nobody – if you have anything to say about the Dictionary, there it is at your will – but treat me as a solar myth, or an echo, or an irrational quantity, or ignore me altogether.'

But we must be thankful that K. M. Elisabeth Murray, who evidently possesses something of her grandfather's powerful will, as well as his family piety, has disobeyed the implied injunction of the old man whose beard tickled her when he kissed her at the age of three and a half. Although the scope of her book is inevitably narrower than the biography of that other great lexicographer, it is without doubt a work of large importance as well as of very considerable entertainment value.

OED +

A Supplement to the Oxford English Dictionary, Volume III, *O–Scz*, edited by R. W. Burchfield
The Concise Oxford Dictionary, seventh edition, edited by J. B. Sykes

A papal visit, a war won, a royal birth (1982), and now Volume III of the *OED* Supplement. *Semestris mirabilis*. The importance of this 1575-page triple-columned instalment of a great masterpiece was dimly recognized even by the *douaniers* of the Côte d'Azur, who charged me 75 francs for its possession, as well as making me pay 400 francs in taxi fares to free it from sequestration. One more volume will bring us to the end of supplementation, and then – since about 450 new words come into English every year – the whole business will have to start all over again. Here are 18,750 words divided into 28,000 senses and, always the great glory of the *OED*, about 142,500 illustrative citations. I know that I am one of the cited, because I had a letter about citing me. I illustrate the word *rhotacismus*.

The stop-press up-to-dateness of the volume is best exemplified by *Rubik's cube*, which was a craze in 1981. The definition is exemplary: 'a puzzle consisting of a cube seemingly formed by 27 smaller cubes, uniform in size but of various colours, each layer of nine or eight smaller cubes being capable of rotation in its own plane; the task is to restore each face of the cube to a single colour after the uniformity has been destroyed by rotation of the various layers.' The next Supplement will have to fit in the 64-cubed sophistication I saw advertised on my recent London visit. The lexicographer's work is never done.

All dictionaries now give *quark*, usually with the pronunciation we assume Joyce gave it (to rhyme with *ark*), but now we know it has to be pronounced *quork*. M. Gell-Mann, who adapted the joycism to physics, makes this clear in a letter (27 June 1978) to the editor: 'I needed an excuse for retaining the pronunciation quork despite the occurrence of "Mark", "bark", "mark", and so forth in *Finnegans Wake*. I found that excuse by supposing that one ingredient of the line "Three quarks for Muster Mark" was a cry of 'Three quarts for Mister . . .' heard in H. C. Earwicker's pub.'

Prang still has no etymology, despite its pretty certain provenance in Malay *perāng*, which means fighting in war. Strangely, *satay* (a Malaysian kebab) is underived from *sateh*, which, in both Arabic and Romanized spelling, signals an audible aspirate at the end. Tone numbers are not given in Chinese derivations. Here begins and ends my nitpicking.

Let us now see what words which seemed too fragile or nonceish to last have entered the eternal canon. We are entitled to call the Queen *Queenie*, since it is not, as it seemed during the sixties, a term of good-humoured contempt but one of affection, like *Queen Mum*, a usage ratified by *The Times* (4 August 1980; 'The dear old Queen Mum is . . . "the best loved lady in the land." '). *Pseud, pseudery, pseudish* and *Pseuds' Corner* are in. *Philly* gets in as a US slang abbrevation for Philadelphia, but surely it is an established British usage as the short form of the name of a processed cheese. We may *psych* or be *psyched* or belong to the *psychedelic* subculture, despite the irregular formation of the latter term. *Queerie* is acceptable for one who is queer. *Pakis* are around, being duly bashed ('wanton physical assault on or other violence directed against Pakistani immigrants'). *In petto* seems established as meaning 'on a small scale', which is a pity.

What words, anyway, ought to go in? When does a nonce word become a genuine neologism, and when is a neologism accepted as a fully paid-up part of the lexis? I invented some years ago the word *amation*, for the art or act of making love, and still think it useful. But I have to persuade others to use it *in print* before it is eligible for lexicographicizing (if that word exists). T. S. Eliot's large authority got the shameful (in my view) *juvescence* into the previous volume of the Supplement. Terms made up for one occasion only – like *apothanein-theloish* (suicidal in the manner of Petronius's Sybil) – stand little chance. The final authority rests on need manifested at least a handful of times. What is interesting about the Supplement is its liberalism: we no longer need separate compilations for slang, argot and cant. The unitary lexicographer is here to stay.

When I reviewed the two last volumes, I pleaded, with little hope, for the inclusion of Dr Burchfield's name in an Honours List. I don't know whether it ever appeared. It seems to me that no man can better honour his country than by systematizing the language of his country. But a dictionary is of little help to a political party, since it clarifies what politicians prefer to remain obscure. Still, if the Upper House has its law lords and bishops (though not Catholic ones), it ought to have its lexicographers too. There will be no more laudable achievement this year than the publication of this volume.

For those unwilling to be made drunk or mad by the intolerable wealth of English as the great *OED* presents it, the *Concise Oxford* (1264 double-columned pages in this new edition) will, as always, serve. No Pakibashing here, and *queenie* limited to homosexuals. Unfortunately, it has to stand comparison with the similarly priced *Collins Dictionary*, which has proper nouns and the International Phonetic Alphabet for its pronunciations and, it seems to me, more elegant definitions. For *cunnilingus* the *Oxford* had 'stimulation of vulva or clitoris by licking', while the *Collins* gives us 'a sexual activity in which the female genitalia are stimulated by the partner's lips and tongue'. Both dictionaries are vague on *fugue* but *Collins* does at least specify repeating a fifth above or fourth below, while *Oxford*'s definition could refer to a canon. The *Oxford posh* is ignorant about etymology, but *Collins* helpfully refers to a probable derivation from *port out, starboard home*. Any etymology, as the late Eric Partridge insisted to me, is better than none.

Collins, too, is more exact in its science. It suffices *Oxford* to define *entropy* as 'measure of the unavailability of a system's thermal energy for conversion into mechanical work; measure of the degradation' – too much of the emotive there, surely – 'or disorganization of the universe.' In the other we end with a formula: '$S = k\log P + c$ where P is the probability that a particular state of the system exists, k is the Boltzmann constant, and c is another constant.' For *phoneme Oxford* has merely 'unit of significant sound in a specified language'. What is meant by *significant*? Collins makes all clear: '. . . /p/ and /b/ are separate phonemes in English because they distinguish such words as *pet* and *bet*, whereas the light and dark /l/ sounds in *little* are not separate phonemes since they may be transposed without changing meaning.' And, while the *ph*-pages are open, *Phrygian* is merely to *Oxford* 'an ancient Greek mode, reputed warlike in character' and the third of the 'church modes (with E as final and C as dominant)' (C? Not B?). *Collins* spells it out: '. . . the natural diatonic scale from E to E.' I shall go on using the *Collins*; the *Oxford* I shall give away.

People as Well as Words

Collins Dictionary of the English Language, edited by Patrick Hanks

W e are expecting more and more from new dictionaries what used to be reserved to encyclopedias – namely, information about proper nouns. Look up *Rolling Stones* in the new *Collins* and you will find

> English rock group (formed 1962): comprising Mick Jagger (born 1943; lead vocals), Keith Richard (born 1943; guitar, vocals), Brian Jones (1942–69; guitar), Charlie Watts (born 1941; drums), Bill Wyman (born 1936; bass guitar), and subsequently Mick Taylor (born 1941; guitar; with the group 1969–74) and Ron Wood (born 1947; guitar; with the group from 1975). Their classic recordings include many hit singles . . .

And the entry goes on to exemplify these and add that many of them were written by Jagger and Richard. The length of the article is an indication of the importance which the age accords to this rock group. The dictionary is much of the age, very now (this adjectival usage is not ratified here, probably rightly). John Braine and Alan Sillitoe, who might have got into a similar dictionary of the sixties, are absent, but Amis, Kingsley, has not yet been superseded by Amis, Martin. The Beatles (1962–70) have to be here, but they are not as much here as are the Rolling Stones. Travolta has not made it yet, but Presley, Elvis has outlasted Dean, James. Monroe, Marilyn follows Monroe, James, and is herself followed by the Monroe Doctrine.

All this reference-book stuff is trimmings; the dictionary has to be judged as pure lexicography, and it is a very fine example indeed of the new lexicographer's craft (it is also incredibly cheap). My own craft, such as it is, entails the almost constant use of dictionaries. Here in Monaco I am not as well equipped as I would like to be. I have an unbound review copy of the *American Heritage Dictionary*, which has lost its X, Y and Z and glossary of Indo-European roots, a 1926 *Webster*, the two volumes so far of the *OED* Supplement, Partridge for slang and Onions for etymology. The *American Heritage* can give me *quark* but not *quango*, which, triumphantly, the *Collins* has, just above *quant* meaning a punt pole and *Quant* meaning mother of the miniskirt. Looking up *miniskirt* I find that that delightful garment, symbol of our long-lost sixties exuberance and prosperity, had to be at least four inches above knee. Above it I find *minipill* – 'a low-dose oral contraceptive containing progesterone only' – and, on the opposite page, *minge* – Brit. taboo slang for the female genitals (of obscure origin). This dictionary is very suitable for a writer trying to keep his English up to date. I have, by dint of getting rid of a lamp that doesn't work, a model of the Santa Maria and the cat, found room for it on my desk. There it shall stay, except when I take it to bed to read.

It is not a narrowly British English dictionary. It recognizes the world status of our language, though it is not always ready to accommodate those transatlantic usages which, sooner or later, replace our own. The parts of *fit* are given as *fits, fitting, fitted*, though the American preterite is *fit*. The solecism *hopefully* for *hoffentlich* gets in, however, as does *ass* meaning *arse* (it is very hard to persuade even educated Americans that the latter word is a real one and an ancient one and not just an affected Briticism). The Malay *stengah* (literally half) in the sense of a half-measure of whisky with soda is not here, though *stinger*, with the same meaning, is. But my other dictionaries, apart from my own usage, prefer a stinger to be a cocktail of brandy and crème de menthe. *Pawnee* gets in as an Indian confederacy but not (Hind. *pani*) as the water that dilutes the nabob's spirits. *Prang* is there to mean crash or explode or explosion, but the probable Malay etymology (*perang* means war) is ignored. *Chopsticks* does well enough, but its etymology cannot match the classic one of the *American Heritage*:

> Pidgin English *chop*, fast, probably from Cantonese *kap*, corresponding to Mandarin Chinese *chi*2, fast, hurried – STICK(S). A loose translation of Cantonese *fai chi* and Mandarin *kwai*4 *tse*, 'fast ones' (originally a boatman's substitute for *chu*4, chopsticks, which is a homonym of *chu*4, to stop, stand still, an unlucky word for boatmen.)

All that information is delightfully useless (or useful if you want to show off in a Chinese restaurant). The *Collins* is very adequate on etymology, but it gives no bonuses.

Still, it gives a lot of words (over 162,000 references and 14,000 biographical and geographical articles), and it lists, in its opening credits, a lot of special contributors. Steve Higgs, in Melbourne Grammar School, concentrated on Australian, and Ron Brown did jazz and Brian Dalgleish metallurgy, while the polymath Ralph Tyler covered not only films and TV and radio but literature, mythology, theatre and the biographies. The editorial director is Laurence Urdang, who once managed the *Random House Dictionary* (another great one, whose last entry, I remembr, is *zzz*, for the sound of snoring). I wish I had the etymology of *Urdang*.

Pronunciation is given in the narrow form of the IPA or International Phonetic Alphabet, which, *pace* the *OED*, is probably the best way of representing speech. One needs the IPA, anyway, to discuss the regional and national varieties of English, as the specialists do very interestingly in their introductions. When, incidentally, are we going to see the symbols of the IPA become part of the normal inventory of the non-specialist printer? If, as I would like to do now, I want to express dubiety about the phonetic representation of the diphthong in *home, go, snow* as a combination of schwa (the neutral vowel in *father, away*) and the slack high vowel of *put, pull*, I can only do it periphrastically. We all ought to know the IPA.

Under *Burgess* you will find two entries – one for a writer and the other for a traitor. I'm interested to note that the pronunciation given for the name contains, in the second syllable, the vowel of *bit* and *pit*. I myself, and those who address me by the name, use the schwa, making that syllable the same as the second one of *purpose*. I am not saying that I and they are right, only that I, certainly, seem to have excluded myself, perhaps through expatriation, from a certain field of usage. I am glad, while we're on pronunciation, to see that my preferred *pejorative* with accent on the first syllable has not altogether been superseded by the too popular *pe'jorative*, that the old patrician–Cockney *awff* for *off* seems to be done for, and that nobody ought to pronounce *girl* as *gal* or *gel* any more. This is a fine dictionary.

Anglo-American

Longman Dictionary of Contemporary English (Editor-in-Chief Paul Procter)

Professor Babara Strang, in her admirable, nay brilliant, *A History of English* (Methuen), distinguishes between three kinds of users of our language. The A-speakers have English as a mother tongue; the B-speakers, found mostly in the former British colonial territories, learn it in childhood and accord it a special status as the tongue of law and culture; the C-speakers are the others, foreigners who study English at school and university and recognize its importance as a medium of world communication. This means that there are a lot of English-users: the A group alone probably comprises 400 million. A lot of users and a massive need for manuals of usage and dictionaries, especially among the B and C groups. English-as-a-second-language is a major industry. In tax havens like Monaco you will find fewer novelists than creators of usage primers – rich men bewildered and sometimes guilty and not often happy at having been thrust out of England by their accountants.

This new dictionary should earn a lot of money. It deserves to. It is all that hard work, imagination, scientific rigour and the sincere consultation of world need can make it. It is primarily for *them*, not us – viz., the C-speakers. It posits for the user an initial maximal vocabulary of 2000 words, and computers have been employed to stop that vocabulary getting above itself. The nudity of some of the definitions would have shocked Dr Johnson. *Net,* which he was only able to define by calling up such words like *decussated* and *reticulated* (the literary artist instinctively making his definition an image of the thing itself), is here 'a material of strings, wires, threads, etc. twisted, tied or woven together with regular equal spaces between them.' What could be more lucid? A-speakers would be wise to buy this dictionary and enjoy an intelligibility of definition they cannot always expect to find in the A variety. Take *entropy*, of which definition 1 in the *American Heritage Dictionary* runs:

A measure of the capacity of a system to undergo spontaneous change thermodynamically specified by the relationship $dS = dQ/T$, where dS is an infinitesimal change in the measure for a system absorbing an infinitesimal quantity of heat dQ at absolute temperature T.

Longman gives:

A measure of the difference between the temperatures of something which heats and something which is being heated.

That's definition 1. Definition 2 is

the state which the universe will reach when all the heat is spread out evenly.

The *American Heritage* will not help you much when you want to understand a statement like 'American literature from *The Education of Henry Adams* to Thomas Pynchon's *Gravity's Rainbow* is a gloomy forecast of human entropy.' *Longman* is right, or bang, on.

This is an Anglo-American dictionary. In definition 3 of *faggot* we have '*AmE* also (*infml*) fag – HOMOSEXUAL' which comes before '*BrE* an unpleasant person (esp. in the phr. old faggot)'. *Street* is illustrated by a beautifully clear representation of its subject, with island/AmE safety island and slot machine/AmE vending machine and hoarding/AmE billboard, as well as our old friend pavement/sidewalk. *Fit* has the weak termination -*ted* in *BrE*, but Americans treat it like *put* and say 'The suit fit him perfectly'. This has its due place in the article on *fit* but the irregular form is missing from the catalogue of irregular verbs which makes up one of the appendices (along with currencies and service ranks). I say this not to be captious but because I wish to emphasize the smooth beauty and professionalism of this lexicographical masterpiece by scratching on it. And, while I'm at it, readers of American fiction who wonder what is meant by 'They loved each other up' must still, as I must, remain in the dark.

All the taboo words are here, and terrible they sound in their C-language clarity: '(esp. of a man) to have sex with (someone, esp. a woman) and '1 (C) VAGINA (C; *you* + N) a foolish or nasty person. A dildo is 'an object shaped like the male sex organ (PENIS) that can be placed inside the female sex organ (VAGINA) for sexual pleasure.' Nowhere do we find the decent near obscurity of Latinate circumlocution. I feel myself to be back in Malaysia with a Chinese boy saying 'What please tuan is angel?' and I reply 'A kind of man like a bird that comes from God.' *Longman* gives us 'a messenger and servant of God, usu. represented as a person with large wings and dressed in white clothes.' Join the A-train of the *American Heritage* and you will arrive at 'An immortal, spiritual being attendant upon God. In medieval angelology, one of nine orders of spiritual beings (listed from the highest to the lowest in rank): seraphim, cherubim, thrones, dominations or dominions, virtues, powers, principalities, archangels, and angels.' No wings, no white garments. C-Engish, of its nature, cannot penetrate far below surfaces. A C-dictionary cannot help much with a Nairobi or Singapore or Stockholm first attempt at Conrad or Henry James.

Pronunciation is given in the symbols of the International Phonetic Alphabet, as it always should be – the narrow form, too. The broad form, as I know from my own second-language teaching experience, causes trouble. If you represent the vowel in *fit* as /i/ and the vowel in *feet* as /i:/ you are as good as saying that the second sound is only the first sound lengthened, which it isn't. Longman consistently gives the diphthong in *oboe* as a combination of the schwa (the neutral vowel of the indefinite article, as in *a boy, a girl*) and the vowel of *put* and *bull*. Try it – especially in *oboe* – and you seem to get the somewhat affected diphthong of the old J. Arthur Rank starlets. Is this refined rendering of diphthongal *o* really the standard for foreigners to follow? Is it really all that common now, except with Her Majesty and retired colonial governors? In exile as I am, I can't really say. But I'm pretty sure that 'going home, Joe?' ought to have some lip-rounding in it.

English as a Foreign Language

A Krio–English Dictionary, compiled by Clifford N. Pyle and Eldred D. Jones

K rio is a lingua franca used in Sierra Leone. The name is derived from *creole*, which must be distinguished from *Creole*. A Creole is, generally but not always, a person of mixed European and Negro ancestry. A creole is a language that derives from extended contact between two language communities. There are grounds (see *Journal of Creole Studies*, Volume 1, No. 1, 1977) for supposing that English is a kind of creole, the product of extended contact beteen Normans and Anglo-Saxons; but normally the term is used only of a tongue made out of an Indo-European and a non-Indo-European language, and both Norman French and Dano-Anglo-Saxon claimed the same Indo-European ancestress. Creoles begin as pidgins (Chinese corruption of *business*), trading languages which are blends of a native structure and an imported vocabulary. The typical transformation of a pidgin into a creole, or new mother tongue, is seen when the bringers of the vocabulary (British or French or Portuguese) force the suppliers of the structure (usually Africans) into a living situation which cuts the latter off from their roots. Slavery is the most notorious of the deracinating devices, and *creole* seems to derive from the Portuguese *crioulo* – a slave born in the master's household.

At the beginning of the nineteenth century the British abolished the slave trade and returned some of the creole speakers of the West Indies to Freetown. Their now native language was a mixture of English and Yoruba, though there were other elements as well – notably Portuguese, which provided the preposition *na*, meaning *in*, and a number of vocabulary items. The British stayed on the West Coast until the middle of the present century, imposing genuine British English as the administrative and cultural medium, but Krio florished and was even exported – to Gambia, Cameroun and Nigeria. Krio has attained the dignity of a literature, a scientific linguistic descriptive apparatus, and this highly professional dictionary.

If my readers have stayed with me thus far, they will now be ready to ask: what has this to do with us, educated people without a linguistic orientation and, for the most part, unacquainted, except for Mr Greene's *The Heart of the Matter*, with the people of Sierra Leone? My answer has to be that users of English ought to know what has happened to English outside England: they have a kind of ancestral responsibility for the spread of their language. Much more important, though, is the matter of evaluation. There are too many people around who regard

African versions of English as primitive, quaint and inefficient – a stricture especially applied to the Black English of the United States. Unsophisticated white stay-at-homes see in such a language as Krio a failed attempt to speak 'proper' English. This is wholly unjust and very stupid. Krio is not a dialect of English, though the lexis is overwhelmingly of English origin. Its basis is native African, mostly Yoruba: its grammatical structure is totally non-English, and it even has, like Chinese, a system of tones which materially affect meaning. Its phonemic system (or scheme of pronunciation) is altogether African and totally consistent. It cannot well be presented in the alphabet we use: a modified form of the International Phonetic Alphabet is employed in this dictionary. Unfortunately, I cannot reproduce the symbols of that alphabet here. We are still not ready to accept it as a regular reading tool – even though Bernard Shaw saw, as early as 1912 and the published version of *Pygmalion*, that no person concerned about language could well get on without it.

Anyway, I select a page arbitrarily to show how the Krio lexis works. *Manpus* for a tomcat and *man og* for a male pig may seem quaint or childishly poetic, but not to an ear attuned to the logical classifying systems of African, and for that matter Asian, languages. *Manyual lebo* is manual labour and a *manyual ogan* is an organ powered by hand-operated bellows. *Maogani* is mahogany, but *manzhe* is (humorously) to eat, *mao* to steal, often mercilessly, or to eat heartily, or to be initiated into certain secret rituals. This *mao* comes from Yoruba. *Mara*, from Mende, means to behave coquettishly or foolishly. If *marabu*, ultimately from Arabic, means a Moslem hermit or monk, then *marabu wachnet* (watch night) means the eve of Ramadan and a *marabu skul* is a school where you study the Koran. A *mangromonki*, or mango monkey, is a child fond of tree-climbing. A child who can claim sailors as putative fathers is a *manawa pikin* (man-of-war picaninny).

The jargon of politics finds its way into the colloquial vocabulary. If *mandet* derives from *mandate* and means authority to act, then you can say: '*U gi yu mandet fo go tok lek dat?*' – who gave you the right to talk in that manner? There are plenty of idioms out of the Christian missions – *Mana from evin* and *mana indi wildanes*; *lov so amezin* – a jibe at persons who display overmuch affection (straight from Isaac Watts: 'love so amazing, so divine'). *Jizos* is who you think it is – as in *Jizos avmasi* (have mercy), *Jizos awa fade*, *Jizyu frend of sina*. *God buk* is the Bible. If you say *God de wit* of a person, than that person is under divine protection. The great opposition is between *God en mamon*.

The reader may now, in spite of good resolutions, feel somewhat superior in the presence of what he must feel as deformed pronunciation and simplistic tropes. He has to be reminded once more that he is not in the presence of a kind of English but confronting a foreign language that knows perfectly well what it is doing. How foreign it may be seen in a folk saying like *Ef uman drim bot snek, i go sun geh beleh*, which means 'If a woman dreams of a snake, she will soon become pregnant,' or *Ef yu drim draifis, da min kowngowsa, oh pikin go dai* – 'If you dream about dried fish,

147

that means gossip, or else a child will die.' I take these two dream interpretations from Professor Ian F. Hancock's compilation, made in Austin, Texas. Hancock collected his folklore from Krio speakers in Canada, Britain and the USA as well as in Sierra Leone. The language has certainly travelled.

This first Krio–English dictionary is a model of lexicographical skill, and its linguistic apparatus is very comprehensive. It is not the work of expatriates but of native Krio speakers, *aliquid novi ex Africa*. I do not expect many of my readers to buy it, or even to consult it in a library, but the fact that it exists should promote a tiny stir of interest in those who, by the mere habit of reading book reviews at all, show some kind of concern with language. There are great linguistic things happening all over the world, as I can confirm from a recent return visit to Southeast Asia. Languages once thought fit only for rice-planters and fisherfolk are modernizing themselves and confronting the semantic problems raised by an age of electronics and cybernetics. These languages are also looking at themselves, drawing on the descriptive techniques made available by men and women in the linguistics department of Western, and now Eastern and African, universities. This is far more important than what the politicians say and the terrorists do, but it never makes the headlines.

Partridge in a Word Tree

A Dictionary of Catch Phrases, by Eric Partridge

Some years ago I was commissioned to compile a short dictionary of modern slang. I finished the shortest and second longest letter sections – Z and B – and then gave up the assignment. I could see that my life would be spent in keeping the thing up to date (*bovver boots* came in just as I'd finished B) and dealing with fractious correspondents who disputed my etymologies. I had admired Eric Partridge before, as a cheerful and industrious one-man lexicographer on the Johnsonian pattern; how much more have I admired him since. I have dedicated a book to him – all I could do. I have no influence in the domain of royal honours or academic awards. Partridge is eighty-three this year* and still industriously putting the living language into big books. His new dictionary is as useful and zestful as anything he has done in his youth. It must have been a very difficult work to put together.

Difficult because a catchphrase is hard to define: how does it differ from cliché or a slang term? Partridge charmingly declines definition; he says that he just doesn't know. He does know, however, that a catchphrase – while it is certainly something that has 'caught on' – is not a phrase at all but a complete sentence. It thus has the shape of a Proverbial Saying, a Cliché or a Famous Quotation. Its special quality resides in 'the context, the nuance, the tone'. One sympathizes wholly with that vagueness and approves Partridge's use of square brackets to accommodate entries that are 'doubtfully eligible . . . yet worthy of comment'. Thus, on the very first page, we have the entry in 'mangled Malay' that is far from a common catchphrase, even in Malaysia: *apa changhol dua malam* – literally 'what hoe two night' ('What-ho tonight?'), though that *changhol* should be *changkul*. It's interesting, it has a right to be there, but so has a lot more service macaronic, like *satu empat jalan* ('one four road') and *shufti kush, shufti zubrik*, which I need not translate. I see now, having made it, that such an objection is not in order. Few objections are in order with such a work. 'Partridge is game,' as his best friend said on the Somme, and we should be thankful for so much rank tastiness. But he will, I know, be delighted to be put right on a few minor points.

Cold enough to freeze the balls off a brass monkey got itself combined with *Too late! Too late!* (marine castration) in the *Rag Rag*, not the Rag-Bag ('. . . the brass monkeys on top of the Kremlin were heard to utter a high falsetto shriek'). *Richard's himself again* came earlier than 1841: it was one of Colley Cibber's contributions to *Richard III*. *Stone Win(n)ick* should be *Stone Winwick*. It was Coriolanus who first said *Alone I did it* (v 114), not Clarice in Sutro's *The Fascinating Mr Vanderveldt* (1906). *Don't tear it, lady* should be properly followed by *I'll take the piece*. Partridge calls it a 'street witticism of rather vague meaning', but it refers to a woman breaking wind. *'E's lovely, Mrs Hoskins – 'e's lovely!* indeed comes from the radio show *Ray's a Laugh*, but it should be preceded by *Young Dr 'Ardcastle? Another day, another dollar* should be answered with *A million days, a million dollars*. These, and one or two others, are quibbles, nothing. I present them to show that I have been reading the dictionary (the best way to read Partridge) like a novel.

But catchphrases tend to breed ripostes, which in their turn breed others, and it is hard to know where to stop. Thus, *Are you a man or a mouse?* is regularly followed by *A man. My wife's frightened of mice*. The retort to that may now be ready. That very foul catchphrase dialogue

*1977.

beginning *Fireman, save my child* is practically a whole blackout sketch. What do we do about those ribald prose recitations which feature the Hula-Hula Bird and the Unga-Wunga Camel, either of which can roll out of a drinker's belch? Then there is *Sister Anna shall carry the banner*, a whole sad story when done in full. If these are not catchphrases, what are they? Possible answer: a catchphrase has to have a situation context; these subsist in the void, random verbal entertainments. I don't know, I'm not sure, nobody can be sure. Catchphrases like *Never mind, it'll soon be Christmas* often fill in gaps at drinking sessions, just as *Put another pea in the pot hang the expense* can be said apropos of nothing. Phatic communion, perhaps, is the term to use here. *Roll on, death* (which can be followed by *And let's have a go at the angels*) has a situation context so wide – being in the services and frustrated by it – that it can easily be extended to encompass the whole of life. Stephen Potter, in his *The Sense of Humour*, recalls a pub landlord whose entire conversation consisted of unrelated and unmotivated catchphrases, from *Mind my bike* (Jack Warner, *Garrison Theatre*) to *TTFN* ('tata for now', Tommy Handley's *ITMA*).

And, indeed, the whole point of a lot of the catchphrases made popular by *ITMA* was their floating quality, their surrealistic freedom from context. One of them was *NCAWWASBE* – a virtuoso effort admittedly, to be picked up only by the few – meaning 'Never clean a window with a soft-boiled egg'. *Don't forget the diver*, with its pendant *I'm going down now, sir*, touched, appropriately, submarine depths in the collective unconscious. Some phrases, like Mae West's classic *Beulah, peel me a grape*, rarely find a suitable context in offscreen life, but they are irresistible as tropes, tunes you can't get out of your head. *Whitey whitey kay*, provoking 'What does that mean?', makes its own context. It means, of course *YTYTK*, which in turn stands for 'You're too young to know' – *ITMA* again.

Some of Partridge's 'utility' catchphrases are very fine. The finest are the coarsest, and the coarsest come from the services. *Surprised? You could have fucked me through my oilskins* has disappeared. Popular among Oxford undergraduates in the 1930s, it clearly has an earlier naval origin. *With thumb in bum and mind in neutral* is given as an Australian army catchphrase dating from the 1950s, but Herman Wouk has it as one of Queeg's insults in *The Caine Mutiny*, thus placing it in the US Navy in the 1940s. *The sun's scorching your eyes out* is a venerable waking call, like *Rise and shine, rise and shine. Hands off your cocks, pull up your socks, orderly room's at nine.* There are a lot of these, like *Out of them bloody wanking pits* and *Shit, shave, shampoo and piss buckets out of the window* and, sinister enough for *The Waste Land*, *You've had your time, I'll have mine.* The army's round-up of 'our brown brothers' is *Sudanese, Siamese, Breadancheese, Standatease*. I note here, as I have always noted, that the demotic creativeness of the spoken language finds no counterpart in the English of the upper class. You have to be downtrodden to make vital catchphrases. In a Paris bar the other day, I noticed the Algerians at it during a card game. '*Je suis un homme,*' said one brown brother, '*pas une omelette.*' And so in England we get *My name's Simpson, not Samson.* Homage to Eric Partridge in his word tree, and may he live for ever and me live to bury him. And let those in higher places take their fingers out and clap on him the public honours he merits. Whoreson zeds, unnecessary letters as they are. (I have finished the last page.)

P.S. Alas, he did not live for ever.

Where They Think They Come From

Morris Dictionary of Word and Phrase Origins, by William and Mary Morris

T his compilation has a foreword from a Mr, or probably Dr, Edwin Newman, who seems to be well known in America, as a dogmatic lunch companion if for nothing else:

> Those of you have heard or read my views on the likely demise of literate English know how strongly I feel about making every effort to preserve precision in communication. True, I learned to curb my criticism of colleagues' conversation when it became evident that, if I failed to do so, I would be doomed forever to have lunch alone. But the battle against inaccuracy, infelicity and downright impropriety in the use of our mother tongue continues, even with an occasional luncheon recess. . . .

The kind of fight in which Mr/Dr Newman is engaged is evidently one which does not concern itself much with language as a mode of social intercourse. Newman, sour over the cottage cheese and Jello, has to listen, probably, to the bizarre mixture of slang and technical terminology that is common at institutional luncheon tables – like 'zeroing in on the parametric nitty-gritty' and 'data schmata, I *like* my theory' and so on. But, on the evidence of his stern preface, he is as likely to promote the 'demise' of the language as any colleague who uses it for self-expression and the hell with inaccuracy and infelicity and downright impropriety, whatever the terms mean. Staid conservatism is as much an enemy of the language as loose slanginess, and barking headrime like 'curb my criticism of colleagues' conversation' is no substitute for wit, energy and inventiveness. Still, Mr/Dr Newman expects to be listened to, if not when eating at least over the coffee, and I hope to God no one listens to him when he says: 'At first glance it may seem odd that a dictionary of word and phrase origins should claim to contribute to the cause of linguistic precision. But a knowledge of a word's history is likely to assure its accurate use.' Ah no, Mr/Dr Newman, not at all.

You will remember Professor Beavis in Huxley's *Eyeless in Gaza*, who, ordering tea for his son, referred to him as a 'young stalwart' and twinkled at the waitress as though she too knew it meant 'foundation-worthy'. The same pedant tells slum children that 'primrose' should really be 'primerole' – a folk-etymological 'howler, like our old friend "causeway" '. Huxley is saying that professional etymologists have nothing to do with the real world of cottage cheese for lunch, and he is right. Once approach usage in terms of word origin and you are lost, everyone else being lost with you. To refuse to use *silly* as stupid because it once meant 'holy', or to call a boy a girl because he was so called in Middle English, is to ask to be designated a nut, and quite right too. Alternatively, of course, you can be a poet, which is a kind of nut.

For it is within the province of the poet to sound the whole range of meaning of a word, fusing the diachronic and synchronic, which is theoretically impossible. When Auden uses *buxom*, the original 'bend' element is there (AS *bugan*) as well as the regular denotations. In poetry words sound all their overtones; poetry is, among other things, the total exploitation of words. We don't expect *buckle* to represent the seventh type of ambiguity in speech, but, since Professor Empson, the famous line in 'The Windhover' will always be about collapsing like a bicycle wheel and, at the same time, clicking on a belt for military action. Auden prided himself on having the best dictionaries money could buy. Etymology is one of the genuine poet's legitimate studies. Edwin Newman ought not to have to concern himself with it, except as a lonely hobby. The book he introduces would be of no use to a poet, who needs the *OED* or William Morris's own *American Heritage Dictionary*. This chatty compilation is here to demonstrate (I quote Newman for the last time) 'that learning the subtleties and nuances of our common tongue can be not only instructive and rewarding, but fun.' That last word hangs strangely from the grim cairn of Newman's prose; it would seem more properly to belong to his table companions. However, here we have 654 pages of it, etymological fun.

William and Mary Morris are both fine professional lexicographers. I have myself, as the sole British member of their usage panel, been happy to assist them with another dictionary. In this one I appear as the apparent inventor of the term *dogmerd* – 'a felicitous blend of "dog" and the common French vulgarism for excrement'. That does not go far enough. *Merd*, surely, is to be found in Sir Thomas Urqhart; *Webster* gives it as a native word, though obsolete. But, more important to me, *where* did I introduce *dogmerd*? Not in a book, I'm sure. In an article, then. When and where? It is one of the limitations of a dictionary like this that it has to substitute amiable chattiness for dry documentation. The Morrises are desperate to make etymology fun, but fun means vagueness, chirpiness, a disavowal of scholarship. Dr Johnson inevitably has to appear occasionally (eighteen times to my computation), and he is sometimes 'Sam Johnson', which makes him less the Grand Cham than a fellow barfly, and on one occasion he is at a literary tea with ladies. The Morrises are determined to make him fun, if not fun of him. And all the fun is, has to be, very American.

The British user of the book finds himself very much on the outside. *Many-splendored thing* has an entry, but we are enjoined to 'note that Thompson, being British, spelled it "splendoured" '. The Morrises can be vague about what goes on in Britain: 'Britain's monetary reform (1971) includes new values for pound, shilling and pence, with the new abbreviation "p." for pennies.' *Bosh* is an oddity, so British 'that one can scarcely think of hearing it from any but British lips'. While the Morrises, very rightly, reject the *Marie est malade* derivation of *marmalade*, they pour scorn on the notion of a Frenchified breakfast for a Scottish queen, which makes them bad historians. They are bad on the Bible, too, presenting Joachim not as Joseph's father-in-law but as Joseph himself in disguise. And Beatrice Lillie did not sing a song about a dozen double damask dinner napkins: she rendered a sketch or playlet.

Where the dictionary is valuable is in its ruminations on the origins of specifically American terms. A dogie is defined by cowboys as 'a calf that has lost its mammy and whose daddy has run off with another cow'. Orphan calves had to subsist on grass and water, too heavy for young bellies, which came to resemble 'a batch of sourdough carried in a sack', hence *dough-guts*, hence *dogie*. This may well be as false an etymology as *Marie est malade*, but it rings plausibly. A ten-gallon hat, or John B. (after John B. Stetson), was originally a Mexican *sombrero galon* – the braided hat of the *vaqueros*. A thank-you-ma'am is a small bump in the road. When a young couple went driving, the man was entitled to kiss the girl when they met one of these bumps. A snollygoster is a shyster, and not, as President Truman thought, a man born out of wedlock, but the origin of *shyster* is not given. The Caesar salad was first improvised by Caesar Gardini of Tijuana, Mexico, and not by 'Prince' Mike Romanoff ('a transplanted New Yorker with a king-size supply of chutzpah') in Hollywood. A gopher is a stage-struck kid who hangs round theatres and does errands – 'Hey, kid, go for some coffee'; 'Go for the papers', etc.

In circuses, an acrobat is a kinker, a convict a zebra, a clem a fight that breaks out when the luck boys or gamblers have knifed or swindled too many suckers. The sucker-enticer is the shill and the rubber man sells bladders, or balloons. In carnival lingo the shill, or stick, is the confederate in the audience of the whizz operator, who lays the note and dupes the marks or suckers. If you travel with a tent show you kick sawdust and live on kinkers' row. The grinder is the spieler who delivers his bally in front of his pitch or concession. A gaffed pitch is a game of chance with a rigged wheel. The cataloguing lust of the Morrises in this verbal area drives out the etymologizing joy, but no matter. American can still be gloriously *other*, when Professor Beavis gloated over fever-frows getting themselves storked.

The dictionary is full not only of American but Americans. The phrase *I never met a man I didn't like* was a saying of Will Rogers, first used by him in Boston in 1920, the jam over a sour misanthropy which expressed itself in growls like *Get lost, kid*. The fine epitaph on a waiter – *Bye and bye God caught his eye* – is attributed to David McCord, fund-appeal expert of Harvard. George M. Cohan gets six attributions – including, apparently, the term *nifty* – and the film about him, *Yankee Doodle Dandy*, was, in the star's own view, the best movie James Cagney ever made. *Tennis, anyone?* was the first and only line spoke by Bogart in his Broadway debut. *Private eye* comes from the Pinkerton letterhead, which showed an all-seeing eye. The Ohio congressman James M. Ashley had a new Western territory named Wyoming, though the word was Eastern and Algonquian. It meant 'big flats', right for a plains state. The original Wyoming was a Pennsylvanian valley, but Thomas Campbell popularized the name in his *Gertrude of Wyoming*.

H. L. Mencken, the great separatist who affirmed the existence of an American language, is mentioned thirteen times. It was he who described OK as 'the most successful of Americanisms', without, any more than the Morrises, being able to give a convincing account of its origin. Woodrow Wilson thought it was Chocktaw Indian – 'Okeh' – and persuaded a record company of the 1920s (the one that first pressed Louis Armstrong) to adopt it as a trade name. Charles Berlitz believed it was really '*Aux Cayes*' in Haiti, a port where the rum was good, that got the word into sailor's slang or gob talk as a generalized expression of approval. Andrew Jackson did *not* use it as an abbreviation for 'Orl Korrect'; he was an attorney and highly literate. Nobody knows about OK, but everybody knows where OKD comes from. It is a Philadelphia expression 'used in conversation by two Main Line women about a third who is not – "she's nice enough, but not quite OKD", or "our kind, dear".'

A genial relaxed kind of dictionary, then, which could have got more words in if it had left out more gossip. I mean, if anyone buys it in the expectation of finding a scientific and near-exhaustive lexicon like the great work of C. T. Onions, then there will be large disappointment. The term *dictionary*, when it describes a book of this size and expense, implies a compendiousness that the Morrises are not out to achieve. Let me, I hope, please this admirable couple by calling it a 'good read' – a term which, though 'very British', is heard much in Manhattan 'three-martinis-for-lunch book-editor circles'. It reminds us that the tapping of the current of word history is, God help us, fun. But it has little to do with learning how to stop the 'demise' of literate English. Let Mr/Dr Newman put a copy in the place of each of his lunch-mates. They will only be confirmed in their view of English as a ball kick around or a thruway or a national park. Precision preschmision.

Wise Brevities

The Concise Oxford Dictionary of Proverbs, edited by J. A. Simpson

This is a very slim compilation, no longer than a short novel, and it is a reduction of the big *Oxford Dictionary of English Proverbs* (third edition, 1970). That extensive work concentrated on the saw or saying up to the end of the seventeenth century, 'the heyday,' says J. A. Simpson, 'of the proverb as a vehicle for expressing unquestioned moral truth.' The concise dictionary is more concerned with proverbs that are in use today, and it reminds us that not all proverbs derive from the remote past, the wisdom of a kind of folk-god murmuring from the mists. There are proverbs being made today, and we know the authors of some of them. Thus, *Work expands so as to fill the time available*, usually known as Parkinson's Law, from the former Singapore professor who propounded it, dates only from 1955 but it is as firmly established as *Many hands make light work* and *Too many cooks spoil the broth*, those venerable scraps of folk sagacity which cancel each other out.

In the *Guardian* of 4 April 1979 we read: 'It takes two to tango. . . . Mrs Thatcher has turned Mr Callaghan down.' The saying comes from a song written by Messrs Hoffman and Manning in 1952, and it has the best qualities of a proverb – brevity, headrime, undoubted truth. *What goes up must come down* (which the dictionary says is 'commonly associated with wartime bombing and anti-aircraft shrapnel') is cited as first appearing in 1939, but its provenance in a popular song of the time is not mentioned. I remember distinctly travelling through Germany in 1938 and getting a lift from an ardent Nazi who sang the song, firehot from Tin Pan Alley: 'What goes up must come down, and baby you've been flying too high.' The proverb has a double sexual connotation not cited here.

Some proverbs survive only in our reading, like *Brag is a good dog, but Holdfast is better* and *When the gorse is out of bloom, kissing's out of fashion* and the obscure *What is got over the Devil's back is spent under his belly*. One proverb was already so wellworn in Shakespeare's time that Hamlet disdained to finished it: 'Ay, sir, but 'While the grass grows' – the proverb is something musty.' Three hundred and ten years later, Bernard Shaw, in *The Doctor's Dilemma*, finished it for him – 'the steed starves'. Some proverbs are dangerous, like *A great book is a great evil* and *The greater the sinner, the greater the saint* (fully illustrated by Mr Graham Greene's better novels) and, most dangerous of all, *The greater the truth, the greater the libel*. One proverb is no longer permitted: *A woman, a whippet and a walnut tree, The more you beat 'em the better they be* (though here the duller 'dog' is substituted for 'whippet').

Some of the best of the newer proverbs are American, and not all from popular songs. *Easy come, easy go* sounds American, perhaps because it became the title of a song, but isn't. Still, admirers of Stan Laurel will assert that it took on an ironic American force in the film *Fra Diavolo*: he and Hardy together lose their life's savings in one banditic swoop, making Laurel say: 'Go easy, come easy' and killing the old meaning. *If you don't like the heat, get out of the kitchen* was coined by President Truman, and John F. Kennedy's father said: *When the going got tough, the tough got going*, which is too ingenious for a true proverb, as is the sickening slogan *The family that prays together stays together*. The American proverb is often hard to separate from the catchphrase – *The best things in life are free* and *If you can't beat 'em, join 'em*. Whether a proverb is permitted cynicism is a matter for argument. *Why buy a cow when milk is so cheap?* subverts the sanctity of marriage, and W. C. Fields's *Never give a sucker an even break* expresses bottomless malignity. But there is altogether admirable commercial wisdom in *If you pay peanuts, you get monkeys*.

The dourer proverbs are most needed when life is hardest, and I am sorry to see that army saws – thrown up by the soldier's tough fatalism – are not well represented here. But with sayings like *The army can give you a kid but can't make you love it* and (of an overweening N C O) *There's many a big spud that's rotten* we approach problems of definition. The West can no longer see the difference between a proverb and a phatic utterance derived from television shows and commercials. The essence of the proverb seems to be the encapsulation of genuine wisdom, and the biblical book is to be taken seriously. But wisdom seems to help nobody in an acquisitive world, and one has to go an Asiatic village to be able to conduct an adult conversation entirely in proverbs. So Malay elders will deal ancient sayings like *The hornbill pairs with his own kind, and so does the sparrow* and *Enter a goat's pen bleating, enter a buffalo's stall bellowing* as guides to conduct. An Asiatic student of English would be unwise to pore over the Oxford book, complete or concise, as a guide to conversational usage.

Still, we learn, if we're interested, how damnably ancient and also exotic is a lot of the English lore we regard as homespun. Socrates first said *Eat to live, not live to eat*, and Cicero followed with *edere oportet ut vivas, non vivas ut edas*. We get *East, west, home's best* from *Ost und West, daheim das Best* and a great deal from the French. There is hardly a tired old bromide in the speech of Sancho Panza that does not find an equivalent in English. Which reminds me that the structural essence of all proverbs is to be found on page 41 of the Eulenburg score of Richard Strauss's *Don Quixote*. Sancho, on the viola, makes two banal statements which remind us that brevity and symmetry are what we look for in a proverb and we will swallow an unacceptable content, or no content at all, for their sake. Life, however, is neither brief nor symmetrical.

Now Quotes

A Dictionary of Contemporary Quotations, compiled by Jonathan Green

Dictionaries of quotations, like the *Oxford* or the *Penguin*, are, we've always assumed, for finding out who wrote *A rose-red city half as old as time* or *Philosophy is language idling*. I can never remember the provenance of the first, and that is why I have the *Oxford*, which enables me to find out in order to pass the information on in an article, but I do know who said the second. Mr Green has a fair amount of him in his compilation, but he says: 'For better or for worse, more people want to hear from Ernie Wise than from Wittgenstein.' I do not know who Ernie Wise is and Mr Green gives me no help in his index. There is a Rabbi Stephen Wise there, but no page reference for him. Some obscure joke is going on: perhaps Ernie is the pet name of the Rabbi, and the Rabbi is here because, like John Cage, he knows the wisdom of silence.

There are other, very contemporary people who have a lot to say to Mr Green and the kind of audience he seems to have in mind. He is not concerned with what, for elegance and incisiveness, has stuck in the converse of the cultivated. His line is mostly Sayings of the Week, except that his week has expanded itself to the thirty-odd years since the war, though, since in that period a film of *The Picture of Dorian Gray* was made, it has been possible to attribute certain epigrams of Oscar Wilde to the late George Sanders.

The contemporary people who provide the sayings are sometimes oddly described. Charles Chaplin is an American film star, Canetti a Bulgarian writer, Anais Nin a French novelist and Raymond Queneau a French historian. The person who seems to be most quoted is Quentin Crisp, a British author best known as a naked civil servant. On the very first page, where The World is being dealt with (the dictionary is arranged acccording to subject, ending with Race and Graffiti), Mr Crisp says: 'Is not the whole world a vast house of assignation to which the filing system has been lost?' I don't know, knowing nothing of houses of assignation. Speaking of this same World, Stewart Brand, described as an American environmentalist, says obscurely: 'You can't blame the baby for the afterbirth.' And Elias Canetti has 'The Earth – a globe carelessly hurled into the Universe to annoy the Heavens.' Arthur Koestler, who has become a British philosopher, regards the universe 'as an invisible piece of writing in which we can now and then dicipher a letter or a word and then it's gone again.'

It is not an encouraging first page: the standard is sub-*Reader's Digest*. But Mr Green seems to believe that the quotable for our age is not the literary, not even the higher journalistic, but the ill-considered bromide of the interview, rendered less bromidic by being inaccurately reproduced by the interviewer. This means that film and pop stars have more to tell us than philosophers and literary artists. Johnny Rotten appears five times, Anthony Powell once; Bob Dylan twenty-two times, Philip Larkin thrice; Rod Steiger eleven times, Doris Lessing not at all.

Mr Green is to be congratulated on catching the very soul, or paraphysical mechanism, of our age. Women speak out, which they don't much in the classical compilations. Marilyn French: 'All men are rapists and that's all they are. They rape us with their eyes, their laws and their codes.' Erica Jong: 'Many women have the gut feeling that their genitals are ugly. One reason women are gratified by oral–genital relations is that it is a way of a man's saying "I like your cunt. I can eat it." ' Couturiers are to be listened to, like J. R. Doube: 'I have called the priest type costume "Ave" after Ave Maria; the other is "Cardinale" after Claudia Cardinale, the actress.' John Crosby says: 'T-shirts are the going form of immortality.' Margaux Hemingway, described as a model, has 'I am totally a people person.' Never so lavishly has the failure of the age to relate words to meaning been demonstrated. 'Gentlemen who wear moustaches are generally obsessive, psychopathic, impotent or have some other sexual problem' (N. Parker).

Instead of the epigram we have the wisecrack. Bette Davis on a passing starlet: 'There goes the good time that was had by all.' Alfred Hitchcock: 'I have a perfect cure for a sore throat – cut it.' Joe Namath, American football star, asked if he preferred Astroturf to grass, said: 'I don't know, I never smoked Astroturf.' Malcolm Muggeridge, with twenty-seven quotes, sustains his suety frivolities about ultimate reality: 'If on Judgement Day I was confronted with God, and I found God took Himself seriously, I would ask to go to the other place.' Randy Newman, an American songwriter, says: 'God is implausible. I wouldn't lay that on my kids, though.' Vladimir Nabokov, listed as a Russian writer, has, God help him, to say: 'God – the contrapuntal genius of human fate.' Bob Hope has 'The good news is that Jesus is coming back. The bad news is that he's really pissed off.' Hugh Hefner: 'I think the essence of Judaic/Christian teaching is very similar to *Playboy*.'

Auden, a British poet with twenty-five quotes, says nothing in verse. Verse is reserved to the pop or rock men, and they say nothing either. Bob Dylan (Hon. Mus. Doc.): 'While money doesn't talk, it swears/ Obscenity, who really cares/ Propaganda, all is phoney.' Mick Jagger and Keith Richard: 'All of my friends at school grew up and settled down/ Then they mortgaged up their lives. . . . They just got married 'cos there's nothing else to do.' There is no memorable verse; indeed, there is no memorable prose; the only memorable things are catchphrases like *Ay thang yew* and *What's up, doc?* and *Wakey-wakeeeyyy* and *How tickled I am* and *I'll give it foive* and *I like the backing* and *You've gotta admit it, lady, I do have a go* and *How about that then, guys and gals?* (a British disc jockey, OBE, one of the breed described by D. G. Bridson as 'the wriggling ponces of the spoken word').

The lack of memorability, of the sharply epigrammatic or tersely elegant or just elegant, makes me wonder if anyone could seriously be expected to use this dictionary to discover the authorship of some statement that haunts the mind. Nothing mind-haunting here. It is not, incidentally, really a dictionary: it only admits the alphabetic arrangement of names within sections that themselves have no alphabetic arrangement. Statements are not alphabetized. It is an anthology, then, mostly of banalities. It is least banal when it is anonymous. I have nothing against the page of graffiti which ends the book. *Give me librium or give me meth!* sits with *Death is the greatest kick of all. That's why they save it till last* and *If voting changed anything, they'd make it illegal*. We're living in a very cynical world, also sentimental, also ill-educated, also vulgar. It is the virtue of Mr Green's book that it shows, in this collection of rabbit droppings, just how sick we are.

Abiding Mystery

The Message in the Bottle, by Walker Percy
From Locke to Saussure, by Hans Aarsleff

Walker Percy is best known as one of the American Southern novelists. Quietly, though, he has been contributing articles on language to learned journals for the past twenty years, and he has at last collected them. Some of them are tough technical going, with exact and arcane terminology and Chomskian diagrams; others present language in terms more acceptable to laymen and novelists. The subtitle is 'How Queer Man Is, How Queer Language Is, and What One Has to Do with the Other' – a showman's spiel which sets up expectations of a kind of freak show. But once you get inside there is only Percy with chalk and blackboard.

The scientist, especially the behaviourist of the American tradition which is also Russian, sees language as a system of signs. 'How like a dog is man,' says Professor B. F. Skinner, palinlogizing Hamlet. A man, like a dog, is supposed to make a purely neural response to a word. A word is a Pavlovian buzzer, no more. Say *ball* to a dog and he may look for it under the sofa. Say *ball* to a man and he may demand the trimmings of syntax, but his response can be adjudged in terms of a physical sign. But, say Percy and others, *ball* to a human being is not a sign but a symbol. It names something, and no scientist understands the process of naming, though it is the primal Adamic act. We can't know the world as animals know it; we can only know it through a system of symbols, which both are and are not the things symbolized. The phonemes that make up the world *pencil* (or *crayon* or *matita* or *Bleistift* or *blyertspenna* or *tuzka* or *karandash* or *moli'vi* or *enpitsu*) are, neither singly nor collectively, at all like that artefact of wood and graphite, and yet the object cannot subsist without being so named.

Naming, as Saussure reminds us, and not only Saussure, is an arbitrary business. *Ball* has an iconic element in it – the lips are rounded – but very few words attempt oral mimesis of the thing symbolized. *Pencil* ultimately means, as Professor Beavis in *Eyeless in Gaza* roguishly puts it, teeny weeny penis; a penis is a tail, but it does not sound like a tail, nor does it sound like a penis. Perhaps it is the hopeless task of the poet to try to restore to language an imagined Edenic innocence in which word and image are the same thing. The moan of doves in immemorial elms, and so on. It is through the wrongheadedness of metaphor (nothing could be madder than to say that all flesh is grass) that the truth about the external world can flash for an instant: rub two lumps of arbitrariness together and you get a spark. Mr Percy is very good on metaphor.

He has a chapter entitled 'Metaphor and Mistake'. Sometimes an error in naming, as with what we call folk etymology, can provoke the thrill of the sense of an authentic mystery. Percy says; 'In Mississippi, coin record players, which are manufactured by Seeburg, are commonly known to Negroes as seabirds.' A black guide in south Alabama told the boy Percy that a particular bird was a blue dollar hawk. Percy *père* said he'd got it wrong: it was blue darter hawk. The lad was bitterly disappointed. Beauty, says the mature Percy, has to be divorced from ontology. *Seabird* is wrong, right, but it is brilliant. *Blue dollar hawk* sets up resonances we can rationalize (eerie conflation of nature and human history; money becomes life; paper grows wings, etc.) but we're still left with what Percy, rightly, calls the Hopkinsian inscape, the moment of truth. William Empson misread Rupert Brooke's 'unpassioned beauty of a great machine' as 'impassioned', and the error proved him, which he is anyway, a better poet than Brooke. Error, Percy concludes, is perhaps another word for that blind chance-taking without which we cannot name anything.

A short while ago I was asked to provide a 'primitive' language for a film about the Stone Age called *Quest for Fire*. The film critic Philip French did not hear much more in the resultant structures than Tarzanian grunts, which was perhaps in order, since, if we have no ear for recurring patterns, any unknown language must sound like noise (though noise doesn't have either morphemes or phonemes, both of which Mr French ought to have detected). The point I want to make is that, in constructing the naming parts of the language, I was too timid to be arbitrary. I called a forest *dondr-dondr*, a Chinese-type duplication of a form of Greek *dendron*, which anyone who grows rhododendrons knows means tree. A stag I called *tirdondr*, sticking to a known form for animal (German *Tier*, English *deer*) and putting a tree on its head: This is the way you manufacture a language, but it is not the way real primitive languages evolved. The overwhelming mystery about language lies in the arbitrariness of naming, the willed error whereby a thing becomes identified in our minds with a thing which it clearly is not.

Professor Aarsleff's book is exclusively for scholars, and it will doubtless get, in the scholarly journals, the kind of review it deserves. Here I can merely say that, in pursuing the history of language study from John Locke onwards, the work inevitably raises the question of the origin of all language. When scripture ruled even free inquirers, it had to be assumed that Genesis told the truth about both the birth of language (Adam naming things) and its confounding with the building of Babel. The tongues spoken by post-Babylonian man – including Leibnitz, Boehme and Robert Fludd – were assumed to retain particles of the Adamic tongue, or, put it another way, it was possible up to the time of the great iconoclast John Locke to think of language not as a collocation of arbitrary vocables loosely attached to mental images of things, but as a system still bearing the maimed marks of its Edenic origin.

Language study was, in a sense, cabalistic. 'If, for instance, the word "gold" could be understood in proper cabalistic fashion, it would give us information about the essence of gold itself.' John Locke, whose great *Essay* was the epistemological manual of the new mechanical philosophy, set his face against such irrationality and paved the road towards today's Tower of Babel, which is a fair term for the many-roomed mansion of linguistics, where nobody agrees with anybody else. Perhaps that goes too far. The linguistic philosophers of whom the great world knows nothing – von Humboldt, Herder, Taine, Bréal, Condillac (most neglected of them all) – have brought us at least to a concern with language as it is here and now (the synchronic approach, the diachronic, or historical, approach leading us only back to Adam, who did not exist) and an acceptance of the essential arbitrariness of words. But the great mystery – which Mr Percy as a novelist, is qualified to bid us bow before – remains.

Big Book

The Art of Biblical Narrative, by Robert Alter
The Great Code: The Bible and Literature, by Northrop Frye

The New Testament sits uneasily with the Old. The two languages are not merely different but not even cognate. Christians stitch the two together with devices of typology and prophecy, but the unity is factitious. Even the Old Testament is less a book than a library – *ta biblia*, the little books, not the big, or good, one. We begin with a man and a woman in a garden and end with revelations, but only in Oscar Wilde. The disunity of what Professor Alter calls the Bible (meaning something different from what Dr Frye calls it) has traditionally been seen in its yoking of art and non-art. In some editions you can see the art quite clearly – poetry set in lines, full of extravagant oriental metaphor and exaggerated cries from the heart, bowels and loins. The rest, mere prose, has been taken as artless. Professor Alter seeks to show that, even when we're being dully enlightened with catalogues of battles or confusing genealogies, the hand at work is rarely that of the mere, as it were, monkish chronicler. There were giants in those days, and some of them were novelists.

Traditionally we have accepted that prose narrative came pretty late into our part of the world (meaning not China or Japan). The epic form was reserved for the telling of stories, and it was only with the loss of credence in epic heroes that the novel began to appear as the anti-epic – *The Golden Ass, The Satyricon, Daphnis and Chloe*. Professor Alter argues that the epic form had all the wrong associations for Hebrew narrative artists: it resounded with mythological assumptions very unsuitable for a monotheistic audience, and it surged and thundered, which was not right for tales of shepherds who became guerrilla leaders. Prose, a fine flat medium capable of subtle ironies, is, when you come to think of it, a rather Jewish thing, and proto-Bellows and Malamuds came very early.

'I am not a Biblical scholar,' says Dr Frye, 'and anyone who was one could say of my Hebrew and Greek what Samuel Johnson said, with far less justice, of Milton's two Tetrachordon sonnets, that the first is contemptible, and the second not excellent.' Professor Alter is not in this situation. He teaches both Hebrew and comparative literature at Berkeley (his recent critical biography of Stendhal is very enlightening) and is in a position to explicate the original biblical texts, whose Nabokovian wordplay and prosodic tricks are not available to those who believe the King James version to be the word of God.

Let us look briefly at Jacob and Esau. Esau is all red hair, thick-pelted, animalistic ('*adom* means red: 'Thus is his name called Edom.'), a hunter, while Jacob is *tam* – mild, retiring, capable of cunning. 'The heart is treacherous,' cries Jeremiah – '*aqov ha-lev*, and Esau is aware of the meaning of Jacob's name – *Ya 'aqov*: 'He will deceive'. Esau, famished from the chase, asks for a swallow of the 'red stuff' Jacob is cooking. The stress is on the brutish: Esau cannot, in his famished state, perform the human office of naming a lentil stew directly. The verb he uses – *hil'it* – is more appropriate for beasts than for men: 'let me cram my maw'. His 'precipitous character' is reflected in the rapid chain of verbs – 'ate, drank, rose, went off'. But Esau is polite enough to use the particle of entreaty – *na* – when crying for food, while Jacob is the strong position of not having to use it when demanding in return Esau's birthright. Literary art, in other words.

One of the pleasures of the literary artist used to be the manipulation of a known narrative formula. Take what Professor Alter calls the betrothal type-scene. Future bridegroom journeys to foreign land, meets girl (*na'arah* – maiden) or girls at well, draws water, girls rush off to announce to father arrival of stranger, a meal invitation is issued, a betrothal takes place. Thus Abraham's servant meets Rebekah, Jacob meets Rachel, Moses meets Zipporah. What joy for the narrative artist when he sets up the same situation for Saul. Saul meets girls at well but does not draw water for them: he asks instead: 'Is there a seer near here?' Yes, there is, and Saul hurries to meet the man 'who will launch him on his destiny of disaster'. The disaster is proleptically presented in the abortion of the type-scene. Art.

This is a ground-breaking book, reminding us that the nature of narrative art is grounded in Judaeo-Christian free will, men and women going their own way, clashing, sinning, and God letting them get on with it. And yet, in the paradox of fiction, the characters are controlled by the narrative artist, who is thus a more stringent creator than the Creator. But this is impossible, therefore free will is to some extent illusory, and the narrations of the Bible have to be illustrative of an emergent pattern long predestined. Look at the professor's index, and you will find James, Woolf, Joyce and Faulkner there, as well as Stendhal (whose prolepsis in *Le Rouge et le Noir* – Julien Sorel foreseeing his own end in an anagram and sun-reddened holy water – is far cruder than the cognate devices of the biblical artists). Historical fiction and fictional invention have been going longer than we thought, and, so long as we learn Hebrew first, we can import the Bible into our creative writing classes.

Of Northrop Frye's book I will say little except that it is excellent. His concern is that of most teachers of European literature – the ignorance of the Bible among students who come to a literary tradition soaked in the Bible. Such ignorance can be expunged only by the reading of the Bible, but few laymen, and not many clerics for that matter, know how to read it. Dr Frye considered an approach based on allusion and texture, which would relate Blake's mere five words – 'O Earth, O Earth return' – to seven direct biblical locations and hence be merely a footnote course. He had to move towards a presentation of 'a unified structure of narrative and imagery', which entails coherence of shape rather than meaning – meaning not being in the province of a scholar who knows little Greek and less Hebrew. But some statements in the Bible – like 'thou shalt not kill' – seem direct enough, transcending differences of *langue* and residing in a universal *langage*. It is the quality of indirectness in that directness (there are evidently times when you may kill) which Dr Frye is qualified to relate to the stylistic corpus of the Bible as a whole. And other things. It is a wise book. Consider this, for instance: 'To answer a question . . . is to consolidate the mental level on which the question is asked.'

Slang with Tenure

1 Crimespeak

Language of the Underworld, by David W. Maurer, collected and edited by Allan W. Futrell and Charles B. Wordell, University Press of Kentucky

The late David Maurer was Professor Emeritus of Linguistics at the University of Louisville. He was one of the pioneers of the study of American cant and argot, starting his work in the wake of H. L. Mencken's *The American Language*, which asserted the separateness of the English of the United States from the tongue of the mother country. While Mencken, who was not a professional linguist, assumed the existence of a unified kind of American English enlivened by regional variations, Maurer sought to emphasize an essential disunity and the absence of a central norm on the lines of the so-called 'King's English'. He believed that the normative approach to language taught in schools and colleges aped a tradition in the motherland that was already fossilized in the eighteenth century, and a reasonable approach to American English might be in terms of American subcultures and their distinctive specialized forms of the language. Two of his former pupils have selected, from over two hundred books and papers and articles published by Maurer, a number of brief glossaries relating mainly to the criminal or subcriminal trades. If we seem to know many of the words already, this is because a whole generation of specialist lexicographers has drawn deeply on Maurer, who never himself pursued the harmless drudgery beyond the glossarial stage, though his *Argot of the Criminal Narcotic Addict*, with its seventy-odd double-columned pages, could be classified as genuinely a pocket dictionary.

It is commonly assumed that there is, in proportion to the population, more criminality in America than in Europe. Maurer seems to accept the assumption and take some pride in it, though it is rather a pride in the linguistic wealth of the American criminal than in his antisocial enactments. European criminals, like English Puritans, found a refuge in the Land of the Free, and the Mafia – which, sadly, has contributed little to the English lexis – has turned America into a hypertrophied Sicily. But some of the organized crime of America finds no counterpart in Europe. The bootlegger and his customers equally defied the Volstead Act, which itself could be glossed as a sort of criminality, and specifically American crime may be regarded as a response to specifically American Puritanism. The moonshiners, tucked away in the Kentucky hills, are technically criminals, but it is easier to accept them as exponents of American individualism. The line is always hard to draw. The point, anyway, is not how specialist argots derive from antisocial trades, but how these argots are generated and sustained by the closed nature of the social groups which used them.

Maurer, we are told, was a man well qualified for this kind of linguistic fieldwork. He was big, tough, broad-shouldered, but never to be mistaken for a cop or a fed. The law used him to instruct its undercover agents in the use of one patois or another, but he found it hard to unteach his pupils the furtive predatory manner of the fuzz or pig (which term, incidentally, is as old as 'China Street pig', used for a Bow Street runner in the late eighteenth century). He himself was always accepted, and the lexical fruits are in this book. He began not with criminals but with North Atlantic fishermen, from whom, working with them at the nets, he garnered not only terms like *gurry* (fish entrails), *dong* (penis), *whore's egg* (a small spiny crustacean relished by Italians) and *put a face on* (spoil someone's good looks) but also peculiarities of verb morphology (*I has seed* but *he have seed; I does* /du:z/ but *he do*). Then he fared inland to engage circuses and carnivals.

A number of the terms he picked up from showpeople in 1931 have now passed into the general American vocabulary, such as *cheaters* (spectacles), *saw-buck* (ten-dollar bill), *century* (a hundred-dollar bill, hence *C-note*), *dip* (pickpocket), *Johnny-come-lately* (greenhorn), *hustler* (prostitute), while others are already dead, such as *jig-opry* (negro minstrel), *mitt* (palmist), *lucky-boy* (lazy young man who lives off a circus girl), and *main guy* (show boss). His list, like all his lists, serves to show how ephemeral much of the argot of a subculture is. All such glossaries tend to be word museums.

Maurer's verbal gleanings from the prostitute's trade fill a mere two pages, and he explains why.

> Argots originate in tightly closed cliques, in groups where there is a strong sense of camaraderie and highly developed group solidarity based primarily on community of occupation. Since prostitution, by its very low position in the hierarchy of the crime world and by virtue of its internal organisation, denies the prostitute all claim to true professional status, it is obvious that professional pride is lacking as a motive for argot.

Moreover, there is in prostitutes, as is evident from their fantasies (some of which, like Dr Johnson's friend Bet Flint, they try to eternize in doggerel), a desire for conformity and respectability. Their language is a poor thing, but it has, or had, phrases like *hair pie*, *public enemy* (a customer's wife), and *Oom Paul* (a customer, not necessarily a Boer, who likes cunnilingus). This must be the only trade which calls on the title of a classic play to designate one of its activities: *She Stoops to Conquer* describes fellatio, which, by the less cultivated, may be called *Way Down South in Dixie*. Maurer persistently confuses sodomy and pederasty. He is not interested in the origins of words and phrases, which makes him no true philologist. Eric Partridge was right to insist on providing etymologies, even when these were tentative or mere guesswork. Maurer gives us no hint, for instance, as to why a hooker who accepts coition up the dirt road is called a *turquoise*, though I presume he knows it's a deformation of *Turkish*.

Before we engage genuine criminals, let us consider the language of the moonshiner, very little of whose terminology can be explicated on a basis of straight translation. It is not enough to define *kerosene liquor* as 'liquor contaminated by kerosene'. We have to know that a teaspoon of kerosene in a 1000-gallon vat of beer will cause all the liquor to taste of itself. When the boiler is fired with kerosene the moonshiner must wash his hands carefully 'after filling the pressure tank, and not allow any of his supply bags to lean against a kerosene drum when hauling them to the still site.' *Horse-blanket whisky* describes a crude liquor made by covering a boiling kettle of beer with a heavy folded horse blanket which is periodically wrung of its condensed moisture. 'This technique is not approved by first-class moonshiners.' To *bulldog* is 'to heat used barrels by setting them against a large oil drum in which a fire is built in order to sweat out the whisky that has soaked into the barrel staves.' Half the glossary is richly technical, the other half has to do with beating the *revenooers*.

The cream of the criminal world are probably the Confidence Men, whose complex skills entail a very precise mastery of conventional language but whose inner argot is colourfully arcane. The victim, as we all know, is the *mark*, but he is also the *apple*, *egg*, *fink*, *savage*, *winchell*, *chump* and (why?) *Mr John Bates*. On him is played the *big con* or the *short con*. The biggest of the big con games is the *payoff*, and the term is shorthand for a whole scenario. A wealthy mark is led to believe that he has been taken into a deal by which a big racing syndicate is to be swindled. 'At first he plays with money furnished by the confidence men, then is put on the send for all cash he can raise, fleeced and blown off.' There is also the *wire*, in which a bogus Western Union official convinces the mark that he can delay the transmission of race results to the bookmakers long enough for the mark to place a bet after the race is run. And so on.

Maurer remembers that, while words are the daughters of men, things – which include criminal activities – are the sons of heaven. Glorying in the plenitude of argot, he at the same time deplores the 'major industry' which sustains it. America and presumably other nations will only learn to deal with organized crime when they understand its nature, which involves knowing its language. This sounds like the usual social justification of an academic obsession: in a materialist society it is often difficult to defend the pure as opposed to the applied study. Liquidate criminality and part of Maurer's occupation, or that of his followers, is gone. When he says '. . . we have seen within the last two decades the mass invasion of a definitely criminal subculture by teenagers (and sometimes preteens) from the dominant culture – an invasion that has played havoc with the criminal's cultural pattern as well as his argot' it is as though he were trembling at the situation of an endangered species. Yet who could deny the nobility of his vocation or do other than praise the results of his inquiries among the jug-heavy, forgers, faro bank men, three-shell game operators, pickpockets and junkies? He was a Greene or Dekker with tenure.

2 Ecofreaks, Etc.

Dictionary of American Slang, compiled by Harold Wentworth and Stuart Berg Flexner

Any dictionary of slang has to be historical – in the sense that slang dates so quickly, especially in America, that the term 'current' can have no meaning in a printed book. This is a second 'supplemented' edition to the compilation which came out in 1960 after ten years of preparation. It is very adequate as a guide to the reading of tough American fiction and punchy American journalism published any time up to 1979, but it may not help the prospective visitor to campus, ghetto or commune who wants to enter armed with the not quite yet shopsoiled. It also has the defect of being, unlike Partridge's great work, indifferent to etymology. Look up *twenty-three skidoo*, for example, and you will find that it first appeared at the turn of the century and was 'perhaps the first truly national fad expression and one of the most popular fad expressions to appear in the US', but you will find no speculations as to its origin. Etymology is notoriously difficult with slang, but Partridge considered, rightly I believe, that guesswork was better than nothing.

There are, or were, a lot of American slang terms based on numbers. *Two and a half* was, in the thirties, a lunch-counter term meaning a small glass of milk, and a *twenty-one* was a glass of limeade or orangeade. *Thirty*, denoting the end of a day's work or death or, as in 'OK – thirty for now' from a Shirley Temple film, simply goodbye, reveals a clear enough origin – the triple X at the end of a telegraph message or newspaper correspondent's dispatch. *Third rail*, as a generic name for a strong drink, comes from the electrically charged third rail of a railroad, and the untouchability of that rail makes the phrase also signify a person not to be bribed. *Thirty-four*, meaning 'Go away', was used by a salesman to another who was interfering with a sale, and *thirty-three*, besides being an order of ground beefsteak, was applied to a customer who would not buy from one salesman and was handed over to another. A *three-letter man* is still, I think, a fag, whose queerness is reinforced by the *three-dollar bill* which is the epitome of phoneyness. (I do not find *ten-four*, the signing-off signal of the Highway Patrol.)

Let us now consider *fag*. When, in 1966, the film actress Shirley MacLaine called me a fag on the strength of my British accent, I was not offended, for I had not pre·iously met the usage. *Fag* to me, and to most of the British I think, is still a cigarette. Wentworth and Flaxner give that as the primary meaning but more or less limit it to the First World War, though they have L. Hughes, in a book published in 1952, representing a 'white boy' passing 'them swell fags around'. *Fag* became a term for a male homosexual in America round about 1920 and it is suggested here that cigarette smoking, being regarded as effeminate by pipe and cigar smokers, started the usage off. A suggestion equally shaky has the British public school 'boy servant or lackey' as a possible origin. And yet almost the next entry has *faggart* or *faggot* as the full form – 'archaic, having been replaced by the shorter "fag" '. It seems likely that *faggot*, meaning a loose bundle, is where it comes from, nor is the term archaic, even in America. The expendable object of fire or hunger, a faggot was to be despised and used. Cigarettes and schoolboys never had anything to do with it.

The Supplement, by Flexner, Sheila Brantley and Herbert Gilbert, gives a conspectus of the preoccupations of the seventies. Drug addiction, dignified into a 'culture', is responsible for *A-bomb*, marijuana and opium rolled into a fag, *Acapulco gold*, a high-grade Mexican marijuana; *acid freak* and *acid rock*; *age out* – 'to teach an age when drugs no longer have the desired effect'; *angel dust*, a powdered form of PCP; *baby-sit* – 'to serve as a guide to someone undergoing a psychedelic drug experience'; *bam*, a mixture of a depressant and a stimulant; *big John*, a policeman; *big Harry*, heroin; *blue flags*, LSD: *caballo*, heroin again; *campfire boy*, an opium addict, and so on to *zonked out*, very high on drugs.
 – An *ecofreak* is 'a vigorous supporter of ecological programmes'. A *faunet* or *faunlet* is a juvenile homosexual object. A *Castro* is a full beard. An *Afro-Saxon* is a black who *Toms*, while a *bad nigger* takes no shit from nobody. A *Barbie doll*, named for a popular plastic blonde gynomorph for children, is a WASP conformist. A number of British terms have gotten over there, including *Beeb* (perhaps used by devotees of the PBS), *brain drain*, and *corksacking*. But I see now that *corksacking* is my own invented euphemism for a term found more in American slang dictionaries than in the American press. I seem to have written the following for the *New York Times Magazine* on 29 October 1972: 'I have already had several abusive phone calls, telling me to eff off back to effing Russia, you effing corksacking limey effer.' Under *eff*, another euphemism, I give the reason, which I had forgotten, along with the abuse, for the abuse: 'This is because I suggested some time ago . . . that America would be better off for a bit of socialised medicine.' Finally, *pudding* – 'the penis, esp. as used for masturbation' – is supposed to have been popularized by the 'Brit. singing group the Beatles'. I do not think we have to accept the speculation that this comes from *pudding head*, and 'the old superstition that masturbation leads to feeblemindedness': *pudding* is an acceptable extension of *meat*. What, besides singing and twanging, were the Beatles doing out there?

English as a Creole

Journal of Creole Studies, Volume 1, No. 1, edited by Ian F. Hancock (University of Texas at Austin), published by De Sikkel, Kappellen, Belgium

This new magazine is dedicated to the study of the pidginization and creolization of language and of Creole societies and cultures. *Pidgin*, which we have always been taught is an oriental corruption of *business* or even *business English*, denotes a contact dialect of mixed vocabulary and elementary syntax, whereby foreign traders or soldiers can communicate crudely with the natives. British troops on duty at the Gibraltar–Spanish frontier would point at the baskets of homegoing Spanish workers and say '*Mungy*?' The workers would reply '*Sí, mungy.*' The British thought it was Spanish and the Spanish thought it was English, which is sometimes the way with pidgins. To what language does *jigajig* belong?

A creole is a sophisticated pidgin, with structures still simple but vocabulary larger, and it can serve as a mother tongue. The word *Creole* derives ultimately from Portuguese *crioulo*, a Negro brought up in his master's house (*criar*, to bring up, from Latin *creare*, create, beget), but it came to connote mixed ancestry in the West Indies, white expatriation (the Empress Joséphine was properly a Creole), eventually a white language adapted to the needs of a people of negroid stock. The terms *pidgin* and *creole* interpenetrate. The speakers of Tok Pisin call their language a pidgin, but it is a mother tongue with a fixed orthography, dictionary, a newspaper called *Wantok* (one talk, or united by speech, hence compatriot, friend), a full-fledged creole.

To those familiar with only the narrowest denotations of the term, the title of Nicole Z. Domingue's article – 'Middle English: Another Creole?' – will come as a shock. Briefly the argument is as follows. The English of *The Pearl* and *The Owl and the Nightingale* and even Chaucer is spectacularly different from the Old English of *Beowulf*. It does not look like a smooth development out of pre-Conquest English, as Tuscan looks like a painless transformation of Latin. The lexica are different. Thomas Phyles says that 85 per cent of the Middle English vocabulary is of French origin. But there are Scandinavian elements as well – words like *they*, *them*, *their* and *are*, prepositions like *till* and *fro*, conjunctions like *though*, possibly the -s ending for the third person singular of verbs. The voiced fricative in *father* seems to mean that English has gone to Old Norse (*father*) and jettisoned the Anglo-Saxon (*faeder*) for this most basic of words. In other words, Middle English could get along nicely without too much Anglo-Saxon.

Then look at the revolution in structure. Modern German has not wished, or been able, to break free from the musclebound grammar of Old German, but shortly after the Norman Conquest English was shedding noun classes, gender, personal verb endings, dual categories. It was trying to turn itself into an analytic language, something very different from the heavily synthetic Anglo-Saxon. This resulted in, or was caused by, or both, a loss of flexibility in word order – 'a likely influence of French syntax, with its SVO and Aux–Main Verb orders in all clauses' (contrast German, or Anglo-Saxon: 'I have taken her to the local meadhall'; 'This is the girl whom I to the local meadhall taken have'). Why did genders disappear? Because Norman French was presenting a different gender system from the Germanic one, and 'gender categories are notoriously difficult to learn in second language learning situations'. The response is to rid get of genders altogether.

Middle English, then, is a language whose sounds are Germanic but whose syntax is, though essentially Germanic, far simpler than the tongues of the grim North could yet decently allow. But its lexicon is mainly non-Anglo-Saxon and has a very large number of Norman French words. This is typical of creoles – adoption of the invading vocabulary but not the invading structures – as are features which don't come from any of the original contributory languages: 'while OE, Scandinavian, and French were all heavily inflected languages, ME has no grammatical gender, only remnants of noun categories, case endings and verbal inflections, and no trace of rounded vowels.' One is not too happy about that last assertion (it refers to front rounded vowels – *u* in *lune*, for instance): how did Chaucer pronounce *vertu*? Reply, reply.

If a creole is an extended pidgin spoken as a mother tongue, we have to establish that a pidgin existed in England at the time of the Norman takeover. But there is no written evidence. There is no talk of the native tongue being corrupted by the foreigner, though there are some thirteenth-century denunciations of Anglo-Norman as 'bad French'. Yet the social situation presumes multilingualism, and multilingualism implies the necessary search for an area of very simple common understanding. There was also what Dr Domingue calls a situation of 'unstable pre-pidgin continua', caused by two hundred years of Scandinavians and Anglo-Saxons communicating with each other 'by reducing severely all features of language which were difficult to learn and along universal lines of reduction'. The native speakers of English could have used the middle part of the continuum – the most pidginized part, the farthest from both Anglo-Saxon and Scandinavian – to address the Norman invaders, accommodating, while they were about the simplifying process, the kind of simplification that the invaders wanted – the hell with your gender categories, for instance. 'Such a situation could have resulted in the formation of a *bona fide* pidgin or pidgins.' Middle English, then, could be regarded as a creole, and not only Duke Ellington but also the anonymous poets of the Middle Ages have produced Creole love songs.

The *Journal of Creole Studies* is equally fascinating when it deals with the

Pidgin French of Vietnam (*luy yang na bat, yang na kot, luy fe be-be-be* = *lui il y en a barbe, il y en a cornes, lui faire be-be-be* = a goat) and the stand-ardization of Naga Pidgin. In *Notes and Queries* Joe Dillard, of North-western Louisiana State University, asks if anyone knows of a similar idiom to the Gullah and Black (US) English 'my love come down', meaning to be sexually aroused. There is also useful advice from Sierra Leone, like *Ef yu keych tu pipul dey ab, chuk pin na banana weys, denh go fashin towgeda sowtey yu pul di komot dey*, meaning: 'If you catch two people in coitus, stick a pin into the end of a banana and they will become fastened together until you remove the pin.' Try that tonight.

Homo Sibilans

Whistled Languages, by R. G. Busnel and A. Classe

Whistling, like riding a bicycle, is best not inquired into too curiously. Think about it, and you cannot do it. It is conceivably older than speech and relates men to birds, otters and guinea pigs. Taboos are attached to it. 'A whistling woman, a crowing hen /Whistled the devil out of his den.' Witches whistle (thrice), also whores. Yet *siffleuses* have achieved as acceptable music-hall art as *siffleurs*. Elizabeth Mann shocked me into awe by whistling a florid Bach top line with fine tone and expression. (The violinist in her father's *Doctor Faustus* has the same gift.) Whistling enables a man to be his own ensemble. I was once able to hum 'Swanee River' and whistle Dvořák's *Huŕhoresque* at the same time but have lost the knack. Dr André Classe, whom I shall come to in a moment, 'once heard Sir Richard Paget perform four-part music with his daughter, both simultaneously whistling and humming.' Whistling is music, but it can also be speech. In this latter form we know it only as something crude or comic – the GI's wolf-whistle, Harpo Marx's urgent revelations to Chico, which Chico laboriously has to hit-and-miss into words.

Whistled Languages deals with a more sophisticated mode of semiotics. Dr Classe is in Glasgow, Professor René-Guy Busnel presides over the Laboratoire d'Acoustique Animale of the Institut National de la Recherche Agronomique at Jouy-en-Josas. They have come together to compile a highly technical account of various kinds of whistled speech – specifically those in use among the Mazateco Indians of Oaxaca, Mexico, the peasants of La Gomera, one of the Canary Islands, and certain Turks. G. Cowan pioneered study of the Mazateco Indian method of communicating 'both at close quarters and at a distance by means of modulated whistles, with the same ease, speed and intelligibility as when using speech in the ordinary manner.' That was in an article in *Language* in 1948. The wonder of this faculty is somewhat diminished when we consider that Mazateco is a tonal language, like Chinese, and to make a whistle-speech out of it is a matter of extracting from the vocal speech continuum those prosodic parameters which come closest to music – tone and duration.

But another wonder supervenes: how can intelligibility subsist when all those elements of language which we are taught to regard as of primary importance are eliminated? It does subsist, as it does with the drum, flute and horn signals of Central Africa. I am reminded of that scene in the Pascal film of *Pygmalion* where Leslie Howard as Higgins played D–E–G on a xylophone and the audience, to its delighted surprise, heard the phrase as 'Throw him out'. But there was a question asked first, and a mere intonation curve is often a sufficient answer. We have to know how Mazateco works before we can understand how whistle-Mazateco works. Few of us have time or inclination.

But in La Gomera we have a dialect of Spanish to be transsibilated, and we can if we wish, like Busnel and Classe, go and hear how the thing is done before modern technology obliterates it. In 1891 R. Verneau published a book called *Cinq Ans aux Isles Canaries*. He described how the peasants of La Gomera whistled at each other over the deep valleys or *barrancos* that cross the island radially. Though Verneau had scientific training, he did not at all observe accurately the technique of the Silbo, as it is called, or the Silbadores, who practise it. This has all now been put right. There are various methods of emitting the basic whistling sound – the fingerless, one-finger, two-finger, knuckle and so on, subtle variations within each category. Busnel and Classe give us a full inventory of the phonemes of Canary Spanish and show how these can be adapted to the whistling technique. Vowels are comparatively easy, but consonants raise problems. Whistled speech is of necessity voiced, so that the voiceless–voiced opposition – /p t k b d g/ – is mainly neutralized. 'It is somewhat startling,' we are told, 'that in practice no ambiguity should result from this.' The making of a plosive with the lips stops the air in ordinary speech. The lips are immobilized in whistling, so that the Silbadores check the air flow by means of the thorax muscle and the diaphragm. 'Alternatively lip closure can be replaced by a glottal occlusion, which seems acceptable to Gomeros at least although we have never observed them doing it, presumably because the glottal stop is, to the best of our knowledge, altogether unknown in the phonetic system of all Spanish dialects, and certainly to that of Canarian.' And so on.

Considering Professor Busnel's position in the National Institute of Agronomic Research, it is not surprising to find here a closing section on whistling in the animal kingdom. Dolphins, for instance, have been trained to 'reply with whistles to acoustic signals of great complexity and to imitate them, copying pitch contours very accurately.' They can, in fact, reach the first human steps of echolalia, through which children learn to use their speech organs. The spectacular achievements of films like *The Day of the Dolphin* are sheer SF. The basis of any future language teaching for dolphins will be through sibilation. As for birds, a blackbird in the Garmaish-Partenkirchen region 'copied whistles that for years a man had used to signal his cat. The model whistled rather roughly four notes between 1 and 2 kHz, with variations of pitch and rhythm. The blackbird transposed the whole motif up a fifth and introduced ornaments as one introduces embellishments in eighteenth-century music.' But the aesthetic gifts of birds do not lead to a closer rapprochement between them and men. It's the mammals that count, especially the dolphins.

Whistled speech is dying out everywhere as telephones and loud-hailers increasingly span valleys. At least this ingenious system of communication has been recorded and is, though not by myself, well understood. This slim piece of xeroxing serves to enhance one's awe at what man, *Homo sibilans*, is capable of doing.

Isoglosses and So Forth

The Linguistic Atlas of England, edited by Harold Orton, Stewart Sanderson and John Widdowson

T he origins of this atlas go back a long way – to 1923, in fact, when the great Joseph Wright, editor of the *English Dialect Dictionary*, complained of the difficulty of classifying dialects of Middle English. It was impossible, he said,

> . . . to fix the exact boundaries where one dialect ends and another begins. Nor shall we ever be able to remedy this defect until we possess a comprehensive atlas of the modern dialects such as has been produced by France and Germany of their dialects. An atlas of this kind would enable English scholars to fix the dialect boundaries far more accurately than is possible at present.

The late Harold Orton, whose child this present achievement must be said to be, heard the words of Wright fifty-five years ago. He and Eugen Dieth, of the University of Zürich, heard other words twelve years later – those spoken by Hans Kurath at the Second International Congress of Phonetic Sciences held at University College, London. Kurath was talking of the historical background of the speech of New England, and he complained:

> Unfortunately the lines leading back to the Mother Country, to England, and to Northern Ireland will remain vague and tentative until a linguistic atlas of the British Isles is made . . ., for the great majority of colonists of the seventeenth century, whose descendants remained the most influential element in America during the eighteenth century and after, did not speak the cultivated speech of London, but various Engish dialects or provincial standards. These we know only very imperfectly through contemporary evidence. They must be reconstructed very largely on the basis of a linguistic atlas of English folk speech of the present day.

War came. In 1945 Dieth resumed a six-year-lapsed correspondence with Orton, speaking of the 'ploughing up of a good deal of the linguistic ground' owing to the enforced wartime mixing of peoples, the impairment of the stability of the English regional dialects, which would be further increased by new habits of social mobility and the influence of radio and television, and the urgency of the need to start dialect-mapping while there was still something to map. By the end of the summer of 1947, Orton and Dieth had produced their first version of the questionnaire for the field workers.

These field workers travelled mainly to English villages with small and stable populations, seeking chiefly men over sixty 'with good mouths, teeth and hearing' who would answer questions like 'What do you call the red-hot things that fall through the grate when the fire is burning?' or 'What is the month before May?' The inquirers were after four things – phonology, lexis, morphology and syntax, resolving into four different kinds of map. Men were found to be more conservative and honest than women – or rather women exhibited an interest in upward or outward mobility that militated against their giving the right answers. Lexically, there was never a wrong answer to give about the fruit on that tree over there, but the way to pronounce *apple* is what the first map of the atlas is about. There is a huge swathe of England, from the Scottish border to the deep Midlands, where the *apple* vowel is the low a of French *patte*, while the higher sound (represented phonetically as /æ/), which we are taught to regard as 'standard', is used in a slender slice of the Southeast (which, however, contains the capital and the ancient seats of learning), as well as in the West Country and the Isle of Man. There are eccentric areas where the vowel is pushed back to the *o* of *hot* and up to the *e* of *get*. We see all this, the product of laborious notation and plotting, on a map of England snaked with black curves and dotted with symbols which represent local phonological variants within an otherwise homogeneous speech region.

Arrive at the word *Tuesday* and you face a phonological variety which no deformation of orthodox orthography is able to represent. The Northwest and the near-entirety of the East are loyal to the Middle English *tiu-*, but there are pockets where *chu-* and *tu-* prevail, and there is a small slab near the Wash where the vowel is frankly centralized (the tongue pushes to the middle of the mouth, where dwells the schwa or first vowel of *apart*). This area of usage waves across at a central Midland region of identical vocalic usage over the waste of regular *tiu-*. Just a hundred years ago, when Prince Louis-Lucien Bonaparte made vicarious amends for his family's execration of England by pioneering English dialect studies, it was noted that to make isoglosses in terms of county and culture did not work. As Stewart F. Sanderson puts it, 'the Prince sometimes found dialect features just where they ought not to be.' Distributions of dialect varieties are, to put it mildly, complicated: there is nothing tidy about these language maps. Devon, for *Tuesday*, contributes a vowel which seems to be a rounded version of the one in *fit*. I have only previously met this in German.

Then look at the map for *coulter*, whose nationwide pronunciation variants cover an immense vocalic and diphthongal field, with no Southeast 'norm' to call them home to the judgement of conventional correctness. And if the Southeast decrees for *worms* a long schwa with no *r* after it, great tracts of the country opt for that historical *r*, as America does, a fricative or a tap or, as in the far Northeast, something *grasséyé*. Almost the entire South and Midlands agree on *sheaf* (Middle English *scef* with a long *e*), but there are areas where the Middle Low German seems to be commemorated with something like *shoff* or *shoof* or even *shuff*. The bewildering thing is the lack of gradation. In the far Northeast you will get as good a *sheaf* as in London, but the train runs south through *sheff* and *shaff* and *shofe* before you hit /i:/ again.

It is, inevitably, the vocabulary of rural occupations, which do not greatly interest the language courts of the capital or the older universities, that provides the richest variety of nomenclature. Take the decayed craft of thatching, for instance. The ropes used in the process are called billy-bands, binder-bands, coconut-bands, hay-bands, hazel-bands, pitch-bands, stack-bands, straw-bands, tar-bands, tar-marl-bands, thacking-bands, thumb-bond, coir-ropes (a borrowing from Malay *kayer*), over-ropes, reeden-ropes, thumb-ropes, thumb-simes. The pegs are rick-pegs, thack-pegs, stack-prods, rick-spars, stack-spelks, rick-sprays, stack-stobs. A donkey is called a cuddy, a dicky, a neddy, an ass, a fussock, a fussanock, a moke, a mokus, a nirrup, a jack nirrup, a bronkus or a pronkus. *Cuddy* is not given as a form used in my own county of Lancashire, but most pubs named for a horse, black, white or grey, are popularly The Cuddy, even in sophisticated Liverpool. Most of England is happy about *gosling*, but the West prefers *gull* and *gib* is to be heard in Lincolnshire. Our Northern *gesling* preserves the Middle English *geslying*, itself from the Old Norse *gæslinger*. Earth closets are necessaries or dikes or dunnekins (dunnies in Australia) or shit-houses or petty-holes. *Petty* is the term I remember as being regularly in use in my Lancashire childhood. A slice of meat seems to be everywhere except in Norfolk, where it is a round, and on the Lancashire–Yorkshire border, where it is a slishe, and in my own region, where it is still gloriously and, I hope, for ever a shive. *Dip*, according to the *bacon fat* map, is mainly confined to Yorkshire, but it was the regular word in my boyhood in Manchester. It seems to be a version of *dripping*, but it was always assumed that it was so-called because you dipped your bread in it.

The morphological section of the atlas shows the changes to be rung on basic forms like *I'm not* and *aren't* and *are you*? The grammar books of the Southeast, decreeing a norm for the past tense of *come*, have closed our eyes to the comparative rarity of *came*. You can travel from Penzance to Hadrian's Wall and hear *come* or comed. Nor does the *-ing* present participle ending have as much clout as print would have us believe. The *laughing* map shows that a syllabic *n* or *in* or schwa plus *n* is universally preferred. When it comes to the verbal noun *writing*, however, there is a lot of *-ing* about and, I would guess, far more Chaucerian *-ingg* than the map indicates.

Devon and Cornwall prefer *we put on the light* to *we put the light on*, which is standard usage nearly everywhere else. The *on Friday week* map is like a harlequin quilt, with its *next Friday* and *next Friday week* and *a week on Friday* and *a week next Friday* and *a week come Friday* and *a week Friday*. What I have searched diligently for is the distribution of a past participle of *get* that corresponds to normative American usage. In Lancashire you will hear *gotten*, as in *Oo's getten eed-warch*. All the varieties of the singular feminine pronoun are present – *she* and *sha* and *shoo* and *her* and *he* and *hoo* (I have yet to hear that aitch). And muryans, pismires, pissy-beds, pissy-mices, pissy-mires, pissy-motes and pissy-mothers are as busy as emmets. Go to the pissy-mother, thou sluggard. Plenty of theeing and thouing, too.

All posthumous honour to Harold Orton, and present congratulations and gratitude to Stewart Sanderson and John Widdowson and their helpers. This is a great book, and it may be only a beginning. As the introduction says.

> The wealth of material in the English Dialect Survey's collections has been exploited and displayed only in small measure in the pages of this atlas. It was Harold Orton's hope, as it is that of his co-editors, that this volume will stimulate a wide variety of further research into English dialects, not just in England alone but wherever the English language is spoken.

Despite the centralizing influence of radio and television, one has reason to believe that the essential inertia which Saussure found in language continues to preserve at least the phonological systems and structures of our dialects. My own desultory researches seem to show, certainly in my native county, that the metropolitan standard has more the function of an auxiliary than of a substitute for native speech. I should have preferred this remarkable work to have been initiated in the University of Manchester than that of Leeds, but at least I can be satisfied that once again the North (a deeper North than that of *OED* Murray) has flamed out with a work of immense linguistic value. That its makers will go unhonoured in those lists that make barons of showmen I take for granted. But it is one of this year's really notable events. The riches of the people's English, not the Queen's, by all roads roam to Leeds.

Teenspeech

The Language of the Teenage Revolution, by Kenneth Hudson

The combination of high price and scant content, quite apart from the title, led me to expect a genuine linguistic treatise – deep structures, phonology, taxemes, morphemes, the whole Chomskian works. But this is sociolinguistics, with the stress on the socio. For teenage phonology, go to Kingsley Amis's *Girl, 20*, where there are, for instance, very accurate notations of teenage assimilation – *corm beef, tim peaches, vogka* – as well as an awareness, which non-phonetic transcription cannot properly convey, that the a-phoneme in *flat* has been pushed back to a central position (see also Barbara Strang's *History of the English Language*) with a Portuguese flavour. None of this particularity in Mr Hudson's book. Indeed, there cannot properly be much about language at all. Teenage communication is minimally linguistic – deafening oneself with pop noise, being violent, touching and clutching, taking drugs are more important than speech – and, where a speech system does exist, it does not easily lend itself to adult investigation. When the young speak, they do not want to be understood by adults; if adults overhear and *think* they understand, they miss the deliberate distortions the young apply to the inherited lexis. Moreover, teenage language changes so rapidly – rapid change being of its essence – that, once you have it recorded in a book, it is no longer teenage language.

Mr Hudson sees the division between the young and the old as beginning after 1945. He could have said that the breakdown of the old class system, of which the so-called teenage revolution is an emanation, began between 1939 and 1945, when a necessarily muffled conflict between the ruling and the ruled was growing in the armed forces, to become unmuffled in the 1945 General Election. If Jack was as good as his master, as Mr Hudson puts it, the young were as good as the old. Full employment for the young meant a specialized consumer market in which the cunning old provided the materials of a lifestyle for the innocent young. A counter-culture was born, and a new semiotic system was part of it. The system has, I think, to be defined negatively: it is more based on rejection than acceptance.

A big point that Mr Hudson makes – far bigger than his central teenage thesis – is the difficulty of investigating language through the traditional machinery of the lexicographer. Dictionaries are concerned with the written, not the spoken, word; moreover, they are highly selective, regarding, say, slang as peripheral to the language. Some words are classed as vulgar or taboo. Ever since Dr Johnson, a dictionary has been a tool of the cultivated and the literary. A major characteristic of our young is their rejection of literature. Their vocabulary is not fed by the past, which has no meaning for them; traditional graces of communication – the exact word, the well-formed phrase – are despised as a property of the old. Speech, what there is of it, is the sole linguistic reality. This, of course, has been held to be true by linguists ever since linguistics began: the written word is a mere ghost of the spoken. Only tape and disc can show us the true state of the language at any given time, but we cling to the belief, as Mr Hudson does, that it is possible to write books about the way we communicate. With the young the lexicographers can do little. They can record lexical items, but these, by the time the long process of preparing a book has been completed, are already part of history. Nor can the particular nuances of teenage talk be easily set down. Somewhat pathetically, Mr Hudson has to make use of an essentially literary device when discussing teenage irony. They take, he says, words from the old and despised and 'put them in inverted commas'. Thus, *charming* is used to damn something which isn't charming, and *chum* is pejorative. The innocent old, hearing these, get the wrong signals.

The language of the young is really an 'anti-language' – defined as 'the special language of people who choose to be outside society'. It is, if you like, a secret code, and its users are always aware of the attempts of the established world outside to break the code. But there is a teenage strategy for defeating this pressure: once the secret password has been learned by the 'enemy' it ceases to be a secret password. There has to be a constant renewal of the teenage lexis: virtue lies not in verbal aptness but in verbal novelty. I tried, back in 1960, to write a novel about teenagers, and, with inexcusable innocence, I amassed a suitable real-life glossary. Then I realized that all this would be out of date by the time the book appeared, so I had to invent a lexis, setting my story in an imagined future. The irony is that, in the United States, a number of teenagers appropriated items from this lexis – words like *droog* and *groodies* and *nadsat* – and thus shoved my future into the discardable past.

As language is taken by Mr Hudson to mean more than speech and its visual symbology (an unfair extension, I believe; the term semiotics exists to cover the entire field of communicative signs), he is able to write a whole chapter on pop music 'as a cultural carrier'. The music is properly nothing and the words even less, but we could use Malinowski's term 'phatic' to describe a listening (or sometimes non-listening) experience which has nothing to do with art and everything to do with proclaiming group solidarity. The chief effect of pop in the bigger world was to force the capital to take the provinces seriously – especially my own industrial North, where the accent was traditionally a joke. 'It became normal,' says Mr Hudson, 'not to belong to London and the South-East.' The Northern pop groups, of whom the Beatles (not typically pop: too literate and unnoisy) were the most popular, were merely following an old tradition: the Catholic North, banned from the professions until 1829, always had to channel talent into entertainment. Mr Hudson is good on the importance of the Liverpool College of Art, which produced an attitude more than artists. It also produced the Beatle couture and coiffure.

But all this has nothing, or little, to do with an inquiry implicit in the book: how do those of us with teenage kids (*children* in inverted commas) break the cultural barrier and establish rapport with these strange creatures we begot? The answer seems to be that we'd better not try. The spirit of divisiveness is strong and not getting any weaker. The teenagers are a mutation. To my generation they seem dull, with a boring pseudo-culture and no ideas. To term their breakaway a revolution is to over-ennoble. But they themselves, if they know the word, probably shove it in inverted commas.

Yidglish

Hooray for Yiddish!, by Leo Rosten

M r Rosten's subtitle is 'A Book about English'. Take title and subtitle together and you get the truth – the manner in which, chiefly in New York, Yiddish has impregnated English and produced a wonderful hybrid which Mr Rosten calls Yinglish and I prefer to call Yidglish. After all, Yinglish could be Yankee English or English expressive of the Yin as opposed to the Yang. The book, a leisurely lexicon which makes one laugh, is a sequel to *The Joys of Yiddish*, which came out fifteen years ago and has sold over 750,000 copies. You should be so lucky.

How far a Gentile or *goy* is permitted to use Yidglish is not a point argued by Mr Rosten. As American showbiz is a Jewish province, it is inevitable that showbiz language, even in Britain, should partake of Yidglish idioms, which include modes of emphasis and inversion as well as calques and straight borrowings from Yiddish. I have heard a distinguished British stage producer say 'We need that like a *loch in kop*' and 'Hamlet he wants to play' and 'Mummerset yet'. The production of plays and films places its participants in situations of stress and despair analogous to those of a whole long-suffering people, and Yidglish provides ironic tropes which contrast dramatically with the agonized cries and lavish curses of the Old Testament. You can rant prophetically in the desert or wail by the waters of Babylon; in the exile of the cities, where nobody listens anyway, you use Yidglish.

Mr Rosten's last book sold well because it was funny, and this is funny too. New York Jewish jokes are the best in the world; here they are in the service of subtle differentiations of usage. Take *Gevalt* (pronounced ge-VOLLT). The obstetrician played cards with Count Rothschild while his countess lay ready to deliver in her bedroom. She screamed, but he calmly went on playing. And again. And again. Only when she yelled '*Gevalt*!' did he leap to his feet and say 'Now'. The Nifkovitzes changed their name to Manders Northridge and dined at the *goy* country club. The waiter spilled soup on Mrs Northridge's lap and she cried: '*Gevalt*! - whatever that means.' Man comes into the world with an *Oy*! and leaves it with a *Gevalt*! You don't have to define *Gevalt*, even if you can.

Some idioms with a Yiddish origin have already been so long absorbed into standard American colloquial that Mr Rosten has difficulty in establishing provenance. 'Go fight City Hall' is clearly, in its rhythm and ellipsis, as well as its hopelessness, Yidglish, as is 'Go talk to the wall'. But this latter is patently from '*Red tsu der vant*'. In 'Who paid you, Lefty? C'mon, *give*', the blunt imperative tells us to suspect, if not certainly know, that it is Yidglish. Love of the laconic has turned *enjoy* into an intransitive verb. Nails (or Nate, or, to his mamma, Nateleh) Koslovsky, a no-goodnick who has been shot by the O'Callahan mob, comes bleeding to death up the stairs. He groans: 'Mamma, I -' She replies: 'Don't talk. First eat; enjoy! Later, you'll talk.' I once gave a reading at the YMHA on Lexington Avenue, and the chairman, none other than John Simon, guardian of pure English, ended his exordium by saying 'Enjoy!' The audience did not, as it turned out, greatly enjoy. 'Excuse the expression' seems to be Yidglish solely by association. Rosten is strong against it: 'No instance of Bronxian, Brooklynian or Lower East Sidean is more genteel (and grating) than this gratuitous apology. Purists say that 'excuse the expression' marks the user as (excuse the expression) *déclassé*.' He tells the story of a lady in a crowded Tel Aviv bus groping for her purse. The man next to her says: 'Lady, let me pay.' She says: 'No, I'll get my purse open.' He says: 'But till you get it open, you already unbuttoned three buttons on my - excuse the expression - fly.'

The use of *shmaltz* is now pretty general in criticism of the arts, though F. R. Leavis, excuse the expression, never employed it. It literally means chicken fat used in cooking or to temper the dryness of chopped liver. 'He delivers a line with enough *shmaltz* to fill a shovel.' It can be a verb as well as a noun: 'She *shmaltzed* up her speech like it was the Fourth of July.' As fat means rich or richness, we can have 'He lives in silk and *shmaltz*.' To marry rich, says Rosten, is to fall into a *shmaltz-grub*. The introduction of the *shm* cluster into English, where it is not native, is more interesting than most of the words it initiates – *shmatte* and *shmegegge* and *shmei* as well as *shmaltz*. The duplicate forms which denote contempt, like *fancy-shmancy* and *Oedipus-shmoedipus* and *data-shmata*, are perhaps unique in their attaching so much semantic weight to a mere bound morpheme (excuse the expression; your response should be *morpheme-shmorpheme*).

But Yidglish is brilliant always in doing so much with so little – an inversion, an intonation – and is remarkable in seeming to carry in every form the whole experience of a race that has learned to respond to tribulation with grim humour. Under *Gezunthayt*! Rosten gives us some apophthegms about health which contain a whole philosophy: 'Too much is unhealthy' – 'Your health comes first – you can always hang yourself later' – 'What a fat belly cost, I wish I had; what it does, I wish on my enemies' – 'When there's a cure, it was only half a disease' – and, from the Talmud, 'Eat a third, drink a third, but leave a third of your stomach empty; for then, if anger overtakes you, there will be room for your rage.'

Englishmen, naturally *goyim*, since there is an assumption that an Englishman cannot be a Jew, despite Disraeli and Siegfried Sassoon, come occasionally into Rosten's stories. A *moyl* or *mohel* is a professional circumciser. An Englishman in New York saw a lone clock in a shop window and went in to get his watch repaired. A bearded man in a skullcap appeared and said he didn't repair watches, or sell them. He was a *moyl*. Then why the clock in the window? 'Mister, what would *you* put in the window?' Another story, perhaps better known, concerns the Englishman in a kosher restaurant who ordered matzo balls in his soup, ate them and said: 'Excellent! Tell me, what other part of the matzo do you people cook?'

A male *goy*, like that Englishman, is a *sheygets* and his mother a *shikse*. The plural of *goy* comes aptly in a reply to the quatrain written, surely, by Sir Walter Raleigh the professor, not – as Rosten thinks – Hilaire Belloc: 'How odd/of God/To choose/The Jews.' It deserves to be set out in lineate glory:

Not odd
Of God:
Goyim
Annoy 'im.

Onomastic

Names, by Basil Cottle

I am always interested to read books written by my exact contemporaries. Dr Cottle is, like me, sixty-six and perhaps wondering whether to regard himself as old or merely middle-aged. He sounds old, but he also sounds fit. He neither drinks nor smokes, and he does not read novels, 'holding with Coleridge that the reading of novels entails over a period of time the complete destruction of the powers of the mind.' So much for those of us who read little else. 'There is so much truth to be discovered and spread that the warpings and speculations of novels fog an already confused scene.' As Dr Cottle's speciality is onomastics or the study of names, he is not averse to an interest in the titles of novels and must be the first scholar to devise what theologians call a criteriology for them. C.P. Snow's are 'big-deal'; Ivy Compton-Burnett's – which he sees as a parade of 'stressful relationships' and not, being no structuralist, in terms of N Conj N – deter him from reading the books to which they are attached ('I am ready not to enjoy these'). Graham Greene ('of whom it was venomously said that he had to be obscene to be believed') gives us a 'glum and restless programme' in his titles, which Dr Cottle does not seem to understand very well, assuming that *A Burnt-Out Case* refers to a shell case and that *The Third Man* ('we have heard enough of *this* phrase') derives from rather than originates the journalistic cliché about a missing diplomat. Dr Cottle ought really to get down to destroying the powers of his mind some time.

If you want the essence of Cottle you will best find it in the *Penguin Dictionary of Surnames* (enlarged edition, 1978), where onomastic truth confronts the inquirer head on and not, as here, through the whimsical mists of belletrism. Dr Cottle's predecessors in this field of charming philology were Ivor Brown and, more especially, the Professor Weekley whom D.H. Lawrence cuckolded, leaving the sad scholar to console himself with *The Romance of Words*. Dr Cottle reveals more of himself than Weekley did or dared to. When discussing the nomenclature of racehorses he has to tell us that the turf is not in his blood:

> . . . the nearest I ever came to it was my being happily awakened by the *tlot-tlot* of exercised horses every morning during my three stays outside Newbridge, Co. Kildare, in 1968–70 – Curragh country, and full of the lore of innocent horseflesh and peccant gambling (*Priest*: Do you know the Credo? *Penitent*: No, Father – what's his stable?).

Well, now we know that Dr Cottle visited Ireland three times. We would like to know what he did there. We know what he did not do. He did not smoke or drink. Nor did he learn about the Catholic Church, which does not regard gambling as peccant.

There is an interesting section on the naming of commercial products, with such fragments of donnish wit as 'What is the use of nature conservancy articles headed "Can We Save the Condor?", when tobacconists advertise Condor Sliced?'. In commerical warfare, he says, the dirtiest fighters are the soap firms, and names are weapons. Rinso is 'a bit joky', but Persil, which is French parsley, is nice if you can forget that *persillé* cheese has a blue mould on it, and Surf and Tide 'share the clean sea with us'. It is true that Omo is meaningless, but it does not sound 'avuncular and trustworthy' to anyone who knows his Dante. Dr Cottle could have given us a fine bit of useless belletristic information here, referring to the *Purgatorio*, where starving Florentine citizens have OMO on their faces – two hollow eyes, cheek furrows and a pen-sharp nose. I'll find you the exact line. No, I won't. At sixty-six one does not willingly get out of one's chair to look for things. I can be discursive too. Dr Cottle mentions a concert-party joke at the Roath Park Lake, Cardiff, of his youth. 'May I kiss your palm, Olive?' Answer: 'Not on your life, boy.'

When he gets onto surnames, Dr Cottle rightly refuses to impinge on his own lexicographical achievement (which, venially, he boosts while denying responsibility for the 'vulgar cover') and concerns himself mostly with the statistics of distribution. There are four kinds of surnames – patronymics or metronymics (Johnson, Madge), place-names (Jack London), trade names (Butcher) and nicknames (Armstrong). Dr Cottle recently faced an audience of 50 people, of whom 20 had the first kind, 15 the second, 10 the third, and 5 the last – the exact population (if you double the figures) percentage for England. Take any page of the *Observer* and you will see how it works out – Blunt, Whitelaw, Thatcher, Jenkins, Foot, etc. (I refer to the front page of the 27 March issue: I get my *Observer* late). It doesn't work out at all, of course, on so narrow a sampling, where the non-patronyms seem to do best. The HMSO *Population Trends* of 1976 shows in order of commonness Smith, Jones, Williams, Brown, Taylor, Davies, Evans, Thomas, Roberts and Johnson. The first three have maintained their positions in this century, but Brown has risen two places, replacing Taylor and Davies, which were once fourth and fifth. White, the commonest name in endogamic Newfoundland, has risen here from 22 to 12. There were evidently once a fair number of tanned men and ironworkers around, but names mean nothing now. Though conceivably the name Thatcher, designating a fine old rural trade, gives more confidence than Foot, which sounds either aggressive or facetious, I do not see either a Chambers or a Philpot forming a government, but you never know. 'In the House yesterday Mr Shufflebottom said. . . .' I can't see it somehow. I knew a lady in Lancashire who referred to herself as 'Shufflearse's missis'.

This chatty tone is catching. But I wish to be rather solemn in considering Dr Cottle's conclusion concerning the name Amerik, which is a version of the Welsh Ap Meuric, or son of Maurice. A certain Richard Amerik, senior collector of customs for Bristol, was 'probably the heaviest investor' in John Cabot's second voyage west in 1498. We have been taught to accept the nominative claim of Amerigo Vespucci as regards America, but Dr Cottle regards this as 'frivolous'. So that huge continent is named for a Welshman. This is a discovery to be prized.

There are a good number of prizable discoveries in Dr Cottle's book, consolations for or consequences of discursive garrulity, and one of them is the failure of the inventors of Scrabble to note that the commonest English letters are E, T, A, O, N, I, – in that order. Too many South American three-toed sloths (the name is Ai) hanging around at the end of the game, says Dr Cottle, who clearly has his vices.

New Light on Language

Modern Linguistics – The Results of Chomsky's Revolution, by Neil Smith and Deirdre Wilson

I t would be fair to assume that readers of this review have a certain concern about language. That is to say, they will consider themselves competent to judge whether a piece of written English is good or bad and are even able to invoke rules to justify condemning a sentence like 'We was proper shagged'. They will be able to recognize a split infinitive but will not be too sure *why* it is wrong. They will be uneasy about a statement like 'Whatever did you choose this book to be read to out of from for?' and perhaps mutter something about the impropriety of ending sentences with prepositions. They will have, in fact, schoolroom memories of prescriptive grammar and notions, sometimes vague, of taste, clarity and elegance. Ask them how many phonemes there are in the word *rhythm* or how many morphemes in *boy's*, or what precisely is the final sound of the first word in *corned beef*, and there will be ignorance or dubiety. Rightly, since to answer such questions correctly presupposes a scientific knowledge of language, and very few of even the professionally literary possess such knowledge.

The science of language is called linguistics, and it is a fairly new science. When I was an undergraduate at the beginning of the war, English studies were divided into lang and lit, mutually hostile disciplines, but lang mostly meant the historical study of literary texts, for which one was equipped with an elementary knowledge of phonetics and the rules of i-mutation and ablaut. Language as a universal phenomenon was not much studied, despite the great pioneer work of men like Saussure, Bloomfield and Sapir and the members of the School of Prague. It would be going too far to say that Modern Linguistics began in 1957, with the publication of Noam Chomsky's *Syntactic Structures*, but it is certain that that book fomented a revolution, and not only in the study of language:

> The effects of that revolution are still being worked out. One immediate result was that linguistics began to be of interest to philosophers, psychologists and logicians; this was largely because Chomsky was proposing to draw conclusions from the nature of language to the nature of the human language-user – conclusions which directly contradicted assumptions currently being made in philosophy and psychology. . . .

Drs Smith and Wilson, whom I quote, put the whole thing directly enough. Their book is, I think, the best general introduction that has yet appeared to a discipline that is of its nature very complex. If it is no easier to read than a manual on the maintenance of the internal combustion engine, that is because linguistics requires its own terminology, and the richness of its referents makes the terminology rich. But their glossary is admirable. The average literate person who, since he uses language all the time, is bound to resent the turning of what he thinks of as the simple known into the complex unknown, may wonder why there has to be all this technical fuss. He utters the word cat and finds no mystery in it. The first sound, which is scientifically represented as /k/, he will find described as a phoneme realized as an allophone. There are innumerable varieties of /k/ (the k-phoneme) and the variety is determined by context. Thus the /k/ of *cat* is different from the /k/ of *kill*, which gives you two allophones. And /k/ has to be described in terms of its features – + consonantal, – coronal, + anterior, – voiced, – nasal, – strident, – continuant. Speech is as complex as metabolism, but the average person thinks he knows speech. He knows it as well as a horse knows neighing.

But to return to Chomsky. His revolution consisted in demonstrating that 'language is a reflection of the human mind, not just in the sense that humans have produced it, can learn it, and do speak it, but in the much more specific sense that language is as it is because the human mind is as it is.' The older belief was that language was an arbitrary set of arbitrary structures arbitrarily discovered and arbitrarily imposed. It was even assumed that human beings were awfully clever in being able to learn languages. We know now that the ability to learn comes early. My son, at the age of ten, knew English, Maltese, French and several dialects of Italian. There is something in us, demonstrated best in early childhood, that predisposes us to acquire linguistic competence, something built into our brains. Chomsky boldly asserted that language was a universal phenomenon and took, whether in Latin or in Eskimo, much the same forms. It was possible to erect universal patterns which contained elements like NP (noun phrase) and V (verb) into which all languages would more or less fit. True, Japanese has no Adj or adjectives, but it can select from a limited number of parameters shared with other tongues precisely what it requires. All languages are more or less the same, and this has nothing to do with the outside world, which language attempts to describe, being much the same wherever we are. As Buckminster Fuller told me recently, the universe is only verbs. But the human brain, which is given to structuring the continuum of the phenomenal world, is predisposed to make its structures classifiable into the NPs and Arts and VPs of the Chomskian tree.

Since Chomsky, professional linguists have been ferociously busy at the work of propounding linguistic rules – not the prescriptive rules of the classroom but laws which have scientific validity. Thus, we pronounce *telegraph* with a stress on the first syllable but *telegraphic* with a stress on the penultimate, and so for *telescope/ telescopic, atom/ atomic* and so on. The old way was to list the pairs, showing the stress-shift but not explaining it. Now we can say: 'Stress in the adjective is regularly attracted towards the syllable immediately preceding the adjective-forming suffix – ic.' Given a new word, say *agronome*, you will know how to pronounce *agronomic*. But how about *arithmetic*? *Arithmetic* with the antepenult stressed is a noun. But the adjective *arithmetic* obeys the general rule. 'Descriptive adequacy here involves providing an explanation for facts at one level of analysis, phonology, by reference to constructs at a different level, syntax.'

The terminology of modern linguistics can be formidable, but it can also be endearingly down to earth. 'A meaningless element which has syntactic but no semantic function' (like *it* in 'It upsets me that he left') is called a dummy. A tough-movement relates the object of an embedded clause to the subject of a higher clause, as with 'It is hard to lasso elephants' and 'Elephants are hard to lasso' (for *hard*, if you wish, read *tough*). Deep structures, which everyone has heard of and knows to be very Chomskian, are now much argued about. Chomsky said that 'John gave a book to Bill' and 'Bill was given a book by John', being synonymous statements, shared a common deep structure. But 'Bill received a book from John' is clearly synonymous with those two and yet, because of a lexical difference, cannot be paired with either in terms of deep structure. Now Chomsky's successors are saying that it's not a matter of the word but of the meaning or, to be exact, of generative semantics. But how about 'John killed Bill' and 'John caused Bill to die'? That has to be thought over.

I sincerely recommend this book, which is very cheap, to anyone who, caring about language, is willing to consider that it may be cared about scientifically instead of, well, sentimentally or aesthetically. Anyone put off by the political overtones of 'Chomsky's Revolution', remembering that Chomsky is a bit of a Marxist firebrand, might like to consider that there may well be a logical relation between radical politics and generative grammar. Language is not an intellectual construct, a hieratic cultural creation, but the property of the people. Nobody is better than anyone else at it.

Babel and Bible

The Language Makers, by Roy Harris
The Language and Imagery of the Bible, by G. D. Caird

In old Mandarin the word *ku* designated a sort of drinking goblet with corners. When this vessel came to be made without corners it was still called *ku*, and Confucius deemed this outrageous – not because the word was no longer appropriate to the thing, but because the thing no longer conformed to the word. This was the doctrine of *cheng ming* which, functioning in our own time, would forbid forms like *tin box*, since a box is essentially wooden. Professor Harris wittily illustrates the implications of the doctrine by adducing the instance of the 'women's liberation lady who legally changed her name from Cooperman to Cooperperson. If she had believed in the doctrine of *cheng ming* she would have had a sex-change operation instead.'

Cheng ming seems to posit a superhuman provenance for language. When letters to *The Times* object to a new usage – *meld* meaning mix instead of show; *hopefully* made to behave like the German *hoffentlich* – they are really invoking a remote Olympian authority, assuming that usage was decreed for humanity by a god in the far past whose bible is whatever dictionary happens to be in the house. Professor Harris's thesis is that 'languages do not come ready-made, any more than philosophies, religions, or forms of government. They are what men make them.' Even the Book of Genesis recognizes this. Adam tells God what things are named, and not the other way round. 'Language-making involves much more than merely the construction of systems of signs. It is also the essential process by which men construct a cultural identity for themselves, and for the communities to which they see themselves as belonging.'

As for making theories of language, or the descriptive systems which are the concern of linguistics, these, we are reminded, are very much the product of the kind of society we are living in. The linguistic inquirer may think he is engaged on objective science, but he cannot evade a heritage of assumptions which have more to do with social needs than with the strict search for truth. *Cheng ming* was a product of the society which Confucius's Analects, in terms of its sustentive moral principles, portray. We are trying to build linguistic doctrines appropriate to an age of 'intellectual malaise, of which the controversy over language can be seen to provide a direct reflexion.' In other words, there is a dilemma in modern linguistics, manifested in a multiplicity of schools. The central question 'What is a language?' remains unanswered.

I am aware, and Professor Harris must be too, that such a question will not greatly concern the majority of readers of newspapers or paper-backs, who think they know what a language is since they regularly use one. But it is often such readers who tend to become dogmatically prescriptive, asserting that this is right usage and that wrong, bemused by the dubious authority of dictionaries and the magic of the printed word. Ours, unlike the Chinese, is an alphabetic society, but the nature of language is essentially auditory. The dead weight of alphabetic tradition nevertheless oppresses even professional linguists. Bloomfield, one of the American founding fathers of the pseudo-science, thought he heard three phonemes in the word *pin*, probably because he saw three letters. (Actually there are four phonemes, since the *p* is immediately followed by an aspirate.) Because we see words on a page, we think that a word has an identity separate from the stream of speech. I would suggest to the reader that, without the aid of a dictionary, he attempt to define the word *word*.

To ask 'what is a language?' is hard enough; to define 'language' is a much tougher task. We are led into semiotics, the nature of communication, the new disciplines of metalinguistics and psycholinguistics and, since we live in the age of Lévi-Strauss, the glamour of structuralism. We seem able to be pretty sure that all systems of communication are based on a duality of forms – vowel works with consonant, morpheme with phoneme, the voiced sound opposes the unvoiced, and so on. Red means nothing as a stop signal without the opposing green for go. The figure-of-eight dance of the queen bee is divisible into two segments. Here the structure of the brain appears to be decreeing form, and not the structure of society. But, as Lévi-Strauss points out, all human structures are the same in origin. As for animals, we are discovering that we share a sign-making capacity with them (the five-year-old chimpanzee Washoe was taught a vocabulary of 130 signs), even though Chomsky and his school insist on the essentially human nature of language.

Professor Harris must forgive my inability to do justice to his book in such short space. I fear its theme is not one which will strike the average cultivated reader as compelling: we have a long way to go before the importance of linguistics is accepted at the non-academic level. But even Academe is slow in according it serious attention: Harris is Oxford's first Professor of General Linguistics, and the chair was established only in 1978. This profound and disturbing book, developed out of the inaugural lecture, is a worthy foundation stone.

Professor Caird is concerned with the exegesis of Holy Scripture at the same university. There are devout people who would hold that the Word of God is not to be defiled by scientific explication (though Professor Caird soothes us by saying that 'this is a book by an amateur, written for amateurs'), and there are fundamentalists in the American South who believe that the Lord wrote in Jacobean English. To these latter Professor Caird will stress the importance of reminding oneself that the Old Testament was written in Hebrew, a language given to spoken rhetoric and wordplay. In Amos 8, 2 'a basket of summer fruit becomes a portent of Israel's end' because the basket is *qais* and the end is *qes*. An almond tree (*shaqed*) is a 'reminder that God is keeping watch (*shoqed*) over his word' (Jeremiah 1, 11). John the Baptist tells the mockers (Matthew 3, 9) that God could make children for Abraham out of the stones there, drawing on the pun *'ebnayya – benayya*, though recorded in Greek. In Isaiah 5, 7 justice (*mishpat*) is sought and oppression (*mishpah*) found. Those who think that Shakespeare may have written the Bible are on the right paronomastic track or trick.

The young people who come to our doors exhorting us to join Bible study groups do not seem to realize they are locating the way and the truth in a translation which has to be inadequate. It is like studying the Sufi philosophy by reading Edward Fitzgerald. Professor Caird warns us of the danger of reading Occidental literalism into rhetorical Orientalisms. St Paul did not mean by 'resurrection of the body' the calling together of sundered bones at the Last Trump. The Day of Judgement may be here and now, in God's time, not at some remote calendar date. The Kingdom of Heaven is not up there but in here: Thy Kingdom came when Christ started his mission.

Professor Caird thinks the *NEB* to be 'incomparably the best of the modern translations', and he ought to know. But he follows Tennyson in referring to attacks on it by a 'chorus of indolent reviewers'. I was one of the attackers and I am *not* indolent. Unless he means, with Tennyson, 'causing little pain'. He encourages us not to take meanings on trust.

Firetalk

You will be seeing soon, I hope, or I hope have already seen (1984), a movie called *Quest for Fire*. The title tells you what it's all about. We are presented with a primitive human society which discovers fire and has to fight for its continued possession. In the old days of the cinema it was possible to dramatize such a subject in fairly fanciful terms. There was no need to pay heed to prehistoric fact or probability. But nowadays we all fancy ourselves as amateur anthropologists and expect to find, even in the most extravagant reconstruction of the remote past, a substructure of scholarship. The trouble is that we too often fail to distinguish between what is an aspect of our own immediate culture and what is permanently built into human behaviour. This is true even when we try to reconstruct the historical past. In the television series *Roots* it was painful to watch natives of West Africa who had never been in contact with white society indulging in facial gestures they could have learnt only in sophisticated Manhattan. Look at Alexander Korda's film about Henry VIII and you see the encapsulated 1930s, not the 1520s. But in *Quest for Fire* you will find, one hopes, a society like ours only in being anxious, predatory and violent. Nor will you hear, as a concession to entertainment values, the kind of fractured English appropriate to being stoned. This is the one film ever made which will not require dubbing or subtitles before it greets the non-English-speaking world. The characters speak a language as unintelligible to Anglo-Americans as to Finns and Albanians. In other words, there has been an attempt to work out how our fire-discovering ancestors might actually have spoken.

Not only spoken but also gestured. Desmond Morris, author of *The Naked Ape*, and a more recent book on how man communicates with his body, was called in during the planning stages of the film to construct a whole lexicon of gestures appropriate to a primitive society. I myself was asked to create a spoken language that should be more than a mess of grunts and snarls. To some extent Morris and I had to work together, basing our collaboration on the theory that speech is merely a specialized form of bodily gesture. Instead of signalling with arms and legs and facial expressions you signal with the tongue and lips and vocal cords. Visible gestures are for the day, auditory ones for the dark. It is probable that man developed speech as a night-time language but found it so efficient that he elected to go on using it when the sun rose. Probable, I say, but I am only guessing. We are pretty much in the dark when it comes to considering the origins of spoken language. The light only dawns when we have written records, but man was very slow indeed to learn how to write. He was arthritically slow in learning how to invent an alphabet.

We know a very great deal about ancient languages like Latin, Greek and Sanskrit, since we have written records. The more ancient language out of which most of our European languages have sprung – called Aryan by some, Indo-European by others – can only be painfully reconstructed through a technique of comparison. I mean that if we compare the forms of a word in a number of old languages which we know sprang from a common source, we shall be able, with a fair degree of accuracy, to reconstruct the original ancestral form. Look, for instance, at the word *to be*, present tense, in some of the older tongues of Europe (and, of course, India):

Anglo-Saxon	Gothic	Latin	Greek	Sanskrit
eom (am)	im	sum	eimi	asmi
eart (art)	is	es	ei	asi
is (is)	ist	est	esti	asti
sindon (are)	sijum	sumus	esmen	smas
sindon (are)	sijuth	estis	este	stha
sindon (are)	sind	sunt	eisi	santi

We can have little doubt that the dead race known as the Aryan or Indo-European people used a word with *m* in it when they said 'I am', and a word containing an *s* and an *m* (or perhaps an *n*) when they said 'we are'. More important, we know they had a verb *to be* – something that Oriental languages like Chinese and Malay seem always to have been indifferent about.

When the producers of *Quest for Fire* came to me and asked for a suitable primitive language, they suggested, having done some philological homework, that something approaching the old Indo-European tongue should be used. But, at the time when man discovered fire, Indo-European had not yet come into existence. (Any more than English existed when Moses led the Israelites out of Egypt.) We are concerned with a very remote past, but a past that is localized in Europe. *Quest for Fire* is set not in Asia or Africa or Australasia but in the ancestral landmass of the Europeans, or the Indo-European speakers. This meant that it would be reasonable to construct a language having more in common with Indo-European than with, say, Chinese or Indonesian. Even the unsophisticated are aware that English and Russian are practically the same language (they of course were in the days when they were both Indo-European) when compared with one of the languages of the Far East. Take Malay (or Bahasa as it is now called) and you will see that it functions quite differently from English. *Saya benchi dia* means 'I hate him' and *dia benchi saya* means 'He hates me': the words don't change their forms, only their positions. English is typically Indo-European in that it relies on the inflection of a pronoun to make its points. 'Him I hate' and 'Me he hates' are a little eccentric perhaps, but word order is less important than word form. Latin, as we see from reading Latin poetry, didn't give a damn about word order. It didn't have to, since the ending of a word showed exactly what was happening. You can write *Puella puerum amat* or *Amat puerum puella* or *Puerum puella amat* and it always means 'The girl loves the boy'.

So the language I was to construct had to behave like Latin or Sanskrit, not like Malay. It had to sound as though it might one day turn into Indo-European. People usually expect what is called a primitive language to be simple, but the farther back you go in the study of language the more complications you find. Simplicity is the fruit of the ability to generalize, and primitive man found it hard to generalize. One word for this man's weapon and another word for that man's weapon, but no word for weapon. It would have been stupid, in preparing a script in an unknown tongue for actors to learn, to be too pedantic about the probable complexity of an ancient language, so I compromised. But I could not compromise too much. If xxx means *man*, then xxxe must mean *to a man*, and xxxis *by, with or from men*.

Structure was not a problem, but vocabulary was. Take this very basic word *fire*. What was I to call it? Our modern Indo-European languages don't help us to dig out an original Indo-European root, much less suggest something older than Indo-European. Spanish has *fuego*, Italian *fuoco*, Portuguese *fogo* and Rumanian *foc*, all of which clearly derive from the Latin *focus*. But the Latin word for fire was *ignis*; *focus* meant the fireplace, the place where all gather to be warm, the living centre of a room – you can see how it took on its modern English meaning. To call a fire a fireplace argues a kind of taboo on naming a thing directly: it is like calling the toilet or jakes the bathroom. If German has *Feuer* and Dutch has *vuur*, the Scandinavian tongues have *eld* and *ild*. Polish has *ogien* and Czech *ohen* and Russian *agon* and Serbo-Croat *vatra*. Modern Greek has *fotia* and Yiddish (an Indo-European language, a derivative of German, though spoken by a people whose ancestral word for fire is *esch*) *sreife*. There's no community of form, which seems to argue that the Indo-Europeans threw up many words for fire, among which a variety of choices have been made by the languages which derive from Indo-European. I decided, somewhat arbitrarily, to have my fire-seekers call the hot bright magic *atr*. This suggests a taboo if we take it that *atr* could be the ancestor of the Latin *ater/atris*, which means black. The atrium was the open main court of a Roman house, so called because it was blackened by smoke from the hearth. Having chosen *atr*, I had to regard it not as a word but as a root – properly *atr-*. If I see the fire it is *atrom*, if the fire sees me it is *atra*, if I am surrounded by many fires these are *atrois*. Very Indo-European – or shall we say very unChinese, very unMalay.

There was once a linguistic concept – put out by Max Müller and sometimes called the 'bow-wow' theory – which stated that words originally all tried to imitate the things they described. If a child calls a dog a bow-wow he is fulfilling this theory, just as when he used to call a railway train a puff-puff or a choo-choo. But the great Saussure said that words were very arbitrary structures, and it is true that the imitative instinct is satisfied by very few words in any language. Moreover, if words are supposed to imitate sounds, there is a comparatively limited field of referents for the linguistic instinct to process. The things we see are regarded as more important than the things we hear. Nevertheless, the imitative instinct seems to be at work in a word like *little*, where the tongue creeps as high as it can in the mouth, making the littlest possible space between tongue and palate. When people roguishly say *leetle*, they are decreasing the space even further. Let us look at the word for moon in twenty-six languages:

French	lune
Spanish	luna
Italian	luna
Portuguese	lua
Rumanian	luna
German	Mond
Dutch	maan
Swedish	måne
Danish	måne
Norwegian	måne
Polish	ksiezyc
Czech	komar
Serbo-Croat	mjesec
Hungarian	hold
Finnish	kuu
Turkish	ay
Indonesian	bulan
Esperanto	luno
Russian	luná
Greek	fengari
Arabic	qamar
Hebrew	levanah
Yiddish	levoneh
Japanese	tsuki
Swahili	mwezi

What you would expect from a good descriptive word for moon is an attempt on the part of the mouth to imitate both its roundness and its elevation. The Latin languages and the Germanic languages and the tongue of the Malay archipelago agree on this. The lips are round and the back of the tongue is high in the mouth. But Serbo-Croat and Polish seem to make a terrible hash of the moon, while Mother Russian very sensibly keeps close to the Latin form. The Arabic (and Maltese) word turns the moon into a rasping scimitar, and Czech has found the term worth adopting. Hebrew, which Yiddish follows, has a word which suggests a ritual involving the moon rather than the moon itself. I have the task, in fitting *Quest for Fire* with a soundtrack, of making a plausible pre-Indo-European word. It has to have a long *u* in it, and there is a majority acceptance of a nasal after it, so why not something like *buuuun*-? I love the moon: *Buuuunan*; the moon loves me: *buuuunu*; I am surrounded by moons: *buuuunois*.

Generally speaking, I found it convenient to make my invented language iconic, or image-containing, sometimes fancifully so, and it seemed reasonable to consult living languages for evidence of congruence between sound and referent. The English word *breast* is very inadequate to depict that most lovely attribute of women, but the Russian *grud-* root is good, and so is the Scandinavian word *barm*. Hebrew *chaseh* is unbreastlike, but Japanese *mune* is fine. General rule: begin with a lip sound, continue with a back vowel, end with another lip sound. This could give you the colloquial *boob* or the eighteenth-century *bubby*. The trick is to obviate laughter on the part of the audience and make the invented word just sufficiently remote to have the auditors puzzled. But to puzzle them means to make the language unintelligible. Yet unintelligibility, without the aid of gesture or context, is the object of the exercise. *Muuv-* will do very well for breast.

Obviously, my language of the firemen has to be limited to what is needful for a film in which there is more action than speech. And, to ease the learning problem of the actors, it is as well to make the minimal vocabulary a kind of box of bricks out of which compound structures can be built. I use the word *tir-* to mean animal. It is cognate with German *Tier* and English *deer* (a good example of particularizing). The word for tree is *dondr-*, which suggests Greek *dendron*. Put *tir-* and *dondr-* together in the form *tirdondra* and it connotes an animal with antlers. *Tirdondra* sounds, to my ear, like the sort of word that might well have existed in ancient Europe.

How about the language of the heart or glands? Vocables signifying pain, regret, or perturbation are to be found in all living languages: *ai* or *aiiii* is very Latin and *oy* very Germanic. Any diphthong, especially if the second element is an *eeeeeee-* sound, will do for both anguish and pleasure. To speak of love or hate may have been difficult for primitive man, but we can conceive of his thinking of a strange affliction, under emotional stress, of some inner organ. With us it is the heart – not the real anatomical one but a kind of heraldic symbol – which is affected; with the Malays it is the *hati* or liver. *Kharrd* will do for the organ, whatever it is. Add *atr-* to it and you have something no stomach tablet can cure.

I think that the film will be understood without the provision of a glossary at the cinema door. There will be no metaphysical discussions or theological wrangles: we are right in at the beginning of human society, with no agriculture and hence no astronomy and hence no gods, with a fear of the dark and a great awe at the mystery of fire. Speech still seems, all these 80,000 years ago, to be an aspect of gesture, and speech and gesture together will make things clear. But it has to be established in what, though promoted as entertainment, is still a serious and even scientific film, that man is a talking animal, that articulate speech is what defines his species. We may agree with Noam Chomsky that there is a speech-making machine in the human brain or, with Claude Lévi-Strauss, that man is a structure-building animal whose most typical structure is speech. But by speech we do not mean Tarzan grunts: we mean syntax, vocabulary, cadence. Man may not be in control of that element which lies waiting to be released in the kitchen matchbox, but he is in total control of talk. That is what makes him man.

So much for my contribution to the background of the film. How is the film itself making out? Let's look for a moment at the book on which *Quest for Fire* is based. It's called *La Guerre de Feu* – Fire War – and was published as long ago as 1911 by the Belgian author J. H. Rosny. It has been popular with European children ever since then, but only as a fanciful romance, not as a genuine exploration into past epochs and primitive forms of *Homo sapiens*. In the book man is a 'noble savage' on the lines of Jean-Jacques Rousseau's untenable dream, and this dream image is hardly acceptable to Darwinians. Still, the book has sold some twenty million copies to date, proving that dreams appeal more than scientific reality.

One of the European children on whom *La Guerre de Feu* had a profound influence was another Jean-Jacques – the Annaud who grew up into one of France's most important film directors. The story pierced his mind and became the undislodgeable furniture of it, but it was a long time before the Rosny myth and his own vocation came together in the aspiration to get the story onto the screen. Jean-Jacques Annaud has made his name, particularly with *Black and White in Colour*. This, a study of French attitudes to their former colonial subjects, worried the French, who decided that they did not want to see it. But it scored a large success outside France and received an Oscar as Best Foreign Film of 1978. His next film, *Coup de Tête*, touched no hollow tooth in the French sensibility, and it made money. It enabled him to live during the two agonizing years which he spent in trying to persuade the money men to finance the filming of *Quest for Fire*.

The vicissitudes of the production would make a film in themselves. All things were potentially ready – a script by Gerard Brach (Roman Polanski's collaborator), my own language, preliminary tuition by Desmond Morris in the gestures of anthropoids, casting that, necessarily, had to avoid the big names and concentrate on serious young actors who would learn totally new modes of acting. A little money came in, and a low-budget production was set up with a small English technical crew. The locations were to be Iceland and Kenya. Then Michael Gruskoff grew interested. Gruskoff is one of the new entrepreneurs, a trendsetter, a creative man in himself, who was responsible for *Silent Running*, *Young Frankenstein* and *Lucky Lady*. When he was in Paris, making *Nosferatu* with Werner Herzog, he met Jean-Jacques Annaud and became fascinated by his project.

Columbia shared his fascination but underwent one of those bewildering sudden changes of management which are the despair of the creative. Having said yes, Columbia now said no, and Gruskoff went to Twentieth-Century Fox. Alan Ladd, who had believed in *Star Wars*, was head of the company and thrust his enthusiasm and authority behind *Quest for Fire*. Then he resigned from Fox. His successor, Sandy Lieberson, fortunately inherited his belief in the project, and the big money began to roll. By the time shooting in Iceland was ready to start, some two and a half millions had already been spent on it, but now problems arose in the shape of Iceland's quarantine laws, the strictest in the world, which forbade the importation of the elephants and lions (to be made suitably shaggy for the film) which the producer was bringing in from Africa. By the special building of a quarantine ship, the promise of total segregation on the sets, and the construction of a special airstrip, the Icelanders were persuaded that their laws would not be violated. The project was now really under way. The team was working on the central tableland of Iceland, far from human habitation except for the small village of Hella. This the team needed so badly for accommodation that they persuaded the villagers to go on a pre-paid Mediterranean cruise for the whole period of the filming. But now came another blow.

The Screen Actors' Guild called all its members out on strike, and every American-backed film project automatically shut down. For eighteen hours a day Gruskoff was on the telephone, trying to drum up finance from the most unlikely sources. At last the Hungarian-born John Kemeny, who runs the International Cinema Corporation in Montreal, stepped in. He had ten million dollars to find, and Fox insisted on the reimbursement of their two and a half million. The negotiations took time. The beasts went back to their zoos, the villagers to their village, the airstrip froze over. But *Quest for Fire* did not burn out.

There has been a bewildering series of changes in location – Iceland to Scotland to Canada – but the integrity of the project has never diminished. What has been most heartening has been the energy and imagination of the actors – as well as their willingness to endure cold, privation, and the discipline of new modes of speech and gesture. Few of them are well known. The doyen of the troupe is Everett McGill, a mid-Westerner who trained in the London theatre, joined the Lincoln Center Repertory, and appeared in *Equus* on Broadway. Rae Dawn Chong, a ravishing Chinese-Canadian who, alas, can show none of her beauty in the raw ambience of primitive life, has done a little television work in Los Angeles. Nameer el Kadi, an Iraqi acrobat, has mimed and danced off Broadway. No stars, but astonishing talent, and a heroic capacity for endurance.

There they all are, then, grimacing in the cutting room, zigzagging the sound track with sounds never before heard by a cinema audience. It is not just an artistic breakthrough: it is a genuine glimpse of our eighty-thousand-year-old ancestors. And if they were not like that, who is to tell us what they were really like? Sometimes one has, against all the odds, an instinct of the genuine in the most outlandish act of the imagination. *Quest for Fire* seems to me to be genuine. And its language in particular, even though I manufactured it myself.

Signals

Working with Structuralism, by David Lodge
Structuralism or Criticism?, by Geoffrey Strickland

S tructuralism got into the news, at least in the quality papers, a few
months ago, as a thing that university students of literature moaned
against and some of their professors had to defend. When students
complain about something, one suspects that there is a great deal of the
defensible in it. What students don't like is academic rigour, especially
in a field like literature, where they expect to be permitted to burble
about beauty and social significance and the effects of terminal tuberculosis on Keats's attitude to love. It was like that when I was a student,
forty years ago. There was no structuralism in those days, but there were
Leavis and I. A. Richards and the close examination of a text as though
it were a frog in a biology lab. The girls who loved Shelley didn't like
that. A new generation doesn't like *langue* and *parole* and narratology and
fabula and *sjuzet* and Roman Jakobson's definition of literariness as 'the
projection of the principle of equivalence from the axis of selection to the
axis of combination.'

This is not a classroom, so I propose to eschew academic rigour in
discussing structuralism. Man, according to Claude Lévi-Strauss, is a
structure-making animal: his brain is so composed that he has to select
from the continuum of external nature a series of opposed signs. Out of
the spectrum he selects red and green, and makes one mean *stop* and the
other *go*. Out of the babble of sound of which his vocal apparatus is
capable, he selects those opposed signs called phonemes, without which
there would be no language. It is in language that the structure-making
impulse is most spectacularly evidenced. Language is a complex structure of signs, and the study of signs is called semiology. This is not to be
confused with semantics, which is the study of meaning. The old
classroom approach to literature was vaguely semantic, but semantics
itself tends to vagueness. I. A. Richards asked what was the meaning of
meaning, and came up with no clear answer. Semantics takes us into
psychology and history and culture in general: it asks too many questions to which not even specialists know the answers. With signs we
know where we are.

Saussure, the father of modern linguistics, was insistent that the relationship of a word (or lexeme or semanteme) to the thing in the outside
world which it signified was purely arbitrary. As Professor Lodge
reminds us, it is only by an arbitrary consensus that *cat*, and not *dog*,
means the furry creature that chases mice. It has seemed to Saussurians,

therefore, that they have more chance of making the study of language truly scientific if they ignore referents, or *signifiés*, or the world outside. Concentrate on the structuring of signs, and you have the chance of generating laws. Now you can see how structuralism may appeal to a mind naturally given to scientific rigour when it comes to studying literary texts. Look at the structures and ignore the question of meaning. This goes too far, of course, and that is why academics like Professors Lodge and Strickland, brought up in a tradition of British empiricism (unlike such Frenchmen as the structuralist Barthes and the post-structuralists Lacan and Derrida), are ready to work in an older critical tradition as well as to consult the claims of the newer discipline. Barthes and Leavis represent, to Professor Strickland, a kind of polarity; yet both are immensely valuable to the student of literature.

Lodge is a writer of fiction, and a very distinguished one, as well as an academic. One of the most interesting chapters of his book is entitled *Oedipuss: or, The Practice and Theory of Narrative*, where he takes a brief story of his own (one commissioned and later rejected by BBC radio) and subjects it to structural analysis. A family is going on holiday, the cat has to be left behind but will be fed by the neighbours, the husband and father must buy cans of cat food. Rushing back in the car with the cat food he accidentally kills the cat. The story, Lodge discovers after writing it, is Oedipal. Oedipus leaves Corinth to avoid killing his father and marrying his mother, and, by doing so, puts himself in the unavoidable position of committing both crimes. The husband-father buys food to keep his cat alive and by this very action kills it. Lévi-Strauss has a fascinating essay on the pure structure of the Oedipus myth (I myself drew on this essay in writing a structuralist novel called *MF*, which only Frank Kermode understood). We're not concerned with morality but with shape. Lodge's conclusion – there is far more to his study than the pure Oedipuss element – justifies, from the horse's mouth, a great number of structuralist doctrines, including the 'paradox that it is not so much man that speaks language as language that speaks man; not so much the writer who writes narrative as narrative that writes the writer.'

Strickland cites Saussure as much as does Lodge, but he counters the doctrine of arbitrariness with a statement of Benveniste:

> between the signifier and the signified, the link is not arbitrary, on the contrary, it is *necessary*. The 'concept' *boeuf* is necessarily identical in my consciousness to the phonic group ('signifier') *böf*. . . . There is between them a symbiosis so close that the concept *boeuf* is like the very soul of the acoustic image *böf*. The mind has no room for empty forms or for concepts without a name.

This is a corrective to extreme Saussurianism and it justifies cautious expeditions in semantics. We want meaning as well as juggling with signs. We want it, to take an extreme example, in the phrase 'Emily-coloured hands', which, though Strickland seems never to have known its authorship, is a typical coinage of Edith Sitwell's. (I take it to mean, though I may be wrong, the rough hands – Emily suggests *emery* – of a scullerymaid.) Meaning may depend less on what the author intends than on the reader's own autobiography, which may include the reading of a Sitwell biography; meaning – as in Empson's seventh type of ambiguity – may mean holding two contradictory significations in one's mind at the same time (like the famous *buckle* of 'The Windhover'). But man is a meaning-seeking animal as well as a structuralizing one. Both these valuable books seek a balance between what certain hot-headed students regard, apparently, as irreconcilable disciplines.

The Language of Food

Some gustatory sensations can be expressed only by metaphor. There is an embarrassing passage in Evelyn Waugh's *Brideshead Revisited* where two young men enthuse about the contents of a noble cellar – 'This is a shy nymph being pursued by a musclebound faun'; 'This is a dawn zephyr flavoured by the effluvium of a distant gasworks' – that sort of thing; I can't be bothered to hunt out what is really said. Sometimes, as in vintners' catalogues, metaphor can be solidified into an acceptable code. When we're told that a claret is noble (paprika too, for that matter), we have a sensation of rare maturity, none of the swillability of what Australians call plonk. A Burgundy can have, like a dog, a good nose. *Pétillant* means more than just fizzy.

It never takes long, when discussing drink or food, to realize the inevitability of drawing on the French language. Many people in Britain or America only properly meet French on menus or in the cookery books of Julia Childs, which means that, for them, the language is circumscribed by the kitchen. What they consider to be the elegance or exactitude of French is derived from the memory of palatal events which can be renewed, either in Paris or in the dining room of a neat professorial home in New Hampshire. French dishes, like pieces of music, can be performed with only minor mutations of tempo and dynamic (read, if you wish, seasoning). The Empress Joséphine, while still living in the Antilles, offered visitors from France classic Parisian dishes adapted to the climate and the availability of herbs and spices unknown to France: these, so strict is French naming, could not be called what she called them. She might have cooked a chicken in red wine, but it was not really *coq au vin*.

I have before me a carton of Spoon Size Shredded Wheat, purchased from the *supermarché* here in the Condamine of Monaco. It has instructions for serving. First, the English: 'Ready to eat whole wheat breakfast cereal. Simply add cold or hot milk and sugar to taste.' Now hear it in French: '*Céréale pour le petit déjeuner composée de blé complet, nourrissante et prête à déguster. Il suffit d'ajouter du lait froid ou chaud et sucre à volonté, et voilà en réserve le plus gros de l'énergie indispensable à une matinée bien remplie.*' Note how the French relates the simple breakfast to life – reserve of energy for an activity-crammed morning. Note how elegant is '*prête a déguster*' – ready to degust, not just to eat. The German instructions do not really bear reproduction – '*Nahrhaftes fertiges Vollweizenfrühstück*' – no, no more: it is as though that *blé complet* had turned into Nackwurst.

The linguistic philosophers of France, especially the late Roland Barthes, have been aware of how the French cuisine relates to the French couture and how both relate to structuralist philosophy. A Parisian dinner is meant to be a single elegant statement, like a well-turned sentence or an outfit from Yves Saint-Laurent. The Anglo-Saxon view of a banquet can be expressed in terms of the history of the world. You begin with soup – water with things swimming in it – then move on to the aqueous kingdom, then to flying creatures, then to mammals. Finally you celebrate man in cheeses and desserts, both products of sophisticated culture. This is the diachronic view, which the French reject. They prefer to see the various courses as syntagms, or sentence components – soup adjective, fish noun, chicken adverb. One might add that they look at clothes in the same way. Every sentence needs a verb, as it needs a noun. Every suit needs trousers as it needs a jacket. Without a jacket you have only a pronoun.

I am not, despite what you may think, joking. The French, in their Cartesian way, are addicted to exact definition which shall also be elegant, while Anglo-Saxon food nomenclature avoids elegance if it can, since pleasure in food is probably sinful. I saw on the menu of a British transport caff the item 'Tinned peaches and evap. milk.' That's exact but inelegant. In French that would have to be something like *tranches de pêches pochées en sirop à la crème américaine*. The British have a quite palatable dish consisting of a pork sausage cooked in batter, but they have to call it toad in the hole, which is disgusting. I even saw Giant Toad on a pub bill of fare. Fish and chips is the finest dish in the world (I ate some last night in a Cambridge fried fish shop, with my fingers out of newspaper, over-seasoned with vinegar. Delicious) but you need the elegance of something like *cabillaud frit aux pommes allumettes* and, of course, no vinegar.

The unavoidability of French in the *cadre* of the cuisine is seen, for a start, in the implements you use. You need a *moulis-légumes* – a vegetable mill which cannot be exactly named in English. You need a *Doufeu* for pot-roasting. You can't call a *bain-marie* Mary's bath, and a *sauté* pan is not a frying pan. You need a *charlotte* mould and a *brioche* mould and a *gras-maigre* sauceboat (for separating the fat from the meat juices). And, of course, you have to have *gratin* dishes. I know all about these utensils, and others, because my seventeen-year-old son has become a *cuisinier* (which sounds better than cook and means more). His tendency to use French terms for the processes of cooking, even when talking English, points to the Anglo-Saxon debasement of our native equivalents. Because *stew* is as full of unsavoury as of savoury connotations – was not a stew a brothel? Does not Hamlet refer to his mother as being stewed in corruption? – it is better to speak of a *ragoût*. But my wife, who is Italian, rejects *ragoût* because the Italianized form *ragu* means a spaghetti sauce. I myself will not speak of a cauliflower cheese chiefly because it was all we British had to eat (if we were lucky enough to get some cheese, if we were lucky enough to find a cauliflower, just after the last war) and give it a fresh start with *chouxfleurs au gratin*. The French nomenclature, at least for Anglo-Saxons, never turns sour. It can turn sour enough for the French, who are no more exempt than the rest of us from horrible cooking.

But, in general, they care about food, perhaps too much for our more puritan taste. Wandering through the woods of France, a paunched senator will see in a wild boar not a bristling forest king but, like Obelix in the Asterix cartoons, a stuffed roast. My wife has just brought in our television magazine, *Télé-Sept-Jours*, and I note an article on a historical programme due tonight on TFI: its heading is *Le Mariage de Louis XIII et d'Anne d'Autriche introduisit le chocolat en France* – the chocolate being the most important aspect of the dynastic match. They gorge with discrimination and enthuse in exact terms which have a certain intellectual coldness. Americans, especially American women, are different.

By this I mean that English will accommodate a catalogue of seventy courses (as when King James I, on progress, ruined many an enforcedly hospitable country lord) but not easily encompass descriptions of pleasure in food without turning sentimental or vulgar. I don't mean just 'Wow' or 'Yumyumyum' (even French children will, saying '*J'ADOOOOORE les frites*', rub their tums and go mmmmmmmm; I mean this sort of thing:

And then once in Paris, in June [what a hackneyed but wonderful combination of the somewhat overrated time-and-place motif!] I lunched at Foyot's, and in the dim room where hot-house roses climbed crazily outside on every trellis, I watched the head-waiter, as skilled as a magician, dry peas over a flame in a generous pan, add what looked like an equal weight of butter, which almost visibly sent out a cloud of sweet-smelling hay and meadow air, and then swirl the whole.

That is from *A Food Lover's Companion*, the section entitled 'P is for Peas' by M. F. K. Fisher. I much prefer Russell Baker:

> The cheese course was deliciously simple – a single slice of Kraft's individually wrapped yellow sandwich cheese, which was flavoured by vigorously rubbing over the bottom of the frying pan to soak up the rich bologna juices. Wine being absolutely *de rigueur* with cheese, I chose a 1974 Muscatel, flavored with a maraschino cherry, and afterwards cleared my palate with three pickled martini onions.

I have seen American women in Paris behave, usually over some dish which could be delinguistified into New England Boiled Dinner, as though they were beginning a sexual transport. I deeply resented the British stewardess on my last British Air flight back to Nice ending her valedictory spiel with *bon appétit*, as though the Côte d'Azur were a ready-laid table. I resent people who use the language of religion in restaurants – like the bloody fool who runs a so-called gourmet restaurant in Wiltshire and rebuked a bishop for smoking at table: 'I would not smoke in your cathedral, my lord. Pray respect mine.'

The French, who appreciate but do not rush into mystical ecstasies, have a profound sense of the danger of extolling what you eat: praise it too highly and you may not get it again. The lack of overt appreciation is a kind of apotropaic gesture: you don't wish to make the gods of food, in their perverted way, withdraw what mere human beings like. Like a thing and you'll lose it: that's the way the gods operate. They have long ears but are somewhat dim-sighted: they will catch the blasphemous 'Those *langoustes* were heaven' but not always see the steepled finger ends drawn away from the kissing lips.

The Americans, with their immense technological skill, have learnt how to turn the language of the menu into a substitute for the taste that is not there. One can tolerate this at dinner but not at breakfast, when one is too weak for fine writing. The insincerity of the 'Good morning!' at the head of the screed is bad enough, but that business of 'two freckle-shelled eggs laid at dawn this very day in our own country hen-runs, scrambled with fresh farm butter to a golden ambrosia, served with crisp crackly crunchy nutty bacon slices cured in the Kentucky hills over fragrant hickory smoke' goes far too far, especially when you have heard the deep-freeze door open on those venerable eggs and caught the whiff of entrenched grease in the skillet. God knows what the audience for the purple gustatory prose is; Americans aren't taken in by it. Perhaps it's for Asiatics like Balachandra Rajan's Nalini in his novel *Too Long in the West*:

> 'I'll have Boston clam chowder,' she said, 'and roast, stuffed, young Vermont turkey. With golden-brown, melt-in-your-mouth Idaho potatoes. And king-sized, tree-ripened California peaches.'
>
> 'We got chop suey,' the girl said, 'and Swedish meat balls and Swiss steak. But we ain't got none of the fancy stuff you're wanting.'
>
> 'Then I'll have a hamburger,' Nalini insisted, doggedly.

'You want it with French fries?'

'I want it,' said Nalini, clenching her pretty teeth, 'with potatoes that taste of American earth, fried in the only way they should be, in butter fresh as a New England welcome. And then I'll have pie like your grandmother used to bake it when America was real and itself.'

Nalini's frustration will only come clear to Americans when they realize how xenophiliac their short-order cuisine is – hamburgers, I mean, which Hamburg would not understand, French fries incomprehensible to the French, English muffins you never see in England. Attribute your lunch-counter staples to Europe and you season them with the spice of the remote. Or perhaps you don't. I was with an American couple just back from Europe. The wife opened a can of Heinz spaghetti, saying: 'Nice to get back to something genuine after all that foreign stuff.'

Learn from the French, who say nothing if the meal is superb but burst into senatorial or Zolaesque invective if it is not. Recover the native puritan spirit, with a brief grace before and after meals (by God, we're lucky to be eating at all), but don't push your luck with prose poems about *tripes à la Caen*. Remember that the primary function of language is to categorize and that it is in order to ransack the dictionary for terms which describe culinary processes but not for the poetry of what Dr Johnson called gulosity. The vulgarity of a lot of writing about food is cognate with the vulgarity of a lot of writing about sex. Certain sensations cannot be described except through metaphor, and the metaphor of sensation is too often the metaphor of mysticism. The Old Testament reminds us that a major sin of the Exodus was to lust after the onions and leeks of Egypt. It also, in the Vulgate version of the Psalms, alludes to the admirable oriental mode of expressing satisfaction in repletion: *Cor meum eructavit laudem tuam* – My heart hath belched forth thy praise. Eructate, but not too loudly. That is better than words.

The Times as Guardian

As I am one of the writers rebuked by Mr Howard of *The Times* for using gibberish, I must tread very carefully. Admittedly, it was not what I wrote but what I said that he, rightly, found fault with. Asked by some interviewer about violence in one of my books, I said incautiously: 'That's what life's all about, isn't it?' Mr Howard describes the phrase *That's what it's all about* as 'a mindless bit of parrot jargon, much in vogue with sports commentators to describe some generally inconsequential fact that has little to do with the matter in hand.' It seems to be in order to roar the line at the end of each verse of the 'ludicrous dance' called the Okey Cokey (which Mr Howard decockney-fies through aspiration), but it just will not do in educated (that is, possessing as one of its parameters correctly placed aspirates) speech.

The trouble about being prescriptive for spoken language is that speech is so swift that both diagnosis and prescription come too late for cure of its diseases. When one speaks one is always horrified at what one is saying, and one goes miserably on, still horrified and horrifically impotent. If one is Samuel Johnson or Bernard Levin (also of *The Times*), one can speak like a book and get away with it, but speech has properly nothing to do with books. Speech is the primary reality, loose, inexact, crammed with solecisms, its grammar atrocious, but it is what human communication is all about. Mr Howard concerns himself, very valuably, with lexical misuse, but it is in the nature of speech to malapropize, spoonerize and appropriate the bad habits of one's interlocutors. I had a man on the telephone from New York only yesterday who kept using *hopefully* as though it were *hoffentlich*. I found myself seduced by the abusage and ended up (horrified, naturally) by saying: 'Hopefully then I'll hear from you on Monday.' But in writing I would not commit that solecism. Hopefully Mr Howard sets out to put people's writing right. He has picked all the words that the average *Times* letter writer would regard as trouble spots, and he deals with them sensibly and learnedly.

As a writer myself, though not to *The Times*, I examined my conscience diligently as I read him. I have not, I think, come out too badly. I have used *charismatic* in only one book, and there I made it apply to the autocephalic early churches that St Paul fulminated against. *Clinical*, alas, I have sinned with, but so has all the world. 'Journalist, advertising copywriters, and other magpies of technical terms have seized this sharp, precise word, and, as usual, got hold of the wrong end of the thermometer.' *Clinical*, which derives ultimately from *klinē*, a bed, has to do with 'smoothing the fevered brow on the lace-edged pillow', but I have used it in phrases like 'He made love to her, coldly, clinically,' and we read in advertisements of bathrooms and kitchens possessing functional, clinical lines. I think that, with me, it has something to do with going to municipal clinics as a child and hearing the clink or clinik of indubitably cold glass and metal. Of course, if you make love to someone clinically you usually do it on a bed, but such an appeal to etymology would not be likely to appease Mr Howard. How, incidentally (another word greatly abused, as here, now), do you get hold of the wrong end of the thermometer?

Gay has become a real nuisance. You can no longer dance the Gay Gordons, and *The Gay Divorcé* (which has 'Night and Day' in it) must be retitled, just like, though for different reasons, *Prancing Nigger*. 'It is a paradox that it has been expropriated by one of the sadder groups of society' (does not Mr Howard perhaps means 'appropriated'?). *Camp* has its uses, but it is too vague. Miss Penelope Gilliatt once wrote of 'camp tat', which is even sloppier than Mr Cliff Michelmore's 'After the bonanza came the crunch'. Mr Howard cannot properly *define* low camp as 'a female impersonator imitating Marlene Dietrich in a seedy nightclub', though he can present such a performance as an example. As for etymology, one lacks written evidence that *camp* derives from what went on in summer army camps in Hyde Park: ' "Going for a bit of camp" is alleged to have been the phrase used by the fops of the time' – the nineteenth century – 'who slipped under the awnings of the tents for assignations with the rapacious and licentious soldiery.' (Why, that might almost be Bernard Levin writing: defenders of the well of English undefiled seem much given to sonorous cliché.) Despite it, though (the written evidence, I mean), *camp* has to come from camp and not, as seems possible to some, the French *camper*. Philip Hope-Wallace read somewhere: '*Monsieur Pont a su camper le rôle de Rigolette avec dignité.*' That to me sounds like regular usage: to set up, establish, fix. The most interesting *camp* in the world is that *campé* by 'Les Girls' in Sydney NSW, who are obviously evoking the spirit of a camp concert party of Anzac days.

As for *ethnic*, Mr Howard neatly says: 'We are all ethnics under the skin.' And not only under it, one would have thought. To make it mean, as in America, 'supposedly lesser breeds just inside the Law' is silly, but Howard is reconciled to it by New Testament koine usage, which makes it mean heathen or Gentile. 'A part of the temple fell down and made a great destruction of *ethnics*' (1375). The pejorative kind of semantic change has always been commoner than the meliorative, human nature being what it is, and Mr Howard shows how *student* is coming to mean irresponsible young layabout, just as *research* can signify the looking up of telephone numbers and the riffling through of old press cuttings. And see what has happened to *theology* in the usage of people like Sir Harold Wilson, who contemptuously fires it at unpragmatic Labour idealogues: 'Let's forget the theology', and so on. Theology to Sir Harold means calculating the number of angels that can dance on a needle point. Readers of *The Times* seem to have established that no theologian has ever concerned himself with such a trivial question (to which the answer has always been known, anyway). *Metaphysical* and *academic* are also used as terms of abuse by pragmatic politicians. But such people inhabit a world whose lexis is as shaky as its motivations are hypocritical, and it is probably true to say that all semantemes used by politicians are suspect. What is *socialism? Democracy?* What is a *Trot?* Because I have never cared for the Joannine reforms, I am regularly condemned as *fascista* in the left-wing Italian press. We come to the end of the line with *truth* and *good*, dangerous value words, says Mr Howard, quoting Auden:

> Leave Truth to the police and us; we know the Good;
> We build the Perfect City time shall never alter.

We need to have rebukes like Mr Howard's from time to time – salutary knuckle-raps to which, alas, only people already concerned about language will respond. For the rest, *nescius*, meaning ignorant, becomes *nice*, and St Audrey is forced to preside over cheap trinkets won at a fair. Language is not, howardever, merely words: it is rhythm, tone, deliberate lexical abuse for aesthetic ends. Communication can survive even the most brutal verbal falsifications, and the history of language, as Mr Howard knows well, is a record of deviation from fixed semantic position. Let Dr Johnson have the last word: 'It remains that we retard what we cannot repel, that we palliate what we cannot cure.' Or was it Bernard Levin who wrote that?

The Language Man

A World of His Own - The Double Life of George Borrow, by David Williams

M ost people, if they know nothing else of Borrow's, know this passage from *Lavengro*:

> 'Life is sweet, brother.' 'Do you think so?' 'Think so! There's night and day, brother, both sweet things; sun, moon, and stars, brother, all sweet things; there's likewise the wind on the heath. Life is very sweet, brother; who would wish to die?' 'I would wish to die.' 'You talk like a gorgio – which is the same as talking like a fool – were you a Romany Chal you would talk wiser. Wish to die, indeed! A Romany Chal would wish to live for ever!' 'In sickness, Jasper?' 'There's the sun and stars, brother.' 'In blindness, Jasper?' 'There's the wind on the heath, brother. . . .'

Or rather they know part of it, the wind on the heath bit, and probably adjudge it overwhimsical. But this is Borrow, the lavengro or man wise in languages, genuinely suicidal, and that is Jasper Petulengro, Borrow's blood brother, ineptly trying to talk him out of it.

Borrow, usually taken to be the back-to-nature boy, odd man out on the Victorian scene, rejecting book learning and the industrial Britain being forged before his eyes, was a complicated creature who suffered from visitations of what he called the 'horrors'. These were not what my namesake in *Candida* attributes to drink or, listening to Marchbanks, poetry. Borrow seems to have suffered from a black incubus of a kind more interesting to the exorcist than the alienist or blood letter, though he himself, blunt and pragmatical, had little interest in either God or the devil. Hence the exquisite irony of *The Bible in Spain*. There are some who, not having read the book, have an image of Borrow the missionary, carting the Protestant word of God all over the Catholic, hence atheist, peninsula, sustained by his faith through fever-ridden plain and freezing sierra. The truth is that Borrow did not give a damn about the Bible.

What did he give a damn about? First, foreign languages. The son of a regular ranker who rose to captain, living in grim barracks miles from anywhere, he escaped into the countryside and met gipsies. More, he learned the gipsy talk. In Ireland after the Napoleonic Wars, whither British troops were sent to keep down a rebellious people growing poor because England no longer wished to import their grain, he learned Erse. Before long he had learned Welsh as well, also what is termed

Ancient British (probably Old Welsh); later he was to learn Cornish. Languages became a passion: he knew, by 1851, all the tongues of Europe and several of the East. The only good thing about the Great Exhibition, which he very reluctantly visited, was the chance to show off his polyglottism in the multinational crowd. He was widely noticed, an immensely tall, spare but muscular man whose hair had grown white in youth, yapping away in Armenian and Turkish and Manchu.

It was Manchu (which Mr Williams ought to have told his readers something about) which got Borrow into his long association with the Bible Society. Manchu was the sort of language that was bound to fascinate Borrow, with its strange Uighur alphabet and its habit of indicating gender through vowel gradation (*ama* is father and *eme* is mother; *garudai* – from the Sanskrit – is a male phoenix, *gerudei* a female one). He needed a job, and he learned the language so that, on behalf of the Society, he could get a Manchu Bible printed in St Petersburg. Russian, of course, was no problem, but the Czar who, like the Pope, did not wish people to read the Bible, was. Borrow loved a fight – whether with the Flaming Tinman or the oppressive State – and he went into Bible-selling chiefly because it was, in countries like Russia and Spain, a pugnacious activity. He loathed the Pope, and a demotic Bible was a stone slung at that Goliath. He had nothing theological against him, merely a detestation of what looked like tyranny. This was not just in the Bunyan–Defoe British dissenter tradition; it was the gipsy in Borrow – perhaps literally: he had a certain swarthiness; his mother may have, during her husband's absences on duty, sought consolation in a dark man's arms. But this is mere speculation, like the reasons for the apparent lack of a Borrovian sex life. The Victorians (and he was Victorian enough) are still, sexually, the strangest people in the world.

The Spain where Lavengro or Don Jorge toiled on behalf of his evangelical masters in London was torn by the Carlist wars. *The Bible in Spain* sets it all down, and very vividly. Borrow was tough, and the Spaniards knew it. They shoved him in jail, but he was soon out again. It was always possible to threaten Spain with gunboats and Lord Palmerston, but the six-foot-three hunk of white-haired British truculence, his man Lopez waiting outside with three hundred Testaments in the donkey's panniers, was a force of nature to be respected. *The Bible in Spain* has been described as *Gil Blas* written by Bunyan. It is the most ironic piece of picaresque writing in all literature – the gospel of turning the other cheek retailed by a giant who pulled no punches.

How do *Lavengro, The Romany Rye* and *The Bible in Spain* fit into our bookish annals? They are sports, they belong to no tradition. Borrow had little interest in literature, though his passion for languages naturally brought him into contact with great unknown bards and fabulists. The passion itself was cognate with that of the supreme lexicographer James Murray, but Murray became a philologist while Borrow never betrayed interest in language families, sound laws, or Proto-Indo-European. He had a photographic memory which enabled him to carry whole pages of exotic vocabulary in his head, but his grammar and pronunciation were probably always faulty: we have evidence that his spoken Welsh, though fluent, was a joke to native Cymric speakers. He marvels that a Welsh hill farmer should call his dog Perro and that *puta* should be the worst term of opprobrium in the Icelandic sagas; he never relates or compares or seeks a community of Aryan origin. A language is a thing in itself, isolated from its sisters and a medium of phatic discourse not of the literary imagination. He gets his prose style from nobody, but he is not without art.

He married a widow older than himself. There was probably no sex in the relationship but there was money, and Borrow became a small land-owner. Here was the source of the double life of Mr Williams's title – the man of property (he made money too out of *The Bible in Spain*, which was very popular) who was fundamentally on the side of poachers, thieves and gipsies. He was happiest wandering on foot, drinking ale in pubs (he was a great believer in the therapeutic powers of ale, even for sick horses), using his fists, being truculent. Mr Williams presents a rich full portrait, though the condensation of so short a book (only 171 pages of text) makes sometimes for hard reading. We needed something longer and more leisurely. But we are sent back to Borrow himself, which is a good thing, and to more entertaining solidities than just the moon and the stars and the wind on the heath, brother.

Ameringlish

Paradigms Lost – Reflections on Literacy and Its Decline, by John Simon

John Simon is a film and theatre critic well known in New York as a man of large intelligence and impossibly high aesthetic stan-dards. 'He looks,' said Gore Vidal to me once, 'as though he had tasted everything and found it insufficiently seasoned.' That does not go far enough. Insufficiently cooked, the materials of bad quality, and in the consumer a chronic hyperacidity. Mr Simon mentions at one point, or more, in this collection of magazine articles an institution called the 'Dick Cavett' show (his quotation marks, not mine: does he regard the name as a somewhat shady pseudonym?). I appeared with him on it once and asked him if there was any film he unreservedly admired. He answered: Yes, Fellini's *I Vitelloni*. I rushed back to Rome to inform the maestro, expecting a gush of amazed gratification. Unfortunately, Fellini had not heard of John Simon. One tends to forget that the Simon writ does not run much outside Manhattan. A Central European fluent in Serbo-Croatian, Hungarian and German before he became a superb practitioner and haughty arbiter of English, he is a typical New York phenomenon. A chastener of American metropolitan taste and now a scourge of bad Ameringlish usage, he is a whipping boy as well for the philistine, a local Savonarola feared and hated and therefore despised. I have suffered from him both as a dramatist and as a novelist, but I bear no grudge. His strictures, aesthetic or linguistic, are usually unanswerable.

Usually though not invariably. In this book I am presented as one 'who is considered by many, not excluding Mr B., a black-belt-champion wielder of words and usage.' Mr B. has, in fact, never claimed any exceptional skill in the management of our lovely but difficult language. The more Mr B. writes the less he finds he knows about writing. Mr B. would never dare, as Mr S. does, to prescribe for the user of English. This is because he works in a creative area where new rules have to be made almost hourly for new problems of expression. Mr S. has the easier task, that of being a kind of draconian elementary schoolmaster to errant journalists, mediapersons and elementary schoolmasters. People must not say 'Between you and I' or use *like* as a conjunction or make *hopefully* do the job of the German *hoffentlich*. They must learn that *media* is a Latin and *criteria* a Greek plural and neither may be used as an English singular. Mr Simon always gives good logical reasons for the avoidance of solecisms. Because, like me, he considers Black English a tongue of deprivation and berates teachers who sentimentally drool over its alleged expressive virtues, he has been condemned as an elitist. Meat-and-potatoes frontiersmen condemn his prissiness, call him a spinster schoolmarm and promise to make his velvet-breeched posterior meet the mud. But Mr Simon fights very courageously in a war he has no hope of winning. Stoically he is forced to accept the Johnsonian position: 'It remains that we retard what we cannot repel, that we palliate what we cannot cure.'

Mr Simon has a signal advantage in not having learned English as a mother tongue. Unlike me, he has not had to struggle to overcome the inheritance of a dialect which, clinging to antique forms and hence historically valid, fails to meet the demands of the normative version of the language – itself a dialect, that of the English East Midlands with anomalous forms which have jumped out of the county of Kent across the Thames. The word *it* one thousand years ago was, in London and hence potentially New York English, spelled and pronounced *hit*, as it still is in Yoknapatawpha County. It had no genitive inflection: the *-s* termination got there through analogy. Am I wrong if I say, as I said as a boy, 'It bark is worse than it bite'? In certain West Country dialects of England *I* is an invariable form ('Give it to Oi'), and this might seem to imply a justification for 'between you and I'. What I am trying to say is that it is very difficult to lay down normative rules. What begin as solecisms often end up as acceptable usage. Before about 1960 it was wrong, in England at least, to say 'Due to fog on the line the train will be late'. When British Rail printed, in 1960, posters with this formerly unacceptable phrase on them, the British were able to jettison 'owing to' as a supererogatory form. T. S. Eliot in his 'Gerontion' used the nonexistent *juvescence* instead of the correct *juvenescence*. The latest supplement of the *Oxford English Dictionary* admits the Eliotian word as one which is endorsed at the highest literary level. Mr Simon invokes both personal authority and the impersonal past, but both sometimes abet what he regards as solecisms. New York cab drivers say 'you was'; Dean Swift said it too.

Mr Simon scorns the science of linguistics because it merely describes what people do with language. He demands, it would seem, prescription backed by a kind of national academy on the French model. But languages do change, even though Mr Simon wants them to stand still, and change is usually initiated at the demotic level, unconsciously following some inner need for regularity and simplicity. When the Normans confronted the Anglo-Saxons they heard a kind of English which, owing or due to the need of an already much invaded people to communicate with the Danes, had shed much of its Teutonic grammatical inheritance and turned into a creole. It was inevitable that Mr Simon, brought up on three highly inflected languages, should wish to cling to what rags of inflection are still left in English. He is right, I think, to insist on clarity and elegance but probably wrong to be too nice about grammar. Fighting change, he is himself a subscriber to changes which were condemned with Simonian heat by men like Defoe, Swift and Johnson. Or Caxton, for that matter. He wanted *eyren* not *egges*, but *egges* won.

Moreover, Mr Simon does not seem to know that what is right for Ameringlish is not so for Britglish and vice versa. In England we use *that* and *which* indifferently: when I write for America I have to be unnaturally stringent with my relatives. Few Americans will accept 'aren't I?', which the British use all the time. *Whom* is dying out in England, where 'whom did you see?' sounds affected. Curiously or not, British visitors to America hear more refinement than seems proper to a tough and revolutionary people, for Americans pronounce their aitches, which the majority of Englishmen don't.

Mr Simon is at his best when he is slating the slipshodness of Clive Barnes and Rex Reed and Barbara Walters. Such sloppiness as they exhibit owes more to slovenly thinking and ill-conceived similes and the malapropistic tendencies of the ill-read than to grammatical incompetence, though, as Mr Simon says, subliteracy rarely manifests itself on one level only. Clive Barnes describes another Mr Simon – Neil of that ilk – as 'walking barefoot on the heart. The heart is his own.' John of that ilk says: 'To walk barefoot on a heart sounds murderously sadistic, and unhygienic besides; to walk on one's own heart must give the giggles even to a contortionist, to say nothing of a prose stylist. And what does such a walk, barefoot or *shod*, mean? Bare-faced shoddiness?' Bare-faced shoddiness, one might say, is a quality rather than a meaning, and Mr Simon's shod is only there for the pun. *Unhygienic?* Dubious, if the feet have been washed. If it is murderous, it does not matter whether it is hygienic or not. It would not give a contortionist the giggles if he walked on his own heart, since he would be murdering himself, presumably masochistically. Mr Simon is the first to admit that he is capable, like the rest of us, of bad writing, but he should not write badly when he is writing of bad writing. Still, he usually writes well. He is one of the few among us who have that terrible duty. What he does not write is, if I may use the term, creatively. It is in poetry and the novel that the real writing problems start, and Mr Simon's prescriptiveness is not very helpful there.

A final point. He does right to trounce the feminists, who behave as though language were a masculine invention devised to put women down. A correspondent to *Ms* magazine wrote: 'I protest the use of the word "testimony" when referring to a woman's statements, because its root is "testes" which has nothing to do with being a female. Why not use "ovarimony"?' This is, of course, absurd, but I cannot help feeling that Mr Simon, who is not above consulting etymology when it suits his purpose, had a brief spasm of sympathy when he read that bit of activist pedantry. The woman, by God, had used a dictionary.

Fair Speaking

A Dictionary of Euphemisms, by Judith S. Neaman and Carole G. Silver

The great Murray and even the great Partridge might have been shocked at the sight of two respectable American ladies digging into the dirt from which euphemisms flower. Meaning of course chiefly the organs and processes of sex and excretion. But it is in these areas that the taboos have proved to be weakest: it only needed Kenneth Tynan to say *fuck* on television in the sixties for decent girls to glory in the language of bargees. The most powerful euphemisms operate in the political field (chiefly departments of defence and strategy) and these are foliating like triffids. The other euphemisms are already mainly of historical interest.

Terms like box, Cape Horn, the golden doughnut, snatch and grumble are no longer needed for what Miss Neaman and Silver term, with lexicographical propriety, the female pudendum. Nevertheless there is something not quite right about *cunt*. The word is iconically inept: it suggests something sharp and aggressive, as Joyce, who uses it only twice in the whole of *Ulysses*, was quick to see. A sowcunt barks, and Bloom finds in the Middle East 'the dry shrunken cunt of the world'. So a variety of euphemisms continues to be used not because of pudeur – the only true reason for euphemizing at all – but because Anglo-Saxon seems to be letting us down. The large number of terms for the penis is again not a matter of shame but of the feeling that no word properly works. *Penis* itself, meaning a tail, is coy. Florio, Shakespeare's friend, who made the first English-Italian dictionary (and a very fine one it is) translated *cazzo* as *pricke*. The Roman tendency to use *cazzo* on all occasions does not inhibit their decorating the concept with a huge fanciful glossary, of which the best item is *dumpennente*, from *dum pendebat*, which comes from the *Stabat Mater* and describes Christ hanging from the cross.

What I am trying to say is that there is a large difference between a true euphemism and a word which presses the expressive button (a word given here for clitoris, which is surely too learned a word for the man in the boat and is not improved by being abbreviated to *clit*). *Breast* is not a good word because it sounds wrong: too many consonants for that glorious smoothness, and the vowel is far too short. You can see why *boob* (not a good word because of its association with fools and errors) developed out of *bubby*. We need a long u as in the Russian *grud*. And *fuck*, despite Tynan's advocacy of the free use of the term even in marital contexts, has connotations of attack which are not always appropriate. Hence *make love*, which decent people prefer, is not really a euphemism.

'Let's fuck, baby', an invitation frequently found in the novels of Ms Jackie Collins, detumesces without benefit of what Rabelais's translator Urquhart calls venerean ecstasy.

Is *gay* a euphemism? I think not. But what are homosexuals to be called? Havelock Ellis, who first used *homosexual* in 1897, never liked the term but was not happy with *invert* either. The terms in use in America for various homosexual or gay activities are less euphemisms than slangy shorthand. The bird circuit is the predatory tour of gay bars; playing checkers is seeking a partner by shifting seats in a male movie house; a meat rack is a gay pickup place; 'What number and what colour?' means 'What sexual practices do you prefer?'; gayola is police payoff by homosexuals. Sodomy, whose connotations of fire, brimstone and Lot's wife, are offputting, had to be called buggery, though that is a libel on the Bulgars, and terms like go Hollywood, kiss or kiss off, kneel at the altar, ride the deck are merely attempts to avoid the legalistic. They are probably true euphemisms.

Race, not sex, has become the great taboo area of our time. It is the one area in which the euphemistic has never operated. All that can be done here is to neutralize what I must call the cacophemistic and throw out terms like *nigger*, *wop* and *sheeny*. But it is still permissible to call Frenchmen *frogs* (taken by the French as a tribute to their culinary catholicism). Nobody has ever liked other races. This leads us to the most interesting section of Mss Neaman and Silver's book, which has to do with making war while pretending not to.

The people who make a fortune out of the instruments of death are to be called the Armament Community, which replaces the Munitions Interests strongly disliked by opponents of the Vietnam War. Total nuclear war has become an All Out Strategic Exchange. The strategy planners are Defence Intellectuals. A nuclear explosion is an Energetic Disassembly, and even a fire may be called a Rapid Oxidation. Troops not competent at killing are put on to BEST, or Behavioural Skills Training (as, in the civilian field, slow learners are named Exceptional Children). We know all about megadeaths, one hundred of which sound rather less than one. One man's guerrilla is another man's Freedom Fighter. Hiring mercenaries is Greenbacking (an allusion to the American dollar). Grave registration is in the hands of the US Memorial Services. If you crash in a military plane Old Newton takes you. *Zapped*, however, is no euphemism. Termination with Extreme Prejudice is a CIA term for assassination.

The CIA (whose special assassination unit is called the Health Alteration Committee) seems to have the best euphemisms. It invented the term Overflight for illegal aerial investigation of neutral territory glossed as hostile, calling them also National Technical Means of Verification, which sounds almost friendly. The Company, as the CIA is called, has Assets (listening posts and monitoring stations), and when it sends out a military operative under civilian cover it terms this Sheepdipping. Protected by the Intelligence Identity enactment of House Bill 5615, he traps Targets who are either Ill (arrested on suspicion) or in The

Hospital (jail). He can perform a Technical Trespass or break-in, and all his investigative Covert Operations feed a huge official network called the Backchannel.

Even when governments are not concerned with the discomfiture of a putative enemy they are apt at hiding realities under the euphemisms long known as gobbledygook. The Nixon administration produced the term Biosphere Overload for overpopulation. Benign Neglect (coined by the Earl of Durham in 1839 to describe England's treatment of Canada) is now used to mean, apparently, letting the underprivileged fight their own way up. Personnel Ceiling Reductions are employment cutbacks. To do a Uey (or U-turn) sounds and is Australian, and it means to change your political point of view. There is nowhere in this interesting little compilation a euphemism for unemployment, but that is surely on its way. Statepaid Temporary Leisure? REST (Right to Earn Statutorily Terminated)? GARDENING (Guaranteed Absence of Re-employment Due to Economic Non-recovery Indicated by Notional Geostatistics)?

Who Said it?

1 Oxquote

The Oxford Dictionary of Quotations, third edition

W inston Churchill is quoted here as saying that it is a good thing for an uneducated man to read books of quotations. He said that at a time when ignorant politicians still felt they had a duty to sound like Burke, but times have changed. Quotation is no longer one of the English vices, and even in 1941 (year of the second edition of the *ODQ*) the ability to spout great sundered lines and then wonder where they came from was dying along with the rest of the patrician past. But I, and a few other recidivists, have cherished the *who said?* game and continued to love the *ODQ* as the ultimate cultural reduction. All the Bible, Dickens and Shakespeare a reasonable person needs is here, the iron rations of literature in a knapsack. If one wanted to get beyond Cowper and Carlyle, the *Penguin Book of Modern Quotations* (in which, wrongly but I'm not grumbling, I am credited with the immortal 'Laugh and the world laughs with you, snore and you sleep alone') was soon available, and one was content to regard the *ODQ* of 1941 as a beloved fossil, rather like the Harvey *Oxford Companion to English Literature* (I mean, who now wants Scott plot summaries and the *Noctes Ambrosianiae?*)

But now the *ODQ* has updated itself. It has cut down on the Cowper and Wordsworth and introduced Auden, late Eliot, Lowell and far too much Christopher Fry. It is very interesting reading, especially for one flu-bound and bedrid and with a limited span of attention, but its additions seem curiously arbitrary. On the other hand, it may be very accurately reflecting the post-1941 situation as regards quotability, which means that important cultural movements have washed over us and left no succulent detritus. There was, for instance, the anger of the young men, and here there is no John Osborne, though Dorothy, Lady Temple, is still with us. All we have of Kingsley Amis is 'More will mean worse' (*Encounter*, July 1960). But surely a lot of Amisian dicta have passed into the language – 'Nice things are nicer than nasty ones'; 'He made his Edith Sitwell face'; 'It was no wonder that people were so horrible when they all began as children' (undoubtedly a misquote, like many quotes, but I need to be put right without searching for *One Fat Englishman*). The very title *Look Back in Anger* is already as venerable as 'It was Christmas Day in the workhouse', but it is not here. And surely some of Jimmy Porter's excretions, like the one about Pusillanimous and the other about swinging on the bloody bells, ought to have got in.

There is some Orwell, though no Newspeak, and 'You have nothing to lose but your aitches' is not here. Five chunks from Graham Greene and seven from Evelyn Waugh seem insufficient, when we have to have twenty-one from Christopher Fry. There is Vladimir's line 'We're waiting for Godot' and two more unimportant bits of Beckett, but where is the murmurous mud or the *merde universelle?* Nabokov is represented only by 'Lolita, light of my life, fire of my loins', and yet most literary people can quote at least the opening of the poem *Pale Fire*. There is nothing of Edmund Wilson nor of Angus, though Harriette continues to give us the exemplary opening of her memoirs ('I shall not say why and how I became, at the age of fifteen, the mistress of the Earl of Craven') and Charles Erwin Wilson says that what is good for the country is good for General Motors, and vice versa. Sir Harold, with his three faint bromides, reminds us that contemporary politicians specialize in lies that are mercifully unmemorable. Edward Heath will go down to posterity as the author of 'the unpleasant and unacceptable face of capitalism.' Who (while the book is open at the Hs) said 'But did thee feel the earth move?'? No, not Hardy but Hemingway; Hemingway said more than that, but from this book you would not think so. Who said 'I cannot and will not cut my conscience to fit this year's fashions'? It sounds like some Marian martyr but was in fact Lillian Hellman to the Chairman of the House Committee on un-American Activities, 19 May 1952. It was, of course, well said.

The writer just above Lillian Hellman should be Joseph Heller, if only for his title: there will soon be a generation unaware of the origin of 'Catch 22', as there is already a generation that misuses the slogan. In fact, Hellman is preceded by Heine, whose formerly final dictum *Dieu me pardonnera. C'est son métier'* is now capped by a prophecy taken from Puntsch's 1966 *Zitatenhandbuch 'Dort, wo man Bücher verbrennt, verbrennt man am Ende auch Menschen.'*

The introduction to this new edition makes an honest statement of policy concerning the demotic quotations of the age of radio and pop song. Catch phrases are not easily attributable and are, anyway, as much a specialized field as nursery rhymes (which you will now have to look up in the Opies or the 1941 *ODQ*): it would have been decent to refer the reader to Eric Partridge, sadly dead this year.* Quotes from the Beatles or the Stones are not, we're told, really separable from the music. 'If the words cannot be said without the tune . . . coming to mind, they are *not* quotations in the same sense as the others.' This means no Cole Porter but it does not mean the exclusion of Noel Coward:

> She refused to begin the Beguine
> Tho' they besought her to
> And with language profane and obscene
> She curs'd the man who taught her to.
> She curs'd Cole Porter too!

If ever there was a quote (which incidentally nobody ever quotes) which was unquotable without the music, this surely is it.

Musicians, if not music, have now got in. Gustav Mahler, seeing Niagara, said *'Endlich fortissimo!'* Sir Thomas Beecham, speaking of Bruckner's Seventh Symphony, said: 'In the first movement alone, I took note of six pregnancies and at least four miscarriages.' We are apparently not yet ready to hear him on *Glorianus* and the Mistress of the King's Musick. Stravinsky, who has produced whole volumes of memorable table talk, is not here however, nor is Schoenberg (who, when told that a soloist would need six fingers to play his concerto, said: 'I can wait').

The cinema, which has provided us with a host of catch phrases, is ill-represented. From *Monsieur Verdoux* we have:

> *Priest:* May the Lord have mercy on your soul.
> *Verdoux:* Why not? After all, it belongs to Him.

* 1979.

Humphrey Bogart is credited with 'Here's looking at you, kid' and 'If she can stand it I can. Play it!', both from *Casablanca*. The latter, a footnote tells us, is often quoted as 'Play it again, Sam'. It would have been reasonable to attribute the misquotation to Woody Allen, who has solidified it into a true quote. Orson Welles, who improvised in *The Third Man* the great line about the peaceful Swiss having produced only the cuckoo clock, should be here between Thomas Earle Welby and the Duke of Wellington but is not. The Welby quote is worth having, though: ' "Turbot, Sir," said the waiter, placing before me two fish-bones, two eyeballs, and a bit of black mackintosh.'

I think I have said enough. Hang on to your 1941 *ODQ* unless you are a library, in which case you will have to have this 1979 one too. But I think the editors of the Penguin modern quote book are more on the ball with the postwar age. Finally, today or the next wet Sunday, waste a little time tracing the following:

Hard pounding this, gentlemen; let's see who will pound longest.
Feather-footed through the plashy fen passes the questing vole.
There is always room at the top.
A rape! A rape! . . . Yes, you have ravish'd justice. . . .
Orthodoxy is my doxy; heterodoxy is another man's doxy.
Ultima Thule.
Well, if I called the wrong number, why did you answer the phone?

2 On the Road

The Travellers' Dictionary of Quotation, edited by Peter Yapp

I t would be churlish to doubt the value of so massive an undertaking as this – a volume of 1022 double-columned pages filled with the observations of travellers on all the visitable sites of the known globe. Misread the title, shoving the apostrophe back a space, and you may take it to be a kind of universal Baedeker, but the book is too heavy to be packed in your luggage. It is essentially a literary compendium to be read like any other dictionary of quotations, very big but very limited. If, for instance, you propose visiting Mali and wish to know what it is like, you will be reminded only that it used to be Timbuctoo and that Byron mentions it in *Don Juan*:

To that impracticable place Timbuctoo,
Where Geography finds no one to oblige her
With such a chart as may be safely stuck to.

So what? Byron gets the stress wrong and says in effect that Mali is unvisitable. One gains much the same impression of Malta, which comes next and is covered a little more lavishly, though there is no quotation later than 28 May 1920, on which date D. H. Lawrence wrote a letter to Catherine Carswell, calling Malta 'a strange place – a dry, bath-brick island that glares and sets your teeth on edge and is so dry that one expects oneself to begin to crackle.' As for the Maltese (for every reasonably well-known location there is a section on the inhabitants), the last word is Admiral of the Fleet Lord Fisher's in 1919: 'Neither rats nor Jews can exist in Malta. The Maltese are too much for them' – a pretty inaccurate observation.

Malta has become a bad place, true, and lost the charm it had for the so-called sixpenny settlers of the 1960s, but it deserves fuller treatment. There is a fair amount of literary material available, including Nigel Dennis's poem on Maltese oranges and his book-length essay on the island, not to mention my own lengthy verse-letter to the late Vladimir Nabokov. And, while we are on to myself, I may reasonably register protest that I am uncited on Malaysia or, having published a whole book on the place, New York. I am limited to things like the following: 'In Monte Carlo, where we have to take amusement seriously, there is not much to laugh at.' On the other hand, I was pleased to read the late William Sansom on the whole principality – 'Cyclamen faience balconies, turquoise urns, gold moorish tiles, a sunbaked hotel called Balmoral, the whorled icing of the Casino with its elegant lavender lamps on Suicide Terrace. . . .' It is not really like that, but what a writer that man was. The value of any anthology lies in its power to fill the gaps of literary ignorance, and Mr Yapp does a good job there. The overall subject matter is perhaps finally irrelevant; it's the temperament of the traveller that counts.

Let us take one restless traveller, already cited above – D. H. Lawrence. In *The Plumed Serpent* he has Ramón say of Mexico: 'It is a country where men despise sex, and live for it. Which is suicide.' In *Mornings in Mexico* he comments on its 'curious, inexplicable scent, in which there are resin and perspiration, and sunburned earth, and urine. . . .' On Sardinia, quite inexplicably, he is not cited at all, and he gets only two little quotes on Sydney, though he is permitted to generalize at some length out of *Kangaroo* on the 'curious sombreness of Australia, the sense of oldness, with the forms all worn down low and blunt, squat.' On Nottingham he is allowed to say nothing, and the county itself is lumped in with Yorkshire for a droll and inaccurate summary from Horace Walpole (1756) and nobody else. Mr Yapp has clearly read vastly, but for so large a project he needed a whole team of readers.

The larger projects within the whole large project comprise such giants as the USA and the USSR, which used to be plain Russia, and no amount of literary research could conceivably do justice to either. Every generalization about America is cancelled out by another generalization. Lenny Bruce may say that nobody likes Americans any more – '. . . we have lost the world completely – because we fucked all of their mothers for chocolate bars' – but he is immediately countered by Paul

Goodman: 'In the modern world, we Americans are the old inhabitants. We first had political freedom, high industrial production, an economy of abundance.' Anything goes, and America ends up by being indistinguishable from Russia or else the place where Dylan Thomas continued his lifelong search for naked women in wet mackintoshes. What happened in Columbus, Ohio? One night the bed fell on Thurber's father. Concord? Thoreau and Emerson were there, but not, apparently, Robert Lowell. Washington DC is, to Dylan Thomas, not a city but an abstraction, whatever that means, but Gore Vidal is not here to say that it has the efficiency of the South and the charm of the North. As for Russia, everything said by Dr Giles Fletcher in 1589 still seems to hold, and the Russe Commonwealth is plaine tyrannicall.

It seems appropriate to end with the Falklands and Gibraltar, on both of which, in their contentious connections, Mr Yapp is up to date, though I am not sure what Alexander Haig meant when he said (of the former, of course): 'This has been a pimple on the ass of progress festering for 200 years, and I guess somebody decided to lance it.' Gibraltar is left to mere visitors or politicians who knew it only as a mere red pimple on the Spanish *culo*. Those of us who lived there and wrote at length about it are not favoured. Kenneth Tynan is. To him it exemplifies 'the uncanny skill with which the British contrive to export their least likable features intact'. Augustus Hare called it 'a beautiful prison' and Mark Twain 'a gob of mud on the end of a shingle'. Molly Bloom says nothing. The most realistic quote is from James Cameron (*News Chronicle*, 1954): 'A current gag in the Madrid cafés is to pass round in a conspiratorial way little packets which when opened reveal a tiny stone and a note saying: "Patriots! Spain has regained the Rock! This bit is your share." ' That gag was still alive in late 1982 when I was in Madrid.

A lot of work went into this compilation, and hard work must, in these days of syndicalist restrictivism, be honoured. If I am dubious about its value, that may be because we seem to be going through a spate of anthologizing. Homosexual Verse, Death, Aphorisms – one wonders what will come next. The moon? Cheese? To be fair to Mr Yapp's comprehensiveness, there is a section not only on the moon but on the sun and the universe itself. And there is a fair postscript from S. J. Perelman: 'I suggested that she take a trip round the world. "Oh, I know," returned the lady, yawning with ennui, "but there's so many other places I want to see first." ' Precisely my feeling.

A Large Italian Job

Enciclopedia Einaudi, Volumes I and II, Turin

T he most arduous commission, not to say bizarre, that I have ever
received was to write the article on THE NOVEL for the most
recent edition of the *Encyclopaedia Britannica*. Arduous because of
the need to be encyclopedic – that is to say, cover the entire field of long
prose fiction (but what is *long*?) systematically yet comparatively briefly;
bizarre because not only were the parameters imposed by Chicago (The
Novel as Life Style; Pastoral Novel; Novel of Apprenticeship, etc.) but
also the word lengths (Definition of Novel, 453; Chinese Novel, 316, or
something like that). I was not quite a writer and not quite a machine.
The work was not excessively well paid, but one got a complete set of the
edition. I had never had a great modern encyclopedia before; previously
I had made do with a second-hand *Everyman's* (bought in Tunbridge
Wells for £4). I thought, naturally, that I knew how an encyclopedia
worked. It was rather like a big dictionary, except that you were not
supposed to be after definitions but miniature courses of instruction.
Still, the alphabetic taxonomy was essential, and you did not expect to
find gaps. One was not so foolish as to look up, say, MATCH and expect
the term to be dealt with under the headings of matrimonial, football,
device of ignition, but it seemed legitimate to demand information on
MATCH under that last designation, since there must be a long and fascinating history of it somewhere, from lampwick to Kruger and after.
MATCH is not to be found either as a heading in the new edition of the
Encyclopaedia Britannica or, so far as I can make out, as a piece of buried
treasure in some article that deals, on some margin I have still to discover, with pyrotechny or pyrogenesis or something.

I understand that it was on this very burning issue that Sir William
Haley, who was to have been in charge of the edition, parted company
with the steely men of Chicago, who had new strong ideas which had
little to do with alphabetic inclusiveness. The new edition, as is well
known, represents a breakaway from all previous editions. There is a
micropedia, which gives you a kind of *antipasto* information and then
shows you where to get a full meal in the macropedia. The macropedia is
a massive collection of courses of instruction alphabetically arranged,
but it might as well not have been so, since the micropedia takes care of
alphabetic arrangement and sends you to numbers (volume and page) in
the weightier compilation. Thus, if you look up VIDAL, GORE in the
micropedia and are dissatisfied with the *amuse-gueule* that you get,
you could be referred to a volume of biography or on the arts. I mention
VIDAL, GORE hypothetically, since he has no entry, though he is

223

mentioned succinctly in NOVEL.

What I am trying to say is that the new encyclopedias do not seem concerned with purveying information in the good old way – ready and rich reference with the referrer expecting, and finding, an almost lexicographical fullness of themes. If I need quick information about a famous person (profession, nationality, life span) or a country (location, extent, population), where can I look these days but in the *American Heritage Dictionary*? Perhaps it is in this very eschewal of alphabetic inclusiveness that the new encyclopedias are proclaiming their seriousness. Perhaps it is in the awareness of their editors that an encyclopedia cannot any more, so rapid are the advances of knowledge, be truly encyclopedic that a disowning of the *appearance* of inclusiveness is part of the new pattern.

I have before me the first two volumes of the *Enciclopedia Einaudi*, edited by Professor Ruggiero Romano. There are to be twelve volumes altogether. The format is admirable, a triumph of Turinese design and of Milanese bookmaking (Monotipia Olivieri). Each volume is toughly cased and is not too tall to be lodged with regular-sized books. The type is clear and there is no columnation. As for contents, consider Volume I, which runs from *abaco* to *astronomia*. *Abbondanza* goes with *scarsità, analisi* with *sintesi, assioma* with *postulato*. There are also *analogico/digitale* and *antico/moderno*. It is a compendium of ideas rather than facts, and some ideas are inseparable from their opposites. The entries are essays of an essentially provisional kind, avoiding the listing of facts but not averse to speculation. The approach is sometimes lateral or medial, with no doorman wearing a museum uniform. Take *Armonia*, for example.

Armonia starts off by mentioning Martin Vogel's book on the ' *Tristan* chord' and, at leisure, gets from that chord to Chailley's representation of historical change in harmony in terms of the components of the 'natural' harmonic series. Problems are stated, but there are no dogmatic resolutions. One is stimulated to read further, but the article itself is no traditional crash course in the subject. I remember, in the army in Gibraltar, being ordered to give a brief course in the history of metaphysics. It was possible to tear out the appropriate page of the *Encyclopaedia Britannica* and conceal it, as a crib, in my military cap. If *Filosofia*, in Volume V, follows the *Armonia* pattern, it will offer no easy capsule summaries; it will plunge into a specific problem and work outward to implied generalities.

In Volume I there is on article on *Avanguardia* – an *idea*, if ever there was one, and it deals with politics as much as with art. Aesthetics is approached, in the same volume, through the opposition of *bello* and *brutto* – with a deliberate evocation of Diderot's article, in the mother of all encyclopedias, on the *Beau*. After the beautiful and the ugly, we can learn about the concept of need (*bisogno*), the nature of the *borghesi* and the *borghesia*, and the diversity of the notion of a *burocrazia*, with Kafka in the opening paragraph.

Looking ahead, I see we shall be able to learn about the poetic, but not the history of poetry, literature but not the novel, sin but not heaven or hell. But, through indirection, we shall find direction out. Jacques Nobécourt, in *Le Monde*, confessed to handling the first volume with a mixture of fascination and timidity – '*parce qu'on ne sait pas, au départ, ce qu'on y cherche exactement ni où la trouvaille va entraîner l'esprit.*' And he described the whole project as an encyclopedia of doubt, not of certitudes, of relatives, not absolutes. In other words, it mirrors the intellectual state of the contemporary world, especially as seen in Italy. I cannot imagine certain of the entries finding a place in an Anglo-Saxon compilation of similar form and scope – *donna*, for instance, *castrazione/complesso*, and *servo/padrone*. But I may be wrong. Ruggiero Romano is reported to have said: 'This is not a drugstore of knowledge' – meaning that you can't walk briskly to the shelf and take what you know you want. You have to browse, open, sniff, and discover that there's a difference between needing and wanting. It is not a shop at all but a very progressive college.

What to Read

The List of Books, by Frederic Raphael and Kenneth McLeish

'A recommended library of 3,000 works,' says the subtitle, and this, as the compilers make clear, has to be purely 'imaginary', since no modern dwelling has room for so many. The public library round the corner has far more, so the Raphael–McLeish shelves are an oneiric compromise erected between two realities. They house also a compromise between personal choice and the dictates of tradition. One may not like the *Iliad* or the *Canterbury Tales* (these two do) but they have to go in. On the other hand the works of Sir Walter Scott are not here, nor those of Calvino, Gadda, Belli or Montale. The emphasis is very Anglo-American, with a few translated 'classics' (*Don Quixote, War and Peace*), but, surprisingly, no room for such useful anthologies of foreign literature as are put out by Penguin.

The books are not classified according to the Dewey system, which cannot easily take in such new categories as Science Fiction (which in my view is not a real category) and the Literature of Feminism. We have also Occult and Paranormal, Media, and Sex and Love. It is a thoughtful and useful taxonomy. If this were merely a library catalogue, it would be interesting enough, but the compilers provide brief tangy or feisty or punchy comments on the books, as well as a number of Baedeker-style symbols – a stylized armchair meaning 'a particular pleasure to read', an exclamation point for 'seminal book that changed our thinking', a magnifying glass signifying 'difficult; worth persevering', a black book to mean major and a white book to mean minor masterpiece (Cervantes is as minor as Camus and Colette and Wordsworth and Yeats, to say nothing of Dryden and Goethe, while Eliot and Donne and Blake·and Catullus are major). Most ingenious of all are a Union Jack and Old Glory, each no bigger than an ant's egg, signalling a special national interest.

Now for some samples of the comments, which are clearly modelled on those of newspaper bestseller lists. Shakespeare.

> 'What can one say? He is an Everest, and all other dramatists stumble in his foothills; the poet of poets, the man of men? All of that, and none of that; he is unique. *Othello* is one of the most accessible of his greatest plays: poetry, form and spectacle are kept in perfect balance.'

And then a recommendation of the Arden edition and apparent ignorance of the great and definitive Houghton Mifflin *Riverside Shakespeare*. Still, no real objection. Now for Dante. 'Dante was one of the greatest medieval poets: worth learning Italian for. Best translation (alas): Sayers.' Lame, wouldn't you say? And if it's alas for Sayers, how about John Ciardi or the three-volume Singleton? Never mind. Edmund Spenser? We ought to read *The Shephearde's Calendar*, since 'the odes of Spenser are the most successfully inventive metrical system in English. Indispensable.' Odes are not a system, and there are no odes in *The Shephearde's Calendar*, only dialogues in a variety of rhyme schemes. But again, never mind.

In the fiction section one gets the impression that novelists did best in their first books and that there has been a falling off since. Wilson, Angus: *Such Darling Dodos* (1950): 'The world of the sensitive middle class and genteel England were never the same again. Nor was Wilson, to our loss.' Bellow, Saul: *The Victim* (1947): ' . . . one of his good early books . . . before *The Adventures of Augie March* (1953) led to fame and fat.' Burgess, Anthony: *The Malayan Trilogy* (1956–59): 'Best, least ostentatious early work of prolific man of letters. . . .' Raphael, Frederic does rather better with *Lindmann* (1962) and *California Time* (1976).

Lindmann is a passionate, compassionate examination of one man's guilt, and racked conscience, for the sinking of a refugee-ship in World War II; *California Time* is a witty experiment, the movie novel (the novel *as* movie) to end them all. Also: *April, June and November, The Glittering Prizes, Sleeps Six* (short stories), etc. See DRAMA (Aeschylus); POETRY (Catullus).

I must start reading, as I am intended to, this Raphael character.

In the drama section, Aeschylus (transl. Raphael) has produced masterpieces (major), as have Euripides, Goethe (Goethe? That unactable *Faust*?), Ben Jonson, Shakespeare, Sophocles. The minor masters are Thornton Wilder and Oscar Wilde. Poor Shaw, Racine, Marlowe, Aristophanes, Beckett, Congreve, Goldoni. Sorry – these Baedeker symbols are hard on the eyes in a fading light – Ibsen and Molière and Chekhov join the minor masters. Bamber Gascoigne's book *World Theatre* gains the award of five symbols. It is a particular pleasure to read, a standard work on the subject, not to be missed, contains a good bibliography and exceptional illustrations. I think this is the most marks any book here gets without being a masterpiece.

There are a few errors which will undoubtedly be corrected in the future editions we are promised. *The Malayan Trilogy* is *not* about 'conscript life in the oriental twilight of empire', William Cooper's *Scenes from Provincial Life* was first published in 1950 not 1961 (it could not otherwise 'precede' the school of Amis, Larkin, etc.) and it is a novel, not a series of 'neat and humorous tales'. *The White/Garnett Letters* are between David Garnett and T. H., not E. B., White. *Finnegans Wake* is not spelt with an apostrophe, and I am always tempted to throw away any book which commits that solecism.

Let me finally record my pleasure that certain books are in which might easily have been out. Crèvecoeur's *Letters of an American Farmer*, for instance, Golding's *Lord of the Flies* (I always suspected he must be a 'Catholic apologist'), David Karp's *The Day of the Monkey*, with just praise for his *One*, Deryck Cooke's *The Language of Music*, Ilza Veut's translation of *Huang Ti Nei Ching Suwen*, Henry Chadwick's *The Early Church*, Bonhoeffer's *Letters and Papers from Prison*. On the whole, this is an estimable and even useful compilation, and a courageous one. There were bound to be errors of inclusion, summation, exclusion, taste, judgement, and it is commendable that there are so few. But the omission of Walter Scott and, for that matter, Manzoni is not easy to forgive.

Being Witty and American

The Oxford Book of American Literary Anecdotes, edited by Donald Hall

James Sutherland's *Oxford Book of Literary Anecdotes*, a marvellous compilation, concentrates on the British. This American counterpart is equally good fun, though perhaps, in its later pages, too drunken or desperate for anything but unease. Archibald MacLeish considers it a better book, 'because American ideosyncracy [sic] is more original, and when it is sad, more poignant.' As *idios* means personal or peculiar or separate (*sunkrasis* meaning a mingling of elements, hence a temperament) I do not see how one idiosyncrasy can be more original than another, but let that pass. I agree, though, about the poignancy, so long as it means getting drunk and suicidal. The final anecdotes about American poets are stories of decline and dissolution. The earlier ones are healthier and, one might say, more British.

With the song 'Yankee Doodle' the music of the great continent is said to have ceased to be colonial and have become American. Literary anecdote seems to start being American with Daniel Webster. The Webster brothers were very idle. 'What have you been doing, Ezekiel?' asked their father. 'Nothing, sir,' was the reply. 'Well Daniel, what have *you* been doing? 'Helping Zeke, sir.' Before this, the early settlers and the American sons of the Enlightenment are anecdotal kin to their cousins. William Byrd (1674–1744) is, in his diaries, Pepysian enough: 'I neglected to say my prayers, which I should not have done, because I ought to beg pardon for the lust I had for another man's wife. . . . Endeavored to pick up a woman, but could not, thank God. . . .' Thomas Jefferson is, despite his slaves, a transplanted Englishman of large culture, to whom John Kennedy, honouring forty-nine Nobel Prizemen in 1962, paid the best tribute: 'The most extraordinary collection of human talent . . . that has ever been gathered at the White House – with the possible exception of when Thomas Jefferson dined alone.'

Poignancy begins early in this collection, and where you would least expect it – with Mark Twain. William Dean Howells tells the terrible story, too long to be considered mere anecdote, of how the great humourist told, at Whittier's seventieth birthday celebration in Brahmin Boston, of the three dead-beats who imposed themselves on a California mining camp as Ralph Waldo Emerson, Henry Wadsworth Longfellow and Oliver Wendell Holmes. Not a titter, only the descent of transcendental ice. Later, Henry James asked Twain if he knew Bret Harte. 'Yes,' said Twain, 'I know the son of a bitch.' The real point of that anecdote is, one presumes, James's unspoken response. There is not, I fear, a lot of wit around.

There is a fine long story about James's brother William. He complained on a train about a child's making the journey hideous with an endless whining singsong. The mother he addressed made no response but a man called him a cad. William asked him to repeat his words on pain of a slap in the face. The man said it again and was duly slapped. The great mild philosopher was now arraigned as a bully, except for one lady whose appearance suggested 'a wider point of view'. At the end of the journey William said: 'You, madam, you, I feel sure, will understand. . . .' But the lady recoiled and exclaimed: 'You brute!' The expected anecdotes about Henry and Edith Wharton are here, though Henry's stricture on *Leaves of Grass* may not be well known: 'Oh, yes, a great genius; undoubtedly a very great genius! Only one cannot help deploring his too-extensive acquaintance with the foreign languages.'

If Whistler is witty it is because he has been sharpened on Wilde. 'Do you think genius is hereditary?' he was asked, replying: 'I can't tell you, madam. Heaven has granted me no offspring.' That seems proper for London but hardly for New York, home of the wisecrack. Dorothy Parker, looking at the row of back-to-the-wall lunchers in the Algonquin, with none facing them, said: 'This looks like a road company of the Last Supper.' At a Hallowe'en party she saw ducking for apples and murmured: 'There, but for a typographical error, is the story of my life.' Her pal Robert Benchley asked a uniformed man at the door of the Trocadero in Hollywood to get him a taxi. The man icily said that he was a rear admiral. 'All right, then,' said Benchley. 'Get us a battleship.' This is not as good as W. S. Gilbert's reply to the man who asked him to call him a cab. 'Very well, you're a fourwheeler.' Damn it, sir, etc. 'Well, I could hardly call you hansom.'

We have met all the Hemingway and Fitzgerald stuff before; it has become folkloric by now. The T. S. Eliot anecdotage is chiefly about cheese and is all London-based. W. H. Auden, another national ambiguity, provides nothing new for those who have read the recent biographers, but it will always be a pleasure to hear that Yevtushenko is the poor man's *Howl* and that Shakespeare was in the homintern. Shirley Jackson (1919–65) had the distinction of being the only writer to use, with success, black magic on a publisher. Alfred Knopf was skiing in Vermont. She made an image of wax and stuck a pin in one of its legs. Knopf broke a leg in three places. There are others in that great house who could have done with the hex, but there are no more Shirley Jacksons. It was her husband who floored Dylan Thomas for making a pass at her and ruining his teleview of the ball game.

The one poet Dylan wanted to meet in America was Theodore Roethke. Roethke went mad, and one wonders at the decency of making a spectacle of him. When driving with Thomas Kinsella he conceived the notion that the Mob was after him and he phoned the police for tommy guns. Delmore Schwartz died in a squalid hotel, his corpse unclaimed at Bellevue. John Berryman drowned himself in Minneapolis. Sylvia Plath took her own life. The world these later Americans struggled through was not that of Jefferson and Franklin. But not all the gossip is grim. Donald Hall, himself a fine poet, has worked hard and well.

Prolefeed

The Batsford Companion to Popular Literature, by Victor Neuburg

When critics complained of what they termed the excessive energy of H. G. Wells, who seldom produced fewer than four books a year, he responded justly that he had little energy and his devotion to writing, a deeply sedentary trade, was the proof of it. My own critics, who find in my output a sub-Wellsian but still damnable superabundance, are best answered in the same way. Only lazy writers write much. Why, anyway, complain of fecundity when God commanded us to be fruitful? The answer was sagely given by one of my *Observer* colleagues a few weeks ago: if you write much you do not give yourself time to meditate; without meditation there is no Literature, only the lower-case variety which is the subject of Mr Neuburg's miniature encyclopedia. God save us from churning out prolefodder; let us be decently costive like the late T. S. Eliot and E. M. Forster and thus prove that, being gentlemen, we are also Creators of Literature.

Arthur J. Burks (1898–1974) was no gentleman. During the 1930s, when he would sometimes have nearly two million words in current publication, he aimed at producing 18,000 words a day.

> Editors would call me up and ask me to do a novelette by the next afternoon, and I would, but it nearly killed me. . . . I once appeared on the covers of eleven magazines the same month, and then almost killed myself for years trying to make it twelve. I never did.

Ursula Bloom, born 1895 and still with us, is clearly no lady. Writing also under the pseudonyms of Lozania Prole (there's an honest name for you), Sheila Burnes and Mary Essex, she has produced 468 books, beginning with *Tiger* at the age of seven. Most of the writers listed by Mr Neuburg are churners, but churning is not necessarily a sad guarantee of prolixity. Frederic Brown (1906–72) churned much but also produced the shortest SF story in the world:

After the last atomic war, Earth was dead; nothing grew, nothing lived. The last man sat alone in a room. There was a knock on the door. . . .

But, says Mr Neuburg, there is a story even shorter: 'As the sun set slowly in the East. . . .'

Was Richard Horatio Edgar Wallace (1875–1932) a gentleman? He ruined himself at the race track, a gentlemanly thing to do, but forewent any claim to be invited to tea in Bloomsbury (not that he would have had time and, anyway, the tea would not have been green) by being able to dictate a whole novel during a weekend. In the 1920s and 1930s, Mr Neuburg tells us, one in four of all books read was the work of Wallace. Everybody, especially the now unreadable Sir Hugh Walpole, looked down on this perpetually dressing-gowned king of the churners, who gave the public what it wanted. What the public wanted, and still wants, is an unflowery style woven out of clichés, convincing dialogue, loads of action. Is the public wrong?

Q. D. Leavis said yes and made a moral tissue of it. I prefer to consider the public half right. Doubtless the public should be taught how to appreciate Henry James, seeing in his tortuosities and subtleties of character both a mirror and a criticism of life, and the public is wrong if it thinks that the difficulty of serious literature is the product of unworldly ineptitude, and that the capacity to tell a plain tale is the greatest of the auctorial gifts. On the other hand, the most acceptable kind of fiction ought to be compounded of Jamesian complexity and Wallacean verve, and the public cannot be wrong if it thinks the novel ought to be a high-powered car rather than a Gothic cathedral. It is totally wrong, however, when it discounts the virtues of well-chosen language and the importance of ambiguity and introspection.

Let us consider the phenomenon of Barbara Cartland, born 1900, author of more than 230 romantic novels with world sales of over seventy million copies. She is the great mistress of contrivance and unreality, with all her heroines virgins, her moral principles stuck somewhere in the age of Richardson, her stereotypical predatory men, her improbable plots, her inert language. She is, to the Malaysians, Turks, Sri Lankans and Filipinos, what modern English writing is all about. She cannot be written off or laughed away. Her books *move*, she has the right narrative stuff in her. She is only dangerous when she convinces her readers that life is as she presents it. This, I think, is the Q. D. Leavis or moral point. Accepted as an anodyne, she can do no harm. The trouble is that life is short and the human imagination needs more than anodynes.

What is implied in Mr Neuburg's book is that popular literature is happiest when it can evade the ambages of language and fulfil itself in some unequivocal visual form like the cinema or television film (consider the current BBC *Beau Geste*, better than Wren) or the comic strip. CASEY COURT is the entry immediately following CARTLAND, BARBARA. This was a full-page panel drawing that first appeared in *Illustrated Chips* in 1902, presented the adventures of back street urchins, and, in its stage form, gave the role of Billy Baggs to Charlie Chaplin. This and *Blondie* and *Andy Capp* and *Jane* are literature in the sense that there are characters, events and *fumetto* dialogue, but not literature in that there is no verbal *récit*. The great public, like bored Alice next to her reading sister, can do without verbal *récit* but not without dialogue. There is no Leavisian literary pundit qualified to condemn *Garth* or *Rip Kirby* or *Peanuts*. Here we are into a different art, usually managed with great skill, that, being a kind of drama, has only a cousinly relationship to literature. For, in the modern age, drama need not be literature, though it is better when it is.

Mr Neuburg's book is useful, but it would be more useful if it were bigger. For it is not possible, without real comprehensiveness, to know whether certain authors are not listed because they are not 'popular' or because room could not be found for them in a mere two hundred pages. We expect Agatha Christie, P. G. Wodehouse and Dennis Wheatley to be here, but are not sure whether Graham Greene, Somerset Maugham and John Braine are to be regarded as popular or not. Probably not, since they are concerned, on however elementary a level, with the aesthetic exploitation of language. But if science fiction is a popular form, where are Aldiss and Ballard? The entries on genres – guidebooks, Gothic novels and so on – are concisely good, and there are odd speculations of value. Was the Susannah story in the Bible the first detective fiction and Daniel a proto-Perry Mason? Is the Bayeux Tapestry the father of the comic strip? There are also some nice odd chunks of information. In Ohio in 1932 a Mickey Mouse film cartoon was banned because it showed a cow reading Elinor Glyn's *Three Weeks*. Leslie Charteris's real surname is Yin, and he is the son of a Singapore Chinese. Maigret's first name is Jules. And so on.

Stars and Us

Astrology and the Popular Press: English Almanacs 1500–1800, by Bernard Capp

The subject is historical, but the resonance of the title is wholly contemporary. Few us of go out of our way to consult the stars, but fewer still actively sneer at the space devoted to astrology in the newspapers and magazines of the people. There may, after all, just be something in it. A loved one *was* considering leaving me. That Number 7 *did* turn out unlucky. She's a real Sagittarian. I share, with other Pisceans, a certain artistic propensity. Astrology has been going on a long time, and why should there not be a correspondence between the motions of the planets and those of our minds, glands and circulatory systems? Serious people expect strange things from the coming Jupiter effect. Don't give him the car keys: there's a full moon.

In the old days, Chaucer's as well as Ptolemy's, the identity of elements in human physiology and the constitution of the planets was unquestioningly accepted. Heat, cold, dry and moisture accounted, in varying mixtures, for the make-up of the soul and the stars alike. It was the astrologer's task to chart the relationship of the planets to one another as they moved through the Houses of the Zodiac (conjunction, opposition, trine and so on) and to predict the consequences for man and nature. Natural astrology concerned itself with the health of the body and the expectations of the farmer; the judicial branch forecast the state of the nation, warned of coming war or famine, or calculated the destiny of an individual through brooding on the stars that reigned at his nativity. Astrology was never in conflict with religion, since it did not deny free will or moral responsibility: man was 'inclined' by the stars, not pushed. One of the greatest astrologers of the fifteenth century was Cardinal Pierre d'Ailly. Paul of Middleburg, a brilliant star-watcher, was made a bishop and designated cardinal. Popes had their horoscopes drawn up. Pius II jailed a man for predicting his death. The forecast was correct, and Pius's successor freed the man and gave him a present.

The annual almanac, which gave brisk astrological information, was an essential tool of the physician or surgeon as well as the statesman. Why should not the ordinary man or woman have it too? Hence the demotic tradition which, later enfolded into the popular press, still subsists in the annual *Old Moore's*. There has been more research going on in this field than we laymen were ever in a position to suspect. Not only research into the astrological almanac as a best-selling phenomenon, as a precursor of that popular press which was to absorb it, and as an index to demotic culture, but also as an influence on our politics, part of the subject matter of our literature, and a unifying codex in a diverse society. As precognition, magic, and even science, the almanac began to lose authority as soon as the Ptolemaic universe gave place to the Copernican, Galilean, Newtonian. The almanac-makers themselves, as popular educators, helped to disseminate the new astronomical knowledge:

> For two centuries almanac-makers had been popularizing new theories on the size of the universe, translating the huge and incomprehensible figures into more concrete images. Thus, Wing in 1732 was continuing a long tradition when he explained that a cannon ball flung into space and travelling at its maximum velocity would take 700,000 years to reach the nearest of the fixed stars. The prognosticators were undermining their own credibility.

The heavenly bodies were ceasing to have an interest in terrestrial affairs. The moon remained, but her potency was part of immemorial folklore and required no sponsorship from the almanacs. But it was the job of these to calibrate her waxing and waning, to guide the sower of seed, to tell the time to a world without watches.

The almanac-maker, as Dr Capp says, became in the eighteenth century an authority mainly on time. George Fox the Quaker confounded his accusers by appealing to a *Synopsis Anni* or an *Ephemeris* or a *Speculum*. 'They looked at the indictment and their almanacs and saw that they had sworn a whole year false. . .they were in a rage again and stamped.' The indictment was squashed. We may say that the old almanac was fractured into the authoritative manual of facts (like *Whitaker's*), the scandalsheet (like the *Newsother*), the Ingersoll watch, the tradesman's calendar, the blood-and-thunder comic, *Tit-Bits, Pears Cyclopaedia*, the parish magazine, the electioneering pamphlet, Lett's Diary, *Superwoman*, and Foulsham's Dream Book.

Still, Old Moore remains. He sold a million copies in 1898, when people, though the 1870 Education Act had taught them to read penny newspapers, were still happy with the rural superstitious prognostics of their fathers. In 1975 his print order ran to one and three quarter millions. There is still an irrepressible belief around that those shining things out there are tied up with wars, earthquakes, and our loved ones walking out on us.

Thanatic

The Oxford Book of Death, chosen and edited by D. J. Enright

'Solicitous friends' – if Dr Enright may be permitted a personal note – 'feared that the "depressing" nature of the undertaking might prove too much for the compiler's animal spirits. The reverse was the case. Or most of the time, for it must be admitted that certain areas – suicide, the death of children – call for more fortitude than others.' What applies to the undertaker applies also to at least this client: the Enright death book is mostly very heartening and sometimes even hilarious. To look death and its concomitants squarely in the skull is to take away a lot of the nastiness. But, going through the contents, one wonders how squarely it has been possible to look at Henry James's distinguished thing: Graveyards and Funerals; Resurrections and Immortalities; Hereafters; Revenants; War, Plague and Persecution; Epitaphs – these indicate the scope of this thanatanthology. The section entitled 'The Hour of Death' is what it says it is about – the hour rather than the instant, the area around the pinpoint of dissolution. Death itself cannot be dealt with from the inside, though in his *Time Must Have a Stop* Aldous Huxley had a valiant shot at it. And no literature, real or sub or letter to *The Times*, can help with the real trouble about dying, which is fighting for breath and losing, and leaving behind a body which discharges its extrements with abandon and makes death disgusting rather than ennobling.

The death of the world, which we have been expecting since 1945 and, to the disappointment of some, not getting, is not really what death is about, any more than gas-chamber statistics or the counting of battlefield corpses is. Death is highly personal or highly familial. Our knowledge of death is usually given us first by our parents, which is mythically appropriate, since our primal parents are said to have invented it. Cats and dogs die and are buried in the garden, but the death of a father or mother is usually a major event seen at close quarters and highly traumatic. We expect to feel guilty, because we, the children, are being made room for, but we do not expect to feel disgusted. The desperate asthma, the rattle, the rictus are so mechanical and depersonalizing, and the collapse of the excretory system, with its aftermath of a ruined mattress waiting days for the garbage cart, is a sub-Rabelaisian joke in very bad taste.

None of that kind of death here, then. The hour of death can be a pretty long one and also pretty remote, far enough off for Yeats to start studying in a learned school till the time of the wreck of the body and for

Jung to be reasonable about it: 'It is just as neurotic in old age not to focus upon the goal of death as it is in youth to repress fantasies which have to do with the future.' And Leopardi, in his *Dialogue between Frederic Ruysch and his Mummies*, makes Ruysch say: 'Then what is death, if it is not anguish?' and a mummy reply: 'Rather pleasure than otherwise. Know that dying, like falling asleep, is not instantaneous but gradual.' A mummy ought to know all about it, but one is not convinced. 'The feeling I experienced was not very different from the satisfaction produced in men by the languor of sleep.' Only one writer seems to come close to the reality as most of us imagine it, and that is Sir John Betjeman:

> And shall I groan in dying
> As I twist the sweaty sheet?
> Or gasp for breath uncrying
> As I feel my senses drown'd
> While the air is swimming with insects
> And children play in the street.

I do not blame Dr Enright for his avoidance of terminal asthma. It is better to be cheerful if one can and cite Winston Churchill, on his seventy-fifth birthday, saying: 'I am ready to meet my Maker. Whether my Maker is prepared for the ordeal of meeting me is another matter.' Or give us Frances Cornford's 'Epitaph for a Reviewer':

> Whoso maintains that I am humbled now
> (Who wait the Awful Day) is still a liar;
> I hope to meet my Maker brow to brow
> And find my own the higher.

Dr Enright gets the painful stuff over early, following 'The Hour of Death' with 'Suicide'. As I once had an attempted suicide in my family, I have been able to assess the practical utility of some of the great arguments against it, the best of which is probably Vernon Scannell's 'Felo de Se.' 'I want to die. I'll hurt them yet,' says the suicide, placing his head 'Gently, like a pudding in the oven.'

> The lampless darkness roared inside his head,
> Then sighed into a silence in which played
> The grown-up voices, still up late,
> Indifferent to his rage as to his fate.

As for the existentialist view that suicide is the ultimate act of free choice, Cesare Pavese – who eventually nevertheless did the deed – advises putting off the decision, 'feeling (or hoping) that one more day, one more hour of life, might also prove an opportunity of asserting our freedom of choice, which we should lose by seeking death.' But, just to both sides, Dr Enright gives us the most harrowing and articulate suicide note ever, one to which it is hard to supply an answer, written by

Bridget and Richard Smith, failed and debt-ridden bookbinder. The husband and wife not only killed themselves but their two-year-old daughter. The year was 1732, and the style shows it:

> We apprehend the taking of our child's life away to be a circumstance for which we shall be generally condemned; but for our own parts we are perfectly easy on that head. We are satisfied it is less cruelty to take the child with us, even supposing a state of annihilation as some dream of, than to leave her friendless in the world, exposed to ignorance and misery.

The rational tone has a curious resemblance to that of the Declaration of Independence. God, framer of the glorious universe, is expected to be rational, meaning reasonable, meaning humane. Some of us feel that there is nothing beyond God, Old Nobodaddy rather, and the suicide's hell may seem to him a highly just terminus, especially if compounded with infanticide. Hamlet's soliloquy, rightly here and seen rather freshly in this context, is everybody's interior monologue on the theme. The inevitable chunk from *Jude the Obscure* is here too ('Done because we are too menny' – would it be less harrowing if correctly spelt?) and Virginia Woolf's farewell to Leonard. The option remains open, but there is a cheating kind of suicide for which Dr Enright might have looked for illustrations – the kind proposed to Eliot's murderee in the cathedral, for example, and, perhaps not yet recorded in literature, the sacrificial visit to Belfast or New York's subway late at night.

The value of a good anthology, whatever the unifying subject, must be its provision of texts previously unknown to the reader. In the section on mourning, which admits both solemnity and satire, there is a fine passage from a dialogue written by Henry Mayhew, or perhaps merely collected by him, in *The Shops and Companies of London* (1865):

> Lady: . . . . I suppose you have a great variety of half-mourning?
> Shopman: – Oh! infinite – the largest stock in town. Full, and half, and quarter, and half-quarter, shaded off, if I may say so, like an India-ink drawing, from a grief *prononcé* to the slightest *nuance* of regret.

We have also 'Graveyards and Funerals' but, regrettably, no wakes, unless Jilly Cooper may be regarded as providing one with the crates of Australian Burgundy discovered under the stairs after her grandmother-in-law's funeral. 'A rip-roaring party ensued and soon a lower middle busybody . . . came bustling over to see if anything was wrong. Whereupon my father-in-law, holding a glass and seeing her coming up the path, uttered the immortal line: "Who is this intruding on our grief?" '

And perhaps there is not quite enough of the death taboo which has replaced the sex one and is dealt with so fully in Philippe Ariès's *The Hour of Our Death*. There are passages from Jessica Mitford's *The American Way of Death* and a brief paragraph from Evelyn Waugh's essay 'Half in Love with Easeful Death', but nothing from *The Loved One*, the only genuine piece of thanatographic fiction we have. The section on animal deaths could have profited from an extract from it dealing with The Happier Hunting Ground. The buglers blowing taps over a canary's grave are better than Brautigan's discovery in a pets' cemetery in San Francisco – 'Here Lies Tweeter/ Wrapped in Silk/ The Little Bird/ Drowned in a/ Glass of Milk' – and probably not less genuine. Dogs do sentimentally best here, but Hal Summers's poem 'My Old Cat' is the most moving, with the creature meeting death in pure hate: 'Well died, my old cat.' Philip Larkin's 'Take One Home for the Kiddies', with its final 'Mam, we're playing funerals now', is revealed as a small classic on a par with Ralph Hodgson's 'Stupidity Street' which, like the one about ringing the bells of heaven and wretched blind pit ponies and little hunted hares, does not bear too grave or Gravesian a scrutiny but one would not be without.

The section about death and children could have been painful, but Dr Enright wisely extends his brief beyond the expected and deals with what children think about death, quoting, for instance, Freud: 'I was astonished to hear a highly intelligent boy of ten remark after the sudden death of his father: "I know father's dead, but what I can't understand is why he doesn't come home to supper." ' There is also John Crowe Ransom's fine poem 'Janet Waking', which dares sentimentality and achieves high dignity. Dickens is not allowed much of a look in: he gets away with a brief visit to the cemetery in *The Old Curiosity Shop* and no more. 'Every time an earth mother smiles over the birth of a child, a spirit mother weeps over the loss of a child.' If that were J. M. Barrie we would be nauseated; it happens to be an Ashanti saying so must be all right.

Dr Enright saves the larger hilarity for the end with 'Epitaphs, Requiems and Last Words'. Nigel Dennis, in an *Encounter* article (November 1961), was very doubtful about the authenticity of famous last words, what with Rabelais being credited with five utterances and Heine with three, all too good to be true. A doctor apparently told Mr Dennis that he had attended five hundred deathbeds without hearing any memorable final line. Most patients confront their Maker doped, anyway, drawing from Mr Dennis the comment 'Just as the pneumatic tyre has driven the straw from the street of the dying, so has the hypodermic silenced the householder.' However, James Thurber is here saying 'God bless . . . God damn', and Ralph Vaughan Williams with his '. . . in the next world I shan't be doing music, with all the striving and disappointments. I shall be being it.' He said this a fortnight before his death, but it is too good to leave out. Of the epitaphs, most are very well known but none could properly be omitted. What is omitted is the pseudo-Homeric one on Margites – 'Him the gods had made neither a digger nor a ploughman nor otherwise wise in aught, for he failed in every art.' I would like this for myself. While I am being personal I may as well offer my father's dying words, which I heard clearly: 'Bugger the priest. Give me a pint of draught Bass.'

Much work has gone into this compilation, and the individual introductions to the component sections are, as we would expect, elegant, modest and very wise. Death is a difficult subject because it is a negation. 'To talk at all interestingly about death,' says the compiler, 'is inevitably to talk about life.' True, because death is the limit of life which defines what life may contain. And what brings death about is contained in life, indeed may be regarded as life itself. The antonym of death is not life but birth, and I wonder whether an *Oxford Book of Birth* will ever appear. I should imagine it would be slim and highly sentimental.

There are two final points to make, neither of them relevant to the other except in so far as they relate to this anthology. One is that, after Shakespeare, Dr Johnson is the most cited author, as he is, without that qualification, in John Gross's recently published *Oxford Book of Aphorisms*. Johnson's approach to death comes closest to that of the average man who was brought up in a faith with an eschatology – sensible about the uselessness of grief, for example, and occasionally hysterical about the judgement (the hysteria, one might suggest, of the guilty masturbator). The other point is that death is becoming, as it rarely was in the past, a thing to worry about in terms of finance. There is an interesting *Times* correspondence here about the cost of coffins, which is perpetually rising, the necessity of buying one well in advance of likely use, and the difficulty of hoarding one in a small flat (one correspondent suggests using it as a cocktail cabinet or, better, buying a grandfather clock instead). People are also frightened of dying these days because of the financial mess their relicts are likely to be in. For the first time in history one has to worry whether one can afford death as one can afford a new refrigerator.

Celebrations

The Book of Days, by Anthony Frewin

This is not the kind of book you can borrow from the library. I think you are supposed to have it on your desk along with the *Concise Oxford Dictionary*. Every page has a date, and under the date is the basic information of the Church Calendar, followed by certain anniversaries of a secular nature. Thus under 29 February we learn not only that St Oswald of Worcester had, in the 1930s, his feast predated to the 28th, but that Leap Year Day was the day of Disraeli's first ministry, the cutting of the St Gothard Tunnel, and the proclamation of the Islamic Republic in Pakistan. Ann Lee, founder of the Shakers, was a leap-year baby, as were Rossini, and the film director William A. Wellman. The novelist E. F. Benson died on the bisextile day along with (much earlier of course) Archbishop Whitgift. Now you know what the book is about; what it is for is a more difficult question.

Confining his anniversaries as he does – one page one day – Mr Frewin has had to exercise great restraint in the presentation of events and to make value judgements of a strongly idiosyncratic nature. He is not going to have the great world outside tell him what is important and what is not; he will make up his own mind about that. On 5 January Charles the Bold was killed by the Swiss at Nancy. Bishop Colenso was excommunicated for his heretical study of the Pentateuch. Pope Paul VI met Athenagoras I in Jerusalem. I think the great world is stepping in a bit there: telephone Mr Frewin at once and ask him how important he thinks the excommunication of Colenso was. For that matter, ask him if he knows what *The Pentateuch* (whose title he italicizes in the manner of a novel) is. But here is, without doubt, Mr Frewin himself: 'Billie Holiday records *When You're Smiling (The Whole World Smiles With You)* with Teddy Wilson and his Orchestra in New York, 1938.' World-shattering, never to be forgotten. On 15 January 1929 we are impelled to note that Luis Russell and his Burning Eight (with Louis Metcalf, Charlie Holmes, etc.) recorded 'Savoy Shout' and 'Call of the Freaks'. I never knew that. Mr Russell is sandwiched between the 1877 collapse of the Dover–Folkestone railway tunnel and the US victory at Guadalcanal.

I have been desperately trying to find a pattern in the fact that Benedict Arnold, Fantin-Latour, Pierre Loti, Schweitzer, Hal Roach, Cecil Beaton and Joseph Losey share a birthday. Mr Trewin neglects to inform us what heavenly bodies rule on 14 January and I am too lazy to find out. Are treachery and artistic talent zodiacally connected? Never mind. Having discovered these anagraphical facts, what am I supposed to do with them? Make lithographs of Icelandic fishermen while thinking of the historical Jesus and watching the Keystone Cops? Again, never mind.

If I were to take this book seriously I could be angry and affirm that the first nights of *Le Sacre du Printemps* and *Salome* were at least as important as the recording of 'Echoes of Harlem' by Cootie Williams and his Rug Cutters. Or protest that Ford Madox Ford didn't have two ds to his middle name, that Anthony Powell was not born in 1808, and that James Joyce did not write *Finnegan's Wake*. But there is no point in getting bad-tempered at a nullity. For a nullity is what this book is, despite the admirable job that printer, binder and illustrator have done on it. Why then review it? As a protest. There are far too many of these well-made nullities about, nonbooks pretending to be books. By their qualities as physical artefacts ye may know them. They are usually triumphs of the bookmaker's craft, and their beauty as mindless *objets d'art* is their only justification. Dr Johnson, patron saint of lovers of real books, tore the heart out of his tomes and to hell with the typography and the binding. Santayana broke his books into their constituent signatures and, when he finished one, threw it into the *poubelle*. But books like *The Book of Days* are articles of furniture, like the duller bestsellers. Unread, they stay in the house like Chinese ginger vases.

Consider the books that many people buy – cookery manuals that rehash other cookery manuals; photograph folios of the beauty of New York black males; sexual postures that everybody has tried already; the book of *Saturday Night Fever*; Garbo in backview; the Queen's corgis; the Queen's horses; British country seats; derelicts of Roscommon. Consider the number of reprints that publishing skill (Mr Frewin is himself a publisher's editor) should be working at. Consider *The Book of Days*.

On the other hand, there is a genuine need for mindless works of chronology. Arnold Bennett used to give his fellow-writers copies of a work long disappeared, of inestimable value to the historical novelist. It tabulated the years and showed what was happening in any given country at any given time. The chronological table in *Pears Cyclopaedia* comes close to that, but it isn't nearly detailed enough. It's years we want, not days. Finally, if you want to expend £7.50 on reading matter try and find an old copy of the great Chambers's *Book of Days*. Mr Frewin rather despises it because of its discursiveness. It gives too much information. It was produced in those innocent days when books were meant to be read.

Baal on the Coast

Moving Pictures: Memories of a Hollywood Prince, by Budd Schulberg

Mr Schulberg appositely if blasphemously labels the parts of his opus Genesis, Exodus, The Promised Land and Kings. The Jewish creators of the American film industry, fleeing the Cossacks, went to New York as small furriers, rag-pickers, consumptive tailors, but were fired by a vision that escaped the Gentile manipulators of the penny arcade bioscope. After the discovery that stories could be told on celluloid, the Zukors and Mayers and Goldfish and Laskys and Schulbergs made the long desert journey west. In California they built temples to a god who was a Baal to their synagogue-going parents. They developed power and wealth and slept with handmaidens; they also conceived a kind of guilt which could best be expiated by gambling lavishly and ineptly. One of the guilty kings was B. P. Schulberg, a literate not to say literary man who reached his royal peak as production chief of Paramount. His son tells the family story. It is a thrilling and depressing one and it covers the years from *The Life of an American Fireman* (eight-jerky minutes of seminal narrative) to, very nearly, *Gone With The Wind*. Budd, a stammering kid with a gift for writing whom Hollywood permissiveness made as puritanical as all hell, ends by going to Dartmouth. His best novel (he has not written many) is about a return to Dartmouth with a film team and a thinly disguised Scott Fitzgerald, who had been hired to write *Love On Ice*. We know that he inherited, if not a crown, some of the family jewels. Perhaps he may tell the rest of the chronicle in another volume.

Readers in search of the lowdown on the stars under contract to B. P. (as he is consistently termed) may be disappointed. Much depends on how old these readers are. I am four years younger than Budd and have seen Clara Bow the It Girl (so named by Elinor Glyn herself) as well as George Bancroft the first sympathetic gangster (a daring creation of B. P.'s). Clara Bow was naturally flirtatious because she had nothing to talk about, and when she did talk it was a Brooklyn whine that could not survive the talkies. Worn out at thirty with drink, she is the female counterpart to Bancroft, one of the stupidest men who ever lived, a pioneer soon overtaken by clever men like Edward G. Robinson, Cagney and Bogart. The young Budd saw wealth which its beneficiaries lacked the taste and education to handle; he saw stars shoot to earth like Lucifer or Cardinal Wolsey; at the same time he saw, because his father saw it first, the possibilities of an art too much treated as an industry, possibilities still to be realized.

Eisenstein came to Hollywood, but no work could be found for him.

Erich von Stroheim, who thought in terms of forty-reel epics (the *Greed* we know is a mere rump of the original concept) had to become a frustrated actor. Marcel DeSano finished *The Girl Who Wouldn't Work* in six days and $20,000 under schedule through cutting the film in his head during the shooting, but he was scared of following up his own success and committed suicide. B. P., who dared to bring such men in, was lucky enough to combine the artist's vision with the toughness of the mere magnate: at the end of the book he has survived the foul ignorance of the finance men and innumerable knives in the back, but the end of the book is not the end of the story. The great sin of Hollywood was not the worship of Mammon; it was the unwillingness to see what film was really about.

Perhaps Budd's neurosis, expressed in his stammer, was the result of his knowing the sordor behind the glamour and yet possessing a child's willingness to be taken in by the glamour. Mary Pickford was an acquisitive little bitch worthy of her mother but still the World's Sweetheart. Fredric March was an actor of high intelligence but he could not leave young flesh alone. Bancroft, who used the word facsimile in every sentence with every meaning but the right one, took truckloads of bootleg scotch on his trip to London but was formidable on screen. Marlene Dietrich brought lesbianism to Los Angeles but glossed it as European sex. Budd saw with sorrow his own father corrupted by the charms of Sylvia Sidney. Zeppo Marx seems to have been the least demented of the colony: frustrated in film, he took to winning at high-stake poker (B. P. lost hundreds of thousands to him). And while Budd saw the millions coming in and was served Cokes by the butler, he brooded on the wrongs done to Mexicans and blacks as well as, outside Hollywood, to the Jews. He became, we may take it, the high-minded young hero of *The Disenchanted*.

On the whole, and despite B. P.'s dalliance, he seems to have been lucky in his parents. His mother was unpossessive and given to causes, none of the ravening *Iss, iss, mein Kind* murderess celebrated in the tale of Alexander Portnoy. The house was crammed with books, many of which both parents had read. B. P., who had started off as a publicity writer and scenarist, knew what made a script good. His son heard him on *Dr Jekyll and Mr Hyde*:

> Don't change Stevenson just for the fun of rewriting him. You can kill a classic with 'improvements.' A big, sprawling novel, say *Bleak House*, you have to pare down to a continuity that will hold an audience for ninety or a hundred minutes. But remember, *Jekyll and Hyde* already has a continuity. We don't have to waste time hammering out a story line. What you have to do is visualize it, think of every scene as the camera will see it and not as you – or Stevenson – would describe it in prose.

Wise words, and Budd seems to have taken them to heart. He has written fine films – including *A Face in the Crowd* (which I have just been re-seeing – in Italian, to little loss), *Across the Everglades* and *On the Water-*

front. Behind his own success as a writer of both books and scripts is the intelligence and strength of will of a pair of formidable Latvian Jewish exiles. Like most Hollywood marriages, the Schulberg one could not last, but the storms premonitory of its breakdown were a kind of lateral electrical charge which fired creation, not self-destruction.

This book can be taken as almost the definitive Hollywood family chronicle. It is, alas, not all that well written: it does not proclaim the devotion to Henry James and Fitzgerald that irradiates parts of *The Disenchanted*. Since he is not obliged to convert reminiscence to literature, Schulberg permits slackness and slanginess, as though acknowledging that the illiterate aficionados of old Hollywood have a right of entry here. He himself is rather the artist as a young bore, but he is surrounded by personages too fantastic to be boring. His flyleaves are decorated by autograph-album entries in the large unlettered scrawl of the stars. 'Follow your dad!' says Adolphe Menjou and, cries Ricardo Cortes, 'Never forget you're a Schulberg.' At a grandfather's age, Budd has at last done something about getting his dad out of his system.

Shmuck

Adventures in the Screen Trade, by William Goldman

Steve McQueen was prepared to appear in Richard Attenborough's *A Bridge Too Far* for three million dollars (three weeks' work) plus the peanuts of a few grand for his entourage and a few more grand for the Palm Springs hovel he couldn't dispose of on the open market. Sylvester Stallone got ten million to write, direct and star in *Rocky III*. Few movies do more than bankrupt their makers these days, but the rewards remain exorbitant. However, there's no real need for envy. When stars don't kill themselves they are ruined by tax and alimony, rarely use their yachts, and drink mostly Perrier water. Universal turned down *Star Wars* and lost a billion. So what? Easy come, easy go. You can't take it with you. Those noughts are only eggs for juggling with. As Goldman, respected scenarist of *All the President's Men, Butch Cassidy and the Sundance Kid* and *Marathon Man*, tells us, 'a million dollars is what you pay a star you don't want'.

Screenwriters are still what Sam Goldwyn called them – 'shmucks with Remingtons' (read word processors now) – but their fees reflect the spendthrift madness of a business that doesn't understand business. Any cash I have in the bank was made not from my primary trade of novelizing but from writing scripts for films that were never made and, so it always seemed at the time of signing the book-length contract, never had any chance of being made. I am just emerging at this moment from the situation of typing a second draft (the first draft is never satisfactory on principle, but it is often identical with the twelfth draft) in a state of mechanical hopelessness. One occasionally has hopes, less occasionally the hopes are fulfilled, but nine tenths of the screenplays written are doomed never to reach the floor. Goldman's book is mostly about this hopelessness, which is a dead sea fruit of other people's megalomania and stupidity. The screen trade is a desperate one.

The sincerity of Goldman's wrath and disgust is never in doubt, but he had no right to expend those emotions in a book so ill-composed that it is an insult to the reader. Damn it, Goldman's enemies lie anywhere but in Brentano's on Sunset Boulevard or in Smith's at Charing Cross. It is a freshman composition in which sometimes the shift key is depressed and, for no special reason except possibly the blindness of the sweat of anger, left so, the word *shit* is the major pejorative, and slack slang dribbles like unwiped mucus. Yet Goldman considers himself to be primarily a novelist who got into screenwriting for the bread and then went into a phase of believing that you could carry a script, without spilling a drop, straight from typewriter to screen. After all, there had been a time when stars were firable and directors merely brothers-in-law, and the producer would, with the respect for the written word of the Central European illiterate, demand that so many pages (repeat pages) be into the can by noon.

Now however director and stars, sometimes one and the same person, regard the screenplay as a thing they could have done better themselves had they had the time. Goldman is right when he says that everybody is silent about what they're *really* getting from the discardable hack – not words but a structure. Perhaps the big men don't even know the concept, let alone the word. Goldman may be a lousy wordman but he has the structural gift, a rare commodity. Of the films of his I have mentioned, we remember few lines but we do recall a shape.

He has been lucky with one of his directors – George Roy Hill, who studied under Hindemith at Harvard and wrote his master's thesis on the music in *Finnegans Wake*. Intelligent as well as an intellectual, Hill could give charmingly cogent reasons for this or that change – like the excision of what seems on the surface an admirable opening to *Waldo*

Pepper: kids dreaming of flying. The *Butch Cassidy* script had a firm enough form to encourage Hill's own innovations – the interlude of a catchy song by Bert Bacharach and a final freeze which is lapidary, monumental and mythicizing. With Robert Redford – who had, till recently, literally the first and last word on any Hollywood project – Goldman was not so fortunate.

He describes the job he did on *All the President's Men* – a worthy and painstaking effort with no distortion of historical fact for the sake of the cinematic *frisson*. Nobody, one thinks, could have done the thing better. But then the wife of Bernstein, one of the two *Washington Post* reporters who put the bomb under the Watergate scandal, herself wrote a script – altogether fanciful, glorifying her husband's sexual prowess, a gross falsification of fact – which Redford, who was producing, preferred to Goldman's own. Redford, like Mrs Bernstein, missed the whole point of the project, which was the telling of certain shocking truths. Here one forgives Goldman's spluttering inarticulate despair: words literally fail him.

Only two personages emerge from the story with large credit, and they are both British. Goldman's praise of Olivier, ill, stoic, heroic in *Marathon Man*, put upon by Dustin Hoffman in endless rehearsal which disclosed both the state of Olivier's physical decay and Hoffman's own fear of his co-star, is a testimony to British professionalism matched by the long account of Attenborough's comparable heroism in his direction of *A Bridge Too Far*. Not even Redford, who took over from McQueen, could impair the gentlemanly patience of one who, while the film was being made, wept with joy at being appointed a trustee of the Tate and thought the knighthood was probably a practical joke. In contrast to these two ennobled perfectionists, the snarling, whining, pampered, analphabetic humanoids of Hollywood emerge as garbage irrelevantly gilded with adventitious photogeneity.

Why, then, work with them? The fascination of what's difficult, the bad-tooth-biting masochism of wanting to see just how far ingratitude can go. And, of course, that mad hope of being the basic creator of a great work of art. It sustains even myself, who have had my own share of suffering. I have been engaged in projects which not even Goldman, with all his proven expertise, could encompass and could, if there were space, a tale unfold which would harrow even his middle-aged blood. I read his book, gulped it rather, with deep fellow-feeling, but I regret that he has so little respect for his reading public that it satisfies him to retail, in hard covers, a mere snarl of jottings. It is not the Hollywood iron that has entered his soul but the Hollywood muckheap.

No Visceral Relish

Genre: The Musical, edited by Rick Altman

In the field of the film musical (*genre* they say here, forbidding and, as it turns out, ominous) I can claim at least a failed though not easily forgettable creative participation. In 1967 I was summoned to Hollywood by Warner Brothers to write the script and lyrics for a musical on the life of William Shakespeare. The producer was William Conrad, the bulky private eye of *Cannon*, and the director was to be Joseph L. Mankiewicz. Those were the days of the hard-ticket movie, and *The Bawdy Bard* (a misleading title soon changed, on my insistence, to *Will!*) was projected as a four-hour extravaganza with an all-star cast. Robert Stephens was to play the lead and Maggie Smith Mistress Hathaway. For the rest, there was a clear and unanimous choice only for Ben Jonson – 'Peter Ustinov, because he *looks* like Ben Jahnson'. I wrote script and lyrics and, while my hand was in, also the music, which survives in a studio recording, but the film was never made. Warner Brothers changed hands and scrapped all existing projects, but *Will!* still haunts the bardophile faubourgs of Hollywood as one of the great impossible dreams. It could have worked. I dream of it regularly in 70-mm Technicolor. Reading this collection of highly intellectual essays on the film musical, I wonder how it would have fitted into the various sociostructural taxonomies.

While conceding that the form is primarily intended to entertain, these cinematic philosophers are concerned overwhelmingly with a *Cahiers* approach, as the titles of the essays indicate. Thus, Robin Wood gives us 'Art and Ideology: Notes on *Silk Stockings*'; Jim Collins 'Towards Defining a Matrix of the Musical Comedy: The Place of the Spectator within the Textual Mechanisms'; Rick Altman 'The American Film Musical: Paradigmatic Structure and Mediatory Function'. Professor Altman teaches French and Comparative Literature at the University of Iowa and is Director of the Inter-University Centre for Film Studies in Paris. He deals in the higher cinematics. From the pages he edits here only the subdued joy of achieved analysis within the cadre of political and structuralist concern suggests that there may well be pleasure to be obtained from the genre. Certainly there is no visceral relish.

Let us, with Mark Roth, look at some Warners musicals of the thirties and see how far they exemplify, or fail to, the spirit of the New Deal. In *42nd Street*, Warner Baxter ('. . . You're going to dance your feet off . . . . It's going to be the toughest six weeks you ever lived through. . . . Not one of you leaves the stage tonight until I get what I want') represents a traditional view of authority charged with a Calvinistic work ethos. Baxter gives orders but is removed from the actual techniques of production. It has to be left to James Cagney, in *Footlight Parade*, to demonstrate the new collectivist spirit. Cagney, like Baxter, plays a producer, but a producer who is also a hoofer and can step into the show when the leading man is too drunk to perform. Here, we are told, is the spirit of the New Deal, with the collectivist added to the Calvinistic. *42nd Street* ends with the weary Baxter, cynical and alone, saying 'Just another show.' Things are as they have always been, 'an alternation of success and failure, boom and bust for eternity'. But *Footlight Parade* ends on stage with the Busby Berkeley production number 'Shanghai Lil', a huge bar fight ending in order and tranquillity, drills, the American flag, even a portrait of Roosevelt. Whether this is a better ending than the other seems not to be the point: social significance is easier to demonstrate than the values of art.

One cannot discuss the great age of the musical without lavish references to Busby Berkeley. He was bound to come in for some hard knocks as an exploiter of female beauty in an age when the eye has become an instrument of rape, and Lucy Fischer has much to say about an exploitative philosophy summed up in Berkeley's 'I love beautiful girls and I love to gather and show many beautiful girls with regular features and well-made bodies.' She concentrates on the crudely titled *Dames*, which versifies the Berkeley creed in a song of Dick Powell's:

Who cares if there's a plot or not, if it's got a lot of dames?
What do you go for? Go to see the show for?
Tell the truth – you go to see those beautiful dames.

It is very grim stuff. 'What we see on the screen is a shot of the Berkeley harem arranged in pyramidal fashion against a complex decor. Imperceptively, the image of the actual women transmutes to that of a photographic representation. And in a parody of sexual entry, the number ends with Powell's head breaking through the image surface.' In what I would take to be a harmless little sequence – Joan Blondell in 'The Girl at the Ironing Board' – we are told that she is ' "gang-raped" by a mass of laundry which slides down upon her', and that the 'overwhelmingly male syndrome' of clothes fetishism (Kinsey, 1953) is imposed unusually (though 'significantly') on a female persona. Nobody saw this in 1934, naturally, but, by God, we see it now.

We come now to the divine Cyd Charisse who, in *The Band Wagon*, according to Dennis Giles, represents 'the mother who possesses a phallus' to the lost little boy who is Fred Astaire. He has lost his star status, but she is secure in hers. Her legs are powerful, and these 'and her mastery of the show-at-hand all tend to lend her virility in the eyes of the fragile, disconsolate Astaire.' Mercifully, however, she retracts her phallus. Astaire metaphorically kills the father–director of the show and Charisse's own lover and 'Charisse deprives herself of her parental status by suffering auto-castration'. We are ready for the show to go on for an indefinite run, meaning erotism without end; 'That's entertainment,' goes the song, and love is part of it. In *Silk Stockings* Cyd Charisse is in the service not of Freud but of Marx, though Robin Wood admits that 'the film's creative vitality cannot reasonably be reduced to its ideological contradictions.' Still, there is a fair attempt at such a reduction. Mr Wood prefers *Silk Stockings* to the Garbo vehicle *Ninotchka* on which it is based because 'Cyd Charisse's discovery, through dance, of her individual physical existence opposes itself to both the state-determined automatism of the film's Communism and the woman-object of its Capitalism.'

The most massive piece of dissection and exegesis comes in Raymond Bellour's 'Segmenting/Analysing', which takes *Gigi* (perhaps a suitable subject since it has a Parisian setting) and splits it into segments, supra-segments, subsegments and syntagma in the service of a demonstration of the aim of the *sous-texte*, which is the resolution of an Oedipal situation. It is beautifully done, but was it worth doing? The assumption, throughout this collection, is that so flimsy a structure as a film musical can bear the weight of all this analysis in depth. The makers of those delectable and brilliantly carpentered entertainments are seen, in the French manner, as the spoken and sung rather than as the speaking and singing, as the instruments of archetype and *Zeitgeist*. We are being told here to use them as indices of Freudian, Marxist and Lévi-Straussian truth, but, in the process, the dancers' legs become paralysed and the pretty little tunes are distorted.

Dante as Rhyme and Rhythm

The Divine Comedy of Dante, translated and introduced by Kenneth Mackenzie, with 111 engravings by John Flaxman

For an English translator of Dante, the agonizing question must be whether to rhyme or not. And the decision to rhyme means the reproducing of the original *terza rima*, since rhymed couplets will sound like bad Pope or Wordsworth's *Ode to Duty*, and alternating rhymes will sound as though the unit is the heroic stanza, not the canto. We ought to remember that *The Divine Comedy*, being written in one Italian dialect, that of Florence, can be translated into others, and Porta did a version in the Milanese dialect which avoided *terza rima*. The opening –

> *Nel mezzo del cammin di nostra vita*
> *Mi ritrovai per una selva oscura*
> *Che la diritta via era smarrita –*

became

> *A mitaa strada de quel gran viacc*
> *Che femm a vun la voeulta al mondo da là*
> *Me sont trovaa in d'on bosch scur scur affac,*
> *Senza on sentee de podé seguitá*

The fact is that *terza rima* strikes the Italian ear with less force than it does the anglophone: the Dantesque music lies in the middle of lines, not at the end. Italian in all its dialects has a multitude of like endings, and prose itself is full of disregarded rhymes. Joyce, in *Finnegans Wake*, mocked the *-azione* endings of bureaucratic Italian in the drone of the twelve old men who say things like 'Our examination round his factification for incamination. . . .'

Rhyme in English is so difficult that it is mostly merely approximated by pop lyricists. Because Symes, in *Nineteen Eighty-Four*, can find only one fitting rhyme for *rod* in his Newspeak version of Kipling, he is sent to Room 101. English rhyme, especially when triple or quadruple, always seems to be a *tour de force*. It sticks out. Yeats and Wilfred Owen felt they had to muffle it into slant-rhyme or assonance – life/waif; progress/tigress. It has always seemed to me that Owen had the most Dantesque movement of all twentieth-century poets: he could present with immense controlled authority true visions of purgatory and hell. Had Owen lived, he might have been the best of all candidates for the translation of Dante, slant-rhyme not seeming eccentric in him. After Owen, T. S. Eliot comes closest to Dante, as in the following from 'Little Gidding':

> In the uncertain hour before the morning
>   Near the ending of interminable night
> At the recurring end of the unending
>   After the dark dove with the flickering tongue
> Had passed below the horizon of his homing. . . .

He substitutes for rhyme an alternation of masculine and feminine endings. This gives a double movement, not triple, and hence only corresponds to Dante in the most general sense of obeying a consistent pattern. The Dantesque atmosphere belongs to a rhythmical gravity of a kind which few English poets have been able to attain. Compared with Dante, even Milton and Shakespeare are eccentric.

I have, I think, read all the rhymed English versions of the *Divine Comedy* – John Ciardi's and Dorothy L. Sayers's are probably the best – but I have preferred, like most anglophones who have done Latin at school, to take him in the original with a crib on the side – specifically in the fine Temple Classics edition. One of the excellences of the new blank verse translation by Kenneth Mackenzie lies in its total literalness: it is a poem, but it is also a crib:

> Midway upon the journey of our life
> I found that I had strayed into a wood
> So dark the right road was completely lost.

Here, in the first line, we see demonstrated the impossibility of conveying Dante's meaning and movement in English rhyme. For that line *must* end with *life*, as the original ends with *vita*, and there is just no appropriate rhyme (or even slant-rhyme) available.

Kenneth Mackenzie is known only, I believe, for his Everyman translation of *Pan Tadeusz*. On the evidence of his large skill, he seemed to the editorial director of the Folio Society the right man for a new Dante. He has spent ten years on his task. He was, until retirement, a Clerk to the House of Commons. I like, in my romantic way, to imagine him living with the reality of Dante while surrounded by those wraiths called politicians and their aneschatological enactments.

I have said that Mackenzie's *Divine Comedy* is a poem, but this does not necessarily mean that Mackenzie is a poet. If he were, he might get in the way of his great original, and his function is to sustain a consistent transparency. He is a very competent versifier (we perhaps need versifiers these days more than we need poets), and he manages a blank verse that is very regular, its iambs always resistant to inversion. There is not one line that echoes 'Tomorrow and tomorrow and tomorrow' or 'Never, never, never, never, never'. His is the blank verse of some minor post-Wordsworthian or, in our own age, the Auden (or was it the

Isherwood?) who composed the soliloquies of *The Ascent of F6*. The idiom is neutral:

> 'O poet,' I began, 'who are my guide',
> Consider if my powers be strong enough,
> Before you trust me to the deep descent.
> You tell how in the flesh Aeneas went,
> While still a mortal, to the immortal world.
> But, that the Adversary of all ill
> Should have conceded him this privilege,
> Seems fitting to an understanding mind,
> Considering the high effect that was
> To spring from him, and who and what he was. . . .'

You will note in the above extract from Canto Two one example of a non-functional, or unintended, or undesirable but unavoidable rhyme, and one example of a couplet with identical line endings. As long ago as John Dryden it was accepted that to avoid occasional rhyme in blank verse was an intolerable artificiality. There has never been any prosodic rule about contiguous identical line ending. In Elizabethan blank verse the device of word repetition deliberately evoked Seneca. Here Mackenzie is not as clumsy as it would appear: the first *was* has schwa in it, the second a full low vowel. Read him aloud and you will find he reads well. His big test comes at the end of the *Paradiso*, and I think he passes it:

> And here the power of heavenly vision failed;
> But now all my desire and all my will
> Like a smooth-running wheel was moved by love,
> The Love that moves the sun and all the stars.

A novelty of this publication is the use of, as canto headings, the engravings made by John Flaxman for a previous, unrealized version of Dante. They are terribly inferior to Blake's Dante engravings, being mild, their sufferings the mere exasperation of a wet Sunday, the raging beasts harmless, and the major concern of the tortured souls the hiding of their genitals when clouds or stipple don't do this for them. They indicate, I suppose, what Dante has mostly meant to the British Protestant middle class – an author undoubtedly important, though foreign, dramatizing an eternity all right for superstitious Papists but mere nasty outmoded myth for children of the Reform. Mackenzie knows what Dante is about. His notes and introduction are admirable. He stresses the importance of the *liberum arbitrium*, how men and women must choose to be destroyed or purged and liberated. And his translation is a translation to buy. The book is beautifully made, and it is far from dear at the price.

Mr Mackenzie would be the last man in the world to absolve us from the reading of Dante in the original. That is a primary duty for all *literati*, and it probably antecedes the duty to read Shakespeare and Milton. This new translation is a valuable crutch for the stumbler and it will give even those xenophobes who set their teeth against the learning of Italian grammar a very fair idea indeed of what Dante is like.

Whan That, Etc.

The Life and Times of Chaucer, by John Gardner

We do not in Britain go in much for scholar–novelists, and when we get them – Iris Murdoch and J.I.M. Stewart, for instance – we find the métiers kept rather sternly apart. True, Stewart's scholarship becomes Michael Innes's pedantry, but you would never dream, reading Stewart on Conrad or Lawrence, that this professor knew the craft of fiction from the inside. Americans are different. John Gardner has been teaching medieval literature for twenty years and making a big name as a novelist in tandem, not on the pseudonymous margin. Though writing about Chaucer as a scholar, he exults in the possession of artistic insights which British academia, probably, would regard as indecently pushy. For instance, he finds Chaucer's later work clumsy, but deliberately so, and speaks of the Manciple 'babbling lines that might serve as a model of art so bad that, finally, it's good.' A sort of novelist myself, I see what Gardner is getting at. He, like me, must have been reviled at times for writing clumsy English and fretted at the code which forbids answering back and saying that the clumsiness was the product of very hard work.

Gardner is speaking very much as a post-Joycean novelist when he talks of Chaucer's 'unreliable narrators'. If there was to be a literary contest among the Canterbury pilgrims, 'someone, after all, had to lose miserably'. But the courage to create miserable losers – in other words, not to give a damn if someone in one's courtly audience finds one's regular expertise lacking – is only given to the very mature (or, to the stupid, decrepit). Chaucer could not have written the *Tale of Melibeus* in his early days, when it was essential to be brilliant all the time. As for the *Physician's Tale*, in which 'Chaucer carefully removes every feature of motivation in his source (a great work by Livy), introduces confusion and plot inconsistency, ghastly padding to fill out lines, and so on.' Gardner thinks the bad-art point would have been made by Chaucer's reading it aloud very priggishly: 'his courtly audience must have been left in stitches'. When people understand that huge chunks of *Ulysses* – and of Kubrick's *Space Odyssey* – are meant to be boring, they may be able to accept the *Manciple's Tale*.

As a novelist, Gardner is surely in order when he presents the infant Geoffrey trying to sort out his *Gestalten*, beginning to

find the world predictable, this morning the same as all other mornings ('For the whichë,' his mother said, 'thankëd be God!'). His ears grew attentive: the sad, ghostly cry of the conch-shell horns on the merchant

253

ships; the lapping of the water; the clean, hard echoes from the wharves of stone. His nose grew attentive: his big stepbrother's funny smell, the fierce, slightly frightening animal smells of his father and uncle Tom, the smell of his mother, as wide and sweet and otherworldly as a meadow. He slept again. . . .

Enough, or too much? I see no harm in it. I would go further and say that this kind of colour is essential if anything like a book is to be made of Chaucer's life. When biographical materials are so scanty, as with Shakespeare even more than Chaucer (Chaucer is our Bach, says Gardner, and Shakespeare our Beethoven: I'm not too happy about that), only a novelist – with his vocational intuition about all people laughing when they're tickled – can be trusted to make something out of little. And as much of the 'times' is made up of Black Prince, Black Death, Lollards, Peasants' Revolt, the only way in which the biographer can sound like something more than a rehash of Warner and Martin is to make soldiers sneeze in the rain and John of Gaunt grow pale when he discovers there is a bubonic rat in the palace.

A character emerges, certainly, and if Chaucer was not really like that, does it matter much? The Gardner Chaucer squares with the poems and is tougher, more learned, more subtle than the plump smiler whom once, untypically, Aldous Huxley berated for not being like Langland, crying 'aloud in anger, threatening the world with hell-fire . . .'. And Professor Coulton said: 'Where Gower sees an England more hopelessly given over to the Devil than even in Carlyle's most dyspeptic nightmares – where the robuster Langland sees an impending religious Armageddon . . . there Chaucer, with incurable optimism, sees chiefly a Merry England' – Merry England being what Jim Dixon cries out on and optimism a disease. But the Gardner Chaucer is not Panglossianly optimistic: he sees that society will survive only on certain conditions and he believes that, in the long run, these conditions will be fulfilled. If Langland sees a field full of folk, Chaucer scrutinizes people of all social stations and evidently cares about them. And the author of the *Pardoner's Tale* was not smiling much.

For whom is this learned, lively, chatty book intended? For an American audience primarily. Medieval pounds are translated into contemporary dollars (£10 = $2400), Middle English pronunciation is presented in terms of the Cisco Kid: 'Boot hombray, thees ees nut yoor peesstol', fourteenth-century London is slightly larger than Muskogee, Oklahoma, and England itself – Chaucerian or Betjemanian – smaller than Florida or Georgia. Americans scared of unhygienic modern Europe must be expected to be horrified at the thought of visiting, even in a book, medieval England, but – though 'trash collection was a problem' – everything smelled fine, and London was 'small and white and clean' (William Morris's words – the poet, not the theatrical agent). There is something American in the debased Kelmscott illustrations – Gardner and Wolf the artist windowed in ornamental letters on the title page, mock-monkish chapter initials – as though to enter

Chaucer's life is no more frightening than to enter the dining room of the Kensington Hilton.

Otherwise I have few complaints. One assumes, perhaps, an American audience, not necessarily a student one, interested in getting back to roots as exotic as though less bitter than Dr Haley's. An English reader will feel something of an outsider yet pleased at the continuity of Anglo-American culture. I'm grateful to Gardner for showing me, what I'd stupidly missed before, that the third cock in the *Miller's Tale* is an obscene ambiguity. I think he's wrong in deriving *trivial* from the trivium that Chaucer studied. *Trivial* surely comes from *trivia*, a crossroads, where vapid gossip was traded. Gardner's students would not find the trivium trivial if they had to follow it, nor would anyone.

Faith in the Bottle

Rabelais, by M. A. Screech

When M. Peyrfitte lamented the Cartesian inflexibility of his nation under the title of *Le Mal Français*, he did not propose, to go along with a demotion of Descartes, a rehabilitation of Rabelais. I have the impression, shared with Professor Screech, that the French do not greatly care for Rabelais. They have to translate him into modern French before they can understand him. But no modern version can work, except the miraculous one of Sir Thomas Urquhart. Encouraged by Urquhart, whose *Gargantua* is often very close to the original, and by the fact that early sixteenth-century French has words lost to modern French but still present as loanwords in English, an English reader can plunge with some confidence into

L'occasion et manière comment Gargamelle enfanta fut telle, et, si ne le croyez, le fondement vous escappe!

He knows, anyway, that he is not reading Racine.

That *escappe* has, in my edition, to be glossed with *échappe*, but I cannot somehow imagine one of the sleek men of French television, much less one of the chic speakerines, reciting with any pleasure that bit about the bumgut dropping out. The Cartesian tradition has taught the French that they are rational creatures, and that fundaments are only to be seen and heard in low entertainments for tourists. The body in Rabelais is neither fed with the *haute cuisine* nor clothed in the *haute couture*. All those tripes and sausages and a newborn child yelling for drink. Even the spirit of *Clochemerle*, a diluted homage to Rabelais, is not now much to be found in France. On the other hand there was, until Goscinny died untimely, having committed the error of visiting a doctor, the *Asterix* series.

Is *Asterix* Rabelaisian? In the sense that Obelix is a kind of giant with great strength and a huge appetite, dedicated to trouncing occupation forces that would eliminate the Gallic (pre-French) devotion to freedom and joy. There is even a magic bottle, filled with a strength-giving elixir, not wine. But the series owed more to *Of Mice and Men*, nostalgia for the forties, and the hyperboles of Walt Disney than to Rabelais's literature of excess. Rabelais has touched British literature – Sterne, Burns, Joyce, even Shakespeare – more than French.

What Professor Screech tries to do in his book is to explain the deeper significance of what the non-specialist reader like myself has always taken to be pure high-spirited scatology. The bumguts, vomiting, rivers of urine, and costiveness that has to be dug out with spades are in the service of a philosophy, even a theology. Dust thou art, to dust returnest, and your lower functions are meant to remind you of it. But even if we read the great four books as entertainment without metaphysical resonances, the gap between Rabelais's age and our own, in terms of assumptions of faith and thought, is so vast that we need annotation of the kind the professor so generously gives. The only trouble with any such exegesis is that it tends to kill spontaneous laughter by telling us what we ought to be laughing at, and why. We do not feel much like laughing when we know that Professor Screech is standing behind us making sure that we laugh in the right places.

We may sum up the fundament or bumgut of what we ought to know before rereading Rabelais something like this. François Rabelais was a Franciscan, also a Dominican, friar. But he was also one of the new humanists, like Erasmus and More. He admired *Utopia* immensely, and makes Gargantua king of a country so-named. There was, among French reformers, great support for Henry VIII's divorce and a corresponding disparagement of the stiffnecked Sir Thomas, but Rabelais remained loyal. We have to remember that England and the other Germanic countries had no monopoly of the desire to cut adrift from Rome, and that there were royal rumblings in France, Rome's favourite daughter, about the need for schism. But Rabelais was a genuine reformer, in that he wanted not merely to clean up the Church but to reinfuse it with that primitive joy that had once made men willing to die for it. Pantagruel is a kind of comic Christ. Wherever he appears he promotes ecstasy. He wishes to redeem the world through wine, which is Christ's blood.

This must sound blasphemous, but Catholic notions of blasphemy have always been different from those of thin-lipped reformists. A monk like Rabelais was suffused with the holy texts; the average monk of the type most despised was suffused with nothing else. It was natural for the words of the gospels to take on tavern connotations. Christ on the cross says 'I thirst' and a man in a bar (or Stephen Dedalus on the shore) may say the same thing, aware of the divine precedent. It is natural to Rabelais to echo Holy Writ throughout his secular narrative. For the secular and the holy were not sealed off from each other, as now. As in Omar Khayyám, the injunction 'drink' must mean more than itself.

Now one of the major themes of the four books of Rabelais is the nature of human communication. When, on a monkish tongue, the language of the Gospels or the mass grows meaningless through overuse or sheer hebetude, then it may be time to consider whether words are, after all, the best mode of conveying meaning. Henry VIII himself referred to a priest who had, owing to a misprint in his Latin text, been saying *mumpsimus* all his life, and when confronted with the correct form, mumbled 'I will not change my old *mumpsimus* for your new *sumpsimus.*' Rabelais is very much contra *mumpsimus*. A lawyer before he became a physician, he considers whether gesture might not be better in court than language which stiffens into formula. The farting and bewraying that fill the four books are to be considered semiotically. Verbal language is turned into a circus.

Literature which revels in language, like this, is not, then, primarily happy with language as other than a mode of phatic communion, the kind of drivel you use drunk in the dark. The long catalogues in Rabelais, the macaronics, the mere show-off polyglottism (as of Panurge when he first meets Pantagruel), the more than Hal–Falstaff abuse – all are in the service of killing verbalism. And yet, we are reminded, all the books were probably meant to be read aloud, glorifying the speech process if casting doubt on its efficacy as a medium of conveying truth. What happens if you read Rabelais aloud? You get very thirsty.

Pantagruel, the giant son of Gargantua, appearing first in a printed book cunningly meant to look like a dull legal manual, takes his name from Penthagruel, a mythical dwarf well known to Rabelais's first readers. He was a kind of devil who threw salt into the mouths of sleeping drunkards and made them wake so parched that they had to get drunk again. Pantagruel is dedicated to slaking the thirst of the world. His chief enemies are the Dipsodes, who seem to glorify their chronic thirstiness. But the joy of drinking is a figure of the joy of Christian redemption. To the superficial reader there would seem to be little enough Christian joy in a work full of gross and cruel jests, like those perpetrated by Panurge (that Barbonnesa tart – ugh), but we have to consider Panurge – who is all urge and nothing else – as a subject for Pantagruelian redemption. And is there not perhaps something morbid about all that gratuitous gloating over faeces? Not really, not when you think of the truly morbid cloacal brooding of Swift. Rabelais, as a physician, had to taste excrement as part of the diagnostic process. That was no age of American toilets. His work is a testament of acceptance. Nothing human alien – that was what humanism meant.

Will in the Women's Room

Shakespeare's Division of Experience, by Marilyn French

In 1980 I was awarded, by the association known as Women in Publishing, a pink marzipan pig as one of the sexists of the year. In 1981 I was informed that I was on the short list for yet another pink pig, but to my slight chagrin I did not win it. I think I am bound to be one of the porcine elect this year, since I have a book by Dr Marilyn French to consider, and whatever I say about it is bound to be wrong. Dr French is a noted feminist, author of *The Women's Room* and *The Bleeding Heart*, a pair of detesticulating or gesticulating novels, as also of a rather useful book (male condescension) on Joyce's *Ulysses*. Now she has published what the innocent will consider to be the definitive feminist introduction to Shakespeare. It is an interesting book and not unoriginal, but, though it comes from a scholar, it is somewhat unscholarly.

By this I mean that Dr French views Shakespeare in a vacuum, without reference to the other dramatists of his time, the historical background, even the Elizabethan stage. Shakespeare is alone, unpreceded by Marlowe, not followed by Ben Jonson or Massinger, and he is made to behave according to a system of Dr French's own devising, one that, perhaps expectedly, is based on sexual polarity. Dr French prefers, at least at the beginning, *gender* to *sex*, in some ways an unfortunate term, since it evokes linguistic accidence – the least dynamic aspect of language and unknown to the tongues of the East – and implies a taxonomy based only metaphorically on the sexes, whereas Dr French means real sexes or, if you wish, literal masculinity and femininity.

In Shakespeare, says Dr French, you find dramatic conflict based on the opposition of the two polar principles. The masculine principle is concerned with domination and killing and legitimacy. The feminine principle is split into two subprinciples, which Dr French terms the inlaw and the outlaw. The inlaw feminine denotes passive virtue, the model to which aggressive man refers when he is guilty about his aggression. The outlaw element is very different: it relates woman to anarchy, subversion, magic, wild nature, dangerous sexuality. Falstaff, instead of being a mound of blubber given to sack, cowardice and wit, is a prime example of outlaw femininity. The France of the *Henry VI* plays is always an outlaw female, and there waiting to dole out castratory witchcraft is La Pucelle. Let us see how the scheme works out with one of the mature tragedies – *Othello*, say.

Here Shakespeare probes 'the consequences of the misogyny upon which Western culture is founded'. Spell that out in simpler terms, and it means that our civilization is based on hatred of women, which I think goes too far. By misogyny Dr French presumably means the frustration of a male-dominated society in trying to subdue women to a pattern of passive virtue. One might add that intransigent males have to be subdued too, but Dr French will reply that such males are really outlaw females. (She does not, by the way, anywhere refer to Alfred Adler.) 'Sex is bestial and filthy; control is an absolute good: females are sexual; males must maintain control of them.' You can desexualize women by idealizing them – which is what Othello does with Desdemona. But ideals are always shaky, and Othello loses his faith in 'inlaw feminine virtues'. Now loss of faith in one area induces a loss of faith in all areas (why?), and the ideals of war, conquest, legitimized aggression die along with Desdemona, so Othello, who embodied these ideals, might as well die too. I take it that Iago, who is a male frustrated of legitimate accession (or the right to military promotion), may also be read as an outlaw female. We need more than this. We need, among other things, the irony of Shakespeare's audience's foreknowledge that Desdemona, being a Venetian, has to be a light woman. We need human weakness and passion and all the things we took for granted before Dr French came along. What we do not need, unless we are Women in Publishing, is simplistic schematization.

How about *Hamlet*? The prince does not really wish to kill the king, since his crime is nothing compared with that of the queen. 'Murder is the extreme of the masculine principle; copulation is the foundation of giving birth, the extreme of the feminine principle. Of the two, copulation without sanctification, by a woman, is the worse crime.' Why, and who says so? According to this thesis, there is no longer any mystery in Hamlet's procrastination. The king is not worth killing: the great task is the chiding of his mother and persuading her to return to virtue. Presumably, Polonius, by reason of his accidental contiguity to the chidden mother, becomes a kind of fleshly extension of her, a symbol of her crime, and he may be slain with impunity, so long as Hamlet's sword pierces the arras first, this being part of the woman's room, which rhymes with womb. After the killing-chiding, Hamlet is relaxed and full of fun: he has done his duty. Of course, there is a good deal of both the inlaw and outlaw female in Hamlet: he is always speaking up for virtue; he is wayward, skittish and subversive. One could go on like this for a long time.

Shakespeare became mature, according to Dr French, when he ceased to be on the side of brutal masculinity and saw the need for its tempering by the inlaw feminine virtues. He never came to terms with the outlaw. 'If his horror of sex, powerful women, and the sloth and bestiality of a Caliban was pathological, the disease was not his alone. It was part of his culture and it is part of ours.' I should have thought that hatred of Caliban was altogether healthy and the detestation of raw sex (the expense of spirit in a waste of shame) a mark of the capacity to love. What Shakespeare was apparently after was 'synthesis, integration . . . the reason for assimilating and valuing inlaw qualities was because they make this life richer, make it, at its worst, bearable.'

Dr French, to male relief, ends by praising Shakespeare as a 'major influence on all of Western culture'. But there has to be a qualification. He saw life in terms of 'polar opposites', and the authority of his work has been instrumental in 'perpetuating the very division he sought to reconcile'. Well, all art is made out of division, but one would hesitate to express this division in terms of accidence. If Dr French's thesis works with Shakespeare (with whom most theses work), it ought to work with everybody. In Marlowe's *Dr Faustus*, masculinity goes to extremes of control, but hell awaits. It is all too easy to see hell mouth as the *vagina dentata* and Helen of Troy as its portress. In music, the dominant seventh may be female and the full close male, but musical syntax is anterior to musical accidence. Dr French is playing with metaphors which, following the feminist vogue, she converts to very shaky plain statements.

Mr W. H.

Shakespeare by Hilliard – A Portrait Deciphered, by Leslie Hotson

The Elizabethans were very American in some ways, particularly in their phonemes and the vague ebullience of their speech, but they had no belief in the intrinsic value of bigness. It is not growing like a tree in bulk doth make man better be. In pictorial art, they loved miniatures more than oversize battle panoramas, and of all the miniaturists they best loved Nicholas Hilliard. A small portrait was a fine thing and a finer thing still if it was embellished with cryptic emblems. The more symbolism you could get into a portrait the more you exalted a representational, hence minor, art into that pseudo-philosophical sphere beloved of the Elizabethans, wherein magic, arithmology and grave moral teaching danced a quirky pavane together. Hilliard fulfilled the rule of 'in less compass, more cunning' with admired exquisiteness. He crammed his narrow space with meaningful tropes which are now mostly dumb to us. Dr Hotson's new book aims at making the dumb speak again.

In 1964 he published a work celebratory of Shakespeare's quater-centennial, in which he proved to his own satisfaction that the subject of one of Hilliard's portraits was Shakespeare's dearmylove Mr W. H., beautiful young Will Hatcliffe, Prince of Revels at Gray's Inn. Dr Hotson admits now with wry honesty that he was not at that time ready to read all of Hilliard's symbolism – the bent leg, for instance, that turned Hatcliffe into Apollo – nor even quick enough of eye to see that the initials W. H. are woven into the circumambient foliage. He is now ready not only to interpret all the symbolic subtleties of that portrait but to deal at length with a Hilliard miniature far more mysterious – that known as 'Unknown man clasping a hand issuing from a cloud'.

Dr Hotson says, justly, that we have to look at any Elizabethan utterance, whether it be plain-seeming speech, a tragedy, or a portrait, with Elizabethan eyes. The Elizabethans, like the Americans, seem to speak our tongue, but as suspenders are braces and homely is ugly, so an income was an entrance fee and horse meat oats. Pictures were never pure representation, and what looks like supererogatory decoration turns out to be coherent, if enigmatic, statement. Thus, whose is the hand that issues from the cloud? It is Apollo's. This we know from the supernatural whiteness of the flesh, from the index finger separated from the other four, from the sevenfold cloud (7 is Apollo's number). And who is the young man who blandly clasps the divine hand? He too, though dressed in the height of Elizabethan fashion, must be a god. Though his face is delicately pink, his hand also is heavenly white. He is, and Dr Hotson overwhelms us with evidence, Mercury. It is enough for now to look at the arithmology. Mercury's number is 4. His day is the fourth day – Wednesday, mercredi, mercoledi, dies Mercurii. It is no accident that the son of Mercury, Autolycus, makes his first appearance in the fourth scene of the fourth act of *The Winter's Tale*. In Hilliard's portrait, the year 1588 happily adds up to 22, and 2 and 2 are 4. The mercurial young man's lace collar is of a four-square design. And so on.

But the young man is only Mercury in a special figure: he is a deathless god but also a mortal Elizabethan. His hat may be Mercury's but it also cost a pretty penny somewhere off Cork Street. If he is mortal, let him who clasps from the clouds be mortal too, though still divine Apollo. Who are these two, besides being gods? There was only one Elizabethan Phoebus in 1588, and this was Will Hatcliffe, lord of the dance, Prince of Purpool, Mr W. H. And who can it be clasping that delicate hand but sweet Master Shakespeare, Mercury of the age?

Mercury? How? Who says that Shakespeare is Mercury? Quite a number of people, it seems. Here is Thomas Freeman of Magdalen addressing the poet with 'Shakespeare, that nimble Mercury thy braine, Lulls many hundred Argus-eyes asleepe'. William Basse's elegy makes 'Wilyam' a *fourth* with Spenser, Chaucer and Beaumont, with a clear arithmological meaning. And does not Ben Jonson state that Shakespeare came *forth* 'like a Mercury to charm'? In 1651, Samuel Sheppard writes for him:

> Sacred Spirit, whiles thy *Lyre*
> Ecchoed o're the Arcadian Plaines,
> Even *Apollo* did admire,
> Orpheus wondered at thy Straines.

The lyre is Mercury's, since it is not Apollo's, nor Orpheus's either. A book published in 1652, *A Hermeticall Banquet, dressed by a Spagiricall Cook*, presents the court of the Princess Phantasia: '*Ovid* she makes Major-Domo. *Homer*, because a merry Greek, Master of the Wine-cellars . . . *Shack-Spear*, Butler. . . .' Mercury was butler to the gods before Ganymede took over. And is not Shakespeare himself making a plain statement of mythic identity when, at the end of *Love's Labour's Lost*, he says: 'The wordes of Mercurie are harsh after the songes of Apollo'? These are the least of Dr Hotson's adductions.

He is a fine detective. We have already seen him at work in *The First Night of Twelfth Night*, where he probed the archives of Italy and Germany – but not of the Kremlin, the Kremlin proving uncooperative – to establish a scene so unforgettable it smacks of the fictive imagination: Epiphany, 1600; Whitehall; the suspicious Russian emissaries; Prince Orsini of Bracciano next to the Queen; Orsino on the stage; ill-willed Malvolio a thin disguise for Sir William Knollys. We believe partly because Dr Hotson overwhelms with evidence, but mostly because we want to believe. Whether the same willed credulity will make the world accept Hilliard's previously Unknown Man as Shakespeare at the age of twenty-four I do not know. We are bowled over with wholly persuasive argument, but I for one remain unconvinced – perhaps because I wish to be. Had the Will of Armada year done enough to earn the title of England's Mercury? Dr Hotson believes he had already achieved the earlier sonnets. 'In his Sonnets Shakespeare relives the outward vicissitudes and inward motions of his friendship with Gray's Inn's boy– "Apollo" in aptest allegory. On Poetry's high scene his beloved Will pacing forth under his royal canopy is King Apollo, and himself the golden god's humble Friend, the Poet Mercury.' I would accept all this, and the much more we are given, if only I *wanted* Shakespeare to look like the Unknown Man.

But this rather vacuous handsomeness, the unemphatic nose, the marmalade beard, the wide-set eyes brooding on nothing say nothing to me of the Stratford poet on the make, while the so-called Burbage portrait says much. *Attici amoris ergo* says the legend beside the held hands – 'Athenians for love's sake'. London was as much New Athens as New Troy, and the Inns of Court were the citadel of Athenian wisdom and wit. But Shakespeare was not an Inn man, although he became – with *Venus and Adonis* – an object of the Inn's adoration. Have we not perhaps here a lost Mercury, even if we assume that we have an Apollo found? A fellow-bencher of Hatcliffe's wrote poetry long gone; he flashed, quicksilver, in a small closed fellowship and then flew away. It is at least a probability.

To me, Dr Hotson's conclusions are the least part of his book. Such gusto, learning, odd discoveries, wit are their own justification. And, of course, that continuing capacity for penetration into the Elizabethan mind which, ever since *The Death of Christopher Marlowe*, has turned raw scholar's notes into music.

What Shakespeare Smelt

The Elizabethan Underworld, by Gamini Salgado

It is well known that many of Shakespeare's images take fire only when they are related to his experiences as an Elizabethan Londoner. Macbeth's 'hangman's hands', for instance, are to be imagined as coated with blood and entrails after the drawing – that second stage of execution between the hanging and the quartering. Shakespeare had doubtless seen at least the Lopez butchery at Tyburn. Whether he was a frequenter of brothels we do not know, but he certainly knew where the brothels were:

> Dwell I but in the suburbs
> Of your good pleasure? If it be no more,
> Portia is Brutus' harlot, not his wife.

Suburbs is a pretty neutral image to us, suggesting Hampstead or Swiss Cottage, but to Shakespeare's contemporaries it meant chiefly Southwark, where the whores or Winchester geese displayed their breasts at the windows of the trugging houses. They were called Winchester geese because the Bishop of Winchester controlled the property there and had done so since about 1100. Traditional Christianity has never seen much wrong in episcopal brothel-keeping. St Augustine said: 'Suppress prostitution and capricious lusts will overthrow society.' St Thomas Aquinas went further: 'Prostitution in the towns is like the cesspool in the palace; take away the cesspool and the palace will become an unclean and evil-smelling place.' Reforming religion usually involves closing down the brothels (Henry VIII had a try at this in 1546). One characteristic of Elizabethan England was a prevalence of vice, to be associated in the Graham Greene manner with the older faith, and an attempt on the part of the ultra-reformists, mainly the Puritan city fathers, to control that vice with whips, branding-irons and prisons.

Professor Salgado's book breaks no new ground, but it is a satisfying compendium of Elizabethan roguery from trulldom to Bridewell and Bedlam, and it is very good on the Romanies or Minions of the Moon. Thomas Dekker, in *Lanthorn and Candlelight*, starts off by being censorious about the gypsies – 'beggarly in apparel, barbarous in condition and bloody if they meet advantage' – but ends up by displaying more intimate knowledge of them than is proper in a moralist. The gypsy women wear 'rags and patched filthy mantles uppermost, when the undergarments are handsome and in fashion'. There were a lot of gypsies around in those days, especially in Shakespeare's own

Warwickshire. They appealed to the villagers, to whom they brought sorcery, colour and tambourines, and a reminder of a wild faith older than Catholicism (though gypsy bands were believed to harbour papish priests in disguise). Ben Jonson glorified them in a masque for King James. Borrow was to write a book pointing out that they had no word for glory in their language, and that the word *merripen* meant both life and death. Poets were interested in their language, which they tended to confuse with the cant of native thieves and vagrants.

> White thy fambles, red thy gan,
>   And thy quarrons dainty is.
> Couch a hogshead with me then,
>   In the darkmans clip and kiss.

The variety of modes of Elizabethan roguery is indicated by the richness of the canting terms used by thieves and sharpers. An apple-squire was a pimp or brothel-servant (like Pompey Bum in *Measure for Measure*). An autem was a church, and an autemmort a female vagrant married in a church. A bene faker of gibes was a first-class forger of certificates. The beak was then, as now, the magistrate. Booze was drink, and a boozing ken an alehouse. Romeville was London, and Romeville booze was wine. A dell was a virgin, soon to become a doxy. A gentry cove was an upper-class man, and his wife was a gentry mort. The figging law was the art of the cutpurse (who had a bit of sharpened horn on his thumb), and, if he failed to budge a beak, he would be cracked on the sconce by the catchpole's filchman. Pigs in fields were grunting-cheats in greenmans, where, as you could see with your own glaziers, the grannam grew. You pulled out your pizzle to pluck a rose. You talked with your prattling-cheat and prigged on a prancer into the dewse-a-vill. You wore a fambling-cheat on your finger. To cut bene whids was to tell the truth. Your crashing-cheats were your teeth, and if you were whipped you clied the jerk.

There were about fourteen prisons in Elizabethan London. The Clink was mostly for offenders against religion, as was the Marshalsea, which also accommodated committers of crimes at sea. There were two Counters in the City and one also in Southwark, and, according to what garnish you could pay the jailer, you were put in the Master's Side, the Knight's Ward, or the Hole. For a weekly charge of ten shillings you could eat at a meal 'bone of beef with broth; bone beef, a piece; veal roasted a loin or breast or else one capon; bread, as much as they will eat, small beer, and wine claret, a quart.' Conditions in the Hole were such as to make a poor man not too anxious to be committed to jail, but to a rich man imprisonment was a darker, more cobwebby extension of ordinary life. There was no shame in it. My Lord Southampton was jailed for putting a venue under the girdle of one of the Queen's Glories, and Ben Jonson was thrown in for killing Gab Spencer (he pleaded benefit of clergy and had his thumb branded with a T for Tyburn) and, later, for helping to write *The Isle of Dogs*. Shakespeare seems to have kept his nose fairly clean.

Life ran very high, and also very low, in those days. If one sometimes has the impression that the secret police are always watching, and that one can be committed for sneezing during a recitation of the Lord's Prayer, one is also comforted by evidence of how inefficient was the arm of the law. Shakespeare summed it all up in Dogberry. 'You shall comprehend all vagrom men; you are to bid any man stand in the prince's name.' One of Dogberry's underconstables says: 'How if a' will not stand?' And Dogberry replies, reasonably: 'Why, then, take no note of him, but let him go, and presently call the rest of the watch together, and thank God you are rid of a knave.' Or: 'If you meet a thief, you may suspect him, by virtue of your office, to be no true man; and, for such kind of men, the less you meddle or make with them, why, the more is for your honesty.' You could get away with murder if you had money. Things, of course, have changed since then.

Sleight-of-Hand Fiesta

Cervantes: A Biography, by William Byron

When, in 1605, the British delegation went to Valladolid to negotiate peace with Spain, they were treated to the mandatory bullfight but also, as a curtain-raiser, to impersonations of Don Quixote and Sancho Panza prancing round in the ring. The characters had already leaped out of a book not yet finished. Cervantes, whose struggles to keep out of jail and earn a living had not yet finished either, must have foreseen grimly the ironic consequence of creating too well: his book would, to many, become a mere verbal prison for personages whose rightful place was some visual medium – a festive cortège (like Macy's Thanksgiving procession), a volume of etchings, the musical stage. There are a lot of people around who, because they weep over 'The Impossible Dream' or the end of Strauss's symphonic poem, honestly believe that they have some time in the past read Cervantes. I think it was Auden who said that nobody had ever read *Don Quixote*.

I have read it twice in English – Shelton and Motteux – and once in Spanish. This is not a boast: I genuinely love the book, as well as the characters in it. This ought to mean that I love Cervantes as a writer, but I have to confess to knowing little else of his except the *Exemplary Stories*. This is the general situation among the British. It is general also to think one knows Cervantes's life on the strength of Chesterton's *Lepanto* and *Man from La Mancha*. The truth is that he did not write *Don Quixote* in jail: it would have been impossible with so much darkness, noise and grim practical jokes: on the other hand, the idea of the book may well have come to him there. That he fought at Lepanto is well attested; what is not so well known is the length and agony of his life in Algiers as a slave of the Turks. There he had to wait for a ransom which never came, attempt escape to Oran which was savagely punished, fight against the tempta-tion to convert nominally to Islam, and still believe in the Christian mission of a Spain which would not find the handful of reales necessary for his manumission. When the money came at last it came in the form of a loan repayable at high interest.

It was a hard life, and Byron recounts it with empathy and gusto. The smells of the age steam from the page, and the prose rumbles like an empty stomach. Byron is a Hispanicized American, and he can recon-cile baroque grandiloquence with zesty slang. The book works, and Spain comes through in all its tarnished finery. Through this Spain Miguel de Cervantes Saavedra wanders, like his family before him, looking for work and occasionally finding it, contriving to live long despite diabetes and omnipresent plague and famine. He died at sixty-eight on 23 April 1616. Shakespeare died at fifty-two on the identical day. Unfortunately, the Spanish and British calendars did not at that time gear, and there was a distance of ten days between them. But history insists on our seeing the British and Spanish glories as somehow complementary, symbolizing this in a terminal contemporaneity. The mad fine fictionizable thing is that they could have met. The British in 1605 were made to sit through a Lope de Vega play; what prevented, except a historical record, the appearance of the King's Men at Valladolid, with Shakespeare, Groom of the Royal Bedchamber, in the cast? Cervantes was certainly there as a kind of official chronicler of the peace.

But, alas, the Spanish knew nothing of the British literary achieve-ment. Cervantes plodded on for years in the Spanish theatre, and nei-ther he nor Lope de Vega was able to learn what Renaissance drama was really about. There was no Marlowe, not even a Kyd, to prime a dra-maturgical genius that was only able to flame very late (at the age of fifty-seven) in the novel. The Philippines were not able to learn from the Elizabethans, but the Elizabethans were not slow to learn from the greatest of the Philippines. Ben Jonson and Beaumont and Fletcher knew *Don Quixote*, and Shakespeare must at least have seen the 1611 Shelton translation (still perhaps the best) on the stalls in Paul's Yard.

But the man who could create Hamlet and Falstaff had nothing to learn from a lean knight and a fat squire.

What Cervantes and Shakespeare had in common was a large humanity, a capacity for compassion, forgiveness and benevolence after long evidence, stitched into the nerves and the very pia mater, of the malevolence of life. Of Shakespeare's own sufferings we know little, but they could never have been as great as those of Cervantes. Byron is very good on these sufferings: where he has no direct documentary evidence he makes highly plausible guesses, and we can believe him all the way when he evokes debtor's jails, the stink and danger of the galley, and the cruelty of the vindictive Mussulman. When Cervantes came to write *Don Quixote* he could have been expected to follow the pattern of Alemán's *Guzmán de Alfarache*, a novel of immense acerbity which met some deep, or even superficial, Hispanic need, since it went into twenty editions in 1604 alone. Byron thinks it might qualify as the most bitter book ever written, the archetypal picaresque novel of 'a rogue boy growing up in a rogue world'. Man is a beast and beastliness is enforced on him by the beastliness of the world. 'God . . . becomes a disgruntled father who will receive the repentant sinner with open arms – but who will not lift a finger to help him, who will stand by in regretful inactivity if the sinner stumbles and falls in the attempt, as he inevitably must. Worse: He deliberately places obstacles in man's paths.' Life in Alemán is hell, and a very well realized one: here is a Zola long before his time.

Cervantes sets a mad emaciated knight on the road striving to do good in a world which has forgotten what good is. Nothing would have been easier than to wring the heart with a Dostoevskian parade of cruelty – Don Quixote as the battered Rocinante of Raskolnikov's dream – but somehow, despite the blood and the broken teeth, the effect is always of high and heartening comedy. A good God exists somewhere, divorced from fat bishops and a sadistic Inquisition, and man strives to know him through the godlike in himself. The ridiculous, for the first time in European literature, becomes a technique for confronting the spiritual. True, Shakespeare had tried it first, but never on such a scale, and Shakespeare terminated an artistic tradition while Cervantes initiated one that is still with us and whose possibilities are far from exhausted.

William Byron's biography is well researched and has a formidable bibliography, but it is addressed to ordinary readers more than to scholars. He might have trusted these readers to take some of the citations in the original Spanish, instead of just the naked prosy renderings that convey no literary quality at all. For instance, Cervantes recited in Seville, before the honorary tomb put up to solemnize the death of Philip II, a sardonic sonnet that excoriated the city and suggested that the king had not been all that well loved. All Byron gives us is the prose content. We need the rhymes and the roll and clatter of the Castilian consonants. And I should like to know how the great Góngora really celebrated the coming of the British peace-makers:

We staged a pageant, pure folly,
And a sleight-of-hand fiesta
For the angelic legate and his spies
Who swore by Calvin to make peace. . . .
We remain poor; Luther was enriched;
And to record these feats, order was given
To Don Quixote, Sancho and his ass.

Picaresque Justice

Henry Fielding: A Biography, by Pat Rogers

'The successors of Charles the Fifth,' said Gibbon, 'may disdain their brethren of England; but the romance of *Tom Jones*, that exquisite picture of human manners, will outlive the palace of the Escurial and the imperial eagle of the house of Austria.' A prophecy fulfilled and more than fulfilled, for *Tom Jones*, as a popular film, influenced the view of the British of themselves more than two centuries after the publication of the novel and made the Americans, though briefly, revaluate the national character of their cousins. There is a pop singer who calls himself Tom Jones, a name supposed to be suffused with blunt virility. There are as yet no singers rechristened Clarissa Harlowe or Tristram Shandy. If *Tom Jones* the novel, despite the strictures of the foreigner Nabokov, is considered still to be the best fiction of the eighteenth century, this has as much to do with the character of the author – our kindly chaperon through two long Everyman volumes of adventures – as with the author's artistic expertise.

We all think we know something of this character, and not only through the philosophizings that, to our unexpected pleasure, hold up the action of *Tom Jones*, *Joseph Andrews* and *Amelia*. Fielding's life divides neatly into acts like one of his own stage comedies: he is a personage who strides across the first half of the Age of Reason in several assumed public functions. After Eton and the University of Leyden, he is a writer of popular stage burlesques, all barbed, some of them libellous. *The Historical Register for the Year 1736*, in which the great Robert Walpole was venomously traduced, led to that infamous Licensing Act which was repealed only in 1968. Fielding, out of a job, took to the law, riding the Western Circuit as an advocate. Then Richardson produced *Pamela*, progenetrix of two centuries of shopgirl romances, and Fielding responded with the parody *Shamela*, in which virtue is debased to 'vartue', a hypocritical commercial commodity. Discovering in himself more than a capacity for satire, Fielding wrote *Joseph Andrews*, which begins as a Richardson skit but then rides under its own steam. The great novelist was born, somewhat to his own surprise, but there was no real career in fiction.

Hence Fielding the magistrate, the Bow Street justice surrounded by the stink and poverty of London slums that Pope and Johnson hardly knew. And then Fielding in decay, ailing with gout and asthma and dropsy and wastage of the limbs, seeking renewal on a voyage to Lisbon, dying philosophically but still writing (the record of the voyage is most entertaining reading), buried at Lisbon, his monument with its florid Latin epitaphs an oddity among the tombs of dull British merchants. One of the most moving passages in the works of Kingsley Amis is to be found in *I Like It Here*, a novel with a Lisbon setting, where the literary cynic pays his tribute to a novelist who never has to be excused on the grounds of changing fashion, who saw right and wrong clearly, who amused and enlightened, who did not huff and puff. Fielding was only forty-seven when he died. At that age neither Defoe nor Richardson had started writing novels.

The standard biography by W. L. Cross is sixty years old. It suffers from a shortage of letters. Professor Battestin has found a number and is looking for more. Professor Rogers's brief biography takes advantage of Battestin's research: in terms of new material alone it has to be commended, but it must primarily be read as a most vivid, sympathetic and humorous evocation not only of a remarkable character but of an astonishing age. The book is very fully illustrated, with, rightly, much Hogarth, since Fielding saw that incomparable social commentator as a brother in art. It is very good on the London theatre, which produced (apart from Goldsmith and Sheridan, who are very much after Fielding) practically nothing we could watch with pleasure today. Addison's *Cato*, perhaps, but not Barnwell's *The London Merchant* or the *drames* of the sentimental Steele. And yet the age produced great actors and, Professor Rogers reveals, one great transvestite actress, Charlotte Clarke, probably a lesbian, the deplorable but vigorous Colley Cibber's daughter.

The kind of work Fielding did for the stage has journalistic virtues. Professor Rogers, always ready with modern instances, has occasion to mention *That Was The Week That Was*, a topical television satirical series that launched people like David Frost. There is a kind of writing that, witty and well made, nevertheless acknowledges itself to be ephemeral, and Fielding, like those BBC lampoonists, was glad to do well what could not, of its nature, last long. It took a very great satirist, then as now, to transcend his topical material, though it was easier to produce lasting satire in Popian mock epic or Swiftian allegory than in a rushed confection for the Augustan playhouse. But we would do well to examine a few of Fielding's burlesques, *Tom Thumb* for instance, to admire the thrust, the sharpness, the good humour which were later to find their more fruitful place in his fiction. His *Rape upon Rape*, admirable selling title, is behind *Lock Up Your Daughters*, a Mermaid Theatre farce and later film which cashed in on the *Tom Jones* vogue of the sixties.

Two literary faculties which were, at first, distinct were later to conjoin in the novels – skill with dialogue, facility with an expository prose that came out in pamphlets and periodicals. But there was also, which the novels never allow us to forget, a huge physical energy. Like Handel, that other formidable figure of the Hanoverian stage, Fielding was a big man, muscular, perhaps capable of amorous and convivial excess but gifted with a prudence and sense of responsibility almost Johnsonian. These two last qualities, allied to genuine good-heartedness, made him a fine magistrate. Unbribable, hence always poor, he saw, master of the *picaresque* as he was, that ill luck, bad environment and desperate poverty pushed the *picaro* to crime more than a love of evil. Some of his judgments were Solomon-like. Three women bearing the same name claimed the same husband. Fielding awarded him to the eldest. He, and his legal brother, desperate at the lack of a police force, dreamed up the idea of a corps which was eventually to be the Bow Street runners. It was not enough to sit in judgment on crime; the prevention of crime came first. A lesser man would have battened on the mess of judicial corruption. Fielding pushed on till ill health dragged him from the bench. His view of the 'trading justices' is incarnated in Thrasher, and of the constabulary in Mr Gotobed, both in *Amelia*.

Though Pat Rogers is a professor of literature, he does not see it as in his province to suggest new aesthetic approaches to Fielding's fiction. It is, after all, good blunt uncomplicated narrative seasoned with honest Augustan moralizing, garnished with body humour and mock-epic cadenzas from which Joyce was to learn:

> Hushed be every ruder breath. May the heathen ruler of the winds confine to iron the boisterous limbs of noisy Boreas, and the sharp-pointed nose of bitter-biting Eurus. Do thou, sweet Zephyrus, rising from thy fragrant bed, mount the western sky, and lead on those delicious gales the charms of which call forth the lovely Flora from her chamber, perfumed with pearly dews. . . .

And so on till we meet Sophia, her of the nacreous nates. But *Tom Jones* and *Amelia* and (superior, I think, to those) *Joseph Andrews* cannot be well understood without some knowledge of the private Fielding and the tumultuous world in which he publicly functioned. Professor Rogers gives us what we need, and in a perky contemporary style, witty, sometimes slangy, which is altogether suitable.

Oddity

Dictionary Johnson, by James L. Clifford

By a kind of legerdemain, James Boswell persuades us that he is telling us more about Dr Johnson than he really is. On 16 May 1763 he met the Grand Cham for the first time, said the wrong things out of enthusiastic brashness, and feared that he'd forfeited the chance of his friendship. He also said that he came from Scotland but couldn't help it. 'That,' said Johnson, 'is what a very great many of your countrymen cannot help.' Boswell's fear, as we know, proved without ground. The greatness of his biography consists mostly in the unique detail of its record of a friendship. We have Johnson the moralist, talker and eccentric. Except for *The Lives of the Poets*, we hardly have Johnson the writer at all.

The fact is that Johnson's great years as a writer had ended before Boswell met him. Between 1749 and 1763 he produced *Irene, Rasselas, The Rambler* and *The Idler* and, most of all, the immense *Dictionary*. This period, a fifth of Johnson's life, takes up a tenth of Boswell's biography. What Boswell tells us is second hand: he discusses the writings well enough but has little to tell us of the life. The filling-in, on a near-Boswellian scale, of the earlier years was the life-work of Professor Clifford, who completed this successor to his *Young Sam Johnson* shortly before his death in 1978.

Professor Clifford is able to give us, with a candour not permitted to Boswell, an account of Johnson's sexual and cloacal life. The latter, indeed, would have been of no great interest to Boswell's contemporaries, who used close stools, shoved them in the closet for the nightly muckman's removal, then forgot them till it was time to remember them. We, with our sanitary obsessions, worry about the lack of a WC in Gough Square and wonder if Johnson ever took a bath. I once had an American student who, assuming that Johnson never did, had fits of nausea even when he read *The Vanity of Human Wishes*. As for Johnson's sex life, Boswell told us what he dared, which was not much. During the period under treatment, Johnson was a married man and then a widower. His wife Tetty who, on the evidence of a solitary portrait, was a woman of considerable blonde beauty – at least before she married him – is in bed at the beginning of the book and, like Mrs Bloom, she stays there, drugged not by amation but by drink and opium. Mrs Johnson's maid attested to Johnson's sexual vigour (as did the young David Garrick, peeping through the keyhole back in Lichfield), but his wife would have none of him. He sometimes caressed her maid, but he pushed her away brusquely when his amorous propensities became overexcited. He seriously aimed at remarriage after Tetty's death, but nothing came of it. When Garrick asked him which were the two most important activities in life, Johnson answered: 'Sir, fucking and drinking.' With powerful appetites for both, he did neither. Morality got in the way. Lying in bed late in the morning, he seems to have yielded to erotic fancies. The shameful initial M appears frequently in his notebooks. The sin of Onan contributed to his chronic guilt, along with sloth.

That a man who made the first real English dictionary single-handed in seven years, while forty French academicians couldn't get theirs done in forty years, should consider himself slothful is hard to accept in an age in which sloth, to judge from the exemplary young, is one of the seven deadly virtues. But Johnson did everything he could to avoid working. He talked. He drank tea. Professor Clifford tells us how much tea he drank. On his travels in Devon, he pushed his cup towards his hostess for the eighteenth time. 'Dr Johnson,' she said, 'you drink too much tea.' 'Madam,' he replied, 'you are rude.' On another occasion his hostess, expecting conversation from him, got only twenty-five words while she had to dispense twenty-five cups. He ate too. Another Devonshire hostess told him there were pancakes for dessert, did he like pancakes? 'Yes, madam, but I never get enough.' She served him thirteen.

This trip to Devonshire in the company of Joshua Reynolds, who was in search of his past, yields much of interest. We must all have wondered why, when asked how he could define 'pastern' as the knee of a horse, he cheerfully, and without the expected elaborate defence, could reply: 'Ignorance, madam, pure ignorance.' The fact is that he was in a country house with a spacious lawn apt for the running of races. A young lady said she could outrun anybody there, so Johnson rose and said: 'Madam, you cannot outrun me.' He kicked off his tight shoes into the air and ran like a rabbit, leaving her far behind. Such a victory made him complaisant. 'Dr Johnson, you are a chronic masturbator.' 'Pure randiness, madam.'

Here too, in Devon, his oddities of behaviour were carefully noted by the rural unsophisticates. He would align his toes or heels to make a V of his feet, and then beat his sides repeatedly with his hands 'as if for joy that he had done his duty'. He would leave the spot and then return to it and perform the ritual all over again. He would go through the motions of lifting barbells, straddle gigantically, press his feet on the floor as though to test it for strength. 'That's Johnson the great writer,' an innkeeper said. 'Oddity they call him.'

The innkeeper got the priorities right: the great writer comes first. Professor Clifford does not need to remind us of the excellence of Johnson's art. The legend of his verbosity, love of the sesquipedalian, moral obscurity, humourless heaviness began in his own lifetime; but it was put about by frivolous journalists and pert misses who never read him. True, his vocabulary was the biggest of his time, but it was amassed not for show but in the drudgery of putting a dictionary together. It was also in the service of verbal exactness. He was learned, but also a born entertainer. Macaulay quoted Sir Hugh Evans in *The Merry Wives of Windsor*, looking at Falstaff in drag: 'I spy a great peard under her muffler; I like it not when a 'oman has a great peard' when discussing *Irene*. His contention was that Johnson, attempting to create a female character, could not keep out the heavy male moralist. *Irene* was, in fact, a dramatic success: it made Johnson money. Far from being dull, it was considered too daringly violent for the first-night audience, who objected to seeing Irene strangled onstage and cried 'Murder!' If *Rasselas* fares ill as light narrative when compared with the exactly contemporary *Candide*, it is still a readable novella and, which few novelle are, full of permanently pertinent wisdom. Johnson could create characters when he wanted – witness the swiftly delineated personages who crowd the pages of *The Idler*. As for humour, Johnson has given the world more belly laughs than Joe Miller.

That world has never taken seriously Johnson's asseveration that only a blockhead writes except for money. But he meant it, and he was right. He suffered all the trials of the hack's life, including the 'patron and the jail' (twice imprisoned for debt, even after he became Dictionary Johnson), and could not, like a monied amateur, dissociate the practice of literature from the agonies of deprivation. That is why, even when granted the modest affluence of a pension ('. . . in England it is generally understood to mean pay given to a state hireling for treason to his country.' He never changed that definition) he wrote with pain, reluctance, and impatient rapidity. The whole of Fleet Street, which is just off Gough Square, ought to regard him as a patron saint. Through the hagiography of both Boswell and Clifford an immensely gifted imperfect suffering human being glooms through.

Pi for Pleasure

Boswell: The Applause of the Jury, 1782–1785, edited by Irma S. Lustig and Frederick A. Pottle

The news of Dr Samuel Johnson's death, which took place on 13 December 1784, reached James Boswell at Edinburgh on 17 December. 'I did not shed tears. I was not tenderly affected. My feeling was just one large expanse of stupor. I knew that I should afterwards have sorer sensations.' This is the eleventh volume of the Boswell journals, and it is chilling to think that we shall not meet Johnson again, except in Boswell's own memorializations. In 1785 he produced his *Tour of the Hebrides*. 'Dined at Malone's with the *jury* on my *Tour*, who applauded it much.' Malone was the Shakespearian scholar who ill-advisedly insisted on stiffening some of Boswell's informal and ebullient prose into the acceptable diction of the time. The *jury* was composed of literary friends of them both. Its applause was not echoed in the literary reviews.

Boswell, as a writer, was well ahead of his period. His concern with the minutiae of narrative, the Flemish-picture approach, was not to the taste of an age which preferred the abstract and general. It was considered indecently egotistical of him to place himself so vividly in the picture. His technique was not well understood, and there are still readers of the *Life of Johnson* who fail to appreciate the intelligence and cunning of the man, who sets himself up so often as a butt for Johnson's wit and Scotophobe raillery, daring ridicule in the cause of art. He knew what he was doing:

I am electric eel to Dr Johnson. Also the boy in the bowling-green who gives him the bowls. Langton said it was a great deal to do this, to be always ready. And he plays with no common bowls. His the long bullets. Great rubs. Often *rides*. Seldom *draws* a cast. But gets to the jack better than anyone.

The Johnson biography is certainly art, and the journals, which are not, yet sometimes read like it. This sounds like Mr Jingle:

'Got into Oxford coach at Old Bailey. . . . My companions sweet young woman, architect (ugly; builder, I believe), jolly, good-humoured man, I know not who. Quite hearty and lively all the way. Only sudden fever of love. Quite sentimental. Pretty riding-clothes, fine hair, sweet voice.

> Gave her my cheap nosegay: a tulip, a white lily, three sprigs of myrtle. Charming creature.

The diarist's candour anticipates the confessional fiction of our own century. If the sexual act is not described, at least it is statistically recorded. Matrimonial bouts are signalled by *pi* for pleasure. The drunkenness is set down by the bottle, the crapulae are inscribed almost in blood. There is a relish for sexual anecdotes. His friend Grindall told him of three cases of self-castration that he knew of directly; the third was 'a German jeweller, despairing love for his landlady. "You bitch, you shall have it one way or other''; threw it at her.'

In the three years covered by this volume, Boswell was attending to his duties as Laird of Auchinleck, practising at the Scottish bar, nursing political ambitions, writing and reading, copulating and carousing, recording Johnson's *dicta* whenever he could get to London. Because Johnson is not in the foreground he is, in a paradox we associate with fiction, more real than in the relentless white light of the biography. He is allowed to retreat behind the pages and get on with his life or death in privacy. Boswell is his own Johnson, and his acts and words are worthy of our attention. In a session with George III he discusses the problem of how to designate Charles Edward Stuart in his *Tour*. He will not have 'Pretender', which may be parliamentary but is not gentlemanly. He reminds the Hanoverian monarch that the Boswells have Stuart blood. George graciously permits the appellation 'grandson of King James II'.

Boswell is mixed up. He loves England but he is jealous for the preservation of all the Scots rights of the Act of Union. He regrets that Edinburgh should be so provincial. 'The coarse vulgarity all around me is as shocking to me as it used to be to Sir John Pringle. Dr Blair accosted me with a vile tone. "*Hoo did you leave Sawmuel?*" ' But he adds: 'What *right* have I to be so nicely delicate?'

Back to *Samuel*. It is this section of the journals which contains the revelations of Johnson's sexual life which Boswell prudently termed *tacenda* and, in the biography, was duly silent about. He and Lowe cross-examine Mrs Desmoulins, young and attractive protégé of Johnson's wife Tetty, who preferred the bottle to sex and, pleading that her bed was too small, kept Johnson out of it. But Johnson toyed with the complaisant Mrs Desmoulins, kissed her, grew terribly aroused but never proceeded to consummation. Sir John Hawkins 'accounted for Johnson's fear of death: "I have read his diary. I wish I had not read so much. He had strong amorous passions.' BOSWELL: "But he did not indulge them?" HAWKINS: "I have said enough." ' Onanism, a foul sin which Boswell seems to have avoided. But Boswell committed other sins of the flesh and, if he did not have Johnson's fear of hell fire, he hardly ever stopped thinking of death.

Being a kind of novelist, he was able to look at death objectively and ponder the mystery of the lack of transition between it and life. He goes to the London hangings, is impressed by the fortitude of the condemned, sees all. George Ward, whose crime was the theft of a basket of linen, 'struggled long. While they were yet hanging, I went to Betsy just by. Imagined the feelings of a desperate highwayman. Said to her: "I have got a shocking sight in my head. Take it out." Her pleasing vivacity *did* remove it.'

Boswell records his dreams, including one almost Raskolnikovian: 'I awaked in horror, having dreamt that I saw a poor wretch lying naked on a dunghill in London, and a blackguard ruffian taking his skin off with a knife in the way that an ox is flayed; and that the poor wretch was alive and complained woefully.' His unconscious had access to the horror of the age; his conscious had the sense to follow Burke's advice and, as far as he could, 'live pleasant'. But he was too much the artist to wish to evade the duties of introspection, and too much the Celt not to suffer from manic depression, which he termed, like the rest of his age, hypochondria.

The standards of editing and presentation are as high as ever, the notes are satisfyingly full. We are reminded, however, that this is American scholarship by occasional flashes of ignorance. Brag, which Boswell plays, is a living game, not merely an 'old one like poker'. Boswell's riding song 'Gee-ho, Dobbin' is surely still sung to children and is far from being 'unidentified'. But these are minor points. We end with Boswell's expense accounts. A dinner at the Swan with Two Necks, Lad Lane, Cheapside, for 2s 3d. Postage 2d. And it took only three days to get the news of Johnson's death in London dispatched to Edinburgh.

Sade, Our Bedfellow

De Sade: A Critical Biography, by Ronald Hayman

I t seems ironical that the Laura of Petrarch's sonnets, which glorify the agonies and transports of love, should be Laure de Sade. But it is not really, since the most notorious member of that ancient and noble Provençal family also specialized in erotic pains and ecstasies. So long as Mrs Whitehouse continues to be zealous on behalf of British morals, so long as it is remembered that the Moors Murderers had a copy of *Justine* in their library, the precise nature of Donatien Alphonse François's specialization will never be known in England. On the Continent it is different. I even found my son, at the age of eight, poring over an Italian comic book in which Donatien was the bewigged and muscular hero. It is always best to have things out in the light. The major horrors of our age have been perpetrated by regimes that banned *The 120 Days of Sodom*.

This book, Sade's masterpiece, is a fictionalized catalogue of sexual perversions, all of which involve torture and some of them death. The *mise en scène* is an impregnable castle in the Black Forest, where four debauchees from Paris – a banker, a bishop, a duke and a judge – spend seventeen weeks in perverse pleasures graduated from the merely revolting to the ineffably evil. It was Sade's intention to describe six hundred perversions, but he only managed to get through the first thirty days – though he made detailed notes for the other ninety. A fairly mild pleasure entails strapping a naked girl to a table and having a hot omelette – to be eaten with a sharp fork – served upon her buttocks. A more advanced one has fifteen girls tortured simultaneously in fifteen ways, while the *grand seigneur* who arranges the *Grand Guignol* watches and waits for orgasm. It does not come easily. It has to be effected through masturbation and the exhibition of two male bottoms.

Disgusting, Mrs Whitehouse? Ah yes, but may we not also consider it pitiable? The creator of these visions was evidently in a state of sexual frustration so intense that no imagined stimulus could procure a discharge. At the same time he was clear-headed enough to recognize, with a clarity never before known, a truth that not even Mrs Whitehouse may deny – that sex and cruelty have much to do with each other. If we were permitted to cool the inflamed expectations that the proscription of Sade encourages, if we were permitted to read him entire, then we should find less pornography than philosophy, anthropology and pioneer sexology. And we should find a good deal of it rather dull going.

Whether we like it or not, we have to accept that Sade was an original thinker, as shockingly candid as Freud and as radical a discloser of psychological truths that the world of the respectable would prefer to remain hidden. The extent of the originality can only be judged against Sade's own time, and it is necessary that we read a good biography before settling down to *Justine* or the very philosophical *Dialogue Between a Priest and Dying Man*. Mr Hayman's is a good terse biography. We follow the young marquis from the days of maternal neglect and grandmotherly coddling, through his distinguished military career in the Seven Years' War, the aftermath of debauchery and a taste for sodomy (a capital offence in those days), the exaggerated Jack-the-Ripper reputation that got him into the Bastille and, when the Revolution started, out again. At first a trusted officer of the new Republic, even a judge, he was always too much of a sceptic to truckle to the Jacobin orthodoxy.

Back in jail as an *aristo*, he only escaped the guillotine when Robespierre fell. Then he was cleared and treated once more as a patriot. He began to publish books considered unrevolutionary and corruptive, was back in jail once more and, finally, committed by his own family to the madhouse at Charenton. 'His only madness is that of vice,' said the medical superintendent. What he did at Charenton in the field of dramatic therapy we know well enough from the *Marat–Sade* play. He also nourished a dream, hardly broken, of ever more massive sexual violence until he died, obese, diseased, but still loved by the young actress Marie-Constance Quesnet, in 1814.

To Sade, a good eighteenth-century rationalist, God was dead. But the goddess Nature was much alive, lavishly and carelessly creative but also wantonly destructive, revelling in earthquakes, storms, floods, volcanic eruptions. We, says Sade, are her children and must do her will. Destruction is behovely, since it is in the service of new creation. Cruelty is a manifestation of impersonal, or prepersonal, energy. Morality means nothing. The first law of life is to accept the world as it is. This meant, presumably, accepting the Terror. Sade was more realistic than Rousseau, and posterity has made him suffer for that. But posterity has also seen the fulfilment of some of his dreams in the Nazi holocausts, the thermonuclear bomb. Disaster movies about earthquakes and the end of the world derive from his scenarios. And who can say he was wrong always to expect the worst of mankind?

Mr Hayman reports from France on Sade's present literary reputation, which, since the advent of Structuralism, is higher than it was. Roland Barthes and Philippe Sollers call his novels great masterpieces, despite their lack of narrative movement, their hollow characters and feeble grasp of the world of physical particulars. Mr Hayman disagrees but considers Sade 'a key figure in the history of modernism, and, above all, in the history of alienation. He was a nihilist before the word "nihilism" existed, anticipating Dostoevsky and Nietzsche.' If you can find Genet and Céline acceptable (and it is in terms of these two modern cathartists of evil that Sade is often now mentioned in France) you will find it possible, perhaps, to follow Sade's career with sympathy as well as fascination. But, however you feel after reading his life, you will not be able to write him off as an evil and discardable lusus. He knew what we have all taken a long time to learn – that sex is not just something that happens in a bedroom.

Janeite

A Portrait of Jane Austen, by Lord David Cecil

'Some people,' says Lord David, 'are well worth knowing even as acquaintances. Jane Austen is one of them. She reveals herself in her letters and records as a personality with a sharp, subtle, agreeable flavour of her own; a personality observant, perceptive, amused, perhaps formidable, certainly intriguing and all the more so because she seems very different from the conventional idea of an author of genius.' *Author*, Lord David tells us, through a corrective letter from the publisher, should be *authoress*: that suffix makes all the difference. I have tried to think of what the conventional idea of an authoress of genius is: George Sand? E. B. B.? Emily Dickinson? Mme de Staël? Brigid Brophy? Perhaps somebody very full of herself and always dragging men into bed. I don't know. I'm sorry the issue has arisen. I'm sorry too that so elegant a piece of bookmaking (the work of Rainbird) should be marred by this and one or two other ugly errors of printing. The book is superbly illustrated, very moving and informative, a work to buy not borrow.

Formidable certainly, not just perhaps. The only shameful advantage we seem to have over Jane Austen is knowing that she died of Addison's disease (failure to function of the adrenal cortex, the symptoms bronzelike skin pigmentation, anaemia and prostration). That I am twenty years and Lord David thirty-five years older than she was when she died represents no advantage to either of us. We have not produced her novels. She remains not only a formidable artist who would demolish both of us (well, certainly me, if she thought me worth demolishing or even taking notice of) in a couple of lines; she testifies formidably to the truth that we have nothing to teach her about how to live the good life, nor, for that matter, anything to teach her age about the right true end of civilization. She appeared in a good time, when patriotism, the Christian faith, courtesy, firm taste in domestic architecture and interior decoration, exactness of language and powerful familial piety conjoined in a classical ambience of certainty that revolution and Bonaparte saved from smugness. The smugness came later, and it was to denounce a certain regrettable coarseness in Jane Austen, meaning a preparedness to mention mistresses and confinements. She was closer to Dr Johnson, whom she loved, than to, say, John Ruskin, who was shocked into impotence by his bride's revelation that women had pubic hair.

Recount Jane Austen's life to a class in an American university, and there will be unseemly expressions of shock that she knew nothing about life, man, meaning like well never slept with a guy and like well was stuck in a crappy old house without an icebox. There are others, less ingenuous, who believe that Jane Austen was cut off from the great world of dangerous public enactments, unaware that she had two brothers engaged in the naval wars against Napoleon, both to end as admirals, and a cousin, Eliza Hancock, whose husband, M. de Feuillide, was guillotined as an Enemy of the Republic. Jane Austen knew everything about what was going on; she merely decided to leave guilt and misery to other pens. It wasn't solely, either, that guilt and misery were going on over the waters; there were enough of the commodities near at home. Consider, for instance, what happened to Mrs James Leigh Perrot, her aunt by marriage.

That wealthy and elegant lady was accused, by a draper in Bath, of walking out with some white lace she had not paid for. It was all a mistake, of course, but information was laid with a magistrate and she was dragged off to Ilchester jail. She might have had to stay there for months pending trial if the jailer had not granted her lodging in his own dirty house. A theft of anything over five shillings was a capital offence in those days. Mrs Leigh Perrot could have been hanged or, at best, transported for fourteen years to Botany Bay. After seven months of nauseating confinement she came up for trial and was acquitted. But she might not have been. Jane and her sister Cassandra offered their companionship in prison and their support at the trial, but Mrs Leigh Perrot said: 'To have two young creatures gazed at in a public court would cut me to the very heart!' Toughness and family loyalty characterized the Austens, but especially Jane. Of the whole incident Lord David remarks:

> On the one hand, it shows how a life as civilised as that of the Austens existed cheek by jowl with a legal system, cruel, inefficient and unjust; on the other, that this system was administered with a sort of ruthless fairness; so that all Mr Leigh Perrot's wealth and respectability could not save his wife from its severity, once its machinery had got into action.

The Tory Anglicanism of Jane Austen is worn lightly in the novels. In private life it was (that word again) formidable, even Johnsonian, and sometimes, as with the Grand Cham, the moral content of the one had to battle with the secular loyalty imposed by the other. The Prince Regent expressed, through an intermediary somewhat like Mr Collins, willingness to accept a dedication. Jane Austen, instead of leaping at the chance, had to decide gravely whether or not to seem to condone his debauchery. As we know, loyalty or common sense won. But it was the only occasion when stern morality took a back seat. Approaching death, she wrote her own prayers. One of them went:

> Incline us Oh God: to think humbly of ourselves, to be saved only in the examination of our own conduct, to consider our fellow-creatures with kindness, and to judge of all they say and do with that charity which we would desire from them ourselves.

Like all novelists with a strong satiric bent, she knew that the gentle pillorying of folly could be construed as lack of charity. No one more charitable, more chaste, more vital, more civilized ever existed. As Kipling recognized, there has to be a heaven to accommodate her.

Victory for Hugo

Les Misérables, by Victor Hugo, translated by Norman Denny

In *Cold Comfort Farm* Reuben says to Flora: 'I ha' scranleted two hunded furrows come five o'clock down i' the bute.' Flora does not well know what to reply – whether 'My dear, how too sickening for you' or 'Attaboy' or 'Come, that's capital.' She falls back on the safe remark 'Did you?' and provokes a storm of wounded pride. That same safe remark has been the response to my boast that I have read the whole of *Les Misérables* in two nights and a day, and I have felt like snarling: 'Don't you know the length of the thing – 1267 pages? Are you unaware of the dullness, the irrelevancies, the preaching, the sentimentality, the improbabilities, the melodrama?' I did not add: 'Also the greatness.' I suppose it has to be a great book since it cannot be a good one. The French, who know Hugo better than we do, admit his greatness and then sigh '*Hélas.*'

Les Misérables is one of the books we all think we read when we were young. Perhaps we saw a film of it or acted in a school play called *The Bishop's Candlesticks*. A fellow-sergeant during the war told me it was about a geezer what stole a loaf of rooty and got followed to his dying day by a bastard of a rozzer. No one ever complained that book and film alike appeared in English with the original French title. That title was pronounced as if it were English. The ingenuous thought it was the story of a man called Les who had the miseries. Having just finished, thank

God, Mr Denny's translation I am fairly sure that I read the whole thing long ago and determined never to read it again, not even for a reviewer's fee. I should like to have known whose translation I read, but Mr Denny coyly refuses to divulge the names of his predecessors. He read one of them, he says, and found it heavy going. He can, as they say, say that again. It was too literal, and it kept everything in. Mr Denny is more merciful. He has been bold enough to 'abridge, tone down the rhetoric, even delete where the passage in question is merely an elaboration of what has already been said.' But this edited version is still damnably long and (to the unconscientious, meaning not the reviewer) highly skippable.

And yet the prosy preaching, the potted history, the pseudo-poetical divagations, the improbable coincidences and the morality-play characterization are all part of the highly idiosyncratic texture. You cannot really afford to miss too much. The strength of the book lies in its weakness, which is an unwillingness to shape and file and, in short, produce a genuine novel. It is so clumsy, and so animated by generous anger, that we take it as a testament of nineteenth-century liberalism rather than as a piece of art. But art is not missing. Jean Valjean and his pursuer Javert are such sturdy, if inhuman, fabrications that, when they fade from the narrative in order to accommodate a treatise on the Battle of Waterloo or on the state of Paris in 1831, we are prepared to be patient and wait for them to reappear. The same goes for the unhappy Fantine, who sells two front teeth so that she shall have a little money to send to the rascally guardians of her bastard daughter; for the daughter herself, Cosette, whom Valjean brings up as his own; for the urchin Gavroche, whose wit does not, it seems, go well into English. He talks too much about 'cops'. The term 'horrid fascination' applies to all these children of misery.

It is said that a good novel ought to disclose its content in its title. *Les Misérables* is certainly about what it says it is about. It is a gallery of wretches who are brought together very very slowly into the contrived unity of a plot. Of these wretches Jean Valjean is the most wretched – cancerous with guilt, as strong as ten horses, saintly, obsessed with charity and justice (these get in each other's way), totally, like his creator, without humour, and yet monstrously impressive. He exemplifies, as does his pursuer, the peculiar abstractness of crime – a metaphysical state which has nothing to do with its first enactment (the lifting of the loaf of rooty). His adopted daughter Cosette begins in the depths of deprivation but ends as the beautiful wife of the noble Marius (who, in the early days of courtship, shudders at the horror of even envisaging, God curse this human lust, the divine shape of her hidden ankle). Nobody lives an ordinary decent middle-class life. You have to be in the gutter or apotheosized to high gentility. *Les Misérables* is nothing like *The Vicar of Wakefield*.

The details of low life are dwelt upon with a thoroughness from which Zola must have learnt. There is no doubt that Hugo knows his Paris of the outcasts – from the lath Napoleonic elephant near the Bastille,

whose cobwebbed interior Gavroche shares with the rats, to the labyrinth of the city sewers. He knows with equal thoroughness the dark pits
of the human soul, but we have only to think of a book like *Last Exit to
Brooklyn* to recognize how unrealistic his depictions of villainy really are.
There are long speeches instead of blood and panting; when blows are
struck they have a mainly metaphysical force. And, of course, there is
absolutely no sexual crime. There are a lot of ragged children about,
which presupposes that the sexual act must have taken place among the
rats, rags and ashes, but people kill for revenge or out of hunger, never
from lust. Needless to say, surfeited as we are with contemporary libido,
we find a certain charm in all this depraved chastity.

The book has been much praised as a chronicle of life in post-
Napoleonic France, complete with neo-revolutionary barricades, but we
have to take it finally as a portrait of one man's soul – that of Hugo
himself, Buonapartist and republican (he wrote the work in exile in the
Channel Islands), poet and humanist, as stagy as Dickens but without
either Dickens's grotesquerie or his humour. Here is the death of young
Gavroche on the barricades:

> Gavroche was seen to stagger, and then he collapsed. A cry went up from
> the barricade. But there was an Antaeus concealed in that pygmy. A
> Paris urchin touching the pavement is a giant drawing strength from his
> mother earth. . . . He sat upright with blood streaming down his face,
> and raising his arms above his head and gazing in the direction of the
> shot, he again began to sing. . . . A second ball from the same musket cut
> him short. This time he fell face down and moved no more. His gallant
> soul had fled.

Possessing Dickens, we do not really need *Les Misérables*. But it is perhaps necessary to read it in order to gain new insights into the meaning
of the term 'literary greatness'. There is a massiveness here which cannot fail to impress, even when we are most ready to reject the unashamed
exploitation of our feelings. The structure holds in spite of every
imaginable fictional fault. It is, in other words, a big book. And it is
frighteningly sincere.

Praising Stendhal

Speaking of Stendhal, by Storm Jameson

'Being a darling of the *élite*,' says a distinguished Yorkshire writer, 'Stendhal has undoubtedly been over-praised.' He goes on to say: 'Just as there is something unsatisfactory and ambiguous about the man himself, so too, in spite of their originality and brilliant technical innovations, his novels offer us too many dubious elements to be accepted as great fiction.' That is J. B. Priestley, and I am inclined to agree with him. Now here comes another distinguished Yorkshire novelist to speak for the Beylistes, to admit that their god is a cult rather than an influence and to talk of 'the love, the complicity, we' (meaning the cultists) 'feel for him', as well as 'the incomparable pleasure of returning again and again to books which have the grace and suppleness of young athletes stripped to run a race.' I have read Stendhal. Commissioned to write the entry entitled '*The Novel*' in the most recent *Encyclopaedia Britannica*, I reread him. I do not propose ever to reread him. Now, if I said that about Shakespeare or even Dickens I should be self-condemned as a being somehow corrupt, one who has had part of his humanity excised; Mr Priestley and Dr Jameson alike, accepting the premise of the cult, will acquiesce in an honest rejection of Stendhal by one who considers that there are more important books than *Le Rouge et le Noir* and *La Chartreuse de Parme*, life being short, to re or reread. Therefore Stendal (as he should be; he took his pseudonym from a German village; the aspirate is owed to an inaccurate memory) is not one of the great. I think this logic is sound.

Wherein lies his appeal to those to whom he appeals? Lord Snow, who, a few months ago, published his own tribute to Stendhal, sums him up in his blunt Priestleyan way: 'For better and for worse, he often speaks to us in the tone of a modern Western man. You can meet him today at literary parties in New York or London, aggressive, abrasive, amusing, rancorous because the great commercial break hasn't yet come.' That commercial break has nothing to do with television. Stendhal said he would get a readership in 1900 or 1930 or 2000. He was very clear-sighted about his own work and, if you examine his life, not really all that rancorous about his small sales. It is this clear-sightedness, a social honesty to match it, and a psychological honesty that granted him (Snow again) 'a knowledge of his own emotional states, above all of his emotional vicissitudes in love, which he studied as coolly and clinically as any man has ever done' that make him attractive to those he attracts. There is also a perennial youthfulness which is supposed to appeal, expressed in gaucheness, social indiscretion, everreadiness to fall in love. There is a lot of the real Stendhal in Julien Sorel, as there is a lot of what Stendhal would like to have been in Mosca.

Dr Jameson's short biography, for it is nothing more, puzzles me a little. She says: 'I have left it too late to write the long book I hoped, many years ago, to attempt.' She does not regret this, since Henri Martineau's *Le Coeur de Stendhal* (1952) says nearly all that has to be said. But we, whose first reading language is English, may beg leave to regret that she has not done what she was always richly qualified to do – namely, produce a slow, ruminative, critical life, with all the books (after all, there are not many) deeply assessed, for these who know Stendhal in English. He loses little in English (he, who adored Shakespeare and even wrote English, though sometimes ludicrously, would have been delighted to concur), and there are good translations of him in the Penguin Classics. As it is, she gives us a rushed life, with Beyle jetting about Europe, that is needful of over scrupulous mastication, and says far too little about the books. Moreover, when she quotes letters and journals, which is often, she quotes in French. She might as well have written her book in French. Before he died, Beyle wrote: '*Je trouve qu'il n'y a pas de ridicule à mourir dans la rue, quand on le fait pas exprès.*' Snow says: 'He speculated whether it would be ridiculous to die in the street. He decided not, provided that he hadn't done it on purpose.' That blunt paraphrase is not less witty than the original.

Dr Jameson's raid on the rich territory of Stendhal's life may be regarded as a kind of testament of a lifelong devotion. Did her Yorkshire reticence forbid the writing of a love letter? Hardly, since her novels, which I have always admired, are marked by a strong and honest emotional content. I should have preferred the kind of directly personal epistle that Mario Muchnik wrote to Michelangelo. The late lamented John Lodwick, in his novel *The Butterfly Net*, came as close as anyone ever did to recreating Henri Beyle (though up there in heaven) as a person to be loved. All we get from Dr Jameson is the odd interjection like 'Dear Beyle' – smiling, affectionate, pitying, head-shaking. Then back to the crammed rushed record.

I wish there were space to develop Mr Priestley's generalization about 'dubious elements', or what I think he means by the generalization. I have only room to suggest that even the most convinced Beyliste must admit to mechanical contrivances in *La Chartreuse de Parme*, to a lack of balance of head and heart in *Le Rouge et le Noir*, to an unbecoming coolness of style which makes the reader uncomfortable when the gales of emotion decide to blow. Everybody knows what the fine things are – the Waterloo scene which taught Tolstoy so much, the marvellous class-hatred of Julien, the wonderful honesty of *De l'Amour*, the charm of Mme Rênal, the incredible Duchess of Sanseverino. He could create fine parts but was less successful when it came to conceiving totalities. Dr Jameson, suggesting that Stendhal was of too rare a blood type to be able to transfuse his qualities into other writers, thinks that Lampedusa's *Il Gattopardo* is perhaps the only novel where the Stendhalian red flows as in its own channels. I wish there were space to say something about that.

Inimitable

The Letters of Charles Dickens, Volume V: 1847–1849, edited by Graham Storey and K. J. Fielding

The energy of the man! In April 1848 he completed the serial publication of *Dombey and Son*. In May 1849 he began *David Copperfield*. Between the two books he wrote the last of his Christmas stories, *The Haunted Man*. He wrote regularly, during 1848 and 1849, for the *Examiner* and, at the end of the period covered by this collection, was planning to start *Household Words* in the spring of 1850. Apart from all this, he was launching the Cheap Edition, acting and stage-managing, speaking in public, begetting sons, helping Miss Coutts to run the Home for Homeless Women, attacking social wrongs at home and defending national rights abroad, identifying with the European revolutionaries of 1848 ('*Citoyen Charles Dickens*'), living a vigorous social life though not, as far as we can tell, womanizing. In addition he produced the 1248 letters of this volume, which is hence as hefty as a Dickens novel. The secret of his output and activity seems to have been unobtrusive organization. He knew when to say no, though he did not say it often. 'Dear Lord Albert Conyngham – I am afraid I am *not* to see a masked ball, just now.'

The letters are better organized than the books, being shorter and unserializable. They have beginnings, middles and ends, which the books do not always have. They are always charming, even when formal: the charm resides as much in the shape of the statements as in the tone, which may be described as modest without self-abasement. You feel you are in the presence of a man who knows his own worth too well to have to push it. As all the letters present the character of the man, one reads them as one reads the fiction and the journalism – in the expectation of quirky flashes that delight as well as that laughing unafraid liberalism which attracted Orwell. He writes as well in French (save for a *Jean Bull* indifference to genders) as he does in *echt* Dickensian. Dickensian is carefully slangy when it has to be regretful: 'My Dear Stone – Hopelessly engaged (wus luck!) and just going out. Ever Affecy. CD.' Sometimes, as in the letters to Forster, it combines concern and facetiousness: 'The sea has been running very high, and Leech, while bathing, was knocked over by a bad blow from a great wave on the forehead. He is in bed, and had twenty of his namesakes on his temples this morning.'

In the Dickens manner, the story of Leech's misfortune builds up into a miniature saga, and you feel it ought to go into a book somewhere. F. M. Evans is told that Leech is 'a ship in distress, in a sea of bedclothes'. Forster learns that the Inimitable has tried magnetism on him, with some success. Mark Lemon hears that Leech is better and is to have a boiled fowl for his dinner. But letters to *The Times* are, though not necessarily brief, highly concentrated and dignified. The one which protests against public executions is a masterpiece. Even so, despite its close argument, it finds room for references to *Macbeth, Don Quixote* and the punitive methods of ancient Egypt. Dickens is happiest when he can let his prose riot like an unweeded garden. But his inner monitor tells him to reserve the vegetative approach to his novels. He may not know when to stop a novel, but he always knows how long a letter should be. This is an aspect of the unobtrusive organization.

When he makes a promise he invariably keeps it. Mrs Jane Seymour Hill, a dwarf manicurist and chiropodist, was greatly distressed by the portrait of Miss Mowcher (*Copperfield*, Chapter 22), which was rightly taken to be a somewhat sinister version of herself. Dickens expresses his own distress at causing distress, makes the novelist's regular excuse that all his characters are compounds of reality, not copies of it, and then says:

> I should be most truly pained if you were to remain under the impression that you have any cause of complaint against me or that I have done you any injury however innocently. I am so sincere in this believe me that rather than you should pass another of those sleepless nights of which you write to me or go another morning tearfully to your daily work, I would alter the whole design of the character and remove it, in its progress, from the possibility of that bad construction at which you hint.

He kept his word. Miss Mowcher does not, after all, help Steerforth to seduce Little Em'ly. In Chapter 32, when she visits David, she is a sympathetic personage. In Chapter 61 she helps in Littimer's arrest and is cheered all the way home. Dickens could not bear ill will.

His ability to balance the claims of art with the desire to inspire universal affection is one of Dickens's many achievements. Even Mrs Seymour Hill's tearful letter (quoted in the footnotes, which are always admirably detailed) has to be more sorrowful than angry, since she is writing to a Man hitherto considered as a Christian and Friend to his fellow Creatures. One would, indeed, like the letters more if there were some big blazing row with Thackeray always going on (Thackeray did not believe the writing of novels was really a gentlemanly occupation and he scorned Dickens's ambition to have it regarded as a reputable profession). But the Dickensian niceness is unremitting, and he seems to be not much nicer to the mother of his children than to Lemon, Macready and the rest. But this is saying a lot about his niceness. The Brotherhood of Man was a bigger thing than marital passion.

This volume, like its predecessors, is a marvel of scholarship. There is not a reference in the letters, however obscure, that has not been pursued to its source. There are also bonuses in the form of such occasional writings as the Appeal to Fallen Women ('If ever your poor heart is moved to feel, truly, what you might have been, and what you are, oh think of it then, and consider what you may be yet! Believe me that I am, indeed, YOUR FRIEND') and the parody on Gray's 'Elegy', which proves, despite the sneers of those who find blank verse in his prose, that Dickens knew as much as any *Punch* man about prosody:

> Here rests his head upon his native soil
> A Youth who lived once, in the public whim:
> His death occasion'd by a mortal Boil,
> Which settled on his brain, and settled him.

Dickens: A Life, by Norman and Jeanne MacKenzie
The Mutual Friend, by Frederick Busch

The main claim to our attention of this new biography of Dickens seems to be the taking into 'full account of many new letters and the considerable research of Dickens scholars during the past twenty-five years.' The portrait it presents is, nevertheless, not notably different from that in, for instance, the late Una Pope-Hennessy's life, the last one which I, who am not a professional Dickensian, seem to have read. I remember that biography well enough to be dissatisfied with odd failures of substantiality in the MacKenzie work – the actual words Dickens spoke and the poem he wrote at the time of meeting Miss Christiana Weller; the boarding up of his dressing room when he decided to cease cohabitation with his wife; the lethal doling of brandy to the injured after the train wreck; the verse prologue to *The Frozen Deep*. This new biography pushes us on on a temporal treadmill, making us powerfully aware of Dickens riding time, but it is harmed by an unwillingness to stand outside time for an occasional space and deliver judgements on a phase in Dickens's development, either as a man or as a writer. It is not a bold book; it lacks flavour. Unfortunately, like all literary biographies since the late fifties, it has to stand comparison with Richard Ellmann's *James Joyce*, where there is wit, exasperated affection for the subject, and a willingness to engage the business of assessing the work as well as the life. Perhaps the lack of a biographical attitude is inevitable in a work written by two people who, though one flesh, cannot always be of one mind and hence are sometimes of no discernible mind at all.

On the other hand, there is a concentration on the Victorian background and Dickens's relationship to it which is of immense value; it is as though the old left-wing stigmatization of Dickens as an unpolitical man, or a man ignorant of Utilitarian theory and the doctrines of reform, is being deliberately countered with an image of an activist to whom the writing of fiction was a secondary métier. We are reminded of how Dickens's primary concern was with rapport with an audience; he had the demogogic urge to *move* his public, sometimes in the direction of impracticable social anger. He was, however briefly and unsatisfactorily, the editor of a daily newspaper. Labile, given too easily to powerful responses to stock collective stimuli, he could yet respond sourly to the Great Exhibition of 1851 and, in *Household Words*, has that Old Year saying:

> I have been a year of ruin. . . . I bequeath to my successor a vast inheritance of degradation and neglect in England, a general mismanagement of all public expenditure, revenues and property. I do give and bequeath to him, likewise, the Court of Chancery. The less he leaves of it to his successor, the better for mankind.

The following March the first number of *Bleak House* appeared. George Orwell, who saw Dickens's politics as naive and his morals simplistic, shrewdly made the point that he could attack wrongs till he was apoplectic and yet leave the wrongdoers unmoved. More, the very targets of his attacks, from bureaucrats to Utilitarian factory owners, were somehow confirmed in their villainy by the very force of his denunciations, whether in journalism or in fiction. The force was always excessive; it was virtuoso and entertaining. Charles Reade, in *Put Yourself in His Place*, could attack 'rattening', or trade union terrorism, very effecvely because his art was smaller than that of Dickens; when Stephen Blackpool in *Hard Times* is victimized by the syndicalists, the union movement is transformed into a force too satanic to be true. Dickens was not without detailed knowledge of and sharp insight into the nature of Victorian society, but he was prevented by his very special verbal gift from being an effective propagandist for reform. This gift, which he was all too willing to put into the service of subversion, insisted on flourishing in a region both above and beneath politics – in a realm of impossible idealism or a kingdom of equally impossible physical appetites. Whether he wished it or not, he was betrayed into art. This is why we read him more than we read Reade.

It is often the claim of new biographies to sharpen the contradictions in genius, to call forth wonder at the coexistence of irreconcilables in the one personality. This book makes no such claim nor, for that matter, any other claim, but it succeeds in presenting a very unified image, or rather one whose disparities are explicable in very human terms. The glandular vagaries of late middle age are enough to explain, if not excuse, the putting away of his wife and the taking of Ellen Lawless Ternan as a mistress. His wife did not do badly out of the exchange; she was past sex and her husband's excessive energy had always wearied her. If we tend to be shocked by Dickens's insistence on justifying his action to the world, we can at least commend what he thought of as his honesty. It is this love affair with his public, from which he must have no secrets, which we find not merely singular in a literary man but quite unique. It was an affair whose progress he was able to gauge, quite uncynically, in terms of monetary returns. There was a kind of logic here: it is the duty of one's family to provide both love and financial security; Dickens's worldwide family kissed him and loaded him with flowers and did not sell him into the slavery of a blacking factory. Nor is there any real contradiction in Dickens's professed solidarity with the poor subsisting with an unashamed ambition to grow richer and richer still. He was, in a way, an example to the poor, a model of self-help. He had not, like Orwell, been born into a world of aitched privilege.

After reading the MacKenzie book, one is newly amazed at a strength of character that, despite the universal worship (qualified, of course, by the acerbity of literary critics who wanted him to keep on writing *The Pickwick Papers* all his life), was never betrayed into great-man postures. He knew he was inimitable, and he made a joke of his inimitability. The kind of adulation he received is never now accorded to writers, only to popstars, and few popstars come well out of the deification. Dickens was corrupted only into an innocence and trust that an artist's relationship with his public cannot well sustain. He could not understand other people's self-interest, and was honestly perplexed by American hypocrisy at the time of his discreet, though eloquent, pleas for universal copyright. It was in his demonic nature to push, be the centre of things, control, organize (though this was mostly in the harmless sphere of amateur theatricals), but his ebullience was admired rather than resented. His viciousness towards printers and publishers, often taken as an aspect of greed or pile-driving ambition, can, at least by his fellow-authors, only be applauded.

The MacKenzies astutely stress a chronic infantilism that could produce great literature but could not cope with the stresses of a marriage. Wisely they keep deep psychology out of their assessment of his character and do not raise the wearisome issue of arrest at the anal-erotic phase. To be frank, very little Victorian literature can be called adult in comparison with what was being produced across the Channel, but Dickens at least understood the child's mind, which few Victorian adults did, and it may be said that it is enough for a novelist to assume mastery of even a fraction of the human psyche. The limitations of Dickens's grasp of what actually goes on in the adult mind are, by our standards, appalling, but few of his contemporaries did better. One young man, writing on *Our Mutual Friend* in the New York *Nation*, saw in it 'the poverty not of momentary embarrassment but of permanent exhaustion . . . so intensely *written*, so little seen, known or felt.' He, being Henry James, was to make the novel a medium for the presentation of known and felt complexities, but with a sacrifice of verve and ebullience that the form, sternly aware of its responsibilities, has never been able to recover.

The biography of a writer is never able to give us an inkling of those seen, known and felt aspects of a writer's life which justify the memorialization of its other aspects – I mean, the things that go on in the study behind the door with its false bookshelves: the scratching of the pen, the tearing of paper, the dictionary, if used, used. We must go to the novelist to learn about novelists. Frederick Busch's little fiction does not dare to guess at the mysteries of the Dickensian creative agony. To read it after the Mackenzie biography is unfair to its author, since the documentary sources remain fresh in our minds and we see their conscious manipulation into what purports to be an imaginative reconstruction. Professor Busch is interested in George Dolby, 'a large bald-headed man with a stammer, whom Mark Twain described as a gladsome gorilla' (I quote the MacKenzies), the faithful assistant of the man he called 'the Chief' on those eventually lethal readings in both Britain and America. Busch sedulously reconstructs the railway journeys through the States, with Dickens wearing a gutta-percha overshoe on the left foot, addressing his stuttering Tapley in terms like 'Really, Dolby, I don't *want* to sleep in any more towns named Utica. *Utica*. Doesn't it sound like an herb you take for your health?' Dickens sounds like a decent, tired, stock member of the British upper class, except for that unaspirated *herb*, which is wholly American. The book is a brave effort that does not, could not, come off. But at least it particularizes where the MacKenzies generalize. Catherine Dickens recalls accurately the dreadful schism:

> He wrote home to direct the old servant, Anne, and Georgina, of course, to see to a certain remodelling of Tavistock House. His little dressing-room off our bedroom was to be changed, the washstands being taken into the bathroom and the doorway between the dressing-room and my room – once it was all called our apartment – separated from the dressing-room by a wooden door, and the recess filled with shelves. The dressing-room was now his bedroom. Where I had slept I once had designated our room, and now it wholly was mine, and mine in such a way as to be nobody's.

Professor Busch brings in a reformed prostitute, one whom Dickens and the rich Miss Coutts have 'reclaimed', to provide statutory scenes of sexuality, though not with the Inimitable. His son Plorn is painfully fellated to the tune of 'You shit-smeared kitchen-maid whore'. There is still room for a good novel on Dickens, though Dickens already seems to have written it, or them. Meanwhile there is the outstanding job of convincingly completing *Edwin Drood*.

Dickens: Interviews and Recollections, edited by Philip Collins, 2 vols.

We have here a synoptic portrait of the Inimitable, made out of impressions not only diverse but divergent. The total effect is one of intense animation, improper for a hall of fame but apt for music hall or cinema. I mean, there is no marble bust of the kind that

Eckermann tried to make of Goethe. Dickens resists still portraiture. The eyes were too animated, the features always in motion. In respect of the extreme vivacity of his face and gestures, Dickens was remote from the stereotypical Englishman of the educated classes – the lord and owner of his face, unmoved, cold, and to temptation slow. To many he looked, if not like a foreigner, at least like an impressionable man who had travelled and absorbed the Latin vocabulary of gesture. Naturally, to many he seemed a vulgarian.

Boston, Mass., which knew all about refinement, found Dickens an unsuitable candidate for the best society. Elizabeth Wormeley deplored his two velvet waistcoats – 'one of vivid green, the other of brilliant crimson; these were further ornamented by a profusion of gold watch chain'. In 1841 a black satin waistcoat was almost the national costume of gentlemen in America: so that Mr Dickens's vivid tints were very conspicuous. Mrs Dickens '. . . showed signs of having been born and bred her husband's social superior. . . .' Richard Henry Dana, author of *Two Years Before the Mast*, saw a man under middle height 'with a large expressive eye, regular nose, matted, curling, wet-looking black hair, a dissipated looking mouth with a vulgar draw to it, a muddy olive complexion, *stubby* fingers and a hand by no means patrician. . . . He has what I suppose to be the true Cockney cut. . . .'

Some of his British friends heard the Cockney inheritance in his occasional 'Lor!' at some new revelation of social injustice. That, otherwise, he was his own Professor Higgins seems evident enough. His English did not offend the Americans, and yet it was wholly acceptable in London drawing rooms: it was clear, classless, an actor's English. Of his skill as an actor we have many testimonies, but the best is that of the young American Kate Field, who attended twenty-five of his readings (which were genuine theatrical performances) in Boston and New York. She takes us through *A Christmas Carol* almost scene by scene: 'Ah, but the best of all is Stave Three! I distinctly see that Cratchit family. . . . Ah, that Christmas dinner! I feel as if I were eating every morsel of it. . . . Dickens's sniffing and smelling of that pudding would make a starving family believe that they had swallowed it, holly and all.' Apparently Dickens disappointed his auditors only when, in the *Pickwick* readings, he arrived at Sam Weller. The mere mention of the name would bring the house down, and then followed a curiously muted and cringing impersonation, as though Dickens were ashamed of his own Cockney blood.

Some find Dickens robust, others frail, some tall, others short, some discern nobility, others plebeian opportunism. All concur in being overwhelmed by a preternatural energy which was destined to consume the frame that housed it. It was not an energy fuelled by big dinners or whipped up by alcohol. Like many novelists who rejoice in cramming the board, Dickens ate little. His wife wrote a book called *What Shall We Have for Dinner?*, in which cream and proteins are paraded to surfeit with no allaying greens, but the diet of her husband is reflected only in toasted cheese, which (without pig's pettitoes) was the great man's one weakness. At banquets he diluted his champagne with water. On those killing final readings he was sustained by sherry cobblers and beef tea. His body was fretted to decay by a dynamism which existed for its own sake. After the success of *Pickwick* he never had to drive himself for money. He was never in Balzac's situation.

According to Paul Féval, a popular French novelist of the day, Dickens admired Balzac, but 'in an uneasy and almost frightened way', finding fault with 'the unchecked inflation of his ego'. His stricture is worth quoting in full:

> 'Balzac and a good few others are marked by criticism, as if it were smallpox. You see them getting over-sensitive, like horses that have been ill-treated. They start as egoists, and then the mosquito-bites of journalism make them neurotic and vicious. I have been spoiled the opposite way; I'm much better liked than I deserve.'

To which Féval adds: 'He was wrong there, but he was not lying. He had nothing false in him, not even false modesty. . . .' And yet there is something more attractive about Balzac's incessant pen-shoving to keep the creditors at bay than Dickens's daily three pages in a genteel family atmosphere at Gad's Hill; Balzac had enemies but Dickens had none (not even Thackeray was an enemy); authors ought to have enemies. And authors ought not to be too respectable.

Orwell was right when he implied that Dickens was, as writer and man, supremely endowed with unhatability. Civil servants adore the Circumlocution Office, and judges chuckle over Serjeant Buzfuz. He attacked, but he could not offend. One can never be sure, reading these innumerable tributes to the Dickensian niceness (even the sour were quickly won over), whether the likability is the product of wanting to be liked or a gift carried around a little too carefully. The most distasteful event of Dickens's career – not so much his separation from his wife as his attempt to justify it in the eyes of his public – is given little space. Even the big biographies are uneasy about it. The great love affair with the world (the Italian papers said '*Il Nostro Carlo Dickens è Morto*'; tough Frenchmen wept; Bostonians blubbered; his death was a universal calamity) depended ultimately on qualities which are not to be assessed either aesthetically or morally. Dickens went further with the doctrine of brotherly love than Jesus Christ himself, and nobody crucified him. 'I'm much better liked than I deserve': that was, despite Féval's contradiction, a statement of truth. Hamlet was right: 'Treat every man as he deserves, and which of us shall 'scape whipping?'

No literary judgement will properly work with Charles Dickens. He created a world and, in his spare time, he created Christmas. These two volumes, beautifully printed in Hong Kong, brief enough to have been bound into a single book, terribly expensive, appear close enough to Christmas to seem a seasonal celebration. Professor Philip Collins has worked hard for Dickens, both as a scholar and as a public reader of his works. This anthology of contemporary cuttings is a true flower garden, or a herbary without aloes.

The Shocker

Edgar Allan Poe, by David Sinclair

Not the least informative part of Mr Sinclair's book is his bibliography. Some of the titles of works on Poe might well have been invented by Mr Angus Wilson – *The Haunted Man, The Forlorn Demon, The Haunted Palace, Glorious Incense* and so on – but the title of Daniel Hoffman's book (1972) is beyond satire. It is *Poe, Poe, Poe, Poe, Poe, Poe, Poe*. The rhythm, of course, is that of Poe's own 'The Bells' – which Rachmaninov turned into a choral symphony – but there is a defiance there, like William Pitt in the House of Commons crying, 'Sugar, sugar, sugar, sugar, sugar, sugar. Who will dare to laugh at sugar now?' Because the French have taken Poe too seriously, Anglo-Americans have been disposed to write him off as an embarrassing curiosity. The Gothic tales are all right, and he did create the first detective fiction, but, my God, the poems. . . .

Yet the poems have outlived their parodies, and certain lines will live for ever: 'The glory that was Greece, /And the grandeur that was Rome' . . . 'The viol, the violet, and the vine' (which meant much to Mallarmé) . . . 'But we loved with a love that was more than love – / I and my Annabel Lee' (indeed, the whole poem) . . . 'Quoth the Raven: Nevermore.' Besides being a classic phrasemaker, Poe was a daring prosodist. Hopkins was born in 1844, five years before Poe died at forty, and he systematized what Poe did instinctively – the organization of the line in terms of the counting of beats, not syllables. 'The Bells' is pure sprung rhythm. Poe has been laughed at for searching out what Rossetti called 'stunning words' – like scoriac, quadrated, tintinnabulation and so on – but he believed a poem should shock, unlike Longfellow and the other Transcendentalists. Revolutionary America had produced a namby-pamby literature. Poe's main faults are faults of excess.

Mr Sinclair's biography is very good on the facts of Poe's life, but it does not go deeply into the work. It is content with telling us that the stories 'show how feeble is our hold upon sanity, how unsure our footing as we search for direction along the perilous pathways of our souls.' It does not ask how the stories relate to the poems, how the Gothic horrors cohere with the strong sweet lyricism. Poe's own answer seems to be technical. He believed that a piece of literature should be consumed at a sitting: that it should be a poem of moderate length or a short story. Now the only materials that would fit into a short story in the pre-Chekhov days were Gothic – the sharp shock and the palette knife loaded with crimson. This is Dickens's line as well as Poe's. To speak of Poe's warning us 'in brutal and uncompromising terms of the evil within, to make us aware that inside each one of us there are demons which might one day rise up and overwhelm us' goes, I think, too far. It will do for a Poe character but not a Poe commentary. Making the flesh creep was a legitimate commercial undertaking, and it was as cool in Poe as in Dickens.

For Poe's life, though wretched enough, was not exceptionally so. It was the life of any writer struggling in a world devoted to commercial values – Chatterton in Bristol, Savage in Old, Gissing in New Grub Street. Poe was an orphan adopted by the womanizing philistine John Allan, who treated him badly, but not as badly as Mrs Savage treated Richard. Thrown out of college, he had to join the US Army, but the military life did not destroy him as it might have destroyed (or so he tells me) Yves Saint-Laurent. Poe became a sergeant major and later went to West Point. He was crossed in love, like everybody, and his bride Virginia, whom he married at thirteen, died of tuberculosis. He himself, according to Mr Sinclair, who adduces adequate medical testimony, suffered from diabetes. He was not a drunkard: a little drink knocked him out. There is no evidence that he habitually took opium; like everybody of the period he may have salved grief or pain with laudanum. He had a bad posthumous press. Griswold, whom Poe innocently made his literary executor, wrote, the day after the funeral:

> Edgar Allan Poe is dead. He died in Baltimore the day before yesterday. This announcement will startle many, but few will be grieved by it . . . he had few or no friends; and the regrets for his death will be suggested principally by the consideration that in him literary art lost one of its most brilliant, but erratic stars.

Rufus W. Griswold, a Baptist minister and literary journalist, was one of those offended by Poe's critical candour, which was considerable. In those days, as now, American writers formed self-protective cliques. When Podhoretz slashed *The Adventures of Augie March*, the New York and Chicago Bellovians said by God they would get him. When Poe attacked *Norman Leslie*, a novel by T. S. Fay, associate editor of the *New York Mirror*, calling it 'the most inestimable piece of balderdash with which the common sense of the good people of America was ever so openly or so villainously insulted', he was surprised to find that he had made enemies. It was typical of American journalism of the time that, when Poe turned Richmond's *Southern Literary Messenger* into one of the best periodicals of the country – using the 'hanged, drawn and *Quarterly*' technique – its owner regretted that it was turning professional: he had started it as an organ for genteel amateurs. It was the slop and sentimentality of America that Poe engaged. Before his time, he was vilified or indulged as a wild man who would write well if he studied the best contemporary models. He was always poor, always in debt. Like any other writer.

It is right to regard Poe's horror tales as so many dredgings up from the collective unconscious. They still provide raw material for such applied art as film and opera: one regrets that Debussy did not live to write his *Fall of the House of Usher* – which would have told us more of Debussy's inner agonies than Poe's. But I think it is wrong to try and find in Poe's own life a commentary on the work. He was a man of intense imagination who chose the Gothic story because it was convenient for his talent. His genius probably lies in his verse, which, despite all the books, has been insufficiently studied. Mr Sinclair's biography is a very useful and honest work which disdains to be 'literary'. There is enough of that quality in his subject.

The Kingdom of Lear

Edward Lear and His World, by John Lehmann

I have been concerned with two failed attempts to make a film out of Edward Lear's life story – the first with Peter Ustinov in the lead, the second with Michael Powell as producer–director. I even have a mouldering draft script, opening with that fine scene in the railway carriage when the old gentleman tells the children laughing over *A Book of Nonsense* that Lear does not exist and Lear himself, quiet in a corner seat, is forced to show the pompous fool the inside of his hat with his name there. The life and the work still, with the minimum of scenarist's invention, cry out to be filmed. There are all the paintings and drawings, Lear's own songs with the composer at the piano, Alfred and Emily Tennyson, Queen Victoria, the travels, the epilepsy, even – for the permissive age is still with us and children must be kept out of the cinema – Lear's venereal disease and probable homosexuality. I remember stating the case for a Lear film in New York before possible backers, but they hadn't heard of Lear. Wasn't he a king or sumpn? *The Owl and the Pussy Cat*? They've already done a movie of that, with Barbra Streisand.

If we can't have a film we can at least have John Lehmann's book, which is crammed with pictures. I have, necessarily, read all the bigger books but am glad to have this. It has as epigraph the Auden sonnet with its fine closing line 'And children swarmed to him like settlers. He became a land', which I think goes too far and, unfortunately, reminds us that Carroll, coming after, is a more fitting begetter of the conceit. The *Alice* books have been filmed, enstaged, televised, disneylanded, have jumped outside literature into myth. Nothing of Lear has done that: he is fixed on the page. We don't have to be nice to Carroll (who, incidentally, is featured in this Thames and Hudson series with a fine book by John Pudney): he has risen above his stammer and parthenophilia and we're never tempted to interpret him in terms of his Regret (Auden's upper case). Lear the nonsense-man asks for pity. The draughtsman of the *Family of Psittacidae* and the *Journals of a Landscape Painter* does not. But posterity, probably wrongly, has decided to put the nonsense first.

Mr Lehmann gives us more than a life. He discusses the drawings and the poems; his exegeses take Freud in their stride, making the nose obsession phallic but, obviously, far far more: psychoanalysis has never yet explained even a minor work of art. He presents the pleasure of the limericks as a composite one: without the drawings – which are of a very prophetic and unVictorian leanness – the rhymes are not much. I think most people only pretend to like the limericks: they feel in their bones that Lear lets the form down by making the last line a feeble near-reprise of the first, and the usual excuse – that repetition expresses the hopelessness of the invariable eccentric set upon by 'They' – is offered because one must not be nasty to poor Mr Lear (who, like Wordsworth's Matthew, is never enough beloved). Mr Lehmann says that the origin of the term 'limerick' is unknown. Am I dreaming, or does the following really exist?

> First give your pork chops to the trimmer, ek-
> Cising the fat. Let them simmer. Ek-
> Ceptional folk
> Eat them smothered in smoke,
> Like the pig-chewing people of Limerick.

The form itself, lyrical not comic, goes back to the Tribe of Ben. Herrick, for instance: 'Her eyes the glow-worm lend thee. . . .'

Mr Lehmann thinks the poems, as formally perfect artifacts, as a quirky kind of romanticism, are to be regarded as worthy items of the Victorian poetic canon. Lear invents places with sonorous names, but Milton's authentic places sound invented. In one poem Mr Lehmann thinks Lear approaches 'the wilder shores of surrealism':

> Mrs Jaypher found a wafer
> Which she stuck upon a note;
> This she took and gave the cook.
> Then she went and bought a boat

Which she paddled down the stream
Shouting: 'Ice produces cream,
Beer when churned produces butter!
Henceforth all the words I utter
Distant ages thus shall note –
From the Jaypher Wisdom-Boat. . . .'

Lear hated many things – big dogs, Germen, Gerwomen, Gerchildren, monks. I see here as clear an anti-Catholic poem as Swift's *Tale of a Tub* is, in its Lord Peter episodes, an anti-Catholic fable. Ignore Jaypher Jesus and look at the parodic transubstantiation. The poems are nearly always remarkable, but I think they are spoilt by nonsense words: the runcible spoon is the one flaw in the otherwise perfectly visualized 'Owl and the Pussy-Cat'. Carroll's neologisms, like Joyce's, are polysemantic and delight through a witty counterpoint of meanings; Lear's are evasive. If both a hat and a spoon can be runcible, runcible means nothing. Even nonsense verse should be more than glossolalia. This paragraph will make me enemies.

I always feel that the inscription on the grave of Lear's beloved cat Foss (whom he so brilliantly draws) does ill justice to that fubsy immortal. Lear says Foss died at thirty-one after thirty years in his service, a lie. Isn't the reality – seventeen years – remarkable enough without the gross exaggeration? The Italian isn't right, either: 30 ANNI needs DA in front of it. These are small matters. Mr Lehmann's admirable book reminds us that Lear's greatness lies in the diversity of his talents. The nonsense got in the way of the exquisite draughtmanship for a long time, as well as the brilliance – prefiguring that of D. H. Lawrence – of the evocation of place in the travel books. We now have to find the songs he wrote. When Lear sang 'Home They Brought Her Warrior Dead' at John Millais's house, the Dean of Carlisle, broken-voiced with emotion, said: 'Sir, you ought to have half the Laureateship!' Perhaps his musical rhythms, which we know nothing about, afford a sort of key to letters like:

Thrippy Pilliwinx – Inkly tinksy pobblebookle abblessquabs? Flosky? beebul trimble flosky! Okul scratchabibblebongibo, viddle squibble tog-a-tog, ferrymoyassity amsky flamsky ramsky damsky crocklefether squiggs.

> Flinkywisty pomm
> Slushypipp

This, anyway, makes a little more sense than that damned runcible.

Nonsense and Wonder: The Poems and Cartoons of Edward Lear, by Thomas Byrom

The rhyme scheme of the limerick is in 'Hickery Dickery Dock' and Ben Jonson:

> The wheel of fortune guide you,
> The boy with the bow beside you;
>   Run aye in the way,
>   Till the bird of day
> And the luckier lot betide you.

But the limerick proper requires more than a rhyme scheme. It must have amphibrachs and anapaests, a first line generally, though not invariably, based on the formula 'There was a(n) young/old man/fellow/lady/person of/called/with place name/personal name/personal characteristic' (probably Noam Chomsky has a more scientific symbology available), and it must retail a bizarre story. The term limerick is said by some to have been applied to verses popular with veterans of the Irish Brigade who served King Louis XIV after the surrender of Limerick to William of Orange. These verses were probably obscene. Over two centuries later the term was officially admitted to the language with the *OED's* definition of it as an 'indecent nonsense verse'. Possibly *limerick* specifically meant an indecent poem, while a clean or innocent or even uplifting poem based on the same scheme of rhythm and rhyme had no name at all:

> There was an old woman of Leeds
> Who spent all her life in good deeds;
> She worked for the poor
> Till her fingers were sore,
> This pious old woman of Leeds.

Verses like this were to be found in *The History of Sixteen Wonderful Old Women*, published in 1821. Lear read limericks like it, but his favourite – the one that got into *Our Mutual Friend* (Chapter 2) – appeared in *Anecdotes and Adventures of Fifteen Gentlemen* (1822):

> There was a sick man of Tobago,
> Who liv'd long on rice-gruel and sago;
> But at last, to his bliss,
> The physician said this –
> 'To a roast leg of mutton you may go!'

Lear took the form of the lyric of uplift and the content of the anecdote of inconsequentiality and created his own nonsense poems out of their fusion. His last line is usually a variant of his first. He is not writing epigrams but, says Louis MacNeice, lyrics. If we are disappointed at the tameness of his endings, it is because we are looking for the wrong thing. Lear's little poems are not, in effect, limericks at all. 'Lear's scheme is more suited to the limerick *as lyric*. It gives a better balanced and more assured statement; we do not anxiously wait for the virtuoso ending.'

Patric Stevenson the poet writes to me, quoting MacNeice, to tell me that he has composed a hundred limericks on Irish placenames using the Lear model. But his publisher is doubtful about the tame or lyrical endings and has asked him to keep 'in reserve a new rhyme to add punch to the last line'. Like this:

An angler who lived at Kinsale
Encountered a bilingual whale;
He swore that it sounded
A Yank as it grounded,
But was, when caught blowing, a Gael.

Is it all a matter of taste, or of upbringing – the capacity or incapacity to enjoy the Lear limerick lyric? Perhaps the shock, or anxiety, associated with the new rhyme of the last line is not to be admitted into the nursery. Those of us of the working class who had no nursery and whose parents were too busy or illiterate to read Lear to us at bedtime first met the limerick as a very brutal form and, when we became acquainted with Lear, naturally regarded his nonsense as a namby-pamby bowdlerization. It is a class matter. To me the limerick is a vehicle of naughty wit, coarse or subtle, and the Lear lyrics MacNeice first met in his father's Ulster rectory have no part in my culture. Still leaving class culture out of it, would Lear's nonsense be any the worse for a kind of punchline?

There was a young Lady of Tyre,
Who swept the loud chords of a lyre;
At the sound of each sweep, she enraptured the deep
Till her toenails got caught in the wire.

But, of course, the point of the verse doesn't reside in the verse but in the illustration. Lear takes 'sweep' in its primary sense and shows his lady (who is no more young than is W. S. Gilbert's Katisha) rushing at the lyre with a broom. Therein lies the humour. Gilbert, incidentally, saw that the limerick without a punchline could only be funny in itself if it got rid of rhymes altogether:

There was a young man of East Cheam
Who one day was stung by a wasp.
When asked: Does it hurt?
He said: No, it doesn't,
But I'm so glad it wasn't a hornet.

Thomas Byrom's admirable study of Lear spends a long time on the limericks, categorizing them, indicating their symbolic Adlerian content, showing how They represent a Gradgrind world that will brook no idiosyncratic fantasies.

There was an Old Man of Whitehaven,
Who danced a quadrille with a Raven;
But they said – 'It's absurd to encourage this bird!'
So they smashed that Old Man of Whitehaven.

It is the 'smashed' that is so terrible here. How did they do it – by hammering him to a pulp, depriving him of his union membership, bribing his bank manager to return his cheques? In a sense they are right to dislike a bird of ill omen and punish a man who domesticates it. But, in another sense, they have not punished him at all, since a quadrille is a dance for four, therefore the man has not danced it, with a raven or with anybody else. Again, perhaps the real meaning of the poem lies in the opposition between a white harbour and a black bird. Byrom rightly points to the contradictory behaviour of They in an 'exceedingly strange limerick'.

There was an old man who screamed out
Whenever they knocked him about;
So they took off his boots, and fed him with fruits,
And continued to knock him about.

The illustration shows a rather gleeful rotund old man leaping in the air, grapes in either hand, while his torturers apply the truncheons. His torturers want to beat him but they do not want him to scream, so his mouth must be stuffed with pulp and juice. But they take off his boots, surely, only so that they may administer the bastinado. They and the old man have certainly come to the kind of understanding between torturer and tortured that Graham Greene's chief of police talks of in *Our Man in Havana*. Torture is sweet, like fruit. An emblem of total submission to torture is the removal of the boots which might inadvertently kick the torturers. In one limerick we come close to the Gulag Archipelago:

There was a Young Lady of Russia,
Who screamed so that no one could hush her;
Her screams were extreme, no one heard such a scream,
As was screamed by that Lady of Russia.

It is undoubtedly unfair to look too deeply into nonsense, but Lear's life, with its Oedipal remorse, its syphilis and demon of epilepsy, as well as its homosexuality, found artistic correlatives of profound symbolic interest to an age obsessed, as his own was not, with symbols. Lewis Carroll's life is a fine quarry for aficionados of sexual deviation, as is John Ruskin's, but, once the obvious Freudianisms have been got out of the way, the *Alice* books have a logic that doesn't have to be related to social or sexual maladjustment. A raven is like a writing desk because both words begin with the same sound and the backs of both referents provide us with the means of writing. You need a surface, you need blackness and a quill. Lear is the lesser nonsense writer because one always feels uncomfortable in his presence: there is something going on that is creepy and unclean.

Even, alas, in 'The Owl and the Pussy Cat'. The owl is the male and somewhat unpractical. He can sing to a small guitar, but it is the cat who steers the boat. When she says 'You elegant fowl' she seems to be apostrophizing the bird as already cooked and on the table. It is she, contrary to the Victorian code, who proposes marriage. We don't know who is asking the pig for his nose-ring, but certainly that ring is a cruel symbol of servitude. In Lear's drawing of the ring-buying, the owl already looks timid and put-upon, while the cat, heavy-jowled and frowning, surveys her betrothed like something soon to be torn and eaten. The owl is wisdom and the cat is the senses, and that terrible world of sex and cruelty is going to prevail. The wedding feast is of mince – which, if it is minced heart, will do for the owl, but it seems already to be an elegant dish of hashed poultry – and, because it rhymes, quince. Quince is only edible when cooked. If sliced, it is still raw and very sour. Quince suggests quim. The runcible spoon is made of the same substance as Mr Lear's hat, pointing to fear and alienation. The landscape of the wedding dance is cold and lunar. The marriage is forbidden, the union of a bird and a mammal is denied by nature, like the union of a man and a man. The cat and owl have had, anyway, to flee the real world to declare their love.

But these frightening elements are finally denied by the illustration of the wedding ceremony – the turkey spreading his benedictory fantail, the cat bowing in submission though with tail erect, the owl looking down on his bride without uneasiness. And the rhythm of the epithalamion banishes apprehension. Its joy is unqualified. The grace of a great light in the sky and an eternal ocean – on whose verge the bridal pair dare to dance – sanctifies all impossibilities. Life is bigger than Victorian England. Nonsense means what we cannot understand. God is nonsense. Evidently we have here a very complex poem.

Byrom's approach to this, and to the other poems, takes into account the necessity of relating them to Lear's strange double life, anguished and joyful, but, quite rightly, concludes that his poetic gift is big enough to justify that kind of analysis. We don't trouble to look for hidden meanings in the literally nonsensical. Mr Lear had a fine ear (he was a musician) and a fine eye (he was a painter), and he had an approach to language which, in a later age, would have related him to the serious experimentalists of expatriate Paris. Byrom's epigraph is Lear's, as it were, allophonic realization of three lines from *Idylls of the King:*

Nluv, fluv bluv, ffluv biours
Faith nunfaith kneer beekwl powers
Unfaith naught zwant a faith in all.

This is the sort of thing that had to be nonsense in Victorian England, but, in Joyce, would be taken for a higher realism. Tennyson himself recognized a gift in Lear that was fundamentally Tennysonian, though it went further than could be permitted to the Laureate of the Antimacassars. It embraced humour, for instance.

The fact remains that it is not possible to have a taste for Lear unless the seeds have been planted in childhood. It is possible to come to Lewis Carroll late and without benefit of an upper-class mother with a silvery voice. I remember, during the war, a sergeant of the Royal Electrical and Mechanical Engineers reading the *Alice* books in the mess with beer and wonder. 'Bloody marvellous,' he said at intervals. With Lear he would have said 'Bloody nonsense.' It is probably the Dong and the Yongy-Bongy-Bo and the Quangle Wangle Quee and even the piggy-wig that offend members of the working class. Those are the vocables of privilege.

Clean and Obscene

The Penguin Book of Limericks, compiled and edited by E. O. Parrott, with illustrations by Robin Jacques

I had thought that the rhyme scheme if not the other traditional properties of the limerick went no farther back than Ben Jonson and his tribe (Herrick, for instance: 'Her eyes the glow-worm lend thee,/ The shooting stars attend thee;/ And the elves also,/ Whose little eyes glow/ Like the sparks of fire, befriend thee.'). But Mr Parrott has heard of a medieval manuscript with the following in it (though it cannot, as he alleges, be of the eleventh century):

> The lion is wondrous strong
> And full of the wiles of wo;

> And whether he pleye
> Or take his preye,
> He cannot do but slo.

Slo meaning slay. The Herrick rhyme scheme is supposed to have been attached to obscene improvisations made in the officers' mess of some regiment after the battle of Limerick, and thereafter two traditions subsisted side by side – the scabrous and oral; the bizarrely biographical, beginning with the formula 'There was a –'. The one about the Old Man of Tobago dates from 1822, and it became the model for Lear's limericks, which nobody really likes but from which all limerick anthologists, with a grim sense of duty, have to make a selection. Mr Jacques has even put the Old Man with a Beard on the cover of this book. It might not have been easy to stick the Young Lady from Ealing there instead.

It is the tameness of the end lines, near-identical with the first ones, that makes Lear's limericks seem so feeble, though Louis MacNeice believed there was a lyric point in this circularity. To all of us now the limerick must rhyme wittily and surprisingly, must make a clean epigrammatical point or else be (back to that officer's mess) obscene. Of course obscenity and wit can go together, as in the limerick by A. Cinna (who, presumably, is not to be torn for his bad verses):

> Consistent disciples of Marx
> Will have to employ private narks
> > If nationalisation
> > Of all copulation
> Leads to *laissez-faire* fucking in parks.

For some reason we feel cheated when the opening formula is eschewed. Bertrand Russell kept to it:

> There was a young girl of Shanghai,
> Who was so exceedingly shy,
> > That she undressed every night
> > Without any light
> Because of the All-Seeing Eye.

We accept the false stress on *was*, as well as the imperfect prosody in general, as characteristic of the form and will take anything so long as the rhymes are right. In general limericks ought to look a little clumsy on the page, like the lyrics of Cole Porter; they are essentially for vocal delivery.

How to arrange an anthology like this? Mr Parrott begins with Genesis and ends with Revelations (sexual revelations, to be precise). He has no biblical pattern in between, but he unifies subject matter. Thus, there is a section of literary limericks, such as (by Victor Gray)

> Said Arnold to Arthur Hugh Clough,
> 'Why I don't instantly stuff
> > Your *Amours de Voyage*

Up my arse, is, it's large.
But I don't think it's quite large enough.'

That is, I suppose, donnish; you wouldn't get away with it in the public bar, but this might go down moderately well in a pub on Duke Street, Dublin:

Riverrun where can you guess?
Finnegans Wake is a mess
    Will you help get me even
    Said left-over Stephen
Yes I said yes I will yes.

With virtuoso performances like Bill Greenwill's version of *King Lear* the limerick form is debased to a mere prosodic pattern, repeated, run on and distributed among voices. Tom Stoppard did something like this in *Travesties*. It doesn't work. The limerick will stand so much and no more. In *Punch* in the late twenties there was a double limerick so horrible that I have never forgotten it:

There was once a girl with a flivver
    And a man with no reason to live.
She sank with her car in the river,
    He filed off his head with a sieve.
        For her car wouldn't run
            And his liver was bad,
        And it's really no fun
            To pretend to be glad
When your liver's no good as a liver
    And your flivver refuses to fliv.

On the other hand the rhymeless limerick works because we are so shocked by the thwarting of our expectations. If the limerick is subversive, the subversion of subversion has its own piquancy. Take this:

An American girl in Versailles
Said: 'I feel so ashamed I could weep.
    Ten days I've been here
    And not gone to the Louvre.'
'Never mind,' said someone, 'it's possibly only the hard water.'

The limick, which bears the same relation to the parent form as the curtal sonnet does to the whole Petrarchan works, is illustrated by some examples of Ogden Nash, such as

A young flirt of Ceylon
Who led the boys on,
Playing 'Follow the Leda',
Succumbed to a swan.

This surely needs an internal rhyme in the third line. Impossible here, but try this:

Two nudists of Dover
When purple all over
Were feasts for the beasts
Who mistook them for clover.

There are, I am glad to see, two limericks by Aldous Huxley which we have previously known only from their openings – 'There was a young man of East Anglia/ Whose loins were a tangle of ganglia' from *Antic Hay* and 'There was a young fellow of Burma/ Whose betrothed had good reason to murmur' from *Eyeless in Gaza*. There are no limericks that I know that are not here, except the ones about the young man from Stroud, the young lady from Leicester (ending 'fester') and the fellow called Dave who committed necrophily in a cave. The one by Norman Douglas about Skinner who took a girl out to dinner is surely only funny when made part of the story about the American who misremembered it as about Tupper and supper and up her and then said: 'For some reason it was all blamed on some poor guy called Skinner.' This book is a fine tribute to all those of us who like brevity as the soul of obscenity, find rhyme witty in itself and would love to join the great limerickizing anonymous. I, naturally, blush at finding myself here. It wasn't I who wrote the limerick; it was a character in one of my novels.

Crossmess Parzle

Lewis Carroll: Fragments of a Looking Glass, by Jean Gattégno, translated by Rosemary Sheed

'Only France matters among the nations,' wrote Ford Madox Ford in *No Enemy*. 'I will resay it as my eyes close in death.' He meant, I think, that the French mentality and the French sensibility seem to form the outer of a set of concentric circles, each of which may be regarded as a national endowment of feeling and thought. Certainly there is a sense in which the French mind *encloses* the British, and the British may learn to understand themselves better when they look at themselves through French eyes.

We have always thought of Lewis Carroll as very British. Does not William Empson, in one of his poems, turn Alice into a kind of Britannia? But now Jean Gattégno, Professor of English Literature in the University of Paris at Vincennes, pioneer of Carrollingian studies in France, shows how a sharp European intelligence can disclose elements in 'the double person' who was 'a single writer' not in accord with our fireside and pudding image of tradition. Lovers of Carroll have wanted him to be merely the Snark and Alice man. Professor Gattégno has gone deeply into the writings 'virtually unknown in France' and, one might add, not much better known in Britain.

More than that, there is a Gallic charm, elegance and piquancy in the very shape of this book. In French it is called *Lewis Carroll: Une Vie*. The English title seems to indicate a fear that British readers may only be able to stomach its formal originality by not taking it too seriously: don't expect profundity here – only magpie shards of mirror. But what look like fragments are delicately fretsawn items that fit together into what Joyce called a crossmess parzle.

What we have in fact is a little Carroll encyclopedia – or, put it another way, an alphabetic taxonomy enables us to enter Carroll's life and thought at any point we wish between *Alice* and *Zeno's Paradox*. It is an approach which reminds one of Michel Butor's in *Mobiles*. We are freed from the conventional tyranny of the paginal treadmill which imitates time as it was before J. W. Dunne, and the technique is altogether appropriate to the subject.

What do we look up first? *Girl-Friendships? Sexuality?* No, leave those till later, though with no expectation of a lubricious gloat. Try, say, *Macmillan's*. Carroll's perfectionist nagging of his publisher is still a legend with the firm, for which he invented, among other things, a system of book-packing and the first real book jacket. It was Tenniel, however, who rejected the whole of the first edition of *Alice in Wonderland*, in which the illustrations were badly printed. Carroll insisted merely on the withdrawal of *The Nursery Alice* because the colours were too gaudy. But there was never any waste in the Macmillan kitchen: what Carroll or Tenniel, Mr Woodhouse-like, would not let the British eat the Americans were always ready to devour. Indeed, what was too gaudy for Carroll was not gaudy enough for them. In Professor Gattégno's swift summation of Carroll as a published author, we get an image of a kind of patron saint of writers – one who attacked overlarge bookseller's discounts with courteous ruthlessness, who insisted on the importance of the *look* of a book, who worked his publishers hard.

Russia? Carroll went there in 1867, his first trip abroad. He wrote a little about it, but had nothing really to say. He never travelled abroad again. *Notables.* Was Carroll a snob? If so, there was ambivalence in his snobbery. He was a skilled photographer and a brilliant storyteller as well as, in the time of his courting the great, a famous author. He didn't mind being accepted as the last but objected to being exploited as the second, and was probably hurt when Lawn Tennyson (the Laureate was actually mowing when they first met) knew him merely as the first. He dearly loved the Salisbury family (hence perhaps the sympathetic portrait of the Earl and Lady Muriel in *Sylvie and Bruno*), but he was never again asked to Hatfield after he 'declined to undertake my usual role of story-teller in the morning, and so (I hope) broke the rule of being always expected to do it'. Touchy and, as he grew older, no great diner-out. *Food?* No separate entry, but see *Sickness and Health*. (A light eater, hence not greatly interested in food, hence able to concoct bizarre or purely cerebral meals in his books.)

Theatre? He demanded reverence for the deity on the stage and condemned Gilbert and Sullivan bitterly for putting 'Damme!' in *HMS Pinafore* and making fun of a minister of religion in *The Sorcerer*. *Trains*. A great part of his life and his books too. But, says Professor Gattégno astutely, 'for Carroll trains are not so much the means to a journey as the substitute for one'. He always travelled with a bag full of puzzles and games, devices for seducing (enticing, beguiling, winning over, attracting) young persons. And so to the first entry, *Alice*, and the question 'Is Alice Himself?' Alice Liddell and Alice in the books are not identical, but there are points of contact. Alice Liddell is frozen in the photographs at seven. Humpty-Dumpty said 'Leave off at seven – but it's too late now.' Carroll wanted to be fixed for ever at an idyllic prepubertal age; the photographs are mirrors. Sex, of course, doesn't come into it.

Sex and little girls. It is incredible to our age that Carroll should not seem to recognize the nature of the *frisson* he gained from kissing big girls (their mothers seem to have assumed that he knew all about it, though), but we take the sexual revolution too much for granted. Of Carroll's innocence there can be no doubt, but this does not prevent his having (see *Sexuality*) a sophisticated capacity for delineating sexual types, from the 'castrating mother' Alice to the nasty machismo of Uggug.

Professor Gattégno's book is vastly informative, stimulating, wise, *spirituel*. A French lady in New Jersey once telephoned me to say that Shakespeare was undoubtedly French, his name being originally Jacques Père. Charles (Carolus) Lutwidge (Ludovic/Louis) remains still a very English Dodgson, but he is shown to be easily marriable, despite his terrible celibacy, into France. And, viewed in the French looking glass, he is much more subtle, various and intriguing than when seen purely, so to speak, cismanically.

Celtic Sacrifice

Selected Letters of Oscar Wilde, edited by Rupert Hart-Davis

Sir Rupert brought out a complete edition of Wilde's letters in 1962. This has gone out of print (rapid going-out-of-print is one of the major diseases of modern culture), but, if in print, would now be very expensive. Moreover, says Sir Rupert in his preface to this selection, there was a lot of repetition there and 'a large number of letters which were included for biographical or other factual reasons and are now on the record.' There is, in Sir Rupert, not only a scholarly gift but an artistic one. His fine biography of Hugh Walpole, which I have read at least ten times, reads like a novel. This selection of letters, having as protagonist a writer a hundred times more important than Walpole, and tracing a perfect tragic parabola, may be taken as a rare instance of life, through the mediacy of a direct record minimally adjusted by an editorial master, taking on the properties of a work of art. This book must be cherished and not allowed to go out of print. It appears simultaneously as an OUP paperback and ought to attract a wide and varied readership.

The story told in Wilde's letters (whose recipients are fully identified and characterized in Sir Rupert's footnotes) is of a brilliant young Irishman, of good professional family, who gains a first at Oxford and then dazzles the London world of art, literature and fashion with exceptional charm, good nature, wit and creative talent. Gilbert and Sullivan produced a comic opera called *Patience* intended to mock the pretensions of what was known as aestheticism, satirizing, in the 'fleshly poet' Bunthorne, the character and art of Rossetti. Wilde was not at that time regarded as more than a potential leader of the greenery-yallery Grosvenor Gallery cult, but D'Oyly Carte and his New York agent saw the advance publicity possibilities in sending Wilde on a lecture tour of the United States before the new operetta got there. Wilde was glad to go and lecture on beauty to New England ladies and West Virginia miners. He did well. His achievement somewhat took the wind out of the sails of the musical satire. The Americans admired him – even the miners, whom he, a six-foot burly Celt, could drink under the table any time. He went back to London and began to create art, not just lecture on it.

He worked hard at all the major literary forms – the novel, drama, poetry, the critical dialogue. The hard work, the genuine scholarship, the strenuous devotion to literature are what Wilde's moral detractors always left, and still leave, out of account. Then Lord Alfred Douglas came on the scene:

My Own Boy, Your sonnet is quite lovely, and it is a marvel that those red rose-leaf lips of yours should have been made no less for music of song than for madness of kisses. Your slim gilt soul walks between passion and poetry. I know Hyacinthus, whom Apollo loved so madly, was you in Greek days.

This was written some time in January 1893. We meet this rapturous tone for the first, if not the last, time. The letters show it to have been directed on only one object. I will never understand homosexuality, but I cannot see in Wilde those properties which Mr Legman, in his recent study of the Dirty Joke, generically bestows on the breed of which Wilde is supposed to be the patron saint. There seems to have been no restless dongiovannism, no fear of the father expressed in the avoidance of women or the queasy act of sodomy in the dark. Wilde was, till Bosie arrived, a good husband, and he was always a good father. He was struck, like Mann's Aschenbach, by a Dionysiac madness. It is something we are ready to find in literature but rarely in life. Wilde's moral decline is not to be judged in terms of sexual inversion, only as a much more sinful waste of time, talent and affection. There are some still living who see much in Lord Alfred Douglas, but all the evidence, and especially the evidence of this volume, point to a Narcissus stupid when not cunning, a liar, a poseur, and a deplorable poetaster. In the summer of 1935 he wrote a letter to a newspaper, complaining that Hopkins's poems (he knew all his work well, he alleged, except the sonnets) did not scan. I, a schoolboy, wrote a furious letter back. I did not know who he was, and my letter was not published. But, whoever he was, he was a stupid poseur. I now know that he was much worse than that.

The long letter to Bosie known as *De Profundis*, written from prison while society gloated at the savage punishment of Wilde's wit and talent more than his pederasty, is a masterpiece of reproach without self-pity or hysteria. The waste of money on Bosie's pleasures is very practically, not sordidly, dealt with (money, to a writer, represents the blood and sweat of writing, and also time bought to shed more sweat and blood), but the main plaint is against the selfishness of that slim gilt soul, which begrudged the time Wilde spent on his trade and pouted for attention. The letter is a confession of sin, but also of innocence. In Wilde, paradox was a substitute for complexity. He was an ingenuous, trusting, good-hearted man; he did not see how Bosie was using him in the battle with his father the Marquis, one of the most detestable aristocrats that England, rich in detestable aristocrats, ever produced. He could not even spell 'sodomite'.

Wilde lost everything, even his talent. He was dragged through the criminal, bankruptcy and divorce courts. His property was seized, down to his school prizes. His children's names were changed, and he lost the right even to see them. But he scrupulously paid his debts, helped fellow-prisoners and warders alike, agitated in round plain pedestrian terms for penal reform. He was a man of great courage and honour, as well as genius, and he was set upon by devils.

It is pathetic to read his final letter, dated 20 November 1900, written to Frank Harris (a rogue who never really got caught up with). It is about the money Harris owes and which Wilde, whose terminal illness is costing him dear, desperately needs. A great and dying artist is enmeshed in the sordor of debts and bankruptcy laws, sleeplessness over money, literary robbers. It is not an untypical story in our literary annals, as Johnson's *Lives of the Poets* reminds us, but Richard Savage's sufferings are small, grey Grub Street stuff compared with the tragic purple of Oscar Wilde. It is a relief to turn back to the early days again and the charm and high spirits of a dashed-off note to Violet Fane:

> Of course I am coming! How could one refuse an invitation from one who is a poem and poet in one, an exquisite combination of perfection and personality, which are the keynotes of modern art.
>
> It was horrid of me not to answer before, but a nice letter is like a sunbeam and should not be treated as an epistle needing a reply. Besides your invitations are commands.

Or that letter to Lily Langtry ('My dear Lil') in which he says

> I am going to be married to a beautiful young girl called Constance Lloyd, a grave, slight, violet-eyed little Artemis, with great coils of heavy brown hair which make her flower-like head droop like a flower, and wonderful ivory hands which draw music from the piano so sweet that the birds stop singing to listen to her.

Our philistine society demands its occasional sacrifice of the innocent and brilliant, and it is usually a Celt who is the *élu*. Drink and guilt got both Dylan Thomas and Brendan Behan, but there has never been a bloodier offering to the Jehovah of dullness than the one recorded in these letters. The French still taunt us with it, seventy years after Wilde's body was interred at Père Lachaise. That tombstone by Epstein is taken as a supreme monument to British hypocrisy.

Port after Stormy Seas

Joseph Conrad: The Three Lives, by Frederick R. Karl

It was in 1924, shortly before Conrad's death, that Virginia Woolf gave, at Cambridge, her famous speech about there being no living English novelist from whom the new writers could 'learn their business. Mr Conrad is a Pole, which sets him apart, and makes him, however admirable, not very helpful.' Of all the judgements on Conrad made by reputable literary figures, this was perhaps the most curious. Especially curious when you consider that H. G. Wells and Arnold Bennett, whom Mrs Woolf dismissed as old hat, understood precisely the nature of Conrad's modernity and saw that, if Conrad's Polishness was relevant at all to his achievement, it was only because he was a deracinated Pole whose second language was French and whose devotion to Flaubert led him to make art where men like Galsworthy (who, also dismissed by Mrs Woolf, appreciated Conrad thoroughly) were condemned to make money.

The most egregious review ever written on Conrad came when, to most of those who understood literature, he was already one of the great English masters. It was written by Robert Lynd and it said:

Had he but written in Polish his stories would assuredly have been translated into English and into the other languages of Europe; and the works of Joseph Conrad translated from the Polish would, I am certain, have been a more precious possession on English shelves than the works of Joseph Conrad in the original English. . . .

'To answer this kind of criticism,' says Professor Karl, 'an author can only hope for the wholesale death of all reviewers.' Amen. The notion that, because English was Conrad's third language (or possibly fourth: Conrad denied knowing German, but his son Borys was surprised to hear him haranguing Prussian officials with great fluency and effect), he could not, despite all the evidence, be very good in it, is a fatuous fallacy that still persists. The fact is that the better he got to know it the worse, or less well, he wrote: when weary, he took the first words to hand, like any Englishman. In his great days he handled an instrument which he knew as a master craftsman and a master mariner, but not as a pedestrian penny-a-liner.

It was not that the Polishness of Conrad was irrelevant to his fiction; it was rather that it was seized on by some as a clue to his difficult originality. Poles were Slavs and so were Russians, therefore Conrad could be explicated in terms of the Slavic soul. Mencken in America always made a great thing of the cymbal-clashing Slav barbarity in Conrad, and Conrad had to reply mildly that the Polish element in him was chivalric, Quixotic and wholly occidental.

In 1899, when Conrad was at work on *Lord Jim* and *Heart of Darkness*, Eliza Orzeszkowa, a Polish novelist, attacked him for deserting his native country and making himself rich through writing in English. The whole betrayal was made worse, she alleged, by the fact that Mr Jozef Teodor Konrad Korzeniowski, who now called himself Joseph Conrad, had the same two outer names as a writer 'over whose novels I shed as a young girl the first tears of sympathy and felt the first ardours of noble enthusiasms and decisions.' This kind of attack is still levelled at writers who put art before patriotism; the allegation of selling out to Mammon usually goes with it, and it was especially misplaced in the case of Conrad, hundreds of pages of whose biography reiterate the weary tale of penury, lack of a readership, illness, despair. If Conrad did desert Poland, it was because there was nothing he could do for that unhappy unfrontiered land. If he gave up the name Korzeniowski (which he never fully did: it was on his Board of Trade marine certificates, his passport, and eventually his grave in Canterbury) it was because it was a name no British book-buyer could confidently pronounce. Nor did he proclaim: 'I was a Pole, now I will be an Englishman.' There is a long and devious odyssey between Berdyczów, where he was born, and the adopted country where, at last making ends meet, achieving a collected edition, rejecting doctorates and a knighthood but hoping vainly for the Nobel Prize, he died worn out and not yet, in his own view, fulfilled.

Conrad might have become an Austrian, but he opted for being a sort of Frenchman. He also opted for being nothing: a genuine suicide attempt in Marseilles left him with a bullet wound on chest and back but no impairment of vital organs within. He took to the sea because the sea was there; the British ruled the sea, so he qualified himself painfully as a

British marine officer. There were too many sailors seeking too few berths, and Conrad never achieved a shipboard appointment commensurate with his qualifications. How he attained his consummate mastery of literary English must remain a mystery to us, an insular people with no compulsion to learn foreign languages. He never, he said, opened an English grammar book, and his spoken English was, by all accounts, thicker even than that of Nabokov (who had the advantage of an English governess and a Cambridge education). But a thorough knowledge of literary French seemed a sufficient way into English. He prepared himself for a day's work on *Nigger of the Narcissus* by rereading a page of *Salammbô*.

Professor Karl wonders whether, if Conrad had settled into the captaincy that was his entitlement, he would have become a novelist. The answer is probably yes. There is a stereotype of the beached sailor who starts to write because he has so much to write about and turns out rattling good yarns. But Conrad had a vocation, and he was highly articulate in his enunciation of a theory of symbolic art which, with the irony that attaches to so much of Conrad's career, was better understood by late Victorians like Wells and Bennett than by either James or Virginia Woolf. He seems to write books about the sea, the Malay archipelago, and the Congo, but he is really writing about the desperate convoluted hopeless heart of man. As he dissociated himself from the movement that contained Pound, Eliot and Joyce (who all read him; Eliot proposed putting 'Mistah Kurtz, he dead' as the epigraph to *The Waste Land* but was persuaded by Pound to reserve it to 'The Hollow Men') so the movement itself relegated him to the dead Edwardian tradition. Now we are well aware of his modernity, yet it is still possible to appreciate him as a rattling good yarn spinner. It was in this latter capacity that he was fêted in America, but now he is a mainstay of American literature courses, profound, difficult, reticulated. And yet it was the unaesthetic Wells who saw his true content before anybody.

It is impossible in a review of this length to do even minimal justice to Professor Karl's monumental biography – the first in twenty years and the first ever to make use of the whole corpus of Conrad's letters, which Professor Karl is editing. This is a book of over a thousand closely printed pages, a model of American scholarship in which not even the most recherché reference has gone unresearched. It tells the story of a very sad man, a hopeless warrior, and of the heroinism of a wife who, like Nora Joyce, suffered not only in herself but for him. I do not know whether her own memoirs of Conrad are still in print, but the time has come to have a fresh look at them and honour her memory. Her cookbook, by the way, is one I regularly use. It is instructive to compare it with Mrs Dickens's *What Shall We Have for Dinner?* The Inimitable fed over-richly; Conrad made do with cunningly fricasseed scrag end. But the money is coming in now, I should think, and nobody in Poland has a bad word to say about its most illustrious exile. As for him, he got what all men, so he believed, wanted: 'Sleep after toyle, port after stormie seas,/ Ease after warre, death after life does greatly please.' Those lines from *The Faerie Queene* are on his tombstone.

Joseph Conrad: Times Remembered, by John Conrad

I shopped in the supermarket, dragged three bags up three flights, peeled potatoes, cleaned Brussels sprouts, put the joint in the oven, washed yesterday's dishes, made the beds, swept the floors, then sat down to Mr Conrad's reminiscences of life at the house called Oswalds.

> The indoor staff, the crew as JC called them, consisted of Arthur Foote, valet/butler, Edith and Florrie Vinten, housemaids, sisters of the chauffeur, and Mrs Sophie Piper who did the cooking under my mother's guidance, and if there were more than three guests for a meal extra help was enlisted from the village.

Jessie Conrad suffered from her leg, so the nurse Audrey Seal joined the crew. There were two fulltime gardeners and the aforesaid chauffeur. Conrad, note, was not a rich author even though he was a great one. This was the way a man of letters in the twenties was supposed to live. One cannot help a breath of envy of the kind that escaped from Auden when he versified about Mozart not having to make his own bed.

These revelations of apparent affluence begin early. Even when the Conrads were at the humbler Capel House just before 1914 there was a Cadillac. A lot of us have picked up from various sources the legend that Conrad sold film rights in all his books the year he died in order to buy a Ford T-model. From 1909 on Conrad seems to have been doing all right. Future biographers of the great man will, thanks to his second son, be able to stress the persona of the small squire. The author is not around at all. He comes to life about midnight when Master John is asleep. Occasionally, stuck on a passage, he gets his son out of bed to play chess. Then, unstuck, he returns to his work, remembering, for resumption of the game in like circumstances weeks later, the exact position of the pieces on the board.

John Conrad has left the record of life with father unconscionably late. There are dead Conrad scholars who would have given much to have this artless chronicle. It seems to have been precisely John Conrad's awareness of his lack of art that made him reluctant to write. But we have had enough of author's relicts showing that they had talent too – Caitlin Thomas, for instance. The virtue of this memoir is its plainness. We have all of the quotidian Conrad, a formidable but far from unlovable figure. It is a monoglot Conrad, since John could not follow him into the ambages of French or Polish, but it is a Polish phrase that gives this book its subtitle or epigraph. In a hotel in Vienna in 1914 Conrad asked John to take a message to some Polish friends who were staying there. The message was '*Ojciec jest tutaj*' – 'Father is here'. Father is very much here.

He never appears in undress. There is none of the polo-necked unshaven slave of the deadline. His maritime career enforced the habit of daily nattiness and an insistence that his sons look and behave like gentlemen. In the manner of a ship's captain he could be forceful in giving orders and rebuking slackness – a present-day employee would have given him notice after an hour – but he never permitted himself more than a damn. When one of the dogs jumped on Hugh Walpole and made him indulge in querulous blasphemy, Conrad was quick with a rebuke. He did not go to church but he never took God's name in vain. He had heard the voice of God too often howling through the rigging.

Conrad imported to his rural ambience the gestures of continental courtesy – stiff bow from the hips and a kiss for the hand of a lady, especially if she were pretty. One day a candidate for a housemaid's position came to the door. Conrad, unwarned, saw merely a young lady – 'Belle [sic] visage – très chic' – and performed the regular ritual. Scared, she fled. He could not tolerate hypocrisy. If a newspaper reporter came and confessed to not having read any of his work, he would say: 'Sir, you are a hypocrite. I don't blame you for not reading my books but don't come here pretending you are terribly sorry because you do not give a damn whether you have read them or not.' One young reporter began an interview with 'Now, sir, you're a Russian, of course – ' He was thrown out. Conrad hated the Russians. He could never forget how the Czarist regime had treated his parents and he expected no regeneration of the Russian soul under communism. The Russians were scoundrels, and there was an end on't.

He did not speak English with so outrageous a Polish accent as some more casual reminiscences have led us to believe. He had an irreparable thetatismus, talking of dis and dat, and he pronounced the w in sword as if he felt it ought to be there. We don't need to be reminded that his mastery of the language was as absolute as Nabokov's, who similarly had his own Slav versions of the phonemes. Walpole, who always seems to have been something of a fool, came in crying: 'Conrad, Conrad, I have here a most excellent dictionary, quite the latest and best and it is for you.' Conrad replied: 'You know, Hugh, I can spell and I can understand English. I may not always speak it very well but I have no need of a dictionary.' John's Latin was not good, and his teachers had, in the pedagogic manner of the day, the notion that his father must have learnt Latin thoroughly since his English style was so exquisite. It was in vain for John to protest that his father had learnt it through the medium of Polish, and that he had gained his English 'before the mast'. When John's master wrote to Conrad asking if this were true, Conrad wrote back saying it was and rebuking the teacher for the solecism 'different to'. English to him was a kind of seamanship: if you did not know it thoroughly you foundered.

We have odd glimpses of his literal as opposed to literary seamanship. He boarded vessels off the Kentish coast with skill, grace and the voice of unmistakable authority. He taught John knots. He wore a monocle not out of affectation but need, but was always twirling it and breaking it against hard objects. When a new monocle was bought and corded for him he would raise hell if it was secured with a granny knot. These are just a few of the minutiae of the daily Conrad which make this record so absorbing. That he was a firm but loving father is attested by one brief observation from the son: he never wanted to run away to sea; he was far too happy at home.

The Edwardian Novelists, by John Batchelor
Joseph Conrad: A Biography, by Roger Tennant

I misread Mr Batchelor's reference to 'Virginia Woolf's famous attack on Wells, Bennett and Galsworthy' and was pleased, till I reread it, that he considered her attack fatuous, which it was. From the 1920s until the 1970s there was a tendency to denigrate Edwardian art and, with it, the Edwardian ethos, or else to deny that 'Edwardian' was a legitimate term of reference. Edward VII's reign was short, true, and it has been convenient to consider the Victorian age as lasting until 1914, but Frank Kermode, in *The Sense of an Ending*, suggests that 1900 is a reasonable watershed, the date of Nietzsche's death and Freud's *Interpretation of Dreams*, of Husserl's *Logic* and Russell's book on Leibnitz. One might add that the loss of the *Titanic*, though strictly a Georgian catastrophe, provides a more fitting close to an age of hubris than a European war. But how deep did Edwardian confidence go?

The age was an age of expanding wealth and, abetted by the monarch, a very non-Victorian licentiousness. But there were profound anxieties about the dispossessed working class, the death of an agricultural society, the growth of the suburbs and, at the same time, the degeneracy of lower-class city dwellers like E. M. Forster's Leonard Bast – one of 'a weak-kneed, narrow-chested, listless breed'. The upper class had an unhealthy obsession with health, and Eugene Sandow begot the dangerous craft of body-building. The 'abyss' of the slums was too close to the wealthy. There was justified fear of war, though whether the enemy was embodied in German imperialism or the Yellow Peril was not clear. The educated were abandoning God, though not George Eliot's concept of Duty as 'peremptory and absolute'.

Perhaps the ideal Edwardian was Arthur Marwood (not in Batchelor's index but present in Tennant's life of Conrad), the 'heavy Yorkshire squire with his dark hair startlingly silver in places, his keen blue eyes, his florid complexion, his immense expressive hands and his great shapelessness.' The description is Ford Madox Ford's, and those who know Ford's Christopher Tietjens will recognize his prototype. Marwood appears also as Mills in Conrad's *The Arrow of Gold*. His humanistic wisdom, immense sense of decency and duty and devotion to tradition belong to a threatened culture, but these virtues have nothing Victorian about them. Ford's *Parade's End*, which, thanks to Graham Greene's impertinent truncation, is a trilogy in Britain though a tetralogy in America, is a book of the 1920s, but it is a superb summation of Edwardian values and, as such, Mr Batchelor assesses it, though incompletely. Marwood–Tietjens reminds us that you can be a good man without believing in God.

Mr Batchelor quotes Ian Watt's neat apophthegm on the Edwardian crisis (to be found in his study of *Heart of Darkness*): '. . . most familiar to literary history under the twin rubrics of the disappearance of God and the disappearance of the omniscient author.' Batchelor is right to see the Edwardian novel as a genre somewhat distinct from its Victorian predecessor and its 'modernist' successors. With Conrad there is, in his heroes, a new loneliness appropriate to an age of spiritual dispossession; at the same time there is an attempt to find a narrative technique which disclaims omniscience. Ford, in *The Good Soldier*, conceivably the best British novel of the century, leaps into modernism with the 'unreliable narrator', the man who tells a story without understanding it. Even H. G. Wells, who boasts that his work is closer to journalism than to Jamesian high art, produces, in *Love and Mr Lewisham*, a novel that demands to be examined in terms of 'carefully wrought dramatic presentation and strategic use of imagery' – very Conradian qualities.

Inevitably Mr Batchelor, in considering Bennett, Galsworthy and Forster, as well as Conrad, Ford and Wells, finds it difficult to extract common Edwardian attributes from them – there is too much overlapping into the age to come – and, being more of a critic than a historian of ideas, he is more concerned with intrinsic literary virtues and vices than with the kind of exemplification that fits a preconceived thesis. But of Forster it may be said, and Batchelor says it, that the faults of the works that come before *A Passage to India* are typically those of an Edwardian liberal. The characters are products of the suburbs – 'the convenient, debased compromise between country and town which is itself a physical feature of the period' – and their sexuality is scared to declare itself. There are whimpers of sexual rebellion – we find them in Galsworthy too – but no real attempt to indent the social order. There is, in fact, in both authors a 'muddled liberalism' typical of writers who, being forced to reject Victorian values (which were still more or less theocentric), have found no substitute in Wellsian science or Tietjensesque stoicism or Bennettian ambition. Batchelor is right to consider Forster overrated. Galsworthy, fortunately, has been overrated only by the Nobel committee and those who have seen *The Forsyte Saga* on television.

I wish Mr Batchelor had had the effrontery to place Virginia Woolf, who thought she had superseded the Edwardians, in the very tradition she attacked. Ultimately the whole Bloomsbury congeries may be seen as the thick rich cream of Edwardian liberalism – clever but godless, disdainful of the children of the abyss, desirous of experiment but scared of the whole hog, discreetly passionate but shamefully sterile. I wish too there had been room in this book to relate the novelists to their fellow-artists, particularly the painters and composers, however briefly. In the music of Elgar, especially the Second Symphony, we are at last beginning to recognize the Edwardian neurosis.

Mr Batchelor's project began with an attempt to 'place' Conrad (who, since he was a foreigner, was not very 'helpful' to Virginia Woolf's scheme of rejection), to save him from the isolation of greatness to which most Conradians condemn him. The little biography of Mr Tennant seeks merely to separate the life from what Conrad made of the life, to give us the exterior current of a writer's existence, all the rest being for the critics. Mr Tennant is an Australian who, as a child in Hobart, played 'on the beach just across the water from where the hulk of Conrad's *Otago* lay dissolving in the mud.' He was led, almost against his will, to a near-identification with Tuan Jim, and from then on was obsessed with the enigmatic seadog. He considers him 'the greatest writer in the English language', which perhaps goes too far, but his devotion has produced a biography commendably brief and warmly readable.

Questioning Kipling

The Strange Ride of Rudyard Kipling – His Life and Works, by Angus Wilson, Secker & Warburg

When he was barely twenty, and the Indian Mutiny was barely twenty years in the past, Kipling wrote a story called 'The Strange Ride of Morrowbie Jukes'. Jukes, a British engineer, falls with his horse into a deep sand crater near Pakpathan, there to live with derelicts feeding off crows and to be taunted by Gunga Dass, a ruined telegraph master, in terms like 'We are now Republic, Mr

Jukes'. The tale is a nightmare of the precariousness of colonial rule, of the 'terrible hidden gulf' – as Angus Wilson puts it – 'between conquerors and conquered'. Kipling, once accepted by those who read him very selectively as the voice of an unassailable white raj, was always a poet of doubt and division, with hysteria not far from the surface. This is, in the words of the title of an essay by another Wilson, 'The Kipling that Nobody Read'.

One of the strengths of this Wilson's study lies in the fact that not only has he read everything, but he seems to know his texts as a pianist knows his repertory: citations are at his fingertips, not on the shelves: no generalization without confirmation through quotation, as Joyce's Twelve probably say. There is an evident delight in reading Kipling's prose which I, for one, would be glad to be able to share: the verse, for me, is a different matter. Edmund Wilson says that Kipling ought to have been a Balzac, and I agree. I feel disappointed that he wrote so many stories and so few novels, and only one of those good. Those volumes of collected tales are a testimony to a kind of failure. Britain had, in her Empire, her one great Tolstoyan theme, and the only writer equipped to express it on the right scale proved not to be a Tolstoy.

Angus Wilson's book does not, as biography, attempt to supersede Charles Carrington's work, though it draws on new information, especially unpublished letters. Its main aim is critical, but no criticism in depth may neglect its subject's life. Kipling told us not to question anything other than the books he left behind, but he was wrong. He might not have been wrong had he, like Shakespeare, produced work which contains its own key to contradictions and ambiguities. We have to look into Kipling's life, whether we wish to or not, to find out why he wrote as he did, especially in those later, sometimes baffling, stories where a 'modern' compression that makes for near-unintelligibility pushes down neurotic hates, and neurotic sentimentalities, that are profoundly idiosyncratic.

There is 'an off-putting philistinism' in him, says Angus Wilson, 'a false dichotomy between action and thought'. Trying to make his art wholly external, he is led to areas of experience where few other authors trod and, one might add, to the deployment of a lexis rivalled only by Joyce (Edmund Wilson says that Joyce could not have written much of *Ulysses* without Kipling's example). Marinetti and the Futurists (so both Wilsons say) were merely playing when they spoke of the glorification of machines. Kipling *knew* machines, or at least knew their vocabulary; he was himself hopeless with his hands and is said to have exclaimed with admiration when somebody mended a castor on an armchair. What nobody has pointed out is that Kipling's need for a larger vocabulary than men like, say, Andrew Lang possessed derived from the enforced cauterization of that side of his brain which had known, at one time, Hindustani better than English. The machine world was a kind of lost Indian Empire.

But, as Angus Wilson makes very clear, this enlargement of subject matter cannot compensate for a 'persistent evasion of introspection'.

There is a fear of self-knowledge which pervades all his work except *Kim*, a novel that Mr Wilson admires more than his American homonym. (Edmund Wilson finds too easy a resolution of the East–West conflict. The question 'Who is Kim?', which Angus Wilson takes for an unusual act of daring, finds too easy an answer, what with Kim's betrayal of his own East to become, like Mowgli, a mere officer of the Raj.) None of the glib terms – Freudian, manic-depressive, unwillingness to face the nature of his sexuality – really help. Angus Wilson, one would think very reasonably, suggests, without believing this to be anything like a final answer, 'a social-historical description of long generations of Evangelical belief ending in post-Darwinian doubt'. And this might well apply also to Hardy and to Housman. Kipling had beliefs though, despite perhaps his finest poem 'Tomlinson', no eschatology. He believed in the white man's civilizing mission, though his trust in the white man's ability to fulfil it received hard knocks from the Americans, the Germans and the Boers. He ended up believing in a particular kind of Britain, and the unfolding of the belief involved a partisan political stance unseemly in a poet. Hardy and Housman admitted despair, but this was a luxury Kipling could not allow himself. The pretence that order exists, along with law and morality, has to struggle with admissible doubt: this seems to explain the near-hysteria that a Pre-Raphaelite concern with good craftmanship keeps tightly boxed.

It is the avoidance of 'further questioning of the source of despair and anxiety and guilt that enmesh so many of his best characters in his best stories' that keeps him 'out of the very first class of writing'. Meaning, says Mr Wilson, the ranks of Dostoevsky, Tolstoy, Richardson, Dickens, Stendhal, Proust. But how does he stand as a poet? Mr Wilson, a distinguished writer himself of novels and stories, does not venture too far away from the prose, and we are still left with that shaky judgement of Eliot's, which makes Kipling 'a great verse writer', or Orwell's shakier one still, that presents him as a superb creator of 'good bad poetry'. Mr Wilson, mentioning Browning, mentioning Kipling's capacity to delineate character with novelistic fullness in poems like 'The Mary Gloster', almost incidentally throws off a possible line of evaluation. But then we wonder why we should bother to evaluate.

For Kipling's best claim to be approached as a great writer lies in the truth that men like Angus Wilson love his work. He is an *interesting* writer; he has an ill-developed capacity to bore as Proust sometimes bores. He is, moreover, an interesting man, with interesting manias and preoccupations. In tracing the strange ride of the man, Angus Wilson has not been content to brood over maps in the study; he has travelled the same roads himself and has brought photographs back to prove it. The illustrations to this book are of great interest, and many of them show things we have not seen before – Northbank, for instance, the Simla house where monkeys raided Kipling's room, first – he believes – identified by Wilson himself.

Sir Edward Elgar makes a couple of shadowy entries in this work, raising, equally shadowily, the possibility of considering the possible value of a possible comparison of aims, failures, neuroses, techniques. Kingsley Amis, in his monograph on Kipling, says, I seem to remember, that it was a pity Kipling and Elgar did not get together. They did, in fact, collaborate on a vapid propaganda song about the Merchant Navy in the 1914–18 war – 'Oh where are you going to, all you big steamers?' I consider Elgar an *interesting* composer in the way that Kipling is an interesting writer: the imperialist stances are subtly qualified with harmonies of doubt, there is a tendency to hysteria which Elgar keeps in check, despite his use of a large orchestra which Richard Strauss was only too ready to exploit to hysterical effect. A term like *greatness* seems somehow meaningless when applied to, or withheld from, both these artists of the age of British expansion and British self-doubt. One of the most laudatory things one can say about Angus Wilson's excellent book is that, far from enshrining its subject in lapidary definitiveness, it suggests other approaches, other books. It reminds us, in John Gross's words, that Kipling 'remains a haunting, unsettling presence, with whom we still have to come to terms.' Still.

Levity and Gravity

G. K. Chesterton: Explorations in Allegory, by Lynette Hunter

Chesterton was, till fairly recently, regarded as a harmless minor man of letters with a nostalgia for medieval Christianity, a taste for beer and nonsense, and a kind of sub-Wildean gift for epigram and paradox. We were told that he wrote too much, like his friend Belloc, and that what he turned out was specious and superficial. It was grudgingly conceded that his novels and Father Brown stories were brilliant, though they lay outside the mainstream of serious fiction. But his status was low: he ranked with J. C. Squire as a versifier and with

Robert Lynd as an essayist. He ignored the modern movement; his criticism was suspect; he suffered from what Philip Guedalla termed hearty degeneration of the fat. His all too caricaturable pout and girth and coxcomb turned him into an amiable monster, but there were some who found his alleged anti-Semitism evil and his Catholicism dangerously reactionary. He was also optimistic at a time when the best lacked all conviction. In a manner he cheated by dying before the Second World War and the Bomb, thus evading moral accountability and the duty of revising his philosophical position. He belongs, we are told, to the past.

It was Jorge Luis Borges, who belongs very much to the present, who suggested that Chesterton be taken seriously as an artist and a prophet. Lynette Hunter takes him very seriously indeed, so much so that the mythical fat man of beer and Christian joy gives place to a very earnest thinker whose entire career was built on an unrockable metaphysic and whose most flippant *jeu d'esprit* finds its hole in the complex jigsaw of a theology that is also an aesthetic and a socioeconomic system. But the major premise is temperamental. Chesterton began by fearing 'impressionism' – the intensely solipsistic view of the universe which, denying external authority, proclaims one man's vision as the only true one. This, according to Chesterton, is what is meant by madness. As an artist, both visual and verbal, he knew the temptations of solipsism in a world without faith; his own psyche, as he tells us in his *Autobiography*, was neurotically sensitive to the encroachments of the devil who is the lord of madness. He sought sanity in, first, the Church of England, later in the Church of Rome. Finding it, he hung on to it, aware that madness was always ready to pounce. The term *mad*, unrefined into the categories of psychoanalysis, never left his vocabulary. 'A man who calls himself the Son of God,' he said, 'is either mad or telling the truth. Nobody ever said that Christ was mad, therefore Christ was the Son of God.' There are still some who see the simplicity of such Chesterton syllogisms as stemming from a kind of madness.

Granted his premises, there is an inexpungable logic in all Chesterton's literary undertakings. Why that early book on Robert Browning? Because Browning accepted God and human imperfectibility, and the latter is given expression not only in his themes but in his technique, which stumbles, dares and fails while Tennyson maintains a thoughtless perfection. Artists must not be perfect, nor must they rival God in seeking to create an alternative universe. The 'mystic artist' fits best into Chesterton's theological scheme – the mediator between the divine and human, the spiritual and material. The world of tangible things has to be loved and respected: it contains the bread and wine through which Christ manifests himself. Art must be sacramental. It must be allegorical. Fantasy and allegory, so easy to confuse, must be rigidly separated, since, while the second is dedicated to revealing the presence of God, the first presents the human creator in total control, devising his own laws and dealing in what, despite the pleasure and sense of release we may gain from his work, is nothing more than blasphemous madness.

This aesthetic sounds grim, while Chesterton's own poems and stories are life-enhancing. What he does is to bring to his theocentric programme certain qualities for which no theory can legislate. The neglected novel *Manalive* could have been as dull as, say, a work of Gower or Lydgate or Henryson without that Chestertonian madness which is really sanity. The hero of the book seems mad, or certainly criminal. He shoots at people, appears to indulge in polygamy, is always leaving home. At his trial he gives lucid explanations. He leaves home for the joy of coming back to it. He keeps on remarrying his own wife to reaffirm the importance of marriage. He shoots at people, deliberately missing, to make them better appreciate the gift of life. The book is all about the wonder of living, and this has never gone down well in an age dedicated to suicide. Chesterton has been accused of eupepsia. It is, when you come to think of it, a strange thing to be accused of. If dyspepsia is the norm, so is blindness or lameness. The trouble with Chesterton, apparently, is that he is not Kafka.

When you start analysing a novel like *The Flying Inn*, a lot of the joy goes out of it. Islam, the great traditional enemy of Christendom, begins its takeover of England by banning the sale of alcohol (marvellous anomaly, since *alcohol* is an Arabic word). Two men and a dog trundle a barrel of rum and a cheese over the land, singing fine songs and keeping the spirit of Christian conviviality alive. What a splendid idea, and how joyful the execution. But look deeper, and you see that the Islamic crescent stands for human growth, or humanistic progress. A schema which goes too far lumps the Jews with the Arabs. Perhaps the very term *mine host* has sacramental overtones. Dr Hunter is good at disclosing the hard bones of theology underneath what seems to be a fantasy but is really an allegory. Unfortunately, the accidents are lost in the concentration on the substance. We forget that *The Flying Inn* is a good read.

The Father Brown stories perhaps present the quintessence of the Chestertonian method. The bread and wine, or wrapped loaf and plonk, of a popular subliterary form are transubstantiated into the most rarefied theology, and the casual reader is hardly aware that he is in the presence of religious allegory. Father Brown, despite his proclaimed innocence, is terribly aware of the potential evil in himself which enables him to solve cases by subjectively re-enacting the crime. Crime is not perhaps the just word, since a crime is an aberration which is not quite evil. The wrongs that the priest confronts partake of blasphemous madness – the setting up of an alternative system of reality. We are down to theological rock bottom in these tales. Confession, repentance, redemption are more important than punishment. The priest usurps the role of the police, and judgement has nothing to do with judges. Yet how light-seeming these stories are, how entertaining.

Dr Lynette Hunter's book is neither light nor entertaining, but it is honest and serious and, I think, useful. It corrects the easy view of Chesterton as a writer who, when not juggling with paradoxes, is a papist bore. But, for anyone who does not know his work yet is ready to be persuaded to try it, no more offputting introduction could well be imagined. One must not expect a critical work on an author to have some of that author's quality rubbed on to it (else we would reject Leavis on Lawrence), but one has a right to hints of that quality in quotation, or, if possible, a kind of stylistic living up to the subject. Reading Dr Hunter, one is driven to forgetting that Chesterton wrote 'The Rolling English Road' or said that ditchwater, far from being dull, was probably full of quiet fun, or began an essay with 'The human race, to which most of my readers belong . . .', or made the terrifying assertion that Man is a Woman. One ought to reread much of Chesterton and, with that satisfying bulk in one's stomach, sip at Dr Hunter's sharp concentrated brew. It is not pleasant, but it will do some good.

Ear and Beard's Point

Cunninghame Grahame: A Critical Biography, by Cedric Watts and Laurence Davies

When Grahame died in 1936 he was widely sneered at. By Malcolm Muggeridge, for instance:

> Like Don Quixote, he needed a crusade, and, if none was available, had to invent one, tilting against any injustice, however decrepit, and buckling on his antique armour to fight for any cause, however shadowy and remote. He had only to know a country half an hour to have a burning sense of the wrongs under which it laboured, and to set about ventilating them. . . .

This is clearly a piece of derogatory writing, but, to readers no longer credulous of the possibility of social progress through the Marxization of the intelligentsia, the justness of the derogation will not be self-evident. Don Quixote is, true, an absurd character – and Grahame was a suitable model for William Strang's etchings for Cervantes; in appearance, apart from a quarter of his blood and all his temperament, he was *hidalguesco* – but we find him more sympathetic than Stalin. As for the tilting – well, Grahame's achievements have never been sufficiently pondered upon. As late as 1975, in an article entitled 'The Genius of Failure', Jeffrey Meyers said: 'Throughout his life Grahame had a gift for involving himself in doomed projects.' Doomed? Let us look at some of them.

Grahame, as MP, polemic writer, and activist once thrown into Pentonville, fought for militant trade unionism, a British Labour Party, an eight-hour working day, free education, nationalization of the major utilities, the liquidation of empire, the end of racism, protection of the rights of animals, justice for women which went beyond the mere winning of the franchise, Irish Home Rule and a Scottish National Party. Shadowy and remote?

Yet one sees what Muggeridge and others were really sneering at. They found something distasteful in the spectacle of a Scottish aristocrat with Spanish blood speaking up for the oppressed in patrician intonations. The cries for justice seemed to belong to romantic literature rather than to the socialist movement. And Grahame had a talent for the heroic posture which appeared only adventitiously to relate to programmes of practical reform. Bernard Shaw admired him, but as a charming anachronism. In *Arms and the Man* he appears as Major Saranoff, a cavalry officer straight from a novelette, crying 'I never withdraw' (Grahame's own response in the House of Commons to the Speaker's rebuke of an inflammatory statement), and he is contrasted with the Sidney-Webb-like Bluntschli, with his lists of figures and scorn of heroism. But Shaw prized Grahame too as a repository of exotic knowledge. *Captain Brassbound's Conversion* owes its *mise en scène*, and even the close detail of its stage directions, to Grahame's record of his adventures in the Maghreb.

He was a man who sought adventure. Inheritor of an ancient Scottish name and a crumbling estate, he went to Argentina with the ambition of working on an *estancia*. He knew the gaucho life, the miseries and bestialities of the pampas, above all he got to know horses. Applying, at the age of sixty-two, for employment in the First World War and hoping to be enrolled as a Rough Rider, he was sent back to South America to buy horses for the British Army. There was irony in the commission. He, who had rescued his own favourite horse from the shafts of a Glasgow tram, who deplored the cruelty inflicted on the horses of the pampas, was sending the creatures to be gassed and gunned in France. He saw the callousness and stupidity of Texas cowboys and had to live through a cinematic tradition which exalted inarticulateness into heroic taciturnity and turned oppressed Mexicans and Indians into a mythic enemy. The hard life softened his sensibilities. The leaders of England were only a kind of sedentary cowboys as ready to order the massacre of Zulus as to yawn at the agonies of the sweated and the unemployed. His response to the sham of British democracy was to assume the stance of aristocratic arrogance – he had a right to the Scottish and hence the British throne, King Robert – and combine it with a fierce compassion for the underprivileged. Yet there was nothing quixotic about all this: men like Keir Hardie and John Burns responded to his encouragement, and eventually there were Labour seats in parliament. But the political realist was best remembered as Don Roberto, with Spanish blood and a Spanish wife, riding flamboyantly in Hyde Park, a man with a taste for scribbling, a romantic neither before nor after his time but out of it.

This biography is also a history book which is a fine terse guide to the political and economic truths of late-Victorian and Edwardian Britain, which had Bloody Sunday in Trafalgar Square (Grahame was there, knocked about, arrested) as well as Elgar's First Symphony, and in which Winston Churchill was always ready to order out the troops even against orderly popular demonstrations and a warship stood by to blast the Liverpool workers. Not all starch and silver teasets and Ranji in to bat and (Elgar in A flat, *nobilmente*) 'massive hope for the future'. The book also takes on the task of adjudging Grahame's literary achievement.

He was never a popular writer, but his reputation was high among his fellow-practitioners of fiction. Conrad loved him and learned from him – particularly how to manage *Nostromo*, which is set in Grahame territory. Ford Madox Ford at one time thought him the best stylist of the day. He conscientiously followed the example of Maupassant, specializing in the short story, too impatient for the grind of the novel, sexually bold, his range of subject wide, with as good an ear for the speech of the kaleyard as for the Texas ranch drawl. He has, I think, at least one masterpiece – the tale of the Arab who has to transport a bowl full of goldfish across the Sahara – and the story of the sailor in the brothel who finds himself preparing to sleep with his own lost wife is better than the Maupassant *conte* (brother sleeping with sister, highly implausibly, in a similar locale) which is regarded as its inspiration. Because Grahame brought the pampas into English fiction he was, and still is, bracketed with Hudson, the author of *Green Mansions* and *Long Ago and Far Away*, equally perhaps neglected and as worthy of revival. It was Grahame who commissioned Jacob Epstein to sculpt the *Rima* memorial for the Hudson bird sanctuary by the Serpentine. Few strollers in Hyde Park know that Rima is the incarnation of Nature in *Green Mansions*; in my youth she was famous as an aesthetic horror to be tarred and feathered. Grahame was being loyal to a dead friend and at the same time demonstrating a sympathy with the artistic avant-garde which was not untypical. He never cared for the smug and established.

He saw the worth of Conrad and encouraged him throughout his career. When Conrad, tired, dispirited, ready for death, knew Grahame was coming to visit him, he perked up and became the Polish dandy to match his friend's impeccably suited hidalgo. He had an eye capable of seeing the importance of the first Post-Impressionist Exhibition. He found nothing in Joyce or Lawrence. An aesthetic inconsistency, an uneasiness about the location of the border between the artistic and the didactic, a surplus of interests and images – these mar him as a writer. It is as a great character that he must live, not as a reformer, writer or explorer. He stood, in the eye of Ezra Pound in his cage at Pisa, for a complex value that 'was not vanity', and he has his place in the Cantos:

> Mr Grahame himself unmistakably,
> on a horse, an ear and the beard's point showing. . . .

This is an admirable biography, meticulously researched and very sharply written, and it should encourage a new generation to see something in Grahame other than eccentricity, mad energy and the endearing absurdities of quixotry.

Perkinsian Job

Edward Garnett – Life in Literature, by George Jefferson

A life *in* literature? Surely rather a life on its periphery. Edward Garnett had very little literary talent: he wrote a bad novel and a couple of unactable plays. He was a fair critic and did good work in persuading the Edwardian and neo-Georgian public to read the great Russians whom his wife Constance translated. But his real talent was that of talent-spotter. As a publisher's reader he had the insight to descry the potential greatness of Conrad and the eventual saleability of Galsworthy. Half-Irish himself, he had the guts to attack the philistinism of the infant republic which rejected Liam O'Flaherty and Sean O'Faolain. He doled out money to needy authors though far from well paid himself by Duckworth or Cape. Given a flawed manuscript of genius, he could say what the flaws were and how to put them right. He lived a life devoted selflessly to the promotion of literature, but being woefully uncreative, he could never be inside it. He was, inevitably, the sort of man whom the establishment wished to honour far more than the genuine creators – a CH or perhaps an honorary D Litt. But, unlike ennobled publishers or canonized copyeditors or beatified literary agents, he knew he was not worth honouring. Deified by writers he helped, he was humble enough and was right to be so.

Garnett may be said to have inaugurated an age in which authors could be entrusted to possess genius but not to put that genius properly to work. He was not a publisher's editor – that functionary only came in with the expansion of the American houses beyond a couple of rooms and a bottle of sherry in a desk drawer. He had neither the office nor dignity nor salary of a Max Perkins, but he did a Perkinsian job. I wonder sometimes whether it might not have been better for Thomas Wolfe to be allowed to go his own way, the prolixity being part of his talent, rather than be neatly tidied up by the great Max. I do not like talk of the great Max, and I am thankful that Mr Jefferson does not speak of the great Edward. We have been, though only tentatively, asked to honour the editorial greatness of Bob Gottlieb, who put Heller's *Catch-22* into publishable shape. There are no painters' editors who tell artists how to improve their canvases, nor are there composers' editors who regard a submitted score as the raw material for tasteful redaction. Wait – there was one. Rimsky-Korsakov made Mussorgsky acceptable to the bourgeois Russian public. Later, of course, Mussorgsky had to be de-edited.

When I submitted my last novel to its American publisher I received a letter from one of the house editors who said in effect: thank you for this unlicked lump; now we can get to work on it. I had to reply: touch one comma, silently correct one deliberate error and I will be over there with my swordstick. I wish the Conrad of *Almayer's Folly* and the Lawrence of *The Trespasser* had had the courage to reflect that the inner monitor was more reliable than the tasteful publisher's appraiser. I do not like the fawning gratitude with which they, and the remarkable Liam O'Flaherty, attest to the sudden seeing of the light after Garnett's pencil has gone to work.

In the Joyce centennial year it is right to denounce Garnett for his failure to see that *A Portrait of the Artist as a Young Man* represented a new direction in fiction and was not an unhandy attempt to fulfil the precepts of Edwardian tradition. The novel, true, was 'ably written', but 'a good deal of pruning' was needed in the earlier part and at the end there was 'a complete falling to bits'. Garnett's reader's report finishes with these words: 'The author shows he has art, strength and originality, but this MS wants time and trouble spent on it, to make it a more finished piece of work, to shape it more carefully as the product of craftsmanship, mind and imagination of an artist.'

Ezra Pound's response is worth quoting in full; or nearly:

I have read the effusion of Mr Duckworth's reader with no inconsiderable disgust. These vermin crawl over and beslime our literature with their pulings. . . . It is with difficulty that I manage to write to you at all on being presented with the Duckworthian muck, the dungminded, dungbeard, penny-a-line, please-the-mediocre-at-all-costs doctrine . . . as for altering Joyce to suit Duckworth's reader – it would be like trying to fit the Venus de Milo into a pisspot. . . .

That is probably unfair to Garnett. Garnett did not see the virtues of impressionism, nor did many of his generation. He had blind spots and could not perceive that his own son Richard's *Lady Into Fox* was a small masterpiece. He found nothing in Ronald Firbank. On the other hand he was one of the two men living who were aware of the neglected greatness of C. M. Doughty's *Arabia Deserta* (one of the three or four books that made your reviewer wish to become a writer). He belaboured Cape until Cape agreed, with misgivings, to publish it. Cape never regretted this, for the other admirer of Doughty was T. E. Lawrence, who brought the publisher his own Doughtyesque *Seven Pillars of Wisdom*. This, of course, became a bestseller.

The man himself was one of the sights of literary London – grey, jowled, a clumsy dancing bear with thick-lensed glasses, over six feet tall, big-boned, a smoker of herbal cigarettes. Virginia Woolf did not like him. 'I felt surely someone ought to put that surly shaggy unkempt old monstrosity (certainly his nails want cutting and his coat is matted with wind and burrs) in the lethal chamber. Ditto of his mistress, the top half Esquimaux, the bottom Maytime in Hampstead – sprigged muslin, sandals.' (Ah, if only her novels were half as good as her diaries.) The mistress was Nellie Heath, a nice complaisant girl. There came a time when Edward and Constance Garnett did not get on all that well together. She fell in love not only with Russian literature but with Sergei Stepniak, who had fled Russia after knifing a general who had had two girl revolutionaries arrested and flogged.

She herself perhaps emerges as the true heroic figure of this engaging biography. With steadily worsening sight and little monetary recompense she toiled away at translating Tolstoy, Turgenev, Dostoevsky and Chekhov. The great British public did not want these writers, and hence the publishers did not really want them either – or it may have been the other way round. One interesting truth emerges from this chronicle, and it is that both publishers and authors are doing better now than in the expansive Edwardian days. No paperbacks, no separate American publication, editions of twelve hundred copies. But advances were comparatively generous compared with the early deutero-Elizabethan age when I first published a novel. I got a £50 advance in 1955, and authors were getting no less when Garnett shone. There was even talk of giving Joyce £100, and the same for his next two novels. Nobody realized, of course, that these would be the totally ungarnettian *Ulysses* and *Finnegans Wake*.

Sleuth

The Quest for Sherlock Holmes, by Owen Dudley Edwards

The author terms this 'a biographical study of Arthur Conan Doyle'. This is not at all the same thing as a biography, and, anyway, only those years of Conan Doyle's life are covered which preceded the launching of the Sherlock Holmes stories. The aim is precisely indicated in the title: out of what elements in his experience did Conan Doyle create a unique fictional character, together with its satellite personages, and what led him to the forging of a genre with few antecedents and no comparable successors? This is a long dense book, admirably executed, and the labour that has gone into it finds its justification in the author's conviction that Conan Doyle was a great writer.

The literary histories do not agree with him. Conan Doyle was not James or Conrad or Wells; he was a 'mere entertainer' (*mere*, for heaven's sake) with no ambition to change the world's thinking, uncover the mysteries of the human psyche, or leave his personal impress on the language. The truth is probably that our standards of literary judgement are insufficient to deal with him, as they are insufficient to deal with Kipling or, on a steeply descending scale, Rider Haggard, Edgar Wallace, Agatha Christie, Barbara Cartland. Professor Leslie Fiedler has published a book called *What Was Literature?*, in which he explodes the old elitist doctrines. Literature, briefly, is defined as what we study in colleges; all the rest is merely a good read. We are scared of the good read.

Conan Doyle is clearly more than a good read. When I stay in London I stay at the Sherlock Holmes Hotel on Baker Street and breakfast in its Ristorante Moriarti. Reaching it via Baker Street station, I note on the escalator walls a frieze of Sherlock Holmes silhouettes. A hotel guest, I observed in full sobriety the other day, came to the Dr Watson Bar with pipe and in deerstalker outfit. No other character in our literature has so taken over a whole location and convinced the unliterary that he had a historical existence. If Conan Doyle was not great what was he?

The late T. S. Eliot read the Sherlock Holmes stories avidly and, for one of the most poignant passages of *Murder in the Cathedral*, lifted a whole chunk of 'The Musgrave Ritual'. He was always promising to develop an aesthetic of the detective story but never did. Literary elitism got in the way. Posthumously, however, he has inseminated a sellout Broadway musical. The barriers are now down. Owen Dudley Edwards is right to labour at the explication of what may fairly be called great genius. His quest is worthwhile.

The full name, we now learn for the first time, was Arthur Ignatius Conan Doyle. The birth was Scottish, the ancestry Catholic Irish, the training Jesuit. John Doyle, the grandfather, was a Catholic gentleman but also a great and innovative British political cartoonist. The father, Charles Doyle, was also an artist, though a failed one. He made an illustration for his son's first Holmes story, portraying himself, mild, bearded, dreamy, unhawklike, as the sleuth inspecting the Baker Street Irregulars. The seeing eye, public or private, was in the family as it is in Holmes, but Charles Doyle obfuscated it with drink. In his son's work it is alcohol that is the enemy; opium may be tolerated. The mother kept the family together and was a great heroine. There is no misogyny in Conan Doyle's books – only an adoration of woman that the feminists may find equally offensive. 'Oh, blind, angelic, foolish love of woman! Why should men demand a miracle while you remain upon earth?' That comes at the end of 'A Sordid Affair'.

Young Arthur went to Stonyhurst, a Hibernian Scot among the scions of the Lancashire Catholic aristocracy. Mr Dudley Edwards sees the lineaments of the college in Baskerville Hall, and suggests a faint Francis Thompson echo ('I fled him, down the nights and down the days') in the Hound itself. If the name Holmes came from Oliver Wendell, the Christian name derived from a Patrick Sherlock who was the dullest of Arthur's contemporaries at Stonyhurst. There were two Moriartys – John Francis and Michael – both of whom won the Stonyhurst prize for mathematics and left more than an onomastic mark on the evil professor: 'At the age of twenty-one he wrote a treatise on the binomial theorem, which had a European vogue.' I go along with Dudley Edwards's less than wholly serious hint that Inspector Stanley Hopkins owes something to Gerard Manley Hopkins, who, before Conan Doyle's time, taught at Stonyhurst. A remote unconscious chime, perhaps, but that is the way the literary mind works.

Mr Dudley Edwards courteously rebukes me for finding in the anticlericalism of *The White Company* a forecast of the British Reformation. He is right when he says that a dislike of priests is essentially Catholic. Conan Doyle left the Church but never came to terms with Anglicanism. The rigour of Holmes's thinking is Stonyhurst Jesuit with a touch of Edinburgh Calvinistic. Conan Doyle's patron saint taught, in his *Spiritual Exercises*, the importance of 'composition of place'. Holmes lives and works in a London very firmly composed, but it owes more to a small and manageable city like Edinburgh than the true sprawling megalopolis itself. Red marl outside a particular post office: it is not a London concept. The grasp of material detail, fostered by Conan Doyle's medical training, is not uncognate with Hopkins's poetic method. Holmes's detectional methods depend on an acceptance of the physical world. In late life Conan Doyle was forced into qualifying the sullenly material with a study of spiritualism. It was a sort of Catholic heresy.

'If there had been no Mahomet, said the great Henri Pirenne, there would have been no Charlemagne. If there had been no *Micah Clarke*, there would have been no Sherlock Holmes.' So affirms Mr Dudley Edwards on page 347 of his crammed and closely printed investigation. Conan Doyle is, we sometimes forget, the greatest historical novelist after Walter Scott, to whom, appropriately as an Edinburgh man, he owed much. *Micah Clarke* is not only a great novel but a profound exercise in historical investigation, and it opens the way to the methodology of Holmes – 'the exemplar of the historian at work'. Meaning that cultural awareness is alike essential to the recreator of a historical situation and the prober into a criminal problem. *A Study in Scarlet* is structurally weaker than many Holmesians care to believe. *Micah Clarke* strengthened Conan Doyle's technique and clarified in his mind the differences between the novel form and the short story: write a symphony and you will the better learn how to manage a nocturne. Mr Dudley Edwards's fine book is essential reading not only for dedicated Holmesians but for all who, rejecting the Leavisian Great Tradition, consider that the creative processes of even the 'popular writer' deserve close study.

Hem Not Writing Good

Ernest Hemingway: Selected Letters 1917–1961, edited by Carlos Baker

I find that the writing of letters gets in the way of being a man of letters. Some authors manage to fuse the opposed claims of letters and letters by practising what is termed the epistolary art, anticipating the posthumous publication of their collected mail and royalties for their relicts. This entails showing a private face in a public place, which is not what letter-writing ought to be like. Auden wrote a sonnet about a literary man who answered 'some of his long marvellous letters but kept none'. That seems reasonable, but my heart goes out to Sir Thomas

Beecham, who never seems to have opened a letter in his life, unless it smelt of money.

Reading Carlos Baker's biography of Hemingway, I was heartened to discover that there were whole drawerloads of unopened mail in his various houses. But now I have this bulky selection (not collection) to attest that he was quite as bad as Lord Chesterfield or Evelyn Waugh. All that can be said in palliation of his cacoethes is that old Hem, in writing to his buddies, did not try to write good. Or not often. 'Every time I write a good letter,' he wrote, rightly, 'it's a sign I'm not working.' But Baker, who has done the expected fine job of editing here, suggests that Hemingstein the letter-scribbler scribbled letters 'as an antidote to the concentration of creativity' or else warmed up or cooled out with an undemanding allotrope of his craft.

'The last thing I remember about English in High School,' wrote Hemingway somewhere, 'was a big controversy on whether it was *already* or *all ready*. How did it ever come out?' Only once did a regular solecism get past his editors: *A Moveable Feast* (orthography, not title, not book) is able to infect high-school students for ever. In the letters there is no tidying up, and there is a free flow that resists all the rules of propriety. Here he is writing to Scott Fitzgerald from Key West, 28 May 1934:

> For Christ sake write and don't worry about what the boys will say nor whether it will be a masterpiece nor what. I write one page of masterpiece to ninety one pages of shit. I try to put the shit in the waste-basket. You feel you have to publish crap to make money to live and let live. . . .
> Forget your personal tragedy. We are all bitched from the start and you especially have to be hurt like hell before you can write seriously. . . .

Add then blunt words about Zelda being crazy and Scott not really being a rummy. It is sound refreshing stuff. There will be readers of these letters who will say, as the High Command said of Hemingway's private army in 1944, that he is trying to turn himself into one of his own characters. But it is rather the other way round. Hemingway's characters talk like Hemingway. You even get here what has been termed Hemingway Choktaw, telegraphese worked up into an idiolect. Thus, as early as 1921 and Chicago, to Grace Quinlan: 'Guy I usually eat lunch with is sick. So talking to you instead.' Probably his most admired phrase was one picked up from an Indian, whether or not Choktaw not recorded: 'Long time ago good, now heap shit.' There is no attempt to modify the direct simplicities for the highly literate. To Bernard Berenson (Dear B. B.): 'Anyway (get out Big Glass) and read it. We all love you very much and let us all go to (I wasn't brave) gether and have fun. God (Gott) BLESS you and our love my true love.'

The Hemingway style is probably the best one for expressing love, whatever he thought love was. The four wives get good manly loving letters with no Keatsian ordure. Adriana Ivancich, in the fall days of 1954, when the old soldier needed delicious incestuous guilt, got things like 'Daughter I love you and miss you so much. You know we were pretty good maybe and with things bad we *never* fought.' She also gets 'Ingrid is the same. Sweet and good and honest and married to the 22 pound rat. This is not jealousy. Maybe he is the undiscovered 42 pound rat. He makes good children anyway.' The rat is Roberto Rossellini. Hemingway is fine on commiseration too. He tells Arnold Gingrich from Key West, 16 November 1934: 'That's certainly a hell of a damned disease you have. . . . I'm damned sorry about it.' And, from the same place, a few months later, he writes, I think, superbly to Gerald and Sara Murphy, who had just lost their eldest child after a long illness:

> Absolutely truly and coldly in the head, though, I know that anyone who dies young after a happy childhood, and no one ever made a happier childhood than you made for your children, has won a great victory. We all have to look forward to death by defeat, our bodies gone, our world destroyed; but it is the same dying we must do, while he has gotten it all over with, his world all intact and the death only by accident.

Hemingway's own death is not directly foreshadowed. But, from Rochester in Minnesota on 4 December 1960, he writes a totally unnecessary letter TO WHOM IT MAY CONCERN, exonerating his fourth wife Mary from complicity in nonexistent crimes. This was the time of final breakdown, when he believed the Feds and the I R S were after him. Also from Rochester on 15 June 1961 he writes to the son of his doctor, George Saviers, a letter that any sick nine-year-old boy would be glad to receive (the boy Fritz was suffering from viral heart disease):

> Saw some good bass jump in the river. I never knew anything about the upper Mississippi before and it is really a very beautiful country and there are plenty of pheasants and ducks in the fall. But not as many as in Idaho and I hope we'll both be back there shortly and can joke about our hospital experiences together.

Fewer than three weeks later he, as Baker puts it, 'unlocked the basement storeroom, chose a double-barrelled Boss shotgun . . . pressed his forehead against the barrels, and blew away the entire cranial vault.'

These letters, essaying no literary effects, are all the more for that a kind of literature – direct, pungent, idiosyncratic, breathing speech more than lamp oil. The character who emerges is the one we already think we know – sweaty and in shorts and cussing readily – but there is no new and unexpected qualification, such as bookishness or paedophilia. The Hemingway of the letters is almost totally likable or likeable.

336

Chip on Shoulder

The Life of John O'Hara, by Frank MacShane

Does anyone, other than the British novelist Mr Braine, read John O'Hara these days? Does anyone, other than Mr Braine, consider him one of the great fiction writers of our century? That he is still around, far from forgotten, is instanced in TV reruns of the film *Butterfield 8* and the success of the *Pal Joey* revival. Some of his stories have been widely anthologised, and everybody knows that he is the father of the forms of *New Yorker* fiction. It is the early work that people know when they know him at all. *Butterfield 8* was his third novel, and *Appointment in Samarra*, perhaps his best, his first. It was for the later work – *The Lockwood Concern* especially – that O'Hara expected the Nobel Prize, though his friends and enemies alike were amused at his presumption. Despised by the intelligentsia, shocking to the straitlaced, his work exhibits the faults of a personality very acutely analysed by Dr MacShane. An Irish lad from Pottsville who never went to a university, he was afflicted by a sense of social inferiority which manifested itself in drunkenness and bluster. Hemingway once suggested to other graduates in the fiction trade that everybody club together to buy him an education at Yale. But O'Hara's touchiness went deeper than a mere sense of social deprivation. Like old William in Wordsworth's poem, he never felt himself sufficiently beloved.

He made loving gestures which, in his view, were not well appreciated. Faulkner got the Nobel and O'Hara was very decent about it. He gave, as a token of admiration, a gold cigarette lighter to the grumpy Southern genius, who merely grunted something and put it casually in his pocket. O'Hara was terribly hurt, since that lighter had been a gift to himself from a prized friend. When Faulkner heard how hurt he was, he merely said: 'The hell with him. I didn't want the darned thing anyway.' When O'Hara had the novel called *The Farmers Hotel* ready for publication, he suggested to Richard Rodgers that he title it *A Small Hotel*. Rodgers said he'd got the *Pal Joey* allusion wrong: the song referred to was called 'There's a Small Hotel'. Like Faulkner, Rodgers had failed to appreciate the gesture of friendly solidarity, the wish to amass subtle tokens of artistic brotherhood. But no one ever quite plumbed the profundities of O'Hara's touchiness.

There was a certain pathos in his deciding to spend his last years in Princeton, New Jersey, where he felt sure he would be cocktailed and dined by the faculty as a distinguished author and invited to Cottage to yarn with the students. But O'Hara did not know Princeton, the most exclusive and excluding foundation of the Ivy League. The closest he got to acceptance by a university was posthumously gimmicky. Some years ago at the University of Pennsylvania I made a television recording in an exact reproduction of O'Hara's study, complete (or that may have been my imagination or my own physical imposition) with the odour of whisky and cigars. Really there was little for O'Hara to repine about. He made a lot of money and was more or less accepted by the rich he so closely observed and analysed in his later fiction. He gained, after various amorous disasters, the love of a good woman, the wife he anomalously called Sister (compare Hemingway's Miss Mary). He had a Rolls-Royce with J O H 1 as its registration number. He was invited to the White House, though he rode thither in the car officially allotted to the much younger John Updike. There was always something to be grouchy about.

Dr MacShane, my old head of department at Columbia, has already brilliantly recounted the life of Raymond Chandler, another writer who took to the bottle and pined, though this was in his widower days, for lack of love. This new biography is a worthy successor to that, and MacShane could, did he not have other arenas of enterprise, become the specialist chronicler of the American literary tortured. He tells the story of O'Hara in a childhood world where factories had notices like NO IRISH NEED APPLY, in New York and Pittsburgh at the journalist's trade – at which, like Hemingway, he was good; through which he learned flow and the dangers of overmuch finesse – and in Hollywood, where Budd Schulberg, author of *The Disenchanted*, tried to engage him in the leftist causes which, in the late 1930s, were animating the celluloid capital. It was here that O'Hara decided he had very little sympathy with the working man.

It is the redneck arrogance of the later O'Hara, the man who had been poor and made it to the top, which repels the more pinkish of his readers. The rejection of syndicalism, which never did anybody any good, and, in the column he contributed to *Newsday*, the brutal support of William Buckley, the Police Benevolent League and Ronald Reagan as well as his pejorative use of the term 'liberalistic' may reinforce his attraction for Mr Braine (one of the few British authors he met on his visits to London). Unfortunately, this polemical coarseness affects his fiction. Louis Auchincloss spoke of the uniform violence of his later work, in which

> the most casual meeting between a major and a minor character will result either in any angry flare-up or a sexual connection, or both. It is impossible for an O'Hara character to order a meal in a restaurant or to take a taxi ride without having a crude exchange with the waiter or driver. Even the characters from whom one might expect some degree of reticence – the rich dowagers, for example – will discuss sex on the frankest basis with the first person to bring the subject up.

This is a harsh observation, but there is much truth in it. O'Hara provided the raw materials for the caricature which others were only too ready to refine, or coarsen – 'a writer', says MacShane justly, 'obsessed with social niceties and crude sex.'

Powerful emotions never yet harmed a writer and, if O'Hara exhibits too little self-control, yet nobody can rightly complain of a lack of libido or of physical energy in his novels. The real trouble is raucous monotony, like the brass playing all the time, and yet, in the early books and especially in the best of the early short stories, there is delicacy enough, the reticence of a man not yet too sure of himself. When O'Hara arrived at a season when he felt he had better be sure of himself (though he had not gone through the hard processes which lead to a genuine inner balance) his concealed tensions jumped out in the disguise of rant and crudeness. It would be unwise to wish to engage his entire *oeuvre*, but *Appointment in Samarra, From the Terrace*, and one of the early collections of stories ought to be known to anyone interested in twentieth-century fiction. As for Dr MacShane's claim that he is 'one of the half-dozen most important writers of his time', that must be taken as a somewhat spurious pretext for producing his biography.

Poor S.O.B.

Some Sort of Epic Grandeur – The Life of F. Scott Fitzgerald, by Matthew J. Bruccoli

'I am not a great man,' said Fitzgerald to his daughter Scottie, 'but sometimes I think the impersonal and objective qualities of my talent, and the sacrifices of it, in pieces, to preserve its essential value has some sort of it,' and there's your title. This is the third full length biography of the author of *The Great Gatsby* (which T. S. Eliot called the only significant advance in the American novel since Henry James), and it comes just twenty years after Andrew Turnbull's. It is better than

Turnbull's only because it has more facts; it is not better written, nor more moving, nor, despite the plethora of dollar signs, more informative. Professor Bruccoli is a Fitzgerald–Hemingway scholar, but scholarship is never a guarantee of literary elegance. When we read, in the preface, 'He is regarded by a certain kind of Twenties buff as having scribbled his masterpieces during the course of a lifelong bender,' we fear the stylistic worst. And when Professor Bruccoli's very first sentence is 'Many of us share Samuel Johnson's admission that "the biographical part of literature . . . is what I love most," because great writers perform the world's most precious and enduring work,' we are smitten not only by a crass illogicality but an apparent failure to understand what literature is. Johnson's *Lives of the Poets* are literature about literature and contain such gems as the one about Milton being a lion that had no art in dandling the kid. Bruccoli is bluff, dysphonious, journalistic, Gradgrindishly fact-loving, but no true biographer. Turnbull's brief book has not yet been superseded.

On the other hand, Fitzgerald's life is so easy to romanticize that there is some point in going the other way and reducing it to debts, sales returns and medical diagnoses. Yet there are few of us who do not prefer to get our image of Fitzgerald from books like Sheilah Graham's *Beloved Infidel* or Budd Schulberg's novel *The Disenchanted*. Schulberg, as Bruccoli's book reconfirms, collaborated with Fitzgerald in 1939 on a film script for Walter Wanger called *Winter Carnival*. The two were sent off to Dartmouth with a camera crew and a ten-page treatment, and Fitzgerald accepted on the flight a gift from Schulberg of a bottle of champagne. This, in Bruccoli's words, 'triggered a Fitzgerald bender'. The story as Schulberg presents it in his novel is one of tragicomic humiliation and one cannot doubt that, despite Schulberg's halfhearted disclaimers, it is all true. I have read this novel about twenty times and I am prepared to read it again.

The trouble with the life of Fitzgerald is that it is a potential novel in itself, and perhaps superior to any of the novels that Fitzgerald himself wrote. 'Epic grandeur' may not be the term for it, but there is a genuine tragedy of waste. In its crass blunt way Bruccoli's relentlessly factual narrative drives home the nature of the waste. Here was a great artistic talent that required sobriety and even an acceptance of Gissing-like near-poverty for its fulfilment, but Fitzgerald was an alcoholic, a spendthrift, and a superstar playboy possessed of a beauty and glamour that only a Byron could support without artistic ruination. For the artist's task is to create beauty, not exemplify it in himself. All poets should look like Pope. And then there was Zelda, spoilt Southern belle, wilful, extravagant and, as Hemingway was quick to recognize, jealous of her husband's talent.

Fitzgerald's novels were never bestsellers in their own time. They brought him critical praise but little money. So he had to dilute his talent in the market of the magazine story, a commodity that no longer exists, and pay wine and sanatorium bills with large cheques from the *Saturday Evening Post* and *Collier's*. Bruccoli shows us inexorably precisely what

Fitzgerald wrote for the magazines and precisely what he earned. As a fellow-novelist I find my heart aching at the waste of fine plot material on ephemeral near-trash and yet envious of the inordinate rewards. That Fitzgerald was able to keep it up over so many years is evidence of his inventive talent: I can think of no living writer who could approach him. But the barrel emptied, word-spinning replaced invention, and only Hollywood was left.

There is an anomaly in Fitzgerald's attitude to Hollywood which, to give him his due, Bruccoli forgets salary cheques to emphasize. He both despised the cinematic medium because it was not literature and hailed it because it was going to take over the function of literature. *The Last Tycoon*, unfinished as it is, is the best Hollywood novel we have, indicative of Fitzgerald's understanding of the medium as it could become though was not yet. On that disastrous trip to Dartmouth Fitzgerald pumped Schulberg, son of the former head of production at Paramount, for inside details of the craft and the business: another reason why they got nothing done on *Winter Carnival*. Joseph L. Mankiewicz, whom I share with Fitzgerald as my first Hollywood director, assured me that the great dialoguist of the novels was hopeless when he had to shed *récit* and rely on speech alone. Fitzgerald survives negatively in movies. Working on *Gone With the Wind*, he insisted on the deletion of 'Scarlett's statement to Ashley that the sash she made for him looks like gold, and noted: "This is technicolor," ' But in *A Yank at Oxford* he had the choirboys singing in Magdalen tower and made Robert Taylor say to Maureen O'Sullivan: 'Don't rub the sleep out of your eyes. It's beautiful sleep.' Romantic to the end. But in American TV reruns those Fitzgeraldisms are cut.

There are new facts, then, a justification stronger than the urge of the biographical artist to produce a new life of a great fictional artist. The trouble is that Fitzgerald is bigger than the facts and lives best in the untruths of anecdote. Bruccoli comes into his own in the appendices, with a full bibliography, a movie treatment of *Tender is the Night* and the complete Fitzgerald financial ledger. Scottie adds an irrelevant chapter of genealogy.

Scott as Hack

The Price Was High: The Last Uncollected Stories of F. Scott Fitzgerald, edited by Matthew J. Bruccoli

Some time ago I was sent the *Collected Poems of Ernest Hemingway* – fortunately not for review. The only justification for collecting those appalling bits of Oak Park High School doggerel and scrawled wartime outpourings to Miss Mary was the scholarly one that transcends literary values and seeks to put the canon to bed. So let it be with these magazine stories of Hemingway's friend. Unfortunately I have to review them.

Have to? Nonsense, nobody has to do anything. Let me say then that there is some point in considering these 785 close pages as a commentary on the life and struggles of a great novelist – financial struggles, sybaritic life – and as a testimony to the truth of Dorothy Parker's observation on Fitzgerald: although he could write a bad story, he could not write badly. It is the good writing here that is likely to infuriate the reader more than the slick pert plots. Fitzgerald should have been getting on with his novels, not wasting his talent on subliterary prostitution.

He was, of course, well aware of this. In 1929 he wrote to Hemingway: 'The *Post* now pays the old whore $4000 a screw. But it's now because she's mastered the 40 positions – in her youth one was enough.' $4000 a screw fifty years after is not to be sneezed at; in 1929 it was one hell of a lot of money. The fifty stories collected here by Professor Bruccoli earned altogether $106,585, less agent's commission. In 1925 Fitzgerald got $11,025 for five stories, while *The Great Gatsby* earned less than $2000 beyond the $4264 advance. In 1934, the year of *Tender is the Night*, Fitzgerald's total income from eight books was $58.35, but eight stories – and the prices were post-Depression prices – brought him $12,475.

The stories were craft meant to subsidize art, but in fact they subsidized high living. It was tempting for Fitzgerald, once having learnt the craft, to despise the merely consumable and consume the rewards with a kind of self-contempt. He threw the money away, sometimes literally – there is more than one tale of his giving thousand-franc notes to the wind while bowling along the Corniche – and the time for writing the novels remained hard-bought. Moreover, he had a public of great size which didn't even know that he was a novelist. It required an integrity that ran counter to the American Way of Life to sustain the role of novelist at all.

The old *Saturday Evening Post* was an aspect of the American Way of

Life. Its regular circulation was about three million and it sold for five cents. It was crammed with work of genuine distinction, and it gave large value for money – eight stories and eight articles to an issue, as well as three serials and a number of regular features. It was not highbrow but it would never publish trash. The problem that any writer found when wishing to contribute to it was that of divining precisely what the editors required. Faulkner and Wolfe were glad to write for it, but their large individuality conflicted with the personality of the magazine. Fitzgerald knew how to subdue idiosyncrasy of style for the sake of readers who had never heard of Henry James: nobody had to reread a sentence to see what it meant or look for a dictionary. At the same time he purveyed an individual flavour: his name meant something. The *Post* did not mean hackwork, nor did it mean formulaic writing. When Fitzgerald grew tired and ill and poor he sought the way of the pattern, of giving the public what he thought it wanted, and then the *Post* ceased to want him. When Fitzgerald was at his commercial peak he was the only story writer who could always give the *Post* precisely what it wanted: that is why the price was high.

What it wanted was Modern Love, the New Girl, Sexual Emancipation as the twenties saw it. Professor Bruccoli kindly gives us some samples of the kind of illustration that went with Fitzgerald's stories. These drawings are of a high technical standard and totally of their time. 'The Adolescent Marriage' shows a weeping flapper, face buried in the davenport, interrogated by a slim shingled mother, grave tuxedoed father filling a pipe by the mock-Adam fireplace. 'Indecision' has a fancy-dress ball – balloons, slim-legged pierrette, clean-jawed man in tails. 'The Love Boat' breathes the romance of a tropical cruise – stars, Kodak girl with skimpy dress wind-pasted to her body, handsome discreet lover. There is the promise of daring and candour, but not too much. It is all a kind of mockery of the Fitzgerald of *The Great Gatsby*. There posterity looks at the twenties; in the *Post* the twenties merely look at themselves.

As for the prose style, here is a specimen from 'A Change of Class':

> He stood up, terribly aware of what he had done. He watched Earl bent over his check book, not knowing that the check would come back unhonored and that the whole transaction was meaningless. And watching the fingers twisted clumsily about the fountain pen, he thought how deft those same fingers were with a razor, handling it so adroitly that there was no pull or scrape; of those fingers manipulating a hot towel that never scalded, spreading a final, smooth lotion –

Barbering is one of the great images of the period, the maintenance of neatness and slickness, the elimination of hirsute nature, while the destructive element is the failure of money, symbolized in the bouncing cheque. As for the high life, it is best sought abroad, where there is no Prohibition. The *Post* reader was aware that Fitzgerald knew all about abroad: it was getting nothing, for its five cents, at second hand:

> Tommy's dinner was not to be at his hotel. After meeting in the bar
> they sledded down into the village to a large old-fashioned Swiss
> taproom, a thing of woodwork, clocks, steins, kegs and antlers. There
> were other parties like their own, bound together by the common plan of
> eating *fondue* – a peculiarly indigestible form of Welsh rabbit – and
> drinking spiced wine, and then hitching on the backs of sleighs to
> Doldorp several miles away, where there was a townspeople's ball.

Fitzgerald's readers would have taken that 'indigestible' as comic decoration, a blasé gesture. We know that Fitzgerald was in Switzerland
coping with Zelda's latest breakdown. The *Post*'s high prices were now
for paying psychiatrists' bills.

'The price was high,' he said, 'right up with Kipling, because there
was one little drop of something, not blood, not a tear, not my seed, but
me more intimately than these, in every story, it was the extra I had.'
What he meant probably was that, however slick or contrived the story,
there was often some image out of memory that carried a heavy weight of
poignant connotation. Dragged into a magazine tale, its true home was a
great novel disregarded by the huge middlebrow public. The price the
Post paid was indeed high, but it was only money. The price Fitzgerald
paid remains incomputable.

Here, finally, is the Modern Girl:

> She was thin, a thin burning flame, colorless yet fresh. Her smile came
> first slowly, then with a rush, pouring out of her heart, shy and bold, as if
> all the life of that little body had gathered for a moment around her mouth
> and the rest of her was a wisp that the least wind would blow away. She
> was a changeling whose lips alone had escaped metamorphosis, whose
> lips were the only point of contact with reality.

It would be otiose to give her name.

Cole Fire

The Complete Lyrics of Cole Porter, edited by Robert Kimball

Gerard Manley Hopkins wrote to Robert Bridges about being 'struck aghast' by a kind of raw nakedness when he read one of his poems with his eyes only. Switch on the ears, he said, and everything was fine. Read Cole Porter with your eyes, and the nakedness is even rawer than with Hopkinsian sprung rhythm. You need the tune and you don't always know it. Moreover, the convention of printing song lyrics as if there were a difference between internal and final rhymes, as if a visual pattern were significant, as if they were *poesy* is terribly wrong. Mr Kimball, a devoted and learned Cole Porter scholar, admits that you have to set the words under the music, but the *Complete Songs* would be bigger than the complete *Ring* and who could afford it? We must be glad to have what we have.

Though, frankly, we only begin to be glad about page 72, where, after two decades of the banalities he assumed the public wanted, the true Porter erupts with:

> The most select schools of cod do it,
> Though it shocks 'em, I fear.
> Sturgeon, thank God, do it –
> Have some caviar, dear. . . .

That is part of the refrain of 'Let's Do It' specially written for the London production of *Paris, 1928*. He wouldn't have got away with 'thank God' in New York. The version of 'Anything Goes' we all know has

> In olden days a glimpse of stocking
> Was looked on as something shocking,
> Now, heaven knows. . . .

Which is uncharacteristically clumsy. Of course, what he wrote was: 'But now, God knows. . . .'

He was always suffering from bowdlerization. His best song, in his own view, 'Love For Sale' was never allowed on US radio. His all too viscerally witty 'The Tale of the Oyster' was cut from *Fifty Million Frenchmen* (1929) because the critic Gilbert Seldes found it 'offensive'. His best-loved song, 'Begin the Beguine' (*Jubilee*, 1935), had as penultimate line 'And we suddenly know the sweetness of sin' until decency demanded 'what heaven we're in'. His most brilliant song,

'You're the Top' (*Anything Goes*, 1934), respectable enough in its eight refrains as then performed, seemed to have lying latent in it

> You're the burning heat of a bridal suite in use,
> You're the breasts of Venus,
> You're King Kong's penis,
> You're self-abuse.

Kimball does not believe Porter wrote this (there's an Australian rhyme in it), but it was the sort of thing it was assumed he did write and people had actually heard (on the road, in a Toronto tryout). The naughtiness of Porter was Huxleyan, Waughish, smart, educated, even intellectual. If he couldn't write about breasts he wrote about *poitrines*. He calls Aphrodite a whore, but only in Greek. Some of the lyrics are in respectable Italian and Spanish. Or not so respectable.

Porter was the son of a wealthy family, a Yale man, a student of Vincent D'Indy at the Schola Cantorum, a kind of playboy who knew harmony and counterpoint as well as he knew Lady Mendl, Sir Thomas Beecham and Elsa Maxwell. His stage songs allude to the smart set but also to Sappho, Freud, Engels, Eugene O'Neill, Bishop Manning, Gandhi, Shelley, *Titus Andronicus*, Pope, Aeschylus. He gets away with being highbrow because he tempers the learning with the highly colloquial, not to say slangy. 'Brush Up Your Shakespeare', which is the most learned song of them all (*Kiss Me Kate*, 1948), is sung by a couple of gangsters, not professors:

> Better mention *The Merchant of Venice*
> When her sweet pound of flesh you would menace.
> If her virtue, at first, she defends – well,
> Just remind her that *All's Well That Ends Well*. . . .

· It's important to remember that Porter was not a song writer in the Irving Berlin sense – a creator of isolated items intended for Tin Pan Alley promotion. He wrote what the musical theatre calls *scores* – that is to say, he did what Sullivan did in *The Mikado*, but he was Gilbert as well. To contrive long ensemble numbers which related to the plot required genuine musical skill of a kind Berlin did not have. Some of his best work, lyrical as well as musical, can only be known to a generation, like mine, which saw the shows – in London, on Broadway, even in Manchester tryouts (*Wake Up and Dream*, for instance, which Manchester knew as *Charles B. Cochran's 1929 Revue*). So the best numbers in, say, *Panama Hattie* (1940) relate to locale and local customs, and one or two are in Spanish. When Ethel Merman sang 'I've Still Got My Health', she sang it in character:

> I knew I was slipping
> At Minsky's one dawn –

> When I started stripping,
> They hollered: 'Put it on!'

And Betty Hutton, in the same show, made 'Fresh as a Daisy' so muscular an exhibition that the words ('Scared as a rabbit,/ Small as a mite,/ Gay as a meadowlark,/ High as a kite . . .') as well as the music are a mere pretext for display. But then Ethel Merman and Joan Carroll sing

> What say, let's be buddies,
> What say, let's be pals,
> What say, let's be buddies
> And keep up each other's morales . . .

and we have something simple and separable whose tongue-in-cheekiness nobody is likely to notice at, say, the London Palladium.

As Mr Kimball tells us, the music publishers did not always do right by Porter. When a show song had many refrains, they were unwilling to separate the vocal stave from the right-hand piano stave sufficiently to get them all in; nor would they stick them on the back page, which they needed for advertisements. So here they all are, with Porter's rhyming ingenuity strained to the limit (top, flop, pop, blop, *de trop*, stop, hop, op, G. O. P. or GOP) but never, as so often with the Beatles, making do with a false rhyme. He was a fastidious prosodist, though, like all lyricists except Lorenz Hart, he had trouble with 'love'.

I don't think, despite Mr Kimball's claim and his admirable industry, there is quite every word here that Porter wrote. Where, for instance, in 'My Heart Belongs to Daddy' (*Leave it to Me*, 1938) is

> I cared a lot
> For a handsome Scot –
> He was a braw heelan' laddy.
> He wore a kilt
> And was awful well-built
> But my heart . . .?

But there is enough to make us regret the great days when popular song could be literate and even intellectual. And, for that matter, tuneful. Hart, Coward and Porter look down in their dinner jackets at a wealth of hair and noise but little talent.

Thin Man

The Life of Dashiell Hammett, by Diane Johnson
Dashiell Hammett: A Life at the Edge, by William F. Nolan

This makes three lives of Hammett I've read in two years. The film *Julia*, in which Jason Robards briefly impersonated him, may have stimulated an interest in the man. The best of his work, I should have thought, is pretty secure, with *The Maltese Falcon* conceivably the best American detective novel ever written. He helped Lillian Hellman to success and was briefly a success himself; he was also an exemplary failure. The parabola of his life is typically American: fame stultifies the creative urge; money means drink means ruin. Hammett had, in addition to the agonies that Hemingway and Fitzgerald knew, the torment of the McCarthy witch hunts, the slings of the FBI, the arrows of the IRS. He died of lung cancer at sixty-six; his condition complicated by smoker's emphysema, pneumonia, and diseases of the heart, liver, kidneys, spleen and prostate gland. He never complained. At his funeral Lillian Hellman said: 'He seemed to me a great man.' He was certainly a stoical one.

Hammett brought to the detective story a factual authenticity which derived from his brief career as a Pinkerton agent. He knew all about guns and fingerprints. Working in San Francisco, about as corrupt a city as any of those United States, Hammett found the doctrine of original sin amply confirmed (the family was Catholic on the Dashiell or De Chiell side). Evil mined society, just as the spirochaete and tubercle mined the body. Hammett was tubercular from an early age and always looked it. Creator of *The Thin Man*, he was a thin man himself, austere, sometimes elegant. He was never syphilitic but was always catching the clap. Life was pretty bad and God had removed himself from the scene. Justice had to be left to men like Sam Spade, progenitor of a whole American tradition of incorrupt private eyes. There was solace in bed or in the bottle, as well as clap and cirrhosis. But the best solace was art.

Hemingway was always talking of 'grace under pressure', but Hammett knew more about pressure than he (he fought in two wars, while Hemingway merely acted the *miles gloriosus*); the stoical grace of Hammett's art is not inferior to Hemingway's, and there were reserves of irony which stopped the unconsciously self-parodic from creeping in. The two men met. Hemingway bent a spoon with his biceps and challenged Hammett to do the same. But Hammett was so secure in his elegant misery that he never had to accept challenges.

It was Hollywood that was supposed to have brought Hammett low. When one's writer–protagonist gets to his suite in the Beverly-Wilshire one knows that Disillusion will soon be stocking the bar and Cynicism

348

cracking the ice. Hammett and Hellman met, fell for each other, and then started a Nick and Nora Charles saga full of sex and scotch and wit and literary allusions. Hammett, no man for acquisitions, drank his salary away but could not dissipate his literary gift: Hollywood needed him as it never needed Scott Fitzgerald. *The Thin Man* bred a series; eventually, after two false tries, *The Maltese Falcon* was magnificently brought to the screen (John Huston saw that no script was needed: everything was in the book). But Hammett succumbed to the devil within. Drunks are always a bore and the drunken Hammett bores monumentally. He could no longer write, but he helped to found the Writer's Union. Remembering what had happened to the Wobblies, no longer resigned to wicked exploitative America, he substituted a kind of political activism for literary creation. The FBI began to look for him but couldn't find him, for, although over-age, he joined the army.

William F. Nolan is, according to the dust jacket, 'the leading Hammett scholar'. Diane Johnson has written a biography of Thomas Love Peacock's daughter and helped Kubrick with the script of *The Shining*. While Nolan is informative about the genesis of the books, Ms Johnson has more to say about the suffering man. Her first chapter shows Hammett in prison. Fifty-seven, toothless, thinner than he has ever been, he must pay the price for contempt of court during the McCarthy nightmare. Released, he faces the tribunal again, pleading the Fifth Amendment when asked if he is a communist. Ms Johnson transcribes the occasion in full. One feels ashamed at belonging to the same cultural tradition as the United States.

The other Hammett biography I have read was by Richard Layman (*Shadow Man*, 1981). The fact that one seems to need all three books to gain a rounded portrait of the subject, as well as the whole of the historical background and a critical assessment of the work, seems to point towards some bigger biography not yet begun. Perhaps only a lengthy study of Hammett and his times can raise the details of the life above the dull and sordid. We are not impressed by the spectacle of Hammett and William Faulkner collapsing drunk on the floor at a Knopf dinner party. The heat cure for clap which Hammett endured rouses no terror or pity: Hammett should not have caught clap. The writer's block – whether in the film studio or the brain – is not calculated to impress British writers who have to regard literary paralysis as a luxury. It is unfortunate that all the Hammett biographies invite comparison with the very good one of Raymond Chandler by Frank MacShane. Hammett was the pioneer, Chandler merely the beneficiary, but there is no doubt who was the more interesting man of the two. Unfortunately, Chandler was not what passes in America for a tragic hero. He grew old and lonely and he drank too much. Hammett was a victim of his own nature and of a corrupt and oppressive phase in American history, and his bibulosity can be turned into a symptom of the sickness of the age. Finally, a writer's life is only useful if it is a genuine *biographia literaria*; these two books are merely horror stories whose subject happens to be a writer.

Thurbing

Selected Letters of James Thurber, edited by Helen Thurber and Edward Weeks

'**D**ear Thurbs,' John O'Hara begins a letter to Helen and James in the fall of 1949: 'By the way what does a thurber do? What is thurbing? "I think I'll go out and thurb the nasturtiums." "That goddam thurbing son of a bitch Ross." "Father, the greeve needs a new thurber." ' There may well be readers of this book who do not know what a thurber does, or did, since there are no more creative thurbers and, in any case, there was only one anyway. There is no plural to phoenix.

That goddam thurbing son of a bitch Ross was the editor of the *New Yorker*, and Thurber wrote and drew for it. Those were the alleged great days of Dorothy Parker, E. B. White, Woollcott, Benchley, and the Algonquin Round Table, when semi-intellectual New Yorkers believed the *New Yorker* to be the finest magazine in the world, meaning New York. To the hardly existent world outside New York there has always seemed to be something parochial about it. Of all its contributors, James Thurber has worn best. His crude but lively drawings, curiously inimitable, had captions which have passed into the language, or at least my language: 'What have you done with Dr Millmoss?'; 'It's a naive domestic Burgundy without any breeding, but I think you'll be amused by its presumption'; 'I said "The hounds of spring are on winter's traces," but let it pass, let it pass . . .'; 'Well, if I called the wrong number, why did you answer the phone?'; 'Unhappy woman!' (dour clergyman rebuking lady in seventh heaven of drunkenness).

'The Secret Life of Walter Mitty' is a fine story, ruined in its film version by the antics of Danny Kaye; 'The Night the Bed Fell' is a brief comic masterpiece; *The Last Flower* raises near-sentimentality to near-nobility. Ross may have been a literary slob who didn't know who Henry James was, but Thurber was a genuine literary artist who not only knew Henry James but actually wanted to make a stage version of *The Ambassadors*. He achieved, with Elliott Nugent, a highly actable play called *The Male Animal*. Most of the *New Yorker* crowd have left a pathetic smear on the margins of the subliterary history of the territory known as C/BA (Coast/Big Apple): they went to Hollywood to sneer and stayed to survive; they drank too much; their fatal Cleopatra, for which the world was well lost, was a wisecrack. Thurber went blind, which was a Miltonic thing to do, and he never succumbed to self-pity. His salvation lay partly in his determined provincialism: he was an Ohio boy who, towards the end of his life, could say, charmingly: 'The clocks that strike in my dreams are often the clocks of Columbus.'

This selection of letters differs radically, in the mode of their presentation, from other American epistolary selections we have had in the last year or so. The Hemingway and Chandler letters alike made big volumes, were as comprehensive as they could be, and formed marginal biographies. From Thurber's letters, and some letters to Thurber, his widow and his editor–friend at the *Atlantic* have tried to fashion a volume that, in humour and elegance, matches what Thurber wrote with professional care and for money. There is no chronological arrangement: the taxonomy is made in terms of recipients. There are also drawings, though not, alas, the one which 'shows a man with an enormous thing . . . saying 'Hello, folks' to popeyed nude women and scowling little nude men' – an indiscretion 'circulated in smoking cars and bars by leering guys'. Thurber's art was always chaste, except for that one regretted scrawl, and the chasteness had something of Columbus, Ohio, about it. You will never meet a dirty word in these letters, any more than you will find ungraciousness or bad temper.

The graciousness comes out in a letter to Kenneth Tynan, who, in 1958, joined the *New Yorker* as dramatic critic. 'I was tremendously happy that the magazine had the good sense to take you on after Gibbs went away into the undiscover'd country from whose bourn no traveller returns except maybe Archibald MacLeish.' His bilious-sounding diatribe about the magazine itself may be taken as a frame for enhancing his sense of Tynan's brilliance and not as a true snarl: 'The present-day editors, caught somewhere between the *New Yorker*'s original naive anti-intellectualism and a curious oversimplified pretentiousness all their own, now and then send me, and most of the rest of us, into screaming orbit. . . .' And the odium was never personal: it was always to do with editorial obtuseness.

A literary man's letters occasionally, with Thurber frequently, rehearse ideas – especially ones that, in decent privacy, ought to be tried out for laughs. Of most American comic writers Thurber justly remarks that 'the lint of the high-school magazine sticks to the blue serge of their talent.' Perhaps his own serge is linty; no harm in trying this out on Ross:

[Fred] Allen plays the lost Livingston, and as the story opens, everybody is talking about him. Orson [Welles], playing Stanley, says, 'You see, it's your show,' to which Allen replies, 'But I'm not even in it yet.' And Orson says, 'That's because you're lost.'

And would this drawing with caption really work? A man says to a dumb-looking woman: 'You complicated little mechanism, you.' This, thinks Thurber, could fit an old drawing captioned 'Where did you get those big brown eyes and that tiny mind?'

He reserves poetry for his incipient blindness. Writing to the eye specialist Dr Gordon Bruce, he talks of religious visionaries who confuse holy visitations with retinal disturbances. His visual illusions include

. . . a blue Hoover, golden sparks, melting purple blobs, a skein of spit, a dancing brown spot, snowflakes, saffron and light blue waves . . . to say nothing of the corona, which used to hallow street lamps and is now brilliantly discernible when a shaft of light breaks against a crystal bowl or a bright metal edge. This corona, usually triple, is like a chrysanthemum composed of thousands of radiating petals, each ten times as slender as a needle and each containing in order the colors of the prism.

Cecity brings him close to Nabokov.

But he is normally given to understatement, finds no great virtue in the Parkerian wisecrack, but relishes the just epigram, as when Edmund Wilson calls Somerset Maugham 'the gentleman caterer' and Hemingway says of another writer's acute ear 'It's the ear of a writer who asks a croupier to give him a list of the expressions he uses.' These are the letters of a decent man without pretensions except to writing as well as he can, friendly, uncantankerous, dedicated to the most difficult job in the world – succeeding in amusing people without really seeming to try.

Rusticant Wilson

The Forties, by Edmund Wilson, edited by Leon Edel

In 1940 Scott Fitzgerald died. He had been a Princeton coeval of Edmund Wilson's, and his unforeseen and untimely end set the great critic, then forty-five, to thinking to his own mortality. He had roistered in his youth, drunk hard and fornicated freely, prolonged unduly his devotion to Marxism, but he had also produced *Axel's Castle*, one of the seminal books of our century. It was time to acknowledge that he was middle-aged and rusticate creatively in the corner of America he loved best – Cape Cod. In 1941 he bought a house at Wellfleet. In 1943 he took a permanent job with the *New Yorker*, writing the long literary reviews which he collected into books. In 1946, having divorced Mary McCarthy, he married Elena Mumm Thornton, a beautiful Russo-German after whose family the champagne was named. He would have preferred to marry Mamaine Paget, but she proposed marrying Arthur Koestler.

These chronicles of a highly productive delayed maturity – Wilson had always been mature in his literary judgements, less so when it came to the important things – have been admirably put together from the holograph ledgers in which Wilson ceaselessly jotted, sometimes at great length. The jottings were usually tidied into published books by the jotter himself, but Leon Edel has performed a posthumous service to an old friend with all the skill and devotion he previously lavished on Henry James. But was it worth it? Those of us who have read the books – *Europe Without Baedeker* and *Red, Black, Blond and Olive*, for instance – must have the impression of a film running back from the dining room to the kitchen, where the raw materials await the processing into a meal we have already eaten. And it is not pleasant to have to see some of the less worthy aspects of Wilson's personality regurgitated.

His chronic anglophobia, for instance. Nobody likes to be disliked as much as Wilson disliked us, even when the dislike is rational. God knows the British ruling class has always been unamiable, but Wilson's determination – visiting rent and weary England in 1945 – to find nothing and nobody to please him (except Mamaine Paget) argues a colonial shoulder-chip unseemly in a cultivated American. When, back home at Wellfleet, some lady professes a love of the British lower-class cuisine – whelks, suet puddings and so on – he is disgusted that her response is not one of disgust. He met both the confirmation and the rebuttal of his phobia in Evelyn Waugh, who pretended that Wilson was a Rhodes Scholar studying Henry James and yet said gracious things about Americans. 'In his well-tuned way – a lovely voice redeems his ugliness –' Waugh said that the Americans were politer than anyone else. To which Wilson has ungraciously to reply: 'Only than the British.'

The author of *The Wound and the Bow* – that brilliant study of the literary trauma – was also the author of *Memoirs of Hecate County*, a book of stories that was a bestseller but also widely banned for obscenity. It is, as you will remember, full of copulatory detail in the tradition of Henry Miller, and, to a European, much of this must seem not merely gratuitous but offensive. It is even more offensive to find in the notebooks meticulous accounts of his sexual encounters with the lady who was to become the last Mrs Wilson: I put my hand here and then I put it there and I shoved it in and I came like a bomb, etc. It is offensive not only because civilized behaviour, which includes the keeping of notebooks meant for publication, depends on reticence in intimate areas, but also because the sexual act, especially with a loved one, is a greater thing than its parts: you do not convey an ecstasy which Virgil thought best described as the 'known flame' through enumeration of orgasms or notation of the physical accidents which are transubstantiated into a theophany. Childish, vulgar, and, one must say, American in the worst sense. Wilson, whose literary taste was mostly impeccable, seems to be one of the sponsors of the American bestseller formula: you gotta have your first fuck on page 15, baby.

Wilson did not produce much fiction, though a good deal of the early part of *The Forties* is devoted to planning a novel which was never written. Yet he does a lot of what novels about novelists writing novels have led novel-readers to believe novelists regularly do: that is, go round notating the autumnal colours of the sumac or the change in the tonalities of the call of the bullfrog. If novelizing is all about getting cloudscapes onto paper, then Wilson has much of the novelist in him, but his brilliant critical insights should have told him that the best novelists, like the painter Turner, invent their sunsets. There are many wearisome sub-Walden pages about the beauties of Cape Cod. There are also two unforgettable notes about rats in Haiti: one rat, clutching an egg in all its four paws, was dragged down the stairs by its tail by another rat; a man, sleeping with his hand dangling on the floor, had the tips of his fingers bitten off by rats, which apparently (at least in Haiti) have a secret anaesthetizing agent which they spit onto the amputable part. Wilson, who was there before Papa Doc, is good on Haiti. He has great hopes for its future. The imperial British have not been there, which is much in Haiti's favour.

Wilson also goes to Zuni in New Mexico, there to see the Shalako ceremonies and the Koyemshi clowns (products of incestuous unions who, according to Lévi-Strauss, whom Wilson does not seem to have read, fulfil the Oedipal pattern by asking daft riddles). If Wilson hates the British he loves the Indians, as we know from *Apologies to the Iroquois*, and it is one of his large virtues that he is willing to bring to a number of unexpected areas of study the hard research and the insight which make his literary criticism so valuable. Not only the Indians but the Canadians, and the Dead Sea Scrolls, and federal taxation, and the Civil War. It is a lively and inquiring mind, and, as Wilson gets into his fifties, it is turned fearlessly also onto intimations of mortality. Everybody seems to be dying or succumbing to self-pity and drink. Dos Passos loses his wife and an eye in a car accident. Joyce and Yeats, two of the heroes of *Axel's Castle*, are dead. Edna St Vincent Millay, whom he had once loved, is growing lumpy and querulous. But Wilson hangs on to life, punishing the whisky, screwing like a rattlesnake, reading, reading and, above all, hating the British.

Mother of Nightwood

The Formidable Miss Barnes, by Andrew Field

I n T. S. Eliot's Russell Square office there were two elegantly framed photographs – one of Groucho Marx, the other of Djuna Barnes. Though it was once proposed that Groucho play the role of Dr O'Connor in a filmed *Nightwood*, the two had nothing in common save Eliot's friendship and admiration. Djuna Barnes was, by the way, well worth photographing and was much photographed by Man Ray: her beauty was considerable and her cloaked chic distinctive. Her picture comes and goes in books on the Paris expatriates of the twenties. More, her own caricatures – notably of Gertrude Stein and Eugene O'Neill – sometimes appear in literary chronicles of modernism. She was a skilled draughtswoman and had first earned her living in New York as a newspaper interviewer who provided her own illustrations and even headlines. For those who have impatiently put aside *Nightwood* and *The Antiphon* as arty blather, it is important to stress that, like Hemingway, Djuna Barnes had come to literature via tough American journalism. But perhaps I am making an untenable assumption. Perhaps *Nightwood*, which seems to be out of print in Britain though not in America, is unknown to my readers. And probably *The Antiphon* has not even been heard of. Who, anyway, *was* Djuna Barnes?

She was certainly one of the Americans who went to Paris in that post-First-War epoch of literary experimentalism which produced, in Gertrude Stein and Hemingway, an anti-cerebral prose very fitting for an age of disillusionment. Joyce was also there, of course, first destroying style and finally language itself. Djuna Barnes admired Joyce without, like so many of the literary *poseurs*, mindlessly worshipping him; Joyce secretly approved of her and even gave her the original manuscript of *Ulysses*. She was strong enough not to be influenced by either the Joycean parodic blarney or the Hemingway tough-guy declarative sentence. If she admitted literary influences at all, these were somewhat remote – *Religio Medici* and *The Anatomy of Melancholy* – but, like Joyce, she had a strong sense of the multiple resonance of language. When Eliot gave her novel the title *Nightwood* she was delighted, knowing that buried in the wood was the Chaucerian word for madness.

Nightwood is chiefly about the destructive relationship between two women. It could have had the same scandalous impact as *The Well of Loneliness*, except that it contains no overt lesbian scenes and, unlike Radclyffe Hall's atrociously written oblique confession, it is unquestionably a work of literature. It is perhaps too literary, very much a cult book. Strangely, though published in 1936, it does not seem dated:

it is rather that its overtones are at last clearly to be seem as those of a self-destructive civilization, and the highly allusive language seems to encapsulate a culture that was, as we now know too well, in grave danger. For all these resonances, it is also a highly personal work, in that it records the strange ménage that subsisted in Paris between Djuna Barnes and Thelma Wood, the silverpoint artist who was also a frightful drunk. Mr Field's biography reproduces some of her work, which seems to me to be brilliant. Evidently, Thelma Wood was not drunk all the time: silverpoint requires great concentration and a slip of the hand can ruin days of work.

'I'm not a lesbian,' said Djuna Barnes. 'I just loved Thelma.' It was one of a number of painful relationships, most of them with men. She never married; she had an abortion at forty-one; she never achieved the safe domesticity that, as Joyce unerringly saw, was the essential base for Dedalian flight and labyrinth-making. A lonely woman, despite her beauty and intelligence, she did her own share of drinking too much. She also smoked too much and was racked by asthma and, later, emphysema. Helped by a bounty from Peggy Guggenheim (far less generous than Harriet Shaw Weaver was to Joyce), she survived into a penurious old age in a New York flatblock in whose court the young practised their mugging. She was brave and refused to yield her purse and bag of groceries to a black mugger who eventually grew frightened by her eyes. She died in 1982 at the age of ninety, in pain but indomitable.

She had been lucky in two respects – that Eliot admired her *Nightwood* and Edwin Muir thought highly of her strange play *The Antiphon*. When Muir and Dag Hammarskjöld were being awarded honorary degrees at Cambridge, Muir could talk of nothing but *The Antiphon*, and he fired the UN Secretary-General to read it and, more, translate it into Swedish. Considered unactable in Anglo-America, it was played with success in Stockholm. Hammarskjöld told an interviewer that his work on Djuna Barnes's behalf was one of the things he was proudest of in his entire career. Eliot said much the same thing. It seems that, having let her death pass by with little notice, we ought at least to conceive the duty of looking at her work. There is not much of it.

That she is difficult there is no doubt, and more difficult in her verse than in her prose. The blank verse of *The Antiphon* was, by a reviewer in the *Listener*, stupidly compared to Christopher Fry's, but it is unslick, deliberately lumpish, not at all smart:

> You'll come roaring up the galleys of the dead,
> The oar-arms banked and trussed upon the bond,
> Crying 'J'accuse!' and hale me by the brows
> And in alarm bark out 'Not this arouse!'
> Guilt has her, let guilt haul her house!

And one quatrain she produced in extreme old age shows her toughness:

Somewhat sullen, many days.
The Walrus is a cow that neighs.
Tusked, ungainly, and windblown,
It sits on ice, and alone.

Dylan Thomas, who was shown *Nightwood* in manuscript by a woman friend of Djuna Barnes who liked sleeping with poets, raved about it and read chunks out on his American tours. He also evidently learned something from her verse, though he lacked the cunning ungainliness she brought to her rhythms. Eliot persuaded her to stick to prose, telling her that she wrote it far better than he did. The point is, I think, that, like Joyce, she broke down the old verse–prose barrier: the term 'poetic prose' is meant to be disparaging, but how can one describe writing in which the verbal engine is going all out? In *Nightwood* she makes concessions to the need for a narrative drive, but the strength of the work lies in its capacity to pack language with conflict and ambiguity. Highly intense, she is not devoid of humour. A boastful male spoke to her of the beauties of the penis, saying that it could even write a sentence on the snow; could a woman's organ do that? A woman, said Djuna Barnes, could at least provide a period.

Pen Pals

Pound/Ford: The Story of a Literary Friendship: The Correspondence between Ezra Pound and Ford Madox Ford and their Writings about each other, edited by Brita Lindberg-Seyersted

There are some, and I am one of them, who hold that the greatest British novelist of this century (I naturally exclude Ireland) is Ford Madox Ford and that the most innovative poet working in

English was Ezra Pound. A new era in English letters (I do not use the term in a national sense) began in the First World War, with the publication of *The Good Soldier* and *Homage to Sextus Propertius*. Since God has been killed by Nietzsche, the God's eye view of fictional narrative had to be replaced by artful limitation, which Ford called impressionism. In *The Good Soldier* the narrator, not being God, does not fully understand the story he is telling. In the tetralogy (or, as Graham Greene would have it, trilogy) called *Parade's End*, time and space become subjective and fluid. This was modernism in prose. In verse, diction became colloquial but very allusive, and shifts of imagery followed the logic of the cinema. Pound swore that Ford was as responsible for the new poetry as for the new prose: a great prose practitioner, he saw that verse could only advance through the abolition of the traditional verse–prose dichotomy.

Ford is not now much read for his poetry, or, for that matter, for his prose. Pound, like Eliot, thought little of the latter, but his classic essay on the prose tradition in verse, reprinted in this book, reminds us of Ford's superb rhythmic sense. Ford had no doubt of the importance of the *Cantos* and fought like mad to get them published in England. His essay on Pound's *Personae* is a brief critical masterpiece and, again, can be read here. A great deal of this expensive book, alas, consists of stuff we can find elsewhere. The correspondence is something else. Ford, like any good man of letters, hated writing them. Pound wrote them all the time, but always in this manner:

> Dear Ole Fordie/
>   GORR dem it!!! Will dew what I can BUT // expected to lexchure in Nov. and it has been postponed till end of this month/ AND . . . heaven knows when I'll git paid AND paid six months rent on March 1st . . . I may git in a chq/ sometime////// Have you any idear WHEN Slipping cott will pay? anyhow here is 600 fr/ that will last over the week end. sint life just wonderful.

On the surface, the two men would seem to have little in common. Ford *né* Hueffer wanted to be like his own Tietjens, a betrayed country gentleman of blond Viking stock walking lordlily over his estates; Pound was a shockbearded Bohemian mocking his Mid-Western ancestry. They met in a general devotion to literature (Ford called himself 'an old man mad about writing'; Pound, young or old, was madder still and ended mad) and in a particular devotion to the culture of the Mediterranean. They were both desperately short of money all their lives, and many of the letters are about publishers slow to pay, magazines going untimely bust, quick loans to tide over. Both earned large vilification. Ford was guilty of a marital irregularity and was too magisterial to keep friends long. He indulged in lying, which he called impressionism, and he had the insolence to volunteer for the war and come back foully halitotic with phosgene. Pound, we are told, was a traitor to his country and deserved to be hanged.

This aspect of the correspondence is, of course, very embarrassing.

But there is little doubt that the non-technical term 'mad' can be invoked to cover Pound's later obsessions, which had more to do with economics – which he didn't well understand, but who does? – than with literature. He fell, quite early on, for Major Douglas's doctrine of Social Credit, as, incidentally, did Eliot: there is a long shameful passage of pseudo-Cockney dialogue in *The Rock*, in which Liza is gleeful about 'Arry's trouncing a communist demagogue (I may have got the names wrong) with applied Douglas. Pound, whose name may have had something to do with it, loathed the banks, and this meant loathing the Rothschilds, who were Jews. He did not loathe America, however much his Rome broadcasts give that impression; he was sick at America's betrayal, as he saw it, of the principles of Thomas Jefferson. Jefferson is the Odysseus of the *Cantos*.

Now Ford, ill and penniless, got a tutorial job at Carmel College in Michigan and, in his longest letters, tries to persuade Pound to take over this job. But Pound snarls queries as to whether there is a printing press there, and would they be ready to reprint Jefferson's works. Ford is reasonable and persuasive, but the Jeffersonian obsession goes on and Pound, from Rapallo, snarls on out of a snarled-up brain. Ford, who suffered in one war, did not live to see the other, which Pound unfortunately did. Had Pound's demented devotion to Italian fascism – which, like international banking, he did not understand – not found an outlet in wartime propaganda, little harm would have been done. After all, Maurice Chevalier and Edith Piaf remain heroes of popular art, despite earning large sums under the Occupation. But haters of modernism were glad to find patriotic reasons for wanting Pound dead. The *TLS* published a long dismissive summation of his work, not his conduct, in which the author said: 'I remember only one thing about Pound. He had a beard, and it looked false.'

Yet, as these letters show, these two men were martyr–heroes. They were fired by such devotion to literature that they would willingly have consigned their own works to the fire if that could ensure the world's appreciation of Conrad or Lawrence or Joyce or, for that matter, Eliot. And this devotion had nothing to do with architectonics, great thoughts, the apocalyptic vision. Literature was something that flashed out in the phrase or the line. Ford found it in the *Cantos*:

> One year floods rose,
> One year they fought in the snows,
> One year hail fell, breaking trees and walls.

Pound found it in a very simple lyric of Ford's, where rhythmic assurance could take mock-archaism in its stride:

> And paper shops and full 'bus stops confront the sun so brightly,
> That, come three-ten, no lovers then had hearts that beat so lightly
> As ours or loved more truly,
> Or found green shades or flowered glades to fit their loves more duly.
> And see, and see! 'Tis ten past three above the Kilburn station,
> Those maids, thank God!, are 'neath the sod and all their generation.

In an age in which British kids on motorcycles thrum along the roads of France with swastikas on their helmets, the treason of Pound is almost forgotten and, grudgingly by some, his greatness is acknowledged. The martyr-master Ford has not been accepted. He is the 'stylist' under the leaking thatch in *Hugh Selwyn Mauberley*, poor, pounding away on the keys, offering 'succulent cooking' from the materials of his own garden. The age of the supermarket bestseller does not want him, but his time will come.

Loving the Unlovable

The Scandal of Syrie Maugham, by Gerald McKnight

Of William Somerset Maugham, Dame Rebecca West has reportedly said: 'I didn't have a great opinion of him myself because although he was amusing, I didn't think he was very clever. And I still can't see why people feel ecstasies over his short stories, which I don't think are very good. In fact, I don't think any of his work is very good. His plays are terrible. If he hadn't been a homosexual, I don't think he would have made it at all.' On BBC television about fifteen years ago, Lord Boothby pronounced, in the presence of Mr Priestley: 'There are only three good British writers – Jack here, Monty Mackenzie, and Willie Maugham. All the rest are bloody awful.' These are two distinguished summations, and the truth, as always, lies in the middle. Maugham has given us all some pleasure. I, like most people, have read everything he wrote. I have found him entertaining but innutritious. He was called Master by mediocrities, and he was assumed to be great because he became very rich. By most accounts he was unlovable. One woman loved him, however, and he never forgave her for it. This book is about that woman.

Syrie Barnardo was the daughter of a notable philanthropist of Italo-Jewish origin who made up for his charity towards waifs by neglecting his own children. She married Henry Wellcome, an American pharmaceutical tycoon who eventually became a British subject, perhaps so that he could be ennobled for his wealth. He was duly knighted. He was a mean and cruel man who made Syrie very unhappy, especially in the bedroom. She met Willie Maugham at a time when he believed himself to be only one quarter homosexual. As Maugham himself put it, they engaged in 'sexual congress with the intention that Syrie should conceive', adulterous conception being a sure way to a divorce. She miscarried, but Wellcome cited him as co-respondent (he could also have cited the founder of Selfridges, but that's another story). The next occasion of sexual congress produced a delightful daughter named, after her of Lambeth, Liza. Maugham played the gentleman and married the mother of his child, but by now he had discovered himself to be only one quarter heterosexual.

It was a charming but dissolute young American named Gerald Haxton who helped him to this discovery. From then on, until the divorce in 1927, Syrie fought Haxton hard for the Master's affection. She was a fine fighter, a woman of beauty, elegance, and imperious manner and voice, but she could not win, even when her husband twitched his nose at the sight of Haxton lying snoring in his vomit. Still, this was not the end of the world. She was a talented woman well able to make her own way, and, while Maugham was merely one writer among many, Syrie had a unique specialization. She was the greatest interior decorator of her day.

I am always dubious about the employment of the term 'great' in comparatively lowly contexts. We hear of great publishers, great literary agents, though perhaps not great plumbers. Gerald McKnight uses the word continually of Syrie. Everybody said she was great. I do not personally believe that to pickle furniture and splash rooms with white is comparable with the discovery of relativity or the composition of *Paradise Lost*. On the other hand, one does not have to live inside Einstein or Milton, and to transform people's daily lives through a revolution in decor is an achievement that merits more than the reward of money (which Syrie was paid, in large quantities, though she lost most of it). The trouble is that those of us who have never been in her snowy salons have to take this alleged greatness on trust. Mr McKnight's book should have been illustrated.

Anyway, she became famous, lived a sexless life among avowed homosexuals, and is memorialized by a white marble bust of Catherine the Great in the Victoria and Albert Museum. 'In the use of her talents,' says Mr McKnight, 'and in the way she intrigued with her "courtiers," Syrie was as powerful as any empress of the bedchamber. Hers may have been only drawing-room battles, but they did much to enhance the face of life. And in one quality she was identical with the great Catherine of all the Russias: courage.' This is probably an absurd similitude. Try comparing Ed Kaufman, inventor of the round waffle, with Napoleon.

Seven years after Syrie's death, Maugham published a blistering condemnation of her under the title *Looking Back*. McKnight talks of 'the intolerable burden . . . of Syrie's undying love lying like a corpse on his conscience', and of a kind of belated rejection of the heterosexual world into which she had drawn him. 'He was pretty gaga, you know,' said A. S. Frere, once of Heinemann, Maugham's publisher. It was Lord Beaverbrook, who made him an unprecedented offer, who talked Maugham into publishing an outburst its author was later to regret. The unreasonable, or gaga, hatred in which, said S. N. Behrman, he was 'embalmed', embraced his own daughter, whose only crime was to be an emblem of Maugham's heterosexual competence. He had adopted Alan Searle as his son and, on the grounds that Henry Wellcome had not denied, even if he had not admitted, legal paternity, he tried to deprive Liza of her inheritance – a considerable patrimony of works of art – so that Searle could take all. The French court found for Liza in her fight with a 'senile and fitfully demented father'. It is a sad and sordid story, and I wish we'd heard the last of it.

An honourable desire to exonerate Syrie from rabid and untenable charges, and to exhibit her as a woman of high morality and solid achievement, has led Mr McKnight to the writing of this brief biography. He writes in a style which used to be termed 'journalistic', meaning clumsy, overblown, occasionally illogical, semantically frequently off-centre, and given to colourful irrelevance. 'In the years immediately following her separation from Wellcome,' he writes. 'Roald Amundsen reached the South Pole; suffragettes rioted in Whitehall; the *Titanic* sank on her maiden voyage, with guests in full evening dress dancing as she went down. . . .' This makes it a 'time of excitement and revolutionary achievement'. Maugham's tongue 'could cut like a razor dipped in acid'. We hear of 'an oriental inscrutability forming over his face like an icecap'. Sue Barnardo 'proudly' wears Syrie's father's signet ring 'with its Latin motto, *Peace with Understanding*'. We hear of 'a team of admirers drawn into Syrie's meteoric tail'. These curious tropes make the book rather charming.

I put it down with some concern about my inability to regard this world of smart and rather vulgar people as in any way important. It resembles the world of the American bestseller *Princess Daisy*, in which the half-minute television commercial is a major art form with its 'great' practitioners, dress and decor are all-important, there is the thrill of sexual scandal, and nobody quotes a line of poetry or philosophy or whistles a measure of Mozart. The Syrie Maugham book is a slight cut above that, since there is an author in it, even though he is only Willie Maugham.

War and the Weaker

Women and Children First, by Mary Cadogan and Patricia Craig

This book is, at three hundred pages, far too short for its subject. That subject is fiction – quality, trash, in-between – dealing with the situation of women and children in the two world wars. As some of the children are sixth-form boys who become trench fodder, the scope is wider than the title suggests. Add to this the fact that some of the fiction is prospective (1901–14) and by far the greater part retrospective (1918–39; 1945–78), and you have a literary and subliterary survey that takes in the entire century so far. It is too much, and Mss Cadogan and Craig would have been better advised to divide their material into two books, each of them larger than this one. It is an American-style project conducted on British lines. Skimp, rush, skim, dash. But it is far better written than anything that could have come out of a US PhD manufactory.

It is always dangerous to approach literature in sectional terms. Pick out the books with women and children in them, and you are ignoring the profounder criteria and, indeed, are tempted to be eccentrically selective. Let me take, for a start, a very sweeping statement that comes towards the end of the book: 'None of the leading writers of the Modern Movement had direct experience of the trenches, and few were concerned with the kind of direct transcription that war writing appeared to demand.' Surely Hemingway was part of the movement? Space is given to *For Whom the Bell Tolls* (the scope is even wider than I've already indicated), but by this time the writers have apparently forgotten about Hemingway. About Ford Madox Ford they seem not even to have heard. *Parade's End* is acknowledged to be a major novel of the First War, and Captain Ford came out of that war gassed. Nor can ignoring the book be justified in terms of its lack of interest in women or children. The heir of Groby? Sylvia Tietjens and Valentine Wannop? The novel is *about* women in wartime to a greater extent than any of the books dealt with here.

Evelyn Waugh's *Put Out More Flags* is mentioned because of the evacuee Connollys, but *Sword of Honour* (Virginia Crouchback, Kirstie and the others) doesn't get a look in. Nor does the perfect exhibit in such a crammed gallery – the *Balkan Trilogy* by Olivia Manning, by a woman about a woman and with war on every page, not to mention the first volume of the same author's *Egyptian Trilogy*, with a most remarkable imaginative participation in the Desert War. This is just not good enough. Even where a book that has to be dealt with is, in fact, dealt with, literary assessment in depth is precluded by the need to get the trash in as well, which, if it has women or children in it, is worthy of the serious consideration we expect only to be accorded high art. Muriel Spark's *The Girls of Slender Means* is a perfect compact allegory of war, but the profundity of its symbolism is evaded. Come on, we have to *move*. So move we do, to *Gem* and *Magnet* and *Girl's Crystal* and *If Winter Comes*.

There is, stirring behind this book, a thesis that has not yet been sufficiently worked out. This has, I think, something to do with the relating of aesthetic values to moral ones. If a man writes a novel which does not take women seriously, can that be a good novel? Is there not at least the danger that, with a subject like the one Mss Cadogan and Craig have chosen, aesthetic virtues may be found when there is a lack of 'sexist' vice? In the new dispensation, will it be possible for a heterosexual novelist to write a good novel in which homosexuals are treated with ignorance or disdain? That the aims of this book are mixed is, I would say, borne out by the granting of four pages to Richmal Crompton's *William* books and a brief paragraph to Doris Lessing. The writers are capable of making very sensible literary judgements, as is shown by their crisp summation of the required content and technique of a bestseller. I wished often they could forget their declared subject and treat a book as a book, whatever was in it. But they have a kind of social purpose as well as a compulsion to get everything in, *Union Jack* and David Jones (not much of him, naturally).

As their book on girls' fiction showed – *You're a Brick, Angela* – these two are happiest with subliterature, which is good for a laugh and can also be presented as socially significant. Buchan's *Greenmantle*, in which the hero has to take a cold shower after being in a woman's presence, and those boys' magazines which preached the duty of getting seen off by the Hun, are alike easy meat. What is genuinely interesting is their discovery that the only good sense that came out of the world of popular magazines in the First War was to be found in new English *Vogue* (the American could no longer be imported, because of shortage of shipping space), which was wittily ironic and gently subversive, recognizing that khaki-knickered grimness was not necessarily the best attitude to war. I was interested too to learn that the *Union Jack Library* (Sexton Blake's Weekly for Readers of All Ages: 1d) could present the Kaiser as a machinating villain in 1908, and that the possibility of an Anglo-German war was a common theme of subliterature throughout the Edwardian period. 'If by 1914 the boys of Britain and the empire were not raring to go and have a crack at the Kaiser it was certainly not the fault of Lord Northcliffe or his authors.'

And the women? Propaganda and popular fiction alike dragged them from the home and the status of bit of fluff to the munitions factory and the wheel of the general's car, the base hospital and the gunsite. The end of war restored them to the hearth, where they could not annoy the trade unions. But progress was slowly made, and it was at length recognized that the hands that could make a bomb could steer a state. We can dig out the story here, but what we really learn about is the multivorousness of Mss Cadogan and Craig's reading.

The Magus of Mallorca

Robert Graves: His life and Work, by Martin Seymour-Smith,
In Broken Images: Selected Letters of Robert Graves 1914–1946, edited by Paul
O'Prey

Martin Seymour-Smith first met Robert Graves during the latter's enforced English exile: the Falangists had driven him from Deyá to Devon, and the Second World War postponed his reconciliation with the Franco regime. Seymour-Smith was only fourteen and 'full of brash questions' about poetry. Graves gave succinct answers. Dylan Thomas was 'nothing more, really, than a Welsh demagogic masturbator who failed to pay his bills'. Stephen Spender was 'a nice chap, but better as a greengrocer than a poet'. T. S. Eliot was 'a very decent chap, really', but had sold out to Anglicanism and published a detestable poetaster named Auden. Ezra Pound? 'Yes, he had met Pound once: in T. E. Lawrence's rooms at All Souls. He'd had a wet handshake and was clearly crazy.' Graves was glad that his future biographer was 'getting to the stage of realising that there are hardly any poets or ever have been; this is the only decent excuse for writing poems oneself, because after all there *is* such a thing as poetry. . . .'

This kind of puerile dismissal of most of his contemporaries might have been excusable near closing time in the Wheatsheaf or Yorkminster, but there is something immoral in the spectacle of a grown man of proven poetic authority corrupting a youth with his own prejudices. On the other hand, Graves was entitled to write off poets in this manner because he knew what made a poet, or certainly a poem, bad. The essay on the Great English Lyric in *The Common Asphodel* is just and devastating. He and Laura Riding, in their *Survey of Modernist Poetry* had pioneered the technique of dissecting a poem before pronouncing on it, a thing that only Dr Johnson and Coleridge seemed to have done before. William Empson – who, of course, was no good – developed this technique in his *Seven Types of Ambiguity*, to, it is generally accepted, the benefit of the art of criticism. It is generally accepted too, even among Graves's strongest admirers, that the magus of Mallorca would have done well to apply to his own work the informed rigour he brought to that of others.

For Graves's importance as a poet still seems to be in doubt. He has produced enough to ensure that (as with Wordsworth) at least 10 per cent of his output has to be taken seriously, but there is not one stanza or even line of his that has become a common quotation among the literary. Pound may have been an impostor, Auden a plagiarist, Eliot a timeserver and Yeats (whom Graves particularly despised) a poseur, but they have all modified our attitude to life and implanted certain ineffaceable rhythms in our brains. Graves does not hug the memory. He seems rhythmically flaccid and has never quite come to terms with the movement of spoken English. His diction has a tendency to obsolete inversion. There are many poems of his which one would not be without – this, for instance, which astounded Eliot:

> Circling the circlings of their fish,
>   Nuns walk in white and pray;
>   For he is chaste as they,
>   Who was dark-faced and hot in Silvia's day,
> And in his pool drowns each unspoken wish.

But his extravagant rejection of the entire corpus of modern poetry in English – with the exception of Hardy, Frost, Ransom and, of course, Riding – put him into a position of dangerous eccentricity demanding from his readers a rehabilitation of taste more appropriate to a cultus than to a decent catholicity.

Of the value of many of his prose writings there can be no doubt. Most of the criticism is admirable and entertaining. The historical novels are very readable, and *I, Claudius* is compelling not only as a television series but as a Korda film that never got itself completed. Of much of his prose output Graves has been genially dismissive. His fine autobiography *Goodbye to All That* was written too fast and very carelessly. He essayed the novel not as a novelist but as a needy hack, thus putting himself outside the canons of fictional art. So long as the books paid the bills, the critics could be ignored. The scholars too could be ignored when they complained about the false anthropology of *The White Goddess*. A lot of the prose was there to subsidize the poetry. Some of the prose was a theoretical justification of poetic practice. The only thing that really mattered was the poetry. Eliot never liked talk of 'poets', preferring himself to be thought of as a man who sometimes produced poems, but Graves took the title of poet very seriously. He was a poet, and therefore he had to write poetry. It was never a matter of his having written poetry and therefore being entitled to the high title. Never was a literary life so loftily dedicated. But perhaps dedication, like patriotism, is not enough.

The life itself is of appalling interest. It is not merely fascinating but filmable. It has prolonged *Sturm und Drang* and ends with a hardly earned tranquillity. Seymour-Smith draws on *Goodbye to All That* and the memoirs of Graves's father (author of 'Father O'Flynn') for the first part, filling in with details previously withheld and essaying psychological interpretations not available to the autobiographer. Graves was a chaste boy with a public-school education who tried, as we all do, to distinguish between love and lust. He loved a fellow-pupil who turned out to be homosexual. War neurasthenia, wrongly termed shell-shock, uncovered sexual guilt which had nothing to do with sexual enactment. At the end of the war (and nobody has given a better account of it from the infantry officer's angle), Graves, a virgin, married another virgin,

Nancy Nicholson, a militant feminist who alleged that the sufferings of soldiers were nothing compared to the sufferings of women. She kept to her maiden name, thus rendering eventual divorce awkward, since the petition *Nicholson* v. *Graves* was not acceptable in law. Children were born, but there was not much love. Nancy was bossy, people felt sorry for Graves. A phrase used by Cantabile in Saul Bellow's *Humboldt's Gift* – pussywhipped – seems appropriate. Graves's postwar life begins with pussywhipping from one woman and continues with it from another.

Graves and his family, having made no money either from writing or from keeping a shop on Boar's Hill, went to Egypt, where there was a professor's job waiting. With them went Laura Riding. She, a young Jewish poet from Manhattan, had tried to boss the Fugitives in Nashville, Tennessee. One of the Fugitives was John Crowe Ransom, whom Graves admired. It was thought a good idea to send Laura Riding off to boss Robert Graves. She turned up in London on the eve of the Graveses' departure and attached herself to the family during the short-lived Cairo venture. Graves's account of his professorial troubles in *Goodbye to All That* is merely diverting: here we learn that he went through hell.

Really it was an anteroom to hell. The real hell began back in London, when the *ménage à trois* was turned into a foursome by the appearance of a certain Geoffrey Phibbs. Up to that point things had not been going too badly. Graves had earned £500 from a popular book on his friend T. E. Lawrence and had put the money into the Seizin Press, an enterprise designed to 'actualize the new thinking, bring some of the right people together, and provide practical examples of how writing should be done. The implied precepts of *A Survey of Modernist Poetry* (published in July 1927) required illustration.' Then Phibbs, an Irish journalist, much impressed by Laura Riding's work, joined the group at what was known as 'Free Love Corner' and helped to initiate hell.

Of Laura Riding, whose influence dominated Graves's life for so long, something must be said, since it is probable that she does not now have many readers. It is enough to examine the poems by which she is represented in Michael Roberts's *Faber Book of Modern Verse* (the first edition) to be made aware of her genuine power. The trouble with her as a person was that she was too conscious of her literary gifts and highly resentful of those who did not appreciate them. She was egoistical and damnably dogmatic. I remember her giving, in Manchester, a fifteen-minute lecture on the nature of poetry and refusing discussion, since she alone knew the meaning of words and her auditors could not be trusted to use them at all. When her *Collected Poems* appeared in 1938 I gave the book, apparently, the only review which she deemed intelligent. She wrote a long letter to my editor praising my appreciation of her 'womanness' (her prose was always shocking) but demanding that her laudations be not published. When, in the same year, I thought rather less highly of Graves's first *Collected Poems*, I was subjected to a dual attack which she, not Graves, insisted be published. I was not merely illiterate,

I was analphabetic. I was also ill-mannered. I had a notion that something very queer was going on in that, as it had now become, *ménage à deux*.

Laura Riding's womanness responded violently to Phibbs, whom she called an Irish Adonis. She tried to thrust Graves back into the arms of Nancy, who did not now want him. Then Phibbs announced that he wanted no more of Laura; he preferred Nancy. Laura's response was to drink Lysol, to no effect, and then to leap out of a fourth-floor window with the valediction 'Goodbye, chaps!' Graves, more prudently, leapt out of a third-floor window. Phibbs ran away. A deformation of the spine, in evidence on her Manchester visit, and a prospect of deportation for attempted suicide were the fruits of the escapade. Phibbs lived in a houseboat with Nancy and Graves's and her four children, whom the father had to support. Graves and Laura Riding went off to Mallorca.

Graves loved her but was denied access to her bed. He put up meekly with her tyranny and probably for a good reason. Her poetic influence was wholly beneficial, even though her potboiling prose efforts were unpublishable, while Graves paid the bills. She resented this. She resented his becoming known while she remained unknown. She overestimated her personal magic and her capacity to arouse lust. She became a prophet and proposed reforming the world. When, with war imminent, she and Graves went to America she, perhaps all too explicably, fell in love with Schuyler Jackson, a man with little learning and no literary talent. She broke up his marriage and became tyrannically submissive to his physical advances. In *The White Goddess* Graves was to write:

> The archives of morbid psychology are full of Bassarid histories. An English or American woman in a nervous breakdown of sexual origin will often instinctively reproduce in faithful and disgusting detail much of the ancient Dionysiac ritual. I have myself witnessed it in helpless terror.

She ceased to be a poet. Mr and Mrs Jackson ended up running a citrus-fruit venture in Wabasso, Florida. It was said to be in a constant state of failure, but this did not prevent their keeping another house in New Mexico. Meanwhile Graves had fallen in love with Beryl, wife of his collaborator Alan Hodge (*The Long Week-End*, *The Reader Over Your Shoulder*), and spent a happy war with her in Devon. It was long before Nancy consented to the onomastic adjustment which would permit the lovers to marry, but eventually things turned out all right. Back to Deyá with a wife, not a goddess who had registered with the villagers as a crazy chain-smoking harpy eccentrically dressed, the founding of a new family, a well-earned creative tranquillity.

The impact of femininity on Graves's life and thinking is clearly, as Seymour-Smith's book makes shockingly clear, not of a doctrinaire nature. He had lived simultaneously with two women of almost mythical assertiveness and had kept, for the sake of his art, his own well-developed masculinity in check. He knew the power of the goddess and submitted to it. Seymour-Smith, on the evidence of professional anthropologists, denies Graves's right to posit a primeval matriarchal system (though saying nothing of the *adat perpateh* in Negri Sembilan) but concedes its validity in terms of the poetic imagination. Laura Riding taught Graves to reject history, which is a masculine toy, but not the self-renewing cycle, which is altogether feminine. The error committed by the hero of *King Jesus* is the denial of the feminine, though his claim to kingship is based on female ultimogeniture. Graves's art, as practised in the pacific years at Deyá, depends on a dual concept of woman. His wife is his nearest and dearest, and the recipient of his best love poems, but she is merely Vesta. The goddess who disturbs into a different creative mode comes capriciously and may not be possessed. Graves's late strange adventures with young women in Deyá are not to be interpreted as senile lechery – though healthy rivalry has come into them, like having a fiancé shoved into the lock-up – but in terms of poetic need.

Meanwhile, on the subpoetic plane, Graves has had to go on earning a living, not merely to pay the bills but to subvent appointments like that as Oxford Professor of Poetry. It is consoling to read that he has suffered financially like the rest of us, maintaining an innocent trust in sharks. Tom Roe, for instance, who bought authors' copyrights and guaranteed them an income, though his real speciality was the floating of phantom companies like the infamous Cadco and passing forged dollar bills (the Swiss police found 200,000 false C-notes in the boot of his Mercedes). When Roe began to steal his authors' money Graves lost 65,000 Swiss francs, though Graham Greene and Northcote Parkinson, shrewder men, suffered too. Graves, again like the rest of us, has expected quick showbiz returns and trusted dipsomaniacs and rogues through personal loyalty. His admirable libretto for a musical on the Queen of Sheba (oversalted food in honour of Lot's wife, the only water pitcher in Solomon's bed chamber, Sheba's thirst leading her thither) was rejected by Lena Horne because she 'didn't dig the lyrics'. Graves was too old to express much satisfaction in the BBC's televisual adaptation of *I, Claudius*, and an earlier contractual screwing ensured that he got no money out of it. It is nearly every writer's sad story, but Graves has kept his primary vocation inviolate – or rather the very nature of that vocation has not tempted the world's bemerding fingers.

Still, his translation of the *Rubaiyat*, which may be taken as inviting the attention of Persian scholars and lovers of 'Fitz-Omar' alike, as well as exhibiting the most mature phase of his pure verse craftsmanship, typified inveterate qualities – genial arrogance, innocence, unscholarliness, and a disturbing incompetence. The Cambridge manuscript provided by Omar Ali-Shah was said (in 1978) to be a forgery, and a literal prose translation was not, anyway, the best material with which to work. Graves, knowing no Persian, ventriloquized for Omar Ali-Shah, condemning Fitzgerald for inaccuracy and sentimentality, but producing himself a very dry paraphrase that could not, as Fitzgerald's version had done, accommodate the rhyme scheme of the original. Thus:

Ah me, the book of early glory closes,
The green of Spring makes way for wintry snow,
The cheerful Bird of Youth flutters away –
I hardly noticed how it came or went

which even I, who am no poet, can improve to

I see the book of early glory close,
The green of Spring make way for winter snows.
The cheerful bird of Youth flutters away –
I hardly notice how it comes or goes.

Martin Seymour-Smith has produced an admirable biography and a shrewd commentary on Graves's work. He goes wrong a little with his account of the establishment of the Mediterranean Institute of Dowling College at Deyá in 1969–70. He says that the Institute had 'a number of regular instructors, of whom the least undistinguished and certainly the least drunken . . . was the over-credulous but personally likeable Colin Wilson.' I also was one of the instructors. I make no claim to distinction but I do to sobriety. I even gave a lecture in a suit and collar and tie, a thing unheard of before in Deyá. Deyá I remember as an overlax place with no garbage collection, a credulity about lunar magic, hippies sick because they had to subsist on fish and red wine and could not get Coca-Cola and hamburgers, a set of *Homage to Catalonia* for class study misdirected to Graves's house and sent, fearfully it was thought, back. That was before the death of Franco. Things may be tougher now.

As a complement to the life, the letters, selected by Paul O'Prey, a young man living in the Graves household in Deyá and working on the sorting of the Graves archives. The poet has consistently cultivated the letterwriter's craft all his long life, editing in a clear bold hand and Indian ink, whose virtue is that it dries quickly, though too quickly (i.e. before it leaves the bottle) in the Mallorcan sun. O'Prey provides biographical links but limits life and letters to the periods of the two wars and the uneasy hagridden pax in the middle. Thus, we have all of Graves the young infantry officer, far less mature than he is made to appear with the hindsight of *Goodbye to All That*, and with that limitation of poetic taste which, in one form or another, was to remain with him all his life. Graves thought very highly of Rupert Brooke and very little of Ezra Pound. In 1915 he writes to Edward Marsh:

A three days' spell in billets gives me the chance I have been wanting for some time, of writing to tell you how truly grieved I am about poor Rupert's death, for your sake especially and generally for all of us who know what poetry is: my Father (dear old man!) said this was a fitting end for Rupert, killed by the arrows of jealous Musagetes in his own Greek islands; but fine words won't help; we can only be glad that he died so cheerfully and in such a good cause. What mightn't he have written had he lived?

In 1946 he writes to T. S. Eliot:

> I am in an unfortunate position about the Pound affair. I agree that poets
> should stick together in the most masonic way. . . . But since 1911 when
> I first read Pound in Harriet Monro's *Poetry* magazine; and since 1922
> when I met him for the first time at All Souls in T. E. Lawrence's rooms,
> I could never regard him as a poet and have consistently denied him the
> title.

That early arrogance of 'all of us who know what poetry is' is a theme
developed, though often in the most amiable way, throughout the
letters.

Denying the bays altogether to Pound, Graves is willing to find that
Martin Tupper, best-selling Victorian figure of fun, is 'a good bird at
times'. Writing to Siegfried Sassoon, he says: 'Future literary historians
will compare your anti-major complex:

> When I am old and bald and short of breath

and elsewhere, with Tupper's sonnet on Army Caste.

> *Hard Routine*
> Sets caste and class each by itself aside.
> You fierce-lipped major, rich and well allied,
> To these poor privates hardly deigns to speak.'

Whether Sassoon was or was not pleased at being compared with
Martin Tupper is not recorded. What is recorded is the cooling of the
friendship between two men who perhaps had little in common except a
war and a talent for verse. Sassoon published in 1928 his *Memoirs of a
Fox-Hunting Man*, unfavourably reviewed by Graves, and in 1930 his
Memoirs of an Infantry Officer, where Graves, under the name of 'David
Cromlech', is presented as 'a fad-ridden crank'. *Goodbye to All That* has
much to say about Sassoon, and very little of it was pleasing to the
subject, who demanded changes from the publisher Cape, and, after
some remarkable long letters to Graves, acquiesced in the closing of a
friendship. Laura Riding, with her insistence on impossible perfection
in both life and work, had a good deal to do with such closures. Here is
Graves to 'My dear Siegfried':

> . . . I suppose my 'talking through someone else's bonnet' is a reference
> to Laura. If you had said straight out that Laura was an obscurantist
> influence on my way of writing that could have passed as an ordinary
> ignorant remark, or if you had said that Laura herself wrote nonsense
> that could have been set against the testimony of other people that she is
> the most accurate writer there is. But you come out with a comic-postcard
> piece of vulgarity which is the counterpart of the lace-Valentine vulgarity
> of your *Heart's Journey*: and that ends it. So, for the last time,
> Yours
>
> Robert

Edward Marsh – 'I am not angry with you Robert dear, because I never could be' (another indiscretion in *Goodbye to All That*) – maintains friendship. Basil Liddell Hart, after a break, resumes it. Graves deeply offends Eliot by alleging that the *Criterion* compromises its integrity for commercial reasons:

> . . . I would not suggest that you vulgarize the *Criterion* to increase the sales and fill your pockets: obviously you are not that sort of person but I do think that you have compromised about it just as far as was necessary to keep it afloat and I think poetry has been compromised just to that extent.

That was in 1927. All correspondence between Eliot and Graves ceased until 1946. Graves reconciled himself to having no literary friends, except of course Laura Riding, but he does not emerge from his letters as being essentially a quarrelsome man. His great quality is innocence, expressed to the world as bumptiousness and indiscretion. These letters are, almost without exception, most engaging. It is a pity that there can be no Graves–Riding correspondence: they were too close to mingle souls with letters. But Gertrude Stein, Laura's literary aunt, writes cosily, and, at the end, we have an exchange with the doomed Alun Lewis, who seemed to Graves to be, as Lynette Roberts was, all right. O'Prey's title comes from the lines

> He continues quick and dull in his clear images;
> I continue slow and sharp in my broken images.
>
> He in a new confusion of his understanding;
> I in a new understanding of my confusion –

he being everybody else.

Miss Shakespeare

Sylvia Beach and the Lost Generation: A History of Literary Paris in the Twenties and Thirties, by Noel Riley Fitch

I have just got back from Vienna, where there is an English language bookshop called Shakespeare and Company. There I stood on a chair and recited from, such as they are, my works. The existence of such a literary oasis derives from the protonymous shop on the Left Bank in Paris which, on 17 November 1919, was founded by an American spinster named Sylvia Beach. It was a new thing to promote books in English in a heterophone capital and, moreover, to exalt a commercial venture into a concourse for anglophone writers and their readers on tour or in exile. But Sylvia Beach's largest achievement was to turn Shakespeare and Company into the most courageous publishing house in the world.

When James Joyce had already, with the serial publication of *Ulysses*, scared off all the established entrepreneurs, she alone was willing to take on the job of bringing out the work as a big bound book. On the face of it, the venture seemed impossible. No English language printer would set it in type for fear of criminal prosecution. Maurice Darantière of Dijon, capital of the French printing world, knew no English and hence had no sense of the dynamite he was handling. That first edition of the boldest novel of the century was bound to be crammed with errors, but to handle a copy, bound in the colours of the Greek flag, is to handle history. This is the real *Ulysses*. All subsequent editions are shamefaced acts of submission to stupid censorship laws which an American spinster had the guts to defy.

Getting *Ulysses* into America was an illegal activity like bootlegging or gunrunning. The British customs authorities at Dover were quick to confiscate and destroy. But the candle had been lighted and it did not go out. Publishing the book, as Sylvia Beach knew well, was not just a matter of sending it to the printers and then sticking it in a shop window. It was an act of faith with wide and dangerous implications. One of these was devotion to the author himself. Dr Fitch, who has written a survey-biography that has both academic and sectarian authority, is a woman who admires Sylvia Beach as a woman, and this entails a less than indulgent attitude to Joyce. If, in Dr Ellman's biography, Joyce's predations on his publisher are a matter for quiet humour, with Dr Fitch they become a pattern of heartless aggression essentially male. Joyce was always courteous to women, but, 'as all women know', says Dr Fitch, courtesy is usually a mask of misogyny. Whining, sending his children round to raid the till, suspecting greed where there was only a desire not to be impoverished, Joyce emerges as a very unheroic figure. Heroinism, to use Carlyle's proleptically unfortunate coinage, is reserved to Miss Beach.

For a misogynist Joyce did extraordinarily well out of women. His patroness Harriet Shaw Weaver will undoubtedly get another biography before long; here her stoic devotion to literature, which meant mostly Joyce, has to glow from the margin. Dr Fitch's achievement is to make Sylvia Beach into a central character of considerable interest, however much the great male names – Hemingway, Pound, Ford, Sherwood Anderson, Eliot, Antheil, Wyndham Lewis, others – impinge. 'Who is Sylvia?' Dr Fitch asks in a coy chapter heading, adding the epigraphs '. . . for Who is silvier – ' from *Finnegans Wake* and 'So you're the little woman who made the book that made this great war' – Abraham Lincoln to Harriet Beecher Stowe – as well as a big chunk from Eliot's *The Elder Statesman* on the agonies of going to live abroad and changing one's name to do so. Who, then, is, or was, she?

She was born Nancy Beach, daughter of the Rev. Sylvester Beach, who served in Paris at the Presbyterian ministry to Americans. The name change was an act of filial devotion; she owed her love of Paris to her father. In the 1914–18 war she served France in the *Volontaires Agricoles*, with bobbed hair and khaki culottes, but Paris called her back from the cabbage patches. There she met Adrienne Monnier, who kept a bookshop on the rue de l'Odéon, which was to be the second and final home of Shakespeare and Company. They became friends and probably more: in Sylvia's life there are no sentimental episodes with men. It was the extra-curricular activities of the Monnier *librairie* that inspired Sylvia to set up her own centre of expatriate culture. For *chez* Adrienne she heard Gide read, Schlumberger, Fargue and Valéry Larbaud. Meanwhile Big Bertha boomed and Adrienne Monnier – 'the strong woman of Gallic letters', as Samuel Putnam called her – offered shelter from one reality and helped promote another, that of literary modernism. Shakespeare and Company started its own parallel promotion with the coming of the peace. Then Sylvia met James Joyce at a party and there was no more peace.

Sylvia was small, boyish, pragmatic, agnostic, short-haired and short-skirted, unflirtatious, businesslike but not really in the trade to make money. She spoke French well, with an American crispness that made even a cliché seem like a coinage. French corrupted her English: 'I'm sick of your histories,' she said to a complaining shop assistant. To American visitors she was a way into the real artistic Paris as well as a voice from New Jersey. She was not easily put upon, except by Joyce; when she indulged the literary giants it was because she had sure taste and sound values: she knew what was going on in the lost generation. This term, which was used to Gertrude Stein by her garage proprietor to excuse the lack of good repairmen, got into Hemingway's *The Sun Also Rises* as an appropriate description of the talentless hard-drinking expatriates. It does not fit many of the habitués of Shakespeare and Company, which was a locale for writers who had found themselves. Joyce certainly was not lost.

Having served France in one war, Sylvia did not desert her in another. In December 1941 a German officer demanded her only remaining copy of *Finnegans Wake*. She would not surrender it and was threatened with confiscation and closure. She hid the stock before she was, as an enemy alien, interned, released, allowed to rusticate until Hemingway arrived to liberate the rue de l'Odéon. But Joyce was dead and a new era beginning. The so-called lost generation was really lost. Shakespeare and Company had done its work.

This is the most comprehensive work we are likely to get on the little woman who made, if she did not write, the book that made a great war. It is competent and readable despite patches of dull writing that are, one supposes, mandatory in a work of scholarship. There are one or two errors. Sherwood Anderson did not write *Tarr* and would not have wished to. The last portion of *Ulysses* is not the Telemachus section. Plodding through many flat if informative pages, I was struck by the inspiration that what Sylvia really needs is a Broadway musical. Plenty of scope there – Antheil pounding his piano in the flat above the shop, Lindbergh arriving to cement Americano-Parisian love, Joyce's lugubrious tenor and Hemingway's ballsy bass, love duets for Sylvia and Adrienne and, for that matter, Stein and Toklas. Nazis. Dr Fitch, or Shakespeare, gives us a fine title.

Living for Writing

The True Adventures of John Steinbeck, Writer: A Biography, by Jackson J. Benson

Hemingway was, and is still, Steinbeck's trouble. When Steinbeck was struggling to become a novelist, somebody recommended that he read Hemingway's short stories. He read 'The Killers' and was stunned. Here, he said, was the finest writer alive; he did not dare to read any more of him. Only when his own reputation was secured with *The Grapes of Wrath* did he feel free to read the rest of Hemingway. He even agreed, later, to meet him. But Hemingway behaved badly, as usual, and, denying that the blackthorn stick Steinbeck had given to John O'Hara was, even though it had been long in the Steinbeck family, really blackthorn, broke it over his own head. O'Hara, who was perhaps on the same level of attainment as Steinbeck, or somewhat lower, had the same truculent and jealous admiration for Hemingway, expressed in denigratory snarls. It was worse for O'Hara, who did not get the Nobel Prize and, unlike Steinbeck, desperately wanted it. But Steinbeck would sometimes pause in his peeling of onions for the 'great chilli' he used to make, take *The Sun Also Rises* from the shelf, and sneer at Hemingway's dialogue. This was not altogether in character. Mr Benson expends 1100 pages on showing us what a nice man Steinbeck was.

Though the Nobel raised him to Hemingway's level in the world's eyes (and to Galsworthy's, Pearl Buck's, and Golding's), Steinbeck remains a worthy rather than an important writer. Neither he nor O'Hara did what Hemingway did – stripped language to the nerve, created a new and very twentieth-century kind of stoicism, entered the stream of European modernism in order to make it American. Mr Benson seems, in his early pages, to be writing about a highly innovative novelist, like Galdós, when he says: 'Early in his career he was interested in trying to imitate the structure and movement of specific musical compositions, as well as more generally trying to imitate certain musical forms.' Whatever his early ambitions, Steinbeck owed his success to a very orthodox kind of fiction with traditional prose rhythms, whose power resided in a subject matter always highly emotional and sometimes topically inflammatory.

Of Mice and Men is, I think, a fine novella (or play with extended stage directions) which succeeds because it dares sentimentality. We remember it best as a film with Burgess Meredith and Lon Chaney Jr ('Tell about the rabbits, George'), just as we remember that saga of the oppressed and wandering Okies, *The Grapes of Wrath*, for the performance of Henry Fonda, and *East of Eden* as a vehicle for the doomed and brilliant James Dean. Steinbeck was always luckier than Hemingway in his film adaptations. He loved the medium and he did good work for it: his *Viva Zapata*! is masterly. He loved it because he had a gift for dialogue but no corresponding talent for a modern kind of *récit*: in film, *récit* is left to the camera. Hemingway's dialogue is less realistic than it looks, but his *récit* is nerve and bone and very original and new.

The Grapes of Wrath was a bestseller because it was a cry of referred pain. The migrants from the Dust Bowl were being wretchedly exploited by the California fruit farmers, who chained them to the company store and kept them only just floating at a level of bestial subsistence. The book looked like radical propaganda of the kind that Hemingway, to the disgust of *New Masses*, always refused to write, but Steinbeck insisted that the endpapers show a reproduction of 'The Battle Hymn of the Republic', whence his title came, and maintained stoutly and ever that he was a Jeffersonian Democrat who detested the very idea of communism. When, in later life, he visited Russia, he was not slow to knock the Soviet system. Sending dispatches from Vietnam, he had to struggle between detestation of the war and loyalty to his President. He was a man of simple honour, and it shows in his books.

When the Nobel confirmed that he had done his best work, Steinbeck began to see that he stood for an outmoded ethic. His later days were spent in a kind of dogged futility, soaking in the Arthurian legends – mostly on the spot, near Cadbury, with the great Professor Vinaver to help him – in order to rewrite them and relate them to the modern age. He couldn't do it, but he tried hard. He was always the dedicated writer, and it pained him that the image of the debased and self-glorifying Hemingway had somehow rubbed on to him. He was supposed to be a hard drinker, but he drank little. He had only three wives. He did not like being famous. Compared with Hemingway, whose fists and corridas and safaris get in the way of his prose, he had few adventures, and the title of his biography rings ironically.

Hemingway, secure in his Anglo-Saxon ancestry, could mock his name into Hemingstein. Steinbeck was assumed by the Nazis to be a Jew, especially when he wrote the anti-totalitarian *The Moon is Down*, a copy of which it was death to possess in occupied Europe. He was in fact a mixture of Ulster Irish and German Lutheran, and the mission of his Düsseldorf forebears had been to convert the Jews to laborious Protestantism. The family settled in Salinas, California, and it is safe to consider Steinbeck a regional novelist whose best work has a Californian locale – the fruit farms with their sweated immigrant labour, the coast at Monterey. California brought him close to the Mexicans, eventually to Zapata. He never felt much inclination to drink of the European stream, like Hemingway. Joyce did not, apparently, excite him. The rural nostalgia of *East of Eden* finds very orthodox expression:

> Under the live oaks, shaded and dusky, the maidenhair flourished and gave a good smell, and under the mossy banks of the water courses whole clumps of five-fingered ferns and goldybacks hung down. Then there were harebells, tiny lanterns, cream white and almost sinful looking, and these were so rare and magical that a child, finding one, felt singled out and special all day long.

I have just published a novella in which, by happy chance, Steinbeck is mentioned. ' "I met Steinbeck," Enderby said, "when he was given, unjustly I thought and still think, the Nobel, oh I don't know though when you consider some of these dago scribblers who get it, think it was an unjust bestowal. There was a party for him given by Heinemann in London. I a.ked him what he was going to do with the prize money and he said: *fuck off*." ' The party goes unmentioned by Mr Benson (who has otherwise recorded every pimple and mouthful). What Steinbeck said to Enderby he really said to me. The rudeness was not typical but Steinbeck was very tired. Before then he had been a very tireless writer. It is a great deal to say of a writer that he lived for writing. Steinbeck did.

Inexhaustible Wells

H. G. Wells and the Culminating Ape, by Peter Kemp

Wells's work, says Mr Kemp, 'is pervaded by responses to life learned in South Kensington.' That sounds typically Britishly parochial, but South Ken was not to Wells what Bloomsbury was to Virginia Woolf: it was the location of the Normal School of Science where, for an exhilarating year, he studied biology under T. H. Huxley. There he learned that the world was to be irradiated and redeemed through science. He became a Pelagian, a utopiographer, the father of the Open Conspiracy, the chief of the Samurai, but he never forgot that he was primarily a biologist. This meant that he was more concerned with the species than the individual, that to him life was a laboratory, and that one of these days the experiment of 'developing the realisation of the species' might really work. And yet his novels are positively Dickensian in their proliferation of idiosyncratic personages, the unbiological egotism of what he called 'the Dolores type' (after *Apropos of Dolores*) was best exemplified in himself, and he ended his life by smashing the laboratory and pouring the species down the drain.

His fascination lies undoubtedly in the conflict between opposed elements in himself: the pre-South Ken past, all deprivation and dyspepsia, remained as alive as the post-South Ken future; a belief in the potentialities of the species warred with a scepticism about the declared aims of individuals who were supposed to be the voices of the species; an honest dour pessimism, perhaps having its origins in his digestive tract, denied his scientific utopianism. A man makes himself invisible but achieves only his own destruction; the sighted man is torn to pieces by the blind; the far distant future is revealed to the time traveller as a biological nightmare in which class differentiations have become genetic ones and the basely strong literally devour the exquisitely weak.

Mr Kemp devotes a long chapter to this theme of devouring. There is far more cannibalism in Wells than some of us have suspected: the progressive have to eat the retrogressive in order to survive. The indigestible meals of boiled ham and pickled salmon are not, after all, Dickensian: they represent the cravings of the empty stomach of a deprived youth. The ultimately digestible – which, in the Wellsian paradox, is also the ultimately emetic – is the body of Wells himself, which is to be cooked in butter with potatoes. The horrible eucharistic feasts of *The Island of Dr Moreau* and the late, brilliant, *Mr Blettsworthy on Rampole Island* are more memorable than the rational meals of Utopian futurism. Wells's characters eat therefore they are. This is good biology, but it reads like strong realistic fiction.

Then there is sex, which keeps the species going but is not notable in

Wells for filling the house with Dickensian families. Sex is a war not at all in the service of biology: Wells seeks primarily from it 'a renewal of energy in the individual' and is very vague about eugenics and family planning. If heterosexual passion is a good, it is not so in any romantic sense. Wells, who first learned about female beauty from allegorical near-nudes representing Britannia, was as ready to couple with the symbolic mother as with Amber Reeves or Rebecca West. 'I am a MALE,' he writes to the latter: 'I have got Great Britain Pregnant.' He does not object to a little hypergamy – 'Temporary elevation of the female . . . makes her ultimate subordination the more gratifying,' says Mr Kemp – but women are essentially nubile infants. The babytalk to Catherine Wells, which makes the *Experiment in Autobiography* so embarrassing, is also used to the raven-haired beauty who became the fearsome Dame Rebecca: she was his 'faifful panfer' and 'Fing I like talking to'. Wells was a sensualist, but this is no bad thing in a writer of fiction.

Not much apparent progressivism, then, in the great progressive. The collective image of the novels is of atavistic meals and of tumbling on unmade beds. If sexual and digestive battles are ineluctable, at least their projections onto the world scene in the form of great wars can progressively be eliminated. Orwell believed that Wells was 'a nineteenth-century liberal whose heart does not leap at the sound of bugles. . . . He has an invincible hatred of the fighting, hunting, swash-buckling side of life.' Not so. Reading what Wells wrote during both great wars we meet a Kaiser-hanging Hitler-eating firebrand. We meet too, and not only in wartime, a somewhat muzzy biologist to whom the human species presents a traditional structure of hierarchies. American blacks are nice, gentle, musical but not very bright; he has a *Stürmer* stereotype of 'the Jew' which he emphasizes the more through his heated denial of it. Presumably both blacks and Jews have opted out of the great biological experiment; the laboratory is an Anglo-Saxon preserve.

What Wells believed he was doing was at variance with what he actually did. He blueprinted rather dull utopias while creating cacotopian visions of great power. He chronicled Victorian and Edwardian social decay the better to show what a scientifically planned society could be like, but it is the fusty maggoty Home Counties of his time that appeal, not the aseptic dream of the future. That he was a great educator there can be no doubt: both *The Outline of History* and *The Science of Life*, which my father bought for me in fortnightly parts, are as enter-taining as they are scholarly, though true historians might doubt the value of scholarship filched from the *Encyclopaedia Britannica*. That he was a powerful egoist, far more dangerous than his friend Bernard Shaw, was the final contradiction of his thesis about the comparative unimportance of the individual. He was drawn, very dangerously, to men of destiny like Stalin. The great pedagogue was always ready to become the great demagogue.

Mr Kemp's bibliography shows how much Wells wrote. It was, we are always told, far too much, and the speed with which he wrote militated against accuracy, grace and even clarity. The volubility and dogmatism were aspects of a lower-class cockiness which Arnold Bennett recognized in himself but learned how to subjugate. Wells was never quite accepted by the great world. He received no honours, not even one of the honorary doctorates with which Lord Snow's career was larded. Cockily, in old age, he wrote his doctoral thesis – back to biology – and grinned at the world in a cap and gown he had fairly earned. The patron saint of all who scribble fast for a living, of all guttersnipes and counter-jumpers who make the literary grade, he remains a vivid presence. Like so many great men, he did not understand himself at all. Mr Kemp's brief book is an admirable exposition of the Wellsian ambiguities and a reminder of his incredible achievement.

Experiment in Autobiography, by H. G. Wells, 2 vols.
H. G. Wells in Love, edited by G. P. Wells

I reviewed *Experiment in Autobiography* when it was first published by Gollancz in 1934. That was an amateur job, for the school magazine. I have reviewed fresh editions of it – professionally, but probably no better – and see no good reason for doing more than merely notice this reprint. To review it would be like reviewing *Paradise Lost* (of which it is a kind of antithesis). There is a piquancy in its reappearance under the Faber imprint, which we may historically associate with literary experiment and the doctrine of Imperfect Man, whereas Gollancz used to stand for Liberal Man and social progress. Wells was always changing his publisher – something to do with snobs like Macmillan not inviting him to dinner for fear this jumped-up counterjumper might steal the spoons – and we must expect the business to continue post-humously. There may well soon be a new edition of *Ann Veronica* from Mills and Boon with a discreetly erotic cover.

Experiment is as readable as ever it was, though the 'picshuas' continue to embarrass and the failed prophecies sadden more than ever. Wells worked for the World State and died just before a more plausible blue-print than his own appeared in Orwell's cacotopian novel. His rational optimism has a lavender smell now. But there is something heartening in this anabasis of a downtrodden Victorian boy, son of a servant, turning himself into the great writer he undoubtedly was. He also became a great lover, but the world and the laws of defamation were not, in 1934, quite ready for his amatory revelations. Too many of the loved and discarded were still alive. The death of Rebecca West enabled Anthony West, her and his son, to tell the truth about one particular relationship. Now G. P. Wells, West's half and legitimate brother, has published what his, their, father wrote about all the women in his life, intended as an appendix to *Experiment* but acceptable as a separate, and possibly major, opus – a *liber amoris* by a rationalist who discovered areas of life where reason didn't prevail.

The book begins with that touching tribute to his second wife Catherine, known as 'Jane', which was first published as a preface to a miscellany of her writings. 'Jane' Wells was the rock of his life, the pedal point over which he permitted himself fantastic sonorities of infidelity: she knew, she was complaisant. But when the doctors diagnosed her incurable cancer, Wells stayed with her to the end, the kind faithful companion he always knew how to be when intellectual and glandular restlessness didn't get in the way. He loved her, he loved his first wife (Isabel Mary, his cousin) for a year or two, he loved Moura Budberg incessantly and without qualification. For the rest, he had affairs.

He pursued women, but he was also pursued by them. He had smooth skin, a sweet breath, a hearty sexual appetite: he always regarded himself as edible ('fried, with potatoes'). He was duly eaten by Amber Reeves and Rebecca West. He had announced himself cheerfully as available for erotic adventure: since the introduction of reliable contraceptives, there was no reason why love shouldn't be enjoyed like all the other sports. So the liberated women of the Edwardian age seized him. Despite contraception, he gave both Amber and Rebecca babies; despite the doctrine of free love, he found women prone to possessiveness and very, if not immediately, resentful of having to compete with a complaisant wife. This was not true of Dorothy Richardson, a considerable novelist who had 'an interesting hairy body', but it was true of most of the others. It was even true of the Elizabeth of *Elizabeth and Her German Garden*, that great teaser of the homosexual Hugh Walpole, cool, rational, progressive and, it seemed at first, totally incapable of jealousy. All women, so Wells discovered, were capable of jealousy, except Moura Budberg, of whom, inevitably, he was madly jealous.

Contemporary authors, alas, don't seem to find strange women in their studies, eager to drag them to bed. Nor do they find, as Wells did once, a young woman clad only in a raincoat ready to slash her wrists if not immediately made love to (despite his being in evening dress and ready to go out to dinner). Life ran very high in those days. What Wells learned was that the high erotic life had to be paid for. It was easier to pay for it in a Washington brothel ('White or coon?' asked the taxi driver. 'Coon,' replied Wells) than in terms of female jealousy, but Wells was always the rational optimist who believed that *Tristan* was really written by Mozart. Not even his experience with Odette Keun seriously disabused him.

For her and himself he built Lou Pidou in Provence (with 'This house was built by lovers' over the fireplace) and learned what it was like to endure the tantrums of an exhibitionist of Levantine culture, a screamer at servants, full of threats to publish Wells's obscene love letters if she did not get her way, good in bed undoubtedly but a danger at the dinner table who could not be unleashed on prim London society ('When you say *Ve*,' she said to Alfred Mond, 'do you mean the Jews or the British?'). When a puritanical guest was vague about what precisely Casanova had done, she enlightened him with one coarse word. Wells gives us virtually a crisp short novel about his tribulations with Odette: it is his best piece of writing here. Sample:

> She talked ever more vociferously of her early life in the 'embassy', of her deep spiritual life as a nun, of her religious experiences, of her marvellous explorations in the Caucasus and North Africa, in regions hitherto inaccessible to refined women (and why), of the books she had written and the books she was going to write, of her marvellous insight into the psychology of peoples and her distinctive descriptive talent, of her great and wonderful love for me. She would contradict me and shout me down if I tried to deflect the talk to any subject but herself. Then she would stage a quarrel with me and forgive me – with a headlong rush round the table to embrace me. Or she would discourse, with vivid particulars, on the wonders of our sexual intimacy.

When Wells's passion for Moura Budberg became known to Odette, she inevitably called her 'Bedbug'. This passion, of long duration, represents, one supposes, the retribution that, in fiction at least, visits the philanderer. Moura, a Russian aristocrat who became a close intimate of Maxim Gorky, withheld nothing from Wells except a willingness to marry him. Her Russian soul and Russian capacity for vodka and slovenliness alike appal him, her untruthfulness wounds him, his inability to divine what precisely went on between her and Gorky drives him mad. He behaves besotted, which he was. She loved him, but unbesottedly. The Wells who adored Moura was not the Wells capable of planning a World State. Wells in love meets demons, and the BSc course at London University taught him nothing about exorcism. This is a fine, moving, essentially comic book.

H.D. and Husband

Bid Me To Live; *Her*; *The Gift*, by H.D.
Death of a Hero, by Richard Aldington

In August 1912, over the cheerful cups in the British Museum tea-room, Ezra Pound scribbled at the foot of one of Hilda Doolittle's poems 'H.D. Imagiste'. Thus a beautiful and gifted girl from Bethlehem, Pennsylvania, entered the history of literary modernism and may be said to have founded a profoundly influential poetic method. The three poems by which she is represented in the *Faber Book of Modern Verse* (1936) indicate the method very accurately: you make an image stand for an emotion and a cluster of images for a complex psychological state. It was a method most spectacularly employed in *The Waste Land* and the *Cantos*. If H.D.'s poetry is more read about than read, this may have something to do with embarrassment about those initials. The name Doolittle is an old and honourable one, but Shaw's *Pygmalion* (another literary event of 1912) rendered it wholly comic. H.D. and Bryher (Winifred Ellerman) became lesbic companions and were also onomastically well matched. Both the initials and the pseudonym seem pretentious and put one off. H.D.'s work and life are altogether different matters.

The Virago people present both *Her* and *Bid Me To Live*, which are very much a poet's fiction, as Modern Classics, and this must seem premature. The first was written in 1927 but not published until 1981; *Bid Me To Live* appeared in 1960. Neither book has had time to settle into the literary consciousness and take on that quality of timeless pertinence which proclaims the classic. But one sees what Virago means. If *The Gift* is no more than straight autobiography, the two brief novels transform autobiographical material into a kind of mythology in a manner so original that a whole tradition could have grown out of it. Certainly Sylvia Plath's *The Bell Jar* seems to find its roots in H.D. In the sense that the content of the two novels relates to certain literary figures who have taken on classic status – particularly Pound and Lawrence – they stand as permanently valuable expressions of a phase in the history of the modern consciousness.

The eponymous heroine of *Her* is really Hermione Gart (a surname as hard to grapple with as Doolittle). She is engaged in 'struggling for an identity' (I have still to discover what the phrase means) after failing at Bryn Mawr and vegetating too long at home in dull Pennsylvania. She is buffeted by the gale of George Lowndes – a thinly disguised young Ezra Pound – who has just blown in from Europe. She is both elated and threatened. She carries the fragile flower of her ego under a bell jar to

Fayne Rabb (in real life Frances Josepha Gregg) and is driven to break-down. Hermione (I do not like that Her: it reminds me of my father bitterly discussing my stepmother) goes through hell and emerges at the end of the winter's tale as H.D. (To underline the mythic identification H.D. had a daughter named Perdita, who appends very revealing memories of her mother to all three of these volumes.)

Bid Me To Live is mainly about the breakdown of H.D.'s marriage to Richard Aldington. We are in the middle of the First World War, Lawrence and Frieda ('old Rico' and Elsa) have come from Cornwall and are staying with H.D., or Julia Ashton, in Mecklenburgh Square. Cecil Gray, the musician and friend of Peter Warlock (comically mythicized in *Antic Hay*, libelled in *Women in Love*), who gave H.D. Perdita, appears as Vane, and Pound is newly named Lett Barnes. The reader is so fascinated by the real life that he has difficulty in taking in the fiction. This is very much a *roman à clef*. Distinguished in its writing, brilliant in its evocation of atmosphere, it will not let itself stand as a dispassionate artefact. It looks out to life, whereas the *clef* element in *Women in Love* and *Aaron's Rod* (in this latter Lawrence has a bad-tempered go at H.D.) is comparatively unimportant. You lose the key in the art.

Death of a Hero, I now see fifty years after first reading it, is another *roman à clef*. George Winterbourne, sacrificed to the old bitch gone in the teeth, is really Aldington, observed posthumously by a different Aldington, and the two women in his life – Elizabeth and Fanny – are really H.D. and Dorothy Yorke. It was H.D.'s brother who was killed in action. I have always liked the novel but always been puzzled by the neurasthenia which drives Winterbourne to submit to a kind of suicide a few weeks before the Armistice: 'He felt he was going mad, and sprang to his feet. The line of bullets smashed across his chest like a savage steel whip. The universe exploded darkly into oblivion.' It is not just the war – Aldington makes this clear – but worry over his wife and his mistress. Yet nothing is shown in the novel, which treats 'free love' lightly and rather humorously, to indicate a neurotic guilt which becomes suicidal. We are evidently in the presence of a profound and inexpressible personal emotion for which the author can find no 'objective correlative'. Winterbourne, just having fallen in love with Elizabeth (physically very much H.D.), sings 'Bid me to live' to the dark London streets. History, not literature, makes this tragically ironic.

For the rest, *Death of a Hero* remains a genuine classic, though not reissued as such. It is not as massive as Ford's *Parade's End*, but, daring to turn personal suffering into art, it is superior to such British war books as *Memoirs of a Fox-Hunting Man* and *Goodbye to All That*, and immeasurably better than *All Quiet on the Western Front*. Its mastery of a diversity of literary 'registers' is quite remarkable. It is comic, angry and lyrical by turns, and it deploys flat documentary reportage to devasta-ting effect when dealing with the daily life and death of the trenches. No book better conveys cold, mud, filth, physical misery. But it is no more a mere 'war book' than is *Parade's End* (though Graham Greene's editorial excision of a quarter of that masterpiece has limited the British edition to a chronicle that stops with the Armistice, ignoring the agonies of the peace). It is a blazing attack on British hypocrisy, as exemplified in the mores of the Edwardian age which produces the hero, as also on the intellectual cowards (their names are disguised but we can see who they are: even Mr Eliot is there, though unfairly) who condoned the slaughter and thought civilization well lost for art.

Aldington's anger never abated, though it became attached to new targets. He ended his days in bitter exile, having incurred Churchill's wrath through debunking T.E. Lawrence in a brilliant biography, and he became one of the great unknowns. There was a time when even Mr Auberon Waugh had to confess to never having heard of him. If for nothing else he deserves our homage for having produced *Death of a Hero*. Its rage – against the old who kill the young, against the governments (not always gerontocracies) which thrive on lies and evasions – is all too terribly pertinent to our own time.

Pipesmoking Monster

The Mystery of Georges Simenon: A Biography, by Fenton Bresler

Simenon has written something like 420 novels and novellas, half under his own name, half under seventeen pseudonyms. There are eighty-four Maigret books. According to a UNESCO survey, he is the most translated writer in the world after Lenin, and he has been read by between 350 and 500 million people. He is a sterling millionaire many times over, but he has never let his money earn interest: that, he says, would be 'capitalism'. To end these statistics, he claims to have slept with 10,000 women. One wonders why he makes the claim, since he regards this as 'quite a normal number – even banal. I know a lot of friends who are in the same situation. When you are hungry, you eat. When you are thirsty, you drink. I would say it is essential.' He admits that 8000 of these women were prostitutes.

I do not quite see where the 'mystery' of Mr Bresler's title lies. Dr Pierre Rentchunk, a Swiss psychiatrist, took four of his colleagues to spend a day with Simenon and eventually published a book called *Simenon sur le gril*. It concludes that Simenon is a fantasist incapable of telling truth from lies – the normal situation with writers of fiction. What is unusual is the compulsion to write, to dash off a novel in a week or so, to rend himself with the effort and then recuperate through animalistic sex. The novels, even the lightest of them, are all about the dark places of the soul. Despite the author's claim that he needed to penetrate people, literally and otherwise, in order to uncover these dark places, the inner agonies – brought in the books to ultimate exacerbation – are evidently, as again is nearly always the way with novelists, his own. Fiction is an introspective craft.

He will always be known for Maigret, a decent pipe-smoking police officer who solves crimes not through modern technology but through an almost sacerdotal knowledge of the human soul. Clearly, Simenon would have liked to be Maigret, but he never had much in common with him except the pipe. Simenon, who confesses to being a psychopath, is on the receiving end of the priest-policeman's ministrations. It may be banal, at least for Frenchmen or Walloons, to sleep with 10,000 women, but Maigret's virtue is his sexual coolness, and his devotion to his wife is clearly something that his creator envies. The story of Simenon's married life is far from attractive.

What is bound to shock the Anglo-Saxon reader is the lack of reticence about sex, marital and otherwise, in Simenon's own memoirs, on which Mr Bresler very cautiously draws. There is a cruel flaunting of infidelity and a brutal notation of the details of seduction. The Teresa who is the common-law companion of his old age was once a maid in his household whom, in a moment of need, he took from the rear while she was dusting the furniture. The orgasms of his second wife Denise are recounted in the unornamented style which is so admired in the novels. He wears women's orgasms like pelts: they are always 'copious' and rarely convincing. Love-making, as opposed to instant copulation, has never been in Simenon's line.

Naturally, and deservedly, he has suffered. Nemesis works sometimes strangely, but Simenon can hardly deny that nemesis exists. God and sex are not mocked. His daughter Marie-Jo conceived an incestuous passion for him which ended in her suicide. Denise became unbalanced and built him a huge mausoleum of a house with eleven servants, including a chef in a toque. The two of them drank too much and screamed at each other. Simenon hurled a dish of spaghetti at the dining-room wall. The children all left, and no wonder. Previously, they had only found content in their father's brief but intense working periods, when he went on the wagon and tried to exorcise his miseries through their externalization into fiction. But what was he miserable about? Presumably about his own share of the human inheritance: man is a mess and he needs art.

The man who depicted the external world so accurately, and with so unGidean a minimum of agonizing art, had very little interest in it. When we take pleasure in his delineation of a Paris that is long gone, we ought to note that it is mainly a physical pleasure – the smell of Gauloises, the taste of *marc* or of croissants dunked in coffee. We're in the presence of the author's sensorium. The emphases, as with Colette, are on small physical satisfactions, rarely with the human issues that exercise Dickensian reformers. There is a powerful egoism totally guilt-less. He accepted the Nazi occupation, living in seigneurial self-sufficiency with his pigs and cows and poultry and wife and maid-mistress, even growing his own tobacco. When Vichy decided that he might be a Jew and had to prove that he wasn't, he set his mother scurrying for exculpatory documents, but, like so many of the French writers he, a Belgian born, joined in complacent brotherhood, he got on with literature with a small l ('For me, Literature with a capital L is rubbish') and awaited the Liberation with little impatience.

Not an attractive writer. A fine writer, though, brilliant at exhibiting the sordors of life with sharp economy, creator of a character as immor-tal, possibly, as Sherlock Holmes, but too cold, unloving and fundamen-tally philistine to be great. Probably, San Antonio, Frédéric Dard, his acknowledged successor, is a bigger man and a more original writer of *romans policiers*. Perhaps Simenon's best book is the late *Lettre à ma mère*, in which, if there is a mystery, the mystery is proved all too soluble. That tough Belgian mother of his was one woman who would yield neither to his virile charm nor to his flamboyant success. He sent her money regularly, but she saved it and sent it all back. She turned up in Lakeville, Connecticut, where Simenon lived after the war in order to turn himself into an American writer, dressed in beggar's clothes and an old corset which she rescued nightly from her daughter-in-law's garbage can. She wanted nothing of his; she didn't really like him. So Simenon had to make himself acceptable to 10,000 women and 50 million readers. Strangely, he has no wish to die. At eighty, with dyed hair and an Italian mistress, living in a small flat while his huge mansion moulders unsold, he reads biographies and thinks. As his untranslated *Dictées* show, he is not much of a thinker.

Mr Bresler's biography is all that solid journalistic research, inter-views with its subject and his wives and children, and a no-nonsense style can make it. It is a worrying book, and hence worth reading. There are good photographs, including one of the young Simenon and the young Josephine Baker, the latter making horrible faces. He possessed her body but I possess her piano.

Intimate Memoirs, by Georges Simenon, translated by Harold J. Salemson

T he reviewer of a translation has properly the duty of comparing it with the original, but I make no apology for not having expended francs and time on 800-odd pages of Simenon in French. I have francs but my time is short, and both are better spent on a new edition of *Corinne* or Sartre's recently issued scenario of his film on Freud. Still, I cannot believe that Simenon in French is as bad as he is in English, American rather. The book exemplifies a problem unresolved and hardly even discussed – how far an American translator is justified in turning a European into an American, equipped with the slanginess and slackness that characterize so much transatlantic hack writing. Not that this particular job deserved, as far as I can tell, more than the attention of a hack. Simenon's aim here is far from literary. He is getting off his chest things which would have been better left on it or, since Simenon has always been considered a distinguished writer, digested into the distinguished fiction that was loved by Jean Cocteau and André Gide.

The title gives us fair warning. Simenon is going to tell all, to let it all hang out, to recount his woes and (in parenthesis) his good fortune, most of all to allay his guilt. But the book itself is something to feel guilty about. It takes the form of a series of revelations addressed to his children, so where we, the strangers, come in is not all that clear. He starts on 16 February 1980 with a letter to his dead daughter Marie-Jo, which begins 'My tiny little girl'. In the course of the loose narration we find him talking to his sons – Marc and Pierre and 'Johnny mine'. He tells them things that the average father would be somewhat embarrassed at recounting to his children, but Simenon the memoirist has always lacked taste and discretion, reserving those properties to the six books a year he calls novels.

There is, for instance, the vulgar candour about his sexual life. The whole world now knows that Simenon has slept with thousands of women. The nature of the sleeping, a term rather inept when applied to rapid connections, is peculiar to Simenon, who seems to penetrate without due preparation and miraculously promote immediate ecstasy in his partners. With his first wife Tigy, from whom he was divorced in 1950, sex and love seem harmoniously to combine. Then comes D. (her full name Dénise is never permitted) and a sexual saga which is grossly delineated. Marital permissiveness goes far, and D. is not above casual troilism. This is Marie-Jo's mother, who appears as a schizophrenic drunkard, a vindictive harpy, a monster crammed with envy of her husband's literary achievements. To the world she presents Jo, as she calls Georges, in very unflattering terms – a tyrant who has appropriated the credit for the slavish work she has performed on his behalf.

She does not quite claim the authorship of the books for herself, but she totters alcoholically on the brink of doing so.

It is while D. is hopping into and out of psychiatric clinics and cashing cheques designed to deplete Simenon's coffers (he is probably the richest writer who has ever lived) that the troubles with Marie-Jo begin. This girl, pretty and not untalented in the modern way – meaning she can write sad little stories, strum the guitar, loosely lyricize in the Brel manner – develops an unhealthy passion for her father. Simenon has by this time assaulted the maid Teresa during her dusting operations and installed her in his bed. Marie-Jo is resentful of this and demands to be the only woman in her father's life. Her father, who has so far baulked at little, baulks at the proposal of incest. Marie-Jo now embarks on courses of action and inaction which have to end in suicide. She is cremated. 'This wedding ring you had begged me to buy for you when you were about eight years old, and which you had had enlarged a number of times, was not taken off your finger.'

Simenon turns into a very old man, with the Menier syndrome, arthritis, prostatic trouble, and sits by the fire with the former maidservant Teresa, who has now become the companion of his decline. One would be tempted to regard this story as tragic if only there were a final awareness of nemesis, of spitting in the beards of the gods, but what is totally excluded from this book is a moral sense, a nostalgia for faith, or even a talent for superstition. It would require a greater writer than Simenon to turn such a story into a study of unsought pain and hard-won reconciliation with the fates. He is not completely frank. The relationship with his mother, for instance, a very grim one, is best learned from his biographers, not from this memoir. There is more self-pity than self-excoriation. He has done his best, he seems to say, he has turned himself into the most popular storyteller of the century, and his wife has wished to scratch out his eyes and his daughter has taken her own life.

The final 150 pages are reserved for what is called 'Marie-Jo's Book', a compendium of her writings from the age of eight to her suicide at twenty-five. They make painful reading for two opposed reasons. If her father had not been Simenon it is doubtful whether they could have been published. The little songs are poignant only in that the girl's situation is poignant:

> A whole world of dreams
> Has gnawed my entrails out.
> I am sinking into nowhere
> Into a pit of fire – (without end)
>
> I'm going back to the void
> Becoming dust once more.
> I ask now of death
> To put an end to my fate.

The pain is real, but real pain does not necessarily make art. Dylan Thomas wrote a heart-rending elegy on a certain Ann Jones, about whom he cared little. That's the way art goes. What Marie-Jo gives her father is mediocre art – 'I'll never have but one Daddy/ He is just terrific' goes one of her cassette-recorded songs – but we are intended to feel that aesthetic considerations would be impertinent, even blasphemous. Don't condemn that man for dancing so badly – after all, he lost his right leg on the Somme.

So we take 'Marie-Jo's Book' as an agonizing testament of an aberration that nothing could cure. A girl ought to love her father and that love ought to be returned, but the gods place certain limits on its expression, except in the slums. In extreme old age Simenon must be pondering what sins he committed during his years of vigour. Perhaps he took sex too lightly and Eros struck back. But no, that's too easy. The final irony is that a subject entered his life which demanded the expression of Sophoclean art. The inventor of Maigret had immense talent but he was no Sophocles.

Death in Utah

The Executioner's Song, by Norman Mailer

Since the self-elected execution of Gary Gilmore on 17 January 1977, there have been at least two more optings for death on the part of condemned American murderers, and thirty-five states have, with the recidivism typical of countries born out of revolutions, decided to reintroduce the death penalty. Archie Bunker is winning. In the circumstances, Mailer's massive study of the Gilmore case is unlikely to have the impact its author expected. All journalism dates, and this is not so much the higher as the longer journalism: 1056 big pages and far too many facts. The value of this sedulous accumulation was presumably intended to rest on the uniqueness of Gilmore's rejection of penal liberalism, but Gilmore has ceased to be unique. Style will not preserve the book, since it has no style. Like Buckingham's *The Rehearsal*, it has insufficient vitality to save it from putrefaction.

This is a Utah story. Utah remains the strangest state in the Union. Beneath the surface of smug quiet fat Mormonism there is a sufficiency of unrest and criminality. Salt Lake City is the only town in the world where, in the last twenty years, I have been stinking incapable drunk. I was drunk because there are no bars. Wanting gin, I had to buy a whole bottle of it at a liquor store. Having three hours to wait for a plane to Kansas City, I found it necessary to finish the bottle and be poured onto the aircraft. Salt Lake City is, to compound the bizarreness, the home of the man who has written my biography. There is something spooky about it. In a state where tea, coffee and tobacco are gateways to sin, the coexistence of creamy confectionery, philoprogenitiveness, belief in the miracles of Joseph Smith, live memories of polygamy, winter sports, and a conviction that death is a plywood door produces a pattern of life that requires great art to make it intelligible. Utah has a great choir and a great, or big, temple, but true art is probably a sin, and literature would show up the wretchedness of the prose of the Book of Mormon. The nearest approach to art is gratuitous homicide.

Gilmore, who had spent most of his thirty-odd years in prison or reformatory, committed, on successive days, two murders totally without discernible motive. He robbed first a filling station and then a motel and, with the sparse cash safely pocketed, shot the unresistant attendant and manager in the head. He was easily picked up, charged and convicted of first-degree murder, then sentenced to death automatically commuted to life imprisonment. Gilmore made history by demanding execution by firing squad, this being the traditional Utah way (his successors have had to endure the four-minute agony of cyanide poisoning), but there then began a profound legal tussle about a citizen's right to choose death when an alternative punishment was available. After all, there had not been an execution in Utah for a long time. To kill Gilmore would be a stain on the state; Gilmore himself would, in effect, be committing suicide.

What makes the whole story very Utah is the unquestioned assumption that Gilmore would step through the plywood door and confront his victims. What would he say to them, and what they to him? Gilmore himself, though not a Utah man by origin, faced such questions seriously, his eschatology being a compound of vestigial Catholicism and halfbaked Vedanta. He'd helped the victims a little, he said, along the road to fulfilment of kharma. His last words before the hidden squad tore into his heart were '*Dominus vobiscum*', as strange in Utah as in the Joannine Church. He had no death wish: he just did not want to spend his life in jail. At the pre-execution party, with Gilmore full of legitimate speed and smuggled liquor, with the loudspeakers blaring country and western and Johnny Cash on the line, Gilmore saw a chance of escape through changing clothes with one of his guests: he would have taken it if the guest had been willing to cooperate, which he wasn't. The man was sane and open-eyed enough, not unintelligent, even a sort of poet. But, despite the long probing of the media – for, this being modern America, the whole thing had become profitable showbiz – Gilmore was not able to come up with a reason for his double killing. Hollywood was interested in him, but he was not interested in Hollywood 'motivation'.

Mailer holds for an instant the frayed thread of a bizarre reason, and this has to do with his love for Nicole, an ordinary pretty brainless girl whom Gilmore volubly worshipped (their exchange of letters is presented as Eloise-and-Abelard-like, even if *fuck* is the basic semanteme). Nicole was a mere golden child, and Gilmore had the experienced criminal's abhorrence of child molestation. Was the double killing a means of paying the con deities for the right to pursue a forbidden love? The solidity of this love survives the sordor of the rest of the story. Nicole smuggled barbiturates into the prison visiting room (in a balloon thrust up her vagina), and the star-crossed pair attempted suicide almost under the noses of the guards. The romantic in Mailer is fatally drawn to this Romeo and Juliet aspect of the case. Shit, it's not their fault if they didn't have Shakespeare to give them the right words, right?

Mailer is too experienced a narrator not to contrive a thrilling enough climax (near the thousandth page) out of the final legal attempt to frustrate Gilmore's unwavering determination to be executed at dawn on a snowy day. A citizen's plea to stop the expenditure of public money on a needless quietus was upheld in Utah but immediately set aside by the Tenth Circuit in Denver, and the Denver judgment was confirmed in the Supreme Court robing room at the very hour when the guns should have been raised. If the decreed hour of execution had been passed, there were no wanting jurists who could rule that *hour* meant day. Gilmore walked as calmly as his leg shackles would allow to the kitchen chair where he was to sit and face a black screen with holes in it, and there he was very expertly sent to the Utah afterworld. But, since writing this book has by now become a way of life to Mailer, there is much more to come: the postmortem, the distribution of vital organs to hospital banks, the continuing story of Nicole–Eloise–Juliet. It is a terribly long book, and it seems to me to have its provenance less in Mailer's fascination with the whole Gilmore case (though this is so considerable as to be morbid, even rabid) than in his continuing desire to avoid the production of a long-promised long novel. Mailer is doing everything to frustrate the fulfilment of his primary vocation.

What we might have expected from *The Executioner's Song* is a Mailerian mystico-astrologico-metaphysical expatiation on the significance of Gilmore – quasi-existential victim–hero – in a culture increasingly selling out to evil, but there is no commentary as there is no style. Mailer has minimally compressed events and sharpened taped you-know-like-man burblings, but he is essentially a faceless minister of confirmable facts without a factoid in sight. He is on the back of the dust jacket, grey-curled, unshaven, pixyish, finger on pondering mouth, but he is only in the book as the final link in a long chain of media exploitation, the anonymous operator who took over from Larry Schiller – the Coast film–TV–book entrepreneur who, since he exhibits a capacity to develop with diarrhoea a shocked conscience, is perhaps the most interesting character in the whole story.

The question must finally be asked: why bother? Granted that every human soul may be worthy of 1056 pages, why should a cold murderer with a certain capacity for love and poetry be deemed worthier of such expensive celebration than the harmless grocer of Gissing's *New Grub Street*? Worthy means newsworthy. Newsworthy means tied up with sex and death. Newsworthiest means committed, like good old Charlie Manson, to gratuitous abominations which give a meaning to terms like theological evil. Mailer may need money to pay his multiple alimony, but he is selling out to something nastier than commerce.

Anal Magic

Ancient Evenings, by Norman Mailer

There is one ancient evening in particular, spent 3000 years ago at the court of Rameses IX. It is the Night of the Pig, a rare occasion for the violating of taboos and speaking out freely: even Isis, Osiris and Horus may be mocked. Presiding over a select dinner party is the Pharaoh himself; his guests are Menenhetet I, an old man of great experience in war, policy and magic, Menenhetet's granddaughter, the beautiful and devious Hathfertiti, and her husband and son. The husband, a somewhat dim and timorous personage, is the Overseer of the Royal Cosmetic Box, not so much of a sinecure as it sounds, since the Pharaoh's maquillage is a reflection of, and an influence on, the condition of the Egypt he rules. The son, who is only six, is familiarly named Meni-Ka, but his full name is Menenhetet II, and he dies and is mummified before the novel properly starts. We meet him in the prologue in

393

the person of his Ka, one of his seven doubles or shadows, and it is his Ka that remembers the evening in full detail and recounts its events with great and sometimes wearisome exactitude.

Rameses IX is a charming monarch, but he is not a good one. He is aware of a fatal inability to control the state: there is corruption in the ministries, and there is even a workers' strike caused by failure to deliver corn supplies. His worthlessness as a monarch will be definitively shown by the failure of the Nile to flood. Already there are hints of a coming palace revolution. On this night of plain speaking he demands to know from old Menenhetet something of the secret of the strength of his ancestor Rameses II, whom, in a former life 180 years before, Menenhetet served as a charioteer, an army general and governor of the harem. We learn, at epic length, of the battle of Kadesh which broke the power of the Aryan Hittites; we learn too that the murderous intrigues of the seraglio make war seem like a game for children.

We learn, in these 709 large pages, a great number of things. Most of all we learn how much Egyptology Mailer has learned in the last ten years. Gold mining, magical ceremonies, priests and eunuchs and concubines, the moods of the Nile, crocodiles, the character of Queen Nefertiti and her son Amen-khep-shu-ef – the whole of ancient Egypt is set before us, complete with its odours and its sexual ecstasies, these two last being given about equal billing. And the secret of power, which the book is chiefly about? This lies in magic, and magic is essentially control of the lower human functions. In a word, magic is anal.

The anus is here sometimes called the ass or the asshole. This is a pity. The word should be arse, which has an ancient ancestry, whereas ass is an Americanism of puritanic provenance. A pity because a novel about ancient Egypt must not sound as though it is written by an American, and this is the only verbal area where Mailer's careful stylistic neutrality breaks down. It is the most difficult thing in the world for the speaker of a new language to mimic an old one, and Mailer has, for the most part, done admirably. Never (except for ass and, I would say, cock) is there a breath of anachronism, but the timelessness of the narrative idiom, avoiding slang, Freudianisms and various forms of hindsight know-ingness, inevitably bores a little until it flares into lurid life with canni-balism and buggery.

Buggery has always been one of Mailer's themes. It shocked in the sixties when, in its heterosexual form, it appeared in the early pages of *An American Dream*. Writing about life in prison, Mailer presented homosexual buggery as a technique of conquest and humiliation. In *Ancient Evenings*, you sodomize the enemy to probe the caves of his strength. Rameses IX sees Egypt as looking like the crack between the globes of the buttocks. Egypt is fertile because of Nile mud, and mud is a form of faeces. Old Menenhetet has, to the shock of the court, eaten bat droppings in order to learn about magic. Khepera, that greatest of the gods, is a dung beetle; the Land of the Dead is his, and in it you must face the worst of faecal odours in order to achieve a passage to the next life. The arse of the Pharaoh excretes magical droppings into a Golden

Bowl (how Mailer, who knows his Henry James, must have worried about that appellation). The sorcery of the anal passage is the source of power.

Clearly, Mailer has not spent ten difficult years on a difficult book in order to demonstrate his skill, not previously disclosed, as a writer of historical fiction. If I can achieve a second, or third, reading of *Ancient Evenings*, I may be prepared to name it as the best reconstruction of an ancient world since Flaubert's *Salammbô*, but Mailer does not want that kind of praise. His concern is with the modern world, with the psychic problems of modern America above all, and he considers that these problems may find a solution through an understanding of the repressed areas of sexuality, with the reality of magic. Our own rationality has failed. Here, he seems to say, is a complex civilization of high achievement based on the irrational, on the radial power of a magic whose centre is both decay and resurrection.

He justifies himself with an epigraph from Yeats's *Ideas of Good and Evil*, in which the poet, always a dangerous thinker, expresses his belief in the evocation of spirits and ends by asserting 'that the borders of our mind are ever shifting, and that many minds can flow into one another, as it were, and create or reveal a single mind . . . and that our memories are part of one great memory, the memory of Nature herself.' Mailer finds his spirits in the gods of Egypt and the power of intercourse between minds in the Egyptian doctrines of death. He also finds, in his imagined world of a post-Mosaic Pharaoh, a location for his own anal obsessions. Six times married, the father of four sons and six daughters, he is fascinated by the sin of Sodom, which is no idle perversion but a source of salt and fire. Strange that, nearly ten years ago, some of us could believe that Mailer was working on a great chronicle of exodus and diaspora. Egypt has proved to be no house of bondage for him but the terrain of the release of his fantasies.

In America this novel – which, whatever its intermittent unreadability, makes the fictional products of our own islands seem all too readably bland – has had a bad press. I don't think it has been well understood. Give it a few years and, like the equally misunderstood *Gravity's Rainbow*, it may well appear as one of the great works of contemporary mythopoesis. It certainly gives us a new look up the anus. On the only occasion on which I met Mailer – at one of Panna Grady's literally fabulous New York parties (literally because the big modern sources of fable were there – Lowell, Warhol, Ginsberg *et al.*) – he said: 'Burgess, your last book was shit.' I can see now that he was paying me a compliment.

Lawrence Elopes

Mr Noon, by D. H. Lawrence

Next year (1985) is the centenary of Lawrence's birth, and it is good to be able to anticipate the celebrations with what amounts to a newly discovered novel of his. A little book called *Mr Noon* was, true, published posthumously as a long story in *A Modern Lover* (1934) and then, in 1968, collected in *Phoenix II*. But Lawrence wrote a continuation of the tale, leaving it uncompleted in 1921. There were good reasons – mostly to do with the law of libel – why he was not anxious to see it published. The manuscripts of *Mr Noon I* and *Mr Noon II* were left with Lawrence's American publisher, Thomas Seltzer. The carbon copy of the typescript of *Mr Noon I* got to the literary agent Curtis Brown in 1934 and was put into print. *Mr Noon II* disappeared until 1972, when it was auctioned, along with other Lawrence papers, by Sotheby Parke Bernet, bought by the Humanities Research Center of the University of Texas, and, somewhat belatedly one would have thought, made available for publication fifty years after *Mr Noon I*. The entity, *Mr Noon* unnumbered, is more than a curiosity. It is, with all its faults – most of them willed, perverse and very Laurentian – quite entrancing. It is as though *Love's Labour's Won* had been unearthed and found quite as good as *Much Ado About Nothing*.

The Gilbert Noon of Part I seems to be based on a certain George Henry Neville, whom Lawrence knew in Eastwood, Notts. He was a schoolmate and eventually a fellow-teacher, but he caused a scandal by having to contract an insufficiently hasty marriage. His child was born less than three months after the wedding, and he had to resign from his post at Amblecote, Stourbridge. Lawrence is less interested in the man himself than in the twin themes of sexual incontinence and provincial sanctimoniousness. His hero is a mathematician and a musician – a highly skilled one, apparently, since he is working on a violin concerto and, in Part II, is assembling the materials for a symphony. Like all provincial young men he spoons, and Lawrence is very informative about spooning. Boys wait for girls after church or chapel on a Sunday evening and then kiss and cuddle them in dark doorways. Sometimes the loveplay demands a sequel, and Gilbert Noon goes the whole hog in the woodshed of the father of a certain Emmy. The father is enraged, reports Gilbert to the governing board of the school where he teaches, and in effect compels his resignation. Reports that Emmy has 'neuralgia of the stomach' get through to Gilbert, who assumes pregnancy. He goes off to Germany to study for a doctorate. There Part I ends.

It is brilliantly comic, pathetic and very sharp in its observation of provincial mores before the First World War. It will stand, as it once had to, well on its own, but it is minor art. With the addition of Part II, in spite of its unfinished state, we have something very like a major novel and one of immense autobiographical interest. For Gilbert Noon is no longer G. H. Neville but D. H. Lawrence. Noon's name was once funny and pathetic, rhyming with spoon and signifying that its owner had reached the limit of his provincial possibilities and must henceforth decline. But Noon in Germany, where Part II begins, is *nun* or now, and Gilbert becomes a creature of urgent immediacies. He turns into a kind of priapic god who upsets an aristocratic militaristic German family, a subverter of the Teutonic order which is stiffening itself to destroy Europe.

The story is an almost unembroidered account of what happened between Lawrence and the wife of H. C. Weekley, his French professor at Nottingham University College. This was the aristocratic Frieda, *geboren* von Richthofen, cousin of the aviator who was to be known as the Red Baron. Lawrence transfers their whirlwind elopement from Nottingham to Munich. Johanna von Hebenitz, married to an English academic in Boston, Mass., comes home to Germany to see her family, sleeps with Noon after a mere two hours of conversation, and then next morning finds, as he does, that the world has changed. She must leave her husband and children and go off with a penniless Englishman.

Johanna's family is in Metz, which Lawrence rechristens Detsch, until 1918 a part of the German Empire, clanking with soldiery and starched Teutonic pride. She and Gilbert want divorce, which in Germany will take three years; the Baron and Baroness revile the low-born Nottinghamshire seducer, appeal to all the gods of stability, succeed only in stiffening the resolve of its subverters, then see their daughter go off into the night – over the Austrian Alps into Italy, where the story leaves fiction and enters Lawrence's travel books, poems and the biographies written by other people.

Lawrence's descriptive powers are at their finest in Part II. How well he captures the atmosphere of a German garrison town, sees into the *gemütlich* German soul which has ruined itself with dreams of order, then takes off into the mountains and forests and flinty kind-cold streams, recording everything – which was his unique gift – as though recovering from an illness and seeing the natural world as for the first time. Johanna, whom we get to know physically as well as any heroine in literature, is adorable but maddening. The intimacy between the bizarrely ill-assorted two is presented candidly but without lubricity. When Lawrence sails off into his harangues to the reader about sex mysticism he knows in time when to tack to our patience. He is never without humour or irony.

His technique is cheeky, even insolent. He is always addressing the dear reader, whom he does not permit to be male, but in no ingratiating spirit. He is ready sometimes to revile the reader's presumed prudishness in front of a WC door. His attitude to the lovebirds is mockingly affectionate. He seems to be wiser about women in this book than in any other, except perhaps *Sea and Sardinia*. Johanna has slept around; the sleeping around has led her to Gilbert but it does not stop with him. She confesses that she has been 'had' by an American friend picked up on their Alpine trek. Gilbert forgives her. Lawrence knows that forgiveness is not in order nor, indeed, is any sympathetic response to what the world calls infidelity. Gilbert has a lot to learn about women and we watch him learning. Lawrence is candidly watching his past self.

It would have been pleasant to have picked up this book as a plain text, in the 'brave red' of the old collected edition, but we have to have it as an item in the emerging scholarly Cambridge edition of the works, with notes telling us what *fleur du mal* means, Goethe's dates, how many pence in the shilling of the ancient discredited coinage, maps, historical identifications of the fictional characters, every fifth line numbered to refer us to the notes. In other words, we are meeting a fine piece of Laurentiana with an earnest chaperone. 'One of these days, dear reader, you may meet this book with an *apparatus criticus* clanking behind it.' Lawrence's cheek didn't take him so far. But it took him as far as chiding the critics in the *Observer* and *Times* who had taken him to task for his lowness in the Part I which he had already seen reviewed. He didn't give a damn, really. Books, he says in Part II, are leaves on the tree of life, to be blown away and forgotten. Life is what matters. This book is full of it.

New from Scotland

1982 Janine and Unlikely Stories, Mostly, by Alasdair Gray

Mr Graham Greene had the kindness recently to describe me as an avid if undiscriminating reader. He was referring to a light-hearted publication of mine, in which I commend a near-century of modern novels to the notice of posterity. It seems I chose the wrong ones, except perhaps for two by Mr Greene. Practically all of my choices have been condemned by various of my fellow-critics, but one remains unmolested, perhaps because my fellow-critics have not read it. This is *Lanark*, by Alasdair Gray, a Glasgow man who has brought to post-MacDiarmid/Linklater/Bridie Scottish literature an experimental verve in which surrealistic fantasy cohabits with dour naturalism. Gray is not merely a writer but a visual artist much concerned with making his books objects of ocular interest as well as, which they primarily are, foamy turgid symphonies or perhaps, since he disdains shapeliness except in his drawings, rhapsodies. He not only illustrates; he confers with and probably bullies typesetters in order to turn the craft of print into an expressive ancillary art.

Look at his collection of stories (which are all, just not mostly, unlikely) and you will see him, and his collaborators, playing the full organ. 'Logopandocy' is not merely attributed to Sir Thomas Urquhart, the translator of Rabelais, but presented in the orthography of 1645 (fifteen years before Sir Thomas died of joy at the accession of Charles II), along with double columns, paragraphs effaced by mice, and other devices which make Urquhart anticipate Laurence Sterne. Gray is not so much innovating as going back to *Tristram Shandy* fantasy, a fictional mode which has frightened everybody except the late and regretted B. S. Johnson and this spiky Glaswegian. As for content, Gray owes only the principle of free fancy to Sterne: his ideas are original enough. Thus, a star falls to earth and a boy puts it in his pocket. Taking it out of his pocket in the classroom, he is asked by his teacher what it is; he swallows it and becomes a star himself. The sun, reminded he is feminine in German, complains of her spots. There is a false history of the Industrial Revolution, lavishly illustrated, and a series of tragic letters from Kublai Khan's court poet.

I note that Gray first published two of his stories in *Ygorra*, the Glasgow students' rag magazine, and I'm not being censorious when I suggest that a good deal of the fun Gray has is pretty much on the student level. The same can be said of Joyce's fun: certain innovative writers have to avoid becoming fully adult in order not to learn the drab world's fear (and the drab world contains publishers) of innovation. *1982 Janine*, which is described as but is not quite a novel, exploits the immaturity of a certain kind of mind and, in doing so, touches the higher play which has been consecrated by Borges. Borges's *ficciones* rest on the abandonment of the traditional contract the writer draws up with the reader: that what is presented is a kind of truth. The Borgesian kind of fictionalist says in effect that there is no truth in fiction, fiction being of its nature a damned lie. Hence you can revise your characters and their actions while in full creative flight: there is the total plasticity of a Joan Littlewood rehearsal without script and no night for the show to be all right on. The action of *1982 Janine* is confined to 'the head of an ageing, divorced, alcoholic, insomniac supervisor of security installations who is tippling in the bedroom of a small Scottish hotel.' His thoughts and fancies range freely. We can accept the thoughts – about Scotland's place in the collapsing world (acknowledgments to MacDiarmid's *A Drunk Man Looks at a Thistle* duly made in a postface), Britain's political mess, a Scottish adolescence – in an autobiographical spirit. The fancies are mostly of a masturbatory nature and they raise awkward questions.

Janine of the title is a fabricated sex object. So is Superb (short for Superbitch), Helga too, also Big Momma. Jock MacLeish (whose father bore the same name as a distinguished American poet) manipulates these creatures according to the dictates of his sado-masochistic needs. This entails the fabrication of shameful scenes which, brought up as we are on the pre-Borgesian contract, we have to accept as a mode of imagined reality and, accepting, reject. Bondage and buggery do here what they did for the Marquis de Sade: stimulate a flagging sexuality. But Sade was a bad fiction writer, though an interesting philosopher, and the outrages performed on Justine are too improbable to do more than make Ms Brophy, or Lady Levey, laugh. But Gray is a good novelist, however much he at times perversely rejects the gift, and what he tells us we have to believe. Believing, we are then told not to believe: this is only one sad man's fantasy. It would be possible to get away with a whole abominable Harold Robbins hunk of sadism through the use of such a disclaimer. In other words, the pornography is presented at second hand, as the narrator's personal property, and it is assumed that it has no power to affect the reader.

Perhaps I am taking this business too seriously. After all, Blake, in *An Island in the Moon*, makes a character stick his head in the fire and run round the room with his hair blazing: then he says that this didn't happen, he was only codding. I cannot help, nevertheless, holding to the view that things described by the imagination have the sort of validity a newsreel gives us. Thus Gray's novel disturbs me. If he wants his readers to be so disturbed – glandularly, not intellectually, and I think he does – I feel like becoming dourly Scottish and thundering about human responsibility. Transpose the whole construct to a level of adolescent play, and it becomes more venial. But it is hard to wade through 345 pages of juvenile fantasy, however mature the technique, without feeling affronted.

Jock the fantasist tries to take an overdose of barbiturate tablets halfway through the book. Then the typography goes less wild than artfully chaotic, with marginal comments, some of them upside down, which make the Triv and Quad chapter of *Finnegans Wake* seem like Enid Blyton. Jock vomits up the poison in *vers libre* then takes four blank pages to recover. Back into his plain narrative stride, he shows what a good novelist his creator or alter ego can be. He does not need the adjunct of pen and ink drawings to make his real personages, as opposed to his sex objects, live. But we end with the question: what is the novel about? I suppose the answer must be: what is Liszt's Second Hungarian Rhapsody about?

On the strength of *Lanark*, I proclaimed Alasdair Gray as the first major Scottish novelist since Walter Scott (with apologies to Compton

Mackenzie and Eric Linklater, and to Mr Greene, laughing sardonically in Antibes). *1982 Janine* exhibits the same large talent, deployed to a somewhat juvenile end. Still, with this book he leaves the parochial press of Canongate Publishing Ltd and enters the big world of anglophonian letters. Read it with misgivings and watch for the next. And, while you're waiting, read or reread *Lanark*.

A World of Universals

Paper Tigers: The Ideal Fictions of Jorge Luis Borges, by John Sturrock

There is no Mao scorn in Mr Sturrock's title. The tigers in any man's fiction are tigers on paper, not tigers in a jungle. Or, if they happen to be in a jungle, the jungle too is on paper. We can never, in fiction, deal with reality, only with representations of it, and the representations are made out of arbitrary signs which denote abstractions from reality. If we are Platonists, we will say that the so-called reality of real tigers is a mere copy of a universal tiger in the mind of God. If we are Nominalists, we will say that only particulars are real, and universals are no more than words. But a Nominalist language would entail having separate words for each of the tigers in the world – that one is *kron* and that one is *grert* – and this could never be handled. Nominalists cannot be fiction writers, since fiction writers use generalities like *tiger*. This makes them Idealists, whether they are aware of it or not. Borges is all too aware of his Idealism, and the glories and limitations of his *ficciones*, as he calls them, rest on this awareness. Mr Sturrock's subtitle, like his title, tells no more nor less than the truth.

Borges, who is now old and blind, has had to wait many years for the still partial acceptance of his importance. He is suspected in Britain, admired in America, analysed in France, not well known in the

Antipodes. He worries naive fiction-lovers by not fulfilling the stereotype of a South American writer. He has spent most of his life in Buenos Aires, but he also knows the pampas (or if he did not, he could, like the rest of us, read *Martín Fierro*). He should write picturesque travelogues about gauchos, nostalgic reminiscences of the Argentinian Eden, like Cunninghame Grahame or Hudson. Instead, he is urban, cosmopolitan and highly intellectual, not to say metaphysical. For long a librarian, he is happy to live in a world of universals, or words.

He has written poems and essays, but never a novel. We may call his short pieces of fiction short stories if we wish, but they are not like O. Henry or Somerset Maugham. They do not attempt to imitate the real world (impossible, anyway, because the real world is too big), nor do they present memorable characters. There are plots, oh dear me, yes, but the plots tend to illustrate metaphysical propositions. If Borges goes to the trouble to paint a vivid background, with a wealth of circumstantial detail, then one has to be on one's guard, for he is being very devious. My favourite story of his is the one about the Islamic philosopher Averroes, who, after a staid symposium with his friends in a brightly realized Granada, goes home to resume his commentary on Aristotle's *Poetics*. He has to define tragedy and comedy but, since he has never seen a theatre, he does not know what the terms mean. He equates tragedy with panegyric and comedy with satire and anathemata. He writes that there are fine examples of tragedy in the Koran. Borges is not going to let him get away with that, so he at once vaporizes him and his vivid background; he ends his story by destroying it. And he concludes:

> I felt that Averroes, trying to imagine what a drama is without having suspected what a theatre is, was no more absurd than I, trying to imagine Averroes, with no raw materials but a few scraps of Renan, Lane, and Asín Palacios. I felt, on the last page, that my narrative was a symbol of the man I was while I was writing and that, in order to write that narrative, I had to be that man, and that, in order to be that man, I had to write that narrative, and so on *ad infinitum*.

Very tricky, most devious. The eponym of *El Informe de Brodie* comes across a tribe whose language has no words for artefacts. They help Brodie build a hut, but they have to call the hut a tree. They would have to call a book a tree too. There is an imaginary planet called Tlön which seems to have been designed by Bishop Berkeley: there is no space or time there, only succession, and the language has no nouns in it, since its speakers have no conception of matter independent of their perceptions. Borges makes a number of imaginary places from enforced limits of ideation. When he constructs the Great Library of Babel, on the other hand, it has to be coextensive with the universe, since it contains every possible book, and the books are made, regardless of meaning, out of every possible combination of the letters of the alphabet. This is a slap in the face of the Nominalists, as is the imagined country whose map 'had the Dimensions of the Empire and coincided with it point for point'.

And there is the man with genuinely total recall who wants to write but cannot, since he cannot create logarithms for his memories. To write his biography would require another whole life.

There are characters who move us, situations of detection (with crime as an arithmological structure) which are as well made as anything by Agatha Christie – whose name comes second only to Bishop Berkeley's in the number of nominal allusions in Mr Sturrock's book. There are writings which are like ghost stories or pieces of science fiction, but the shocks, being intellectual, are far more disturbing than anything pure Gothic could contrive. We may, if we are reared on fiction with a 'message', ask why we should read work so blandly labelled by its author as *inutil*. Mr Sturrock gives the answers – delight in intellectual play, wonder, the stimulus of an incredibly creative mind. His book is a methodical survey of Borges's *oeuvre* and a lucid analysis of his metaphysical gamesmanship, but it refuses to satisfy our curiosity about the man himself: the man becomes the author, and the author is defined by his books, which we had better read.

Borges and I, along with my fellow-townsman Alistair Cooke, addressed the Shakespeare Congress in 1975 at Washington DC. He delighted, as was to be expected, in the conjunction of two identical names, saying that he called himself the Burgess of Argentina. This was so I should call myself the Borges of Great Britain, but I would not rise to the temptation, onomastically accurate though the boast would be. At the Argentine Embassy, where there was a reception for him, there were so many listening functionaries about that he and I conversed in Anglo-Saxon. The man is certainly the author. When he is around he creates Borgesian situations.

Taking Canada Seriously

The Rebel Angels, by Robertson Davies

Whatever may be said about the universality of art, literature is a national product and great literature should be held to be a national glory. But the British have built a Commonwealth and are disposed to take pride in an anglophone literature produced anywhere in the world where the mystical unifying power of the British Crown is acknowledged. This means that the British are jealous of the North American achievement in literature south of the Great Lakes and the 49th Parallel and worry about the lack of achievement in the Dominion of Canada. Canada got in early with the colonial novel (her first novelist was a Richardson, but the muse of fiction decreed that there could not be two great Richardsons), but she never produced a Hawthorne or a Mark Twain. The Chicago Nobel Prizeman Saul Bellow was born in Montreal, but unlike the admirable Mordecai Richler, he decided to join the stream of United States Jewish fiction writers. Among Canadian WASP novelists who have remained loyal to the culture of the Commonwealth, Robertson Davies, at the age of sixty-nine, stands out as internationally important and undoubted Nobel material. I hope they are reading his work, and this article, in Stockholm.

Readers of Davies's Deptford Trilogy (*Fifth Business*, *The Manticore* and *World of Wonders*) knew they were in the presence of a sharp intelligence and a well-stocked mind. Perhaps Davies's wit and learning militated against his general acceptance, and those same qualities may limit *The Rebel Angels* to the kind of audience that prefers Nabokov to, say, Michener or Wouk. On the other hand, Davies avoids rarefaction: wit and learning are bonuses added to earthiness and even sexiness. One of the great fictional characters of all time is Mamusia, gipsy mother of Maria Theotoky (heroine and part-narrator of this novel), who restores fiddles by bedding them in manure, foretells the future, scorns book-learning, and laces the coffee of an eligible suitor of her daughter with her daughter's menstrual blood (extracted from a sanitary towel with a garlic-squeezer).

The setting of *The Rebel Angels* is a Canadian university named for St John and the Holy Ghost but called Spook for short. Having learned that Robertson Davies is Master of Massey College in Toronto, prospective readers may groan about university novelists being able to write only university novels. But if one wishes to write about the universe, as Davies does, one may as well choose a place where the universe is studied. The best fiction, I always think, should embrace the gamut between eschatology and scatology, and this is what *The Rebel Angels* does. Perhaps the bequest of John Parlabane ('sometime of the Society of the Sacred Mission') sums it up: 'I leave my arse-hole, and all necessary integument thereto appertaining, to the Faculty of Philosophy; let it be stretched upon a steel frame so that each New Year's Day, the senior professor may blow through it, uttering a rich, fruity note, as my salute to the world of which I now take leave, in search of the Great Perhaps.'

The *grand peut-être* is, of course, Rabelais's, and one of the big themes of the novel is an unpublished manuscript by that master, part of the huge untidy Cornish Bequest, greeted with awe and then stolen. *The Rebel Angels* is in the truest sense of the term Rabelaisian, mixing the taste of food and wine and the rapture of physical love with the equally sharp joys of intellectual inquiry. There is theological speculation too – Maria's surname Theotoky means 'bringer of God' – and this inevitably brings in obverse approaches to the ultimate – blasphemy, heresy, magic, rebel angels.

The most notable of the rebel angels is Brother Parlabane, lecher, sexual invert, disrupter of order, schismatic, a 'shabby monk, his spectacles mended at the temple with electrician's tape'. It is against his predatory interest in her research that Maria has to fight, along with her frank lust for her professor, another rebel angel named Hollier. But away from the university intrigues, which end in murder and suicide, thrums the ground bass of the wisdom of Maria's mother and her uncle Yerko, who live in an old house with *gadjo*, or non-gipsy, lodgers. 'The house stank; a stench all its own pervaded every corner. It was a threnody in the key of Cat major, with . . . modulations of old people, waning lives, and relinquished hopes.' But the gipsy quarters have their own life-enhancing richness, expressed in one of the great feasts of fiction, a Boxing Day dinner with Yerko babbling about Bebby Jesus, whom he has discovered at fifty-eight for the first time at a nativity play put on in New York at the Metropolitan Museum. He believes that the magi brought Gold, Frank Innocence, and Mirth. *Sancta simplicitas*, says Father Darcourt, the guest who drinks the coffee laced with menses.

But Darcourt, though, being Anglican, he is only a priest in a Pickwickian sense, does not marry Maria; or rather he marries her and the heir to the Cornish fortune, who provides a fine apologia for matrimony:

> The sex-hobbyists go on tediously about their preoccupation without ever admitting that it is bound to diminish as time passes. There are people who say that the altar of marriage is not the bed, but the kitchen stove, thereby turning it into a celebration of gluttony. But who ever talks about a lifelong, intimate friendship expressing itself in the broadest possible range of conversation? If people are really alive and alert it ought to go on and on, prolonging life because there is always something more to be said.

The plot is not easily summarized but the meaning of the book is clear: we must learn balance through the intelligent consultation of law and tradition and the equally intelligent use of the inchoate doctrines of the rebel angels. In other words, the work celebrates humanism, not a popular philosophy in an age which prefers the dangers of hubris.

One may ask in what way this wise, profound and joyful book is specifically a piece of Canadian literature. Meeting its author, as I have done, and listening to his urbane cisatlantic eloquence, one may ask in what way he is a Canadian. It is perhaps enough for him to have been born in Ontario and, as a citizen of the Commonwealth, to have felt London and Oxford to be part of his cultural birthright. To live in Canada and learn to be philosophical about its long harsh winters, as about the greater ebullience and guilt south of the Lakes, is with the addition of great literary talent, enough for a Canadian writer. I do not believe there is such a thing as a national literary dialect; I recognize only idiolects and, in the idiolect of Robertson Davies, am aware of a powerful individual voice.

But there is an attitude to life which makes him Canadian. There is none of the suburban whining which marks the contemporary English novel, the sense of being in at the end of things. Nor is there any of the sexual neurosis which disfigures so much of the fiction of the United States. The maturity and balance remind us that Canada is coeval with its southern neighbour; the vivacity is proper to a nation whose future lies all before it. With Robertson Davies the Canadian novel may at last claim to be taken very seriously indeed.

The Last Capote

Music for Chameleons, by Truman Capote

By chance, a copy of the late John Kennedy Toole's novel *A Confederacy of Dunces* got into my hands while I was finishing Mr Capote's latest, and too long awaited, volume of stories and sketches. Both authors were born in New Orleans, still the most interesting city in America, and both have an ear for New Orleans speech. Here is HER, from Capote's 'Hidden Gardens': 'Bastard. Nigger bastard. Fact is, you never had no mother. You was born out of a dog's ass.' Here is Jones in the Toole novel:

'Times changin. You cain scare color peoples no more. I got me some peoples form a human chain in front your door, drive away your business, get you on the TV news. Color people took enough horseshit already, and for twenty dollar a week you ain piling no more on. I getting pretty tire of bein vagran or workin below the minimal wage. Get somebody else run your erran.'

The difference in literary talent cannot well be assessed. Toole committed suicide in 1969 at the age of thirty-two. His mother gave to Walker Percy in 1976 a faint carbon copy of his one novel. Whether he would have produced an *oeuvre* one cannot, of course, say. On the strength of his surviving book he has to be considered a great original comic talent. I will say no more about it for the moment except to affirm its high quality. It is not Mr Capote's fault if its bright light dims his own rococo candles. It is just unfortunate that two New Orleans writers should be published at about the same time, the one a Mississippi pharos untimely doused, the other a bayou *feu follet* that had been flickering intermittently for a long time and so had to be taken for a star.

This volume is fine, OK, good reading. But it is preceded by a foreword which presumes our acceptance of Mr Capote as a major artist who, after early successes and intense struggles with his agonizing métier during a long silence – but not a long withdrawal from public notice – has at last come through to the pared Miltonic style of maturity, with something important to say and a right to the reader's hushed reverence. What Mr Capote believes to be a large innovation, and one that naughty Norman stole from him, is the genre called faction or facfiction, in which reality is treated in the manner of a novel. Reality seems to be necessarily limited to the world of violent crime, as witness 'Handcarved Coffins' in this volume, the best-selling *In Cold Blood* – on whose royalties Mr Capote must mostly have been living since 1966 – and the epigonal *The Executioner's Song*, which Mailer published, to applause and the Pulitzer.

What seems implied in Mr Capote's aesthetic is that journalism is superior to inventive literature because it records life as it is lived, or taken, and because it demands the straight plain style, which is superior to the 'denseness' in which Mr Capote excelled in his early (torrid and luxuriant, as is fitting for Louisiana) work. The fact is that the mere reporting of events is, for one committed to the literary art, a bit of a comedown. You have to believe, because it actually happened. You don't have to enforce the reader's belief through art. 'Handcarved Coffins', the longest piece here, is written mostly in dialogue, and it is a plain account of a series of linked American crimes, whose perpetrator is suspected but never caught. It is excellent journalism, but it needs a prefatory apology from an artist of Capote's proved calibre, not an exordial flourish.

It is not for me to complain about Mr Capote's interest in murderers, or Mr Mailer's for that matter, except to say that the mind of a murderer (treated here in 'Then It All Came Down' – Capote chatting with the multiple killer Robert Beausoleil in San Quentin) is not proper material for the literary man – who, almost by definition, is an amateur in things of the real world – unless he can transmute it into literature. I could not help regarding 'Handcarved Coffins' as admirable material for Conan Doyle: it cries out for the handcarving of high craft and sometimes it almost gets it, but then Mr Capote remembers his purely reporting mission.

In 'Derring-do' Mr Capote recounts his narrow escape from San Diego, whose sheriff had a warrant for his arrest for evading a subpoena order. He was to give evidence in the Beausoleil retrial, but he had promised the killer not to make any of their conversation public. At Los Angeles airport, whence he proposes flying to New York, he spots tough guys with snap-brim hats watching for him, but he is lucky enough to spot Pearl Bailey also and, disguised as one of her chorus boys, get on the plane unrecognized and make his getaway. Here we are, I think, supposed to admire Mr Capote himself, keeper of his word to a murderer, theatrical associate of Miss Bailey as well as friend, artist capable of real-life adventures in the Hemingway manner. Mr Capote the writer is not terribly important here.

This is the trouble with Capote's long literary silence – abortively near-broken with *Answered Prayers*, a syndrome of his situation – and his fame as one who, having written well, deserved the friendship of the great and, having written profitably, was able to travel the world. The glittering vicissitudes have to be used in his writing, but the result is autobiographical glamour rather than art. On the other hand, there is little here that one reads without pleasure, and some of the 'Conversational Portraits' are small gems. In one of them – 'A Day's Work' – Capote goes round with Mary Sanchez, a cleaning woman or lady, from apartment to apartment. He smokes her roaches but does not seem to help with the chores. At the end of the day they enter a church, and Mary prays for all her employers. T.C. says: 'I'm praying for you, Mary. I want you to live forever.' It is the sentimental touch which makes 'Moon River' a not inapposite theme-song for the film of *Breakfast at Tiffany's*. Another 'portrait' – 'Hello, Stranger' – is an altogether admirable story about a man who is near-ruined because he finds a message from a teenage girl in a floating bottle, answers the message, and is betrayed by his own concerned innocence. But the story has to be told in the Four Seasons Restaurant (whose rack of lamb last December was distressingly tough), to show how Capote goes only to the best places.

The title story is about an aristocratic lady of Martinique whose piano-playing attracts the chameleons. It is a pretty idea, and it makes a pretty title, but the big thing is that it is true. It also enables us to see the suave Capote, traveller, who had a good friend murdered in Fort de France, drinking 'iced mint tea slightly flavored with absinthe'. Truman Capote became his own best piece of art.

Life after Murder

A Confederacy of Dunces, by John Kennedy Toole

I don't know whether this novel bore that title while Toole was hawking it round the publishing houses of New York. Nobody wanted it. I like to think that, when he had recorded the final rejection (from, I understand, the biggest of the publishing mavins), he reread these words of Swift: 'When a true genius appears in the world, you may know him by this sign, that the dunces are all in confederacy against him.' There was his title ready made, but it now had a privier relevance than to anything contained in the battered typescript. Toole, in despair, killed himself. This was in 1969, and he was only thirty-two.

In 1976 Toole's mother delivered 'a badly smeared, scarcely readable carbon' to Walker Percy, who was teaching at Loyola. Percy read it with reluctance, 'then with a prickle of interest, then a growing excitement, and finally an incredulity: surely it was not possible that it was so good.' It was and is possible: it is very good, and those publishers were egregious dunces. Even with Percy's raves, it seems that it was not possible for the commercial houses to change their minds. The book was published by a scholarly press – that of Louisiana State University at Baton Rouge. I know nothing of its adventures in Britain before achieving publication with Allen Lane. I can only say I am glad the British are at last permitted to read it.

Toole was a New Orleans man, and his book is a picaresque tale about his city. It has a mad knightly figure as hero, the fat and flatulent Ignatius Reilly, devoted to junk food and Boethius but to nothing else. He lies in bed in a flannel nightshirt, living off his mother's welfare cheques, but occasionally goes out to batter the modern world. He even gets jobs, but he ruins the firms. As a hot-dog vendor he eats up the stock. He goes to cinemas to jeer loudly at the films. He hates homosexuals but has no noticeable heterosexual drive. Things have gone bad with the world since *The Consolations of Philosophy*. 'With the breakdown of the Medieval system, the gods of Chaos, Lunacy, and Bad Taste gained ascendancy,' he writes on one of his Big Chief tablets.

One of the exemplars of the world's degeneracy is the Night of Joy bar on Bourbon Street. This is run by Lana Lee, who sells nude pictures of herself to schoolkids. She likes to have them taken with a few classy scholarly accoutrements – a stick of chalk, a blackboard, a globe. Some day she must find her a book someplace. The book she eventually finds is Ignatius's lost *De Consolatione Philosophiae*. When Ignatius chances to see, on his hot-dog round, the photograph of a poor scholarly woman reduced to earning her bread in the nude, his sympathy and rage find patristic expression. Everything comes together in the Night of Joy bar – Aquinas and striptease, Abelard and Patrolman Mancuso, whose mufti, on sergeant's orders, is ballet tights and a yellow sweater. At this same bar works Jones, a black with dark glasses hidden in a Cloud of Unknowing smelling of pot or twitch fires.

He comes for a job. 'A po-lice gimme a reference. He tell me I better get my ass gainfully employ. . . . I thought maybe the Night of Joy like to help somebody become a member of the community help keep a poor color boy outta jail. I keep the picket off, the Night of Joy a good civil right ratin.' Lana Lee sees this as a present left on her doorstep. 'A colored guy who would get arrested for vagrancy if he didn't work.' Twenty dollars a week, but Jones has to take it. 'I come in regular, anything keep my ass away from a po-lice for a few hour. Where you keep them motherfucking broom?' Lana says: 'One thing we gotta understand is keeping our mouth clean around here,' to which Jones replies: 'Yes, *ma'am*. I sure don wanna make a bad impressia in a fine place like the Night of Joy. Whoa!'

This is the kind of book one wants to keep quoting from. I could, with keen pleasure, copy all of Jones's dialogue out and then get down to the other characters. Apart from being a fine funny novel (but also comic in the wider sense, like *Gargantua* or *Ulysses*), this is a classic compendium of Louisiana speech. What evidently fascinated Toole (a genuine scholar, MA Columbia and so on) about his own town was something that A. J. Liebling noted in his *The Earl of Louisiana*: the existence of a New Orleans city accent close to the old Al Smith tonality, 'extinct in Manhattan', living alongside a plantation dialect which cried out for accurate recording. At the same time Liebling emphasized the not-quite-American qualities of New Orleans, fascinating to any visitor but never, before Toole, properly exploited in literature. 'The Mediterranean, Caribbean and Gulf of Mexico form a homogeneous, though interrupted, sea.' New Orleans, we see at last, needed a novel like this, but apparently the New York publishers didn't.

But the genius of the book lies in its election as main character of a broken-down but terribly vigorous maverick who, seeming to be an invader in a space ship from Galaxy G F9's version of the Middle Ages, is in fact a true, if only inventable, product of a Catholic culture, where old France lives a ghost existence (real absinthe, real coffee), jazz combines the primitive and the ultra-sophisticated, the *haute cuisine* mingles its scents with the acrid reek of the hot-dog stand, and the eccentricities of an Ignatius Reilly merit the madhouse only because his momma thinks it kinda a good idea to hand her son over to care and protection. But Ignatius gets away. A girl gets him off to New York. In a hurry. 'My mother may return with her mob,' cries Ignatius. 'You should see them. White supremacists, Protestants, or worse. Let me get my lute and trumpet. Are the tablets gathered together?' ('Gems of nihilism,' comments Myrna, flipping through the sheets of a Big Chief.)

Let's give the last word to Jones, who loses his job at the Night of Joy after Patrolman Mancuso's raid on it. A bar friend says 'Things can always be worse off,' and Jones says: 'Yeah. You can say that, man. You got you a little business, got you a son teachin school probly got him a bobby-cue set, Buick, air condition, TV. Whoa! I ain even got me a transmitter radio. Night of Joy salary keepin peoples below the air-condition level.' Jones forms a Cloud of Knowing round himself. 'But you right in a way there, Watson. Things maybe worse off. Maybe I be that fat mother. Whoa! Whatever gonna happen to somebody like that? Hey!' But Toole didn't live to write about the fat mother in New York.

Wicked Mother Russia

The Radiant Future, by Alexander Zinoviev, translated by Gordon Clough

About twenty years ago I translated, for the money, such as it was, a rather inferior French novel and dared to improve it by a tarting up of trope and image. I glumly read reviews which praised, in their ignorance of the original, these additions as typical of French genius and the sort of thing that British novelists could not do. Since then I have been dubious about trying to assess translations without access to the original. I think it is probably safe, however, to judge Zinoviev through Mr Clough's version, since we are more concerned with ideas than with style, structure, personages and the regular content of fiction. I have no doubt that non-Russophones will rejoice, as so many rejoiced over *The Yawning Heights*, to find yet another fearless exposé of the Soviet system from one who has suffered from it. We all love horse's-mouth confirmations of our prejudices. I must confess, in my naiveté, that I get something of a sour taste after reading such nest-bemerdings as *The Radiant Future*. I have been to Russia and think I like the Russian people. The impression one gets with so many émigré attacks on the system is that there is nothing left in Russia but the KGB and the self-serving functionaries, along with a shortage of toilet rolls and an excess of potato blight. We're getting a lot of the hard-hitting heroic stuff but not much about the lives of the people. Zinoviev was one of the Soviet Union's leading philosophers till Brezhnev revoked his citizenship, and his quasi-novel is about the tribulations of a Soviet philosopher. I should like a streetsweeper to defect and write a novel about the tribulations of streetsweepers.

Inevitably this book is compared in the blurb to *Animal Farm* and *Nineteen Eighty-Four*, masterpieces which it in no way resembles. No Russian defector has yet come within a hundred versts of the imaginative power of Orwell. Orwell's greatness lay in his capacity to encapsulate certain political truths in homemade myths. Zinoviev merely tells us what has been going on, and what has been going on we already know. On the level of subsistence, nothing can touch Winston Smith's vivid if vague sense of having been cheated – with wretched canteen stew, abrasive soap, bad cigarettes and a shortage of razor blades. On the mental and spiritual levels Orwell went too far. He posited an oligarchy of brilliant creative intelligence, dedicated to the systematic exploitation of ignorance and bodily fear. We knew, from our experience of the socialism under which Orwell wrote, that Ingsoc, or Sovietism, would not be quite like that. The trouble with the Russia which Zinoviev has left behind is dullness more than terror, the victory of mediocrity and the fear of intelligence. It is the greyness which Zinoviev catches, but it is no revelation.

He imagines a 'great permanent slogan' erected in Moscow 'where the Avenue of Marxism–Leninism meets Cosmonaut Square.' It says LONG LIVE COMMUNISM – THE RADIANT FUTURE OF ALL MANKIND! This monolithic structure, very shoddily made, soon becomes a rendez-vous for whores, pushers and meths drinkers. In an apartment near to it lives the Head of the Department of Theoretical Problems of the Methodology of Scientific Communism, the narrator of the story. What we must expect to see, having been given this collocation, is an erosion of the protagonist's own ideological monolith. Orwell would not have stooped to such obvious symbolism. What is heartening about the erosion is the number of intellectual termites prepared to nibble, from our hero's own children to his friend Anton. Whatever Sovietism has suppressed, it does not include the sharp dialectic of the young. The mediocre professor, deprived by new doubts of his old single-minded ability to climb through betrayal of his colleagues, fails to be elected to the Academy. The situation, when you come to think of it, is not very different from that of freer societies – certain universities in England and France, for instance, which had better be nameless.

Soviet Russia, as Zinoviev presents it, is a typical modern state in its proliferation of bureaucrats, or of professors anxious only for tenure. Solzhenitsyn is presented not as the outrageous voice of freedom so much as the man of talent who shows up the mediocrities and hence has to be expelled. Mediocrity is rewarded and is able to afford to build the alternative Russian society, which is hyperbolically consumerist and, in the madness of things, the conceivable custodian of all that is most valuable in the West. Well, at least a taste for good food and wine, the higher pornography, jewels and mink, no cheating of the senses anyway. And no guilt about privilege either, since this is one of the end-products of a democratic revolution.

There are some very good things in this book, though there is nothing specifically novelistic about them. If there is a lack of dramatic action, there is no shortage of people sitting down to say things like 'Every nation has a certain coefficient of productivity. That is a characteristic of its historical individuality. Take the Germans: almost every German individually is stupid and blinkered. But collectively they are a nation of geniuses. Almost every Russian taken individually is a Lomonosov. But collectively we are glaringly mediocre' and 'The Revolution, the Civil War, collectivisation, the innumerable purges, the Second World War, they have all shattered Russia as a nation. Russia ceased to exist long ago, and will never exist again.' Unfortunately you cannot make a work of fiction out of good sayings alone. I fear there will be a tendency among reviewers of this book to praise it for qualities that don't matter a damn in a novel. Solzhenitsyn has been adored for the same reasons that may elevate Zinoviev into a literary giant.

Ironically, the novel seems to get really started on the last page, when the protagonist faces his failure.

> I stood for a while in the square, and then retraced my steps. I have begun
> to drag one leg a little. And my heart troubles me from time to time. But
> that's of no matter. It's the attacks of constipation that are the worst.
> Those old piles. God knows! Here we are, flying to the moon. People say
> they can cure cancer now. But they still can't cope with these miserable
> piles!

Novels are made out of piles more than dialectic. What a beginning that
ending would have made.

Red Conversion

The Turn-Around, by Vladimir Volkoff, translated from the French by
Alan Sheridan

I saw copies of *Le Retournement* around in 1979. I even dipped into
somebody's copy and was put off by what seemed to me to be very
convoluted prose. The French felt differently and bought 230,000
copies. *Le Matin* said: 'Without doubt the most astonishing book of the
season . . . in truth one of the strangest of these past fifteen years' (why
this numerical exactitude, my old? What of strange appeared in 1964?).
Europe I spoke of 'the intrusion of God into a novel of espionage', which
may or may not have been intended as a recommendation. The novel
has now been translated into fifteen languages. Of its author *Newsweek*
says: 'Some critics speak of him as a latter-day Dostoevsky. Others call
him a new Graham Greene and the French answer to John Le Carré –
only better.' The novel is dedicated to Greene. As in Dostoevsky there
are God and ikons and Pauline conversion. Like Le Carré Volkoff
deals with the ineptitudes, wranglings and internecine betrayals of the

Intelligence Service. In fact he is nothing like any of them. If he tries to resemble anyone at all it is that other xenophone Vladimir, who despised Greene, Dostoevsky and popular espionage fiction.

The translation is sound and it conveys the clotted arthritic movement of the original, a tempo that Nabokov made tolerable because he was a great poet. Here is the hand of Marina Kraievsky:

> Her hand was small and chubby; it was fleshy and fineboned; the three middle fingers were rather too short, the little finger and thumb rather too long: this gave her hand a rounded effect, so that when seen from the front it resembled her face, whose little, flattened-out sister it might have been – a satellite, endowed with its own luminosity, the hand-version of a common subject whose face was the face-version. Each of our cells, they say, contains our whole body in *in potentia*: in Marina, this microcosmic homogeneity was evident at a glance.

As you can see, such a style is not in the service of swift narration, yet the genre to which the novel belongs is supposed to be cinematic in speed, laconic in description. But that is an aspect of M. Volkoff's trickery. He seems to be telling a spy story, but his real aim is to retell the tale of Saul's being stricken blind on the road to Damascus. The novel is a kind of sacrament, if you like – bestseller dry bread as the accident of a shining theophany.

Lieutenant Volsky, a Franco-Russian like his creator, is in the Army Reserve and seconded to French Intelligence. Asked by his superior officer what he is on at the moment, he dare not say *nothing* so he invents an operation called Culverin. The aim of this is to get the new counsellor at the Soviet Embassy to join the French side. This man, Popov, is a major in the KGB and the officer who controls a high agent called Crocodile. Marina Kraievsky, a Franco-Russian actress, is persuaded to try to seduce Popova at some danger to herself, since the major's sexual mores are known to be extravagant and even lethal. She does not seduce him, but God or Bog does. Making a professional rendezvous at a Russian Orthodox church, Popov finds himself able to reconcile his godless career with a search for the ultimate, since the Leninist dialectic forbids stasis. So he explains things to himself; in fact, he undergoes a genuine Pauline turn-around, makes his confession (at great and fully reported length) and receives communion. The French now have him in a way they never expected, but because of problems of compartmentalization – Popov somewhat confusingly overlaps with an operation called Greek Fire – he has to be eliminated. His messy death I find implausible, but M. Volkoff apparently sees it as necessary to his structure.

One might expect such a story to be disfigured with piety, but M. Volkoff is a cool French intellectual and will not admit conventional sentimental religiosity. What evidently appealed to the French in the book was the piquancy of reading a spy novel that was also a highly cerebral experience. But French cerebrality goes along with French sensuousness, and that means particularity, the notation of sense data, often at some length. Popular spy fiction, when you come to think of it, is not sensuous at all (we take for granted that it is not intellectual). There are plenty of machines, lovingly described, but machines are generalizations. Their handlers tend to be generalizations too. *Chez* Volkoff love is reserved to pigments, rain, sensations of cold and dirt, smells and flavours. Mother Russia is mainly a gustatory reminiscence to her exiles – native caviar (though Paris prefers Iranian) and black bread with a taste of the earth.

The story is told by Lieutenant Volsky himself, aided by magnetic tapes and his own imagination. To equip a functionary of French Intelligence with the skills of a not quite Nabokovian novelist may seem implausible, but Volsky has literary ambitions and so have many of his colleagues, and he refers to intelligence operatives as 'novelists' – meaning men who see an operation as a closed and shapely structure, try to control their personages but don't always succeed, and use imaginative insight to fill in gaps. At the same time Volsky or Volkoff is obsessed – quite in the Le Carré manner – with administrative exactitude, often to the extremes of tedium – form-filling, file-falsifying, and the disposition of petty cash. You can see what French reviewers meant by 'strangeness'.

But to bring theology into a spy novel is not quite so strange as *Europe I* seemed to think. It was done a long time ago by Chesterton, and Volkoff seems to have read a novel of my own called *Un agent qui vous veut du bien*. If we take the genre more seriously than, frankly, it deserves, we can only flesh it out with political philosophy, which leads to Manicheism – an eternal war in the heavens of which cold war is a copy – and, in the last analysis, the enigmatic God whom Popov finds in a garage converted to a church.

The Winds of Chelsea

Neighbouring Lives: A Novel, by Thomas M. Disch and Charles Naylor

Chelsea is a London borough built on the north bank of the Thames. Sir Thomas More lived there, and those who have seen the film of Bolt's play *A Man For All Seasons* may have retained a veracious image of rural green, river taxis and the tinkle of cowbells. It ceased to be an appendage of the city and became London's artistic, even genteelly bohemian, *quartier*. More recently its King's Road turned into the centre of gaudy youthful fashion and the ancient pubs were loud with rock. In the later days of the reign of William IV, when this novel begins, it was ready to become a fashionable residential area for the lettered but not for the rich, who clustered mostly round Belgrave Square. It was Thomas Carlyle, known as the Sage of Chelsea, who helped to initiate its seedy distinction. The book starts with the arrival of the great Scot, poisoned (as they used to say) with constipation and porridge, and his wife Jane at Cheyne Walk in 1834. A work more scholarly than genuinely fictional, *Neighbouring Lives* keeps the Carlyles at its centre, but it introduces us also to Leigh Hunt, John Stuart Mill, Browning, the Pre-Raphaelites, others, all of whom either lived in the area or, drawn by the dyspeptic Sage, came for a visit. Even Chopin came for an hour or so, visibly dying but deigning to demonstrate that Mrs Carlyle's piano was out of tune.

Samuel Butler once said: 'How good of God to make Mr Carlyle marry Mrs Carlyle, thus making two people unhappy instead of four.' It is not in the nature of this novel (and, incidentally, how do *two* people write a novel? I look forward sometime to a Disch–Naylor disclosure of procedure. If collaboration makes the writing of fiction quicker and easier, why then, teach me how to collaborate. And, of course, somebody else) to dig into the sexual lives of the Carlyles. Tom is something of a tyrant, as well as a martyr to his Aryan herology and the convolutions of his craft, but the sweet intelligent Jane is only conventionally submissive. Her letters survive, and are drawn on, to show a bright gossipy talent. It does not seem too bad a life, if we think of Leigh Hunt's disastrous ménage, the mess of Rossetti's amours, and the prolonged adultery of John Stuart Mill. It is in connection with what the latter allowed to be done with the first part of Carlyle's *French Revolution* that I have vague doubts about the exactness of Disch–Naylor's scholarship. The manuscripts are represented as having been burnt to a crisp. The authorities I have consulted inform me that Mill's cook used them as pie-bottoms.

As, in some Broadway musical, we notice the libretto delicately moving towards some show-stopping song, so here, with Leigh Hunt sharing the Carlyles' supper porridge and learning that Jane can also be Janie, Jeanie and Jenny, we prepare ourselves for the only good poem that poor Hunt wrote: 'Jenny kissed me when we met'. She did, or does, too. Hunt, grey, ill, dying, a failure, is saluted affectionately by Jane, and the show stops for that song. The whole Hunt episode is well done, though the family squalor is a little underplayed. Indeed, the squalor generally is subdued as in deference to modern American susceptibilities. I remember Tietjens's outburst in *Parade's End*: 'I tell you it revolts me to think of that obese, oily man who never took a bath, in a grease-spotted dressing-gown and the underclothes he's slept in, standing beside a five-shilling model with crimped hair . . . gazing into a mirror that reflects their fetid selves and gilt sunfish and drop chandeliers and plates sickening with cold bacon fat and gurgling about passion.' That, of course, is Rossetti.

Messrs Disch and Naylor are in love with the Victorian age, and they are right, but their love is of a kind that blots out the grosser blemishes of the beloved. Theirs is a very bland book. If we want the wretched filthy London which was the background to Carlyle's thunderings and the neo-realism of the Pre-Raphaelites, we must go to Dickens, who does not visit Chelsea, or, in modern fiction, to John Fowles's *The French Lieutenant's Woman*. The very devotion which they expend on their multiple subject matter makes for a reluctance to move on, clip, slash, subordinate detail to the élan of true fiction. But true fiction is what this book is not – though novelizing real people does not obviate the urgency of the fictional method in the hands of genuine novelists. Messrs Disch and Naylor are concerned with giving us a kind of painless history lesson, with a unification of place rather than of plot. Some of us prefer to get our history straight.

Still, there are things here we are glad to have. Carlyle comes, with the silent but ironically smiling Jane, to see Hunt's new picture – Holman, not Leigh. He shakes his stick at *The Light of the World*. '. . . This – this Christ! It is naught but inane *Grimmsmärchen* make-believe and untruth, the which to fabricate and bring-to-view is a heinous occupation for a painter who would respect his own soul.' Carlyle is the most caricaturable of our great writers; wisely, Disch and Naylor let him caricature himself. But, hearing his costive borborygms, we can't help wishing for a copy of the long-out-of-print *Don't, Mr Disraeli*, by Brahms and Simon, in which the comic potentialities of the whole Victorian scene are unblushingly exploited. Morris, Rossetti and Burne-Jones drinking beer in Cremorne Gardens, Swinburne visiting George Meredith, Lewis Carroll and his Alice – a minimal change of approach, and they could all be hilarious. All we are permitted is an affectionate smile:

The atmosphere today was that of spring. Swinburne could almost feel the altered tilt of the earth under his feet – though, in truth, the difficulty was rather to be attributed to the ill-laid pavement under foot and the glass of wine he'd taken with his lunch. Shopfronts fairly whirled before him; clouds hurtled by in the contrary direction. *Such* a gusting wind: already it had taken his hat, but no matter, one could enjoy the wind more without it. And here, already, was Hobury Street.

And Swinburne is only here because Hobury Street is in Chelsea.

This is a substantial book. When we come to the end, with Miss Jo Hoffernan saying goodbye to Chelsea and offering her beauty to Monsieur Courbet, an inferior painter to Jimmy Whistler but more reliable as a man, we have a final glimpse of the Sage. He already belongs to another era. In 1867 we are preparing for the modernity of which Whistler is a portent. It is evidence of the skill of the duumvirate that they should be able to present both the movement of history and the changelessness symbolized by London's river. Impressionism and aestheticism may be coming, but the ageing Carlyle is further ahead of his time than Wilde: he will be the final reading of Hitler and Goebbels in the Berlin bunker. And west of Cheyne Row, just by Battersea Bridge and the same residential block as Whistler, the great Turner lived, the most modern painter of them all. This book is a fine tribute to that most creative region of London, and it is an admirable rendering of its most creative time. It is not, however, a novel, except in a Pickwickian sense.

Irish Hero

Tom Moore, by Terence de Vere White

William Hazlitt thought little of Moore's *Irish Melodies*:

If these national airs do indeed express the soul of impassioned feeling in his countrymen, the case of Ireland is hopeless. If these prettinesses pass for patriotism, if a country can hear from its heart's core only these vapid, varnished sentiments, lip-deep, and let its tears of blood evaporate in an empty conceit, let it be governed as it has been. There are here no tones to waken Liberty, to console Humanity. Mr Moore converts the wild harp of Erin into a musical snuff-box.'

True, and yet not true. Hazlitt, like so many English men of letters, had no feeling for music: his other art was painting. He saw Moore's verses on the printed page and found too much missing. What was missing, of course, was the animating tune. That Moore, despite Hazlitt's strictures, knew precisely what he was doing is attested by his undying popularity. Every anglophone alive knows at least twenty lines of Moore by heart. As for Ireland, she has Yeats, but Tom Moore is still her national poet.

Moore's prophetic ear heard Yeats reciting his own poetry – intoning and moaning ridiculously as though he were Ossian. He noted that poets with no musical ear tried to bring an inept substitute for music to the lyric chanted as opposed to *chanté*. Yeats heard nothing in Moore. Joyce heard much, but, like Moore, he was a light tenor who could play his own accompaniments. If Yeats wrote words for music perhaps (perhaps meaning not at all), *Chamber Music*, like the *Irish Melodies*, is very little without tunes. Moore had pre-empted the best Irish tunes, which Joyce would have been glad of; all he could do was to dream-distort those tunes, and Moore's words, in *Finnegans Wake*:

> If you met on the binge a poor acheseyeld from Ailing,
> when the tune of his tremble shook shimmy on shin,
> while his countrary raged in the weak of his wailing,
> like a rugilant pugilant Lyon O'Lynn. . . .

In one of his letters to his bass son Giorgio, Joyce sets out an admirable Moore programme, with sensible hints as to how the songs should be sung. He also, through Stephen Dedalus, resents the Dublin statue of Moore:

> He looked at it without anger; for, although sloth of the body and of the soul crept over it like unseen vermin, over the shuffling feet and up the folds of the cloak and around the servile head, it seemed conscious of its indignity. It was a Firbolg in the borrowed cloak of a Milesian . . .

The Dublin Corporation had placed the statue above the city's largest public urinal. Leopold Bloom thinks this appropriate: 'Meeting of the waters. Ought to be places for women. Running into cake shops.'

Any singer of Moore's songs – and this means anybody who has ever been on a works outing or in a pub with a piano – knows how singable they are, and if he does not suspect how skilful, that is precisely what Moore intended. The near-banalities, the tarnished elegances, are deliberate, since the meanings must not obtrude overmuch, but there is often a tiny epigrammatic felicity:

> Then awake! – till rise of sun, my dear,
> The Sage's glass we'll shun, my dear,
>> Or in watching the flight
>> Of bodies of light
> He might happen to take thee for one, my dear!

This, from 'The Young May Moon', has to be heard, not just looked at. The prosodic cunning can only be taken in when the song is sung, since to Moore the music always came first. The lyric beginning 'Believe me, if all these endearing young charms' has as its fifth line in the first stanza 'Thou wouldst still be adored, as this moment thou art'; the fifth line in the second stanza is 'No, the heart that has truly loved never forgets'. 'Adored, as' is weighty, the junction of two phrases. When we come to the repetition of the musical passage, we expect also a repetition of the verbal pattern, but instead we get the considerable force of 'truly': without benefit of marked sforzando, it soars and descends a fourth to 'loves' with an impact that mere recitation could never achieve. This same song ends with one of Moore's delicate, almost apologetic, altogether satisfying similes:

> No, the heart that has truly loved never forgets,
> But as truly loves on to the close,
> As the sun-flower turns on her god when he sets,
> The same look which she turn'd when he rose.

Hector Berlioz, who had received this song as well as kisses from the lips of the great Patti, thought that Moore had achieved something here that Shakespeare had missed. Shakespeare, it may be added, missed all the way to capture the pub singer's ear. We may sing Ben Jonson at closing time, but never 'Take O take those lips away'. Nobody seems to understand what Shakespeare's lyrics are getting at. Moore always hits.

He hits softly. Hazlitt wanted Moore to shout out words of Irish defiance in London drawing rooms (and thus, as Hazlitt sometimes was, be thrown out), but Moore's way was one of delicate insinuation so far as the inflammatory libertarian themes were concerned. As Terence de Vere White says, 'The tocsin does not sound in *The Minstrel Boy*, or if it does, not so loud as to shake the teacups; but it was a considerable achievement to have brought Ireland's story into those London lives.' On the other hand, 'Let Erin Remember', made Emmet wish he were at the head of twenty thousand marching men. The Irish Government, despite the persuasions of Professor W. T. Trench, refused to adopt this as the Free State's national anthem: one may set up a statue over a urinal, but one must not allow a poet to write the official songs of the people.

Mr de Vere White's biography presents a lively enough picture of the Milesian Firbolg. Firbolg means 'man of the bag or belly' and denotes the first inhabitants of Ireland, a kind of dark dwarf. Moore was five feet and looked more boyish than dwarfish, not handsome but very animated, anxious – as a salon singer and a popular poet – to please, but not as servile as the urinal statue suggests. He was concerned about his own, as well as Ireland's, honour. He read Jeffrey's raking of his *Epistles, Odes and Other Poems* in the *Edinburgh Review* ('He may be seen in every page running round the paltry circle of his seductions with incredible zeal and anxiety, and stimulating his jaded fancy for new images of impurity') and challenged his critic to a duel. While waiting for the pistols to be loaded, the two men became friends. It was not possible to dislike Moore, and Moore, though he did his best, found disliking difficult. For all that, he had a certain scurrilous skill in satire. Leigh Hunt skimpolishly wrote a holier-than-thou book on the dead Byron, blaming Moore for accepting Byron's manuscript *Memoirs*, and Moore replied with '*The Living Dog and the Dead Lion*':

Nay, fed as he was (and this makes a *dark* case)
With sops every day from the Lion's own pan,
He lifts up a leg at the noble beast's carcase,
And does all a dog so diminutive can.

However, the book's a good book, being rich in
Examples and warnings to Lions high-bred,
How they suffer small mongrelly curs in the kitchen,
Who'll feed on them living, and foul them when dead.

Moore's association with Byron, which began with a note on the abortive duel in *English Bards and Scotch Reviewers*, seemed to some fitting: both poets had a reputation (more deserved in the greater poet) for stimulating jaded fancy with new images of impurity. Moore certainly went further in his occasional verse than the new post-Jacobin temper of bourgeois England considered proper. In staid Norfolk, Virginia, he addressed the wife of the British consul thus:

But oh! 'twould ruin saints to see
Those tresses thus, unbound and free,
Adown your shoulders sweeping;
They put *such thoughts* into one's head,
Of deshabillé, and night and bed,
And – anything but sleeping!

His long poem *The Loves of the Angels*, whose theme sounds safe enough in the Book of Enoch (the angels of the Lord becoming enamoured of the daughters of men) caused rumblings about irreverence and impiety in *Blackwood's* and elsewhere, so that the author, frightened, thought of making the angels Turkish and turning God into Allah. This would have brought the mythology into line with that of *Lalla Rookh*, in which only the *British Lady's Magazine* found 'immorality, impiety and voluptuous vice'.

Nobody reads *Lalla Rookh* today (though I seem to remember a Hollywood film whose highbrow hero named his yacht for it), but everybody read it in 1817. Edgar Allan Poe, who had something of Moore in him, said that Moore was the most popular poet in the world. The Czar of all the Russias and his Czarina took part in a stage adaptation of it; it was read, so Henry Luttrell reported, in those Mussulman regions best qualified to judge of its scenic authenticity:

> I'm told, dear Moore, your lays are sung
> (Can it be true, you lucky man?)
> By moonlight in the Persian tongue,
> Along the streets of Ispahan.

Stendhal read it at least three times. The author made thousands out of it, but he had no delusions about the real location of his talent: '. . . In a race into future time (if *anything* of mine could pretend to such a run), those little ponies, the 'Melodies' will beat the mare, *Lalla Rookh*, hollow.' *Hollow* is the just word: *Lalla Rookh* was laboriously put together out of books in big libraries. Moore, like many men of auditory talent, did not have all that much interest in the external world. He made appropriately ecstatic noises when confronted with Mont Blanc, but his work shows few signs of keen observation (even that sunflower image seems not to derive from looking around gardens), and the Grand Tour (again he made the right noises) was his most easterly trip.

He was, in fact, precisely what he does not seem to be in the legends of his drawing-room triumphs and the easy rhythms of his songs – a very bookish person. He was, despite an apparent irresponsibility that was really absent-mindedness (he would regularly turn up at the wrong house for dinner: he was never disabused by his hosts, a tribute to his qualities as a guest), the right sort of person to entrust with a *History of Ireland* or a biography of Sheridan. Mr de Vere White thinks his life of Byron is the best biography since James Boswell. His prose style is firm and elegant; he marshals facts sternly. His early *Letter to the Roman Catholics of Dublin* is lucid and bold, condemning the Irish for sinking 'so low in ecclesiastical vassalage as to place their whole hierarchy at the disposal of the Roman Court'. He married a Protestant girl whom he loved, but his Catholicism was less nominal than, say, Ernest Hemingway's. Although he earned his money from infidel London, he died in the faith.

He died also an Irish hero. His visits to Ireland were marked by popular enthusiasm of a kind never before, nor since, accorded to a poet. As Mr de Vere White says, Yeats's Nobel award was followed by a quiet dinner in the Shelbourne. When Moore attended the theatre, the rising of the curtain was always held up until he had spoken a few words. Yeats is without doubt the greater poet, but the ability to speak to all hearts in song – on the levels of mystical patriotism, romantic velleity, wholesome family emotion, and always memorably and elegantly – denotes a kind of greatness that may be extra-literary; but what then does *literary* mean?

Mr de Vere White's biography performs a service not before performed in books on Moore. He demolishes the base charges levelled at the poet after his death by John Wilson Croker, who spoke of Moore's 'delirium tremens of morbid vanity' and cast doubts on his marital fidelity. The whole book is an informative, witty and affectionate tribute from one Dublin literary man to another. Ireland's troubles are seen grumbling in the background of the elegant Whig dinners, but the English reader may salve his conscience once more by reflecting that, without the imposition of the Saxon tongue on a Gaelic people, there would have been none of the literature which has been the Irishman's blazing medium of resentment and defiance, as well as, against Ireland's rebellious will, uniting the wronger and the wronged. Moore may be a minor part of that literature, but those who sing him are not much concerned about an Anglo-Irish aesthetic hierarchy.

All Too Irish

The Pleasures of Gaelic Poetry, edited by Seán Mac Réamoinn

Like most people with Irish blood I have at times started to try to learn Gaelic but, for various reasons, soon given up. The best-known primer in England has sentences like 'The priest has tied a string to the left crubeen of the pig', not very useful over champagne cocktails in the Shelbourne. The phonetic notations in the most recent book published in Dublin don't seem to accord with what people actually say. The spelling is a nightmare – too many phonemes chasing too few letters – and even the reformed orthography of 1948 – which simplifies *claoidim* to *cloím* and *tosnughadh* to *tosnú* – is no real help. The ebullient and erudite editor of this book of essays tells me that the spelling is logical, but I am not yet convinced. I once married into Wales and saw logic enough in written Cymric, but Irish Celtic defeats me. There is a character in H. G. Wells's *Soul of a Bishop* who suggests that the anger of the Fenians had something to do with their difficulties with their native language. That goes too far perhaps; I can speak only of my quite disinterested frustration.

To learn the Gaelic tongue, whether of Scotland or Ireland, in order to converse in it has more to do with the claims of nationalism and romantic atavism than with communicative need. The Scots and Irish speak English. But there is the matter of a great literature, ancient and modern, which cries out to be read in the original. Seamus Heaney, in his fine essay on early Irish nature poems, talks of their 'cleanliness of line . . . the tang and clarity of a pristine world full of woods and water and birdsong'. *Rorúad ráth,/ ro-cleth cruth,/ ro-gab gnáth/ gingrann guth* is clearly not adequately rendered by 'Fern clumps redden/ shapes are hidden/ wildgeese raise/ wonted cries'. The wordplay is not there, the chime of trill and velar plosive, light high vowel, dark low one. Mr Mac Réamoinn might consider bringing out a near-scholarly apparatus which breaks up some of the poems in this present book into morphemes and phonemes, showing accurately how they sound and function. In a little book I published some years ago, *Language Made Plain*, I did this with a Welsh poem. It's not a way into using the language but it helps an understanding of the way it works.

We've all heard of *The Midnight Court*, and some of us have read it in translation (Lord Longford, Frank O'Connor, David Marcus, even, partly, Brendan Behan). Cosslett Ó Cuinn's essay on the masterwork is an essential introduction to those who haven't tackled it, but it saddens by telling us what we're missing by not knowing an Irish in which 'the words are really winged, shooting out in parabolas in all directions like tracer bullets'. The vitality of the original, which, alas, we have to accept on trust, is attested by an oral and manuscript life which lasted for a hundred and twenty years before it got into print. 'The Irish Censorship Board,' Mr Mac Réamoinn tells us, 'never got round to banning the original, but Frank O'Connor's splendid translation was, quite disgracefully, put on their list.' So much for the State's attitude to a national treasure. But things have changed.

The poets dealt with in these essays – Piaras Feiritéar, Daibhí Ó Bruadair, Aogán Ó Rathaille of Kerry, others – exhibit a quality to be described, technically not romantically, as bardic. Shakespeare may be termed the Bard, but Ben Jonson, who loved his genius while deploring his slipshodness, knew better what bardicity was about. To be a bard is to exercise a traditional craft, to serve an apprenticeship to it and later to advance it. The tradition is essentially Celtic, like the term itself, and Gerard Manley Hopkins, who read Welsh poetry and imported some of its techniques to English, is perhaps our greatest non-Celtic bardic practitioner. There is a limitation of theme – Hopkins's ideas are painfully orthodox – but a willingness to expand technique to the limit. Read Hopkins in French or Italian and you will be unaware of the bardic quality. Read any of these Gaelic bards in English and you may wonder what the fuss is about. Poetry, as Mallarmé said, is made out of words, not ideas.

But the ferocity of Ó Bruadair sometimes gets through in Michael Hartnett's versions, his anti-clericalism, for instance – 'ye lie befuddled in sops and puddles/ suffering, fasting, pissing in straw' – and his contempt for the English language, which he calls simpering (béarla binn) and squeaky. And John Jordan conveys something of the power of Ó Rathaille – his 'blend of defiance and impassioned stoicism' (Timonesque, Philoctetean), his capacity to 'provoke a tingling in the blood':

> Take warning, wave, take warning, crown of the sea.
> I, O'Rahilly – witless from your discords –
> Were Spanish sails again afloat
> And rescue on our tides,
> Would force this outcry down your wild throat,
> Would make you swallow these Atlantic words.

There is one Scottish poet here, and he is far from being among the dead. Somhairle Mac Gill-Eain, or Sorley Maclean, handles a Gaelic not too remote from Irish, though it no longer has the identity of the era when the Irish too were Scots. As Hugh Macdiarmid dragged the Scottish English of Dunbar into the age of Marxism and machines, so Mac Gill-Eain writes a Gaelic wholly modern. '*Eadh Is Féin Is Sàr-Fhéin*' is to be translated as 'Id, Ego and Super-Ego', and in the poem of that title '*Tha Freud 'na bháillidh air a' choille*' – 'Freud is factor of the woodland'. In the poem called '*Aig Uaigh Yeats*' – 'At Yeats's Grave' – we have the lines '*le dealbh na té oig álainn/ ann an teilifis gach raoin*' – 'with the picture of the young beautiful one/ in the television of each field'.

A living language, then, but its poetic exploitation is, as Seán Mac Réamoinn recognizes with Celtic stoicism, a fierce art practised for and by the few. That Irish children are made to learn their native language in school is no guarantee that they will rush to read or hear their native bards. English has conquered everyone, though the Irish have cunningly conquered English: they ought perhaps to be satisfied that they have produced the world's greatest playwright, poet and novelist in the last hundred years. But poetry is too precious a commodity to be allowed to die merely because it is forged in a minority medium. Buy this book and learn something of a powerful tradition of art. Then, like myself, consider the prospect of, for the good of one's soul, wrestling with the language.

Murmurous Mud

Samuel Beckett: *A Biography*, by Deirdre Bair

This is very much an interim biography, like Gorman's of Joyce. A telephone report from Paris today affirms that Beckett is alive and well and drinking. Mithridates, he died old. When the ultimate job is done, I doubt if Dr Bair will be doing it. We shall need the art and wit of a Richard Ellmann. Her big book (736 pages) is merely informative, scholarly and absorbing. Considering Beckett's known aversion to invasion of privacy, it is a remarkable achievement. Joyce, it will be remembered, laid down precise instructions for Gorman – a piece of devout hagiography was required, featuring an unusually prolonged martyrdom. Beckett said he would neither help nor hinder. Not to hinder is, apparently, to help a great deal. The portrait seems excruciatingly precise – anal cysts, glaucoma, palatal lesion and all. Beckett told Dr Bair that he knew she would write a satisfactory biography but that he would not read it. I understand from Paris that he has read it with masochistic attention.

Beckett's books and plays posit a Cartesian division between mind and body. (His first published work, the poem *Whoroscope*, is a kind of gorblimied life of Descartes.) Those heroes and heroines on their last, or nonexistent, legs, assert a powerful identity in spite of the wreck of the flesh. It is the kind of work one might expect from a lifelong invalid. His biography shows that Beckett was always an athlete, a well-coordinated car driver and motorbike rider who could smash the machine but emerge whole, an excellent swimmer and fine cricketer – the only Nobel Prizeman to be mentioned in *Wisden*. His body has always been spare and tough, able to take any amount of punishment from drink and cigarettes. But one notes a kind of self-flagellancy. A worshipper of Joyce, he took to pretending he had Joyce's feet, which were small and dainty and pleased their owner: he crippled himself with unsuitable shoes. But the body's main pains, and its Oblomov lethargy, seem to have most to do with Beckett's complicated relationship with his mother.

Both parents belonged to a wing of the Irish Protestant ascendancy: the name Beckett is Huguenot in origin, and Beckett's expatriation from Dublin to France could be interpreted as satisfying a nostalgia of the blood (whereas Joyce got to Paris because it was the only place left to go). Beckett's father was extrovert and adored. His mother, gaunt, somewhat mannish, an insomniac who roamed the house at night and sat to breakfast red-eyed, a compulsive driver of servants, possessive of her sons, undevoted to her husband till he was dead, was an incubus who rode Sam till the end. His ailments were psychosomatic, but they would not yield to analysis. Writing has been his best cathartic, but the purge has usually been debilitating. Exhausted by prose, he took to plays. *En Attendant Godot*, which he tends to disparage, was put together as a kind of verbal game. Godot, he insists, is neither God nor flesh nor fish. In other words, Godot is red herring. Travelling by air to London, Beckett heard the pilot say: '*Le capitaine Godot vous accorde des bienvenues.*' He wanted to get off at once.

It has been a hard life and it has begotten a profound stoicism. But it has not been the hard life of a gutter-bred O'Casey or shabby-genteel Joyce. Beckett went to Portora, Oscar Wilde's school, and not to Paddy Stink and Mickey Mud of the Christian Brothers. He is a Trinity man and became a Trinity lecturer. Joyce's pleasure in his company probably had something to do with the prestige of his background. Brendan Behan never learned to understand that Beckett was not his kind of Irishman. Irish was Irish, and if you're Irish come into the parlour, but the flabby drunk with Erse on him was not the cup of tea of this wiry, scholarly, reticent, tennis-playing intellectual aristocrat. Brendan always regarded Beckett as a soft touch: first the lecture on the evils of drink, then the handout. The hard life of the French Resistance, the repeated rejections of the major publishers, the continued abuse of his work (despite the Nobel or because of it) – these have confirmed a native habit of silence and indifference but also augmented a native generosity. Beckett is one of the most generous men alive.

Harold Pinter, who has learned a lot of dramaturgy from Beckett, recalls a long night's boozing which ended up with onion soup in Les Halles. Pinter found himself prostrated with dyspepsia. Beckett went off for half an hour and Pinter thought he had been deserted. Beckett came back with bicarbonate of soda. Pinter believed this saved his life. The heartburns of all fellow-dyspeptics will go out to Beckett. Beckett gives money away very liberally. He needs little for himself. When he was fifty-five and she sixty-one, he married, for testamentary reasons (compare Joyce and Nora), Suzanne Georgette Anna Deschevaux-Dumesnil, old companion of the Occupation. Her part of their apartment is loaded, in the bourgeois French manner, with evidence of affluence; his part is monastic. They communicate mainly by telephone. One doubts, somehow, that there will ever be a revelation of love letters on Joyce-to-Nora lines. Beckett's love letters are his plays and novels. The Swedish Academy's citation was right: he 'has transmuted the destitution of modern man into his exaltation'.

It is somewhat eery to find that the ancient *faible* of Lucia Joyce continued, long after her father's death and the end of Ellmann's record. Time stopped for her, and Beckett remained the young hawklike man who shared the master's silences and, after his rejection of the demented girl's advances, was icily told not to call again. Beckett's devotion to Joyce continues, and his own artistic perfectionism, in the study and theatre alike, is its best expression. He works himself and his actors to the limit. The account of Billie Whitelaw's creative ordeal with him is one of the most remarkable chapters of this book.

Favourite Novel

My literary tastes and standards have changed hardly at all in the last forty-five years. I was both disqualified and castigated when, in a school essay competition, I declared that James Joyce's *Ulysses* was my favourite book. Disqualified because the book, being banned, did not officially exist; castigated for dirty-mindedness. Now, making the identical declaration, I will be sneered at for the banality of my choice. Everybody knows now that *Ulysses* is the greatest novel of the century. It would have been better to intrigue readers with A. F. Mordrick's *Last Innings* or Giulia Febbraio's *L'Impossibilità* (translated by Edna Watkin as *If She Had Only Thought*). But *Ulysses* it has to be, because *Ulysses* it is. It and the poems of Hopkins have meant more to me, as a writer and as a private person, than I can well hope to express.

It is true that, when as a sixth-form boy I smuggled the fine Odyssey Press edition of *Ulysses* into England, I was primarily delighted with the obscenity and the frank sex, but this was swiftly generalized into huge pleasure at the total candour of the book. Not just the candour of Bloom in the outside toilet and Bloom proposing masturbation in the bath, but a candour of rejection of traditional modes of literary communication. Joyce in effect was saying that the depiction of life as it is really lived cannot be achieved in neat periodic sentences and the puppetry of an author (like Thackeray) smugly in control. What looked to the first readers of *Ulysses*, brought up on Victorian fictional techniques, like careless half-formed writing was, in fact, total literary candour. There had to be thought and feeling and impulse and velleity matched by a mode of expression that did not look literary at all. The characters' stream of consciousness had to be presented directly to the reader; new ways of conveying taste, indigestion, lust had to be devised; and the author had to seem to withdraw himself from his work, leaving his prerogative of shape and control to the large, not always realized, symbolic structure that enclosed the action, not to the action itself.

Not that there could, if the novel was to be a realistic presentation of daily urban life, be very much action. Most popular traditional fiction had concerned itself heavily with plot, but plots don't exist in the normal dull living of ordinary people. Joyce is candid about the dullness, and his substitute for exciting events is the excitement of a variable prose style that is almost hysterically responsive to the content of what it has to describe. Take the hero to a maternity hospital, to see how his wife's overdue woman friend is getting on, and the prose becomes ditheringly interested in the process of gestation and tries to mime it. It can only do this by presenting the gestation of English style from King Alfred to

Carlyle and after, and we have to see Bloom battling his way through thickets of Malory, Sir Thomas Browne and Dean Swift. This is Joyce's action, like the mimesis of a fugue in the Ormond Hotel and the peristaltic impulses that animate the lunchtime chapter. All these stylistic devices are justified by the subject matter of the sections where they operate, but the subject matter itself is much influenced by the myth adumbrated in the title. For this is a modern Odyssey; each chapter corresponds to an episode in Homer; contemporary urban man is heroic. Bloom, the Dublin half-Jew, an advertisement canvasser with an unfaithful wife, has to battle with Lestrygonians, a Cyclops and a Circe. He wins through but he is crowned with no heroic laurels. He goes to bed and prepares for another dull day.

The average reader of fiction, who likes his prose style decently transparent, will have no truck with a novel in which the style is opaque or iridescent, imitates a symphony or a political poster, seems simple only when it is parodying simplicity, and, whatever it does, is always so very much *there* – a big dog nuzzling or trying to push us over. But the rest of us like to remember that literature is made out of language, and that language should be glorified, not made servile and near-invisible as in a novel by Lord Snow or Iris Murdoch. A sculptor rejoices in stone, a painter in pigment, Joyce in words. But there is no verbal self-indulgence. Bloom and his wife and Stephen Dedalus – who is Joyce himself at the age of twenty-two – do not get lost in the prose. We have seen them on stage and film, as large as life if not larger: they are made full-blooded and muscular through the strenuous dialect of life and myth, or life and language. We know no fictional character better than we know Bloom; we have never had so naked an exposition of the female temperament as, in the final monologue, his wife gives us. This may be a retelling of myth or a demonstration of the possibilities of language, but it is still a novel.

And yet it is not quite a novel. I have lived long enough with *Ulysses* to be fully aware of its faults, and its major fault is that it evades the excruciating problem that most novelists set themselves: how, without blatant contrivance, to show character in the process of change, so that the reader, saying goodbye to Mr X or Miss Y, realizes that these are not quite the people he met at the beginning. There is, in every non-Joycean novel, a psychological watershed hardly discernible to the reader; without the imposition of a journey to this watershed fictional character can hardly be said to exist. In *Ulysses*, whose action covers less than twenty-four hours, there is no time for change. Indeed, nothing happens of sufficient gravity to induce change. The ordinary man Bloom meets the extraordinary youth Stephen and then says a goodnight which is probably a goodbye. Molly Bloom dreams of Stephen as a kind of messianic son–lover. Whatever happens in the novel, it does not happen today. It ends on the brink of tomorrow, when something may possibly happen, but tomorrow never comes. That is the novel's major fault.

It is a fault so massive that it can only be compensated for by exceptional virtues, and these virtues I have already hinted at – the epic vitality of the scheme, the candour of the presentation of human life as it really is, the awe-inspiring virtuosity of the language. Add to these the comprehensiveness of the urban vision it provides. When we visit Dublin we carry that vision with us; it is more real than the flesh-and-blood or stone-and-mortar reality. We cannot, I suppose, finally judge *Ulysses* as a work of fiction at all. It is a kind of magical codex, of the same order as Dante's *Divine Comedy* (in which hell, heaven and purgatory go on for ever and nothing changes). But, in the practical terms in which writers are forced to think, it is a terrible literary challenge. To call it my favourite novel is, I see, shamefully inept. It is the work I have to measure myself hopelessly against each time I sit down to write fiction.

Joyce as Centenarian

J ames Joyce was born in 1882, on 2 February, the Feast of Candlemas or the Purification; Igor Stravinsky was born in the same year, on 17 June, the day after Bloomsday. The Irishman and the Russian alike became Parisians. In 1913 Stravinsky's *Le Sacre du Printemps* caused a riot at the Paris Opera House. In 1922 Joyce's *Ulysses*, publishable only in Paris, caused a worldwide riot. The two men, who apparently never met, were fathers of revolution in the arts. One hundred years after their nativities, there are people around who say that they can't stand this modern stuff, meaning what they have heard or heard of or seen of one or the other or both. But Joyce and Stravinsky are no longer modern; they are as much classic artists as Goethe and Beethoven. Yet it is their function to continue to disturb.

I leave the celebration of Stravinsky to the musicians. In commemorating Joyce's centenary, I have to approach him not merely as a reader or as a fellow-writer working, to some extent, in his shadow, but as one who, while still a boy, recognized a temperamental kinship. I was brought up in a lower-middle-class Catholic-Irish ambience in

Manchester. Dublin, where Joyce had the same kind of upbringing, was closer to us than London, and not merely geographically: it was a Catholic capital, while London was a heretical one; it was the port where our relatives embarked to pay us visits, usually with illegal Irish Sweep tickets stuffed in their bloomers. Joyce was dim of sight and given to music; so was and am I. I began to lose my faith at the age of sixteen, and it was then that I first read *A Portrait of the Artist as a Young Man*. The great sermon on hell scared me back to conformity, but I could not resist the slow but ineluctable divestment of the peel of faith, and it was to *A Portrait* that I frequently returned to find a magisterial justification of my apostasy.

Of course, according to Joyce, you were really only permitted to abandon the Church if you found a spiritual substitute for it, and it was only art that provided such a substitute. In art, which to Joyce meant literature, you could find priests and sacraments and even martyrs, but art gave you your reward in this world, not just a promise of pie in the sky. So, since I could not be a good Catholic, I had to become some sort of an artist, and I fought against the English side of my upbringing to learn to understand how holy art really was. To the Protestant English, art has always been a somewhat amateurish affair: you don't build a book as you build a bridge; you let it accumulate, like hash. The rigour of Joyce was something new, and his devotion to literature was somehow unclean and Parisian. Oscar Wilde, another Dubliner, had ended up in Pére Lachaise, and he had always been burbling about how art was above bourgeois morality. Look where art, meaning pederasty, got him.

When Joyce produced *Ulysses* it was promptly banned everywhere except Paris. This, to the bourgeoisie, confirmed the equation of art and dirt. No British or American printer had been willing to risk jail by setting up the abominable text, and it had had to be given to a printer in Dijon who knew no English. The book was published by the American owner of a Paris bookshop, and it was sent through the mails to such as relished highly wrought literature, or dirt. Winston Churchill bought it, but Bernard Shaw did not. It was seized by the customs authorities at New York and Folkestone and sequestered or burned. The ban was still in force when, in 1934, my history master smuggled the Odyssey Press edition out of Nazi Germany and lent it to me.

The sexual candour of *Ulysses* is nowadays nothing in comparison with the multiple orgasms of Miss Jackie Collins or the fretful impotence of Mr Harold Robbins. The mouthfuls of obscenity uttered by Privates Carr and Compton in the nighttown episode are kid's stuff, even to maiden ladies who see Mr Pinter's plays on television. And it was clear, even to a lubricious seventeen-year-old like myself, that the sex and obscenity were aspects of a programme of realism very remote from pornography. Joyce had taken a day in Dublin – 16 June 1904 – and set down in their uncensored entirety the thoughts, feelings and acts of three not quite representative Dubliners. Leopold Bloom, the advertising canvasser of Hungarian-Jewish origin, eats breakfast and then visits the toilet. He has a satisfactory movement, a dose of cascara having eased his slight constipation of the days before. On the beach later in the day he is erotically excited by the sight of a girl's lifted skirt, and, while the fireworks of the Mirus bazaar let off sympathetic whizzes and bangs, he masturbates. Towards the end of the book Molly Bloom menstruates. The outrage of menstruatrices like Virginia Woolf and masturbators like E. M. Forster was considerable, though decently contained in Bloomsbury locutions. One would have thought that Joyce, and not Sir John Harington, had invented the water closet.

Joyce set down life as he honestly saw it, and it did him no good. The Bloomsburyites did not like what they termed coarseness, and they were not pleased either with Joyce's comic–epic glorification of the lower middle class. *Ulysses* was considered by communists to be a reactionary book, and Joyce was plaintive about it. 'There's nobody in any of my books,' he said, 'who's worth more than a hundred pounds.' But the reactionary charge, raised also against Eliot's *The Waste Land*, which appeared in the same year as *Ulysses*, had more to do with the parade of erudition, and a technique that did not lend itself to easy intelligibility, than with the subject matter.

Erudition is easily obtained: it is available in public libraries and it costs nothing; nevertheless, since neither the workers nor the middle class particularly want it, it is regarded as an unwarrantable imposition in a novel: a novel should be *a good read*. *Ulysses* is not *a good read*. Joyce plays terrible tricks with the English language. He separates out, like curds and whey, its component Latin and Teutonic elements. He parodies every writer from the Venerable Bede to Thomas Carlyle. He turns one chapter into a textbook on rhetoric. Another is made to behave like a *fuga per canonem*. The last chapter has no punctuation marks. And, when these games are not being played, he gives us stretches of raw thought and feeling in the form of *monologue intérieur*:

> O sweety all your little girlwhite up I saw dirty bracegirdle made me do love sticky we two naughty Grace darling she him half past the bed met him pike hoses frillies for Raoul to perfume your wife black hair heave under embon *señorita* young eyes Mulvey plump years drawers return tail end Agendath swoony lovey showed me her next year in drawers return in her next her next.

But, as we know now sixty years after the publication of *Ulysses*, the difficulties of experimental writing like that are not so great as they seem. If we have read the book attentively up to this masturbatory point, we shall recognize every motif of the ungrammatical flow. Joyce loves mysteries but does not like them to go on too long. He hides the keys in drawers which themselves have no keys. He is not always easy, but he is never impossible.

There was a time when Joyce excited rage for making the prose style get in the way of the narrative. Nowadays we are more inclined to take pleasure in the manner of his exalting – through myth and symbol – ordinary people into epic heroes, even if exaltation means also shoving them up on to a music-hall stage and making them go through a comic act. The real Ulysses of Homer has a rock hurled at him by a one-eyed giant man-eater. Bloom, the new Ulysses, is assailed by a drunken Irish chauvinist who can't see straight enough to hit him with a Jacob's biscuit tin. Bloom, reviled as a Jew and mocked as a cuckold, ends nevertheless as a king in Ithaca, whose location is No. 7 Eccles Street. He is also ourselves, and we too endue the crown of absurd glory.

The world has forgiven Joyce for the excesses of *Ulysses*, but it is not yet ready to forgive him for the dementia of *Finnegans Wake*. Yet it is difficult to see what other book he could well have written after a fictional ransacking of the human mind in its waking state. *Ulysses* sometimes touches the borders of sleep, but it never actually enters its kingdom. *Finnegans Wake* is frankly a representation of the sleeping brain. It took Joyce seventeen years to write between eye operations and worry about the mental collapse of his daughter Lucia. He got little encouragement, even from Ezra Pound, that prince of avant-gardistes; his wife Nora merely said that he ought to write a nice book that ordinary people could read. But clearly *Finnegans Wake* had to be written, and Joyce was the only man dedicated or mad enough to write it.

It is about an innkeeper living in Chapelizod, just outside Dublin, who seems to be called Mr Porter. In his dream he becomes Humphrey Chimpden Earwicker, the Nordic Protestant invader of Catholic Ireland, a man who carries the hump of a kind of incestuous guilt on his back, expresses his guilt in a stutter, and turns himself into the whole generality of sinful man. His wife Ann is all women, and she is also Anna Livia Plurabelle, the river Liffey, and, by extension, all the rivers in the world. Her consort, who stitches his initials HCE into the text like a monogram, is the great archetypal builder Finnegan and also all the cities which he builds. Their daughter Isobel is all temptresses. Their twin sons, Kevin and Jerry, or Shem and Shaun, represent the eternal principle of opposition – sometimes Cain and Abel, sometimes Napoleon and Wellington, sometimes (God help us) Brutus and Cassius disguised as Burrus and Caseous or butter and cheese. Identities shift, space is plastic, time is the year 1132, which is no time at all, merely shorthand for the circular process of fall and resurrection (to count 11 on our fingers we have to make a new start; 32 feet per second per second is the rate of acceleration of falling bodies). The narrative is cyclical and never ends. The language is a Babylonish dialect of Joyce's own invention, made out of all the tongues he had learned in exile and regarded as suitable for recounting a universal dream.

There must be many people, and they of the most literate, who have opened the book and groaned wretchedly at what they found:

> . . . nor yet, though venissoon after, had a kidscad buttended a bland old isaac: not yet, though all's fair in vanessy, were sosie sesthers wroth with twone nathandjoe. Rot a peck of pa's malt had Jhem or Shen brewed by arclight and rory end to the regginbrow was to be seen ringsome on the aquaface. . . .

It looks like nonsense, but it isn't. Joyce never wrote a line of nonsense in his life. Here is Jacob, who is James or Shem, the younger son or cadet, but also a cad, putting on a kidskin and duping his bland-blind old father Isaac into giving him his blessing, and also Parnell wresting the Irish leadership from Isaac Butt. Susannah, Esther and Ruth are present, all loved by older men (as HCE loves his own daughter), as well as Stella and Vanessa (who both had the name Esther) loved by a Jonathan Swift who is Nathan and Joseph in one. And then Shem and Shaun, cloudily refashioned into the sons of Noah glued together, await the brewing of whisky at the rainbow's end. There's too much here, of course, but to complain of excess is a little ungrateful. Most writers don't give us enough.

Clearly, Joyce, though a man of the people, did not set out to be a popular writer. Nevertheless his centenary is being celebrated with rather more enthusiasm than, in 1970, the literary world accorded Charles Dickens, who did set out to be popular. The celebration will achieve its greatest intensity in Dublin, where there are still people who call Joyce a blackguard and revere his father as a great gentleman (compare the situation vis-à-vis Lawrence *père et fils* in Eastwood, Notts). It is very hard not to celebrate Joyce in Dublin, in any year and on any day of the year, because, like Earwicker–Finnegan himself, Joyce has created Dublin. He has turned it into a place as mythical as Dante's Inferno, Paradiso and Purgatorio all in one. At the same time he has stressed its physicality and given the stamp of an enhanced reality to its streets, pubs and churches. When we drink Guinness in the Bailey or Davy Byrne's, we are borrowing Joyce's tastebuds, and when we walk on Sandymount strand it is in Joyce's broken tennis shoes. Joyce couldn't live in Dublin, but he couldn't leave it alone. His obsession with the minutiae of its life and its speech forces all who read him to become Dubliners themselves. No other writer has so made the soaking in of a locality the primary condition for understanding his work.

Ulysses begins in a Martello tower which still stands. The Odyssey of Bloom can be checked with a map and timed with a stopwatch. Even *Finnegans Wake*, the most recondite and rarefied book ever written, has a precise *mise en scène* – Chapelizod, south of the Phoenix Park, where Earwicker's pub may be identified with the Dead Man (so called because customers would roll out of it drunk to be run over by trams). The solidity of place is matched by the solidity of character. Leopold Bloom is so three-dimensional that no amount of linguistic tomfoolery can obscure him. Earwicker's sad stutter sounds clearly through all the mazes of dream. There are some celebrants of Joyce who can ignore the tortuosities of style and concentrate solely on the flesh and blood and their confining geography. Unfortunately, there are far more who revel pedantically in the style, the structure and the symbolism. The secret of appreciating Joyce lies in not letting him go too much to one's head. He is not, after all, John Jameson.

Joyce has been posthumously lucky in having the best biography of our century devoted to him. This is Professor Richard Ellmann's book, a wonder of fact, wit and qualified affection. Ellmann is entitled to draw our attention to such ingenuities as the asymmetrical bookends of the opening and closing words – 'Stately' and 'Yes'. He is similarly entitled to show that Buck Mulligan's mock-transubstantiation at the beginning of the work is contradicted by Molly Bloom's real menstruation at the end. But there are too many scholars – and they will be in Dublin in force on 16 June this year – who treat both *Ulysses* and *Finnegans Wake* as mystical codices, showing no interest in the Ascot Gold Cup (which comes around Bloomsday) and little taste for Guinness. Joyce is, so this centennial ought to show, probably at last becoming the property of the people and not the thesis writers.

To other, unscholarly, writers like myself, Joyce is the novelist's novelist, although neither *Ulysses* nor *Finnegans Wake* can properly be termed a novel. If fiction is the art of fitting the sensations and emotions of life into a structure which shall have some of the shapeliness and autonomy of a piece of music, then Joyce is all our daddies. We can study him on the structural level, finding the principles of symphonic development cunningly exemplified in the 'Oxen of the Sun' and 'Circe' sections of *Ulysses*, and on the nuclear level of the phrase. These are pieces of distinguished writing:

A wise tabby, a blinking sphinx, watched from her warm sill.

The bungholes sprang open and a huge dull floor leaked out, flowing together, winding through mudflats all over the level land, a lazy pooling swirl of liquor bearing along wideleaved flowers of its froth.

He foresaw his pale body reclined in it at full, naked, in a womb of warmth, oiled by scented melting soap, softly laved.

Under their dropped lids his eyes found the tiny bow of the leather headband inside his high grade ha.

For 'ha' read 'hat.' Sweat has erased the 't'. John Gross has pointed out that other fictional characters have conventional headwear: only Bloom has a ha. Yet we have here less literary eccentricity than a concern with reality. Joyce's language is always anchored to its referents. At the same time it achieves a certain melodic independence, reminding us that Joyce was a tenor who, if he'd stuck to singing, would have outsung Count John McCormack.

The man himself, improvident, given to drink, exiled, silent and cunning, vocal, convivial, devoted to his family, lacking in what Hampstead would call good taste, lanky, seedily elegant, half-blind, dead untimely at fifty-nine, lives on in anecdotage, but the essence of his personality – eccentric and yet conventional – is totally contained in his works. His preoccupations are there – the social stability which finds its best expression in the lower-middle-class family, language as man's supreme achievement. He has left his voice to the world under the hiss and scratches of a pre-electric recording, reciting parts of his two greatest books with skill but a sacerdotal intonation that was perhaps to be expected. Intended for the Jesuit priesthood, he built a church of his own – an ecclesia on Eccles Street. His books are confessional, leaving out no sins but making no excuses. His eucharistic function is the conversion of quotidian bread into beauty, which Thomas Aquinas defined as the pleasing. He does not please Mrs Barbara Cartland nor Lord Longford, but he reminds us that life is a divine comedy and that literature is a jocose and serious business. He has left us in *Finnegans Wake* a little prayer which sums up his attitude to life. It is a very reasonable attitude.

Loud, heap miseries upon us yet entwine our arts with laughters low.

Joyce and Trieste

If you drive north from Venice you will eventually come to Trieste. It has, because of its history, acquired a non-Italian aura to those who have merely heard about it or noted its position on the map, but, entering it, you will have no sensation of leaving Italy. There will be copies of *Telegiornale*, Cinzano and Campari in the bars, Agip garages and the confections of Motta. Address the Triestines in Italian, meaning the version of the mother tongue used on the radio or TV, and they will understand you, though their version of Latin has an x in it, unlike Tuscan or Roman, and they turn the Latin aitch into a g. A letter survives from young Lucia Joyce to her father James, beginning '*Go una bela bala*' – 'I have a lovely ball' – and that *go*, which is *ho* on radio and TV, is a typical Slav mutation. The Russians say that Gemingway was not gomosexual. Trieste is partly a Slav-speaking town, which is why the neighbouring Slavs of Yugoslavia have wanted it for their own.

You will see plenty of blondes and redheads around, as in the Venice of the Titian who glorified auburn tresses, and you will find, in some of the taverns, newspapers attached along their spines to tough wooden laths, as in the coffee houses of Vienna. There are odd hints, though not many, that this city once belonged to the Austro-Hungarian Empire. As for James Joyce, you will find his stay celebrated in a street named for him – Viale Joyce. There is also a street named for the great Triestine novelist Italo Svevo, whom Joyce discovered and persuaded to publish. His finest novel is *Senilità*, made into a fine Italian film, and Joyce provided the English title – *As a Man Grows Older*.

When Joyce left Dublin in 1904 with Nora Barnacle, the uneducated Galway girl who bore his children and belatedly became his wife, he went first to Pola, which was in Austria. It is now called Pulj and is in Yugoslavia. When Pola became suspicious of foreigners, he moved from the Berlitz School there, where he taught English, to the sister establishment in Trieste, which was also in Austria. He liked the place, which was a kind of Adriatic Dublin, only bigger. It was the chief sea port of Austria-Hungary, with its mouth open for the engorging of oriental trade. He found his English-language pupils chiefly among naval officers. Being full of sailors, it was a convivial town, and Joyce drank more than he earned. It was full of Jews, who were more welcome there than in other cities of the Empire, and Joyce was able to dream up a Leopold Bloom with an authentic Jewish background – difficult to do in Dublin, where the Jewish population is small (according to Mr Deasy, in *Ulysses*, it is nonexistent). Leopold Bloom is more a Triestine figure than a Dublin one.

It is useless to go piously around Trieste seeking out the taverns from which Joyce emerged drunk and incapable, often spending the night in the gutter. He was in all of them, but some of them are no longer there. His various lodgings are still around – 3 Piazza Ponterosso, 31 via San Nicolo, 1 via Giovanni Boccaccio – or were when I was last in Trieste. More important are the ever-living landmarks which Joyce saw – the terraced slopes which start at the Gulf and climb towards the Carso hills; the Città Vecchia, or old city, dominated by the Cathedral of San Giusto (whose feast day, 2 November, Joyce remembered all his life); the new town, built on land reclaimed from the Gulf by the Emperor Joseph II in the eighteenth century, handsome with wide streets and spacious buildings. Outside the city are the ruins of the castle of Duino, to which it is believed Dante paid a visit, and the modern castle where Rainer Maria Rilke wrote the *Duineser Elegien*. Closer to the city than Duino is the castle of Miramare, built by the Archduke Maximilian before he went to Mexico and participation in the sad story we know from the old Paul Muni movie *Juarez*. As they return by rail up the coast, it is the sight of the white marble of the edifice that makes Triestines feel sentimentally glad to be home. Joyce learned to feel that way.

In Joyce's day, there was a powerful nationalist movement among the Italian-speaking Triestines which almost exactly paralleled the situation of the Irish. This made Joyce feel at home. It is the strong Italian-speaking element of the city which has prevailed against history's long efforts to make Trieste French, Illyrian, Austrian and, at the end of the Second World War, a province of Tito's Yugoslavia. In 1947 Trieste became briefly an independent state – a Mickey Mouse state or *stato Topolino*, as the Italians called it. American and British troops held the zone against the threat of Tito's tanks. Now the territory is indubitably part of the Italian motherland, and the Yugoslavs seem to sulk about it. The Yugoslavs are, historically, all children of Veneto – the lion of St Mark is embossed on all the stonework of the coast – but they pretend to have forgotten their Latin inheritance. When you drive across the frontier, the customs men will say: '*Alles in Ordnung*?'

Trieste has lost its old grandeur as a port. It no longer serves the commerce of a great empire, and it may be regarded as the torpid terminus of free Europe. The collapse of Austria–Hungary in revolution and repartition after the First World War has ended in a glum and not over prosperous communist structure in which democratic Trieste can play no part. Still, there are always ships in the harbour, as well as a new brand of foreign sailors – Indians and Pakistanis. But the wealth of the commercial city draws increasingly on the Italian hinterland.

The shops are smart and busy, the people well dressed and lively. The restaurants serve fine Adriatic fish – far superior to what you get out of the Mediterranean and second, perhaps, only to the fish of the North Atlantic. The Aquario, with its pet penguin Marco, is one of the finest in Europe. If you are looking for the charm of Florence or Siena or the baroque magnificence of Rome, you will not find them here – in respect of the lack of architectural interest you may dub the city 'non-Italian'. But 'Italian' has little true meaning and may not be used as an analogue of 'American', which has a true meaning. Trieste is itself as Venice is itself and Bolzano, where they speak German, is itself. National unity is a political fiction in Italy. The town is characterized more by warehouses and insurance offices than baroque churches and statuary. The girls are mostly exquisite, Titianesque without the Titian opulence. There is chic and animation and no lack of lively talk. The drunkenness is mostly an importation of the sailors.

Though both Joyce and his master Henrik Ibsen first met the South here, that tolerant softness which tempered their natural rigour, the North is ever-present in the turbulent wind called the Bora (derived from the Latin *Boreas* which we read of in the Roman poets). With polar ferocity this great wind rages through the streets in winter and knocks one over. In the summer it scarcely mitigates the huge heat. Joyce knew it, and we can still visualize his lanky underfed frame wrestling with its rude strength.

If we mostly visit Trieste to see the environment where Joyce wrestled with the first chapters of *Ulysses* and Svevo completed *Senilità* and *Zeno*, we would be unwise to view those two great novelists as solitary sports in a city not much given to the arts. For both Joyce and Svevo were more citizens of an empire than of a mere city. The Austro-Hungarian Empire produced great art, from Haydn and Mozart through Beethoven to Richard Strauss, from Metastasio to Rilke and Hofmannsthal, and *Ulysses*, though completed and published in Paris, is a product of a huge culture whose centre was Vienna but whose extremities touched the Adriatic. *Ulysses* may be about Ireland, but only Trieste could have given Joyce the impetus – turbulent and cosmopolitan – to start setting it down.

A Truer Joyce

James Joyce, by Richard Ellmann, new and revised edition

I was repatriated from Brunei in 1958 to be told that I probably had an inoperable brain tumour and might, with luck, live for a year. I was determined to live long enough to read two books, both of which appeared in England in 1959 – Nabokov's *Lolita* and Ellmann's biography of Joyce. Whether the prognosis was founded on an error of diagnosis or the books had a profoundly therapeutic value I shall never know; I know only that I have lived long enough to read both many times. Twenty-three years ago Nabokov seemed to be an ageing disciple of Joyce: now we know that his literary ancestor was the Bely who wrote *Petersburg*, and that Russian novelists were playing with symbolism as early as the first Bloomsday. But it would have seemed reasonable to find Nabokov among the innumerable artists with whom Joyce shared a Paris exile. He was not in the first edition of the biography but he is here now. Nabokov proposed a lecture on Pushkin, and Joyce, fearing that nobody would turn up, turned up himself to ensure that the young Russian had at least one audient. This is a newly unearthed instance of Joyce's kindness, not in the least incompatible with an intense egoism. There are other discoveries – though not one I still long for: evidence that Joyce, a bank clerk in Rome, read Belli (not to be confused with Bely). The greatest literary biography of the century has not, which would be impossible, become greater, but it has – in the Joycean manner – become, through the accretion of more and more detail, truer.

I do not have the 1959 edition with me, and I must rely on memory to spot the changes. For every one I have overlooked I will buy Dr Ellmann a Cork gin in any Dublin bar he cares to nominate. I will buy him Cork gin anyway, the least I can do. One change that should have been effected concerns Joyce's birthday – 2 February. This is certainly Candlemas but it is not also St Brigid's day, which comes the day before. There is a charming story about newly churched Mary granting Brigid precedence in honour of Ireland.

It is now revealed that Joyce pronounced Ulysses as Oo-liss-eez. There are no second thoughts about the extent of Joyce's drinking, but the post mortem in Zürich disclosed that his liver was normal, helping to confirm my belief that, of the Celts, only the Welsh have hepatic problems. The canard about Joyce's taking a drink with Georges Belmont and the Rev. Pinard is now modified: he merely drank pinard. The story about Joyce I like best rests unchanged, but a long footnote now blunts its point. Somebody praised Flaubert to Joyce as the supreme stylist. Joyce, spotting a copy of *Trois Contes* under his arm, asked to see the book. He ignored innumerable infelicities in the body of the book and concentrated merely on the first and last pages. On the former he found *envièrent*, which he said should be *enviaient*, since the action described was continuous. On the latter he objected to the use of *alternativement* as applied to three persons carrying the head of John the Baptist, since that adverb is reserved to two people only. Now the pedants, including the lexicographers, say that Flaubert was right, which is a pity. I do not like Joyce's linguistic competence to be thus diminished.

There are several great things about this book. The first is the excellence of the style, with which Ellmann has not tampered, recognizing – unlike mere revising novelists like Waugh and Fowles – that it could not be improved. It is an ideal medium for expressing exasperated affection, it is often funny and it is often moving. Thus, in Trieste Joyce spent a 'gentlemanly morning, an industrious afternoon and a chaotic evening'. The ending is superb: 'In whatever he did, his two profound interests – his family and his writings – kept their place. These passions never dwindled. The intensity of the first gave his work its sympathy and humanity; the intensity of the second raised his life to dignity and high dedication.' The account of Nora's funeral brings tears: '. . . a priest delivered, after the Swiss custom, a funeral speech at the grave, and described her as "*eine grosse Sünderin*" (a great sinner). Few epithets could have been less apt. She was buried in the same cemetery as Joyce but not next to him, for the space was already filled. The casualness of their lodgings in life was kept after death.'

The second great thing is Ellmann's consistent skill and insight in relating the most trivial details of Joyce's life to his work. Joyce's uniqueness partly lies in the glorification of the casual and the everyday: the novelist should celebrate the ordinary, he said: only the journalist dealt in the extraordinary. So when Joyce, drunk, sings a Triestine drinking song beginning *No go la ciava del porton*' ('I don't have my front-door key') Ellmann is right to relate this to Stephen Dedalus, who has surrendered the key to the Martello tower to Mulligan, and to Bloom, who has left his key in his other trousers. Joyce ignored nothing, and his biographer follows him. Prezioso aspired to be Nora's lover and said '*Il sole s'è levato per Lei*.' Soon, in *Exiles*, the maid was to say to Bertha: 'Sure, he thinks the sun shines out of your face, ma'am,' and Bloom to Molly on Howth Head: 'The sun shines for you.' Joyce's art was literally scrupulous, the art of the crumb brush, but in crumbs lay epiphanies.

Next I must praise Ellmann's profound knowledge of Joyce's own works, probably unequalled among scholars. He seems to know them by heart, so that fragments spring up to illustrate the life, just as scintillae of the life illuminate the work. *Finnegans Wake* seems to be simplified into party-game autobiography. Joyce liked the manager of the Euston Hotel, Mr Knight, and called him a 'knice kman'. Ellmann knows that 'Knight, tuntapster', is lurking in *Finnegans Wake*. The trivialization of the *Wake* (to which Joyce would have added the quadrivialization) makes it accessible, and its accessibility discloses its greatness. Twenty-three years of Joyce scholarship since the first publication of the biography have not thrown up a finer scholar than Ellmann, to whom has been granted in addition the most unscholarly gifts of wit, grace and compassion.

Since 1959, with the growth of the feminist movement Nora Barnacle's heroinism has been exalted without assistance from Dr Ellmann. There is even a documentary film about her. Joyce is not now disclosed as treating her any better, or worse. Like Blake, he did not desire an intellectual helpmeet and his view of woman remains 'perfectly sane full amoral fertilisable untrustworthy engaging shrewd limited prudent indifferent *Weib. Ich bin der Fleisch der stets bejaht.*' German scholars will note his deneutralization of the flesh. That Nora was remarkable we know, and now know again more luminously, but nothing about her conforms with the liberated view of woman. The lineaments of gratified desire shine more, since Ellmann cites now from that bundle of incredible teleerotograms that Joyce sent her from Dublin. She remains, like Joyce's mother, one of the great models of woman tied to male genius.

There are a lot of new photographs, and we have lost, regrettably, some of the old ones. There are a couple of stills from the home-movie sequence some of us recently saw in Dublin: how powerfully charming the pseudo-married couple were, and are. We see Nelly Joyce, put-upon Stanislaus's wife, and very lovely she is, was. We see Joyce's funeral in the Swiss snow, and the enigmatic death mask. That death was no more than a mask is the renegade Joyce's very Catholic message. He is more there than ever in this wonderful redaction of one of the masterpieces of the age, whose publication must be considered the crowning event of the Joyce centenary.

The Muse and the Me

Joyce's Voices, by Hugh Kenner

Professor Kenner's original and entertaining study of, chiefly, *Ulysses* fulfils in an exemplary manner the Quantum desideratum: '. . . a richness of detail and insight within about one hundred pages of print. Short enough to be read in an evening and significant enough to be a book.' It is a reworking of lectures given at the University of Kent in Canterbury to honour the name of the other St Thomas. As I myself am due soon to deliver the Eliot lectures there, despair at being able to emulate Professor Kenner's erudite elegance clouds my admiration. Kenner's own admiration for Eliot had, inauspiciously for the occasion, to be clouded by his need to reject a famous pronouncement by Eliot about the 'mythological method' in *Ulysses*. The mythic element in that book, says Kenner, rightly I believe, is not important. Imaginative writers deal in the particularities of putting sentences together, not with deliberately evoking vague and ancient and irrelevant entities. *Ulysses* is called what it is, but what if, like one of Stephen Dedalus's greenly green unwritten epiphanies, it had been called *P*? Would anyone have suspected that Homer was tapping his way along Grafton Street?

It is useful to invoke Homer in the particularity of the opening of the *Odyssey*: 'Sing to me, Muse.' In an epic, and in an epic novel, there are two creators at work – the Muse and the me. The Muse in *Ulysses* is a mad androgyne of incredible talents – word-mad, pastiche-mad, symbol-mad. The me has a humbler function, that of pushing along a narrative with a plain *récit* – or as plain as the Muse will allow. That Joyce is primarily a master of uneccentric totally economical descriptive prose has never been sufficiently acknowledged. This prose is not, however, a crass insensitive instrument merely apt for saying what time it is or whether or not it is raining. It is very sensitive indeed to the character it is carrying along, and it tends to be coloured by what that character, if he thought about prose at all, would regard as *appropriate* prose.

Wyndham Lewis attacked Joyce for what he considered to be banality. He picked on a sentence in *A Portrait of the Artist as a Young Man* – 'Every morning, therefore, Uncle Charles repaired to his outhouse but not before he had greased and brushed scrupulously his back hair and brushed and put on his tall hat' – and pronounced: 'People *repair* to places in works of fiction of the humblest order.' Precisely, and fiction of the humblest order is what Uncle Charles, if he were a fictionwriter, would write. 'Repair' and 'brushed scrupulously' are there because Uncle Charles is there. The girl's popular weekly style is in

Nausicaa because Gerty MacDowell is there. To allow the *récit* to be inflected by the presumed literary taste of the human subject is what Professor Kenner very usefully calls 'the Uncle Charles principle'.

He finds the principle operating in *Eumaeus*, where Bloom has earned not only the coffee and bun of a conspicuous hero but also the right to be presented in the style he himself might choose if he ever managed that 'sketch' (or more than a sketch) 'by Mr and Mrs L.M. Bloom'. Look how it begins:

> Preparatory to anything else Mr Bloom brushed off the greater bulk of the shavings and handed Stephen the hat and ashplant and bucked him up generally in orthodox Samaritan fashion, which he very badly needed.

Professor Kenner asks us to note, what probably few of us had noted before, that the opening chapter of the whole book is recalled in a ghostly manner: there is 'buck' for Mulligan and 'brush' and 'shaving' and a wraith of the whole blasphemous aubade. The Muse is not very hard at work now (the science figured in the chapter is navigation: the wheel is locked on to the star: the ship seems asleep), but she has a vague idea that Bloom is trying to write a book and the only book she has in mind at present is one called *Ulysses*. The presiding theme of that opening chapter was *theology*: it gets in here in a muddled way with 'orthodox Samaritan', which defines Bloom's father's faith in terms of its antithesis.

But back to this rejection of the mythological rationale of a book which, after fifty-odd years of exegesis, it seems at last we are beginning to understand. Joyce talked much of Bloom's odyssey and cunningly persuaded his friends to talk more, but he was only concerned with finding pretexts (or the kind of excuse a man offers for the party-behaviour of a drunken wife) for the stylistic ports of call of his wandering muse. The Sirens feebly justify a chapter in the form of a fugue, but the true justification lies elsewhere. This is the hour when Blazes Boylan shall take possession of Bloom's bed, but Bloom and Molly have accepted that this boor who knows all about managing is coming to talk about managing a concert tour: Bloom allows his consciousness to be flooded with music, and the Muse gives him more music than he, or any reader, needs.

Again, if the Muse wants a free fantasy of the kind we associate with Mulligan's 'Dottyville', whose patients have GPI, she will find her best pretext in the goddess Circe, who gives men syphilis or (Joyce's brilliantly unscholarly etymology) 'swine fever'. In Molly's final monologue you will find a reference to General Ulysses Grant (whose original first name, incidentally, was Hiram, suggesting that His Majesty, in Joyce's world, could quite readily embrace the Irish Republican Army): may Ulysses grant permission for this apparently insane concatenation of structures. All fits in, see? Words spoken by L. Bloom.

The final argument against the sedulous Hellenization of the island is symbolized by one of Professor Kenner's illustrations – a photograph of the bust of Demosthenes from Trinity College Library. This Demosthenes, says Kenner, 'has a strikingly Irish look: you will see that face in the street outside'. You will, too. Joyce's eyes were altogether on 16 June 1904 in a city concerned very little with truth – whether of myth, history, or human character – but much concerned with words. *Ulysses* is full of lies, deceptions, illusions: words have very shaky referents. But, thanks to the Muse, that insane professional, we have some very solid verbal artefaction. And that's no myth. This is a most stimulating book. *This one*, I mean.

Irish Facts

A Colder Eye: The Modern Irish Writers, by Hugh Kenner

Hugh Kenner is Professor of English Literature at Johns Hopkins University. His blood is Welsh, Scottish and English, though the latter may really be Cornish. He is thus enough of a Celt to qualify for an understanding of the Irish, and, though one of his specialities is modern Irish literature in English, he has become enough of a Dubliner to know that the regular concerns of the literary specialist – which have much to do with the aesthetic and historical evaluation of texts – avail little in an ambience which distrusts art and has a very fluid notion of historical truth. So a book about the Irish modernists – Yeats, Synge, Joyce, O'Casey, Beckett and others – has to be approached Irishly, in a haze of drink and anecdote and those Irish Facts which are, by the most rigorous standards, lies. His book is dedicated to the memory of L. P. B. , a half-Jewish advertising canvasser who lives in Dublin but never existed.

In June 1982, a plaque was unveiled at 52 Clanbrassil Street, Upper, fulfilling the proposal in *Ulysses* that the house in which Bloom was born 'be ornamented with a commemorative tablet'. One old lady told the press that 'the Blooms didn't live there at all. They lived down that way.' Professor Kenner says: 'So Irish Facts multiply still, and it's fair to say that Dublin remains obsessed with the writers it doesn't read.' On Bloomsday 1982 *Ulysses* was virtually imposed on Dublin: the entire text was read out on the radio, though rendered unavailable to mere visitors with hotel radios, and the characters of that book paraded the streets (I think I saw Professor Kenner got up as Father Conmee SJ). Dublin did not seem to care very much: Who de hell's dat fella now wid de stick and de black hat on him, bloody fool disruptin de traffic dere ought to be a bloody law.

Professor Kenner has a thesis, and it may be said to have its source in a Joyce text. Stephen Dedalus listens to the Prefect of Studies of UCD, who is an England convert to Jesuitry, and says to himself: 'The language in which we are speaking is his before it is mine. How different are the words *home, Christ, ale, master* on his lips and on mine! I cannot speak or write these words without unrest of spirit.' A number of scholars have tried to explain why Joyce, or Stephen, chose those particular words. My own suggestion that they cunningly exemplify some of the main differences between spoken Dublin and London English apparently will not do. Now that Joyce himself, when I briefly visited him in 1938 (I was then a student of phonetics), admitted that I was right and the semantic content didn't matter a damn cannot really put Professor Kenner out. After all, we may be in the region of Irish Facts, though Kenner seems to assume I am English (I am far more Irish than he will ever be), and other people's theses will be accepted by the American professor only when they suit his book.

His own thesis is that to the Irish modernists the English language is a strange imposition on a Celtic-speaking people which has to be remade under a new dispensation. Thus, despite its being part of the refrain of Joyce's favourite song, *ale* is foreign in a land where a man named Guinness burned hops by mistake, and *home* may be an Englishman's castle but it is for an Irishman 'the shelter from which he might momentarily' – meaning, I take it, at any moment – 'be evicted'. In other words, Irish writers 'cast a cold eye' on what is to most of them a native language – none dealt with here, except Flann O'Brien, was brought up on the Gaelic – and refashion it either ironically, like Joyce, or, like Synge, according to the syntax and rhythms of the tongue of the peasants. This, I think, is an acceptable notion though not a new one. The new notion is that the essence of International Modernism was generated out of the ear, like Gargantua himself (this makes Kenner's title somewhat inept), and that the Irish fashioned out of English a medium that had nothing to do with the English literary tradition. Joyce destroyed English and Beckett turned his back on it. Yeats, who was a kind of Englishman, had a more difficult job, especially as he had, at first, hardly any Irish audience, but he graduated from Celtic airy-fairy (to please his Anglo-American readers and gain him the Nobel Prize) and forged a highly individual idiom out of his bitter soul.

It would have been un-Irish to develop this theme with scholarly rigour. The pleasure to be gained from Kenner's book lies in the marginal comments and footnotes (he comes close there to Dame Helen Gardner on Eliot and Messrs Warner and Marten on English history) and in the odd dangerous speculations which no decent professor ought to propound. Thus, the text of *Finnegans Wake* is a corpse rich in maggoty life. It is deliberately made out of an inert periodic English (I was regarded as mad when I suggested that Joyce found his sentence templates in Sinclair Lewis, but Joyce admitted to having read *Babbitt*) in which the syntagms are scintillant multiple puns: the *Wake* is genuinely a wake from first to last and the mourned body, in the worst wake tradition, is made to join in the fun (I once saw a corpse brought into a Chapelizod pub and have a pint bought for it). This is Kenner at his best.

Last summer in Cesena, Fritz Senn, a Germanophone Swiss who is perhaps the greatest Joycean of them all, asked his audience (which was mostly monoglot Italophone) to look at the first sentence of *Ulysses* and note how it begins with 'Stately' and ends with 'crossed', thus, in miniature, setting out the poles between which the narrative of the book sparks – the secular order and the ecclesiastical. Kenner takes this up and goes even further, expatiating on the various meanings of 'plump' (which is what Buck Mulligan is) and finding arithmological significance in sentences of eleven words (11 being the symbol for resurrection). All this is very much in order, but one wonders what would happen if the microscopy lavished on Joyce were transferred to, say, Harold Robbins, especially as the structuralists tell us that the text writes the author. Joyce is not yet plucked raw, but he soon will be.

There are errors. The 'th' in the stage-text representation of *true* as 'thrue' does not contain an aspiration: the Irish *t* is dentalized, the English alveolized, and a dental *t* is close to a *th*. Wordsworth did *not* declaim in Northumbrian. Verlaine did *not* write 'Le buste survite [*sic*] à la cité'. Anthony Burgess did not use the made-up word *droob* in his *A Clockwork Orange*, nor did he provide the work with a glossary. Irish impressionism affects Kenner's scholarly exactness. But his book is full of good things – the debt Beckett owes to Synge and to the Yeats–Pound neo-Noh plays, the importance of the poetry of Austin Clarke and of Patrick Cavanagh (a real peasant, not an Abbey Theatre one), the bloody wonderful hopelessness of Ireland. Our one English pope, Nicholas Brakespear, perhaps did right in handing Ireland over to the English. Ireland needed its sorrows and its writers needed the language of the invader.

Gloopy Glupov

The History of a Town, by M. E. Saltykov-Shchedrin, translated by I. P. Foote

Saltykov, who died in the same year as Browning and Hopkins, is hardly known to the British public. There may be readers of his novel *The Golovlev Family*, an unrelievedly gloomy record of decline and ruin in the Russian landowning class, but his satires – which he wrote mostly under the pen-name Shchedrin – have not, till Mr Foote came along, been available in English. In 1871 Turgenev praised this present book in a review in English for *The Academy*, but he warned that its fortified wine was unexportable. I do not know the original, but I can well believe that Mr Foote had difficulty in preparing this version, which reads extremely well. Saltykov seems to belong to the stylistic tradition which produced Bely's *Petersburg* and, for that matter, Nabokov's *Ada* – 'robust, idiomatic . . . richly allusive,' says Mr Foote. I take the original to be somewhat Rabelaisian. If Mr Foote reads more like Motteux than Urquhart, it is partly volitional, a desire to 'ease and clarify' so that the modern anglophone reader will more readily take the satirical points.

There is really only one point, the inability of Mother Russia to govern her children sensibly and liberally. Saltykov's mock-chronicle of the travails of a town under a succession of governors is set a century before the time when he wrote it, but he had his own era very much in mind. The book is popular in present-day Russia, where the regime bosses apparently fail to see that Saltykov was making a timeless, not a historical, point. There is, he seems to say, something in the Russian soul which evades governability of the democratic sort. Tyranny or anarchy, take your choice. There has to be the knout, and the only social contract is one between the whippable and the whipper. For forms of government let fools contest: whoever lays the knout on best is best. The town governors whip in the name of feudalism or the enlightenment or the classless society, but they still whip.

Gloopy, or *glupiy*, as those who have seen Mr Kubrick's *A Clockwork Orange* may remember, means stupid. The town Glupov, which is a microcosm of the whole of Russia, is hence the town of the stupid, Dumbville or Daftchester. Saltykov sings it in the manner of *The Tale of Igor's Campaign*, mock-epically, and tells of the earliest inhabitants, the Headbeaters, so-called 'because it was their habit to beat their heads against anything that came in their way.' There are other tribes whom they subdue and unify – the Lop-ears, the Pot-bellies and so on (the catalogue is very Gargantuan) – and then they attempt, with no success, a measure of social organization. They make dough by mixing flour in the Volga, cook porridge over a fire in a bag, exchange the local priest for a dog, put a flea in chains, erect poles to hold up the sky. They clearly need someone to look after them, so they go in search of a prince. In 1731, a year as achronological as the 1132 of *Finnegans Wake*, the Imperial Government appoints the first governor. Between that year and 1826 there are twenty-one. They are a pretty bad lot.

Thus, Foty Petrovich Ferapontov 'was so fond of entertainment that he allowed no floggings to take place unless he were present. In 1738 he was torn to pieces by dogs in the forest.' Ivan Matveich Baklan, seven feet seven, direct descendant of Ivan the Great (the bell tower in Moscow), 'broke in half in the great gale of 1761'. Dementy Varlamovich Brudasty had a clockwork head. Basilisk Semenovich Borodavkin died in 1798 while attending a flogging: 'given the last rites by a chief constable'. Ivan Panteleich Pryshch had a head filled with forcemeat.

Ugryum-Burcheev, the penultimate governor, has the most radical ideas. He wishes to reduce the ramshackle jigsaw town to geometrical order. This entails total destruction of the existing buildings, but it also means that the river too, which disdains geometry, must be brought under government control. The governor dams it and creates a flood. He sees this as an ocean and dreams of cramming it with warships. But nature has her own way, the dams crack, the river resumes its old course. 'The elements were not obedient, at every step there were gullies and ravines which barred the way to speedy movement; magical things took place before your very eyes, none of which were mentioned in the regulations or individual instructions. One had to get out!' Ugryum-Burcheev marches the Glupovites in a straight line to a perfectly flat plain, there to establish the Euclidian city. But then there are apocalyptical earthquakes and the sun grows dark and the bells ring of their own accord. Ugryum-Burcheev says: 'There will come . . .' and then vanishes. We know what will come: 'One after me who will be more terrible that I.' He has said this before 'with a kind of austere modesty'.

Saltykov, writing more than a century ago, has the gift of prophetic vision. But what makes him a nineteenth-century innocent is his assumption that governors are as mortal as governed and can burst, die drunk, or be eaten by dogs of the forest. He cannot conceive, as Zamyatin and Huxley and Orwell, less innocent, would be able to, of an unkillable self-perpetuating system in which cruelty is an aspect of policy, not just human nature. Moreover, though this book is full of fictional skills, it is not fiction in the manner of *We* or *Animal Farm*. There are monsters and a hundred-headed rabble, but there are no characters. We cannot feel for anybody as we can for D-503 and I-330 and Winston Smith and Boxer. Nevertheless, these annals of Glupov deserve, indeed demand, to be included in any course on cacotopias.

A Nevsky Prospect

Petersburg, by Andrei Bely, translated, annotated and introduced by Robert A. Maguire and John E. Malmstad

In his introduction to the as yet unpublished correspondence between Edmund Wilson and Vladimir Nabokov, Simon Karlinsky calls *Petersburg* 'a novel without which Nabokov's literary origins would be hard to imagine'. Nabokov himself said: 'My greatest masterpieces of twentieth century prose are, in this order, Joyce's *Ulysses*; Kafka's *Transformation*: Bely's *Petersburg*; and the first half of Proust's fairy tale *In Search of Lost Time*.' Edmund Wilson, like Dr Johnson, was always a person very dangerous to disagree with; Nabokov's judgements tended to the flighty. Nevertheless, his claim for Bely's book ought at least to be granted the courtesy of an examination. This has not been possible for most of us up till now. The pioneering translation of John Cournos (1959) bears, we are told, little resemblance to the original. There has not been a Soviet edition for more than forty years. This American rendering, with its fearsome battery of notes, probably gives all that English can give when unanimated by genius. The man for the job was, of course, Nabokov himself, but he preferred to expend his limitless ingenuity on *Eugene Onegin*, thus initiating that classic row with Wilson. We must be thankful for what we are given, but, if we really wish to test Nabokov's assertion, we have no alternative to tackling *Petersburg* in Russian.

The real name of Andrei Bely ('Andrew White') was Boris Nikolaevich Bugaev. He began to publish in 1902, while still a student at Moscow University, and adopted a pseudonym to spare his father, prominent in government, the embarrassment of the son's scandalous association with the Symbolists. It is important for us to know that the period of modernism in Russian art came very early. Stravinsky said of Russian music: 'It was new just *before* the Soviets.' In the novel, word-play, surrealistic fantasy, ambiguity, parody, recondite allusion were going strong while Britain was lauding the originality of E. M. Forster. *Petersburg* first appeared in 1916, six years before *Ulysses*. When people talk of Joycean elements in Nabokov, they are referring to symbolist properties that Joyce may himself have heard about in Zürich from Russian exiles (probably not Lenin). The things that Nabokov has done for English prose stem really from a comparatively conservative Russianism.

Bely constructs a most complex verbal artefact about a simple thriller theme. The scene is, of course, St Petersburg (which most of its citizens called Petersburg, honouring its royal founder more than its patron saint). It is autumn, 1905. Nikolai Apollonovich, an impressionable student, has become involved with revolutionary terrorists who order him to assassinate a high government official with a time bomb. The victim is to be Apollon Apollonovich, Nikolai's own father. There is suspense enough here, with the bomb ticking away for twenty-four hours, Nikolai torn by conflicting loyalties, the reader as much on the edge of his seat as Bely, always ready with new symbolist diversions, will allow. Indeed, the thriller properties render it unfair for the reviewer to disclose the ending. But the book is really about something bigger than an assassination plot. It is about Petersburg itself and, by implication, the condition of Russia in 1905.

Here is a great city with a culture the whole world knows of, vital, innovative, and yet it dithers, it doesn't know its future, it's not sure of its identity. Japan has beaten Russia and taken away Port Arthur, there are strikes and mutinies, revolution is coming, there is no solidity. The city liquefies, stone melts, the Bronze Horseman (Peter the Great's statue) gallops through the streets. Language is inadequate for expressing the simplest notions; it too has decided to disobey those morphological and semantic rules which symbolize the human order. A city in doubt, disarray, turmoil is the true protagonist, not Nicholas or his father Apollo. An East of arbitrary mysticism confronts a West of geometry, as they did in the city-builder Peter himself. But the geometry deliquesces along with civic authority; time is spatial and space temporal. Only the ticking bomb, warning of destruction, holds together, like a metronome, the centrifugal dissonance.

The memory holds the book like two disparate narratives – one a short story (for the plot is little more), the other an ever-expansive cosmic history, for, Bely being a Symbolist, the city has also to be the universe. The emotional turmoils of the characters are not engaged analytically: they engender metaphors of atomic and solar cycles, and, inevitably, they deflect or expand or destroy the structure of language. The narrator, a nameless eccentric who has read the whole of Russian literature and tries to nail the flying carpet to the parquet with fixed points of allusion, is not trustworthy, but he is less untrustworthy than anyone else. He quotes the newspapers accurately, though, as in *Ulysses*, he sometimes allows the newspaper format to take over. The book *looks* strange. It is also meant to sound strange.

Bely was insistent that the reader should be a listener, that the sonic patterns were a clue to the whole structure, but we cannot listen unless we learn Bely's Russian. The book is not translatable, any more than is *Harry Ploughman* or *Finnegans Wake*. If, having read this decent English rendering, we frown in perplexity at Nabokov's judgement, we shall have to conclude that the greatness is wholly resident in the language. And, remembering that the primary task of literature is diversion, a great deal of the fun also. The empirical Comte of Apollon confronts the categorical Kant of his son, but we have to know that in Russian the two names sound the same. On Nevsky Prospect we see 'apples of electric lights' – *'yabloki elektricheskikh svetov'*. An apple is a *yabloko*, and the man responsible for those lights was Pavel Nikolaevich Yablochkov – his surname derived from the diminutive *yablochko* – little apple. Every word resounds, but the harmonics are wholly Russian. Even Hamlet is a little *kham* – boor, lout, throwing a new glimmer onto Chekhov's paralysed aristocracy. *Petersburg*, as Nabokov recognized, is the one novel that sums up the whole of Russia. To appreciate, even to understand it on the primary level, we have to be Russian. The fact that Soviet Russia is so slow in bringing out a new edition may be taken as a small testimony to its importance.

Solzhenitsyn as War Poet

Prussian Nights, by Alexander Solzhenitsyn, a narrative poem translated from the Russian by Robert Conquest

It is a sin not to admire Solzhenitsyn, but I have not yet found anywhere a theological injunction to like him. Nearly every book he has written was born in pain or privation or prison. He is reported to have dismissed the greater part of Western literature as an ineffectual witness to the human condition, since the West has not known enough suffering. We have to treat with respect this narrative poem he produced in 1950, since he composed it in his head while serving his sentence of forced labour, but I refuse to be bullied into considering it a masterpiece.

> Open up, you alien country!
> Wide open let your gates be thrown!
> For, approaching, see how boldly
> Russia's battle-line rolls on!

During the war there were men in British sergeants' messes who would recite, or bardically declaim to the rhythm of popular song, similar lines about epic events of the war:

> South of the border,
> Down Montevideo way,
> There on the river lay
> The German pocket battleship Graf Spee. . . .

Nor is the doggerel tone solely to be found in the translation. Robert Conquest is a very considerable poet in his own right, but he has here submerged his skill and taste to match the original. Readers who know no Russian may be assured that they are getting something as near literal as dammit.

> *Shest' desyat ish v vetrozhoge*
> *Smuglish, spo-veselish lits.*
> *Po mashinam! Po doroge!*
> *Na Evropu! – navalis'!*

This reads literally: 'There were sixty of them, wind-burned, dark-skinned, maliciously high-spirited of face. Into vehicles! On your way! Into Europe! Attack!' And in Conquest's translation:

> There were wickedly cheerful faces
> Sixty of them, windburned, black.
> Into your vehicles! Get moving!
> Into Europe now! – Attack!

The poem is about Solzhenitsyn's own experiences when his battery joined in the invasion of East Prussia in January 1945. Three weeks after the start of the offensive, the author was arrested by, of course, his own people. Looking back, he meditates on the coincidence that the line of advance was the same as that of Samsonov and the Second Army in 1914. The story of Samsonov's defeat is the main theme of *August 1914* – a novel highly praised but, I would guess, little read – and it is certainly the most moving theme of this poem:

> . . . all the pain
> And all the shame of that campaign.
> In the dark cathedral-gloom
> Of one or another reading room
> I shared with none my boyish grief,
> I bent over the yellow pages
> Of those ageing maps and plans. . . .

When the author is most subjective he is most moving. A tune of Sarasate keeps going round and round in his head – sensuous, abandoned, symbolic of the irresponsibility which tempts him and to which his troops yield. But we may say that there is a vicarious surrender. The wanton killing of women and children, the firing and looting are fully detailed, and the relish of the ravagers and ravishers is matched by the relish of description. It may have been a sacred historical duty to produce the three volumes of *The Gulag Archipelago*, but it could not have been done without a certain sado-masochistic propensity. Solzhenitsyn is never slow to dwell on the brutality meted out to women. As for the pious justification of the troops' behaviour, does not the official handout say: *'Nye zabudem! Nye prostim! Krov! za krov'* – 'Do not forget! Do not forgive! Blood for blood!'?

The poet's yielding to the lust for loot is harmless and touching and provides a fine cadenza. A writer long forced to write on bad Soviet paper with watery ink, he surveys the riches of a post office due to be fired – *'Trista tri karandasha . . . Kox-i-nor, pochtenniy Faber . . .'* – three hundred and three pencils . . . Respected Fabers, Koh-i-Noors . . . – and loads his truck.

> Who should I blush in front of? Who?
> Anyone who points the finger
> – Go live in the USSR!

Prussian Nights is not – we may take this for granted even before reading – a poem analogous to such recent Soviet film epics as *They Fought for the Fatherland*, which, with its stereophonic bombardments, kept me awake at the last Cannes Festival I was at. It is unofficial art, its bitterness turned in the wrong direction: an officer who felt like this was certainly due to be hauled off to the Lubianka. As a deliberately brutal ballad-like celebration of the start of the last phase of the war on the Eastern Front, it has its – mostly subliterary – virtues. It is the sort of thing that wars spew up, mostly anonymously, but it has its moments of distinction:

> Through a rent in the smoky sky
> The clock, surviving through it all,
> Measures the time as honourably
> Between the others and ourselves,
> Those who've come and those who've fled,
> With the same ever-even tread,
> Only the ancient hands' fine lace
> Is trembling slightly on its face.

It is that 'honourably' – *'chestno'* – honestly, frankly, with integrity – that reminds us of the presence of a real writer behind all the noise, slang, swilling, burning and rape.

Dorogoi Bunny, Dear
Volodya . . .

The Nabokov–Wilson Letters 1940–1971, edited by Simon Karlinsky

I remember vividly receiving the four volumes of Vladimir Nabokov's annotated edition of Pushkin's *Eugene Onegin* (a title Nabokov
was quite ready to pronounce as though he were addressing a barman) and wondering at the mad devotion expended on it. It was like *Pale
Fire*, Kinbote devouring John Shade to the very caecum. Bidden review
it, what could I do but praise? Then I read Edmund Wilson's bitter
attack in the *New York Review of Books* and Nabokov's spirited reply. I
scuttled, like others, out of the crossfire, leaving it to the giants. What
most of us missed in that battle was the incidental avowal of a twenty-
five-year friendship. Mr Wilson felt for Mr Nabokov 'a warm affection
sometimes chilled by exasperation', a sentiment fully reciprocated: 'In
the 1940s, during my first decade in America, he was most kind to me in
various matters, not necessarily pertaining to his profession. . . . We
have had many exhilarating talks, have exchanged many frank letters.'
And here those letters are, admirably introduced and annotated by
Professor Karlinsky. At no point is there evidence of the coming terrible
breach. Frankness, yes, but always affection, eagerness to meet again,
mutual admiration, love to and from the family.

They had so much in common. Wilson was the sole non-academic
American who could claim a devotion to Russian literature which went
beyond Tolstoy and Turgenev. He and Nabokov had Pushkin in common, and yet it was over Pushkin they parted. Both knew French literature well. Both wrote books first banned, later hailed as trailblazers of
sexual candour: *Memoirs of Hecate County* the one, *Lolita* the other.
(Wilson was unaccountably prissy about *Lolita*.) Wilson could even
claim a layman's interest in lepidoptery: some of these letters had cutout
butterflies in them which whizzed out on the automatic release of a
rubber band. If they failed to achieve a totality of rapport, the fault was
probably more Bunny's than Volodya's.

For Wilson had become so Marxist that he was blind to the unpartisan
interpretation of Russian history that Nabokov was superbly qualified to
give him. He could not or would not see that an émigré like Nabokov
was not bitter at the expropriation his family had suffered (along with
the minor matter of a father assassinated) but angry at the failure of sixty
years of growing liberalism under the monarchy. That liberalism could

have culminated in a parliamentary democracy; instead it was blown out at one puff in a needless and cruel revolution. Wilson was brought up on a New York variant of the nineteenth-century Russian view of literature as an instrument of social change (something that the Soviet regime, far from inventing, merely took over) and saw in Nabokov's writings an evasion of politics – his Russian, at that time, being inadequate for tackling the not yet Englished *Invitation to a Beheading*. On the other hand, the author of the seminal *Axel's Castle* was unlikely to confuse the literary with the tendentious. And yet these letters sometimes show a baffling blindness to the excellence of Nabokov's prose.

Wilson cannot be blamed for not knowing, in 1940, when Nabokov arrived in America, that this debonair penniless European was already established as a major Russian novelist, though the term émigré was a damning one among the Manhattan Leninists. But he can be blamed for not comprehending Nabokov's literary method, for taunting him with lepidopteral wordplay, a kind of post-Joycean frivolity, when Nabokov was merely working in a long-established tradition of finding out truth through examining language. There was Bely's *Petersburg* behind him, a novel of pre-revolutionary provenance, and a tradition of symbolism older than that dealt with in *Axel's Castle*.

Nor could Wilson well appreciate Nabokov's general attitude to literature. Nabokov saw certain revered Anglo-American figures, like Henry James, as mere etiolated versions of Turgenev. He could not stomach Faulkner. He was willing, on Wilson's recommendation, to teach *Bleak House* at Cornell, but he had to invoke the memory of his father reading Dickens aloud in the golden pre-Lenin days. Jane Austen, whom Russians cannot understand, he at length accepted and found useful when annotating Pushkin and writing *Ada* (there is a deliberate evocation of *Mansfield Park* in that novel). But his attitude to books was summed up in the phrase 'a book is either for the bedside table or the waste-paper basket'. Wilson read out of duty, which Nabokov never did. The letters are full of genial failure to come to terms. Though both, probably rightly, saw little in Solzhenitsyn, Wilson found *Doctor Zhivago* a searing masterpiece and Nabokov considered it tripe.

The real division between them, which one sees in these letters first as a hairline fissure, later as a gulf, was occasioned by their attitudes to prosody. Nabokov refused to understand Wilson when he spoke of secondary stress in English polysyllables; Wilson was a long time coming to realize that the only stress in a Russian polysyllable is a root or tonic one. The letters show that Wilson's Russian was never much more than a reading instrument, apter for Leninist documents than the subtleties of Pushkin's verse. He attempts what he calls a clerihew (though it has six lines) in a Russian which even I can see is full of errors. Nabokov, from whom he could reasonably expect help with the language, was never able to put himself in the place of a foreigner who finds some aspects of Russian grammar, like the Russian soul, perversely baffling. As for prosody, Nabokov could be as pigheaded as Wilson. They slammed each other with rubber iambs and anapaests and finally fought a bloody duel over the body of Onegin.

So the correspondence comes to an end, except for brief nostalgic exchanges charged with bewilderment as to how this estrangement could ever have happened. True, Nabokov's circumstances changed radically after *Lolita*. He went back to Europe and could no longer be helped with the offer of a review, a story in the *New Yorker*, or a $500 lecture. Wilson grew crochety and unreasonably vindictive (see *Upstate*) towards old friends. Nabokov seems always, on the evidence of these letters, to have been reasonable and conciliatory. After all, it was not he who made the big public declaration of disaffection: he merely, with remarkable good humour, defended himself.

These letters, most informative about the state of literature in our age, are primarily about an epic relationship between two very quirky temperaments: the book reads like an epistolary novel. I have nothing but praise for the erudite and always helpful editorship and for the beauty of the lay-out (though Weidenfeld & Nicolson must merely bask in glory reflected from Harper & Row). Thunder, in autumn Montreux where I write this, has just begun to iamb and anapaest overhead. The great prosodic battle is now going on in heaven.

Poor Russian Writers

Lectures on Russian Literature, by Vladimir Nabokov

On 10 April 1958, Vladimir Nabokov, then teaching at Cornell but already famous or infamous as the author of *Lolita*, offered his views on the Soviet literary situation. Being more given to particularities than to general vapourings, he cited a passage from *The Big Heart*, written by a certain Antonov and serialized in 1957:

> Olga was silent.
> 'Ah,' cried Vladimir, 'why can't you love me as I love you?'
> 'I love my country,' she said.
> 'So do I,' he exclaimed.
> 'And there is something I love even more strongly,' Olga continued, disengaging herself from the young man's embrace.
> 'And that is?' he queried.
> Olga let her limpid blue eyes rest on him, and answered quickly: 'It is the Party.'

Poor Russian writers. They have never been free. Today they are, unless they choose exile, committed to using literature as a medium of Party Propaganda. Were they any better off in the nineteenth century, when the Czar and his secret police leaned over them as they wrote? They were sent to the salt mines for an unconsidered word that might be construed as hostile to the regime, or, like Pushkin, they could be killed in a duel arranged by the forces of orthodoxy. But they had access to that greatest of all literary joys – saying the dissentient thing in the guise of the harmless. The forces of oppression were brutal but stupid in those days. They are still brutal, but they no longer seem to be stupid.

When Czarist orthodoxy was being undermined by the new voices of revolution, the poet or novelist was in a very awkward situation. One part of the reading public reviled him if he did not, as Dostoevsky did, uphold the eternal values – Czar, Holy Russia and the Greek Orthodox faith. The other half reviled him if he did not, in the manner of Gorki, write proletarian literature which aided the masses in their struggle for liberation. If a writer merely wished to write of young love and spring flowers, he was upbraided as unrealistic and escapist. Choose the State or the masses – there was no other choice. In time, as Nabokov neatly puts it, the Hegelian opposites fused into the final synthesis – the State speaking in the name of the masses.

The lectures that Nabokov gave during his American exile were on the two halves of his literary endowment – first, the English and Americans; now the Russians, specifically Chekhov, Dostoevsky, Gogol, Gorki, Tolstoy and Turgenev. His attitude to them will not please those progressive souls who believe that literature should found revolutions or speak out for an existing stability. Literature, according to Nabokov, is not a matter of the collective or even the individual soul. It is a matter of the exact notation of the physical world. It is a matter of grace, wit, ingenuity, dandyism. It is, in fact, the kind of thing we find in *Lolita*, *Pale Fire* and *Ada*. The permanencies are not political nor even religious. They are the taste of food, the smell of newly washed muslin, the dark hair curling on Anna Karenin's white neck.

Nabokov holds up Tolstoy as the terrible example of a supreme artist who decided, after writing two towering masterpieces, that art was immoral. What was important was man's soul, spiritual regeneration, the putting off of the concerns of the flesh. Such things are too vague to have meaning, and, in Tolstoy's renunciation of life, we see foreshadowed the collective renunciations of abstract Sovietism. Marxism is an abstract system, and it can be forced to be relevant to literature only by robbing literature of its essential properties – the delightful chaos of the world of the flesh, the mind's irrationality. Tolstoy too embraced abstractions, and he became a foolish old man who condemned the achievement for which even the Soviet Union is impelled to honour him.

Dostoevskians will find Nabokov's disparagement of their master deeply discouraging. He takes *Crime and Punishment* and, with unerring acuity, finds in one brief passage the core of the novel's insufficiency as a statement of human values. Raskolnikov and Sonia sit together: she has been reading from the Bible about the raising of Lazarus. 'There they were, the three of them,' says Dostoevsky: 'the murderer, the prostitute, and the Holy Book.' But, says Nabokov, we never see Sonia in action as a whore, and her sin was forgiven two thousand years ago; Raskolnikov, on the other hand, whose crime we have seen in all its bloody detail, is not yet forgiven and is perhaps not even forgivable. To collocate the two in the same implied region of moral values argues a gross insensitivity. It is, in fact, insensitivity that is the overwhelming fault of Dostoevsky – to prose style, to moral values, to the God-given variety of the exterior world. He would, thinks Nabokov, have made a useful playwright, but the plays would have been too long.

And what are the virtues of Turgenev? They are not many: he was not a great artist, but he was the first Russian author to take note of sunlight and shadow. He had what Dostoevsky did not have – a devouring interest in the surface of the earth. Tolstoy had it too, and Tolstoy had something else – the ordinary reader's sense of time. Time is plastic (or Bergsonian) with Proust; in Tolstoy it can be related to the events reported in newspapers: you can date the events in *Anna Karenina*, you find no day unaccounted for, you find no distortion of time to serve the exigencies of the plot. Spatial and temporal reality are what Nabokov seeks, not the borborygms of the Russian soul (whatever that is) and not the involutions of fantasy.

But wait – he adores Gogol, and what could be more fantastic than

The Nose or *The Overcoat*? True; but fantasy does not excuse vagueness. Gogol's world is exactly observed. It is also made out of an intensely physical love of the Russian language. And here comes Nabokov's main, and agonizing, point. You cannot read Russian literature in translation.

> You will first learn the alphabet, the labials, the linguals, the dentals, the letters that buzz, the drone and the bumblebee, and the tse-tse fly. One of the vowels will make you say 'Ugh!' You will feel mentally stiff and bruised after your first declension of personal pronouns. I see no other way, however, of getting to Gogol (or to any other Russian writer for that matter). His work, as all great literary achievements, is a phenomenon of language and not of ideas.

The viability of translation, he believes, is an illusion and always was. Tolstoy seems translatable enough, but in *Anna Karenina* we read: 'Enchanting was the firm-fleshed neck with its row of pearls . . . enchanting her animation, but there was something terrifying and cruel about her charm.' But the row of pearls in *zhemchug*, her animation is *ozhivlenie*, terrifying is *uzhasnoe* and cruel is *zhestokoe*. *Zh* after *zh* after *zh*. The beautiful Anna is enclosed for ever in a forest of buzzes.

Cruel? Crude?

Lectures on 'Don Quixote', by Vladimir Nabokov
Nabokov's Novels in English, by Lucy Maddox

'I remember with delight,' said Nabokov, when he had become the self-exiled author of *Lolita* and was vaguely scornful of his academic days, 'tearing apart *Don Quixote*, a cruel and crude old book, before six hundred students in Memorial Hall, much to the horror and embarrassment of some of my more conservative colleagues.' The Memorial Hall referred to is at Harvard. Guy Davenport, who contributes a foreword to these lectures, sees in the building 'a consummately quixotic architectural rhetoric' derived from the worst dreams of Scott and Ruskin, a good place for the demolition work of a fastidious ironist. I know the building myself and, brought up on Manchester Town Hall, never found much wrong with it. But, in a foreword to Nabokov on Cervantes, it has to become a symbol of false chivalric visions, the kind of thing that Connecticut Yankee of Mark Twain's would gladly have dynamited. Nabokov's colleagues at Harvard, who probably just saw the place as a place to teach in, had the wrong line on *Don Quixote*: they were Tennysonian men who had constructed their own sunny Spain and idealistic hidalgo. Nabokov was there to put them right.

Almost his first job was to show his students what a windmill was like and how to name its parts. Windmills, he said, were something new in Cervantes's Spain, and it was understandable that a homekeeping hidalgo should think it something to strike a lance at. He emphasizes the obscurantism of Spain, how it was stuck in the Middle Ages and, like the imaginary England of Keith Roberts's *Pavane*, was amenable neither to science nor to humane ideas. We read into Cervantes's attitude to his own creation too much of the age of *The Impossible Dream*, assuming that he loved the mad knight and was shocked at the way a new unchivalric Spain was treating him. It was not like that at all, says Nabokov. Cervantes shared the pleasure in bone-cracking japes that was rife under Philip (who could see no humour in letting his empty suit of armour review the troops) and thought it excellent fun to see Don Quixote's teeth knocked out. A cruel book, then. Also crude?

Well, yes, in the sense that it is ill put together, is full of irrelevant novellas (a bad influence on *Pickwick Papers* and, indeed, on Angus Wilson's *Last Call*) and lacks almost entirely the true novelist's interest in the outside world. Cervantes's geography, demonstrates Nabokov carefully, is all wrong, and so is his perception of nature, which comes out of pastoral romances and not from direct observation. Instead of filthy cowherds and sun-scorched rock we get pretty Damons sighing for Phyllis and rosy landscapes full of rills. The characters are stock types, even Sancho Panza, who is nothing more than a red-nosed auguste full of stock quips, thin legs belying a fat belly which is no more than a stuffing of cushions. Dickens, we know, worked in a tradition of stage melodrama, and so did Cervantes. Both were failed dramatists. The excellence of *Don Quixote*, affirms demonstrating Nabokov, lies in its dialogue: Cervantes knew that part of the craft, but he couldn't put a plot together. We are prepared now to have the mad knight knocked as an improbable confection, but Nabokov has to admit that here is a real creation. He undresses him as carefully as Humbert undresses Lolita, observing hair and moles with a lepidopterist's eye, counting teeth and examining diet (chiefly pies made from the flesh of beasts that have ventured too far and fallen over precipices, appropriate food for the knight who should have stayed in the pasture).

Whatever Cervantes intended, his hero is credible, admirable, and a personage more real than early-morning news-readers and front-bench politicians. Quixotry is stupid, but there's nothing wrong in faith, hope and charity. What has happened, of course, is that Don Quixote has stepped outside the boundaries of fiction and become a creature beyond his creator's control, like Falstaff and Hamlet and, conceivably, Emma Bovary and Jim Dixon. When the British peace team came over to Spain in the first years of James I's reign, actors were already portraying the thin knight and fat squire for the benefit of visitors who knew who they were (English was the first foreign language to get them and it got them early). When New York's Puerto Ricans parade they are usually in the procession. You don't have to read the book to know them, and not many people have, though a lot of people think they have. Nabokov has read it with a terrifying thoroughness.

Dr Maddox has read Nabokov the novelist in English with a thoroughness not quite so terrifying, though she has learned from her subject how to nitpick at the text. Pnin, she says, would not have been happy with the factual inconsistencies in his story (he is a great one for checking railway timetables in *Anna Karenina*) and would have wondered how his narrator, who hardly knows him, knows so much about him. But, except for *The Real Life of Sebastian Knight*, she finds great fictional excellence in Nabokov, an admirable accuracy in his recording of the external world, and a superb sense of design. It is this meticulous structuring of the novels that causes, she thinks, such difficulties for the characters. 'Nabokov's people are consistently frustrated by the sense of living on the edge of meaning, of being part of a complicated pattern that they get only glimpses of but that must surely make wonderful sense to someone, somewhere.'

But this, of course, is the paradox of all fiction. A character, to be acceptable as more than a chess piece, has to be ignorant of the future, unsure about the past, and not at all sure of what he's supposed to be doing. The author knows everything, and we know he knows, and that tends to diminish our power to accept his creations as real people. If you structure as solidly as Nabokov does, there's no semblance of free will: all is predestined: life is a Geneva watch or a Geneva sermon. One way out of this impasse is to make the chief character tell his own story, which is what almost invariably happens in Nabokov, and thus seem to be in control of everything except the end. But with Nabokov, as with Joyce, you can tell from the rhythms and the choice of words who is really in charge.

Dr Maddox is best on *Pale Fire*, which she puts first in her survey. Despite the quirky shape of the book – a long poem and a set of notes – there is an acceptable rationale in putting the narrative in the hands of a kind of madman who, since he misunderstands everything, both fulfils the role of Fordian 'limited viewer' and allows us, knowing better than he, to be satisfied with that and not to start worrying about the author's omniscience. It could be said, incidentally or finally, that without some kind of madman – Humbert is manic enough – Nabokov couldn't write the way he did. Only a madman could be obsessed with language and visual exactitude to the extent that Nabokov's narrators are. But this means that Nabokov himself was mad, and so perhaps are all novelists. This is a line I would be very frightened to pursue.

Gigs and Games

A Perfect Vacuum, by Stanislaw Lem, translated from the Polish by Michael Kandel

L em is the other great Pole of our time, scientist, philosopher, futurologist, novelist, trickster, very different from John Pole. His new book is the first book reviewed in this book of imaginary book reviews. Lem as not-Lem reviewing not-Lem as Lem, or perhaps Lem[1] enclosing Lem[2], or the other way about. The title of the book means that it is a book 'about nothing'. In that the books reviewed do not, and cannot, exist, the reviews cannot exist either. Nor can my own review exist. Let us pretend that it does.

There is a long review of a novel called *Gigamesh* by Patrick Hannahan (Transworld Publishers, London). It is an Irish novel that attempts to outdo both *Ulysses* and *Finnegans Wake* (which real Lem, or his translator, inexcusably spells with an apostrophe). The whole action of the novel covers thirty-six minutes, the time taken to convey Maesch, a criminal GI from his cell to his place of execution. Hannahan requires 395 pages to tell his story and another 847 to annotate it. This apparatus criticus, achieved by hooking up computers to the twenty-three million volumes of the Library of Congress, presents a totality of reference which, thinks Lem, will displease the professors since it gives them nothing to do. The very name Gigamesh, an alambdakismic version of Gilgamesh, mythic Babylonian hero, contains GIG, the rowboat in which Maesch used to drown his victims, having poured cement on them, GIGA (billion, signifying the magnitude of evil in a technological civilization), GAME (the game of a manhunt), GIGolo (Maesch's trade as a youth) – more, much more. If, argues Lem, Mel, Elm or whoever it is, there is great literary virtue in the Joycean puzzles, it follows that *Gigamesh* contains the ultimate literary virtue and, morever, it provides solutions for its puzzles.

Sexplosion, by Simon Merrill (Walker & Company, New York) is, Lem tells us, the story of the great sex crash of 1998, when the public, 'in an instinctive feeling of revulsion', rejected the erotic.

> The specter of extinction hung over humanity. It began with an economic crisis compared to which the one of 1929 was as nothing. The entire editorial staff of *Playboy*, in the forefront as ever, set fire to itself and died in flames; employees of striptease clubs and topless bars went hungry, and many leaped from windows: magazine publishers, film producers, huge advertising combines, beauty schools went bankrupt; the entire cosmetic-perfume industry was shaken, as was lingerie. In the year 1999, there were thirty-two million jobless in America.

Food replaces sex. Gastronomy is divided into the normal and the obscene. From Denmark are smuggled pornoculinary magazines of unimaginable grossness (eater in bondage, fingers sunk into garlicked spinach, sucking scrambled eggs through a straw). Funny, Lem, but Aldous Huxley did it before you, so did Woody Allen – the pornography of Jews eating ham and lobster. And now I begin to suspect Lem a little. These non-books are not impossible. Lem himself might have tried them but thought it safer to review them instead. Bet-hedging.

I mean, Alfred Zellermann's *Gruppenführer Louis XVI* is not impossible, and I wouldn't have minded writing it myself. Siegfried Taudlitz leaves the ruined Reich and makes for South America with the SS treasure, there to set up the court of Louis XVI which, since he has not studied history, he does not know very well. He has, for instance, to name the members of his court after French wines, which he does know. A good and plausible black comedy which Lem was too lazy to write and has ensured that no one else may write either.

Lem is too constructive a writer to be able to demolish through absurdity. Besides, literature can now take absurdity in its stride. In his review of Mme Solange's *Rien du tout, ou la conséquence*, we meet the *anti-roman* to end all. Fiction lies, because it is fictitious; therefore let us create a verifaction of denials: 'He was not born, consequently he was not named either; on account of this he neither cheated in school nor later got mixed up in politics.' What is left? Only language, which, 'having come to realize that it represents a form of incest – the incestuous union of nonbeing with being – suicidally disowns itself.' But, in the course of his review, Lem refers to Borges, who can beat anybody at this non-book game. How about Menard, who wrote *Don Quixote*, word for word the same as Cervantes but, because produced in the twentieth century, inevitably different? Cervantes can write about history as the mother of truth, and this is a mere rhetorical flourish. Let

Menard, contemporary of William James, do it and the context, hence the meaning, is totally changed. Lem seems to be signalling that we are not having fun after all: we are making serious investigations into semantics, ontology, epistemology and the rest of the dangerous entities.

There is also the story of *U-Write-It*, a literary erector set which gave you an abridgement of classic novels like *Karenina* and *Crime and Punishment* and encouraged you to take the characters and manipulate them in ways unforeseen by the original authors, making Anna Karenina fornicate with the footman and not with Vronsky or Raskolnikov escape with Sonia to Switzerland. The pleasure you were supposed to get from this was obscenely brutish: '*U-Write-It* allows you to acquire that same power over human lives, godlike, which till now has been the exclusive privilege of the world's greatest geniuses!' You could canonize vice and besmirch virtue. But the public was too ignorant to know who Jane Eyre (available for the brothel) or Natasha (who could be horribly married to Svidrigailov) was. Total neutrality, no thrill. Also, said a Swiss critic, 'the public is grown too lazy to want even to rape, undress, or torture anyone itself. All *that* is now done for it by professionals. *U-Write-It* might possibly have been a success had it appeared sixty years earlier. Conceived too late, it was stillborn.'

You have some idea now of the games Lem is playing, but towards the end they become not literary, which is easy, but philosophico-scientific, which is hard. At the very end, and at some length, we have the new cosmogony of Professor Alfred Testa, summarized by him in an address delivered on the occasion of his receiving the Nobel Prize. This new cosmogony has its beginnings in the work of a Greek, Acheropoulos, a non-person discussed by a non-person, who believed that the Universum is the work of protocivilizations engaged in a Game. 'Science,' says Professor Testa to the King of Sweden and the rest, 'currently sees the Universe as a palimpsest of Games, Games endowed with a memory reaching beyond the memory of any one Player.' Here we have, among things, a scientific justification for Lem's own ludicity. We are also back to St Thomas, who thought it possible that God had created the world in a ludic fit. The point about Lem's games is that they are more serious than other people's seriousness, but we had better not take them seriously.

He is one of the most intelligent, erudite and comic writers working today, and one wonders what he is doing in Poland (*is* he in Poland?). He is well acquainted with the free West and evidently in close contact with his translator, who is superb. Or is he perhaps also that translator? It's a pity he is by nature so sceptical. Hastily ordained, installed, red-hatted, he would do well in the Vatican.

The Boredom of SF

Why is most science fiction so damned dull? There are various possible answers. You practise the genre if you have fancy but no imagination. Bizarre things matter more than such fictional staples as character, psychological probability and credible dialogue. There is usually an atmosphere of evasion of real-life issues, occasionally qualified by dutiful lip-service shibboleths about human freedom and the embattled ecology. Content counts more than form. You are encouraged, despite the examples set by Ray Bradbury and H. G. Wells himself, still the best of the esseffers, to see yourself as working outside the literary tradition, which is artsy-shmartsy, and belonging to a category of near-popular sub-art, meaning bad typewriterese on coarse paper.

SF plots are easily devised. We are a million years into the future, and the world is run by the Krompir, who have police robots called patates under a grim chief with a grafted cybernetic cerebrum whose name is Peruna. There is a forbidden phoneme. If you utter it you divide into two identities which continue to subdivide until you become a million microessences used to feed the life system of Aardappel, the disembodied head of the Krompir. But there is a phonemic cancellant called a burgonya, obtainable on the planet Kartoffel. You can get there by Besterian teleportation, but the device for initiating the process is in the five hands of Tapuach Adamah, two-headed head of the underground Jagwaimo. Man must resist the System. The Lovers, who amate according to the banned traditional edicts of Terpomo, proclaim Love. Type it all out and correct nothing. You will find yourself in the Gollancz SF constellation – along with Bob Shaw's *Ship of Strangers*, Richard Cowper's *The Road to Corlay*, *The 6th Day* by W. J. Burley, and *Roadside Picnic* by Arkady and Boris Strugatsky (genuine Russians translated into genuine American by Antonina W. Bouis).

Though *The Road to Gorlay* is not bad, if not so good as Kingsley Amis's *The Alteration* and Keith Roberts's *Pavane*, which also posit a world in which the Roman Catholic Church rules England tyrannically. Thought has gone into it, there is an attempt at characterization, there is ingenuity in the notion of a waterlogged Britain of the year 3000 which has become seven island kingdoms. *Roadside Picnic*, on the other hand, which is about the Zone in Canada, where mysterious alien visitants leave debris of an advanced technology that fetches very high prices on the black market, is an excruciatingly brutal piece of writing, or translation. Theodore Sturgeon, in his introduction, tells us of a planet of Iron Curtain SF of immense size and density as yet unknown to the West. If this is a specimen, I remain unenticed. I remember a Soviet Writers' symposium I once attended whose SF specialists said, ha ha, the only trouble with their genre was that they could not keep up with the reality. But the real reality, as the Neapolitans would put it, is totalitarian injustice and the technological advances are a mere surface frippery. That SF should be a universal subliterature, ignoring the real world of police and censorship, is not a point in its favour. It is, I say again, evasive.

Ship of Strangers is about the space survey vessel *Sarafand*, which gets stranded in a distant galaxy where everything, including the *Sarafand*, is rapidly shrinking to zero size. Why not minus size while the author's hand is in? *The 6th Day* is very plainly and decently written in the old Wells style. The members of a scientific expedition in the Galapagos Archipelago are transported into the far future, when the human race has self-destructed and a kind of highly intelligent octopus has taken over. Can humanity, in the form of these, and other, chronic argonauts (Wells's original title, by the way, for *The Time Machine*), be persuaded to start all over again? No. Man is too violent a creature. Once you get into violence you get out of SF, save for the technical trimmings. In other words, SF writers sooner or later have to resort to the clichés of the adventure yarn. Robert Silverberg's *Capricorn Games* also belongs to the Gollancz SF galaxy but it is, for some reason, 30p dearer than its yellow fellows. The stories have quality and a few Borges touches – doubt of the viability of the form itself, for instance; a narrator from the future admitting that he is only signs on paper. There is also fine writing: 'At my back sprawls the sea, infinite, silent. The air is spangled with the frowning faces of women.' There is 30p worth of fine writing.

Robert Sheckley's *The Alchemical Marriage of Alistair Crompton* (Michael Joseph) has a beautiful cover by Peter Elson, and it also has humour – not a common commodity in the genre. The eponym is the chief tester of Psychosmell Inc., which makes psychotropic perfumes, and a cured schizophrenic who hates being whole and *robotniy*. The missing bits of his personality are leading separate lives on distant planets, so he sets out to recover them. This is, as they say, fun. *A Billion Days of Earth* (Dobson) is not fun. Its author, Doris Piserchia, 'known for the vivid dream-like quality of her prose', was trained as an educational psychologist, something of a recommendation in a novelist. It was always said that William, not Henry, should have taken up quality fiction. Here is some of Ms Piserchia's dreamlike prose:

> The Gods hurried into their ship, and then there was only Vennavora remaining outside. She stood in the doorway, faced the sky, spread her arms, and with tears coursing down her cheeks, she said: 'Oh, Earth, you have become a scourge. You will go down in the record of the heavens as a world to shun. Killer of Its Babes will be your name. . . . Farewell to the sweet winds and streams of your body, goodbye to the sky and the sun, to the paths in the mountains and the sparkling rain. Wherever we go, we will never find our home. It has cast us out.'

Then they get the hell out to the stars.

Last, there is the old master Brian Aldiss. *Enemies of the System* (Jonathan Cape – cheapest and best of the lot, note) is about the Ultimate State a million years hence and a trip by some of its more prestigious members to Lysenka II, a planet where the bestial inhabitants are degenerate capitalist humans. The utopian specimens of *Homo uniformis* are forced to find, against their will, virtues in these filthy flesh-eating mammalians and are drawn into being what the title says. It is too short a tale to say what has to be said, but it contrives to be rich, allusive, full of real people and unfailingly interesting. It is not, then, real S F.

Laughs

Eastward Ha!, by S. J. Perelman, and *The Most of S. J. Perelman*

Here in Monte Carlo, where we have to take amusement seriously, there is not much to laugh at. Any loud laughter heard spilling over the balconies of the *troisième étage* of 44 rue Grimaldi will usually be manic and occasioned by the latest royalty statement. True, on Sundays Monte Carlo TV collaborates with Westward TV to give us *British Hour*, with Tommy Cooper saying 'I alluz call my wife dere, she as these antlers growin on er ead.' But if I need a real laugh I have to get the Paris *Herald–Tribune* and read Art Buchwald on the back page. Or reread Leo Rosten's *The Joys of Yiddish*. Only New York Jews, who cling to taboos and anxiety like the tablets of the law, continue to know what humour is.

That's why, in bed on the floor (my only luxury is my address; I cannot afford French furniture), suffering, the other morning, from malaria and bronchial asthma, I was pleased when all this Perelman came with the 6 a.m. *courrier*. But, having read 776 pages pretty well nonstop by 5 a.m. the following morning (cable from New York: CAN

YOU REVIEW BEST OF BERNARD LEVIN 1500 WORDS REPLY SOONEST),
I felt that I wanted a damned good cry. I had been fed full of fun and felt
heavy. Perelman is funny but heavy, like the Montreal Jewish prizeman
Bellow.

Of course, it is not fair to Perelman to read so much of him on the floor
in one go, with an intermission for two boiled eggs and a quart of
Twining's English Breakfast. The late Donald Tovey's admirable *Essays
in Musical Analysis* were always mentioning Dr Johnson's friend Edwards
and cheerfulness breaking in, and in an embarrassed footnote Tovey
warned us that these were really programme notes and should not all be
read at once. Now, Perelman is amazingly non-repetitive (only the word
lagniappe keeps breaking in), but the rhythms of his *récit* – his dialogue is
a different matter – are terribly unvarious. What we need is a few *New
Yorker* columns, well broken up by advertisements, and then breathing
space till next time.

In Cannes, in 1972, I asked Groucho Marx what he thought of
Perelman. Too literary, he said, too allusive. If he wanted literature he
preferred to go to old Tom Eliot. And then he was back on to the good
days, with hookers at two bucks a throw. Perelman *is* allusive. He has a
cat that has read *Ulysses* and goes 'Mkgrnao'. Proust and Gide do brief
and ghostly softshoes. Perelman conceives of himself as having a sort of
duty to literature:

> Anybody who chanced to be flatboating down the Sunday book-review
> sections lately, poling his way through such nifties as *Bismarck: A New
> Synthesis* by Dr Stauffer, or *A Deciduous Girl of Old Williamsburgh*, by Sara
> Leamington Latrobe, probably wound up the day in a darkened room
> applying vinegar poultices freely to his forehead.

You can see the pen poised. Is it full enough? 'Poling his way *warily*',
perhaps. Possibly 'to his *febrile* forehead'? It is school-magazine
funniness, with some brilliant sixth-former weighing the exact import of
the delicious bit of slang that is the locus of the fun.

Perelman is, like Groucho himself, at his best when he takes the
figurative literally. 'How about a spot of whisky and soda?' asks Snubbers, and Littlejohn, Snubbers's man, 'brought in a spot of whisky on a
piece of paper which we all examined with interest.' And the soda?
You've guessed it. 'I took it to please him, for Gabriel's cellar was
reputedly excellent. A second later I wished that I had drunk the cellar
instead. Baking soda is hardly the thing after a three-hour bicycle trip.'
He is at his better than best when he writes dialogue. In 'Waiting for
Santy' Riskin, filing a Meccano girder, 'bitterly', says: 'A parasite, a
leech, a bloodsucker – altogether a five-star nogoodnick! Starvation
wages we get so he can ride around in a red team with reindeers!' To
which Ruskin, jeering, replies: 'Hey, Karl Marx, whyn'tcha hire a
hall?' Two turkey vultures cling to a snowy crag outside Los Angeles,
and one says: 'That sure was a delicious scenario writer. You'd have to
go all the way to Beverly Hills for one like him,' while the other replies:

'Listen, that bad I don't need *anything*.'

This last bit comes from a travelogue called *Westward Ha!*, and *Eastward Ha!* is a new book that completes an inevitable diptych. (Diptych-shmiptych, I know I got oil.) Mr Perelman's tripnick journals make me uneasy because I don't know what to believe and what not. I mean, strange things happen in Bangkok anyway. And a Colombo passport control officer *could* have said: 'I've been stamping passports for years, but I'd just like to say that yours is one of the prettiest I've ever seen. It's done with real taste – not like *some* I could mention. May I ask who did it?' Get a humorist into exotic parts and he's not in real control, not like back home, where one can be *fairly* sure that Moss Hart would not *really* be ejected from Schrafft's for not consulting the management about the casting of *My Fair Lady*.

But 'Paris on Five Dolors a Day' is fine, with Giscard d'Estaing and his council of ministers preparing a memorable reception for the American, 'to sustain the nation's highest traditions of hospitality and *la gloire*'. And Giscard says: 'So let us adjourn to our midday feed. Quaffing the good red wine of France, we can be certain that this longtime visitor to our shores will find our fiendishness unchanged, all the torments a Torquemada could invent still bugging him.' Paris brings out the funniest in Perelman, as she does in Buchwald. And really, you know, all of Perelman is very good, really, though a bit slow and a bit old-fashioned.

Groucho gave me a souvenir Romeo and Juliet, which I duly encased in plastic. It fell to pieces on the day of his death, when I was in Barcelona and prayers for his soul were said in Catalan. Groucho's humour still exercises linguistic philosophers. Perelman's is, like the little books of Frieda Lawrence's first husband, merely philology.

The Smile, Not the Laugh

The New Oxford Book of English Light Verse, chosen by Kingsley Amis

'I must now attempt what I hardly had to think of at all . . . while putting this anthology together,' begins Amis, putting the thing, even the syntax, honestly; for definition, which he has to attempt, always succeeds exemplification, though convention insists on putting it first. He thinks, and probably we think, that light verse is a recognizable commodity. On the other hand, W. H. Auden thought so too, but his *Oxford Book of Light Verse*, published forty years ago, is very different from Amis's. 'Danny Deever', the Kipling poem which Amis rightly considers 'one of the most harrowing . . . in the language', got into Auden's collection because it fulfilled a requirement that seems now to be doctrinaire – that, to be termed light, verse should be based on the life and language of ordinary people. Blues and ballads thus also got in, despite their very unlight themes of murder and treachery. But this limerick could not have got in, because ordinary people do not know Latin:

Whenever a fellow called Rex
Flashed his very small organ of sex,
   He always got off,
    For the judges would scoff,
'De minimis non curat lex.'

It is in Amis, and few of us would think that it should not be. It evokes a smile, which all light verse does, and the smile is evoked by neatness or absurdity or gentle obscenity. The smile is good-natured: we need not be scared of testing our reaction to such writing with a shaving mirror. We might be scared of our reflections while reading Swift's scatophobic lines on Celia, or some of Pope's Epistles, so it is safe to call such verse heavy. Lightness needs heaviness as a foil. Lightness also needs immense technical skill, which heaviness often does not. As Amis says, a concert pianist is allowed a quota of wrong notes, but a music-hall juggler is not permitted to drop anything.

Aldous Huxley, whose *Texts and Pretexts* Amis does not admire, and whom he considers to have been tin-eared and humourless, points out somewhere that converts to Catholicism often take to light verse. He was thinking of Chesterton, J. B. Morton and Belloc (who was not a convert), and I think his implication was that the order and neatness on which light verse depends are a reflection of a neat theological orderliness. Take it further and say that light verse takes certain civilized standards for granted, which heavy verse need not. We expect the heavy verse of our own time to eschew neatness, wrestling as it does so often with profound moral issues: regular rhyme and rhythm would seem frivolous. The result is that a lot of contemporary traditional-style verse seems light when it is probably not, a hymn strophe, for instance, being a vehicle for irony or the pain of emptiness. Amis's own Dickensian-Cockney version of Baudelaire's 'L'Albatros' seems more bitter than the original:

> Theyve ardly got im on the deck afore,
>   Cackanded, proper chokker – never mind
> Es a igh-flier – cor, e makes em roar
>   Voddlin abaht, is vings trailin beind.

If our own age cannot produce light verse, except of the technically brilliant kind found in Hart, Porter, Sondheim, Noël Coward (his 'Mad Dogs and Englishmen' is here), all of whom depend on the prosody enforced by song, the Victorian era was preternaturally rich in it. The heavy poets, like Tennyson and Browning, were so skilled in traditional prosody and Browning was so skilled at rhyme, that the light men had to set themselves high standards. There was a lot of parody about, and the parodist has to be cleverer than his original. There was a lot of nonsense too – the best of it in Carroll, the worst in Edward Lear – and it had not yet been exalted into surrealism. The nonsense comes early in Amis, just after Shakespeare and Ben Jonson:

> I grant that rainbows being lulled asleep,
>   Snort like a woodknife in a lady's eyes;
> Which makes her grieve to see a pudding creep,
>   For creeping puddings only please the wise.

That long poem by Anon sometimes seems too Chomskian to be Jacobethan. In his notes Amis says that doubts have been expressed as to its authenticity. Meaning that it was not written by Anon? Or that it was not written when it seems to have been or that it does not really exist? If it did not exist it would have to be invented. The book is almost worth buying for it alone.

English is English wherever it is, and American readers need not fear that the contribution of their own great luciferous land to light verse is neglected. The trouble is, apart from attested Americans like Frost and Phyllis McGinley, to know who the Americans are. P. G. Wodehouse? Auden? T. S. Eliot? It seems not to matter, since there is a heartening community of techniques and targets. The best parodic Longfellow is to be found in two Englishmen – Lewis Carroll and John Betjeman. Walt Whitman ('Me clairvoyant,/ Me conscious of you, old camarado') is adequately taken off by Chesterton. An American hero is decently served by the very British E. C. Bentley:

'No, sir,' said General Sherman,
'I did not enjoy the sermon;
Nor I didn't git any
Kick outer the Litany.'

Public figures, groups, races, whole nations may be knocked,
but it is usually with good humour. Even here, when Wynford
Vaughan-Thomas shudders his way back from the Antipodes:

A Maori fisherman, the legends say,
Dredged up New Zealand in a single day.
I've seen the catch, and here's my parting crack –
It's under-sized; for God's sake throw it back!

But no country is knocked worse than England, whether in Daniel
Defoe or W. S. Gilbert. And yet it is all done with rubber ham-
mers. Once earnestness steps in the light goes out. That light is
flickering badly in the eighties, bemused as they are by earnestness, but the past, on the evidence of this fine collection, is all
ablaze.

Women Have So Much

Literary Women, by Ellen Moers

I have to confess to an initial resistance to Dr Moers's book. '. . . The
written word in its most memorable form, starting in the eighteenth
century, became increasingly and steadily the work of women.' Did
it, by heaven? I read the book and cried: By heav'n, it did (blank verse
by courtesy of E. B. B.). The claims Dr Moers makes for the predominance

of the female voice in Franco-Anglo-American literature – after Richardson had demonstrated what that voice sounded like – are so strong that her occasional snubs to the male seem particularly ungenerous. Ted Hughes, for example, is 'a grotesque figment of the Plath imagination'. The continued elevation of Plath (I still find it hard to accept this brutal ATS usage: Austen, Bradstreet, Cather, Dickinson – all present, ma'am) to literary sainthood, though conducted here on the margin, is a symptom of what is wrong with feminist literary studies. They employ special, divisive, standards, like blacks, homosexuals and SF pundits. Within feminist limits Plath has to be great, like E.B.B., Mme de Staël, and Mrs Beecher Stowe. The big hermaphroditic world of literature may be permitted to think differently.

It is the virtue of Dr Moers's thesis that it forces her to take seriously what a wider and more demanding standard would have told her to ignore, or at least skim over. *Aurora Leigh* is still highly readable, but it cannot be compared with *The Ring and the Book* (*not* highly readable) as literature. This has to do with talent, not sex. Victorian Anglo-America thought that Mrs Browning's verse novel was the greatest thing since Shakespeare. This meant (what ordinary literary histories tend to ignore) that it was influential, and Dr Moers finds that it influenced Emily Dickinson, who was a very large talent indeed. Some of her poems make a new sense when, as it were, they are inserted as arias to break the endless recitative of *Aurora Leigh*. There is also the matter of George Sand, whose impact on a whole generation of Englishwomen who wanted to write novels was immense. Few in Anglo-America read her now, but everybody reads *Jane Eyre*, whose author worked under George Sand's shadow. Adultery was the great Sand theme. '*Jane Eyre* and *Wuthering Heights*, and in a more guarded way even *Villette* are all adultery novels; but the strongest work by a Brontë on the marriage question is *The Tenant of Wildfell Hall*.' If her readers can be persuaded to take a new look at disregarded Anne, Dr Moers will have earned at least 10 per cent of her advance.

Dr Moers is forced to make use of the awkward term *heroinism* coined by Carlyle, whose only drugs were tobacco and porridge. Her chapter on 'Performing Heroinism' is devoted to a book now not much heard of – Mme de Staël's *Corinne*. The twenty-six-year-old Elizabeth Barrett pronounced it immortal; it deserved 'to be read three score and ten times – that is once every year in the age of man' (for *man* read *woman*). Dr Moers admits that it is a somewhat silly novel, though its author was the woman of genius *par excellence*. The heroine is a beautiful bluestocking madly adored, borne in triumph through the Roman streets, laurel-crowned for her gift of eloquent rhapsodizing. Here begins the heroine as great actress or singer (not great writer: writing is an activity hard to dramatize). She is the first explicit brunette of literature, born of the sun, impulsive, Latin, in conscious opposition to her blonde rival – coolness, north, reason, tranquillity, home, stable society – who takes away her man. It is in this buried novel that themes were presented that animated books as diverse as *The Mill on the Floss, Jane Eyre*, Sand's *Consuelo*, Cather's *Song of the Lark*. The point here, as elsewhere, is that women writers have learned almost exclusively from each other and that the pupils are often remembered when the teachers are not. One aspect of *Corinne* was reversed for ever by Anita Loos, but Mme de Staël was behind her. The performing heroine is, of course, still with us; she upstages the mouse-governess but rarely wins. Maggie Tulliver speaks of 'the dark unhappy ones' that she wants to avenge, mentioning Scott's Rebecca (Scott had read *Corinne*). Miss du Maurier's dark Rebecca is evil and exorcized by the fair-haired mouse. But Mme de Staël set up the basic opposituon.

We're given ample evidence that – once *Pamela* and *La Nouvelle Heloïse* had been absorbed – women's literature was able, and still is, to sustain itself without male interference. Women have particular aptitudes and had particular privations forced upon them that conditioned and condition their mode of writing. Dr Moers does not mention one thing that male novelists envy their female counterparts – their skill at rendering the surface of life textures and colours. This author is colourblind, which women never are, and he does not know how to dress his women characters. Women are practical: Henry James is vague about trade and income, but Jane Austen is as sharp as a little needle when it comes to entails, interest and prize-money. Victorian spinsters, like Christina Rossetti, knew about male-female physical contact only from brother-sister horseplay in the nursery: you'll see this allegorized in 'Goblin Market'. Mary Shelley had after-birth traumata, and Frankenstein is a myth made out of these. It was women who cared about slavery and industrial oppression (*Uncle Tom's Cabin, Mary Barton*) because women are too maternally compassionate to allow vague theories about economic necessity to justify inhumanity.

As epigraph to her chapter on 'Women's Literary Traditions and the Individual Talent' Dr Moers has this, from the other Eliot:

> We dwell with satisfaction upon the poet's difference from her predecessors, especially her immediate predecessors: we endeavour to find something isolated in order to be enjoyed. Whereas if we approach a poet without this prejudice we shall often find that not only the best, but the most individual parts of her work may be those in which the dead poets, her ancestors, assert their immortality most vigorously.

Eliot wrote *his* not *her*; Dr Moers's pronominal adjustment has been made slyly and silently. When women have so much, is it fair to give them more? We are back into that profitless arena where the feminist regards even grammar as a male conspiracy. *His* is, in the context of that kind of generalizing prose, of common gender; it contains *her*. Unfair? It is more unfair to make *her* do the containing since it is unsanctioned by the usage that has made the male particle neutral. Dr Moers has a brief skirmish with French grammar too. Her book is so absorbing, sensible and informative that one can only regret this *chairperson* kind of frivolity.

A Pox on Literature

The Horror of Life, by Roger L. Williams

Tertiary syphilis, as my readers will not need reminding perhaps, comes, when it comes at all, about ten years after the initial infection. About two thirds of syphilitics miss it, especially if they are women or coloured. It is believed, though without solid evidence, that it attacks the sedentary more than the active. This means that writers and composers, granted that primary lesion, are prone to it.

Paresis, as it is generally called in preference to the old GPI or general paralysis of the insane, is characterized by symptoms of bewildering variety, confirming the description of syphilis as the Great Imitator or, because of this very wealth of its ultimate manifestations, the Aristocrat of Diseases. Paresis involves a meningoencephalitis which marks its onset by personality changes, mild at first but growing steadily worse. There is irritability, failure of memory and judgement, insomnia, slovenliness, aggression, confusion, delusion, manic depression, epileptiform convulsion, slurred speech, incontinence, emaciation, sensational psychosis, finally death. The act of careless bohemian love, anonymous, quick and uncondomized, is proved not to have been worth the trouble or money.

Dr Williams's book is about a number of nineteenth-century French writers who caught syphilis and probably died of paresis. They are Baudelaire, Jules de Goncourt, Flaubert, Guy de Maupassant and Daudet. A similar book could probably be written about nineteenth-century British writers, including such unlikely victims of syphilis as John Keats and Edward Lear. People were not so frightened of the disease as we are. Few physicians saw the connection between cerebral degeneration and the primary chancre: when the secondary stage of the infection had healed, it was generally assumed that everything was over and lightning would not strike the tree again. This was Baudelaire's belief. One could even rejoice at picking up the pox: it was not merely an innoculation; it advertised one's virility to the world.

The thesis of this treatise could be regarded as very American (Dr Williams is Distinguished Professor in the History Department of the University of Wyoming) in that it is unwilling to accept, in the European manner, the parallelism of soma and psyche. The long tradition of American behaviourism rejects analysis of the soul, since this can only be done through introspection and one cannot generalize for humanity out of what one finds in oneself. Watson in what he called psychology and Bloomfield in linguistics and B. F. Skinner in whatever his discipline is prefer to deal in what can be seen and measured, not in metaphysical speculation.

Williams's starting point is the immense pessimism of nineteenth-century men of letters, a pessimism which retrospection seems to show as historically unjustified, since their age was an age of great progress and achievement. One can explain the pessimism to some extent in terms of various social and political failures, especially in France – post-Napoleonic depression, the rise of the horrible bourgeoisie who hated art, the breakdown of a traditional order in which the writer had been a kind of aristocrat (or perhaps rather it had been that the aristocrat was a kind of writer). But Dr Williams would rather look at the physically examinable, and he finds in the author's disease the roots of what his book cover calls, with an admirable eye on the market, the horror of life.

He does not, in fact, see syphilis as the sole cause of this manic disaffection. There are other predispositions, some of them neural or psychic, but when Flaubert starts losing teeth and hair and vomiting (probably from mercury poisoning, the old cure for syphilis being as bad as the disease) he finds solidities he can latch on to.

The most sensational of all the sick literary lives was that of Maupassant, who died mad at forty-three and whose hatred of God, man and nature – manifested in literary productions which give us immense pleasure: how is that to be explained? – spring from a kind of mother fixation as well as a terror of the cold. He was a bull of a man much given to boats and riparian dalliance, but he had bad circulation. He had other things too, including a Chinese-style priapism which enabled him to copulate, usually in public, six times in a row, the secret being his failure to detumesce. This, of course, like acne and the common cold, can be a symptom of tertiary syphilis, which Maupassant most certainly had.

We have met these biographies before: Dr Williams has merely stressed the morbid in obedience to his thesis. The shock comes from the special emphasis, most shocking in the instance of Daudet, whose *Lettres de Mon Moulin* – which my poor son has had to read at school, like his poor father before him – seems to be the work of a good innocent man and perhaps even a virgin. Daudet differs from the hate-filled Baudelaire and Maupassant in being gentle to fellow-sufferers from the disease of life. Syphilis in him did not engender misanthropy.

One of the big literary movements of the nineteenth century is called Naturalism, a kind of deterministic view of life owing something to a misreading of Darwin and the new materialism of men like Wundt, seasoned with the pseudo-Hinduism of Schopenhauer. The view, which you find in Hardy as well as Zola, of man being set upon by forces bigger than himself, the will of the universe crushing the individual, may be regarded as having a wholly metaphysical provenance, but it would be convenient to diagnose it in terms of such a disease as paresis. For that matter, the doctrine of the Fall, which Baudelaire espoused, thus earning, in Eliot's essay on him, the status of crypto-martyr, can all too easily be seen as a morbidity which drugs can palliate if not cure.

I consider Dr Williams's book to be useful, as well as deeply, that is to say morbidly, fascinating, but I feel that Flaubert and the rest would have written as they did if the Aristocrat of Diseases, in good bourgeois fashion, had ignored them.

Sahibs

Dreams of Adventure, Deeds of Empire, by Martin Green

When Mrs Leavis was working on *Fiction and the Reading Public*, she asked various novelists who they thought their readers were. P.C. Wren, author of *Beau Geste*, replied: 'The bulk of my readers are the cleanly-minded, virile, outdoor sort of people of both sexes, and the books are widely read in the Army, the Navy, and the Public Schools, and the Clubs. . . . Although I now make a good many thousands a year, I still am not a "professional novelist," nor a long-haired literary cove. I prefer the short-haired executive type.'

Wren, though apparently unsure of the sexual dichotomy, was at least aware of a division in literature best expressed in terms of caste and class rather than aesthetic values. When we say, having perhaps reread *Beau Geste* in a state of convalescent debility, that it is a bad book, we probably justify the condemnation by referring to stereotypical characters, lack of psychological penetration, cliché, artificial plot contrivance and so on. If we were more honest, we might say that we didn't care much for cleanly-minded, virile, outdoor sort of heroes, adventure under tropic suns, simplistic codes of honour, the civilizing or liquidating of truculent barbarians. In other words, we reject what Mr Green calls the fiction of the brothers. Which means not only writers of tripe like Wren, but the novelists of whom he was an epigone – Rider Haggard, John Buchan and – the father of all dreamers of adventure – Daniel Defoe.

It is the fiction of the sisters that mainly makes up what Mrs Leavis's husband called the Great Tradition – the domestic scene rather than the open spaces, with the complexity of love (a female invention), most action sedentary or cubatory, heart and intelligence more than muscle and instinct. This, and nowadays one must be quick to say it, does not mean just Jane Austen and George Eliot and the rest of the brilliant women: it means *yin* rather than *yang*. As both these are necessary to a harmonious universe, it would seem that the most harmonious, and hence the greatest, fiction should synthesize them. So *War and Peace* ought to be, which it probably is, greater than *The Golden Bowl*, and Conrad, which he probably is, the supreme novelist of the modern period.

Mr Green does not enter into such arguments. His concern is with the development of a kind of Anglo-American literature which expresses the national attitudes appropriate to empire building. Defoe, about 1700, has all the qualities of this kind of 'modernism'. A Whig, a dissenter, a believer in technical education and modern languages, a failed entrepreneur (like his brothers Scott and Mark Twain) but a vigorous exponent of mercantilism, he produced straightforward journalism without classical allusions or Latinate prose. This no-nonsense technique, with its emphasis on things, commodities, processes, he brought to his fiction, and the finest of his fiction is *Robinson Crusoe*. Against Defoe we must set Jonathan Swift, who stood for the classical rather than the modern side, who detested Defoe, and whose greatest book is a satire on the novel of adventure. The literary establishment of the Age of Enlightenment was in the hands of men like Swift, Pope and Johnson: the upstart Defoe was, to them, as P. C. Wren was to Mrs Leavis. And yet they could not match the success of *Robinson Crusoe*, and *Gulliver's Travels* continues to be read as though it belonged to the Defoe tradition.

Why this constant and consistent devaluation of the novel of adventure, the fiction of the frontier in America and of empire in Britain? Guilt, Mr Martin thinks, has something to do with it. The material of the adventure story is soiled and immoral; it has to do with grab, windfalls of gold, the shooting of natives with Crusoe flintlock or Kipling Gatling. Britain and America alike grew rich through exploitation and unjust mercantilist laws: best not to think of these things or, at least, not make literature out of them. This preparedness to ignore the sources of material wellbeing has earned the British the French taunt of hypocrisy. In literature it has generated a set of standards highly questionable but rarely questioned. Convert *The Four Feathers* or *The Last of the Mohicans* or *The Thirty-Nine Steps* into a film, and even intellectuals will watch it with appreciation. The books themselves remain the cheap sweets one munches on the sly, mere kids' stuff.

Even giants like Sir Walter Scott rarely get on to university syllabuses. In his own day, as Defoe had his Swift, so Scott had his denunciatory Coleridge. Thinking over the content of Scott's novels, which are not exactly in the Defoe tradition (though Scott edited and collected Defoe's works), one wonders how they can belong to an 'opposition' literature at all. For the themes are romantic, historical, patriotic, and there is no celebration of Whig mercantilism. It is best to see Scott as providing his age with an image of aristocratic militarism, a sort of spurious pedigree for the new nabobs. Mark Twain alleged that the spirit of the American South was the creation of Scott, and a deplorable one, with phoney chivalry living off slave labour. Twain himself, whose *Pudd 'nhead Wilson* Leavis praised, goes right back to the Defoe tradition in *A Connecticut Yankee at the Court of King Arthur*, where the world of things, techniques, processes is imposed on a dark age, and Camelot is, in fact, colonized. Sandy is a fair Girl Friday. The American hypocrisy which, for a time, would not admit Twain to the Valhalla where the transcendentalists basked in bliss, is a fair counterpart to the British attitude to Kipling. Kipling is still, in John Gross's words, 'a disturbing presence'. Writing of empire, he ought not to be good; unfortunately he is.

Mr Green's main point is well taken, but he probably covers too much ground in the making of it. There is evidence of wide reading but some of it is secondary (A quotes B quoting C in D), and he is necessarily superficial and summary in some of his considerations. Nor should he have allowed a statement like this to get by: 'Stubbs and Freeman . . . refurbished Anglo-Saxon art and taste; made Beowulf and Caedmon great poets.' But it is in the scattering of so much incidental information that much of the fascination of the book lies. Thus, there is a potted history of the Sarawak Brooke family and a reference to the part that Admiral Austen, Jane's brother, played in the suppression, in 1851, of Malay pirates on the White Raja's behalf. This is in the course of a discussion of the influence of Conrad's adulation of the first Brooke on *Lord Jim*. Green is critical of Conrad's long works and wonders whether the *yang* of the adventure yarn blends with the *yin* of the philosophy and psychology. He raises a number of admirably stimulating points for literary discussion and then moves on, with great rapidity, to the next.

What, he finally asks, can we do about this great body of adventure fiction which, from Defoe to Ballantyne and Henty and Buchan, the Leavisian canon will not accept? He suggests that we read it without shame – 'there is no need for the old defensiveness, the old ignorance' – and, if we wish to systematize our reading into courses of study, we can soft-pedal the aesthetic and play up the social and historical. 'British Studies', he thinks, on the analogy of Black Studies, would make an acceptable college course. The reading of all John Buchan's works could be as pleasurable and guiltless as the practice of soul cookery or bongo-playing.

Young Man's Anger

A Better Class of Person: An Autobiography: 1929–1956, by John Osborne

When I read an autobiography written by someone far younger than myself and reflect that I am far from ready to start writing my own, I am less ready to rebuke the precocity than felicitate on the possession of a sharper memory than my own and sharper things to remember. There is also the matter of achievement, since only the achiever expects the world to be interested in his life. Mr Osborne has achieved much: on 8 May 1956 (also his father's birthday and the anniversary of the end of the Second World War) he presented *Look Back in Anger* at the Royal Court Theatre and, so the theatrical historians say, inaugurated a renascence in the British drama. As art is a mirror of one-self and oneself is one's life, so it is right to want to know about the life of Mr Osborne. But even if Mr Osborne had remained a small repertory ASM with fumbling plays unperformed, his life would be worth read-ing. It is a quite remarkable record of a phase of social history seen from a lower-middle-class angle. It is engaging and compassionate – his plays have never been so described – and it has a narrative verve which sug-gests that, had not Mr Osborne succeeded so well on the stage, he might have become a fine novelist in the picaresque tradition.

I must now modify that statement about the quality of his plays. There *is* compassion in them, but it is a compassion inseparable from a particular kind of nostalgia. Mr Osborne is nostalgic for Edwardian England, as his description of Billy Rice in *The Entertainer* reminds us. Billy Rice owes something to his maternal grandfather, an ebullient publican who breakfasted off 'half a bottle of 3-star brandy, a pound of porterhouse steak, oysters in season and a couple of chorus girls all year round.' The spirit of Grandpa Grove still hovers over Brighton. 'Ozone in Eastbourne was spermatozoa in Brighton, burning brightly like little tadpoles of evening light across the front. Whenever I have lunch in Brighton, I always want to take somebody to bed in the afternoon. To shudder one's last, thrusting, replete gasp between the sheets at 4 and 6 o'clock in Brighton, would be the most perfect last earthly delight.' The joy of Brightonian life is summed up in Mr Osborne's idol Max Miller (of whom Archie Rice is a pale failed carbon copy), insolent, ithyphallic, adorable and a real pro.

Mr Osborne was a sickly child. He discloses a compassion for his young ailing body which has no aftertaste of self-pity. He is always objective. The description of his being battered in the playground is more a tribute to the foul energy of his brutish assailant than a mewling over his own pain. He fainted regularly at the fictive pain of the cinema screen. That his mother, a barmaid of virtuosic skills (four bottles in one hand, four glasses in the other), was unsympathetic, and even more unsympathetic to his dying father, sets off no whine of reproach. She has her own fascination for him, that of the potential artist. 'Her lips were a scarlet-black sliver covered in some sticky slime named Tahiti or Tattoo, which she bought with all her other make-up from Woolworth's . . . She had a cream base called Creme Simone, always covered up with a face powder called Tokalon, which she dabbed all over so that it almost showered off in little avalanches when she leant forward over her food.' Sick and insufficiently coddled, Osborne was always on the side of life. There was a time when life was summed up in an image which remains with me too – the archetypal feast of the comic papers: a monstrous mound of mash with ithyphallic sausages thrusting up from it. Such an image would have had no appeal for Evelyn Waugh, nor his eldest son.

After bad schools (and the badness is thoroughly Edwardian) Mr Osborne went to be educated by Fleet Street – the *Gas World* and the *Miller* (sacred name) – but then, via the Leatherhead amateur dramatic society, he became a young man of the theatre. Here we become very attentive. He learnt his various crafts the hard way, untutored by RADA or the OUDS, recognizing early that theatre was what *worked*, even with an audience of a dozen pensioners with umbrellas and the off-season sea wind howling outside, not a matter of higher aesthetics. He toured with *No Room at the Inn*, an inferior play which *worked*, understudied three male parts, got the scenery out of the goods van in the freezing dawn, sat with the prompt book, entered the world of ageing queers and the screaming egos of actresses, was told authoritatively by one of these to study Pinero, since Pinero *worked*. Here Mr Osborne forgets some of his compassion. When he has it in for somebody he has it in. Lynne Reid Banks, for instance, 'later author of a book and film called *The L-Shaped Room*, and fearless campaigner against dog shit in public parks. . . . Lynne was unspeakable (she may have unconsciously prompted me years later when I wrote a line in *Watch it Come Down*, describing an indiscriminating lecher: "Some people will put it in a brick wall").'

Success with work if not with women will be recorded in the next volume, which I beg Mr Osborne to get finished as quickly as he can. The later chapters of this record his first marriage (failed), unspeakable engagements with wretched companies, the dole, kitchen-work which confirms for Mr Osborne the outstanding realism of Mr Wesker, an inferior play which *worked* and netted him nine pounds, and then the completion, if not the production, of *Look Back in Anger*. On his way to triumphant dramaturgy, Mr Osborne takes time off from wry narration to comment, laterally or negatively, on an aesthetic he shares only superficially with Pinero or Rattigan. He is dubious about the great god Construction. 'It appeared to mean the construction of an artefact like a carriage clock, which revealed its beautiful precision to all, particularly for the benefit of those who were obliged to write and explain its workings to their readers.' He was ordered by an agent to learn 'the Newtonian principles of theatre embodied in *The Winslow Boy*. The most perfect play ever written, he roared. I was also, oddly, directed to the feet of the Master; but Coward on Construction seemed pretty wobbly.' Mr Osborne went the way we know, with anger a substitute for symmetry, but the anger itself not all that unsymmetrical.

Tripe?

Best Sellers – Popular Fiction of the 1970s, by John Sutherland

D r Sutherland quotes me, correctly, as saying that much popular fiction is 'poor art, and life is too short to bother with any art that is not the best of its kind.' Thus I seem to deliver a 'bluff dismissal' of practically all the subject matter of his survey. I made that prissy statement in, I think, 1965. Now I take it back. A good deal of my spare time in the last decade has been beguiled by the reading of authors like Puzo, Forsyth, Higgins, Kyle, Ludlum, Hailey and Irving Wallace. I do not read Iris Murdoch or Margaret Drabble. I offer no excuse for an increasingly systematic neglect of the best contemporary fiction except one that some of my fellow-novelists may appreciate – the fear of being influenced. I do not feel that a reading of *The Godfather* or *The Devil's Alternative* is going to affect either my style or my content. But I have to admit to a slight sense of shame when I queue up at an airport bookstall to pay for *The Amityville Horror* or *Eye of the Needle*. Such shame, as this admirable brief treatise implies, is misplaced. A lot of bestsellers are 'fun books', and God knows we all need a bit of fun in our lives.

What, though, *is* a bestseller? I notice sporadically that my own most recent novel is on bestseller lists in Britain, but that does not make it a *Princess Daisy*. It is only in America, where the term came into being in the 1890s, that there is a hard-eyed commercial concept, the formulation of a genre which makes the bestseller something very different from what merely happens to sell well. A book on the British lists may have achieved a sale as small as 20,000 in hardcover. Look, however, at the *New York Times Book Review* for 30 December 1979, where the American fiction bestsellers of the 1970s are listed. Puzo's *The Godfather* achieved 292,765 in hardcover, 13,225,000 in paperback. Even Erica Jong's *Fear of Flying*, which comes at the end of the list, managed 100,000 in the dear form and 5,700,000 in the cheap. This is the real thing.

Cunning analysts are able to tabulate the ingredients which make a bestseller, but the far more cunning deity who grants free will to the book market ensures that bestsellerdom may never be decreed in advance. It is easy enough, long after the event, to say why Richard Bach's *Jonathan Livingston Seagull* (an appalling book, and not even fun) sold 3,192,000 in hardcover, but, when it was submitted to publishers, it had everything against it – it was very brief, it was illustrated, and it was about birds. Erich Segal's *Love Story* (ten million in paperback) was also brief, and it was sexlessly sentimental in the manner of Ethel M. Dell. If it were possible to know how to write a bestseller there would be no bestsellers.

What Dr Sutherland does, after his general exposition on the whole bestselling phenomenon, is to take certain genres, and the acknowledged masters of those genres, and relate them to popular imaginative needs. A writer whose entire output I have read is Arthur Hailey (he has now, apparently, given up writing in order to enjoy his millions), and I can see clearly what people get out of him. In all readers of fiction there is a certain puritanical hangover which denies value (or perhaps it is sanctity) to a mere work of the imagination. To be instructed is holier than to be entertained, and Mr Hailey instructs. He tells us how a hotel or an airport or a banking system works. He spends a year on research and regards the construction of a novel as the smallest part of his labours. But there seems to be a moral implication in this flooding of his readers with facts. We small people are increasingly set upon by the big collectives, and we want to enter those rooms marked private to confirm our suspicions of tyranny, roguery and corruption. Hailey seems to be performing a public service. He entertains too, of course: there are bedrooms as well as boardrooms. What he does not give us is subtlety either of character or of language. The lack of subtlety seems to be the chief bestselling parameter.

Harold Robbins – whom I find totally unreadable – has cognate inside information, chiefly about the world of tycoonery or jetsetting which his own millions qualify him to enter. But in his books we meet exemplarily the nastier aspects of bestsellerdom – gratuitous sado-masochism and the spirit of the vendetta. When Mickey Spillane (no longer such a bestseller as he was) said on television that he sold because he dealt only in sex and violence, he was at least being honest. Robbins, also on television, once said that he was actuated by ethical aims – to show up the badness in the world. This is a hypocritical claim as old as *Jonathan Wild* and *Moll Flanders*, and people still pretend to fall for it. But there are more and more readers of nastiness prepared to admit to the nastiness within themselves.

It is in their capacity to cater to the sado-masochist in all of us, with a necessary bone or two thrown to the dogs of morality (the desire for wild justice, ecological concern, the cause of racial or sexual equality) that the more brutal bestsellers sell best. What Dr Sutherland is rightly pleading for is a willingness on the part of academic bodies (his own book is a serious piece of academic research, financed by the UGC) to take the bestseller seriously as an index of popular fantasy and even social and familial preoccupation. These novels about children who rape their mothers and kill their fathers and are justly cracked with a coalhammer reflect a genuine ambiguity in family life. Despite all the doctrinaire verbiage of the women's liberationists, the typical woman's novel is a 'bodice ripper'. *The Thornbirds* even had to indulge in ornithological fancy to symbolize a still lively female masochism (thornbirds transfix themselves with thorns and sing sweetly before they die). Bestsellers indulge in a far from Jamesian simplification of the human psyche, and life is presented as cruelty and revenge, but life for the majority is far from Jamesian. Hence these books which literature rejects but the unliterary 99 per cent of the population embraces. They deserve close study.

Glumly, I find myself briefly in the real (i.e. American) bestselling world with *A Clockwork Orange*, a novella totally ignored until Kubrick filmed it (my agent was even unwilling to present it to a publisher). By most people the film is regarded as the primary object and the book as a mere memorandum of a visual experience. This is generally true of bestsellers and it is the best proof we have that they have little to do with literature – viz. the aesthetic exploitation of the word. But that the bestseller is already replacing literature is certain, and Dr Sutherland's book may be taken as one of the first of an inevitable series of scholarly treatises. It is serious and it is objective, meaning that there is no whiff of Leavisite frivolity or disdain.

Lovers' Contracts

Adultery in the Novel, by Tony Tanner

Vladimir Nabokov, in his posthumous *Lectures on Literature*, says: 'Any ass can assimilate the main points of Tolstoy's attitude towards adultery, but in order to enjoy Tolstoy's art the good reader must wish to visualise, for instance, the arrangement of a railway carriage on the Moscow–Petersburg night train as it was a hundred years ago.' The good critic, one might add, must be able to demonstrate a relationship between adultery and railway trains. It is the virtue of Tony Tanner's book that it looks for the expression of the great theme of social breakdown – 'Contract and Transgression' is his subtitle – not merely in plot but in image and rhythm. Text and texture are all; all the rest is for moralists and anthropologists.

Most great traditional fiction is about the breaking of social contracts. In our own age society lacks authority, and contracts are not worth the paper they're written on; the novelist has lost a large portion of his inherited subject matter. Professor Tanner says, rightly, that 'a novel like John Updike's *Couples* is as little about passion as it is about marriage: the adulteries are merely formal and technical. Adultery, we say, no longer signifies.' It ceased to signify with works like *Lady Chatterley's Lover*, in which adultery is virtuous, representing an extra-marital contract embracing nature but rejecting society. The contracts of lovers are loose: they 'bind but till sleep', said John Donne. Transgression against them does not bring the world to an end. Madame Bovary's tragedy lay in the discovery that the adulterous relationship had the same potentialities as the marital one, though the woman's rights were phantasmal, unprotected by custom, morality or religion. Such works as Flaubert's have, in the post-Lawrence age, a purely historical validity. If we find *Madame Bovary* moving, it is out of a nostalgia for a stability that no longer exists – or, if you wish, a pathetic search for a new stability (that of passion, not an aspect of marriage) which has to be doomed.

Professor Tanner deals at length with three novels – Rousseau's *La Nouvelle Héloïse*, Goethe's *Die Wahlverwandtschaften*, and Flaubert's masterpiece. Rousseau's book is not about adultery – rather the opposite: Julie and Saint-Preux begin as lovers but are turned into a married couple. When Wolmar, Julie's surrogate father, bids the bride and groom kiss in the arbour which witnessed their free, uncontractual, embraces, Saint-Preux laughingly says: '*Julie, ne craignez plus cet asile, il vient d'être profané.*' The marital kiss has introduced a new element – the paternal, which stands for society – and has rendered profane the place of free love. This is very romantic, altogether Rousseau, and it reminds us that literature is never really at home with marriage, unless it breaks down or is the mere conventional destination of the plot. Yet Victorian fiction, which was great enough, would not tolerate adultery. Dickens deals with the shattering of contracts other than marital. Meredith's verse novel *Modern Love* was, despite the tragic end of the transgressor, considered immoral. Patmore's *Angel in the House*, a very static lyrical performance, was unjustly set against it. True aesthetic judgements didn't enter into the matter.

The unwillingness of the novel to deal with marriage points to its essentially subversive nature. Children need parents, especially mothers, and the married state is essential to the stability of society. But there is nothing kinetic in it, say novelists, and the structuralists even find the death of language there. As the lecherous priest in Boccaccio told the simple married woman, the husband has become the closest relative, and cohabitation with him is incest. Language has to open out from the incestuous situation – vocabulary limited, private semantics – and dare exogamy and adultery. It is the woman, as always, who suffers. She is tied to her biological function and the impoverishment of language. She is right, imply the novelists, to want to break away, but in doing so she harms society and earns the condemnation of the father as well as the husband. French society found *Madame Bovary* immoral, despite its heroine's bad end. It saw that that bad end was occasioned by the consequences of her false logic (adultery will combine passion and stability) and not by the anger of God.

These are thoughts that occur to one while reading Professor Tanner's very interesting and detailed, perhaps too detailed, treatise. He cites everybody but he has much of his own to say. His examination, in the most interesting third of the book, of the text of *Madame Bovary* elucidates patterns which were not clear before. It is amusing to compare his treatment of the famous hat of Charles Bovary with Nabokov's in *Lectures on Literature*. Nabokov, the practising novelist with his eye on the external world, draws a little picture of the hat and finds in its 'layered' complexity an anticipation of the wedding cake. Tanner suggests that the hybrid nature of the hat forbids its realization: there is a small innutritious feast of language there, with no possible referent in the real world. In other words, Bovary is being shown, while still a schoolboy, as incapable of bridging language and reality and hence predestined, despite his goodness and his genuine capacity for love, to drive Emma to seek a whole relationship elsewhere. When 'le nouveau' gives his name as *Charbovari* – a holophrastic or ungapped utterance – he is showing that he will be unable to deal with the gaps of married life: 'Gap-incompetence would be one way of describing the ultimate source of Emma's malaise. . . .' There is a good deal of this subtle (over-subtle?) exegesis.

In only one of the three novels chiefly dealt with is there real adultery. In *Die Wahlverwandtschaften*, to put it crudely, two married people fulfil their thalamic duties while thinking of other people (a matter of elective affinities). Still, Tanner seems to be right in selecting this particular trio of novels, as he is right in subsuming under his general term a whole constellation of family themes, including several ambiguities. The family itself is that ultimate ambiguity, perhaps: '. . . it has to destroy itself in order to reconstitute itself: continuity involves dissolution.' He passes too quickly, and I would say slightingly, over *Ulysses*, where we see an exemplary piece of ambiguity. Molly Bloom's adultery is necessary (a) to enable Bloom to have his superiority asserted on a basis of lack of marital privilege, (b) to open the way for the entrance of a son-messiah-lover. Adultery has sometimes to be tolerated, even welcomed. It is always forgivable. Both Tanner's cover design and frontispiece (Blake the one, Rembrandt the other) show the Woman Taken in Adultery. Christ did not think too badly of this most creative of sins.

What Makes the Novel Novel

Origins of the Novel, by Marthe Robert, translated by Sacha Rabinovitch

This book came out in the original French in 1972, and it is already a little démodé in intellectual Paris. British readers will find it suggestive and even startling. Madame Robert asks why some of us write and the rest of us read novels, and she is not satisfied with a merely anthropological answer. It is not enough to say that love of a story is deeply embedded in human culture: there has to be a good shaky Freudian reason.

Rightly, I think, she begins by stressing the novel in the novel. It is 'a newcomer to the literary scene, a commoner made good who [which, surely] will always stand out as something of an upstart, even a bit of a swindler. . . .' We remember, if Mme Robert, being French, does not, what Jane Austen says in *Northanger Abbey*:

> 'And what are you reading, Miss – ?' 'Oh, it is only a novel!' replies the
> young lady. . . .' 'It is only Cecilia, or Camilla, or Belinda': or, in short,
> only some work in which the most thorough knowledge of human nature,
> the happiest delineation of its varieties, the liveliest effusions of wit and
> humour are conveyed to the world in the best chosen language.

Despite that vigorous defence and others like it, the novel is still somewhat on the defensive. Being a not easily definable genre, it has to take in
Princess Daisy as well as *Princess Casamassima*. It is more easily debased
than the sonnet sequence or the epic poem. 'It knows neither rule nor
restraint.' Mme Robert finds support for her view for its unclassifi-
ability in the *Encyclopaedia Britannica*, which says 'it is too vast, varied
and amorphous to be considered as a genre or a literary form.' That is
from the last edition but one. The latest *Britannica* article is by your
humble reviewer and tries to be a little more stringent.

A little more stringent, but it doesn't get much beyond a notion of
large-scale storytelling. I accept with Mme Robert that storytelling must
always have the connotation of mendacity and, in many languages, is
actually a euphemism for lying. Lying is evasion. We lie to evade punishment or shut out reality. We are getting close to Freud.

The child views his parents as deities, omnipotent, immortal, infinitely venerable, protective and loving. When he discovers that they are
imperfect human beings he sets up a barrier against reality. He believes
that they are not good enough to be truly his parents; the real parents are
elsewhere and he himself is 'an adopted child to whom his true parents
– royal, needless to say, or at least noble and influential – will eventually reveal themselves and restore him to his rightful status.' Here,
Mme Robert suggests, is the basis of one kind of fiction. There is
another kind which has its origin in the Oedipal situation. The mother is
sexually desired, but her desirability – meaning whorish availability –
involves her fall from a former divine status. If the child still wants
parental divinity, he won't find it in his real father, who is brought low
along with his mother and is a subject for easy elimination. He must
posit an unknown father who is godlike, and he himself must be an
illegitimate offspring of his. In other words, the two basic fictional heroes
are the Foundling and the Bastard.

The Foundling dreams of the impossible. He sets up imaginary kingdoms, pastoral Edens, Utopias. He appears massively in the first great
European novel, *Don Quixote*, where he converts himself into a noble
being performing godlike services for the human oppressed. The world
of reality, personified in the Priest and the Barber, cannot touch him. In
Robinson Crusoe, the first great English novel (though, in conformity to
the view of the novel as a debased form, its author had to deny that it was
fiction), we have another Edenic situation, but the hero has to advance
from the position of Foundling to that of Bastard. Don Quixote, being
old and mad, is under no obligation to change; Crusoe, young and sane,
has to learn how to enter the world of mature people, who are all
Bastards.

The Bastard, after all, has come into his doubtful inheritance through sexual knowledge, which will lead him eventually to the responsibilities of fatherhood. When Man Friday comes on the scene, Crusoe turns himself into a putative father, performing the main paternal task of turning ignorance to knowledge. He calls Friday 'son', and 'thanks to this boy he has brought into being and on whom he practises his new-found realism, the shipwrecked mariner of life can gradually retrace his steps to the civilized world: thus he gets ready both to take his place among men and, as befits this denizen of the fairy tale, to get married.'

Mme Robert seems, on the basis of the various exemplifications of her thesis, to regard the novel as essentially a masculine form – a tale written by a man about men. Even in her long chapter on Flaubert she has more to say about *La Tentation de Saint Antoine*, very much a Foundling fantasy, than about *Madame Bovary*. Because Flaubert once said '*Madame Bovary, c'est moi*', Mme Robert is ready to see something of the Bastard in poor Emma, whose tragedy is surely that she is set upon by a Foundling and a Bastard. There are plenty of Foundlings and Bastards in novels written by women from George Sand to Iris Murdoch, but they are rarely in the centre of the stage. Once Mme Robert generalizes her thesis into statements like 'the novel is dominated by this dialectic between the acceptance and the negation of reality' we are altogether with her, but we have said that sort of thing ourselves. And when she more or less identifies the 'Family Romance' with the novel, who is going to deny that all fiction is about leaving families and going off to found, circuitously, new ones?

Mme Robert considers that 'the Bastard's great venture into Western fiction' is all, or nearly, over. The Foundling has got the better of him. Since Joyce and Proust the novel is 'free to express nothing but the narcissistic giddiness of its own writing and even free to claim that this is the only respectable aspect of its vocation.' That sounds like a dig at the *nouveau roman*, which is already old hat. Mme Robert seems not to have read enough American fiction. In Roth and Bellow the Bastard is still very much around and he appears to have come to terms with the Foundling.

Believing in Something

The Picturesque Prison: Evelyn Waugh and his Writing, by Jeffrey Heath
The Will to Believe: Novelists of the Nineteen-Thirties, by Richard Johnstone

Waugh, being dead and probably great, has now to submit to the kind of close critical analysis which, if the grave unguinnessed Dublin seminars are anything to go by, is rendering Joyce's centennial year so gloomy an occasion. Since Waugh has a long way to go before he achieves a centenary, the right to uncomplicated enjoyment of his work has only just begun to be assailed by the academics, but our literary children, if we have any, are going to be paled around with so much learned exegesis that joy in reading *Decline and Fall* will seem as irreverent as eructating in church, if there are any churches.

I am not grumbling at Professor Heath, who comes early on in the scholarly series, and whose examination of Waugh's symbolism is both sensible and useful. But when, in *A Handful of Dust*, Mrs Rattery appears as the goddess Fortune, ruler of the 'faithless modern world', with her five huge trunks representing the five continents, we have cause to fear the future. Somebody is going to write a thesis on Mrs Rattery, or even on the significance of her saying that patience is a heartbreaking game. Professor Heath, whose name means a large open plain with sandy soil and scrubby vegetation, is heathery with potential subjects.

Some of them are admirable so long as they are not taken too far. For instance, the furniture of the Moslem world provides Waugh with emblems of treachery: Ivor Claire, who seems to personify English virtue, is first seen wearing a turban and lying on a sofa of Turkey carpet. He also wears slippers, an oriental affectation shared by Mrs Stitch and Corporal-Major Ludovic. From such hints we can expect the eventual disillusionment of Guy Crouchback, who enters the war in optimistic innocence but reads the signs of betrayal too late. 'Claire is not a crusader but an infidel.' The classical imagery of *Officers and Gentlemen* is pretty explicit (Hookforce can hardly enter Crete without expecting to meet the Minotaur – German ruthlessness or British ineptitude or both – in the labyrinth), but Heath rightly uncovers Homeric anticipations on the Isle of Mugg, where the Laird is Dis: he has a smoky castle, loves hellish high explosives, and owns 'infernal brutes' of dogs.

Heath's title refers to a persistent symbol he finds in Waugh's novels – the 'lush place' wrongly loved or longed for by heroes whose innocence is not admirable, such as Tony Last's Hetton, Scott-King's Neutralia, William Boot's Boot Magna, or the ambiguous Brideshead, which seems to some critics to be the Catholic Church itself and to others a fleshly snare or earthly paradise. The tension in Waugh himself between the austere practice of the faith and the adolescent arcadianism of Oxford, which provided him with aristocratic friends and tempted him with the pleasures of British paganism, is what makes his character interesting if infuriating and his books fascinating. The tension is resolved in the prose style, which symbolizes the authority of the Church Triumphant but is also a derivative of Protestant (or Deist) Augustanism. Heath praises this style, as we all do, but there are grounds for supposing that it is not fitting for fiction, where Augustanism should only be parodic and the tones of the *récit* highly tentative. In other words, Waugh writes too well for a novelist.

Drawing on unpublished material in the archives of the University of Texas, Heath attempts to illuminate the novels, especially the masterpiece *Sword of Honour*, with references to Waugh's own life, especially his life as a soldier. It is interesting to moralize over the parallelism of Waugh's own escape from Crete and that of Guy Crouchback, but this is not the critic's business. There is altogether too much of this *roman à clef* preoccupation going on, and we had better remind ourselves of Waugh's own insistence that his books were things he had made and not commentaries on his life. On the other hand, since he subscribed to the Thomistic aesthetic of art's not being an end in itself but a way to God, the later books will never make complete sense unless we relate them to a rigorous Catholicism which was not an authorial pose but an ontological reality. Attach this to *Brideshead Revisited* and we can begin to reassess its art. Otherwise it must baffle and, in baffling, seem inept.

Richard Johnstone's brief book deals with Waugh finding his faith, and also Graham Greene. It deals also with Edward Upward's and Rex Warner's seeking security in communism and George Orwell's righteous scepticism about what he thought of as cognate faiths. The 1930s, so Johnstone believes, was the great age of the Quest. Postwar England was the place where, according to Auden, no one was well. The old order had collapsed and writers had to rejoice in building something on which to rejoice. That Orwell could see little difference between the flight to Catholicism and the intellectual embrace of Marxism looks like a gesture of sanity: salvation lay in being a country rector watching walnuts grow or in accepting British pragmatism – working-class decency and beer without chemical additives. To submit to the dogmatism of a rigid system (political or religious made no difference) was the way of death.

There are grounds for supposing that Johnstone is wrong in considering both kinds of conversion between the same covers. He says:

A reason why religious belief – Waugh and Greene's Catholicism, Isherwood's Vedanta – survived the thirties while political commitment as a rule did not, is that religious belief more easily allowed scepticism and faith to co-exist. Once adopted, the religious belief could be left almost out of sight, occasionally making its presence felt, but for the most part remaining in the background, a safety net against despair. Political belief on the other hand claimed the foreground. . . .

If political belief claimed the foreground, it was because Soviet Marxism insisted on the propagandist function of literature. If religious belief survived, it may be because it is attached to the eternal and not the expedient. It is false to imply that either Waugh or Greene ever wished to shove their faith 'almost out of sight'. If faith and scepticism can co-exist, which is highly arguable, this is because faith is a personal matter and political allegiance collective and subject to enforcement. To call faith a 'safety net against despair' is a gross underestimate of a positive radiance that only made Waugh despair of the world that would not accept it.

States of Grace

A Little Order, by Evelyn Waugh. A Selection from His Journalism, edited by Boast Gallagher

The compilation was worth making, and Professor Gallagher, who teaches English at the James Cook University of North Queensland 'in tropical Australia' (the blurb), has made it well. There is probably an implied piquancy, which Waugh himself might have been quick to exploit, in the insistence on North Queensland's tropicality. With the collapse of a great metropolitan culture it is meet that some of its fragments be cherished in one of the barbarous territories that languish under Capricorn.

The title comes from Matthew Arnold – 'to introduce a little order into this chaos' – and it is meant to chime neatly with the title of Waugh's volume of autobiography, *A Little Learning*. Waugh disclaimed scholarship and even termed himself 'ill-educated'. He was an unsystematic reader and he compensated for areas of unabashed ignorance with eccentric advocacies. Thus, Ronald Knox's *Enthusiasm* he regards as 'the greatest work of literary art of the century'. He reserved humility for his private devotions and preferred elegant scorn to reason. He despised so many things, turning his despications into exquisite pieces of verbal craft, that it could not but be evident that he was attempting to make a virtue of inirradiable pigheadedness. In a sense, he was made for a particular kind of journalism.

It may be said that he wrote too well to be a journalist, even though periodicals like *The Month* do not disdain the odd piece of silver-veined Newmanian prose. But the Waugh style was not meant for scholarship and one may doubt sometimes if it was really meant for fiction. A work of fiction should be, for its author, a journey into the unknown, and the prose should convey the difficulties of the journey. Compare Ford Madox Ford's *Parade's End* with Waugh's *Sword of Honour*. Ford is often clumsy; his sentences stutter; deliberate banalities jostle with brilliant felicities: the prose is struggling to cope with the mysterious and unpredictable. Waugh's book – which very nearly does for Waugh's class and generation what Ford's undoubtedly did for his own – is created, as it were, out of a known position, that of orthodox Catholic morality, and the style – witty, terse, controlled – corresponds. That style fits best in some of the admirable occasional pieces collected here, where Waugh is making aesthetic, ethical or eschatological pronouncements and always making them superbly well.

The finest essay is that entitled 'Half in Love with Easeful Death', published in *The Tablet* in 1947. It deals with the necropolis of Forest Lawn (transformed, in *The Loved One*, to Whispering Glades) and it begins:

In a thousand years or so, when the first archaeologists from beyond the date-line unload their boat on the sands of Southern California, they will find much the same scene as confronted the Franciscan Missionaries. A dry landscape will extend from the ocean to the mountains. Bel Air and Beverly Hills will lie naked save for scrub and cactus, all their flimsy multitude of architectural styles turned long ago to dust, while the horned toad and the turkey buzzard leave their faint imprint on the dunes that will drift on Sunset Boulevard.

Waugh here is being a kind of Gibbon. He is admirable when he puts himself into an unknown future or, as he sometimes does, with the Church Triumphant in Heaven, and looks down – shaping in his head periods whose elegance is too civilized to be uncompassionate – on the folly of human aspirations. One could quote him indefinitely on California: '. . . they set up a tradition of leisure which is apparent today in the pathological sloth of the hotel servants and the aimless, genial coffee-house chatter which the Film Executives call "conferences". ' How unfair, how true. How exact (straight from the Seven Deadly Sins) that *sloth*.

Professor Gallagher has arranged his materials under five headings: *Myself* . . . ; *Aesthete*; *Man of Letters*; *Conservative*; *Catholic*. The selection of brief essays on fellow authors does not seem to argue a wide range of tastes, but we have to remember that this is journalism and not a systematized literary conspectus. Still – Saki, Belloc, Wodehouse, Galsworthy (whose style, strangely, he has no bad word for) are evidently the writers Waugh *wanted* to write about. And Max Beerbohm, of course. His condemnation of James Joyce's later experiments – on the grounds of their lack of 'lucidity' – is a lucid enough signal of an unworthy narrowness. But he is too dedicated a literary craftsman not to be capable of profoundly tenable judgements on his fellows. Cyril Connolly writes pretty sentences but has no sense of 'structure'; this disqualifies him from writing books. To Stephen Spender, being a poet means 'going to literary luncheons, addressing Youth Rallies, and Summer Schools, saluting the great and "discovering" the young, adding his name to letters to *The Times*, flitting about the world to Cultural Congresses.'

His judgement on Graham Greene's *The Heart of the Matter* is primarily a theological one. Scobie wills his own damnation for the love of God. This is 'either a very loose poetical expression or a mad blasphemy, for the God who accepted that sacrifice could be neither just nor lovable.' Waugh is stern in his review, but in his fiction he yields to Greene's enchantment, if only vicariously. Guy Crouchback is asked if West Africa was really as *The Heart of the Matter* presents it. 'It *must* have been like that,' he replies. Waugh is never quite sure where aesthetics ends and theology begins, or it may be the other way round. His unhappiness at the *aggiornamento* of the Catholic Church seems to derive chiefly from wounded taste, but one sympathizes. A pop mass is a blasphemous idea, perhaps because Waugh says so.

The subject matter of some of these essays is dated – Youth after World War One, for instance, a great topic for the daily rags – but the fine workmanship of the prose has paid dividends of total readability. Natural wit, the striving for grace, the rhythms of authority make this book literature.

Magic and Elegance

The Coup, by John Updike

T. S. Eliot said that meaning was only one of the parameters under which a poem should be considered, and perhaps not a very important one. Meaning, in fact, could be thrown like a bone to the dogs of reason while the construct did its irrational work, a kind of burgling of the unconscious. With John Updike's new construct the plot is a small bone for worrying, while the circumambient meat is red, veiny, yellow-fatted. Here, Towser, is the bone. Good dog.

There is an imaginary African territory called Kush (low Arabic, I seem to remember, for the female genitalia), very large though small for Africa, landlocked, south of the Sahara, agonized by drought. Its dictator is Colonel Hakim Félix Elleloû, a former soldier of the colonizing French and student of a small Wisconsin college. He is a Moslem and has the statutory four wives, observes the five daily *waktu* and keeps away from alcohol. He is driven round in an air-conditioned silver Mercedes. He rules over a hungry state which officially professes a kind of Islamicized Marxism and houses in bunkers at its borders the *équipe* of a Soviet missile. Hakim, or Félix, detests America but is haunted by it. America generously unlades megatons of junk food for starving Kush. Hakim scornfully rejects it. He even incinerates a whole mountain of breakfast crispies with the American functionary assigned to its delivery on top, a stoic strawberry. But, whether he will or not, American influence creeps in, American knowhow prevails, and junk food, served to the accompaniment of Patti Page and Fats Domino on dining-booth-operated juke boxes, proclaims the ineluctable consumer revolution. When Hakim goes into exile as a short-order cook the five-year-awaited rains come. He ends in Nice on pension, writing his memoirs in the style of John Updike, whom he imitates with exceptional skill. In his alternation of first and third person narration he also imitates John Fowles's *Daniel Martin*. It is a remarkable prose performance and highly poetic.

It is many years since I last reviewed a novel – novella, rather: *Of the Farm* – by John Updike, but I have read all his prose works, not always however in English. I have bought them in Italian and French and picked up the odd paperback in English while on brief but lonely academic missions to the United States. If I have not read as much of his poetry as I should have liked, it is because publishers in Paris and Turin seem to shy at its translation, and it is not much around in American drugstores. But I am told, I think without malice, that to read his prose is to read his poetry, and I am prepared to believe it. The copy of *The Coup* that I have been sent is an uncorrected proof, and I am severely enjoined not to quote from it 'without comparison with the finally revised text', which does not seem, at this moment of reviewing, to be available. This emboldens me to set some of Mr Updike's prose as verse, making such small emendations as are necessary to regularize the rhythm:

The *piste* diminished to a winding track,
Treacherously pitted, strewn with flinty scrabble
That challenged well the mettle of our Michelin
Steel-belted radials. Distances grew bluish;
As we rose higher, clots of vegetation,
Thorny and leafless, troubled with grasping roots
The rocks. In the declivities that broke
Our grinding, twisting ascent, there were signs
Of pasturage: clay trampled to a hardened
Slurry by hooves, and also excrement
Distinguishable still from mineral matter,
Some toppled skeletons of beehive huts,
Consumed, their thatches, as a desperate fodder.
Aristada, which thrives on overgrazed
Lands, tinged with green this edge of desolation.

The boundaries between verse and prose are, in our age, most uncertain. I am happy to find in Mr Updike's work an undoubted traditional verse movement modestly disguised as prose, rather than the opposite, which we find too often in vaunted slim volumes. This is a fat volume, and it is full of poetry of a beautifully recognizable kind on a large number of subjects – the African landscape in all its aspects, the shoulderblades of women, the refrigerator snack after the hour of love, the blood gush at the severing of a head, Pepsi and Coca, hideous malty Ovaltine, leather, a fly's flight. There is a large lyric love of the surface of the world, in which the practice of visual notation conjoins with a great verbal gift – perhaps the greatest in the United States (of which Switzerland, by courtesy, was one) now that Vladimir Nabokov is dead. The only trouble with the practice of this gift in the novel is that it may reverse priorities, making the static examination more important than the thrust of plot, but I cannot really be sure that the swift movement of narrative should come first, especially when it is the most prized aspect of the brutal or sentimental bestseller.

Wyndham Lewis was another considerable novelist who was also a visual artist. He proclaimed as a fictional virtue that exterior point of view which turned characters into well-wrought automata, reluctant to relinquish the cubes of space they were set in. The eating of a shrimp on toast in *The Apes of God* seems a massive mechanical undertaking effected with wheels and levers of solid Edwardian manufacture. Updike avoids that heaviness, but he is committed to a Lewislike stasis which springs from the same lust to describe at length, missing out no wart or follicle. But he is so lyrically joyful, even when presenting a bloody act of execution (Félix committing regicide), that he seems weightless. Nevertheless he is committed also to a kind of poetic unit, a verse paragraph that, in certain contexts of action and even speech, seems excessively long. And there is a basic melody which seems to require otiose adjectives:

> . . . a poster of Elvis Presley in full sequinned regalia, Marilyn Monroe from a bed of polar bear skins making upwards at the lens the crimson O of a kiss whose mock emotion led her to close her greasy eyelids, and a page torn from that magazine whose hearty name of *Life* did not save it from dying. . . .

That *hearty* is surely unnecessary (and perhaps, in his correction of the proofs, Mr Updike has seen it to be so, but I am prepared to bet not), yet without the adjective the prosody falters. His music insists on richly periodic sentences and a formal balance of epithets. This does not apply in *The Coup* solely to the *récit*: his Africans talk like books, though his Americans can be earthy enough. If this, and his other imaginative prose works, can be designated novels, then we have to expand the boundaries of the form, making it accommodate a tissage of lyric utterances whose pretexts are fictional events.

But there is more than poetry in Mr Updike: there is thought – close, basic, original, civilized, terribly intelligent. Ideas, not actions, are the foil to his lyricism. Félix, for instance, insists that French literature more than French political thought is the colonialist's gift to Africa – the dryness of Ronsard and the ironic hopelessness of Villon. (It is hard to imagine an African thinking thus turning himself into a dictator.) Mr Updike is fascinated by religion and, as *A Month of Sundays* showed, can preach an astonishing sermon:

> It may be that in the attenuation, desiccation, and death of religions the world over, a new religion is being formed in the indistinct hearts of men, a religion without a God, without prohibitions and compensatory assurances a religion whose antipodes are motion and stasis, whose one rite is the exercise of energy, and in which exhausted forms like the quest, the vow, the expiation, and the attainment through suffering of wisdom are, emptied of content, put in the service of a pervasive expenditure whose ultimate purpose is entropy.

Entropy – magic American word, as old as Henry Adams and as new as Pynchon. Félix and his fellow Moslems brood on the significance of an Allah without attributes (no attributes = no God?) with a relish matched only by their readiness to quote the Koran. The *surahs* are cited in English, implying a concern with the semantics of what the Prophet preached – whereas my own Far Eastern experience leads me to believe that non-Arabic Moslems regard the texts as mere tongue-curling and fishbone-clearing cantrips. There is too much intelligence as there is too much eloquence. There is, one might say had one the courage, too much Mr Updike and too few personages realized from their own distinct withinness as opposed to their miraculously rendered (especially with the four wives) physical attributes. But no attributes = no people.

And what, for the Book Club member who doesn't give much of a damn about poetry, can this novel offer? A nostalgic evocation of the hopeful fifties, pre-Watergate Nixon and a look back at Ike. The African or Black American consciousness as caught by a white man. A very shrewd and well-informed summation of the impossibility of a rapprochement between Third World need and American generosity. All those cornflakes and the goats' udders dry. A fury of agricultural thaumaturgy, the grazing grounds plucked to nothing by cattle which forget how to wander. American goodwill unqualified by awareness of the terrible depths of the human heart (this is before My-Lai and *Time*'s shamed rediscovery of the principle of evil). The novel is bound to fail as dialectic, since its principal voice as it were *contains* America, foreknows most of the answers, submits at the start to a kind of hopelessness. And the hopelessness is fulfilled at the end, as we know it has to be, by the cheerful American conquest of Africa. American technology is far superior to Soviet. Even the decollated head of the late king of Kush, which speaks prophecies in a cave much visited by tourists, is heavier than it need be, since it is packed with Russian electronics: it would be feather-light had it been US-transistorized. The Russians are lumpish and suspicious, the Americans are light-stepped and eager.

That *The Coup* (a name combining eagles and doves) is, beneath the elaborate and lovely poetry, a true statement about neo-colonialism one cannot doubt. But it is an even truer statement – though self-confessedly distilled through reading as much as observation – about the intractabilities of Africa, the brute facts of geography (or the *National Geographic*, to which Mr Updike pays due acknowledgement), and the terrible inequality in the distribution of the world's resources. It is finally a sour-mouthed hymn to the United States, where men are so fat that they must jog and cut down on peanut butter – thus impairing Kush's sole export – and, whether we like it or not, the patterns of our age have been, and are still being, forged. Africa, and the world, will be saved by American technological lust and junk food. But all this is nothing compared with the brilliant verbal celebration of surfaces. If Mr Updike does not feel inclined to temper his poetic ebullience to the end of producing what James and Conrad called a novel, that is his own affair. Faced as we are with a flood of American junk fiction, in which the lexis is mostly street obscenity and the events orgasms, perhaps we ought to be grateful for such self-indulgent magic and elegance.

Garping

The Hotel New Hampshire, by John Irving

This new novel by the author of *The World According to Garp* is at present No. 1 on the American bestseller lists and thus demands our respectful attention. However superior our literary tastes, it is always foolish to deny respect to an inferior novelist (inferior to Joyce, Conrad, Lawrence, James, etc.) who has discovered a means of making money out of fiction. We can ignore the formulaic trash of Harold Robbins and the rest, but we cannot write off a writer like John Irving, who is literate, ingenious and original. He clearly has something to offer the American masses; we must see what that something is.

The Hotel New Hampshire has three main ingredients – an American family, the city of Vienna, and a great deal of violence. These ingredients have already been exploited in *The World According to Garp*, and clearly had something to do with its success, both critical and commercial. But they were already present in an earlier novel, *The Water-Method Man*, which was merely respectfully noticed and modestly consumed. The Garp book sharpened the violence to the Grand Guignol limit (e.g. stationary car hit with act of fellation proceeding in it; penis bitten off at the root) and sentimentalized the family element. For Americans, and indeed for us, this may well be the best of both fictional worlds. Vienna is there partly because Mr Irving once lived in Vienna. To transfer action thither is (a) a substitute for character development, (b) exotic titillation, (c) a means of intensifying the violence by transposing it from the American private to the European public zone. Or it may just be that Mr Irving is, as the song puts it, in love with Vienna.

Garp looked out from the fastness of his family onto a filthy world. The head of the Berry family, in this new book, seeks security for his loved ones in a clean well-lighted place, the hotel of the title. There are three versions of the Hotel New Hampshire – the girls' school which the family transforms, to good comic effect, in the state which gives it its name; the refurbished Gasthaus Freud in Vienna; a rape-crisis centre in Maine. But a hotel is never a sanctuary: it has to welcome in the filthy world in order to survive. The Berry family finds it difficult to survive.

Consider what happens to it. John Berry, who tells the story, is in love with his sister Fran. Fran is the victim of gang rape. She also has a lesbian affair with another rape victim who hides from the world in a bearskin. Brother Frank is a homosexual. Lilly, a dwarf, kills herself because she fails as a writer. Mother and little brother, whose name is Egg, are killed in an air crash on their way to Vienna. The father is blinded by the bomb of Viennese terrorists, whose attempt to blow up the Opera House is foiled by the family. There are several other assorted deaths and maimings, as well as a healthy dollop of dirty sex. One whole floor of the Gasthaus is the preserve of prostitutes, while another houses the terrorists, and both are committed to human degradation. John Berry and his sister get over their incestuous passion by indulging it to the painful limit. John learns how to kiss from a beautiful black rape victim whose teeth were knocked out by a lead pipe – ah, the voluptuous joy of those deep dark caverns, etc.

For all this, the tone of the book is, like the Garp one, farcical. Irving is adept at setting up complex situations in which all the comic bombs ignite simultaneously – a 'black' equivalent to Thurber's innocent 'The Night the Bed Fell on Father', Frank Berry does a taxidermist's job on the family dog Sorrow, a prodigious farter in life, and the snarling corpse keeps turning up in people's beds or hidden by shower curtains; finally it is the sole floating record of the air crash which kills mother and son. Irving rubs animals and people out without compunction, and the lack of emotion has to be interpreted in terms of the *vis comica*. I don't think one can play around with disaster and grief in this way. Certainly one can't play around with them at such inordinate length.

For the novel is far too long to accommodate characters and situations which one can only accept as the material of anecdote. None of the characters has an interior life: in his denial of the existence of human entities as more than bundles of nervous responses Irving is very much in the contemporary American existential tradition. Evidently the country that produced Hawthorne and James no longer wishes to believe in the human soul. Discontinuity, random parades of shocking events constitute the phenomenology of American popular fiction. There is no underlying morality. There is gratuitous violence and there is a brief compassion indistinguishable from sentimentality (which is itself a form of gratuitous violence), but there is no probing at the root-canals of a sick society. Indeed, *The Hotel New Hampshire* is itself a typical product of American sickness, as is its evident popularity. In Vienna you take whipped cream, or *Schlagobers*, with your coffee. Irving is always bringing up the phrase 'blood and *Schlagobers*'. It is a fair description of an intermittently diverting but ultimately tedious novel.

Hitler Lives

The Portage to San Cristobal of A.H., by George Steiner

I f A.H. is still alive, having consigned a double to death in the Berlin
bunker, he is ninety-two – a not impossible age. Take ten years off,
and you can have the not incredible image of a fierce old man still
believing in the German destiny and misusing the divine gift of language
to hypnotize, justify, and set the whole damnable process to work again.
The theme of Hitler's reappearance has appealed to a number of practitioners of popular art – there was even a Garth cartoon strip, very well
done, in the *Daily Mirror* back in the fifties. The most recent popular
novel on the subject was Philippe van Rjndt's *The Trial of Adolf Hitler*
(1979), in which sound researches into international jurisprudence, and
very shrewd insights into the psychology of contemporary German,
helped to produce a wholly convincing scenario. It is instructive to compare it with Dr Steiner's novella. Van Rjndt's book is a compelling read,
no more. Dr Steiner's is literature.

Literature is the exploitation of language, and language is a major
Steinerian concern. No living scholar is better endowed to deliver – as
Steiner has already delivered in works like *Language and Silence* and *After
Babel* – speculations about the nature of language which, being daring
and disturbing, go far beyond the depositions of mere Chomskyites.
Steiner is not a cautious descriptivist. Moreover, he is polyglot: he
knows *languages*, which most professional linguists do not. A thesis he
once held strongly was that, after Auschwitz and Buchenwald, language
was finished – it could no longer express human outrage – and that
German in particular had been burned out and gutted by the Nazis. He
admired Beckett, who seemed to recognize that language had become
useless and made literature out of its mere rags before finally specializing
in the rhetoric of silence.

Steiner's sense of hopelessness about language has, in a heartening
paradox, always been expressed with great eloquence in his didactic
writings. His admirers have never been in any doubt about his ability to
deploy language in the manner of a creative artist, but he has been consistent, ever since the brilliant *Anno Domini* of the sixties, in evading
creative responsibility. The eloquence of the teacher is one thing, that of
the novelist another. Yet *The Portage to San Cristobal of A.H.*, a remarkable
exploitation, indeed explosion, of many kinds of English, serves to illustrate the thesis of the main essay in *Language and Silence* – that in the presence of evil words misbehave, syntax falters, the lexis of the senses
becomes confused.

A team of tough young Jews finds Hitler alive among the Amazonian swamps and, in a nightmare of pain which the language exactly mirrors, carries him towards civilization. That civilization meanwhile, in Germany, Russia, England and the United States, prepares dubiously to receive the father of evil. We are reminded, in a paragraph four and a half closely printed pages long, of the nature of this evil, a litany of names and atrocities which the syntax stumbles under. We are also given a reminder of the theology of evil: 'All that is God's, hallowed be His name, must have its counterpart, its backside of evil and negation. So it is with the Word, with the gift of speech that is the glory of man and distinguishes him everlastingly from the silence or animal noises of creation. When He made the World, God made possible also its contrary. . . . He created on the night-side of language a speech for hell.' When coherence comes, at the end of the narrative, it is in mouth of evil.

Teku, an Amazonian Indian, recognizes the power in the eyes of the ancient broken A.H. and makes him a chair. In the clearing, while the team awaits the arrival of the helicopters, the articles of attainder are read out and the seated defendant delivers, with terrifying and plausible eloquence, the justification of his acts. As expected, he blames everything on the Jews, but in a manner far more closely argued than the verbiage of *Mein Kampf*. The Jews did wrong, he cries, in creating an omnipotent God. 'You call me a tyrant, an enslaver. What tyranny, what enslavement has been more oppressive, has branded the skin and soul of man more deeply, than the sick fantasies of the Jew? . . . The Jew invented conscience and left man a guilty serf.'

'The white-faced Nazarene' and 'Rabbi Marx' are as responsible as the Old Testament prophets for 'the blackmail of transcendence'. Hitler had to kill the Jews 'to burn out the virus of utopia before the whole of our western civilisation sickened.' The world acquiesced in the Holocaust, being secretly glad of the coming of the exterminator. But, from the Jewish point of view, that Holocaust was a blessing, since out of it was born the free state of Israel.

As for evil, Hitler's record is blameworthy perhaps but not excessive. The Belgians killed twenty million when they raped the Congo. The British housed the Boers in the first concentration camps. Stalin slaughtered thirty million: 'he had perfected genocide when I was still a nameless scribbler in Munich.' And yet Stalin died peacefully in bed while 'you hunt me down like a rabid dog, put me on trial (by what right, by what mandate?), drag me through the swamps, tie me up at night.' The plausibility is unbroken by any words of the prosecution. The Reich begat Israel, 'the vacuous day-dream of Zion' became a reality, the men of war of the Jewish state should honour their old tormentor as a father. These are Hitler's last words before the helicopters come.

We have here a very fearless book. It encloses no debate but bids the debate now start. But, being a work of literature, its aim is not didactic. It claims the same right as the plays of Shakespeare to find an eloquence for evil which evil is too stupid to find for itself. That evil is becoming increasingly attractive as a concept to even men of goodwill (the term is common enough in journalism now: yet it made its first appearance in the popular press in *Time* after the My-Lai massacre) is attested by the growing fascination of the figures of the Nazi regime. They have become eternal myths in death. In life they were just misguided men. Orwell, in 1942, writes of sending Hitler, with a bag of bearer bonds, to become the bore of a Swiss *pension*. He is far from being a bore in Steiner's astonishing book. He has become the dark archangel of a new liturgy.

Hitler's England

SS-GB, by Len Deighton

I have been impressed by Len Deighton ever since he was greeted as the mere successor to Ian Fleming. Apart from his virtues as a storyteller, his passion for researching his backgrounds gives his work a remarkable factual authority. I don't know the world of espionage, but I do know that of show business, and his *Close-Up*, a brilliant study of a film actor in decline, seemed to me quite faultless in its delineation of every aspect of the cinema, from camera technique to tax evasion. With *Bomber* and *Fighter* he established himself as an expert on a period with which, since he was born in 1929, he could not be expected to be directly familiar, at least not as an adult. Yet the authority of these books seems absolute.

In his new novel he plays the daring trick of imagining Britain under the Nazis. It's a trick we've all played in the privacy of our imaginations, but few of us would know how to acquire the factual knowledge that gives solidity to the nightmare. Deighton being the sort of realistic writer he is, the nightmare is both more and less frightening than it is, or could be, in a free fantasy of absolute tyranny. The occupying Nazis are human beings, vulnerable men with problems. The occupied Britons are not, except for the small force of the Resistance, particularly heroic.

Occupier and occupied are preoccupied with the business of contriving some sort of coexistence. One can hardly doubt that London in the early winter of 1941, with Hitler's head on the postage stamps and the swastika flags waving in Whitehall, would have been pretty much as Deighton presents it – granted the near-unacceptable premise that Great Britain would have signed an armistice with its invaders.

The image of Nazi Britain is conveyed more or less peripherally. Deighton is telling a story about the murder investigation conducted by Detective Superintendent Douglas Archer of Scotland Yard. To concentrate on an unchanged routine and admit the changed scene on the margin is a fine authenticating device: a spring and summer have passed since the armistice, and things are already being taken for granted. Work goes on. Whitehall 1212 is the telephone number of Kriminalpolizei, Ordnungspolizei, Sicherheitsdienst and Gestapo. Feldgericht der Luftwaffe is in Lincoln's Inn. Archer's boss is Gruppenführer Fritz Kellerman of the SS, a genial paternal rogue given to fishing (he subscribes to the *Angler's Times*) and the art of survival. Can Archer, whose job is to combat civil crime, be regarded as a Nazi collaborator?

It would have been easy to pile on the concentration camp atrocities – and irresistible to the manufacturer of an eight-hundred-page blockbuster on Deighton's general theme – but the most horrible thing in the book is what the Resistance does to one of Archer's policemen. The profiteer who sells Chippendale to the generals and feasts them on caviar is one of a conspiracy to get King George VI out of the Tower (where he languishes on Himmler's orders) and convey him to the New World, which, for political reasons, does not particularly want him. Nothing is simple as in a morality play. The Abwehr and the SS detest each other, and British patriots must exploit the fact. Everybody, British and German alike, fears the Gestapo. The Germans are not always efficient. Hitler is potentially suicidal, rejecting atomic research even when it is clothed in astrological and cabbalistic mumbo-jumbo. 'The Americans will make the bomb,' says Standartenführer Huth to Archer, 'and win the war that will begin the moment they are ready.' Then, having been too clever and evoked enmity in Gruppenführer Kellerman of Scotland Yard, he goes off to face a firing squad. The Englishman, who has at last let patriotism get the better of duty, remains available at Whitehall 1212.

We end with the future unsettled. There is no European war, and Hitler and Stalin remain friendly. The Russians have even been allowed to dig up Marx's body in Highgate Cemetery in order to send it to Red Square, though a fine act of terrorism disrupts that ceremony. The King is shot during the escape operation in which Archer participates, and presumably Queen Elizabeth II will be proclaimed in her New Zealand sanctuary. We do not know whether Pearl Harbor is going to be attacked or not. It is not Deighton's purpose to rewrite the whole history of the world from 19 February 1941 on. What we are given is a slab of time and a quality of life which might all too easily have been realized – not too good for the British Jews, tolerable for most of the others, admirable for the spivs and puppet Cabinet. Vera Lynn sings 'We'll Meet Again' and Flanagan and Allen 'The White Cliffs of Dover'. Cigarettes are damnably dear on the black market. Churchill, it seems, was shot making the V-sign. The Mirabelle is reserved for high officers of Air Fleet 8 headquarters. There is no blackout. Fried turnip slices are sold in the streets. The beer is watery. Business as usual and life going on. This is one of Len Deighton's best.

The Mystery of Evil

Sophie's Choice, by William Styron

Mr Styron's new novel is set in Brooklyn NY in 1947, with flashbacks to Auschwitz–Birkenau. The comparative innocence of postwar American society is personified in the character of the narrator Stingo, a twenty-two-year-old Southerner who wants two things very badly – to write a great novel and to get laid. To achieve the second is quite as difficult as to encompass the first. Installed in Yetta Zimmerman's boarding house, which is painted pink (the very colour of American innocence: the paint is cheap army surplus), he tries to write while hearing the noise of vigorous humping from the room overhead. Nathan, a Brooklyn Jew of immense charm, various learning and unpredictable temper, is carrying on an affair with Sophie, a ravishing Pole of Catholic anti-Semitic background and a recent American immigrant. Stingo falls for them both, two beautiful people who are as doomed as Tristan and Isolde. For Nathan is mad, and his madness is exacerbated by drug-taking. And Sophie, who survived Auschwitz, is suffused with guilt. Bound to each other tempestuously in *Wuthering Heights* fashion, they end, in the Pink Palace as they call it, poisoned by cyanide, locked in each other's arms, with the phonograph playing Bach.

All fictional plots sound, in bald summary, comic or melodramatic, and I am doing a disservice to Mr Styron's intelligence and skill, which means to the cunning of his style and structure, in thus merely stating what the novel is basically about. A novel, like a painting or a symphony, is about itself, but fiction is condemned, which the other arts are not, to deal with the real world, which means, when it is important fiction, history and the philosophical resonances of history. Three phases of history grind at each other in this book: the seventies look at the late forties, and both look at the German nightmare, which, it appears, we are only just beginning to be equipped to understand in the eighties – if we ever are at all. The one-word theme of the novel is evil, but there is no obsession with evil. The death-camp flashbacks, whether presented through Sophie's imperfect English or the author–narrator's imaginative reconstructions, have as foil the Brooklyn summer, Coney Island, the childish joys of American abundance, and the comedy of Stingo's attempts to get laid.

Coming so close after the television series *Holocaust*, it would appear that the book is cashing in on a reawakened popular fascination with Auschwitz and the rest of the Nazi horrors. The million-dollar advance and the persistent first place in the American bestseller lists seem to confirm a hard-eyed commercial exploitation of the story of the death camps, but *Sophie's Choice* goes deeper than *Holocaust*, by its mass-medial, pictorial, non-philosophical, essentially sectarian nature, was able to or wished to. Thus, Nathan, the Brooklyn Jew, is a product of tolerance and wealth (as is the Brooklyn Heights princess who frustrates Stingo's first major attempt to get laid), and it is Sophie, the blonde Germanophone Catholic, who has the Auschwitz number tattooed on her arm. It was not only the Jews who were slaughtered, but the Slavs and gypsies and nuns and priests and Aryan intellectuals. And the Southerner Stingo–Styron, who eventually writes a novel about Nat Turner, sees black slavery as a precursor of the metaphysic that animated the Nazi camps – which, we are reminded, were intended as a new kind of community with a new kind of economy and ethic. Stingo is able to support himself as an artist because his grandmother sold a slave, (named Artiste) and left the money in gold to her grandchildren. Poland, Stingo sees, with its intolerance and outmoded chivalry, is not unlike the South.

Sophie, a young married woman with a son and daughter, is picked up by the Gestapo for trying to take illegal meat to her consumptive mother. This results in her and her children being sent to Auschwitz–Birkenau at a time when the gas chamber was not reserved solely to the Jews. A drunken SS doctor gives her a choice: either her son or her daughter can be saved. Sophie makes her choice and sees her daughter, clutching her flute and her teddybear, go off to be killed. She lives with the agony of that choice, and Styron observes in the evil of its imposition something so close to absolute evil that it can only be followed by a kind of redemption. The mystery of evil is the mystery of the universe. Its resolution can be found in human love, but it is a pity that, as in so much contemporary American fiction, this has to be expressed here in the explicit terms of getting laid. Stingo eventually gets his lay and gets it, extravagantly, from Sophie just before she goes off for her *Liebestod*. But, since physical explicitness is the whole heart of the novel, one ought not to complain about this plethora of nakedness, sweat and sucking.

For Styron is at his best in such evocations as that of life in the household of Höss, the Auschwitz commandant who employs the polyglot Sophie as a secretary, where every detail is horrifyingly plausible. It is the ordinariness, dullness, vulgarity of a polity based on evil that strikes home, down to the overfurnished parlour and the kitsch on the gramophone. And in the background we are aware of Simone Weil saying that this is what evil is like, dull not Luciferan, and Hannah Arendt commenting that with the driving out of even ordinary animal pity there comes self-pity: poor Höss, racked with migraine, wondering how to reconcile the demands of German industry for more Jewish slaves and those of Himmler for total annihilation. The Jews are a terrible nuisance.

The American critics have commented adversely on Styron's prose, with its orotundity and lushness (the 'amok flambeaux' of the New England fall, for instance). Critics are not always ready to see that a style is as much a character as any of the walking creations of a novel and that, especially when the author himself is withdrawn and leaves things to a narrator, it is entitled to extravagance and even eccentricity. According to the critics, practically every novelist has a bad style (meaning, perhaps, not Barthe's *écriture dégré zéro*), and the greatest have the worst – Faulkner, James, Dickens. Styron's style is 'Southern', meaning rich, leafy and odorous: it is given to superabundance rather than Hemingway leanness (but the Hemingway style is now regarded as bad), and it is typically seen here:

> . . . The Maple Court did not obtain a cabaret license, and all the bright angular chrome-and-gilt décor, including sunburst chandeliers meant to revolve about the giddy dancers like glittering confections in a Ruby Keeler movie, fell into disrepair and gathered a patina of grime and smoke. The raised platform which formed the hub of the oval-shaped bar, and which had been designed to enable sleek long-legged stripteasers to wiggle their behinds down upon a circumambience of lounging gawkers, became filled with dusty signs and bloated fake bottles advertising brands of whisky and beer.

I have nothing against this. The lushness of the whole novel offsets the starkness of the main deposition, the bad apple among the leaves of life.

Sophie and Nathan are very much characters in the round, especially Nathan: Sophie suffers from a mode of communication which no author could manage well – an insufficient English which, nevertheless, must encompass the whole rich nastiness of nightmare. The main faults of the novel, and they are not great faults, are two. First, Styron too often forsakes narrative in order to expatiate professorially, retailing information cerebrally where he should convert it to action or dialogue. Secondly, like most long American novels, *Sophie's Choice* was designed so that parts of it could be published as self-contained pieces of fiction in American magazines. The account of Stingo's attempt to get laid on Pierpont Avenue is appallingly funny and brilliant in itself, but it is so very much *in itself* that it contributes little to the main narrative drive. But, after all, one could say much the same about parts of Dickens.

Fire and Order

Setting the World on Fire, by Angus Wilson

Take Westminster Abbey. Imagine just behind it, extending as far as the church of St John's, Smith Square, a great mansion called Tothill House, complete with formal gardens and huge park. This was once monastic property and it was granted by Henry VIII the Reformer to the Tothill family. The Tothill family saw it pass, through the female line, to the Mossons. At this moment it is in the possession of Sir Piers Mosson Bart, the famous stage director. He had a younger brother, Tom, who died heroically in 1969 when a new Catesby conspiracy tried to set the world, or certainly the Ministry of Defence, on fire. Piers called Tom Pratt, because of his devotion to Sir Roger Pratt, part-architect of Tothill House. Tom called Piers Van, because of his passion for Vanbrugh, who designed the Great Hall of the house. In this hall is a massive fresco of the fall of Phaeton, who nearly and literally set the world on fire. This frightened the boy Tom, who, with an instinct for classic order, was destined to follow the law. This overjoyed the boy Piers, who, with a love of baroque, was destined to transform the British theatre. Both, in their different ways, had incendiary designs on the world.

While still a sixth-former at Westminster School, Piers–Van plans a production of Lully's *Phaethon* in the Great Hall, incorporating the fresco into the decor and even into the action. This does not come off despite the long planning. The boys' mother, widow of Lady Mosson's younger son, announces that she is carrying on an affair with a regular officer of the Royal Electrical and Mechanical Engineers whom she cannot marry, since he already has a wife who is a Catholic. She also confesses that she was engaged in the affair while her husband was fighting and dying in the Second World War. Lady Mosson, an American and a Christian Scientist, is scandalized. Her surviving son, Sir Hubert Mosson Bart, bachelor and banker, is also scandalized. Surrounded every day by both classic and baroque stability, they are locked into a mock-stability which is pharisaic. Great-grandfather Mosson, in his nineties, dies a few hours after Mrs Mosson's scandalous revelation after having, on Piers–Van's priming, disclosed at too great length for his feeble condition an ancient scandal of his own.

The errant daughter-in-law is forbidden further visits to Tothill House. The loyal sons are cut off from the two kinds of order until the deaths of Lady Mosson and her son. But the production of *Phaethon* does eventually take place, in 1969 when Piers–Van has inherited the estate and established himself as a great man of the theatre. It is followed by another production – one of a play based on Tothill involvement in Gunpowder Plot, a mere cover for a latterday plot, one designed to set the world, or Westminster, on fire. This is where you came in.

My summary, inevitably inadequate, must give the impression of a novel brutally systematized. The brothers' reciprocal nicknames, symbolizing two modes of sensibility in art as in life, are not very plausible. The ambiguities resident in the very notion of order are rubbed in. The Kaiser's and the Führer's views of order killed two Mossons and set the world on fire. Lully composed for the Sun King, whose fire fed a court as dull as an old people's home. Baroque is lively but tends to vulgarity; the Prattian classicism is derivative and denies an organic order killed by the Reformation. There is a fine ebullient character, Marina Luzzi, a Turinese heiress, betrothed to Sir Hubert briefly and improbably, who stands for the denial of any kind of order. She wants chaos; she finds most things 'boaring' (I do not see, incidentally, in what way this differs phonemically from 'boring'). The distinction of the novel, and it is a very distinguished novel, lies in its capacity to transcend the systematic. Its personages are glowingly alive. The virtues of nineteenth-century fiction are here, as they always are in Angus Wilson, but wedded to a complex symbolism very artfully and always convincingly managed.

This, in fact, is very much my idea of what a modern novel ought to be. It is a piece of engineering but also a living organism. It is very solid, you can walk round it. The solidity is in the ambience, both real and imagined: you feel you know Tothill House, its hall and its gardens. The flowers in that garden are no mere impressionistic blur: they are named and listed. Lady Mosson thinks the name *Malmaison* inappropriate to a rose in a house over which the God of the Christian Scientists lovingly presides. She has to be told its provenance. Josephine, rose-lover, lived at Malmaison: we get the whiff of history and another kind of destructive order. We are never far away from the past, but the past is always solidified into tangible actualities.

The mastery of craft will be most evident to readers in those shocking set scenes at which Mr Wilson is so adept. Marina Luzzi, having seen herself as the new mistress of Tothill House, proposes the death of the formal garden, the end of the garden party which symbolizes a structured society, the quelling of all that is 'boaring'. But then she lets out, in his mother's presence, nasty revelations of her fiancé's perverted sexuality: 'Do you think I want to see your white bottom anymore – "Make it red, Marina," Get 'er to do it. Go back to your prostitutes. I 'ave done enough for you.' So chaos is averted, but only so that pharisaism can go on prevailing. Sir Hubert ends whipped to death in the slums of the East End. It is one of those briefly reported horrors we have met before in Angus Wilson – the offstage nastiness complementary to the big scene in which, as in slow motion, a world is observed falling to pieces. There are plenty of analogues here to what is unforgettable in *Hemlock and After*, but this new novel proclaims, as it should, a greater mastery of organization.

The two strains in Angus Wilson – Dickensian ebullience, the face of British society hirsute with perverts, grotesques and beleaguered men of good will; the need to create situations somewhat hysterical and only just within the borders of credibility – have not always satisfactorily harmonized. I admire *The Old Men at the Zoo* but see it as two books yoked with violence into one – one all realism, the other all grand guignol. In *Setting the World on Fire* we have a rapid melodramatic finale which, different in pace as well as content from what has gone before, nevertheless seems not merely to blend with but to explain the earlier leisurely realism. The book is about a group of people, but it is also about the whole world being set on fire. It is superb entertainment and social criticism but it is also a poem about the fire in human beings – the source of warmth and the civilized craft of cookery (one of the themes) but also the means of self-destruction. It is a moving and disturbing book and a very superior piece of art.

Nobel Humility

The Paper Men, by William Golding

Mr Golding's hero–narrator is a highly regarded British novelist named Wilfred Barclay. He is white-haired and white-bearded, given to booze but not self-praise, and I should imagine that he is nothing at all like his creator. Novelists often use novelists as the protagonists of novels because novel writing is the trade they know best, but they usually go out of their way to avoid the imputation of self-portraiture. Golding is a nice man while Barclay is a nasty one. Barclay recognizes that he is one of the breed described by the title, a creature who has forfeited various of the traits of amiability in order to spin words. The reality of fiction is not the reality of reality. Barclay has been good at lechery, though he is getting too old for it now; he has not been good at love. To be just to him, he does not love himself all that much, and he is not flattered when a young American academic, Rick L. Tucker, enters his life with a burning desire to be his biographer.

Much of the brief book is about Barclay's attempts to avoid Tucker, who pursues him all over Europe with camera, tape recorder, and total recall. A great deal of this is funny, and the story begins with a fine comic scene with Tucker burrowing into Barclay's dustbin for precious self-revelatory manuscripts, while Barclay, who thinks a badger is scavenging there, flesh-wounds him with an airgun. We can, we think, relax. Golding is not being grim about human evil, he is colloquial, profane, more concerned with the human comedy. Writers will appreciate the situation more than mere readers. American specialists in the work of British authors do not necessarily like or even understand the work. It is mainly a question of grabbing a specialization before others get in there. Alroy Kear in *Cakes and Ales* rightly says that American scholars prefer living mice to dead lions – 'That's one of the things I like about America' – and they naturally prefer the mouse itself to its mere pawprints. Hence Tucker's biographical lust and its object's distaste. Barclay wants to be left alone.

But Tucker tracks him down in the Swiss Alps with a document granting biographical rights which he wants the novelist to sign. He also brings his wife with him, a delicious girl upon whom Barclay looks with the impotent lust and foreboding that the old men on the walls of Troy felt when the sinuous Helen appeared. Not without reason, for she seems to be offered to Barclay as a bribe. He resists, but he cannot prevent young Tucker from saving his life when the rail of an alpine path gives way and his hands clutch tenuous roots and soil above the abyss. In the description of Barclay's physical plight we get the brilliant word magician of *Pincher Martin* briefly at work. Then we go back to the loose colloquial, the curiously out-of-date slang, the American English that sounds parodic.

As this is Golding, the possibility of falling into a spiritual abyss has to be prefigured in Barclay's moment of alpine danger. What Barclay likes better than paper is stained glass, though churches hold nothing of the numinous for him. But he is taken unawares in a cathedral by an image of Christ and he collapses. Behind Rick L. Tucker is a man we never meet named Halliday, a billionaire who is financing Tucker's research, and we have to wonder for a moment whether Halliday (holy day, Sunday, *Man Who Was Thursday*) is God. It doesn't matter, because the rest of Barclay's story is secular and nasty and, unlike Mountjoy in *Free Fall*, he catches no image of redemption. He turns Tucker into a dog, making him yap and lap Swiss wine from a saucer. He is indifferent when his former wife dies of cancer. Although he has probably not read Mr Golding's last novel, he becomes obsessed with what he terms rites of passage. One of these rites is the burning of all his papers on the lawn. Another is the setting down of this chronicle. He does not finish it, because Tucker seems to kill him in mid-lexeme, nay in mid-phoneme.

When a piece of fiction seems banal but its author is distinguished and universally honoured, we are compelled to take second and third looks at it, prepared to be convinced that the banality is a kind of code or a new mode of profundity or elegance we are too stupid to perceive. I would, I think, reading this book with an innocent eye and assuming that it was a first novel, be glad to find large promise in it, patches of descriptive brilliance, a rough humour which experience might refine, a capacity for manipulating symbols, considerable energy. But Mr Golding is presented to us, and not only by his publishers, as the living British novelist whose work 'is most likely to survive'. He is also Britain's first Nobel laureate in fiction since Galsworthy, and this is taken, in the Faber blurb, to be 'the final recognition of Golding's genius' (come; how about the OM?) and the confirmation of 'what has already become generally accepted' – to wit, his unique greatness. It would seem to me that, with right British modesty, Golding has deliberately produced a post-award novel that gives the lie to the great claim. He is a humble man, and *The Paper Men* is a gesture of humility.

Misoginy?

Stanley and the Women, by Kingsley Amis

I
t is exactly four years since Kingsley Amis last gave us a novel, and
that has been a long time to wait. None of us is getting any younger,
time is short and so on, and, despite what lady reviewers tell ageing
male novelists about the necessity of taking time off to *think things out
thoroughly* before blowing Schimmelpenninck smoke over the noisy keys,
we ought to be pushing on with the job. I was a little annoyed with
Russian Hide-and-Seek when it came out in 1980, but it has now settled
into the Amis II corpus of hypothetical fiction and makes a reasonable
companion for *The Alteration*. The new book makes a reasonable com-.
panion for *Jake's Thing*. It is, I think, very good, very powerful. Lady
reviewers will express whimsical wonder that the great lessons of the new
feminism have not sunk into yet another obdurately piggish male brain.
They've sunk in all right. Women wanted the big division, and by God
they've got it.

The narration is in the hands of Stanley Duke, the advertising manager of an unnamed daily paper. He speaks with a SW16 accent and
says *yeah* like his Anglo-Saxon forebears (*yes* is only a truncated *gea
sothlice*). He drinks a lot and is fond of cars. He has achieved that
hypergamy which was one of the big themes of the fiction of the fifties
(*Lucky Jim*, for instance), and his upper-class wife Susan is assistant
literary editor of the resuscitated *Sunday Chronicle*. By his first wife Nowell
('Noel was her name but she or her mother had just not been able to spell
it. There were cases like Jaclyn and Margaux and Siouxie where no one
seriously imagined that was right, but this was different. Nowell was like
Jayne and Dianna and Anette where somebody had been plain bleeding
ignorant') he has a son, Steve. This son goes mad.

The woman doctor who looks after his case is named Trish Collings,
one of the most dangerous females in the whole Amis canon, since she
allows personal vindictiveness to colour clinical procedure. She naturally terms Steve's illness a schizophreniform disorder, and, equally
naturally, blames the father for the son's inability to find himself, whatever that means, finding a lay collaboratrix in Nowell. A more experienced male specialist, Dr Nash, thinks Shakespearean terminology good
enough: 'For to define true madness what is it but to be nothing else but
mad? Not bad. Not bad at all.' Dr Collings lets Steve, further deranged
with chemical therapy, out of the hospital into the big world,
presumably to spite the father, where he tries to warn the Arabs of a
cosmic biblical conspiracy and gets duffed up in good Qaddafi fashion
for his pains. He also apparently draws a knife on his stepmother, but

there seems to be some doubt about this. Susan probably did it herself to get her stepson put away and to regain Stanley's inevitably wandering attention. She goes off, knowing that Stanley suspects this, saying:

> '. . . I don't know how I've put up with you for so long, with your gross table manners and your boozing and your bloody little car and your frightful *mates* and your whole ghastly south-of-the-river man's world. You've no breeding and so you've no respect for women. They're there to cook your breakfast and be fucked and that's it.'

Dinner too, a genuinely gross Stanley might have added. Not that Susan is ever shown cooking his breakfast.

The question arises: since madness has come into the story, are women to be considered mad? Dr Nash finally thinks not: 'They're all too monstrously, sickeningly, *terrifyingly* sane. That's the *whole* trouble.' Their sanity is directed to a very clear end. Cliff Wainwright, Stanley's GP friend, also from south of the river, puts the situation trenchantly: 'If you want to fuck a woman, she can fuck you up.' Stanley adds: 'They used to feel they needed something in the way of provocation, but now they seem to feel they can get on with the job of fucking you up any time they feel like it. That's what Women's Lib is for.' And Cliff says: 'It's getting worse now they're competing on equal terms in so many places and find they still finish behind men. They can't even produce a few decent fucking *jugglers*.'

None of this stern stuff is coming straight from the mouth of Mr Amis. This happens to be a novel, and all the men in it happen to have had, or be having, a rough time with women. Bert Hutchinson, Nowell's second husband, has either to be drunk or pretend to be drunk all the time. Stanley thought he was doing all right with Susan, but look at him now. Even Dr Nash is having, and has had, some undefined trouble or other. Cliff Wainwright's wife has small space to be abominable in, but she makes good use of it. Such women as have hardly any space at all seem all right, like one of the nursing sisters and the Dukes' cleaning lady, who does a better take-off of Susan's posh accent than Susan does of the SW16 one. And there is a nice Ulster woman journalist named Lindsey (ominous, I should have thought) who wears very clean spectacles, except in bed. She seems to be all right, so far.

Jake's Thing, which does for sexology what this one does for schizophreniform specialists, ends with a soaring misogynistic ode; *Stanley and the Women* gets into misogyny fairly early on but gives itself plenty of breathing space for targets other than upper-middle-class Englishwomen (which is what the term *woman* is shorthand for), though where Stanley's life gets fucked up there is often a woman, or else a foreigner, behind it. There is a wonderful party on a Thames houseboat in a high wind at the turn of the tide; everybody is sick, and it is the husband's fault for not holding the boat steady or something. None of the men, except decent Stanley, is much cop either, really. Stanley's editor (compare *Girl, 20*) is deranged and mean. Bert Hutchinson, drunk, has to be dragged into the house from Stanley's car on a kind of carpet arrangement with a handle at one end. The mad Steve spouts on about electronic world conspiracies in much the tone of allegedly sane American students. The things of men, except cars, are not much better. A fruit machine in a pub broadcasts 'at top volume an extract from a harmonium sonata every time anything happened and part of the soundtrack of a Battle of Britain movie in between.' One infallible test of sanity, says Dr Nash, is being able to laugh at something funny. You can try out your sanity on this book.

It is beautifully written, meaning that the dialogue sounds for the most part as though its speakers had never read a book in their lives, and the *récit* is an exact analogue of somehow getting through the day, fuck it. When are critics going to learn that Augustan elegance may be all right for Church Triumphant satire but won't do for genuine fiction? This is Amis *père* at his best. May he not leave it too long before the next one.

The God of Job

The Only Problem, by Muriel Spark

First you must look at the back of the jacket, which reproduces a very beautiful painting by Georges de la Tour (by courtesy of the Musée Départemental des Vosges collections, Epinal). It is of Job's wife visiting her suffering husband. He, a youngish man with what looks like a false beard, sits naked and apparently unblemished. The potsherd on the floor has probably scraped him clean. He looks up at his wife in mild bewilderment, while she, a beautiful young woman in a beautiful gown, says something to him - perhaps 'Curse God and have done with it - you'll feel better that way' - while holding a candle which, as in a cinema film, gives more light than it ought to. Mrs Spark describes the picture at great length and almost impels a visit to the Vosges to look at it.

Her main character Harvey Gotham goes to see it often. He is a Canadian whose father made a fortune out of tinned salmon, and he lives a reclusive life in the Vosges in order to be near the picture and to write a treatise on the Book of Job. The title of the novel seems to refer to the great enigma which a belief in the God of Job poses – how can a benevolent deity see so much human suffering unmoved? Or why should he be so ready to cause it? Or why, when taxed about it by the archetypal sufferer, should he evade the issue and thunder impertinently about man's impertinence in raising the question when he, man, is a mere creature ungifted to create the ha-haing horse or Leviathan, who seems to be a mixture of the whale and the crocodile? The only problem is raised again for the thousandth time and finds no solution.

The story starts unportentously enough. Harvey's wife Effie, who is as beautiful as Job's wife and, indeed, not unlike the de la Tour version of her, shows very minor symptoms of irresponsibility. On a motor trip through Italy, she steals some chocolate from a motorway *supermercato* and justifies the theft in the boring terms of youthful anarchy. The great international combines are stealing from the poor, so let us, the well-off, steal from *them*. Harvey's reaction seems excessive, but studying the Bible has made him prophetic. He leaves Effie at once. Effie has a baby by a man called Ernie Howe. Effie's sister Ruth, who looks like Effie and hence also like Job's wife, leaves her actor husband, who used to be a curate and was always like an actor acting a curate, and brings herself and Effie's baby to live with Harvey. Harvey's prophetic soul proves to have been on the right track: Effie graduates from stealing chocolate to becoming a member, perhaps the leader, of a terrorist gang operating, perhaps to spite Harvey, in the department of the Vosges. She murders. The police move in on Harvey and grill him.

Harvey finds himself in a Jobian position in that he feels guilty in maintaining his innocence. He holds a press conference and, like God, the newspaper headlines shout irrelevancies which are meant to sound like logic. He is a rich man, hence he is playboy. He is studying religion, hence he is a guru. Playboy guru – what could sound more suspicious? Such is Mrs Spark's quiet skill that we ourselves, who, thinking highly of Mrs Spark, must also think highly of any man who devotes his life to explicating the Book of Job, come to find Harvey's preoccupation manic, meaning criminal. For instance, he writes to his lawyer about Effie's demands for alimony, but only as a prelude to raising a point about the identity of Leviathan. The world's realities have ceased to be theological. The police, rightly concerned with putting down terrorism, are less concerned – every man to his trade – with the causes of terrorism, which can perhaps only be considered in theological terms. The Book of Job is in everybody's family bible, and it raises very profound questions about the roots of evil and suffering, but it has become the highly suspect obsession of a guru playboy who has inherited a fortune from tinned salmon (Leviathan has been sliced and pickled).

Effie herself is, like God, something of an enigma. She is both ubiquitous and nowhere, except in that painting by de la Tour. The police affirm that she is in the Vosges, busily terrorizing, while Harvey's Auntie Pet, over from Canada, swears she saw her naked in a Californian commune on television. Effie is shot by the police and Harvey has to identify the body. She seems to look like nobody except Job's wife. To believe that she is really Effie relieves Harvey of the necessity of believing she was naked in the sack with another man. She is, one supposes, one of the nobodies of contemporary violence, a brainless tool of a tool. Without her painted prototype she would hardly exist at all.

Things look as if they are going to end well enough for Harvey, but, knowing Mrs Spark's propensity for a kind of Church Triumphant gratuitous vindictiveness, I should not be surprised if one of the blank endpages is printed in invisible ink and, in a particular light, will some day disclose that God has mindlessly struck him with boils. As things are, he seems to be still in the Vosges, having written his Job study, made Ruth pregnant and decided that he is going to live another hundred and forty years. He already has an adopted daughter, Clara, whose mother was a terrorist. He is going to have another two – Jemima and Eye-Paint. These were the names of Job's second and third daughters. The third was in fact named Box of Eye-Paint – Kerenhappuch. God continues to bestow very enigmatic gifts. What will a girl called Kerenhappuch turn into?

Mrs Spark constructs and writes as she always did – with great cunning and economy. She sometimes appears frivolous but is in reality very profound. Heaven knows how many *sous-textes* the percipient critic will find here. Even odd throwaway lines have large resonance. The curate who was an actor, now an actor playing curates, says: 'I remember hearing a producer say to a script writer, "It's the man who writes the cheque who has the final say in the script. And I'm the man who writes the cheque." One still hears that sort of thing. He had yellow eyeballs.' So, presumably, has God.

Raw Matter

Finding the Centre: Two Narratives, by V. S. Naipaul

I n his novel *Small World* (a work whose profundity is belied by its
lightness of tone), David Lodge presents a novelist who has been suffering from writer's block ever since a computer analysis of his
idiolect disclosed that his favourite word was 'greasy'. He is able to earn
a living by fashioning TV fodder, a matter of plausible dialogue only,
but the capacity for hearing the rhythms of a *récit* has been lost because
he has been made self-conscious. The breaking of the block is difficult
enough for any writer who suffers it, but the breaking in at the start, the
generating of a rhythm rather than the recovery of one, entails agonies
which must seem at the least to be pretentious posturings to the mere
plain reader. When a man considers himself to be a writer before he has
written a publishable word, which was, from his boyhood on, Mr
Naipaul's situation, the moment when the courage to type out the first
sentence arrives is momentous. It is always a matter of rhythm more
than lexis, and the rhythm releases that self-knowledge which foretells
the subject matter, style and tone of a whole *oeuvre*.

Thirty years ago Mr Naipaul was sitting before an old BBC typewriter with a wad of the special non-rustle paper which is used for radio
scripts. A Trinidad scholarship had sent him to Oxford, and, down from
Oxford ten months previously, he had the ill-paid job of preparing a
weekly literary programme to be beamed out to the Caribbean. In a
room in the Langham Hotel reserved for freelances – 'to me then not a
word suggesting freedom and valour, but suggesting only people on the
fringe of a mighty enterprise, a depressed and suppliant class' – he
dared to peck out the sentence: 'Every morning when he got up Hat
would sit on the banister of his back verandah and shout across,
"What happening there, Bogart?" ' He pushed on, singlespacing to
grant a better idea of what the thing would look like in print, and ended
up with a publishable story. He had a rhythm, and he had the lives of the
Port of Spain Indians. The memory of that moment has, in 'Prologue to
an Autobiography', one of the two pieces that make up this book,
primed a recall, unprocessed into fiction, of his own early life.

A reissue of his first major novel, *A House for Mr Biswas*, has an introduction by Mr Naipaul which covers some of the main ground. We see
now how much of Mr Naipaul's own father there is in Mr Biswas – not
the supernumerary digit and the lethal sneeze perhaps, but the literary
ambition and the small journalistic career. It is a comic story, but it is a
loving one. Naipaul learned something from his father that his father
learned from his editor – Gault MacGowan of the *Trinidad Guardian*:

'Write sympathetically.' The young Naipaul took his father's occupation for granted. 'It was years before I worked back to a proper wonder at his achievement.' What he then saw was that his father had fulfilled in his own way the destiny that Indians wish to reserve to one member of the family – the breaking out of the world of bare subsistence (small farmer, labourer in the canefields) to become a pundit. Mr Naipaul *père* found his guru in MacGowan; he signed his columns 'The Pundit'; in a community where writing was not considered an occupation he became a writer – at a starting salary of four dollars a week. Moreover he became a writer with a writer's conception of truth, which is not quite the same as the journalist's. The exterior world had to be moulded to the needs of the imagination. The pundit reported: '. . . his voice was his own, his knowledge of Trinidad Indian life was his own; and the zest – for news, for the drama of everyday life, for human oddity . . . – became real.' All that was to be eventually needed was the bigger fulfilment in the son – major novelist, Nobel candidate.

What, among other things, *A House for Mr Biswas* did was to release Trinidad from its tangled net of vulgarized exoticism, rum and calypsos, and to show its reality. One of the tasks of the novelist is to purvey imaginative human geography if he can. The strength of the book lies in its characters and their setting; but it rests in the memory, until restored by a rereading, as a very individual verbal artefact – an artistic arrangement of truth retailed by a special voice. Accident led Mr Naipaul away from the novel to the kind of skilled reporting to be found in *An Area of Darkness* and *The Return of Eva Peron*. The gentle humour of the Caribbean books was expelled by a sense of the grimness resident in what is called the Third World. *A Bend in the River*, which I consider to be Naipaul's best novel though I seem to be alone in that judgement, shows the reality of one aspect of modern Africa, and there is hardly a smile in it. 'The Crocodiles of Yamoussoukro', which is the second of the two 'narratives' in this book, is about the Ivory Coast and more particularly its capital, Abidjan. At the end of an autoroute 'that would not disgrace France itself' lies the presidential palace. Next to it is an artificial lake in which man-eating crocodiles, not previously to be seen in the region, 'speak at once of danger and of the president's, the chief's, magically granted knowledge of his power as something more than human, something emanating from the earth itself.'

That sounds like novelist's material – the conjunction of French rationalism and 'night and the forest'. But Naipaul is using the narrative technique – selective reporting, the selection of personalities and images – to the mere end of showing what he saw. 'Wood fires between stones burned below aluminium pots. One girl was sweeping up wet, nasty-looking rubbish with a broom made from the ribs of long coconut leaves. A few feet away a woman was using a pestle to grind aubergines in a little bowl set in the ground; and there was a neat child's turd near by.' You see the Ivory Coast and you hear it too. Mr Niangoran-Bouah, for instance: '*Le monde des blancs est réel. Mais – mais nous avons, nous autres africains noirs, nous avons tout cela dans le monde de la nuit, le monde des ténèbres.'* It would be too easy to say that that is what Mr Naipaul's travel essay is about – the absorption by the African of the taboos and man-eating crocodiles of the rational techniques of the white man – but the uneasiness which is in the aftertaste of the essay has to do with the swallowing capacity of the dark continent. A memorable passage in *An Area of Darkness* expressed the panic of Naipaul at the prospect of his Indianness – not his secure place in Western society as a scholar and a respected writer – qualifying him for being absorbed into the huge brown anonymity. He swallowed Trinidad and elegantly regurgitated it in his distinguished fiction. The rest of the world will permit only the nibbling of Naipaul the brilliant reporter.

Both the pieces in *Finding the Centre* are offered, Mr Naipaul tells us in his foreword, as exemplifications of the 'process of writing' and they 'seek in different ways to admit the reader to that process'. In other words, here is how material is gathered and here is how the imaginative faculty begins to work on it. The bigger end – that of the autobiography or travel book or novel – is not yet accomplished, but some time it may be. As for the people in both narratives, they seemed to be 'trying to find order in their world, looking for the centre'. That seems to be a facile summation; we need no traveller from the Ivory Coast to tell us this. What Mr Naipaul is really doing is practising his craft, and practising it well, without having to submit to the burden of the artistic shape. This is in order for what may be termed the book of the interim. *A House for Mr Biswas* reminds us that he has bigger things to do.

Patriotic Gore

Lincoln, by Gore Vidal

I n an afterword to his novel *1876*, Mr Vidal confesses to a 'deep mis-
trust of writers who produce trilogies', having just completed one
himself, but, not yet presumably having contemplated a novel on
Lincoln, regards tetralogists as being 'beyond the pale'. He does not say
why, but I suspect that he considers the spreading of a single theme –
American history, for example – over a long fictional sequence as an
indication of creative impotence, an inability to invent. In an essay in
Matters of Fact and Fiction, he upbraids certain bestselling authors for preferring 'fact or its appearance to actual invention. This suggests that
contemporary historians are not doing their job if to Wouk and Solzhenitsyn falls the task of telling today's readers about two world wars
and to Forsyth and Trevanian current tales of the cold war.' And if to
Mr Vidal falls the task of telling of an earlier war and its hero, one ought
to be making a similar assumption about the failure of the professional
recordist, when no period in history is better documented than that of
the American Civil War, and no hero better served than Abraham
Lincoln – from the twelve-volume biography of Hay and Nicolay to
Carl Sandburg and beyond. Why write the book at all?

There's a good commercial reason. As I write, *Lincoln* heads the *New
York Times* bestseller list. It is not what Mr Vidal calls 'quality lit', being
as plainly written as anything by Mr Wouk, eschewing – except for a
couple of paragraphs in the final chapter – anything like a consideration
of the complexities and ambiguities inherent in the character of either
Lincoln or his times. As Mr Vidal says of Mr Wouk's *The Winds of War*,
'his reconstruction of history is painless and, I should think, most useful
to simple readers'. What skill there is in the novel resides precisely in the
reduction of a tangle of complexities to a not overlong narrative in which
the simple reader will learn the basic facts about Lincoln and the Civil
War – namely, that Lincoln was no more against slavery than Washington and Jefferson had been, and that the Civil War, which was
wasteful and inefficiently fought, was waged for an abstract idea – the
conservation of the Union.

The novel of the period which raged effectively against slavery is not
even mentioned, probably because Uncle Tom has taken on the wrong
resonance among progressives, and in spite of the fact that Lincoln
greeted its author with the words 'So this is the little woman who made
this great war.' Readers who expect Simon Legree and large battle
scenes out of *Gone With the Wind* will be disappointed. There is no
sensationalism and, despite the multiplicity of brothels in Washington,

no explicit sex. But we do learn the etymology of *hooker* (General Hooker's girls). Mr Vidal is mainly concerned with a metaphysical question – the Union and the sustention of the Union – and it is this obsession with the Union which makes Lincoln bizarrely impressive and even, in his quiet way, manic. But it does not make him much of a figure for fiction.

Mr Vidal, to his credit as a fiction writer, does his best with the long lean ascetic figure unblessed by self-doubt, cursed with constipation, a born politician but totally incorrupt, unless the blazing faith in the Union be a form of corruption. This corruption is discussed belatedly in the last chapter, where, at a reception at the Tuileries, John Hay, formerly Lincoln's secretary and prospective co-author of his biography, meets a character from *1876* – the wholly fictional Charles Schermerhorn Schuyler. Hay, placing Lincoln above Washington, says that he had a far more difficult task than the first president: 'You see, the Southern states had every Constitutional right to go out of the Union. But Lincoln said, no. Lincoln said, this Union can never be broken. Now this was a terrible responsibility for one man to take. But he took it, knowing he would be obliged to fight the greatest war in human history, which he did, and which he won.' And then Schuyler speaks of Bismarck: 'Curiously enough, he has now done the same thing to Germany that you tell us Mr Lincoln did to our country. Bismarck has made a single, centralized nation out of all the other German states.' We, with the gift of hindsight, are thus made to wonder whether Lincoln did the right thing.

And yet, in the body of the book, this mystique of the Union is not fully explicated. There are hints that it may be a geographical concept, finding a logical conclusion in the annexation of Canada as well as Mexico, servant or master of a new technology of railroads and telegraphs which makes devolution obsolete, history working through the apparently insentient Lincoln to bring about the modern America whose fat rump is ready for the taws of Mr Vidal. We need a poet somewhere in the book who can display prophetic insight, but all we have is a rather humble Walt Whitman looking for a job and the transcendentalist authoress of 'The Battle Hymn of the Republic'. It seems to be part of Mr Vidal's brief to depoeticize to the limit. This is, of course, essential for a commercial enterprise.

The setting is Washington and environs. Mr Vidal leaves the log cabin and rail-splitting to legend and begins his story with Lincoln's arrival in the capital for his inauguration. The author's affection for a city which he has described as having the charm of the North and the efficiency of the South is as evident here as elsewhere. It is very well rendered, with its canal described twice as 'odiferous' (an obsolete term which Mr Vidal likes, since he uses it also in *1876*), its fried oysters and spittoons, mosquitoes and fever which everybody catches – even Lincoln, though only once. The presidential home which Mrs Lincoln inherits is a mess of dirt and dried tobacco spit, but she soon puts it right. She spends too much, gets into debt, cooks the books, eventually goes mad. She also has Confederate connections. The suspicions which attach to Caesar's wife never touch Caesar: Lincoln's heroic stoicism is matched by total integrity. Inevitably, supporting characters such as Chase, the State Treasurer but always in money trouble, have more of the interest proper to fiction. Sprague, the 'boy governor' of Rhode Island, is of exceptional interest. Through his marriage to Chase's daughter, Chase's own fortunes improve, but Sprague's fortune depends on the illegal, indeed treasonous, importation of cotton. This is the real stuff of fiction, though it is also fact.

To give himself an opportunity to invent, Mr Vidal takes the character of the young David Herold, whom history hears of only in connection with the Booth conspiracy, and builds him up, though to little purpose. He works as a dispenser and delivery boy in Thompson's drugstore, which, in the interests of dramatic compression, is placed closer to the White House than it actually was. David is a supporter of the Confederacy who acts as a spy, crossing the Potomac with impunity to make his deliveries and passing on coded messages. Both Mr and Mrs Lincoln need laudanum, and Lincoln also needs a massive weekly purgative: the opportunity to poison the President seems always to be there and yet not there. Booth shoots him, without crying *'Sic semper tyrannis'* (we are in the wrong market for a quote from *Cato*), and David fails to kill Secretary of State Seward. There is too much of David: he is not interesting enough to justify the space allotted. He is really there to feed Mr Vidal's hunger to invent.

He, one of the most inventive novelists modern America has produced, must have felt damnably oppressed by the need to follow history. It must have been especially oppressive when the moment approached for the re-enactment of a scene that is so historic that it seems already to have been invented. When Gettysburg is first mentioned, we settle in our seats and prepare not only for the Address many of us have by heart but for a chance to judge the author's ingenuity in washing it clean of its sentimental accretions. Mr Vidal comes through remarkably. He does not give us what we know – 'Lincoln's final tinkered-with draft' – but what Charles Hale of the *Boston Daily Advertiser* wrote down. And he breaks it up with clever dramatic insertions:

'We are met on a great battle-field of that war. We are met to dedicate a portion of it as the final resting place of those who have given their lives that that nation might live.' Seward nodded, inadvertently. Yes, that was the issue, the only issue. The preservation of this unique nation of states. Meanwhile, the photographer was trying to get the President in camera-frame.

As for the assassination, this is flat and even perfunctory – something that happened and had best not be brooded upon. Mr Vidal spends a good deal of care on the background and character of the assassin, but the more we learn of him as an extrovert actor the less we are able to accept him as an avenger of the stricken South. The final words of the book are:

'It will be interesting to see how Herr Bismarck ends *his* career,' said Hay, who was now more than ever convinced that Lincoln, in some mysterious fashion, had willed his own murder as a form of atonement for the great and terrible thing he had done by giving so bloody and absolute a rebirth to his nation.

This turns Booth into a mere shadowy device of expiation and the final scene in the theatre a yawning attendance at mass rather than a catastrophe of world-shattering proportions. 'Rebirth to his nation' is probably, knowing Mr Vidal's cinematic background, a deliberate device to evoke the 14th Amendment, the carpetbaggers and the Klu Klux Klan. The interesting, or Vidalian, things are often on the margin in this novel, and all the rest is history sedulously followed and minimally dramatized. It is a novel not of great battles but of telegrams about them arriving at the White House.

So that the novel itself seems only to be a device for awakening wonder at the historical actuality; it points out at history without heightening it through art. In this respect, *Lincoln* belongs to that popular and very American pseudo-fictional genre which Mr Vidal, concentrating particularly on Mr Wouk, condescendingly accepts as wholesome if simplistic teaching but condemns for pretending to be a kind of literature. Irving Stone has written on Michelangelo, Freud and Darwin in much the same way ('Sighing, he lighted a fresh cigar, and wrote his title: *The Interpretation of Dreams*'). James A. Michener has made a vast fortune out of blockbusting history tomes, well researched and indifferently written, which are presented as novels. There is something in the puritanical American mind which is scared of the imaginative writer but not of the pedantic one who seems to humanize facts without committing himself to the inventions which are really lies.

In putting himself beyond the pale as a tetralogist, Mr Vidal is in danger of making the wrong sort of reputation for himself – the popular recorder of American political history, and not the brilliant scabrous fantasist of *Myra Breckenridge* or the revivifier of the remote past as in *Julian* and *Creation*. His recent *Duluth* remade the geography of the United States, created a new kind of eschatology (when you die in Duluth you go into a television series called *Duluth*), and smote American mores hard through every technique available to modern fiction. *Creation* was a remarkable attempt to depict the age of Darius, Xerxes, Buddha, Confucius, Herodotus and Socrates. Both highly sexed satire and imaginative penetration of ancient history should be enough for him, but he cannot leave American politics alone. I am not altogether sorry that he has written *Lincoln*, since this ghost has sent me back to the flesh and blood reality, but its writing could have been left to any bestselling American who, short of a subject, found Honest Abe as good as any.

Inky Islands

Literary Landscapes of the British Isles: A Narrative Atlas, by David Daiches and John Flower

In the days of *Scrutiny*, when it was the thing to disparage Sir Walter Scott, it was said that people read *Waverley* and *Old Mortality* and so on because the reading evoked memories of pleasant vacations in Scotland. This may have been, and may be still be, true, but, as Dr Daiches reminds us, it was the reading of Scott that sent people to Scotland in the first place. And there is no doubt that a large number of visitors to Dublin go there because of *Ulysses*. This used to bewilder even the Irish Tourist Board, but the adaptable Dubliners have already learned to behave (on 16 June anyway) as if Bloom were still masturbating on Sandymount Strand and the Earl of Dudley (William Humble Ward, not, as Joyce has him, plain William Humble) opening a charity bazaar. Dr Daiches takes us on a Bloom's tour of the city and is so topographically thorough that he is able to ask why Master Patrick Dignam, living in Sandymount, is sent as far as William street to buy a pound and a half of porksteaks. He will not mind my correcting him on a point of sartorial detail. Father Conmee's socks are thin, not thick.

This whole book, a charming and useful one, acknowledges the truth that, though God and citybuilders are primarily responsible for the scenery of our lives, it is the poets and novelists who give places souls, just as Conrad created the sea and Walton the English rivers. Michael Drayton's *Polyolbion*, unmentioned here, is worth going back to some time as our first literary exploitation of geography, but Dr Daiches is rightly concerned with the *big* names. Mr Flower's task has been to draw the maps. We get not only Chaucer's London and his pilgrims' route (Deptford–Greenwich–Dartford–Rochester–Sittingbourne–Ospringe–Boughton–Canterbury) but also his World, with Irlaunde and Engelond perched above Flaundre and Britaigne, Affrike and Egipt and Surrye and Arcadye looking on to the Grete Sea, and Ruce and Tartarye glooming away in the east. We watch London expand and turn to Shakespeare's, Johnson's, Dickens's and, for me anticlimactically, Virginia Woolf's. Dr Daiches is, however, fully entitled to work out exactly where Mrs Dalloway lives (in the neighbourhood of Dean's Yard at the southwest corner of Westminster Abbey).

There is a crossword puzzle interest in checking London walking tours with fictional characters like Mrs Dalloway, just as there is in plotting Bloom's odyssey (or Odysseus's, for that matter), but is there much more to it than taking the *Thom's Directory* or the *A to Z* out of the author's own hand and naively marvelling that a kind of magic can be made out of brute cartography? 'Crump left Regent's Park, passing Bedford College on his way to Baker Street. He turned right on to York Street, crossed Gloucester Place and then turned left on to Upper Montagu Street. Ethel was waiting for him in Bryanston Square. He gulped in unpleasurable anticipation.' My God, Meldrum's *Distempered Guest* is crammed with accurate Londiniana. So it should be, streetwise anyway: he got it all from the very *A to Z* you're looking at.

Dr Daiches is very good on Bath, or Aquae Sulis (the Romans identified the British Sul with their own Minerva), and may send readers back to *Humphry Clinker* and *Evelina*, not to mention Jane Austen, who lived there for a time, with an enhanced capacity for appreciating the Bath mythology which, when you come to think of it, has a fair part to play in our classical fiction. Angelo Cyrus Bantam, for instance, who welcomes Mr Pickwick as

> '. . . the gentleman residing on Clapham Green . . . who lost the use of his limbs from imprudently taking cold after port wine; who could not be moved in consequence of acute suffering, and who had the water from the King's Bath bottled at one hundred and three degrees, and sent by waggon to his bed-room in town, where he bathed, sneezed, and same day recovered. Very re-markable!'

Charles II and his court went to Bath to look for a cure for the Queen's sterility, his own fertility not being in doubt, and thus initiated the Bath cult of the Age of Elegance. But Shakespeare got there first, leaving, apparently, uncured of whatever he had:

> I sick withal the help of Bath desired,
> And thither hied, a sad distemper'd guest;
> But found no cure: the bath for my help lies
> Where Cupid got new fire – my mistress' eyes.

Dr Daiches is also good on the Lake District and the Brontë Country and Hardy's Wessex, all of which sections are lavishly garnished with great chunks out of the authors celebrated. My own region of Lancashire is richly and depressingly dealt with in a chapter entitled 'The Blackening of England,' and then come Scotland (not as much as one might have expected from so good a Scot, biographer of Burns, Scott and Stevenson as well as whisky) and Dublin. But the really solid work comes at the end.

This is a self-contained atlas and gazetteer which fixes 236 British literary figures not only in their places of birth, but also in their schools, main working areas, vacation spots, and tombs and memorials (sometimes, but not often, museums). The maps suggest ideas for a new kind of Landorian imaginary conversation. At Torquay, Elizabeth Barrett Browning, Edward Bulwer-Lytton, Sir Richard Burton, Charles Kingsley and Sean O'Casey all, at one time or another, resided. Put them all together in a bus going to Brixham (to see Flora Thompson or the invading William of Orange) and see what they say. One point the gazetteer neglects to make (but you can't have everything) is that Thomas Fuller, the *Worthies of England* man, was born at Aldwinkle St Peter's while John Dryden was born at Aldwinkle All Saints, halves of the same small Northampton village. I see John Fletcher at Rye, but not Henry James. Dylan Thomas is lonely at Laugharne, his nearest literary neighbours being Landor and himself at Swansea. Isolated at Stinchcombe, Evelyn Waugh joined Sydney Smith at Combe Florey. And so on. Are there any fascinating conclusions to be drawn? Does one kind of soil breed a better kind of writer than another? No. It's just nice, for some reason, to know where people were when they were trying to make, impossibly, a living out of literature. And to reflect that the British Isles have produced a great number of great writers. About whom the great British public doesn't give in general a great big damn. Unless they're adapted to the great big little damn screen.

Anglophilia

Literary Britain – A Reader's Guide to Writers and Landmarks, by Frank Morley

Frank Morley is the youngest of the three famous American literary Morleys, all Rhodes Scholars, men to whom the Atlantic was a mere river long before TWA bridged it, with Christopher promoting the cause of literature in English as a supranational unity in New York, Felix editing the *Washington Post*, and Frank helping to found Faber and Faber in London. The intention of writing this book was with him back in the twenties: now, in his eighty-first year, he has fulfilled it. As a kind of literary dragoman to American visitors to Britain, usually more anxious than their cisatlantic cousins to see where Keats wrote his 'Ode to a Nightingale' or the Brontës died, the young Frank Morley developed early a devotion to literary shrines. But his book is more than a record of haphazard rucksacked pilgrimages. It is intensely personal but it is rigorously systematic.

'Britain,' he says, 'is an island in which a wonderfully active life developed, partly because six arterial roadways to and from London provided for quick circulation of whatever was lively in spirit.' Road, and later rail, communications in Britain have traditionally been ahead of the Continent, and this partly explains the existence of a national literature as opposed to, as in Italy for instance, a bundle of disparate regional ones. Keats spoke of poets in Greece 'leaving great verse unto a little clan': the writers in Britain who spoke only for a clan were never great: Burns's Lallans was not slow in being known in London. The stagecoaches of Regency days made the *Edinburgh Review* a national periodical. Although Wordsworth, Mrs Gaskell, Crabbe and Hardy, to name only a few, wrote about regions, they wrote about them for the nation. Mr Morley is right to think in terms of arteries and the great beating heart of London, itself a region in, say, Lamb and Dickens, of an essential unity underlying a diversity owing more to individual genius than to the various *genii locorum*.

But, because of this very pull to the heart, it becomes difficult to make a meaningful relationship between places and authors. Thus, Shakespeare was born in Stratford, but the honouring of that somewhat philistine town seems impertinent when we consider that Shakespeare had to leave it to make his name in London and went back there at the end to die not as a playwright but as a small country magnate. What have mere birth and death to do with life? The Bankside is true Shakespeare country: why bother to go to Stratford at all? To travel north or west in search of the inspiration of *Wuthering Heights* and *The Mayor of Casterbridge* is in order, but such intense regionalism is rare in English letters. Books are mostly written in the Home Counties by men and women recalling a Welsh or Lancashire childhood.

Let us see how Mr Morley deals with my own city of Manchester. Harrison Ainsworth was born there and is best remembered for *The Tower of London* and *Rookwood*. De Quincey got out quickly and wrote an essentially London book called *Confessions of an English Opium-Eater*. Frances Hodgson Burnett was born in Salford and wrote *Little Lord Fauntleroy* in a log cabin in Tennessee. George Gissing came to Owens College from Yorkshire and his novels about the downtrodden are all set in London. Francis Thompson, from Catholic Preston, was another adoptive Mancunian who was quick, like De Quincey, to get to London and the adoption of the opium habit. The only great work to be actually written in Manchester was *Jane Eyre*, but that had to be finished in Haworth. Mrs Gaskell, whose husband did some extramural teaching at Owens College, wrote feelingly about the sufferings of cotton operatives in novels like *Mary Barton*, but she is best remembered for *Cranford*, which is about Knutsford. Mr Morley does not mention either Howard Spring or Louis Golding. *Shabby Tiger* and *Magnolia Street* are probably now not much read, but they were bestsellers in their day. If Manchester had its own *Ulysses* it might gain the metaphysical aura that neither Engels nor the *Manchester Guardian* were able to give it. Dublin is the luckiest of towns: drop an obliterating bomb on it and it would still be alive.

Having used the vague term aura I might as well apply it to Mr Morley's deeper purpose, which is to remind us that it is only literature, which contains history, that is able to confer a more than statistical reality on a country. William Blake turned England into the giant Albion as Joyce turned Dublin into the sleeping Finn. Mr Morley imposes a living template of the imagination on an inert landmass of fields and conurbations. Britain, like ancient Rome, is finally what has been written in it and about it. To bow the head at Laughane or Chalfont St Giles or Bockhampton or Dove Cottage or Sandycove may seem empty and fanciful, since no special grace will descend there, but the metaphysical aura is real and reminds pilgrims that one of the human tasks is to convert matter into spirit.

Mr Morley's book gains from his own lifetime of acquaintance with writers, especially T. S. Eliot, whose *Four Quartets* is perhaps the classic attestation of the spiritual properties of place. The Eliot family came from East Coker in Somerset, a few miles south of Yeovil, and its founder was Sir Thomas Eliot, author of *The Governour*. In the poem 'East Coker' the last of the Eliots has the phrase 'And to shake the tattered arras woven with a silent motto'. That spelling of *arras* was on the insistence of Geoffrey Faber, who would not accept Eliot's *arasse*. But in *The Governour* we find 'with riche arasse or tapestrye', and it was this which the last Eliot wished to evoke. The modern spelling always rankled with him.

If we love 'The Lake Isle of Innisfree', we ought to consider whether Innisfree *is* the right place to pay homage to the poem. For on the crowded Strand one day Yeats heard 'the sound of a little water-jet balancing a wooden ball in a shop window' and at once caught an image of a cataract in Galway 'with a long Gaelic name'. Later, on a Sunday morning, looking at 'the osier-fringed Chiswick eyot in the Thames', Yeats found the poem coming to him. And Mr Morley remembers Joyce saying: 'Yeats, funny fellow, calls himself Yates, it's really Yeats.' This seemed to be an obscure dig at the poet's claim to be of Ireland's landed gentry. The book is full of odd revelations of this kind.

But its distinction, apart from the quality of the writing and the exactness of the information, lies in the radial organization, as though Britain were really Quarles's purple island. We take the Great North Road (on which Mr Morley has already published a book), the Dover Road, the Portsmouth Road, the Bath Road, the Holyhead Road and the Manchester Road and hear quills scratching on and off them. But the highways which take us away from London also draw us back there, to the printing shops and publishers, the literary life, and, most of all, to the language. Nothing could seem less centripetal than the literature of Britain, but its strength is ultimately that of a unified nation with a strong and settled metropolis. Our literature is made not out of dialects but out of idiolects. Mr Morley's topographical tribute to its various greatness is very lovingly done.

Wandering Through the Grove

The New Grove Dictionary of Music and Musicians, 20 vols., edited by Stanley Sadie

Tennyson said something about the repetition of a common word turning that word into a wonder. Literary men and women who know something about music occasionally shake themselves awake from the torpid acceptance of all that sound that nowadays surrounds us – never has there been so much music, and so much of it imposed upon us – to marvel that it should all have its provenance in a piano handspan of twelve notes and an assortment of noises. Next year (1982) is James Joyce's centenary (*Grove* will remind you of this: there are literary men there as well as musicians) and I have devised a musical version of *Ulysses* in celebration. I have spent the last two months in orchestrating the music, and, on my resumption of literary work, I am struck by one great difference between the two activities: for writing words I need a dictionary, for writing notes I have to assume a total knowledge and control of the medium. This is because I am not dealing with meanings. And yet, writing music, I am presumably trying to communicate. What is the nature of the communication?

This is a question asked more by littérateurs than by musicians. If a musician were to worry about the semantics of his art he might well be struck dumb: as with riding a bicycle (Johnson could see no bicycle would go: you bear yourself and the machine as well), you must not let consciousness intrude too much. When, as a boy of fourteen who thought his future lay in musical composition, I pored over the old *Grove* (a second or third edition of the original) in my local reading room, I had enough of the musician's instinct to take it for granted that Beethoven expressed recognizable human emotions: how this was done was not for me to inquire. Sir George Grove himself wrote the Beethoven article, as he had written a few years previously a whole book on the Beethoven symphonies, and he was full of the assumption that music dealt in love, anguish, triumph and visions of heaven. Bernard Shaw, in a memorable article on the Beethoven book in the *Saturday Review*, praised Grove for avoiding technical twaddle about the subdominant ('which I could teach to a poodle in two hours') and rhapsodizing in the manner of 'The lovely melody then passes, by a transition of remarkable beauty, into the key of C major, in which it seems to go straight up to heaven.' Beauty? Heaven? In what way beautiful? How to heaven? The nineteenth century did not ask these questions much. If they did not wish to ask them, preferring instead to concentrate on the poodle twaddle of modulation via the Neapolitan sixth, nevertheless Victorian musicians accepted that a symphony discoursed personal emotion and could attain a vision of sublimity. In Victorian Britain music was heard in terms of morality and promoted among the children of utilitarianism as a device of temperance and uplift. The original *Grove* is a typical expression of the educative urge of the day, the work of a musical amateur (as Murray of the *OED* was a philological amateur) as well able to supply a dictionary of engineering or of biblical geography as to oversee a compendium 'from which an intelligent enquirer can learn, in small compass, and in language which he can understand, what is meant by a Symphony or Sonata, a Fugue, a Stretto, a Coda' and so on. Music was enlightenment and a kind of religion.

Our views of the morality of music have changed, as our views of so much else have changed, since 1945 and the beginnings of the revelations of the true depths of Nazi infamy. The Germans were for long regarded as the most musical people in the world, and they did not cease to be musical – though the repertory was reduced on racist grounds – when they became Nazi. George Steiner has an essay in his *Language and Silence* in which he wonders at the mentality of the death camp commandant who could, after a day supervising the liquidation of Jews, go home to weep tears of pure joy at a broadcast Schubert trio or a recorded Schumann lied. His wonder is misplaced if we consider that the nineteenth-century musical aesthetic was wrong, and that the feelings engendered by music have nothing to do with Kant or Goethe or the New Testament. We can thrill to the *Meistersinger* Prelude as Hitler did, but the imagined referent of the emotion had better not be too closely considered. The Nazis could hear in the last movement of Beethoven's Ninth Symphony an expression of Nazi aspirations. Those aspirations are no more present in the music or, indeed, the words than are visions of Christian democracy or of white supremacy in Smith's Rhodesia, which used the *Ode to Joy* as a national anthem. Freud feared music because it was too close to the id. St Augustine was 'torn between three attitudes to music: exaltation of musical principles as embodying principles of cosmic order: ascetic aversion from music-making as carnal; and a recognition of jubilation and congregational song as respectively expressing the inexpressible ecstasy and promoting congregational brotherhood.'

I quote here from F. E. Sparshott's essay on the aesthetics of music, noting the happy accident of taxonomy which places acoustics and aesthetics, or sound and the meaning of sound, close together in the very first volume. Sparshott's approach is diachronic, as is everybody's approach to everything (look up TROMBONE to find which pedal notes are practicable and you plunge into history rather than immediate need), but he ends with his own questions:

A final problem arises not within music but on its borders. The edges of the arts are becoming blurred. Can and should we continue to think of music as an art distinct from all others, or should we once more face the prospect that, as Roger Bacon and Wagner suggested in their different ways, the future of music lies within some comprehensive form of aesthetic activity? It is a problem on the frontiers of philosophy and sociology, for it may be that music as we have known it is proper to a phase of civilisation that is passing away.

We have, in fact, despite the pondering of individual aestheticians, come no nearer to a common understanding of what music tries to do and, moreover, the notion of what we call music is becoming confused. The phase of civilization represented by *Grove I* was both too sure of itself and too limited in its definitions. We are in the Cage age, in which the hieratic pretensions of music to be superior to mere natural noise are being questioned, and the presentation of a fixed measure of silence can be an acceptable auditory experience. We have things in the new *Grove* which its superseded great-grandfather had, despite the claims of democracy and the expansion of the Empire, to regard as too far away from Beethoven to take seriously – the music of the dance hall and the popular theatre and the gongs and noseflutes of people in loincloths. We have great stretches of ethnomusicology and articles on jazz and pop and popular musicians. In that vastest expanse of any musical compendium – B to Petros Byzantios – Irving Berlin tinkles in the key of F sharp, the only key he could manage, near to Berlioz, and the Beatles (the late John Lennon, by the way, did *not* produce *In His Own Write* in the seventies) precede the troubadour-Beatriz de Dia. There is, in the whole twenty volumes containing over twenty-two million words, a brilliantly informed comprehensiveness mostly touched by the tentativeness of an age not so sure of itself as the expansive time of *Grove I*.

It is as well, when first probing the utility of a new and massive compendium, to test it in an area vaguely eccentric. Last August my friend John Sebastian died. He was an American harmonica player of repute, and for him I composed two works with guitar accompaniment – a bagatelle and a sonatina. More recently I have composed for two harmonica players still happily with us – Tommy Reilly (he and I played an unnamed rhapsody on my sixtieth birthday and on television) and Larry Adler. Both Adler and Reilly have brief but flavoursome entries, but John Sebastian is not there. The article on the harmonica tells us how the instrument works, its range, who manufactures it. It does not tell the prospective composer for the instrument what chords can be played on it. Under the biography of Villa-Lobos there is mention of a harmonica concerto – it was in fact commissioned by John Sebastian – but there seems to be no means, under either his entry or that of harmonica, of mentioning that his cadenza for the instrument was unplayable and had to be rewritten by the performer. Now this is obviously an instance of my asking too much, but only the comprehensiveness of the new *Grove* would tempt me to ask at all. Another performer, for whom I wrote a song in the *Bahasa Negara* of Malaysia, is the soprano Cathy Berberian, who gets a mention in the article on Luciano Berio (they were married; he wrote much for her) but no entry of her own. One of the finest of the younger American composers is Stanley

Silverman (whose latest opera was favourably reviewed in Britain). He and I produced an Oedipus cantata performed in New York. He is not in the new *Grove*, though Bob Dylan and Elvis Presley are. Is it I who put the kiss of documentary neglect on musicians with whom I have associated? You cannot have everybody, but it seems you have to have every minor Nordic teacher and folk-song collector whose name ever began with K.

But musicians happy to see Krengel, Krenn and Krenz may well grumble at space wasted on Eric Fogg, who worked for the BBC North Region and committed suicide. He was a Manchester composer who wrote a bassoon concerto in D for Archie Camden. I am interested in minor British composers, having aspired to be one myself, and am generally satisfied with the way the new *Grove*, if not the musical world without, deals with them. If Sacheverell Coke is not here, Josef Holbrooke is (much quoted for his use of banks of saxophones in Forsyth's *Orchestration*) and also Cyril Scott and Dame Ethel Smyth. On Havergal Brian a judgement is made which is applicable to most of the figures of the British musical renascence – that the fresh and idiosyncratic are juxtaposed with the banal and conventional. The major British composers are well covered, but we do not find in their entries the same concentration on tangibles as we find in the articles on Mahler and Bartok and especially Hindemith – music-type illustrations of compositorial procedures, the physical nature of their styles. I realize that Imogen Holst has a sort of monopoly of her father, but I should have liked, for a change, a non-filial view, with examples of his superposed fourths (which, not being much of a Mahlerian, I had not till now realized were to be found in Mahler) and the triadic daring of the *Hymn of Jesus* and the *Choral Symphony*.

The articles on Mozart (a specialization of the editor, Stanley Sadie, who had better be congratulated now though in parenthesis and recommended for the next honours list), Beethoven, Wagner and the rest can hardly be overpraised. They are not merely informative, they are sometimes thrilling in the manner of literature. If musicians write so well, and incidentally show so much knowledge of literature, it seems in order to plead once again for literary people to know something about music. I can imagine modern Stendhalians who will read Philip Gossett's essay on Rossini with great delight and then become worried when they meet his analysis of the 'slightly tipsy Offenbach cancan' which, in an F major context, 'first deploys a curious melodic D flat and finally rings out a truly bizarre F sharp.' There are, as I well know, many men most learned in opera who cannot even read a score. T. S. Eliot, who, as a man whose work was set to music and who wrote about the relationship between the two auditory arts, has an entry here, loved the later Beethoven quartets and yet probably did not know much about the Neapolitan sixth. If we want to know what a Neapolitan sixth is, what does *Grove* tell us?

It tells us that it is the first inversion of the major triad built on the flattened second degree of the scale. It usually precedes a V-I cadence and it functions like a subdominant. If I were trying to explain it to a non-musician I would, after telling him that it is called Neapolitan because it was popular with the eighteenth-century Neapolitan school – Scarlatti, Pargolesi, Cimarosa, others, bang out an F-major triad on the piano, root position, meaning F in the bass, and then slide the A, C and F which occupy the right hand up to the black keys immediately north of those three white notes (there's your Neapolitan sixth) and then slide back again. The function of the chord? In Beethoven certainly to effect fairly remote modulations. The earlier works change from key to key by the fairly mild process of adding a sharp or a flat; the last quartets modulate by sliding by semitones: that is where the Neapolitan sixth comes in. I cannot put it any more simply in words, but I can show it on a keyboard. The 'intelligent enquirer' of Grove's 1879 foreword could not, in fact, get much from a compendium. Music cannot be explicated in words. *Grove* does not provide a musical education from scratch. You have to be pretty far gone in music before you can use *Grove* at all.

It is no good looking up *Tristan und Isolde*. In Percy Scholes's *Companion to Music* you will find a summary of the plot, act by act; in *Grove* you will have to read the whole article on Wagner. But *Grove* will tell you all about the *Tristan* chord, which may puzzle literary men who consider they have a claim on the opera. And yet without knowing something about this chord – the opening chord of the Prelude: F–B–D sharp–G sharp – you cannot hope to know much about the genesis of modern music. E. Kurth wrote a whole book about the 'crisis' in romantic harmony which the *Tristan* chord engendered, and so did M. Vogel (*Der Tristan-Akkord und die Krise der modernen Harmonielehre*). The article *Armonia* in the Enaudi *Encyclopedia* starts off with the chord. Its mystery lies in the fact that it has a place in traditional functional harmony and yet the first sounding of the chord seems to imply the breakdown of tradition. This brings us to atonality and twelve-note composition. The article by George Perle Lansky may be regarded as typifying the clarity of exposition and depth of scholarship (confirmed, as in every entry, by a most comprehensive bibliography) which characterize the new *Grove*.

The article is, as it has to be, wholly technical. It begins: 'The dissolution of traditional tonal functions in the early years of the 20th century gave rise to several systematic attempts to derive a total musical structure from a complex of pitch classes that are not functionally differentiated.' If we want this to be translated into 'human' terms we must go to O. W. Neighbour's article on Schoenberg, where we all see a photograph of Schoenberg, in Tyrolean costume, scraping a cello with the rest of the Fröhliches Quintet (*c.* 1895), the first fiddler being Fritz Kreisler. We may read about physical hardship as well as eventual racial persecution, the reluctant necessity to create a new musical language against all the odds, the sympathy Schoenberg felt for those who could not go along with him. You will also meet the personal elements in the music: 'The trio of the scherzo incorporates the popular melody *O du lieber Augustin*, the words of which end with the tag *Alles ist hin*, as a private reference to his wife's liaison with Gerstl.' The biographies of most composers – perhaps with the sole exception of Rossini – are pretty wretched reading. Penury, sickness and lack of understanding are perennial elements; our own age introduces the particular villainy of the Nazis (who drove out the Aryan Christian Hindemith as well as the Jews) and the dubious refuge of Hollywood.

But the film music which Schoenberg could not compose ('Are you trying to save my life by killing me?') was written by others, some of them also distinguished exiles, and it has earned at last the tribute of a most absorbing survey by Christopher Palmer and John Gillett. Here we learn that, for *The Devil and Daniel Webster*, 'Herrmann used the sound of telegraph wires singing at 4 a.m. to characterise Mephisto and had the overtones of C printed on the negative in the form of electronic impulses so that when the film was projected a phantom fundamental was produced,' and that underscoring the action of animated films is known as 'Mickey-Mousing'. While we are in this area of music brought to the people, we may note that pop and popular music are carefully distinguished, though the long article with the latter title sees acid and punk rock and the rest as part of a continuum beginning with Pinsuti, Denza and Balfe and perhaps even earlier. It is refreshing to find such objective and literate treatment of phenomena like Elvis Presley, who started with the kind of material Bill Haley had used but 'was a much better musician and a more dynamic personality, and in his singing style, gestures and stage deportment . . . often emphasized the sexual implications of rock and roll more than other white musicians had dared.' And so, after the Jaye Consort of Viols, to jazz, surveyed by Max Harrison, whose seriousness of approach is confirmed in his final quotation from Schoenberg: 'The higher an artistic ideal stands, the greater the range of questions, complexes, associations, problems and feelings it will have to cover; and the better it succeeds in compressing this universality into a minimum space, the higher it will stand.'

This is fine history and excellent discography, but it might have been better for a few music-type illustrations and a closer consideration of jazz harmony, which is a kind of instinctual impressionism, and of the 'blues scale', whose flattened thirds and sevenths Harrison finds to be 'in no way specifically African, nor negroid, still less exclusively American.' I find no entry for symphonic jazz, so I must learn about *The Rio Grande* under Lambert (another neglected British composer) and the *Rhapsody in Blue* under Gershwin. Charles Schwartz, in his two columns and a bit, finds the Jewish *frailach* in Gershwin's rhythms and disillusions us by telling us that the opening clarinet glissando of the *Rhapsody* was not the composer's own work but a joke of Paul Whiteman's clarinettist Ross Gorman. Proportions are always just. Gesualdo follows shortly after Gershwin and is given twenty-one pages, more than three of them devoted to lavish extracts from his madrigals. Stravinsky, according to Lorenzo Bianconi, misunderstood Gesualdo, as did Lowinsky, who assigned the eccentric Prince of Venosa to 'an imaginary, heroic history of visionary prophets'. Bianconi finds in him 'an exhibitionist and at the same time secretive individualism . . . socially and historically conditioned by his melancholy evasion of history and society.' Gesualdo, as is perhaps too well known, murdered his wife and her lover in the act and then retired to cultivate a style too advanced for Wagner, let alone the seventeenth century as we think we know the seventeenth century.

Indeed, browsing in *Grove* shakes one's complacent view of Western musical history as a straight progressive line, exhibiting, with the adoption of once forbidden tonalities or brass instruments with keys, ever more efficient modes of expressing states of feeling or building allegories of divine order (if music is really concerned with these things: we don't know and we shall never know). A small Scandinavian composer whose name begins with K is using Stravinskian discords while Grieg is selling bonbons filled with snow (Debussy's metaphor). Even Dvořák, in the Ninth or 'New World' Symphony, is using consecutive secondary sevenths before history properly allows (that second movement incidentally, was intended to be in C, but Dvořák had found chords suitable for getting from E minor to D flat), and Puccini, whom history tells not to administer musical shocks, shocks with the bare fifths of the third act of *La Bohème*. And Gesualdo uses processions of unrelated triads in what looks like the manner of Vaughan Williams but, of course, is not. Even when the chromaticisms of Purcell's early anthems and string fantasias sound 'curiously modern', Jack Westrup, in his admirable essay on the composer, tells us that 'they are a logical extension of the practice of his immediate predecessors, particularly Locke.'

Over a hundred pages are given to opera – a substantial book in itself, with a team of expert authors too numerous to list here, though the editor is among them. The literary lover of the form need fear no technicalities. The strength of the survey is indicated by the firmness of its definitions and by its willingness to plunge at once into exemplification. 'Music can strengthen, subtilize or inflect any words that are uttered on the stage. It can also carry hints about words or feelings that are left unexpressed.' Examples? The accompaniment to the aria *'Le calme rentre dans mon coeur'* in Gluck's *Iphigénie in Tauride*, where the uneasy throb of the violas 'contradicts the singer's words and instructs the listener that his calm is illusory.' The new theme in the closing scene of *Das Rheingold*, which tells the auditor that an idea has just struck Wotan – great and noble but as yet unspecified. Duets of lovers or conspirators in thirds, sixths or octaves to show unity of sentiment or purpose. And one of the major problems of the form is adumbrated in the general preamble: should primacy be given to the word or the music? Two operas have taken this question as their theme – Salieri's *Prima la musica e poi le parole* (1786) and (1942) Strauss's *Capriccio*.

We know where the true primacy lies – in dramatic success. The greatness of Verdi and Puccini was never wholly musical. Both knew as much as their librettists, if not more, about the dramatically feasible. Mozart, too, knew more than Metastasio but was not big enough to prevail over the Laureate of the Empire. And, in pursuing dramatic success, composers are not to be subjected to the analyses of textbook musicians shockable by irregularities. Jean-Jacques Rousseau is not thought much of as a musician, but he deserves his long entry in *Grove* because *Le Devin du Village* and *Pygmalion* inaugurated respectively the age of the *opéra comique* and the tradition of the melodrama. Daniel Heartz tells us of weak part-writing, parallel fifths in *Le Devin*, but rightly adds: 'It is needless to ask whether a work of genius such as this opera is ''good'' – it held the attention of several generations and continued to form musical tastes to the time of Berlioz.'

One is glad to see that another literary man is considered in his role of musical amateur – Ezra Pound, reviewer of music as 'William Atheling' for the London *New Age*, one of the founders, through his Rapallo concerts in the 1930s, of the modern cult of Vivaldi and, above all, innovative composer of the opera *Villon*. Among the music critics honoured by inclusion, Bernard Shaw leads all the rest in a lively two columns from Robert Anderson which not only summarizes the achievement of 'Corno di Bassetto' but also indicates the musical provenances of some of the dramatic effects in the plays – the mixture of Wagner and *Die Zauberflöte*, for instance, in the fourth play of *Back to Methuselah*. Shaw's master Samuel Butler, who believed music had stopped with Handel, produced, we are told in a brief dismissive essay, very frigid and worthless pastiches of his idol. Shakespeare, who was not Shaw's master, and on whose connection with music whole large volumes have been written, is granted only four pages. Of Shakespeare's own presumed musicality little is said. The two themes which appear solmized in respectively *Love's Labour's Lost* (C-D-G-A-E-F) and *King Lear* (the first four notes of Addinsell's big tune in the *Warsaw Concerto*) are not mentioned, neither is his imperfect understanding of the term 'jack' in the sonnet on his lady playing the virginals nor his vivid use of a lute-tuning metaphor in *Macbeth*. But 'his shrewd assessment of music's power to contribute to drama' is not neglected. It influenced Goethe in *Egmont* and *Faust* and, more interestingly, Verdi's and Boito's *Falstaff*.

Of the immense and lightly carried scholarship in the articles on old music I will say nothing. Indeed, there is nothing more to say about the whole great achievement, a masterpiece of Britannico-American collaboration with notable contributions from Europe. The quality of production is very high, with fine and always relevant illustrations and no typographical error that I have been able to spot. The computer's presence is indicated only by its ignorance of morphemes. Longish monosyllables like *schemes* look like polysyllables to the electronic eye and undergo line-end hyphenization. This is an innovation we have to get used to.

Sir George Grove has, as he has to have, his own brief entry. To call the new *Grove Grove* at all may seem merely an act of national piety. A man once boasted that he had possessed the same axe for forty years, except for three new hefts and five new blades. Still, we may accept a kind of mystical continuity and find in this astonishing compendium the fulfilment of an aim essentially Victorian. I understand that the new *Grove*, which represents on the part of Macmillan – the original publisher and the true blazon of continuity – an investment of more than three million pounds, will have to last us for fifty years. It is doubtful whether in 2031, western or universal man will have come any closer to an understanding of what music is or what it does. The new and presumably still vaster *Grove* that will come out then will be another monument to a sustentive mystery.

Shaw's Music

There are nearly three thousand pages of Shaw the musicologist, and I have finished reading them with no notable sense of fatigue. This is remarkable, since there is nothing more tiring than the company of a man whom vegetarianism and teetotalism have rendered horribly energetic, who would never bring any essay to an end if it were not for the pressure of space, and is never in the wrong – or, if he is, takes care to put himself in the right in a later footnote. Shaw on music is endlessly readable because he is endlessly knowledgeable. He is also remarkably prophetic. Some of the things he was saying about music and musicians a century ago, eccentric in their time, are commonplaces today. As a Wagnerian, and a partisan of the 'music of the future', he was ready for Schönberg before Schönberg was born. When (in Volume III) he at last heard the Five Orchestral Pieces, he had evidently been awaiting them since *Tristan*, and he could even forehear the final note of the last of the pieces. He foretold a British musical renascence while British academics were churning out pale imitations of *Elijah*. He was not surprised by Debussy's whole-tone scale, and he speculated as to whether Debussy had been brought up next to an organ factory, since organ pipes are tuned on a whole-tone system. His blind spot was Brahms, but after all he was a Wagnerian.

Non-musical Shavians have generally assumed that their idol was able to sustain so unstaunchable a flow of musical journalism through verbal trickery, egotistical bluff, and a background of domestic vocalism and scrambling through operatic scores at the piano. He had, in fact, a very thorough musical training, though he despised the academies. Like all of us musical autodidacts, he taught himself the elements with the Novello primers. He knew the entire terminology of the craft but took no pride in it. He liked to pretend that Elgar, of whose greatness he never had any doubt, did not know what the supertonic was, and it was to Wagner's credit that he ignored the rules about consecutives and could not write a fugue (though in fact Wagner did write one, and a very good one, in the *Meistersinger* Overture).

Time was quick to prove Shaw right about the futility of an academic training. A great number of the British oratorios (with dismal libretti by provincial journalists), pseudo-symphonies, tone poems and rhapsodies which he noticed in the *Star* and the *World*, were dry and professorial, and they used fugue as a substitute for inspiration. A good two thirds of the works he dutifully heard have sunk like the lead they were. He is unerring in his spotting of structural weaknesses, and his scorn for the level of literary taste of Victorian composers, as well, naturally of Victorian literary men is eloquent but at the same time good-tempered. There is never any bile in his writing, this all having been absorbed by fruit and nuts, and if he is called ass he smilingly responds with idiot. And, indeed, only the idiots called him ass.

A lot of music critics have no practical knowledge of the making of music, and one very famous critic, who has an amusing battle with Shaw in the indulgent correspondence columns of that age of cheap paper, was even to extol the conversion of music into a purely subjective experience. This was Ernest Newman, himself to replace Shaw as the leading British Wagnerian, who once sympathized with a composer for forgetting the limits of the violin strings and giving them notes below the low G. Shaw has no use for this interiorizing of music. He is to the fore in the controversy about the changing over to French pitch, and full of advice to clarinettists about how to adjust their instruments. He worries, along with Elgar, about how to strengthen the orchestral bass, and is learned about obsolete boomers like the ophicleide (which Shaw's suicidal uncle had played). He knows all about the voice, having been taught it by the great Lee of Dublin, and is ready to tell Jean de Reszke, the famous cigarette smoker, all about head notes.

His main task, though, is to chasten taste, and his taste is faultless. Too many of his readers believe that even the feeblest sacred cantata is superior to the strongest secular piece by virtue of its being about God and his prophets. Shaw wades in, fearless of charges of blasphemy, to assert that Elijah and Jeremiah and St Paul are bores and Sigmund and Sieglinde, though incestuous lovers, are not. His eye is always on art which, in the Oscar Wilde manner, he appraises with the rigour of the moralist.

I once briefly as a boy met Shaw at Malvern (he was not gracious; I wanted his autograph and he said I could never afford it), and I can't help considering him as a great man of my time. It is something of a shock to find him so firmly placed among great historical musicians. He was a mature man when Wagner died (he remembers his erratic beat as a conductor, his sour neuralgic look, and the relief with which the Philharmonic hailed his replacement by Richter); he saw Dvořák and Clara Schumann and wrote for an Oslo paper on Grieg's first London recitals. He saw through Cowan and Mackenzie but found merit in MacCunn's *Land of the Mountain and the Flood*, which, ninety years after its first performance, has at last become popular. He deplored, predictably, the 'working out' section, 'which Mr MacCunn would never have written if his tutors had not put it into his head. I know a lady who keeps a typewriting establishment. Under my advice she is completing arrangements for supplying middle sections and recapitulations for overtures and symphonies at twopence a bar, on being supplied with the first section and coda.'

Shaw was no composer himself. Dr Laurence, who has done the expected fine job of editing, reproduces a setting of Shelley, done by the young Shaw, which Samuel Butler would have sneered at. Shaw reserved musical structure, along with an operatic spectrum of voices, for his plays. *Back to Methuselah* is his *Ring* and *Man and Superman* his *Don Giovanni*. How important a musician Shaw was this collection at last testifies.

Ludwig Van

Beethoven, by Maynard Solomon

Musical composition, more than any other creative activity, shows how far the imagination can function independently of the rest of the human complex. A writer's arthritis or homosexuality or sweet tooth will often come through in a spring sonnet. An armless sculptor cannot sculpt well, no matter how prehensile his toes. A blind painter cannot paint at all. Frederick Delius, blind and paralysed, produced fine music. Beethoven, deaf, cirrhotic, diarrhetic, dyspnoeal, manic, produced the finest, and healthiest, music of all time. This is not, of course, to say that the composer's art operates totally in its own autonomous world. Delius found it necessary to tell his amanuensis, Eric Fenby, that those long-held D-major string chords had something to do with the sea and sky and the wind arabesques could be seagulls. Gustav Mahler put trivial hurdy-gurdy tunes in his symphonies until Freud, between trains, told him why. Although Beethoven's music is about sounds and structures, it is also, in ways not easily demonstrable, about Kant and the tyrant at Schönbrunn and Beethoven himself, body soul and blood and ouns. To read Beethoven's biography is to learn something about what his music is trying to do. Not much, but something.

Maynard Solomon's book is the latest in a long line dedicated to telling the truth about Beethoven as Schindler would not see it and as Thayer, who had to rely heavily on Schindler, was not able to see it. It was only in 1977, at the Berlin Beethovenkongress, that Herre and Beck proved that Schindler had fabricated more than 150 of his own entries in the Conversation Books. Moreover, the hagiographical tendency of many biographies got in the way of presenting the squalor, the clownishness, the downright malice, the drinking and drabbing. It was not right for the composer of the Ninth Symphony and the last quartets to vomit in crapula and frequent brothels. Solomon has no desire to 'fashion an uncontradictory and consistent portrait of Beethoven – to construct a safe, clear, well-ordered design; for such a portrait can be purchased only at the price of truth, by avoiding the obscurities that riddle the documentary material.' At the same time he is prepared to call on Freud and, more, Otto Rank to elucidate the obscurities.

Beethoven was named for his grandfather, a *Kapellmeister* at the electoral court of Cologne, and identified with him, going so far as to wish to deny the paternity of Johann Beethoven and to acquiesce in the legend that he was the illegitimate son of a king of Prussia – either Friedrich Wilhelm II or Frederick the Great himself. He denied his birth year of 1770, despite all the documentary evidence, alleging and eventually believing that he had been born in 1772. His contempt for the drunken, feebly tyrannical, not too talented court tenor who was his father seems not to have been matched by a compensatory devotion to his mother: after all, he was prepared to put it about that she had been a court whore. Beethoven wanted a kind of parthenogenetical birth proper for the messianic role he envisaged for himself. He would willingly turn a woman into a mother if she was too young for the part. That he regarded mothers as supererogatory is proved by his turning himself into the father of his nephew Karl, execrating his sister-in-law as the 'Queen of the Night', pretending that the Dutch *van* of his name was really *von* so that he could use aristocratic clout in the courts to dispossess the poor woman of her maternal rights.

He broke free of Viennese musical conventions to assert a new masculine force, appropriate to the Napoleonic age, which should be characterized by rigour of tonal argument and a kind of genial brutality. The legend about his dedicating his Third Symphony to Bonaparte and then tearing up the dedication page after the assassination of the Duc d'Enghien is still to be accepted as true, but Solomon makes it clear that Beethoven was strongly drawn to the tyrant. Vienna's musical talent assembled at Schönbrunn to welcome the conqueror, but Beethoven alone was not invited. He resented this. He arranged a performance of the *Eroica*, expecting Napoleon to turn up. Napoleon did not turn up. Beethoven was not altogether the fierce republican, the romantic artist shaking his fist at despots. He owed much to his aristocratic patrons; he dreamed of receiving honours at the Tuileries. He had his eye to the main chance. He liked money. He was ready to sell the same piece of music to three different publishers at the same time and pocket three different advances.

He also had his ear, even when it was a deaf one, to the exterior world of sonic innovations. When Schönberg was told that six fingers were required to play his Violin Concerto, he replied: 'I can wait.' Beethoven did not want six fingers, but he did want a pianoforte – once called by him, in a gust of patriotism, a *Hammerklavier* – that could, there and then, crash out his post-rococo imaginings. The fourth horn part of the Ninth Symphony was specially written for one of the new valve instruments: Beethoven knew a man near Vienna who possessed one. He was a great pianist and a very practical musician. His orchestral parts were hard to play but not impossible. Impossibility hovers, like a fermata, above the soprano parts in the Ninth, but sopranos were women, mothers, sisters-in-law.

It is only through the vague operation of analogy that we can find in a symphony like the *Eroica* – a key work, the work that the composer believed to be his highest orchestral achievement – the properties of the Kantian philosophy and the novels of Stendhal. This music was necessary to the age, but not because of its literary programme. One attaches literary programmes at one's peril to Beethoven's work, even when he says of the yellowhammer call of the Fifth: 'Thus Fate knocks at the door.' Give Beethoven a text and he does more than merely set it. *Fidelio* is a free-from-chains manifesto typical of its time (though more in Paris than in Vienna), but it is also vegetation myth, with Florestan as a flower god, woman most loved when the female lion becomes the faithful boy, mother into son, the composer himself incarcerated in his deafness. It is, as well, much more, and the much more is not easily explicated. The music works at a very deep psychic level, subliterary, submythical, multiguous. When Donald Tovey said that the *Leonora* No. 3 rendered the first act superfluous, he spoke no more than the truth. With the American Solomon's excellent book (though not as excellent as our own Martin Cooper's) we know a little more about the man but nothing more about the mystery of his art. That was to be expected.

Beethoven and the Voice of God, by Wilfred Mellers

Ten years ago Professor Mellers published *Twilight of the Gods: the Beatles in Retrospect*. Two years ago came his *Bach and the Dance of God*. Now Beethoven is in on the theodicean act. But, of course, he always was. It has never been enough for Beethoven to have spun notes for money and diversion: he has always purveyed the struggle of the soul in the direction of the divine vision. The latter term has to be used in a Pickwickian sense, since the Nazis, who had a better claim on Beethoven than the Christian democracies, presumably found in him a spiritual uplift appropriate to the Final Solution. We know what God does not mean to Professor Mellers. He says: '. . . I am not and never have been a Christian, and . . . I subscribe to no creed religious or political.' The God he finds in Beethoven is an eclectic entity – illuminist, Blakean, masonic – but, since music cannot propose anything except self-referring structures, he has to be concerned with exalted motions of the mind induced by music. The Mover has to be outside his scope, but, through the free use of metaphor and a wide range of literary and theological citations, he persuades himself that a kind of ultimate reality shines through.

Anybody who loves music has to be worried about the romantic assumption that it contains meanings expressible in words. When Professor Mellers deals, as he does brilliantly, with the *Missa Solemnis*, he is on safe verbal ground. Beethoven is setting the words of the Latin mass and is clearly searching for musical patterns which are metaphors of those words. He is also a good Freemason like Mozart, making use of symbols associated with the rituals of the craft – like the three opening 'knocks' – and sonorities (clarinets, bassoons, strings of major thirds) associated with Freemasonry. There is even a masonic key – E flat. It requires, of course, an extreme eclecticism to reconcile Catholicism with Freemasonry, since the Church has traditionally condemned secret societies, but music can effect the reconciliation because its meanings are not explicit. Where there *are* meanings in the music itself, as opposed to the word set, these, surely, are imposed rather than immanent. 'The "goal" of the Mass, tonally, is G major, which for Beethoven as for Bach is the key of blessedness,' says Mellers. Again, 'B minor, for Beethoven as for Bach, is a key of suffering, whereby a synthesis between God's D major and Man's B flat major occurs and, "for the time being", finds haven in G major's benediction.' I find this very hard to take.

The musical journalist Hans Keller, one of whose modes of musicological argument is dyspeptic bad temper, said, on the occasion of the 150th anniversary of Beethoven's death, that Ludwig van was conceivably the greatest thinker of the nineteenth century. He did not mean by this that Beethoven, in his spare time, worked out a coherent philosophy that makes Kant and Hegel look like schoolboys: he meant, I think, that Beethoven's musical structures exhibit an intellectual strength analogous to that of the inspired metaphysician. If I say that this sounds to me very much like nonsense, I shall have to submit to a Kellerian knockdown argument of coarse abuse. It seems to me that the task of musicologists is to exhibit and explain musical patterns and not to confuse the analogy with the identification. Mellers does not try to turn Beethoven into a metaphysician, but he does try to exhibit him as a mystic. Let us see what he does with the great piano sonata in C minor and major, Op. 111.

After an admirable technical description of what happens in the opening bars of the Arietta, we get this: ' "Garlic and sapphires in the mud/ Clot the bedded axletree": but only momentarily, since parallel thirds and sixths, thrusting up in this fastest version of the boogie rhythm, end the variation of the apex of the Arietta's ecstasies. A Corporeal music has transcended time and the body.' Later, true to the spirit of 'Little Gidding', we have: 'After a baptism in the waters, a scorching in the pentecostal fire, and a *conjunctio oppositorum* of earth and air.' The sustaining pedal is down, and we hear the blur of bells. If we have at all been seduced by Mellers's combination of exact technical analysis and mystical exegesis, we can break free from him when he quotes Herbert Whone's *The Hidden Face of Music* with approval: 'If a man is able to resonate himself he becomes a thing of beauty, as we find indicated in the French *belle*. . . . There is worldly strife (which we see reflected in the dialectic of the Latin words *bella* and *bellum*, beautiful and war. . . . The bell begins to ring for joy when a man finds his own way back to pure being.' Add to this a fancied derivation of *bell* (cognate with *bellow*) from Hebrew *B* and *el*, signifying the Being of God, and you will understand why so much musicology has a bad name.

I would never go so far as to assert that music has no relevance to human experience and that it is no more than a string of tensions and releases, some stronger than others, but I would suggest that it is ultimately undescribable except in terms of its physical content. The oboes and bassoons play a semibreve F-major chord and the strings ppp rush up and down in staccato semiquavers. There's nothing wrong with that. When the chord becomes an expression of ecstasy and the semiquavers are the impotent assault of minor devils on Mansoul, then I get worried. I should imagine that the tensions and releases of Beethoven have as much to do with visceral problems as with the fight towards the ecstatic vision. We do not know what music 'means', but there is no harm in looking for tentative literary analogues if these assist appreciation of the sheer sounds. To approach Beethoven with the aid of Martin Buber, Descartes, Meister Eckhart and Nietzsche seems to me to be a presumptuous stepping outside of the musicologist's province. On the other hand, Professor Mellers's purely musical analyses of some of the Beethoven sonatas are perfection, and I recommend his book for those alone. His title, however, is clearly blasphemous.

The Nine Symphonies of Beethoven, by Antony Hopkins

Having dealt with No. 8 in F major, before engaging the heavy work of analysing No. 9 in D minor, Antony Hopkins, perhaps needlessly but certainly with a decent sense of proprieties, justifies or excuses what he feels may be regarded as 'a somewhat frivolous approach to what is unquestionably a masterpiece'. He means this sort of thing: '. . . the strings buzzing anxiously as the woodwind search for a triad that refuses to materialise. (How can it when they are coupled in pairs? Triads need – "lesh think . . . *three* notes".)' The slanginess perhaps encourages the slackness of 'coupled in pairs', as if things could be coupled any other way. I have to regret these occasions on which Mr Hopkins lets himself down. They do not come often but they are shocking when they do come. Discussing the opening bars of the last movement of the *Eroica*, he says that they are an impressive-sounding hoax, 'roughly comparable to the late and lovable Tony Hancock giving us a few lines of *King Lear* by way of a warm-up. "This should impress the natives," Beethoven seems to say as he lets loose a torrent of semiquavers in the strings.' That is unworthy because it drags a great universal artistic experience into a region of insular cosiness. Who in Seattle knows what Tony Hancock was?

And yet I cannot but approve of the anthropomorphic approach, which was Sir George Grove's and also Sir Donald Tovey's. But Tovey would quote a few bars of Bruckner and say 'Here is Sir Charles Grandison's drawing room.' This is a cut above Hopkins's ' "Did you say KNOCK-KNOCK-KNOCK?" ask the strings incredulously. "YES WE DID!" reply the other instruments. *Strings*: "Oh . . ." (*quietly*) *Wind and brass*: "Hum . . ." (*pensive*).' In fact this imagined colloquy does suggest what is happening in the orchestra, but only on a surface which robs the exegesis of dignity. But Hopkins's search for comedy is incessant, except when 'The tempo changes to *Poco Andante* and a divinely beautiful variation ensues.' The finale of the *Eroica* may be both comic and divinely beautiful, but it is much more besides. If it is about anything it is about Prometheus, a fact which Beethoven spells out by blatantly borrowing from his own *Prometheus* ballet music. The humour is heroic, suitable for a relaxed conqueror, but not one who is playing postman's knock.

The problem of how to write about music is still with us, and, as Hopkins says:

It seems to me that there are two approaches to analysis; one is to apply the chilling hand of the anatomist, applying the correct labels according to musical terminology – 'here the subject is inverted in augmentation over a pedal-point on the mediant' etc; the other is to describe what happens in less abstruse terms – 'the string chords increase in intensity as horns and trumpets pound out the all-pervasive rhythm.' I detest the first method and avoid it insofar as I can; inevitably I am often guilty of the second. However, both are merely descriptions of events and as such do not necessarily interpret what is happening.

Yet, saying that, he does not at all allude to a method genuinely opposed to the technical one. An orchestral score might well carry indications like *intensificandosi* and *martellando* (hammer or pound out). It seems as if for the moment he is ashamed of stating what the true alternative is. It is, of course: 'The bassoons hiccup drunkenly and the first violins utter a prim protest, while the muted violas, less exhibitionistically, croon what sounds suspiciously like a version of "Show Me the Way to Go Home".'

Hopkins is a composer himself, and he knows that long work on a full score generates an anthropomorphic approach to the various instrumental groups. I do not mean that the composer visualizes violinists and oboists; I mean that, in Disney fashion, he endows the instruments themselves as tonal entities with a kind of thwarted free will. The trombones cut into a flute solo, and it seems rude and angry though (since they are totally under the composer's control) only factitiously. The trumpets have been quiet for a long time: time they said something. Before long the score becomes a kind of cartoon zoomorphic drama. But this drama is parallel to the true drama of the music. It is this surface cartoon which too often takes over in detailed musical analysis – and not only in Mr Hopkins's painstaking, generally enjoyable and often enlightening commentaries. There is in many professional musicians, however, an unfortunate tendency to the schoolmasterish or choirmasterly. I remember the *Musical Times* of the thirties and its references to the 'bonny stroke' of Handel's 'Laughter ho-ho-ho-ho-ho-holding both his sides' and 'spunky tunes' in Haydn's finales. Worst of all, I remember the late Dr Herbert Howells rebuking me for not at once spotting that a particular chord was the Neapolitan sixth. 'Come, come, don't you eat ice cream?' I was at the time mature and even bearded. I swore something and knew I had failed.

Mr Hopkins is at his most valuable when he is, forgetting for the moment to be colloquial and breezy, absorbed in technicalities. The First Symphony in C major begins, as all the world knows, with a dominant seventh on C. Traditionally the opening bars of an opening allegro should state the key of the whole work vigorously and unequivocally, and here is Beethoven suggesting that his symphony is really in F, not C. This has been taken as an example of Ludwig van's spunky quirkiness or perverseness. Hopkins shows that the whole first movement is based on chains of dominant seventh-tonic assertions of keys that are not C, and that the opening surprise is an announcement of intention. Similarly he takes the C sharp in the first movement of the *Eroica* – a surprising shift on the part of an E-flat bugle call – and relates it to the D-flat section of the coda, asking us, without facetiousness, to marvel at an enharmonic mystery. It is precisely when he is dealing in augmentations on mediant pedals that he is at his most brilliant and instructive.

He cites Beethoven's notebooks and shows how initial banalities are transformed, by hard work as much as magic, to pregnant themes. He has a very sharp eye and ear for odd three-note wisps of accompaniment (as in the finale of the Fifth) which are turned into bursts of lyricism or energy. The other side of him, the desire to communicate in human terms, blends admirably with the technical anatomist when he comes to the *Pastoral*. Here he has Beethoven's own imprimatur to find the rustic *cornamusa* or *ciaramella* in the first bars and to suggest that themes burgeon like leaves in what follows; to invoke Beethoven's own interest in the tonalities of streams and rivers and justify the muddiness of the bass chords at the opening of the second movement; to impose chronological time on musical duration and suggest that the storm takes place at night and the shepherd's song is heard on Sunday morning.

As a composer and conductor Hopkins is aware both of Beethoven's occasional miscalculations (second violins unsupported and inaudible) and the difference in numbers and balance between his orchestra and ours. Beethoven's apparent ineptness – or misogynistic cruelty – in giving his sopranos long high-held As is excused by reference to the semitone difference between his A and ours. Sing the killing A in the Ninth Symphony as A flat (though only experimentally, not, God help us, in the concert hall) and it becomes easy enough. Hopkins is full of practical knowledge. The three horns still approach the trio of the Scherzo of the *Eroica* with some trepidation: at least the first horn, who has to play an uncovered high E flat, is not happy about it. Hopkins's triumph is, like Beethoven's, the long and intricate Ninth. His references to the Choral Fantasia, in which the piano tries out instrumental recitative in preparation for the speaking basses of the last movement of the Ninth, are relevant and helpful. His last words combine tellingly the coolness of the analyst and the elation of the mere listener: 'Immense descending scales in the strings seem to draw curtains over the biggest stage in the world, the sopranos climb to a top A for the last time, the orchestra scampers to a finish, proclaiming the glory of D major to the last. It is the tonal goal of the entire symphony from the first groping elusive dominant to the ultimate triumphant affirmation of the joyous tonic.' All that we need after this is an extract from Grillparzer's funeral oration: 'The last Master of resounding song, the sweet lips that gave expression to the art of tones,' etc. etc. Hopkins celebrates the living artist in a way that that artist, once he had had Tony Hancock and football choral singing explained to him, would probably have approved. This is a book of very considerable value. If it does not obviate our need to read Tovey, it renders Grove's treatise unnecessary. It contains Grove's spirit but much more.

A Gap in Our Musical Education

The Hurdy-Gurdy, by Susann Palmer with Samuel Palmer

S amuel is the son and Susann the mother. Samuel is an instrument maker. He made a hurdy-gurdy with which the mother fell in love. This book, exhaustive as to both text and (very beautiful) illustrations, is a pledge of love. In a brief foreword Professor Francis Baines (composer, leader of a consort of viols, hurdy-gurdy player) reports that 'the Victoria and Albert Museum, London, say that scarcely a day goes by without inquiries concerning hurdy-gurdies. That can mean only one thing – that it is high time there was a book about them. And here it is.' He might have said more – that the book is a labour of love and so on. For my part I do not think we shall need another book on the hurdy-gurdy for a long long time. What we may need is a brief demonstration on radio or television of hurdy-gurdy-playing – the sound, that is, as opposed to the mere technique. Mrs Palmer is as exhaustive on the technique as on the history.

The very name of the instrument lends itself to a pejorative view of both its sound and its social status. Etymology? 'C.18,' says the new *Collins*: 'Rhyming compound, probably of imitative origin.' The name seems first to occur in Bonnel Thornton's 'Ode on St Cecilia's Day' in 1749:

With dead, dull, doleful, heavy hums,
  And dismal moans,
  And mournful groans,
The sober hurdy-gurdy thrums.

Before that it had more dignified names – symphonie, sanfoigne, chamfogne, cymphan, syphonie, chyfonie, cyfonia, phonphogne, fonfonia. There seems to be a Joycean conflation of *symphony* and *chiffon* in some of those terms, the cloth or rags connoting the beggars who played the instrument, though perhaps primarily the cloth covering of the strings which ensured sweet hushed tone. This brings me, perhaps belatedly, to what the thing is and how it works.

It is a stringed instrument with a handle. The handle turns a hidden wheel against which the strings vibrate. There is a manual keybox whose keys operate tangents that shorten the strings and thus discourse melody. The keybox has black keys which produce a diatonic scale and white keys for chromatic inflections. The better class of hurdy-gurdy – like that used once by the French aristocracy – had or has two octaves; the lowlier or rural version had to be satisfied with one and a half. There is a tonic drone, as on bagpipes; a tonic-dominant drone is possible too. The effect, so far as I can judge, is of a one-stringed fiddle accompanied by a viola or cello playing on two open strings. I am assured that the sound is endearingly simple and altogether charming.

Its appearance is well recorded in pictorial art. A twelfth-century carving on the cathedral of Santiago de Compostela shows two kings or angels operating one hurdy-gurdy – sensible division of labour: one for grinding, the other for playing. In the eleventh-century York Psalter King David's harp is accompanied by a recognizable cymphan or phonphogne. And so, in almost unbroken succession, up to 1979, with a picture of Samuel Palmer himself churning and fingering a very lovely hurdy-gurdy with a smile of quite religious rapture. Perhaps the most famous reproduction of the instrument is to be found in Hieronymus Bosch's *Hell*, where a miniature demon turns the handle but nobody attacks the keyboard. We may term this an apodemoniosis of a humble and harmless discourser of melody which gave much innocent pleasure during several centuries.

I can have nothing but praise for a book which fills in, so eruditely and charmingly, a gap in most people's musical and social knowledge. Admiration, too, for the publishers, who assuredly have produced no bestseller. What is now called for, I think, is a visit to Samuel Palmer's workshop in Whitechapel and a demonstration of fonfonia-playing. His mother has done him proud.

Highly Vocal

The Counter Tenor, by Peter Giles

Alfred Deller, the counter tenor whose artistry has done much to rehabilitate a reach of the male voice too long neglected, was, in the 1950s, waiting to go on at the Royal Festival Hall. He was standing near Sir Malcolm Sargent and the leader of the orchestra. The latter, who had better remain anonymous, said to Sargent, all too audibly: 'I see we've got the bearded lady with us.' Sargent, according to Peter Giles, 'the epitome of the English Gentleman, affected not to hear and is said to have brushed some imaginary dust off his sleeve.' The anecdote indicates a prejudice against the high male voice which is based on the pitch of the speaking voice as an index of sex. As James Bowman says in his foreword to this book (himself a distinguished follower of Deller), 'The fact that we sing at a higher pitch than the other adult male voices does not instantly make us a peculiar breed apart – distant relatives of the castrati. There is no "mystique." We are just singers who, for one reason or another, have preferred to develop the upper reaches of our voices, and this has become a natural means of vocal expression.'

Mr Giles, rightly, spends some time in his book – the first ever on the counter tenor – dealing with the phenomenon of the castrato or *everato* (properly *evirato* – devirilized or emasculated). The image of papal shears snipping off testicles to ensure the continuation into adulthood of a fine boy's voice is not strictly accurate. Kingsley Amis's novel *The Alteration* is historically correct in presenting the owner of the voice as possessing the legal right to accept or reject the proposed operation, right too in his ironical denouement, where the hero becomes what he has voluntarily rejected through a disease of the testicles. A lot of Italian castrati swam into fame through a morbid accident. As for those boys who put music before the joys of sex, it was usually a matter of dosing them with opium, placing them in a warm bath, then snipping the lifelines, so that the testicles eventually shrivelled away. It was a voluntary matter, and the *potestas clavium* never came into it.

It is necesssary to spend some time with the castrati before dealing with the counter tenor, since those 'brilliant artificial voices' eclipsed for a long time the natural falsetto or counter tenor. There was a castrato in the papal choir as early as 1562, but the last of the Sistine falsetti, Giovanni di Sanctos, died in 1625. England clung to the counter tenor until the castrato, with all things musically Italian, became popular in the time of Handel. Henry Purcell was himself a fine counter tenor. Incidentally, the last of the papal castrati, Alessandro Moreschi, who died in 1924, made some gramophone records in 1903–4. It is not a great voice, and the quality of the recording is inevitably poor, but the castrato sound is at least available to those interested or, like Mr Amis, fascinated by the phenomenon.

There is not, despite the stupidity of that orchestral leader, as much prejudice against the counter tenor today as there would have been in, say, the Victorian era. Pop singers favour the higher, or even falsetto, reach of the voice; unisex has been, in some ways, a healthy solvent of a crass and brutal polarity. When Alfred Deller's voice erupted on the air or the concert platform, it was an older generation of musicians that was disturbed, not the possessors of an innocent ear. The exploitation of the higher reach of the male voice springs from no mental or physical morbidity. In theory, anyone can restrict the vibration of his vocal cords to a single segment, thus ensuring a high range which can take advantage of the vibration of an adult sounding chamber – not possible to boy altos.

We accept the four-part mixed chorus – S A T B – without being altogether satisfied with it. Female and male voices do not blend well, any more than (to push the range downwards) trombones blend well with the bass tuba. Wagner saw or heard the need for total homogeneity in his wind sections – hence the development of the heckelphone to complete the family of oboes, and the bass trumpet and the contrabass trombone to ensure a uniformity of tone in the brass. The church choir, with its trebles and male altos, may be regarded as one of the fruits of St Paul's misogyny, but the oratorio tradition, related to the operatic, accepts the two sexes not only because drama involves sex but because female voices are adult and hence powerful. Yet the female alto has an unfortunate woolliness and the counter tenor, which theoretically could replace it, is probably the sound which composers hear in their brains when they pen the second choral line. Unfortunately, there are not yet enough counter tenors around to be massed chorally. The counter tenor, like the castrato, is a rare and brilliant solo phenomenon, and it might have been even rarer had not Michael Tippett heard the late great Deller in Canterbury and given him the encouragement he needed. We are thankful to have his voice preserved for all time, granted perhaps its finest exploitation in the Oberon role of Britten's *Midsummer Night's Dream*, written specially for Deller. And we are thankful that he had followers like James Bowman, John Bowman, Paul Esswood, and Peter Giles himself.

Giles's book is brief, but it has some of the qualities of a comprehensive guide to counter tenordom or ship. There are photographs and a discography, an account of the counter tenor in history, and an admirable appendix on 'The Counter Tenor as an Artistic Phenomenon'. He considers the essential 'Englishness' of the type of voice and relates it to the 'love of *line*' which Nikolaus Pevsner extols in his Reith Lectures collected as *The Englishness of English Art*, the cult of idiosyncrasy, and the persistent conservatism which, by some paradox, emerges occasionally as the new and even shocking. Dunstable showed European composers of the fifteenth century how to accept thirds and sixths, officially dissonances, as an aspect of the native love of the independent vocal line, a traditional contrapuntalism which persisted while Europe was trying to think horizontally. Giles finds an 'ultra-linear' property in the high male voice:

> It is decidedly otherwordly, inhabiting a strange unreal world somewhere in the head, indefinably more than falsetto. It is eccentric and irrational: men do not normally sing as high as women, therefore who but the English would favour over many centuries a purely natural voice which does? The counter tenor is itself the result of English conservatism. Its continued existence stems from English reluctance to embrace the new or recognise when the game is up, the battle lost!

Shaw, in *Man and Superman*, has a counter tenor in his infernal quartet. 'Ah, here you are, my friend,' says Don Juan to the Statue. 'Why don't you learn to sing the splendid music Mozart has written for you?' The Statue replies: 'Unluckily he has written it for a bass voice. Mine is a counter tenor.' Should we take that 'unluckily' seriously? For a decidedly otherworldly visitant a decidedly otherworldly voice might have been in order. Let us imagine that invitation to supper soaring over the trombones. But, alas, Mozart was historically unable to think in countertenorly terms.

Artist and Beggar

The Letters of Claudio Monteverdi, translated and introduced by Denis Stevens

When Monteverdi started writing the letters in this volume. Shakespeare had just produced *Hamlet*; when the letters ended, with his life, the London playhouses had been closed and the Civil War was already raging. The music of England during that period was remarkable, so remarkable that Europe did not despise it. But the music that Monteverdi was composing – in Mantua, Venice and Parma – was revolutionary. Its place in the history of Western music is comparable with that of Wagner and Schoenberg. Monteverdi invented opera – specifically *opera seria*, though he had *opera buffa* also in mind. In instrumental usage he was moving towards the concept of the modern orchestra. He was using, to the annoyance of some of his contemporaries, unprepared discords in his vocal writing. He was founding the baroque tradition, replacing a rigid mode of counterpoint with one more melodic and freer-flowing. On even the shortest list of supreme composers his name has to appear. And yet this superb artist was a slave to giddy patrons, a man trying to present images of order in an age notably disordered, subject to indigence and fear (at least on his son's behalf) of the Holy Inquisition, always forced to fulfil the postures of humility before men unworthy to rule his bar lines.

It is something of a shock to find that Monteverdi and Mozart – separated as they are by an epoch of vast historical changes – yet share, almost without even the smallest variation, the same situation of grovelling for patronage, turned into disregarded journeymen summoned at a finger click for the composing of carnival dances or masses or operas or *Te Deums*. The great change in the situation of European composers occurs with the advent of Beethoven, the first free musician, who had indeed patrons but was prepared to treat them abominably, who wrote pretty well what he wished, who never had to endite elaborate self-scourging epistles ending with 'Forgive me, I beseech you, for so much inconvenience, while with all my heart I make a most humble reverence and kiss your hand. . . . Your Most Illustrious Lordship's most humble and most grateful servant' (Monteverdi to the Marquis Alessandro Striggio, at Mantua, 8 July 1628).

In a letter to the same nobleman (18 December 1627) Monteverdi writes that his son Massimiliano has been in the prisons of the Holy Office for three months, 'the reason being that he read a book which he did not know was prohibited'. What is notable about the attitude of the distraught father is the lack of anger. Later he writes to the Marquis: 'I understand from your most considerate letter that you happened to speak personally to the Most Reverend Father Inquisitor (a favour so great that it makes me blush). . . .' No blasting of the cruel cleric to hell: that would be a later, post-Beethovenian, luxury. We cannot blame anybody or anything, but we have to confess that, after four hundred odd pages of most eloquent self-abasement, we grow angry ourselves at the expenditure of so much epistolary skill on the making of elaborate reverences.

What, on the recommendation of this very fine translator, we have to do is consider these letters as pieces of music. The architectonic instinct of Monteverdi is expressed here, as much as in his madrigals, in the organization of periods which have the effect of counterpoint. In perhaps the only letter which expresses subdued rage at wounded dignity (a just rage, since Monteverdi was now at the peak of honour and not far from death) the shaping skill is at its peak – 'much more rhetorical in style,' says Stevens, 'than the majority of them, and so planned that the subject of the exordium is separated from the main verb by nearly half the length of the letter.' Monteverdi was by now Director of Music at St Mark's and servant of the Most Serene Republic of Venice. A bass singer in the cathedral choir, Domenico Aldegati, spoke insulting words in public, saying:

> The Director of Music belongs to a race of big cut-throats, a thieving, cheating he-goat, with many other wicked insults, and then he added: 'And I call him and whoever protects him an ass, and so that each one of you can hear me, I say that Claudio Monteverdi is a thieving, cheating he-goat, and I am telling you, Bonivento, so that you can go and report it as coming from me.'

(Bonivento was at the time paying out money to the singers given to him by the nuns of St Daniele for a vespers service.)

One thing may be said of the various nobility to which Monteverdi so humbly (and yet with a kind of structural dignity) writes, and that is that they were all musical enough to be worthy of detailed technical accounts of what Monteverdi was trying to do in his commissioned music. Some of the revelations of artistic problems are absorbing. What should be done, in a kind of masque of the months, to represent the goddess Discordia? As a discord was, of its nature in those distant pre-Schoenbergian days, only justifiable in terms of resolution on to a concord, it was not possible to write her music as consistent dissonance. Therefore it was not strictly possible for her to have a harmonic accompaniment for her song. Perhaps the song should be speech? Nay, perhaps even a kind of *Sprechgesang*? If Monteverdi thus foreshadowed *Pierrot Lunaire*, at least in intention, he was also willing to anticipate Strauss's *Don Quixote* by suggesting that the sounds of zephyrs and tempests be handed over to the brass and woodwind. His imagination was incredible, but it was always held in check by the commission on hand, the exigencies of singers' and instrumentalists' talents, and the subtle acoustic problems of the various places of performance. Today's composers are totally free. There is nothing they dream up that cannot be done. But freedom, though a fine political concept, is not really of much use to the artist. Monteverdi exemplifies the paradox of the muse in chains and yet soaring.

The frontispiece to this book is the reproduction of an oil painting of the composer done by Domenico Feti and to be seen in the Galleria dell' Accademia in Venice. It is a very remarkable portrait. The upper half of the face is that of Samuel Beckett, brooding on but writing nothing of the *merde universelle*. The ears reach out for sound like radar dishes (at least, the ear we can see does that). But the total effect, long hidalgo nose and grey beard and mustachios, will do for Don Quixote (did Strauss have this picture in mind when he wrote his 'theme of knightly character'?). It is a portrait of the archetypal artist set upon by the stupidities of the world. All Monteverdians will buy this admirable volume, a work of astonishing care and scholarship, but all concerned with the place of the great musician in a setting not quite worthy of him (apart from the irrelevancies of wars and disease and highway robbers) should at least dip into it.

A Poet at the Opera

Prime Alla Scala, by Eugenio Montale

It is not necessary for a poet to know about music, but it helps. If Swinburne had not been tone deaf, he might have realized that it was not within his province to contrive pure patterns of euphony: there was another art that could quite satisfactorily exploit the allure of sound. Dr Johnson, who got on well enough without a liking for music, encouraged his literary successors to regard it as either noise or angels, but certainly incapable of discoursing sense. The tide turned with Browning. The two great literary productions of 1922, the seminal works of our century (both of which, it may be argued, owe something to Browning) rely heavily on music. There is as much Wagner as Shakespeare in *The Waste Land*, and *Ulysses* showed that the sentence could be an analogue of the musical phrase, the fugue could be imitated, and that the total structure of a novel could learn from sonata form.

James Joyce was a tenor and, had he not been diverted by literature, he might have been a great one. Montale was gifted with a fine baritone voice, and he might have attained professional status with it if his singing master, Ernesto Sivori, had not died untimely. He remained a musician and, between 1954 and 1967, contributed regular very well-informed articles on opera to the *Corriere d'Informazione*. There are certain ignoramuses who assume that to be Italian is to be musical anyway. To these it must be said that there is no such a thing as an Italian. There are, for instance, Neapolitans, who assume, as black drummers with rhythm, that they are naturally endowed with the singing gift, and there are Romans, who make no such claim. Italy is probably less musical than England, and audiences at La Scala, Milan, are regrettably limited in their operatic tastes. If opera, which does not include Wagnerian music drama, is the national art, it is because southern Italian life is operatic. That Montale, in this collected volume of his musical writings, is nearly always at the opera, and not listening to symphonies or quartets, must not, however, be ascribed to the limitations of Italian musicality: as a singer and poet, he was naturally interested in a form which uses words to a musical end.

It is the regular Scala repertoire that Montale usually witnesses, along with such comparative novelties as the *Abu Hassan* of Weber, *Il Convitato di Pietra* of Dargomizhsky and Bellini's *Il Pirata*. When an opera is so neglected that a performance becomes a novelty, the fault usually lies in the words. Of the Bellini work he says: 'Romani's execrable libretto . . . seems to have touched the imagination of the composer only in respect of the part of Imogene . . . the other characters are respectively a baritone and a bass, not a couple of living personages.' Montale admits that the libretto of Verdi's *Nabucco* is '*incomprensibile*', but he finds a primordial power in the music. In an article called '*Parole in musica*' he faces up to the problem of the composer's poetic taste, often severely lacking, admitting the mystery of expressive excellence surviving critical rejection of the words set. 'The truth of the matter is that genuine poetry already contains its own music and will not tolerate any other'; it is poetic intention, realized through the musical setting, that comes through despite the banality of the words. Verdi is one of those who '*si contentano della situazione espressa in parole*' – not the *parole* themselves.

As befits a potential Nobel Prizeman already internationally acclaimed, Montale discloses an international musical, and literary, appetite. He praises George Gershwin, suggesting that if ever the United States should produce a genuine national operatic tradition, that same Jacob Gershovitz must be seen as '*il Glinka, l'iniziatore*'. The libretto of *The Rake's Progress* fascinates him, but, before the triumphant premiere at the Fenice in Venice, he doubts whether its diversity of styles – ranging from *Il Mikado* of Sullivan to *La Terra Desolata* of Eliot – can be matched musically even by Igor Stravinsky. At the performance – at which the composer–conductor bounces like a '*burattino di gomma*' and has a look of Benedetto Croce doubled over an ancient codex – the libretto seems to lose much of its modernist savour but gains in stylistic coherence. Then he wonders if it is less a matter of style than of technique – entities which Stravinsky likes to confound.

He is sympathetic to Walton's *Troilo e Cressida*, but finds the music basically insular, Latin only in its aspirations. He sees Britten's *Giro di Vite* or *Turn of the Screw* at Venice and finds its '*atmosfera viziata*' not far distant from that of Graham Greene (he is always ready with a surprising analogue: Gershwin's *An American in Paris* suggests

Hemingway's *Fiesta* to him), though he surmises Britten to be not a Catholic but a '*cristiano–pagano troublé*', an artist who needs to fish in dirty waters.

Montale writes a graceful journalistic prose unsullied by musical technicalities. He is not comparable with *Corno di Bassetto* in that he lacks the daring to anathematize the mediocre and is a little too ready to be pleased. He dutifully, against the grain one would think, accepts Wagner but finds few Italian voices able to cope with him. He is urbane, catholic, a delight to read, and it is to be hoped that this exhaustive collective of his *ritratti* will soon find an English translator. Apart from the distinction of its author, the book is an admirable guide to the whole operatic repertory.

Words Without Music

The Opera Libretto Library

I entered literature out of music, and quite by accident. I wished to write an opera on a fantastic tale I had discovered in Burton's *Anatomy of Melancholy* (Pt 3, Sec. 2, Mem. I, Subsec. I – the one about the young man who puts a ring on the finger of a statue of Venus and finds himself married to the goddess) and, encouraged by the examples of Wagner, Berlioz and Tippett, attempted my own libretto. It was far too long, so I converted it into a play. The play was too long, so I ended up with a novella. I found that I was no longer a musician but a writer of fiction.

I have never since tried again to rival da Ponte or Hofmannsthal, though Luciano Berio asked me to make an eight-page libretto which should combine *Il Trovatore*, *Rigoletto* and *La Forza del Destino* and yet confine characters and action to a kind of shelfwork of boxes. The brevity desired seemed excessive, but Berio was right in implying that no libretto can be too brief. Mozart suffered agonies from Metastasio's *Idomeneo*, which was terribly wordy and yet could not be cut without danger, since Metastasio was the Imperial Poet. It is no use, in our own day or just earlier, pointing to Wagner as a composer who approved long libretti and justified them in the musical execution. Wagner thought of himself as a poet (he is, incidentally, the poet most cited in *The Waste Land*) and wanted his audiences to admire the words as much as their setting, but there is not one of his operas which would not benefit by the lopping of about half the text. Here is the Landgrave in *Tannhäuser*:

> Minstrels asembled here, I give you greeting.
> Full oft within these walls your lays have sounded;
> In veiled wisdom, or in mirthful measures,
> They ever gladdened every listening heart.
> And though the sword of strife was loosed in battle,
> Drawn to maintain our German land secure,
> When 'gainst the southern foe we fought and conquered,
> And for our country braved the death of heroes,
> Unto the harp be equal praise and glory!

And so on, for another twenty lines. All that was needed was something like: 'Welcome, minstrels. You've sung of war. Now sing of love.'

The realization that, in opera, music is doing the real talking, while the words, like the titles of anecdotal paintings, merely specify the subject of the sonic discourse, has come late to librettists, though even non-literary composers have always had a vague idea of what they wanted. Montagu Slater's libretto for *Peter Grimes* is a model of brevity. 'Young prentice come,' sings Grimes. 'Young prentice home.' Wagner would have written something like 'Now that thou, who wouldst learn the skills and agonies of my ancient hard-won craft, art arrived here in this populous town after enduring the rigours of a lengthy journey. . . .' When Britten's orchestra starts its rumbling, the chorus merely sings 'Storm?'

But da Ponte knew all the tricks, and too few of his successors saw his greatness. From *Don Giovanni* you can learn two things – good colloquial Italian thoroughly viable today, and the capacity of that naturally prolix language to combine, in the hands of a master, the witty and the eloquent with the laconic. *Don Giovanni* is perhaps, with Verdi's *Falstaff*, the greatest opera we have and it is not just because of the beauty of the music. *Der Rosenkavalier* comes close, but even Hofmannsthal could be self-indulgently expansive. I have just been commissioned by the New York Met to convert *Der Rosenkavalier* into a novella (in my end is my beginning). I thought I would have to expand. I find that mostly I have to contract.

In this curious volume you will find no Hofmannsthal and only the one masterpiece of da Ponte. It is curious because it is not really a planned unity with a named editor but a mere stitching together of various libretti, in the original with translations, from various printed sources with a large and disconcerting typographical variety. All Wagner is here except *Rienzi*. There are *Faust, Fidelio* and *The Magic Flute* but also *Mignon* and *Lakmé*. *Cav* and *Pag* rub shoulders with *La Gioconda* (there's a bad libretto for you) and *Aida*. *Hansel and Gretel*, which has a very reasonable libretto, is here to remind us that Engelbert Humperdinck was no mean pop musician. In practically all instances the English translations are damnable.

Of course, the damnability is partly the result of the translator's having to follow the stresses and durations of the music. I had the task about fifteen years ago of translating Berlioz's *Enfance du Christ* for a Christmas television transmission. This is an oratorio not an opera, but the problems are no different, especially when rendering recitative. The French has '*Jésus*' with an accent on the second syllable; the English equivalent reverses the stress. What does one do? One changes the notes. This has evidently been done in the English translation of *Pelléas et Mélisande* which has recently earned such praise, and it is thoroughly legitimate. In practically all of the translations in this volume – all of them hackwork, pre- and sub-sub-sub-Audenian – there is a slavish adherence to the beat of the music though very rarely an understanding of the primary and secondary stress elements in English. Moreover, there is a Wardour Street jargon which rarely fails to be dismally comic. Here is Germont in *La Traviata*:

> Some day, when love hath colder grown,
> And time's broad gulf yawns wider;
> When all the joys of life have flown,
> What then will be? Consider!

Fidelio begins with Jacquino singing:

> At last, my idol, we are alone,
> And can have a pleasant chat together.

Hans Sachs sings after Walther's Trial Song:

> Ha! What a flow
> Of genius's glow!
> My Masters, pray now give o'er!
> Listen, when Sachs doth implore!

The way out is not to cling to the original. If the mass has been (mostly atrociously) vernacularized, opera should not, because of the ineptitude of libretto translators, claim a superior right of exemption. If we go to the opera we have a right to know what is being sung on the stage, and there was never any substance to the argument that English is not a singable language. Not singable, when we have *Dido and Aeneas* and *At the Boar's Head* and *The Rake's Progress*? Auden showed that Mozart's libretti could be translated superbly. The Arts Council or the various British opera trusts could do worse than organize contests for translations of the old warhorses of the repertory. Larkin and Amis would do well (Amis, incidentally, still owes me an opera libretto). Then the curtain would no longer have to go up on either

> *Blaue streifen*
> *stiegen im Westen auf*

or

> Bluish stripes
> are stretching along the west.

Operatics

Romantic Opera and Literary Form, by Peter Conrad
Literature as Opera, by Gary Schmidgall

R ichard Wagner coined for his own works the term 'music-drama', and Peter Conrad considers it to be an oxymoron. 'My argument is that music and drama are dubious, even antagonistic, partners and that opera's actual literary analogue is the novel.' There is sense in this. In opera, and most especially in Wagnerian opera, there is little room for dramatic action. The actors have to sing, not fight, make love, or indulge in aggressive stichomythia. Arias are single soliloquies, duets, trios and sextets multiple ones. To sing a thing takes longer than to say it, implying a kind of novelistic space for introspection. The orchestra, especially the Wagnerian one, stands for a huge complex of unspoken thought and feeling, often in contradiction to what is being phonated up there on the stage. Freud was uneasy about music, though a Viennese, since music was close to the id. The novel is the place for the id; the stage is all prancing egos.

Shakespeare was a key figure in that process which turned rococo opera into nineteenth-century music-drama. The romantic composers, from Berlioz to Verdi, saw Shakespeare as a novelist forced, by the cultural and economic circumstances of his time, to work in the theatre. They couldn't rewrite his plays as novels, but they could at least orchestrate them. Boito and Verdi made of *The Merry Wives of Windsor* the enacted novel on Falstaff that Shakespeare wasn't allowed to write. None of us doubt that the opera is superior to the play (as, in a smaller figure, *The Boys from Syracuse* is better than *The Comedy of Errors*). The Boito–Verdi Falstaff is no mere rutting buffoon. He is a knight and a soldier. The throbbing complexities of his mental life are all there in the orchestra. A hack job has been turned into a masterpiece.

Mr Conrad believes the culmination of the novelistic introversion of nineteenth-century opera was the symphonic poem. Human voices get in the way of introspection, which must be left wholly to the orchestra. Berlioz, in his *Roméo et Juliette*, indeed uses voices but not for the protagonists. Romeo and Juliet become orchestral instruments. Eventually Richard Strauss was to claim an unlimited capacity for novelistic mimesis without uttering a word. The whole of Cervantes's novel is in that fifty-minute set of orchestral variations, cello as the Don, viola as Sancho Panza, sheep, windwills, monks, madness all present. It takes a page or so for a novelist to show a character dying. Strauss does it with a single cello glissando.

Literature becomes music. Can music become literature? Mr Conrad shows how both Goethe's and Auden's dissatisfaction with Schikaneder's confused libretto for *The Magic Flute* drove them to the writing of sequels whose intellectual dignity, wit and allegorical consistency should match the genius of Mozart. In other words, the music *suggests* a literature that isn't there. Auden wrote libretti because he saw opera as the last refuge of the high style. It is outside Mr Conrad's thesis to consider how far the reduction of the music-drama to the symphonic poem can be logically followed by the expansion of the symphonic poem into the novel. My own feeling is that the future of the novel may well lie in its willingness to absorb the lessons of symphonic form.

But, as Mr Schmidgall reminds us, 'the study of literature and music is a sadly neglected field.' Professors of literature either hate music or despise it. Their opposite numbers in the music department can at least *read* literature, while they themselves regard a score as so much technical gibberish. As both literature and music use sounds set in forms characterized by such properties as exposition, development, climax, denouement, it would seem logical to study them together. Few students of *The Waste Land*, to my knowledge, are made to listen to Wagner. Shakespeare scholars are unexcited by the presence of an original six-note theme in a speech by Holofernes in *Love's Labour's Lost*. The ground where the two disciplines meet most amicably (or at least with the appearance of amity) is opera. Mr Schmidgall's book takes works for the stage from Handel to Benjamin Britten and examines the nature of the marriage, or forced yoking, between the two kinds of sound.

There have been a great number of operas based on libretti which had nothing literary about them. When an opera fails to survive it is usually because of a literary, rather than musical, insufficiency. It is not enlightening to examine the texts of *Oberon, Semiramide* and *Louise*. Great operas have a great literary provenance, like *Otello, Don Giovanni* and *Death in Venice*. The question Mr Schmidgall sets himself is: how far can the adaptation to musical form enhance an existing work of literature?

Many will say that there is usually a diminution, rather than an enhancement, of aesthetic effect. We have Thomas Mann's novella, and that's that. Let Visconti put it on the screen, and we have only the picturesque externals. Let Britten set it to music, and the notes get in the way of the words, there is a mere stylization of the *mise en scène*, at best the lily has gilt on it. The answer might be that words try to do what music alone can – that the non-Aschenbach world of sensuality that Tadzio evokes is preverbal; that the cholera that hits Venice is only expressible through the irrationality of organic noise; that Aschenbach's conflicts can be conveyed synchronically in music, but only diachronically in words. What music has and literature does not have is counterpoint. To get it into literature entailed the disruptive punning of *Finnegans Wake*. Literature can only *try* to be music; music can enclose literature. This brings us back to the symphonic poem.

Mr Schmidgall regrets that contemporary music is tearing itself away from the word. The avant-gardistes of Beaubourg in Paris want to explore the possibilities of music as sheer sound, to perform a brutal surgical operation on the sphere-born harmonious Siamese twins. And, he says, even with composers who don't despise words, there is no urge to accommodate operatic form to contemporary literature. This tends to confirm the lowbrow's view of opera as a dead scene, full of unreal, irrelevant, romantic posturing. But Mr Schmidgall forgets Michael Tippett, as he forgets Hindemith's *News of the Day* and, for that matter, Menotti's *The Consul*. I myself, who have suffered both sonic disciplines, have produced an operatic version of *Ulysses* called *The Blooms of Dublin*. *Ulysses* is unique in having a professional soprano and a near-professional tenor, as well as a host of good amateurs, in its dramatis personae. But nobody wants my *Singspiel*. Opera houses are not yet ready despite Peter Hall's production of *Moses and Aaron*, for the onstage blatant prancings of the id.

Wagner in Brown

The Diary of Richard Wagner, 1865–1882, edited by Joachim Bergfield, translated by George Bird

This is the famous Brown Book, given by Cosima von Bülow to Richard Wagner for the notation of his feelings about her in absence, or rather its contents, the original being calf-bound, jewel-studded, metal-locked. Those contents are for the first time published in their entirety. Wagner being Wagner, there is as much cosmos as Cosima, as well as poems for King Ludwig, attacks on anti-Wagnerians, scraps of music and, as a bonus, those Annals out of which *Mein Leben* was written. There is also the first outline of *Parsifal*.

Cosima was the second of the three illegitimate daughters given to Franz Liszt by the Comtesse Marie d'Agoult. She married Hans von Bülow, pianist, conductor, Wagnerian, Liszt's favourite pupil, but Wagner cuckolded the patient von Bülow and had two children by Cosima before she could get a divorce. One of these children was Eva, named for the heroine of *Die Meistersinger*, and it was Eva, who became wife of the notorious Houston Stewart Chamberlain, who bequeathed the book, her mother's own bequest to her, to the Richard Wagner Gedenkstätte in Bayreuth. Like many another pious relict of a great man, Eva was not happy about granting even 'trustworthy persons' the right to gloat over his weaknesses or indiscretions, so she destroyed fourteen pages of the book, pasted over another five to ensure illegibility, but, in recompense, carefully inked over some pencil entries for their better preservation. Cosima herself destroyed nothing written by Wagner, except some of the letters he wrote to Mathilde Wesendonck. There have been very few female relicts of great men who were or are not in some measure enemies of the whole truth.

In 1865, when Wagner pens his first entry on the lines of 'I love you with an ultimate love', the lovers were separated for the first time: Cosima had to go with Hans to Hungary, calling in Austria on the way. Wagner writes: 'Ah, what madness! What madness! And that fool Hans who wouldn't let you go to Penzing and showed you the shops of Vienna instead!' (Wagner had lived in Penzing, a suburb of Vienna, from 1863 to 1864: Cosima had wished to see his lodgings, already sacred.) 'Can one believe it? Can one believe it? And this, if you please, is my one friend! Ah, foolish hearts! Blind eyes!' and so on. It will be seen that Wagner has a rather one-sided notion of friendship. As for love, it finds what one has to term very Teutonic expression (meaning full of references to eternity and destiny and the soul), and not only to Cosima. In 1864, when Wagner had already vowed deathless devotion to her, he was writing to young Mathilde Maier in most affectionate terms – 'My dearest love. . . . go on loving me. . . . With heartfelt kisses from your R. W.' On 18 August 1865 he has an entry in the Brown Book about Cosima's jealousy. Eva carefully pasted this over, but Dr Bergfeld has kindly unpasted it. 'Good morning, naughty child!' writes roguish Richard, 'What a nasty letter you wrote me yesterday! And now poor M. M. has to come in for it again!' *Und so weiter.*

In 1869 Wagner and Cosima, with tiny Isolde and Eva and Siegfried on the way, were happily bedded down in the house in Tribschen. Now, at fifty-five, Wagner purrs like a great cat, madly joyous, and is able to compose something quite unWagnerian. It is a cradlesong with the words

Schlaf, Kindchen, schlafe;
im Garten geh'n zwei Schafe:
ein schwarzes und ein weisses. . . .

If baby will not sleep the black sheep will bite him, her, it. The music is in simple four-part harmony (leading note moving the wrong way) and it is penned in his characteristic clear strong script. This became part of the *Siegfried Idyll* which was played on Christmas morning, also Cosima's birthday, 1870, heard by Nietzsche and beautifully staged by Visconti in his Ludwig film. From now until 1882, the year before Wagner's death, the Brown Book can be used not for plaints to the distant beloved but for verses, schemata, aphorisms. The verses include

Heil! Heil dem Kaiser!
König, Wilhelm!
Allen Deutschen Hort und Freiheitswehr!

and the aphorisms such banalities as 'The oddity of the genius in this world can be very well judged of from the stupid questions he is asked.'

I have just been reading Ronald Hayman's excellent *Nietzsche: A Critical Life*, where we see the Tribschen ménage from the outside and are compelled to compare the two men as thinkers, if not as composers. (Nietzsche's musical *oeuvre* has recently been played through in Milan: he is always competent, very unoriginal but quite unWagnerian). In the glow of Nietzsche's first adoration, Wagner seems an intellectual giant. The Brown Book shows a glib and fluent poet, always ready with a birthday ode for Ludwig, and a mediocre thinker. He reads widely but unsystematically; he has halfbaked progressive ideas; he is a sort of Colin Wilson with musical genius.

But get Wagner away from *Seele* and *Schicksal* and on to the interpretation of his own art and he becomes authoritative and absorbing. Perhaps the person who meant most to him was the *Heldentenor* Ludwig Schnorr von Carolsfeld, the first Tristan, who died young and is the subject of a fine eulogy which Wagner put into the Brown Book and later into the *Neue Zeitschrift für Musik*. 'The orchestra disappeared vis-à-vis the singer, or, more correctly, seemed to be included in this perfor-mance.' Wagner is shrewd and lucid and practical when he talks of the new *Uebermensch* kind of singer who, 'under the inevitably acknowledged leadership of German musical art' (viz. Wagner), will require intellect as well as voice. But we always seem to be on our guard when reading Wagner, fearful that, even when discussing the range of the Wagner tuba, he may suddenly turn abstract or chauvinist or, eye on the main chance, exalt the 'high-minded Sovereign' who was really a hysterical boy.

Perhaps Hitler, another high-minded adorer of Wagner, has made us oversensitive to the proto-Nazi elements in the prose and poetry, if not in the music. The music is harmless, I think, even when Hans Sachs is telling the guilds to honour German art: there is more dangerous imperi-alism in the 'Pomp and Circumstance' marches than in the 'Entry of the Masters'. The fantastic anti-Semitism which Wagner was, in 1882, to impose on the plot of *Parsifal* but which is not yet present in the outline of the Brown Book, leaves that gorgeous score untouched. If we excuse Wagner's anti-Semitism on the grounds of Meyerbeer's success in Paris and his own failure there (which turned all the French into Jews), we have to excuse Nazi genocide on the same grounds – the artistic failures of Hitler and Goebbels and their envy of brilliant Jewish painters and playwrights. Wagner ought at least to have been suspicious, as a univer-sal artist, of his own racist theories. But our trepidation in turning these pages derives from an unfair hindsight. If I saw that biting black sheep as an SS officer that is not Wagner's fault.

The translation seems adequate, but I don't think Schopenhauer's *Vorstellung* should be rendered as 'conception'. The book itself is neces-sary to Wagnerians, but it is not, meaning the man himself, all that attractive. Wagner is too arrogant and high-souled for British tastes, insufficiently Pooterish. But that's true even of Goethe.

All Too English?

An Elgar Companion, edited by Christopher Redwood
Elgar the Man, by Michael De-la-Noy

I prepared for the writing of this review, apart from reading the books, by listening to a recording of Elgar's Second in E flat played by the USSR Symphony Orchestra under Yevgeny Svetlanov. The question I was asking was: is Elgar exportable? Or, more pertinently, could the music of a neurotic conservative Edwardian make sense to the children of a failed socialist revolution? Judging from the scant applause at the end, the work had not made much sense. The interpretation itself strikes me as being insufficiently tentative and nervous: the first move-ment sounds like rejoicing in Red Square, with the odd quiet interval of brooding on the beauty of the personality of Lenin. This may be over fanciful. Perhaps if I had come innocently to the disc and been told the performance was British I might have accepted it (although knowing it was not Boult in charge), but I would have known that the brass instru-ments were not made in the West. The socialist economy has achieved some damnably tinny trumpets.

The truth is that Elgar used to export – to France and Germany as well as to Czarist Russia. The Germans saw the greatness of *Gerontius* before the British did (that execrable first performance – fully recounted in both books – was a huge setback). Elgar had a number of Continental decorations as well as the OM and (the donors knew he had no son) a barren baronetcy. His alleged insularity seems to be a myth of late manufacture. If he is all-English, one wants to know how exactly. Can racial elements reside in pure sound that does not set out to evoke Ancient and Modern or clodhopping on the village green? Neville Cardus, in this excellent *Elgar Companion*, compares Mahler and Elgar, finding in the former personal emotion that might be embarrassing if we are British, in the latter emotions appropriate to public celebration – a king's death, a victory in the Transvaal. Plenty of musicians hear the dropping of Worcestershire pippins in *Falstaff*. I know that Elgar is not manic enough to be Russian, not witty or *pointilliste* enough to be French, not harmonically simple enough to be Italian and not stodgy enough to be German. We arrive at his Englishry by pure elimination. That he was a great composer (hence of international significance) we ought to have no doubt.

The *Companion* is an anthology of reminiscences and assessments we have read before, but it is good to have them together. The Enigma of the *Variations* gets thirty-two pages, complete with 'Auld Lang Syne' in the minor trying woefully to be a counterpoint to the great noble theme.

The man who devised ciphers in the First World War liked his mysteries. The Violin Concerto has an epigraph from Le Sage's preface to *Gil Blas*: *'Aqui està encerrada el alma de. . . .'* Mr De-la-Noy thinks that soul belonged to Alice Stuart-Wortley, whom Elgar called 'Windflower', and that the guilt of the widower Elgar (though all widowers are guilty, being murderers) had much to do with his capacity for loving everybody except his own wife.

Mr De-la-Noy's biography is notable for being the first to be written since the death of Elgar's daughter Carice Blake in 1970. Rosa Burley's sometimes bitchy memoir, already written then, could not be published: 'it quite simply contains comments and judgements upon Elgar and his relations with his wife that no daughter would have wanted to read.' This new biography, which draws on that memoir as on others, is very candid about the relationship. Alice Elgar, older than her husband, idolized his music in a manner both encouraging and embarrassing, especially to strangers, sent the chilled Elgar to bed with seven hot water bottles and woolly bedsocks, but does not seem to have accorded him more substantial comforts in bed. Elgar could be passionate enough in his music, but Lady Elgar never fired his passion. There was a curious *ménage à trois* that lasted many years, in which Dora Penny – the 'Dorabella' of the *Variations* – stayed up with the composer till all hours while his wife retired early, but the piano seems to have been banging away all the time (it comforted Lady Elgar and probably reassured her) and there is no record of Dorabella's being thrown to the floor.

Elgar's sexual life remains dimmer than that of Shaw – the close friend who emerges, in both books, as the only man not of the family who never doubted Elgar's greatness. He wrote to Jaeger (Nimrod) in affectionate terms which did not preclude the odd 'darling', but there was no homosexuality there: Elgar went along with the judgement of his second royal master, who thought that 'men like that shot themselves'. There was no bohemianism in Elgar's life, though there was much manic depression. Although he became a public figure who pretended that music was bosh and only dogs and horses worthwhile, he could behave like a failed poet nail-biting in the Yorkminster. Some of his public pronouncements, especially those attacking British philistinism, gave grave offence, and his professorial tenure at Birmingham – in a chair specially endowed for him – was a disaster. The nastiness of the great man, given the *una corda* treatment by previous adoring memoirs, especially that of the violinist W. H. Reed, comes out here, but the great man's greatness is not seriously diminished.

The greatness, as always with artists, lies only in the art, which may be termed patrician and plebeian but hardly at all middle clas. As a man Elgar was a typical victim of the British class system. His father was a tradesman and he himself began his career as a poor teacher and orchestral player – a ragged usher and a damned fiddler. His craving for state honours was pathetic: he wanted the barony that only Britten among composers got, and got when he was dying. He wanted intimacy with the royal family, though he knew that neither Edward nor George cared a damn about music. His sense of victimization, which could come out even when he wore his state kneebreeches and flashed his medals, found the inevitable economic expression: he was a poor man considering the necessity of taking up violin teaching again even in honoured middle age. It seems true that he did not have much money, but, like Mozart in Auden's poem, he never had to make his own bed and there was always a team of servants, including a cook and a valet-chauffeur. It was no paranoia that made him brood on neglect in his old age. The seventieth birthday concert had a wretched attendance. Mr De-la-Noy is too young to remember his death in 1934 (that was a bad spring for music: Gustav Holst and Frederick Delius also died), but I remember that the popular papers remembered him only as the composer of 'Land of Hope and Glory'. But his work is secure now, except, bafflingly, on the Continent.

Hans Keller, who cannot often be trusted to show much more than well-informed bad temper, said a perspicacious thing in 1957: 'Continental audiences will come to understand Elgar's innovations *via* Britten, just as a twelve-noting pupil of mine has come to understand Wagner *via* Schoenberg.' Keller is right to see Elgar's genius as innovative. Perhaps the Second Symphony was too revolutionary for the baffled Soviet audience on my record of Svetlanov and his tin trumpets.

S. Without G.

Arthur Sullivan – A Victorian Musician, by Arthur Jacobs

A French *philosophe* recently pointed out that, while the French love triplets (*Liberté, Egalité, Fraternité*, for instance), the British prefer pairs – eggs and bacon, Fortnum and Mason, Crosse and Blackwell, *Dieu et Mon Droit*, Burgess and Maclean, Gilbert and Sullivan. It is rarely that a writer dares devote a book to the latter half of this last doublet or couplet, and Dr Jacobs, having done precisely that and at length too, in doing it demonstrates why. For what of Sir Arthur Sullivan's still stands without the prop of William Schenck Gilbert's inspired dementia? Very little, alas. There is the hymn 'Onward, Christian, Soldiers'. The sacred song 'The Lost Chord' can only be performed parodically or recalled in Jimmy Durante's disc about the guy who found it. The big choral works – *The Golden Legend, The Martyr of Antioch* – provoked ecstasy when presented at the triennial Leeds Festivals, but nobody hears them now. The macaronically named *Overture di Ballo* and the incidental music to Shakespeare get an occasional hearing, but even in the Savoy operas, Sullivan is being so transformed as to be robbed of his essence. The recently acclaimed Joe Papp version of *The Pirates of Penzance* retains little more than his melodic line, and the various travesties of *The Mikado* have syncopated even that out of easy recognition. Yet Sullivan in his day was considered to be England's answer to Mozart, Mendelssohn, Spohr and Weber, all impeccably packaged into one moral tasteful essentially Victorian whole. England, having done well enough in literature and conquered a large part of the earth with Birmingham guns in order to make it accept Manchester goods, needed a great composer. Sullivan, it seems, was the only man available.

The mention of Spohr in that list above points to the fallibility of aesthetic judgement. Gilbert makes his Mikado propose punishing music-hall singers by making them hear 'masses and fugues and ops by Bach interwoven with Spohr and Beethoven'. Few had any doubt of Spohr's greatness. Occasional performances of his works on the radio have recently surprised listeners with their revelation of a masterly almost Mendelssohnian talent, but no revolution of standards could place him with Beethoven or Bach. Yet, knowing the shakiness of some contemporary judgements (the Beatles, Andy Warhol, Christopher Fry), we must not deride the Victorians for thinking too highly of Sullivan. British music had been occluded by the great Germans who followed the Hanoverians to London, and what listeners heard in Sullivan was the revival of a native quality lost since Purcell, allied to a technique learned in Leipzig and hence not to be despised by Europe.

The trouble was that the musical establishment was not content with accepting that great musical skill could sometimes find its best expression in the lighter forms. The British proletariat was being kept out of mischief by being formed into brass bands and choral societies, and the huge choirs of the provinces had to be further uplifted by being made to sing oratorios. The duty of British composers was to provide these; if they could, as a sideline, produce the odd symphony so much the better: the moral power of Beethoven was well known and the English, being a more moral people than the Germans, ought to produce symphonies morally if not musically better than his. Poor Sullivan was dragged by an imposed sense of duty, which soon became an inner conviction of responsibility to his own talent, into fields where his deficiencies were nakedly exposed. This did not happen in his prime, but it began to happen when the real British musical renascence began – with the advent of the brilliant, self-taught, neurotic, ambiguous Elgar. Sullivan, though he died young (at only fifty-eight), lived to see it.

Dr Jacobs' very detailed biography – which draws lavishly on Sullivan's letters and diaries – records successes and failures in areas where superficial readings of his career have taught us to believe otherwise. None of the Savoy operas did as well as Cellier's *Dorothy*, which is now forgotten. Sullivan's solitary excursion into grand opera – *Ivanhoe* – flopped only because D'Oyly Carte overexposed it. Comic operas that Sullivan composed with librettists other than Gilbert – *Hadden Hall*, for instance – did not do noticeably worse than the mythic collaborations. Sullivan made a lot of money and gambled much of it away. His career must be accounted an overall success, however posterity is forced to judge it. He gave the Victorians what they wanted and, apart from musical fulfilment, he got a lot out of life – close friendship with royalty, acclaim in Germany (where the future Kaiser would quote from the First Lord's song in *Pinafore*), the willingness of France to pamper him for money if not for music (France still cannot understand what all the G. and S. fuss is about) and, not previously disclosed, a satisfactory if adulterous sexual life with the American beauty Mary Frances Ronalds.

Inevitably, with his attempt to concentrate wholeheartedly on the life and career of Sullivan, Jacobs cannot permit Gilbert to upstage him. There is no room for Gilbert's wit, scabrous and otherwise, though there has to be plenty of room for letters between the two men, if only to show what a fine letter writer Sullivan was, as well as an outstanding diarist. His writings confirm what others said about him – that he was good, kind, urbane, courteous, and a terribly hard worker. Anyone who has ever produced an orchestral score will appreciate what Sullivan's labour was like – the long nights with twenty-odd-stave paper, dotting in his notes with exquisite neatness and the speed of shorthand, his fingers stained with incessant cigarette smoking, always – like Mozart – fighting to meet a deadline.

Unfortunately there is no space in this book to do more than indicate generally the greatness of Sullivan's talent, as opposed to his genius. The genius is in the melodies, which we all know by heart; the talent lay in what the orchestra was doing while the melodies looked after themselves – the odd sly touches like the citation of a Bach fugue when the Mikado mentions the 'ops', the contrapuntal brilliance, the capacity to make even the accompaniment to a patter song live its own organic life. Offenbach's scores are dull. With the coming of the Broadway musical orchestration became an affair of hacks (except for Kurt Weill). No composer of light music has ever, except for Sullivan, brought to it the loving attention to detail which could only be learned in the tough serious school of the symphony and oratorio. *The Mikado* is not just superb entertainment; it is exquisite craftsmanship of an almost Mozartian order. When America pirated his works, Sullivan was pained because he knew what New York and Boston audiences were missing, hearing as they were nothing more than a vamped pit-band transcription of the vocal score. If Sullivan was not a great composer, at least he was technically equipped to become one.

Unfortunately he was a Victorian. This meant that he had to be respectable, and musical respectability meant abiding by harmonic rules and formal restrictions sanctified by Higgs, Prout, Goss and other pundits the world has forgotten. He realized what Wagner had done in the opening bars of *Tristan*, but he did not dare to follow that path. Gilbert's librettos – more subversive and sexually perverse than the audiences guessed – were his substitute for musical daring. When he dared, he could always go back to the Leeds Festival or dash off a religious motet, but the daring was, anyway, only vicarious. Bernard Shaw, most brilliant music critic of that age, saw what was going on:

> He furtively set *Cox and Box* to music in 1867 and then, overcome with remorse, produced *Onward, Christian Soldiers*, and over three dozen hymns besides. As the remorse mellowed, he composed a group of songs – 'Let Me Dream Again', 'Thou'rt Passing Hence', 'Sweethearts', and 'My Dearest Heart' – all of the very best in their *genre*, such as it is. And yet in the very thick of them he perpetrated *Trial by Jury*, in which he outdid Offenbach in wickedness, and that too without any prompting from the celebrated cynic, Mr W. S. Gilbert. . . . They trained him to make Europe yawn; and he took advantage of their teaching to make London and New York laugh and whistle.

Whatever he achieved, he did his best work with the celebrated cynic. Chiefly, probably, because Gilbert was the most accomplished lyricist who ever lived. The moral pundits would have preferred him to work with the Poet Laureate, whose comic fairies were to sing this sort of thing:

TITANIA: Nip her not, but let her snore.
            We must flit for evermore.
1ST FAIRY: Tit, my Queen, must it be so?
            Wherefore, wherefore should we go?
TITANIA: And you dare to call me Tit?
            Tit for love, thou naughty lob,
            Wouldst thou call my Oberon Ob?

The author of *The Bugger's Opera*, whose obscene cast list finds a place in Joyce's *Ulysses*, would never have ordered his musician to set such innocent dirt. The gust remains dual, as in Crosse and Blackwell. Dr Jacobs must write a companion book on Gilbert and, later, bind it with this.

A Short Short While

The Days Grow Short: The Life and Music of Kurt Weill, by Ronald Sanders

Both the title and the dust-cover photograph – Weill rehearsing *One Touch of Venus* with Mary Martin perched on the piano – seem to promise or threaten the man of Broadway more than the man of Berlin and Brecht. That may well be the way Weill would have wanted it. When Walter Huston sang 'September Song' in *Knickerbocker Holiday* and brought the house down, there was, in Maxwell Anderson's lyric, a quiet celebration of change: the long long while or *Langeweile* from May to December contradicted the composer's name, which means short while. Weill wanted to be a man of the New York musical theatre; he wanted to be an American. This entailed ceasing to be the kind of subversive German who could write a *Dreigroschenoper* or a *Mahagonny*. When Louis Armstrong sang 'Mack the Knife' it was with 'corrected' harmonies: the abrasive became bland. Broadway did not exactly ruin Weill. To the end he remained ingenious, inventive and highly professional, the only stage composer who scored his own scores instead of giving them to a hack. Listen to one of those scores, however, and you hear the Broadway sound more or less imposed by the Musicians' Union. Then listen to the *Dreigroschenoper* prelude, with its harsh wind and harmonium: that is the real Weill. It is America more than the liberated Germanies that, since his death at fifty in 1950, has vigorously promoted the real Weill. There are no revivals of *Street Scene* or *Lady in the Dark*. 'September Song' remains a classic pop single (with the words usually wrong: *I'll* instead of *I'd*) but its provenance is forgotten and authorship disregarded. Weill is, as he must be, bracketed with Hindemith, not Gershwin. His jazz is *schmutzig*, not *schmalzy*. He is probably one of the great twentieth-century European composers.

It is assumed, chiefly by those, meaning most of us, who have no chance to hear Weill's purely instrumental works, that without Brecht he would have been nothing. It is truer to say that Weill was essentially a vocal composer, a *Singspiel* man who adored *The Magic Flute* and needed strong lyrics and librettists. In Brecht he found the poet he needed: that Brecht needed Weill is less certain. Indeed, it is probable that, if he had promoted his own musical talent beyond mere guitar-strumming, Brecht could have composed the two major operas entire. He knew music: he delighted in such unfingerable guitar chords as C-sharp minor and E-flat major. The tune of the 'Alabama Song' and the opening bars of 'Macki Messer' are his. But the increasing didacticism of his work for the stage demanded less music and more rant. The trouble with music is not merely that it cannot be political: it transcends faction and expresses abiding human situations which show up political propaganda as mere verbiage. Brecht saw the city of Mahagonny as the doomed capitalist state; to Weill it was merely a place where people were greedy.

Weill had already been long settled in America and was making application for citizenship when Brecht, after exiled sojourns in Prague, Sweden and Finland, suddenly appeared in New York and asked Weill's approval of a proposed all-black *Threepenny Opera*. Weill took fright at once. He did not wish his old communist associations to be known in the Land of the Free. He was a true musician in that he had no intellectual pretensions. If America held up to him the mirror it presents to all exiles, it was to show him that he was a Jew – something he had not much thought of before – and to remind him that he was the son of a cantor. Weill wrote liturgical Jewish music and a huge score for an American extravaganza about the sufferings of the diaspora, but Broadway taught him to be the kind of Jewish composer that Gershwin and Irving Berlin already were – drawn to the yearning music of black slaves, not the funkier jazz that fed the Berlin collaborations with Brecht, and very ready to deracinate and commercialize it. Hitler taught many renegade Jews to recover their heritage: such a recovery did not necessarily make for better art. It was a bad thing for Weill to wish to forget that he was a German.

Brecht's presence and even absence serve to supply the image of an intellectual rigour which would otherwise be lacking in this account of Weill's career. The American phase of it is altogether too showbiz. The source of *One Touch of Venus* is Anstey's Victorian novella, not Florilegus or *The Anatomy of Melancholy*. Over Weill's grave Maxwell Anderson recited words that, along with the music, are inscribed on that grave:

> This is the life of men on earth:
> Out of darkness we come at birth
> Into a lamplit room, and then –
> Go forward into dark again

– schmalzy, very inferior to the moving original of Bede's *Ecclesiastical History*. Weill's American career was a kind of higher schmalz. Lotte Lenya, his brilliant wife, found as little to do in America as Brecht himself: only with the American rediscovery of the great early works was the magic of her voice appreciated; her skill as an actress found an outlet only in films like *From Russia with Love*. Brecht, having covered himself with glory as a witness before the McCarthy committee, went back to dirty decadent Europe. If Weill had lived to a reasonable age it is doubtful whether he would have yearned for the days of his greatness: it was more important to be a good American than to be a distinguished international composer.

Ronald Sanders is a good American himself. A specialist in Jewish cultural history, he is well qualified to stress the ambiguous relationship between Weill and his cantor father and pick out the ancestral elements in the music. On the other hand, he is not able to do for that music what his subtitle seems to promise. The Busonian elements in Weill are important, but we have to be shown what they are in specific illustrations. There is nothing here set out in music type; there is not even the most superficial formal analysis of any of the instrumental works. It is not, in fact, a book for musicians but for aficionados of Broadway. Nor is it well written. It is alternately ponderous and breezy and there are some very exotic syntactical structures. Mr Sanders is, however, kind enough to express a debt to the work of David Drew and the 'monumental study of Weill' that he has still to complete. We must go on waiting for that work: Mr Sanders' book only serves to whet the impatience of Weillians.

Hitter Out

Drum Roll, by James Blades

Jimmy Blades has been heard by nearly everybody in the world. It was he who, on African drums, beat the V for Victory signal of BBC radio during the war. It is he who makes the noise when, at start of a J. Arthur Rank film, Bombardier Billy Wells is seen striking a gong. Serious musicians know his *Percussion Instruments and Their History* (Faber & Faber), the definitive work on the subject. After fifty years in the business, he is the doyen of British percussionists. His autobiography goes, wisely I think, unedited. An American editor would have tidied up the solecisms and destroyed an ebullience very rare these days in the memoirs of showbiz personalities, who often think they have a duty to literature. This story of the life of one of four brother drummers, from rags to circus to cinema pit to, at length, virtuoso of the Bartók sonata for pianos and percussion and special effects adviser to everyone (including Benjamin Britten), is a great delight.

Orchestras are built on injustice. The flautist carries a little case around, while the percussion player has to be responsible for four kettledrums, bass drum, side drum, tubular bells, xylophone, marimba, vibraphone, triangle, tam-tam, Chinese blocks, whip, tambourine and, if he is playing in Hindemith's *News of the Day*, typewriter, anvil for Wagner or the *Gurrelieder*, wind machine for *Don Quixote* and the *Sinfonia Antartica*, and many more. I recognize that, in full symphonic orchestras, there is some division of responsibility in the kitchen department, but the burdens are still heavy enough. In chamber orchestras, like those used by Britten in his later operas, the weight of providing a great deal of the 'colour' falls on one man. It has usually been Jimmy Blades, a Puck-like figure, non-smoker, teetotaller, vegetarian, a demon for work.

Beethoven, until he arrived at the 'Turkish music' in the finale of his Ninth, was content with a tonic and dominant on the kettledrums. There are many who say that the multiplication of percussive colour that came in with Wagner and, more so, with Richard Strauss has done music no good. This view is based on a very primitive notion of what percussion is about: it is not pure punctuation, italicizing, the adding of exclamation marks; it is a mode of expression as old as music itself, and some of the 'new' refinements we find in Boulez and Stockhausen are really returns to old, and very subtle, percussive devices from civilizations that the music of the Enlightenment chose to ignore. The percussion department may be at the back of the orchestra, but the importance of Jimmy Blades's department is frontal enough, and his autobiography ought to be accorded at least as much respect as Yehudi Menuhin's.

His story covers the whole musical field, from the Saturday-night gig to grand opera, and its evaluation of the musicians met on the way is highly democratic. The composer of *The Dream of Olwen* is a fine musician, and so is Stravinsky (whose *L'Histoire du Soldat*, thinks Jimmy, has a really admirable percussion part). Charlie Kunz, with whom Jimmy often played, is another fine musician, and thus a myth which has baffled me from the start is perpetuated. The tale was told in Manchester of Artur Schnabel's being refused admission at the artist's entrance of the Free Trade Hall and, on saying who he was, being told: 'I don't care if you're bloody Charlie Kunz, you can't come in here.' Charlie Kunz, by all accounts a delicate, delightful, generous man, was a schoolgirl-type player of popular sheet music as written. His popularity was immense. He is duly here, among the giants.

But it is not Jimmy Blades's job to evaluate according to the higher aesthetics. A practical musician has to think of the end with which he is presented, and for which he is paid, and to judge musicianship in terms of how efficiently that end is attained. A professional player will do as well for the eight bars of 'tabs' music he is given in the music-hall pit as he will for *Wozzeck*, and his judgements on the music will have more to do with practical playability than with spiritual transports. Some of the musical problems with which Jimmy Blades has been faced – chiefly in the devising of expressive sounds for films or for Britten's later operas – may strike the highbrow mere listener as trivial, but of course, from the view of a serious professional, they are not. When Chaplin was affixing soundtracks to his newly edited early films, he wanted 'a "tick tock" effect to dramatize the situation where an officer was intently watching the second hand of his wrist watch awaiting zero hour'.

'Not wood blocks – something really sinister', I was told. The sound that most pleased C. C. was when I placed a small cymbal on a small kettledrum and a larger cymbal on a large kettledrum, and struck the cymbals gently with coins. The difference in the size of my cymbals and the resonance of the drums produced a rather uncanny tick-tock. 'I'll have thirty seconds of that,' said the maestro.

Jimmy is equally fascinating when he describes the contrivance of that memorable heart beat which is to be heard in the battlements scene of Olivier's *Hamlet*. A stethophonic recording of a real heart was 'like someone consuming thick soup with a rhythmic intake', so finally Vivian Leigh's fur coat was draped over a bass drum and Jimmy prodded with his finger tips. In one of the first TV commercials, Jimmy earned £12 by crinkling a five-pound note in his hand in rumba rhythm, successfully simulating the sizzle of sausages. For the ultimate in fascinating triviality, take the progressive inflation which has overtaken the coin throb on kettledrums in the penultimate variation of the *Enigma*. It used to be pennies, then it went up to half-crowns, now it's 50p pieces. Jimmy does it with guilders given to him in Holland by an Old Fagin-like man who remembered his wartime V signal.

The non-musical reader of these memoirs will be amazed by the amount of work done – in the days when the tax situation made hard work worthwhile – by the professional musicians of England. The average working week of Jimmy Blades – film studio to dance-band dais to recording studio to symphony concert – called for a stamina and a devotion to duty that are now probably outlawed by the unions. Ending his book at the age of seventy, Jimmy asks for another twenty-five years to do the things he still wants to do. I would like to hear him play the percussion score I wrote for the Minneapolis production of *Cyrano de Bergerac* – sizzle cymbal slowly raised out of water, kitchen-utensil glockenspiel, cymbal placed on chromatic kettledrum and soft-rolled while the drum emits a slow glissando. He has probably done these things, and more. He has also banged out a melodious book.

The Maestro Heresy

I know what the notes mean just by looking at them. I can read an orchestral score with as much pleasure as a novel – probably more. Probably more because the eye has more to do, the seat of human engagement is sealed off, I'm away from the world of sex, violence and politics, I'm into an empyrean of pure form. Being a sort of musician, I am, I think, immune to the heresy which afflicts the pure music lover – that of making the mere interpreter of music into a god. Opera singers from Tetrazzini to Callas and beyond have been called *diva* – goddess. This indicates the scope of the heresy. The rewards for the *diva* have been manifold and extravagant – the harnessing of her coach to the adoring shoulders of those made delirious by her high Cs, the drinking of champagne from her sweaty slipper, the fan club and the private jet. Then there are the conductors, of whom Karajan may be taken as the prime living, though ageing, example: body servants await while the applause deafens, ready with beef tea and a change of shirt; the airport has been warned, the police are ready to keep the roads to it clear. All this for the man who wags the stick. All that for the vocal machine which doesn't understand all that well what it's doing. Meanwhile the composer, who is, if not a god, at least married to the Muse, is elbowed out of the way by the photographers.

We celebrate this year (1982) the centenary of the birth of Igor Stravinsky. He was a very great composer who feared the cult of the interpreter. There was a time in his career when he wanted to hand over his piano music to a mechanical instrument, to keep the interpreter out. He insisted that his tempi be sustained mechanically, without expressive rubato, that his dynamic marks be scrupulously observed, that 'expression' as a superadded spice be omitted from the plain meal of his music. He adored no singer, violinist or conductor – these were the mere necessary conditions for turning musical thought into physical reality.

When I was a boy I used regularly to go to the concerts of the Hallé Orchestra in Manchester. This orchestra was, at that time, the finest in Europe, though concert subscribers prevented it from giving of its best by denying it such expansive experiences as playing *Le Sacre du Printemps* or Schoenberg's Five Orchestral Pieces. The orchestra was forced to stick to the two Bs, Beethoven and Brahms with occasional bloody chunks of butcher's meat out of Wagner – otherwise audiences would stay away. On one occasion, to my joy, a performance of an advanced work by the Russian Mossolov was announced. I turned up and, to my chagrin, could not get in. Artur Schnabel was playing the *Emperor Concerto*, and the Mossolov had been merely sneaked into the programme because, with Schnabel playing, it would not harm the box office. But I did not wish to hear Schnabel and the *Emperor*: I knew that damned concerto by heart. I wanted Mossolov, though those who got in did not. There was another occasion when a student from the Manchester Royal College of Music played, to a near-empty house, the little-known piano concerto of Frederick Delius. That, to me, was worth all the visits of Schnabel and Horowitz and Rubinstein put together. I became convinced that the adorers of the great interpreters were philistines, and I have not since been seriously shaken in that conviction.

Let me be honest and admit that it is not enough just to read the music of a symphony or oratorio or song cycle and, hearing a kind of ideal performance inside one's skull, consider that one has had a genuine musical experience. Beethoven was limited to this purely cerebral audition, and a stupid school of musical thinkers once existed, headed by the critic Ernest Newman which asserted that what was good enough for Beethoven was good enough for the rest of us. Music, said Newman, should be what John Keats called a matter of hearing ditties of no tone: the sensual ear was a labyrinthine snare which vitiated the purity of what the composer had put on to paper. There was a British music critic named Cecil Gray who wrote a cantata based on Flaubert's *La Tentation de Saint-Antoine* which he did not wish to have performed, lest gross external sound should sully the ghostly purity of it. There was a very well-known work by Bernard van Dieran, the *Chinese Symphony*, which every London musician knew from the score but no one ever heard and, so far as I know, no one has ever heard in the sixty years since its composition. It used to be thought that Bach wrote most of his works for the sake of writing them and, without the benefit of performance, shoved them into a drawer to be forgotten. All this goes too far.

I would be foolish not to wish to go to a recital of Schubert lieder by Fischer-Dieskau. *Die Schöne Müllerin* has to be heard: we need the physical impact of the sounds, and emotion will not be easily stirred otherwise: the notes on the page cry out for incarnation in the vocal cords and the chords of the keyboard. But why Fischer-Dieskau and not some well-meaning tyro from a music school? Because, we believe, Fischer-Dieskau has a profound insight into the structure of the music and the manner in which this relates to the meaning of the words. Because he possesses a superb physical instrument and the intelligence to control it. Because he subdues his personality to those of the poet and the composer, concerned only with presenting a generalized emotional complex which each of his hearers shall recognize as part of his own actual or potential human experience. But the fact remains that he is no more than the discardable medium through which Schubert is made flesh. Compared to the composer he is nothing. It is conceivable that a vocal machine could be programmed to deliver a lied with scrupulous adherence to the written expression as well as the written notes; no *Schubert-maschine* is remotely conceivable.

But what admirers of Fischer-Dieskau get from his performance is, of course, the personality of the singer himself – warm, intelligent, *sympa-*

tisch, recognizable – yet I doubt whether one is justified in saying 'Let us go hear Fischer-Dieskau sing' rather than 'Let us go hear some lieder – ah, I see Fischer-Dieskau is singing them, good.' For there will come a time, even with the most intelligent and modest singer, when he will feel a certain superiority to his composer and start taking liberties with him. He will consider that, knowing more about singing than the composer ever did, he can put the composer right on certain points; that the composer, living and dying in the pre-Freudian age, did not understand himself as well as he thought.

As the lied represents a kind of house halfway between music unapplied and music attached to the service of the opera house, a speck of forgiveness is possible for the personality cultist. For opera, above all the branches of music, has depended on the singer's capacity for projecting elements beyond the mere words and notes. But, before going to worship a particular *Heldentenor* or *diva*, we ought to remember Mozart's attitude to the singers he had waiting for him in Prague when he went thither with the half-finished score of *Le Nozze di Figaro* or *Don Giovanni*. These were to him no more than imperfect instruments, childishly self-assertive, not so talented as they thought they were, swollen by applause, ready to tolerate the composer only because he gave them the materials for self-glorification. They were to be coaxed sometimes, sometimes bullied, but the great thing was to subdue their egos without their being aware of it. For to Mozart, sighing, singers were only necessary evils.

It's inevitable that I should want to diminish the glory of the mere interpreter, since I have for the last thirty-odd years practised an art which doesn't depend on interpretation at all. With the novel nothing – save the printer's errors – stands between the giver and the taker. The critics are, of course, ready to interpret for the reader and tell him what he is really reading and what the author, without knowing it, really meant, but there's no obligation to read the critics. As soon as I have brought such narrative gifts as I have to a medium – such as film, stage or television – which depends on interpreters, then I have gone through hell. It is bad enough to have to cope with the ill-informed egos of actors, but there is that new, very twentieth century, phenomenon the director to deal with, who has produced the 'director's theatre' and the *cinéma d'auteur*. Some years ago, I remember, I was asked to write a definitive essay on Stanley Kubrick, who had made a film of one of my novels. It was assumed that I would be honoured to follow around my own interpreter with a tape recorder, conceding that he was more important than the primary creator: no insult was intended, but umbrage was taken. If Shakespeare were alive today, he would be asked to take time off from *The Tempest* to write an epic poem on the first interpreter of Hamlet – Richard Burbage – or even on the clown Will Kemp.

But back to music and a word about conductors. The conductor was once a man who kept time from the harpsichord. With the development of the romantic orchestra he acquired a dais, a stick and limitless authority. But the Russian Revolution showed that he was not indispensable:

the first Soviet orchestras did well enough without an imperious stick-wagger. For that matter, even in the democracies, there are seasoned orchestral players who find it safer to ignore the beat and perhaps give only a little attention to the expansive gestures which mean *stringendo* or *allargando*. The music, they feel, if accurately played will make its own impact. A conductor is, properly, a man who has little to do after rehearsal: he should no more take the centre of the stage than the theatrical director. Pierre Boulez, whom I admire, demonstrated the truth of this with his *Le Sacre du Printemps*. His gestures were minimal and served as mere reminders of what had been decided in rehearsal. His concert performance had none of the flamboyance caricaturists and philistine patrons of the arts adore.

If I approach reverence to any conductor who ever lived, that conductor can only be Arturo Toscanini. He fulfilled the first duty of a head of orchestra by converting a heterogeneous body of men and women into a single instrument. He trained the CBS orchestra, he knew by heart the scores he interpreted, and his interpretations were little more than the end-products of endless lucubrations on the meanings of the composer's notes, tempi and expression marks. When you hear Toscanini's Wagner or Beethoven you are, you believe, as close to what the composer intended as it is possible to conceive. Follow Toscanini with the score, and you will be impressed by his total fidelity to what is printed there. When Toscanini took his bow, you were expected to applaud the music, not the man. The cult of personality could never be applied to him: he left both Italy and Germany when those countries' regimes were based on such a cult. Thank God we have him preserved on record.

In a sense he represented the fulfilment of a directorial tradition which had, of necessity, been started at Bayreuth (and which Toscanini would have continued had he not violently disagreed with the Nazi racial policy which excluded Jews from the theatre there). No conductor could assume responsibility for a Wagner score unless he knew it *technically*: this meant a knowledge of every individual orchestral line and a capacity to teach the sometimes baffled players how to approach their parts. My father never tired of telling his own father's story about Hans von Richter conducting the Hallé in a rehearsal of *Siegfried's Journey to the Rhine*. The first horn player said his part was unplayable. Richter, who knew no English, asked for a translation, then for the cornist's instrument. He took a mouthpiece from his pocket and then played the passage with ease and panache. He handed the horn back and the rehearsal continued. There was never again talk about Wagner's unplayability. This was great conducting.

Of the instrumental soloists I know, I admire most Yehudi Menuhin – chiefly for his humility not only towards the mysteries of his instrument, but towards the music he plays. I was a little younger than he when, as a boy wonder, he first played Elgar's concerto under the composer himself (who at that time was, in response to British philistinism, professing more interest in horse racing than in music). The boy was an evident prodigy: he not only knew the notes, he seemed to know what the work was about, but the fact that a mere bare-kneed urchin could understand the curlicues of the mind of a complex and neurotic composer probably proves that music has no real content other than mere notes, and that learning to play a musical instrument well in extreme youth is a sign that there is not much in it. Yehudi had to outgrow the prodigy phase and, as a mature man, be accepted not with wonder but with affection. He turned himself into a conductor and was right to do so – he if anyone, knows the problems of string players and precisely what a string section can do. Well, not exactly precisely: he has spoken to me of the unknown territory up there on the E string, he has disclaimed mastery, he retains his own sense of wonder in the presence of the music he performs. He is the perfect instrument for a composer.

It is, alas, singers who, like actors, exhibit the least humility of all performers and, like actors, earn the most adulation. The disease goes back a long way and was endemic among eighteenth-century castrati; hence it may be taken to indicate a lack of something. Perhaps the disease is less prevalent than it was. There was a time when Caruso and Tetrazzini, grown gross physically, were above seeing the disparity between what they looked like in opera and what the public was expected to believe they looked like. They became bigger than the works they performed in; the composers shrank to mere providers of fodder; the exhibition of high Cs was more important than characterization or expression. If their day is past, nevertheless there are still opera subscribers around who cling to their old philosophy; let us go and see Stronzo or Cazzi in *Falstaff*; not – let us go and see *Falstaff* and trust that the singers, whoever they are, are adequate.

There remains a humbler musical sphere where it is not possible to separate the singer from the song – that of jazz, where the performer is also the creator. There is also the world of the popular song, where everything seems to depend on the performer's charisma and the rewards are higher than even those of a Karajan or Bernstein. It is more reasonable to line up for a Sinatra or Streisand recital than for a Fischer-Dieskau one, since the music they sing is actually given, through their interpretations, the substance it fundamentally lacks. They are scrupulous about putting across such verbal meaning as the lyrics have; they will not, in 'September Song', substitute 'I'll spend with you' for 'I'd . . .'. They will convey the nuance of the comma in 'Lady, be good'. But some of them have inherited from the old opera gods and goddesses a damnable condition of swelled head. Who said, peeling an unripe banana, 'I'll give ya three minutes'? (I was proud, getting my hat, of saying 'Two minutes too much.') Who turned up at Nice Airport and, finding Prince Rainier not there to meet him, cancelled his Monaco engagement? Who is three hours late for rehearsal?

But, back on the subject of real music, let us learn a sense of proportion vis-à-vis the masterpiece and the maestro, reflecting on the possibility that when a performance is merely adequate the greatness of the work performed may shine through all the more clearly. When we talk of Karajan's Mahler or Bernstein's Stravinsky we're rejoicing in a superaddition, as though the composer himself were not enough. I never enjoy Shakespeare more than when schoolchildren perform him: bring in your Olivier or James Earl Jones and you've interposed an animated curtain between yourself and the Bard. In Italy, the least musical country in the world (ask the shade of Toscanini), you can see most clearly, in a kind of caricature, where the adoration of the performer can lead. At the Scala, Milan, during a performance of *Madama Butterfly*, there was respectful silence while Scotti sang; when the orchestra played alone, the conversation happily buzzed. Aghast, I cried 'Shut up!' and was asked to leave. No music lovers, these English. I met Scotti afterwards and she sympathized. I don't think otherwise I would have remembered her name. She would have sympathized with that too. Like myself, she cared about Puccini.

My readers will, I know, now be saying 'Nonsense: without the interpreter there is only silence; anyone who can convert silence into meaningful sound has wrought a miracle and deserves homage.' This view can only come from music lovers who can't read music. Do they feel the same about interpretations of Shakespeare or Ibsen, whom, presumably, they know how to read? Apparently, yes. The maestro heresy has, in our age, attached itself to the drama, and names like Peter Brook, Jonathan Miller and Joe Papp are granted bigger billing than the dramatists they interpret. Their status would be unintelligible to the great actor–managers like Irving, to whom the notion of interpretation and, more particularly, interpretation by a non-participant in the drama would contradict all tradition. In Shakespeare's company, the Lord Chamberlain's (later the King's) Men, Richard Burbage presumably decreed cuts and moves, but he was primarily an actor, which Papp and Brook and Miller are not. Once the director cuts himself off from personal participation, he dreams dreams and has visions. He reads Freud and Jan Kott, he remakes his play from the outside. The playwright becomes raw material for the expression of a philosophy or a sociology. Or else he is pitied for not having lived in the present and so must be brought up to date. I recently saw the Papp production of *The Pirates of Penzance* and mourned over the death of Sullivan's orchestra and the inaudibility of Gilbert's words. But it is Papp who is filmed and G. and S. merely truckle to his image of Victorian England. The historical perspective, indispensable when we see Aeschylus or Sophocles, dissolves into a Freudian or Marxist overview. Stage directors no longer defer; deference is left to the ignorant dead.

Come, sir, be reasonable: without direction there is no play. Similarly, without translation there is no Dostoevsky or Proust. Alas, all too true, but translators preserve for the most part a decent subservience to the master whom they render (except for Sir Thomas Urqhart, who virtually remade Rabelais): there are no maestro translators. Instead, some will say, there are mere hacks, cursed alike by penury, ignorance and a lack of style. As one of the lesser translated, I know this to be true. But it is better perhaps to have one's meaning and style traduced than to be the raw stuff of somebody else's virtuosity. I once wrote a novel in which a character yawned. Instead of merely saying that he yawned, I made him utter the vocables 'War awe warthog Warsaw', which sound like yawning. My German translator promptly turned the noises into 'Krieg Ehrfurcht Warzeschwein Warschau', where there is no yawning. There is incompetence, but it is more acceptable than creative virtuoso performances, in which the translator becomes bigger than his author.

We cannot read every book in the original, we are not all competent to turn our inner imagination into a well-lighted stage with brilliant actors walking across it, few of us can read music. But we can still deplore the contemporary glorification of the interpretative maestro. The singer is not greater than the song, nor is the conductor above the symphony. Somerset Maugham's Alroy Kear says: 'The Americans prefer a live dog to a dead lion. That's one of the things I like about the Americans.' It is probably America, so much concerned with the present and palpable, that has done most to deify the interpreter: it may have something to do with the Hollywood star system, in which actors became gods and writers were merely schmucks with Remingtons. But the rest of the world has not been slow to regard Shakespeare and Beethoven as ghosts and Bernhardt and Bernstein as the living artistic reality. It's time to view the maestri as what they really are – schmucks with batons and voices.

Anybody Can Conduct

True. It requires no very special skill to get up on a podium and lash an orchestra to life. It is much more difficult to be a bus or train conductor. After all, you don't really need a stick-wagger up there. The early days of the Soviet Union were inflamed by such a spirit of equality that they got rid of the one man with the baton who enslaved one hundred blowing, scraping and banging to his will. Russian orchestras didn't noticeably play worse, though the percipient observed how the principal first violin or concert master (as Germans and Americans call him) became more self-assertive and wagged his bow about instead of setting it to his strings. There was, in fact, a reversion to the state that existed before conductors came along. *Somebody* had to keep the orchestra together, but not somebody *up there*, stick-wagging.

Naive music lovers love conductors for various reasons, few of which have much to do with music. A conductor provides visual relief from too much listening: he is a kind of one-man ballet. He is known to be richer than mere fiddlers and flautists, and this gives him star status even if he has little talent. Karajan, who conducts the Berlin Philharmonic, travels about in a private jet and, old as he is, looks glamorous, as Beethoven might have looked had he been successful. The admirers of conductors believe they could do the job themselves moderately well (compare the attitude rock lovers have to rock singers: success is a matter of luck, not genius: this is very comforting), and to some extent this is true. The orchestra has been playing the *Mastersingers* Prelude for years. The conductor drops dead of a heart attack. You, a member of the audience, are ordered to mount the podium. Give the downbeat. The orchestra starts to play. It plays well. But it plays well in spite of you. It knows the damned thing backwards. If it were a matter of a first performance of a new work by Berio or Boulez or Messiaen, the situation would be altogether different.

Watch Pierre Boulez conducting Stravinsky's *Le Sacre du Printemps*. He seems to do nothing except make unemphatic gestures. No flamboyance, no leaping in the air, no hair-tearing, no brow-mopping with a snowy handkerchief. What he is doing is *reminding* the orchestra of what he has taught them in rehearsal. There's nothing much for him to do now. The work has already been done, and now it's up to the players to discourse the notes in the manner he has, in rehearsal after rehearsal, imposed. But before the rehearsals there were months of work quite as important, in which the conductor was alone with the score – reading it, learning it, pencilling in expression marks. He had to decide on tempo – how fast, how slow. On deciding just how loud fff is, and how soft ppp. The composer's expression marks are never very exact. What does *allegro con fuoco* mean? Fast and fiery. But how fast? And what has fire to do with blown wood and scraped catgut?

When an amateur conductor is given charge of an orchestra, the work performed will always be something the players already know well. A symphony by Beethoven – preferably the Fifth. *The Flight of the Bumble Bee*. Give the downbeat to start the thing off, and, like the man who first conducted Berlioz's *Benvenuto Cellini*, you can get your snuffbox out. If the work is Debussy's *L'Après-Midi d'un Faune*, you don't even need the downbeat: just nod at the first flute, saying: 'Start when you feel like it.' What the amateur conductor can't do, even with a work excruciatingly well known and a great bore to the orchestra, is organize balance, make sure the wind are not swamped by the strings and the brass by both. Composers like Beethoven gave the trumpets f and the flutes f in a *tutti*, thus ensuring that the flutes wouldn't be heard. The good conductor puts that right. He puts it right in rehearsal. At the performance the trumpet remembers that he must play mf and the flautist that he must play ff or even fff.

Many people think that the conductor's main job is to beat time. There is something in this. Downbeat, leftbeat, rightbeat, upbeat. But many conductors are very erratic about time. I was at a rehearsal once in which the conductor (very famous, but I had better not mention his name) lambasted the players unmercifully. 'Strings unforgivably ragged,' he yelled, 'and woodwind as pallid as lard. Brass brutal. A disgrace. But I'd better not say any more, or you'll have your revenge at the concert.' A little man in the back row of the second violins spoke up. 'Yes,' he said, 'we'll follow your beat.' What, then, was the orchestra getting out of this celebrated maestro? Chiefly his feeling for the music, expressed in his eyes and grimaces, his body language, the curious illusion that he himself was playing the music on a human keyboard called the orchestra. He *cared* – that was the important thing. A lot of orchestral players *don't* care. They do the job, get paid, are more concerned about union restrictions than about an agonized Beethoven or Schubert. My old violin teacher played in the Hallé Orchestra in Manchester. He *hated* music, so he told me, but fiddling was the only job he could do. He needed a conductor to infuse him with a temporary love of music. All the rest was technique.

Orchestras need conductors, then (whether they wag a stick on the rostrum, nod from a solo pianoforte, or move their head and shoulders from a violin desk). They need them at rehearsal; they don't necessarily need them on the night. But it is wrong for music lovers to rush to buy tickets because Maestro Stronzo or Pferdscheisse is up there. The music comes first, and badly conducted Beethoven is better worth hearing than well-conducted Victor Herbert. Beethoven can more or less look after himself; kitsch has to have glamour spread all over it, like peanut butter. You yourself can, with confidence, get up there, take the stick, give the downbeat and launch the players into 'The Star Spangled Banner'. But you can't do it with Stravinsky or Schoenberg. You just can't spare the months of preparatory solitude and the hours of arduous rehearsal. Conducting is, finally, an art which goes on behind locked doors. What you see in the concert hall is hardly worth seeing.

Witch in C Major

Fair Ophelia: Harriet Smithson Berlioz, by Peter Raby

T he actor–manager Samson Penley put Shakespeare on in Paris in 1822, though little could be heard over the crash of hurled sabots and little seen through the rain of eggs, coins and cabbages. The sight of Desdemona being smothered appalled Parisians brought up on Voltairian classicism, and they cried *'A bas Shakespeare! C'est un lieutenant de Wellington!'* Honest anglophobia got mixed up, in a thoroughly French non-Cartesian way, with an aesthetic which, as Stendhal clearly saw, was on its way out. Romanticism was awaiting its cue, but Penley gave that cue a little too soon. In 1827 Paris, which had by now become unreasonably anglomaniacal, what with volumes of Scott and Byron on salon tables and Windsor soap and lavender water by the washbowls, was ready for a company whose actors were drawn from Covent Garden, Drury Lane and the Haymarket. *Hamlet*, with Kemble in the lead, was billed for 11 September at the Odéon, and – despite the mockery of the *Courrier des Théâtres*: 'Parnassus drowned in the Thames', tragedy by John Bull. . . . "Molière mocked or the Parisians and the English," farce by Milord London' – the occasion was anticipated with interest and even eagerness.

It was Harriet Smithson as Ophelia who set Paris on fire. The daughter of an acting family of no great note, English by blood but Irish by birth, she was already established in Britain as a useful all-round actress, graceful and beautiful but no Mrs Siddons. To the French, unused to an uninhibited style of acting which the British had long taken for granted, she was a revelation. 'By the time Harriet spoke the final words. "And peace be with all Christian souls, I pray heaven. God be with you," ' Mr Raby tells us, 'there was hardly a dry eye in the house, and men reportedly stumbled out of the auditorium unable to watch further.'

Practically the entire French romantic movement was in the theatre: Hugo, de Vigny, Delacroix, de Musset, Deschamps, Sainte-Beuve, Barye, Huet, Boulanger, Gautier. There was a young musician there, too, Hector Berlioz, who was later to say:

Shakespeare, coming upon me unawares, struck me like a thunderbolt. The lightning flash of that discovery revealed to me at a stroke the whole heaven of art, illuminating it to its remotest corners. I recognised the meaning of grandeur, beauty, dramatic truth. . . .

He was only twenty-three, not only dangerously young but also dangerously susceptible, and he had difficulty in separating the impact of Shakespeare from that of Miss Smithson. She was, of course, unattainable, a goddess, the Muse, and he was merely a struggling composer spurned by his philistine family. But it is no exaggeration to state that the thunder flash of the vision of Harriet–Ophelia turned him, almost overnight, into the greatest composer of the age. He tried to cathartize the obsession into music and produced the *Symphonie Fantastique* – a brilliant, wild, botched confection in which Harriet, rarefied into the Beloved and desecrated as the Evil One, floats transfigured as the first ever leitmotif over orchestral noises intended to match the verbal impact of Shakespeare.

With the catharsis the obsession with Harriet might have ended. Berlioz fell for the pianist Marie Moke, more poetically known as Camille, and proposed marriage. But Camille deserted him for the M. Pleyel of the pianofortes, and Berlioz Shakespearianly cried out on high heaven, purchased a gun, intended a *Hamlet*-like massacre. He calmed down, seduced a girl on the *plage* at Nice, and wrote the *Roi Lear* Overture. There the whole story of tempestuous passion might have given way to a decent professional career of bar-ruling and note-spinning had not Harriet reappeared in his life. She was back in Paris, unsuccessful in repeating her former triumphs, and, by chance, attended that remarkable concert of 9 December 1832, in which the *Symphonie Fantastique* and *Le Retour à la Vie* (a weird romantic hotchpotch of music and monologue) were presented. The risen composer wooed the fading star with a symphony orchestra. At length they married. It was a great pity.

It is always a great pity when myth has to melt into the Monday of quarrels about bills over ill-made coffee. Berlioz was first an enchanted husband, then a contented one, then a disillusioned one. Harriet was a bad housekeeper and an imperfect mother. She never spoke French well. She grew fat and took to drink. Berlioz was unfaithful and she was whiningly jealous. At length, having lost the power of speech, she fell into a decline and died. Though Berlioz mourned: 'I loved Ophelia. Forty thousand brothers/ Could not, with all their quantity of love,/ Make up my sum,' he had the honesty to admit that his true residual emotion was pity – pity for a decayed body and a failed vocation. Disillusioned with the too too solid Harriet, he never became disillusioned with Ophelia or Juliet. The fire of that first vision remained with him and produced the best Shakespeare music in the repertory.

It is a sad but illuminating story, and Mr Raby tells it briefly and well. He ends with a thoughtful chapter on the historical importance of the romantic image as embodied in poor Harriet. She brought Berlioz's genius to a blaze, inspired Fantin-Latour, impelled both Hugo and Musset, perhaps even Rimbaud – '*O pâle Ophélia! belle comme la neige!*' – to make the vision of a drowned girl driven mad by grief into one of the central icons of French romanticism. She is in the paintings and lithographs of Delacroix, bare-breasted, wide-eyed, recognizably

Harriet. That she was probably a very good actress is easily forgotten in the tulle and mist of her deification. Those first-nighters at the Odéon wished to be enchanted, but they were no fools. If we have difficulty in dating the start of British romanticism – Ossian? Chatterton? The *Lyrical Ballads*? – we have no such problem with the cognate movement in France. The French had to discover Shakespeare, and they discovered him on 11 September 1827, his spirit, passionate but not really erotic, incarnated in a dark-haired Irish girl. Turn on the cassette player and, in a few bars in C major, she is back with us.

His most ambitious novel to date . . .

ANTHONY BURGESS

THE KINGDOM OF THE WICKED

This is an extraordinary account of the first years of Christianity, recreated in vivid and meticulous detail.

"Burgess takes hold of an immense theme with magnificent mastery. Detail and dialogue are incredibly vivid; one hardly knows which to praise most".

LITERARY REVIEW

"All Burgess's skills are in evidence here: his ornate imagination, his fascination with words, his sly wit, the prodigious energy . . ."

LONDON STANDARD

"His unassuageable energy can do nothing other than celebrate the energy of life itself".

SUNDAY TIMES

"Both reader and author have marvellous fun".

SUNDAY TELEGRAPH

0 349 10439 5   ABACUS FICTION   £3.95

Also by Anthony Burgess in Abacus:
ENDERBY'S DARK LADY

The Periodic Table

'One of the most important and gifted writers of
our time . . . an extraordinary and fascinating book'
Italo Calvino

'We are always looking for the book it is *necessary* to
read next. After a few pages I immersed myself
gladly and gratefully. There is nothing superfluous
here, everything this book contains is essential. It is
wonderfully pure, and beautifully translated'
Saul Bellow

'I was captivated, but also knew that no words of mine
would do this book justice. Nominally it is prose;
in actuality, it is a narrative poem of magical quality'
Frederick Dainton,
NEW SCIENTIST

'This is an extraordinary book, eccentric in
construction, protean in genre, grandiose in its
intellectual ambition, and profoundly moving in the
delicacy and depth of its engagement with tragedy'
SUNDAY TIMES

'One of the most important Italian writers'
Umberto Eco

0 349 12198 2   ABACUS FICTION   £3.95

OUT NOW IN PAPERBACK:

Foreign Affairs

BY

ALISON·LURIE

WINNER OF THE PULITZER PRIZE FOR FICTION

"Brightly lit, fluently shaped, the story is a ballet that dances rings round the English way of life"

MAIL ON SUNDAY

"There is no American writer I have read with more constant pleasure and sympathy over the years. FOREIGN AFFAIRS earns the same shelf as Henry James and Edith Wharton"

JOHN FOWLES

"Alison Lurie is not only the most elegant novelist in America today – she is also one of the strongest"

OBSERVER

"A brilliant novel – her best . . . witty, acerbic and sometimes fiendishly clever . . . a triumph"

PAUL BAILY THE STANDARD

"FOREIGN AFFAIRS is warm, clever and funny"

THE TIMES LITERARY SUPPLEMENT

"Alison Lurie is a writer of extraordinary talent . . . she is perhaps more shocking than she knows – shocking like Jane Austen, not Genet"

CHRISTOPHER ISHERWOOD

FICTION   0 349 122156   £3.50

ALSO BY ALISON LURIE IN ABACUS:

LOVE AND FRIENDSHIP
THE WAR BETWEEN THE TATES ·
THE NOWHERE CITY

The No 1 Bestseller

HAWKSMOOR

PETER ACKROYD

WHITBREAD NOVEL OF THE YEAR

WINNER OF THE GUARDIAN FICTION AWARD

"A brilliant achievement, funny and horrible in turn" James
Fenton,
The Times

"With consummate formal control, he has created a
fictional nightmare, combining the genres of thriller, ghost
story and metaphysical tract . . . Its nastiness illuminates
modern evil as well as testifying to the author's brave way
with the unspeakable" Marina Warner,
Sunday Times

"Mr Ackroyd is a virtuoso writer whose prose is a
continual pleasure to read . . . An unfailingly intelligent
work of the imagination"
New York Times

0 349 10057 8   FICTION   £3.95

Also by Peter Ackroyd in Abacus:
T. S. ELIOT
THE LAST TESTAMENT OF OSCAR WILDE
THE GREAT FIRE OF LONDON

Also available from ABACUS paperback:

FICTION

HAWKSMOOR	Peter Ackroyd	£3.95 ☐
TOKYO WOES	Bruce Jay Friedman	£3.50 ☐
INDIFFERENT HEROES	Mary Hocking	£3.95 ☐
EASE	Patrick Gale	£3.50 ☐
THE AERODYNAMICS OF PORK	Patrick Gale	£3.95 ☐
MR WAKEFIELD'S CRUSADE	Bernice Rubens	£3.50 ☐
CRUSOE'S DAUGHTER	Jane Gardam	£3.95 ☐
EVE	Penelope Farmer	£3.95 ☐

NON-FICTION

THE PERIODIC TABLE	Primo Levi	£3.95 ☐
FLAME INTO BEING	Anthony Burgess	£3.95 ☐
TO BEAR ANY BURDEN	Al Santoli	£3.95 ☐
THIS SPACE TO LET	Ray Lowry	£2.95 ☐
SCHUMACHER LECTURES 2	Satish Kumar (Ed)	£3.95 ☐
THE TRUE ADVENTURES OF THE ROLLING STONES	Stanley Booth	£3.95 ☐
THE FIRST DANCE OF FREEDOM	Martin Meredith	£3.50 ☐
BEYOND THE DRAGON'S MOUTH	Shiva Naipaul	£3.95 ☐

All Abacus books are available at your local bookshop or newsagent, or can be ordered direct from the publisher. Just tick the titles you want and fill in the form below.

Name _____

Address _____

_____

Write to Abacus Books, Cash Sales Department, P.O. Box 11, Falmouth, Cornwall TR10 9EN.

Please enclose a cheque or postal order to the value of the cover price plus:

UK: 60p for the first book, 25p for the second book and 15p for each additional book ordered to a maximum charge of £1.90.

OVERSEAS & EIRE: £1.25 for the first book, 75p for the second book and 28p for each subsequent title ordered.

BFPO: 60p for the first book, 25p for the second book plus 15p per copy for the next 7 books, thereafter 9p per book.

Abacus Books reserve the right to show new retail prices on covers which may differ from those previously advertised in the text or elsewhere, and to increase postal rates in accordance with the PO.